Praise fo[r]

T

Goodreads Choice Awards 2019 Finalist | Starred reviews in *Booklist, Library Journal,* and *Publishers Weekly* | Named one of the best books of the year by *Reader's Digest,* The New York Public Library, *The Washington Post,* LitHub, PBS.com, *PopSugar,* and *CrimeReads* | Included in *HuffPost*'s "Best Book to Give as Gifts This Year" and *Good Housekeeping*'s "Best Books to Give as Gifts This Season" | One of *Newsweek*'s "Books to Curl Up With This Fall" | One of *Buzzfeed*'s "13 Thrillers We Couldn't Stop Thinking About in 2019" | Included in *O, The Oprah Magazine*'s "23 Chilling Thriller Books That'll Keep You Turning the Page" | A *Library Journal* "Essential Title" of 2019

"A superb suspense writer . . . Ware is a master at signaling the presence of evil at the most mundane moments . . . Ware pulls out a stunner on the penultimate page that radically alters how we interpret everything that's come before. Brava, Ruth Ware. I daresay even Henry James would be impressed."

—*Fresh Air*'s Maureen Corrigan for *The Washington Post*

"Let's just say that if you've got an Echo, you're going to unplug it as soon as you finish the book . . . What Ware does beautifully is infuse *The Turn of the Key* with a creepy Gothic sensibility. For all of the novel's contemporary touches—particularly the house's malevolent smart technology—she has delivered an old fashioned horror story, peopled by children with 'eyes full of malice,' a dour housekeeper straight out of *Rebecca* and an inscrutable handyman."

—*The New York Times Book Review*

"Ruth Ware—one of our favorite thriller writers—is bringing down the house . . . Read it for a fast-paced ride."

—*theSkimm*

"This appropriately twisty *Turn of the Screw* update finds the *Woman in Cabin 10* author in her most menacing mode, unfurling a shocking saga of murder and deception."

—*Entertainment Weekly*

"A clever and elegant update to James's story . . . Surveillance and home technology slot easily into the conventions of horror: They bring the sense that your environment is invaded and controlled from afar, and that you are never quite as alone as you might wish . . . *The Turn of the Key*, and novels like it, point to a new reality. We are all, constantly, haunted."

—NPR

"Henry James via *Black Mirror* . . . While the ambiguity in James's masterpiece is 'ghosts or madness?,' here it is 'ghosts or glitch?' Unlike *The Turn of the Screw*, however, Ware picks a lane, deploying a satisfyingly dizzying parade of twists and reveals without leaving much unexplained."

—*Los Angeles Review of Books* (*LARB*)

"Diabolically clever. Twisty and creepy, *The Turn of the Key* is Ruth Ware's best book yet. Read with a blanket nearby, because you will get shivers up your spine."

—Riley Sager, *New York Times* bestselling author of *The Last Time I Lied*

"A ghost story for the twenty-first century, a propulsive gothic thriller with characters you'll really care about. With this book, Ruth Ware proves she's the true heir to Wilkie Collins. Creepy, engrossing, and oh-so-hard to put down."

—JP Delaney, *New York Times* bestselling author of *The Girl Before*

"Pure suspense, from the first gripping page to the last shocking twist."

—Erin Kelly, bestselling author of *He Said/She Said*

"Ruth Ware has been called the Agatha Christie of our generation . . . *The Turn of the Key* is a great read. You're going to enjoy it very much."

—*New York Times* bestselling author David Baldacci for his "Hot Beach Reads: Guilty Pleasures, Popular Books" pick as part of the *Today Show*'s "Best Summer Reads of 2019, according to Top Authors" segment

"If you've never spent a long weekend devouring a Ruth Ware thriller on a hammock, this is the summer to start. Her fifth novel, *The Turn of the Key*, is set in the Scottish Highlands and is as compulsively readable as you would expect a Ware book to be."

—*CBS WATCH!* magazine

"Chilling."

—*Minneapolis Star Tribune*

"Readers, you'll want to sleep with the lights on (and your Alexa off) after reading this spooky tale from Ruth Ware."

—*Bookish*

"All of Ruth Ware's books have been creepy and deeply mysterious, in other words . . . awesome! But I think this might be her best one yet."

—*Get Literary*

"*The Turn of the Key* is a brilliantly crafted, chilling suspense thriller. Clues are seeded through the tale like poisonous plants that you only recognize when it's far too late. Trust no one in this novel except Ruth Ware—she has come up with a totally compelling tale once again."

—Jane Casey, award-winning author of *The Burning*

"Superb as expected . . . Lovely echoes of *Turn of the Screw* in a contemporary thriller. A masterclass in tension."

—Sarah Pinborough, *New York Times* bestselling author of *Behind Her Eyes*

"Ware's mastery of the traditional mystery merged with the twisty psychological thriller never fails to impress!"

—*LitHub*

"A classically spooky thriller involving a potentially murderous nanny and a smart house gone wrong in the Scottish Highlands. Ruth Ware is a No. 1 *New York Times* bestselling author, and her fans are legion and loyal."

—*Vox*

"Truly terrifying! Ware perfects her ability to craft atmosphere and sustain tension with each novel."

—*Kirkus Reviews*

"Over the course of four explosive novels—*In a Dark, Dark Wood, The Woman in Cabin 10, The Lying Game*, and *The Death of Mrs. Westaway*—Ware has established herself as one of the best mystery writers working today, and her streak remains unbroken with this, her fifth novel."

—*B&N Reads*

"In Ware's latest book, *The Turn of the Key*, she delivers a novel full of twisted tension that will have readers looking at technology a little bit differently . . . It solidifies her spot among the greats."

—*Bustle*

"Are you attached to your Alexa? Do you control various aspects of your home from your smartphone? Prepare to be creeped out. Ruth Ware's latest thriller, *The Turn of the Key*, tells the story of a nanny in a smart home that turns downright harrowing."

—*Bookish*

"Breathlessly atmospheric, *The Turn of the Key* is a deliciously creepy mystery . . . Ware's twist on a classic is sure to be a hit for fans of psychological thrillers."

—*Shelf Awareness*

"Straddling the line between horror and thriller, this novel will delight fans of both genres."

—*Bookpage*

"Ware cleverly puts a high-tech spin on [*The Turn of the Screw*'s] gothic foundations of spellbinding menace set in a remote cavernous mansion with mysterious locked doors and a spooky garden . . . Ware's James-like embroidery of the strange and sinister produces a *Turn of the Screw* with cellphones and Teslas that will enthrall today's readers . . . it will not disappoint."

—*Booklist*, starred review

"Ware does a good job of creating tension . . . But above all, Ware skillfully lays the bread crumbs to the novel's satisfying conclusion . . . [that] leaves readers with one final, haunting question, one that will stay with them long after they turn the last page."

—*Publishers Weekly*, starred review

"Ware hits another one out of the park. Fans of hers or anyone with a taste for the disturbing will stay up late devouring this."

—*Library Journal*, starred review

"A lot of fun on a crisp autumn evening."

—*Christian Science Monitor*

"Ware at her eerie best."

—*Newsweek*

"The cast of characters includes an unsuspecting nanny, a creepy housekeeper, and a hunky groundskeeper amid the mists and heather, crumbling stone walls and creaky attics. What more could you ask for?"

—*Reader's Digest*, "Best Books of 2019"

"The definition of 'unputdownable' . . . [and] a terrifically clever reimagining of *The Turn of the Screw*."

—*Refinery29*

"Compulsively readable from the very start . . . *The Turn of the Key* is full of dizzying plot twists and revelations, but one thing is very clear: in Ware's version, we are the ghosts. What human beings are capable of, including what we can accomplish with our technology, has the capacity to turn us into monsters"

—*BookBub*

THE TURN OF THE KEY

RUTH WARE

SCOUT PRESS

New York London Toronto Sydney New Delhi

Scout Press
An Imprint of Simon & Schuster, Inc.
1230 Avenue of the Americas
New York, NY 10020

This book is a work of fiction. Any references to historical events, real people, or real places are used fictitiously. Other names, characters, places, and events are products of the author's imagination, and any resemblance to actual events or places or persons, living or dead, is entirely coincidental.

First Scout Press trade paperback edition May 2020

SCOUT PRESS and colophon are registered trademarks of Simon & Schuster, Inc.

For information about special discounts for bulk purchases, please contact Simon & Schuster Special Sales at 1-866-506-1949 or business@simonandschuster.com.

The Simon & Schuster Speakers Bureau can bring authors to your live event. For more information or to book an event, contact the Simon & Schuster Speakers Bureau at 1-866-248-3049 or visit our website at www.simonspeakers.com.

Interior design by Jaime Putorti

Manufactured in the United States of America

10 9 8 7 6 5

Library of Congress Cataloging-in-Publication Data is available for the hardcover.

ISBN 978-1-5011-8877-0
ISBN 978-1-5011-8878-7 (pbk)
ISBN 978-1-5011-8879-4 (ebook)

For Ian,

with more love than I know

how to put into words

3rd September 2017

Dear Mr. Wrexham,

I know you don't know me but please, please, please you have to help me

3rd September 2017
HMP Charnworth

Dear Mr. Wrexham,

You don't know me, but you may have seen coverage of my case in the newspapers. The reason I am writing to you is to ask you please

4th September 2017
HMP Charnworth

Dear Mr. Wrexham,

I hope that's the right way to address you. I have never written to a barrister before.

The first thing I have to say is that I know this is unconventional. I know I should have gone via my solicitor, but he's

5th September 2017

Dear Mr. Wrexham,

Are you a father? An uncle? If so, let me appeal

Dear Mr. Wrexham,

Please help me. I *didn't* kill anyone.

7th September 2017
HMP Charnworth

Dear Mr. Wrexham,

You have no idea how many times I've started this letter and screwed up the resulting mess, but I've realized there is no magic formula here. There is no way I can *make* you listen to my case. So I'm just going to have to do my best to set things out. However long it takes, however much I mess this up, I'm just going to keep going and tell the truth.

My name is . . . And here I stop, wanting to tear up the page again.

Because if I tell you my name, you will know why I am writing to you. My case has been all over the papers, my name in every headline, my agonized face staring out of every front page—and every single article insinuating my guilt in a way that falls only just short of contempt of court. If I tell you my name, I have a horrible feeling you might write me off as a lost cause and throw my letter away. I wouldn't entirely blame you, but please—before you do that, hear me out.

I am a young woman, twenty-seven years old, and as you'll have seen from the return address above, I am currently at the Scottish women's prison HMP Charnworth. I've never received a letter from anyone in prison, so I don't know what they look like when they come through the door, but I imagine my current living arrangements were pretty obvious even before you opened the envelope.

What you probably don't know is that I'm on remand.

And what you cannot know is that I'm innocent.

I know, I know. They all say that. Every single person I've met here is innocent—according to them, anyway. But in my case it's true.

You may have guessed what's coming next. I'm writing to ask you to represent me as my solicitor advocate at my trial.

I realize that this is unconventional and not how defendants are supposed to approach advocates. (I accidentally called you a barrister in an earlier draft of this letter—I know nothing about the law, and even less about the Scottish system. Everything I do know I have picked up from the women I'm in prison with, including your name.)

I have a solicitor already—Mr. Gates—and from what I understand, he is the person who should be appointing an advocate for the actual trial. But he is also the person who landed me here in the first place. I didn't choose him—the police picked him for me when I began to get scared and finally had the sense to shut up and refuse to answer questions until they found me a lawyer.

I thought that he would straighten everything out—help me to make my case. But when he arrived—I don't know, I can't explain it. He just made everything worse. He didn't let me *speak*. Everything I tried to say he was cutting in with "My client has no comment at this time," and it just made me look so much more guilty. I feel like if only I could have explained properly, it would never have got this far. But somehow the facts kept twisting in my mouth, and the police, they made everything sound so bad, so incriminating.

It's not that Mr. Gates hasn't heard my side of the story exactly. He has, of course—but somehow— Oh God, this is so hard to explain in writing. He's sat down and talked to me, but he doesn't *listen*. Or if he does, he doesn't believe me. Every time I try to tell him what happened, starting from the beginning, he cuts in with these questions that muddle me up and my story gets all tangled and I want to scream at him to just *shut the fuck up.*

And he keeps talking to me about what I said in the transcripts from that awful first night at the police station, when they grilled me and grilled me and I said— God, I don't know what I said. I'm sorry, I'm crying now. I'm sorry—I'm so sorry for the stains on the paper. I hope you can read my writing through the blotches.

What I said, what I said then, there's no undoing that. I know that. They have all that on tape. And it's bad—it's really bad. But it came out wrong; I feel like if only I could be given a chance to get my case across, to someone who would really listen . . . do you see what I'm saying?

Oh God, maybe you don't. You've never been here, after all. You've never sat across a desk feeling so exhausted you want to drop and so scared you want to vomit, with the police asking and asking and asking until you don't know what you're saying anymore.

I guess it comes down to this in the end.

I am the nanny in the Elincourt case, Mr. Wrexham.

And I *didn't* kill that child.

I started writing to you last night, Mr. Wrexham, and when I woke up this morning and looked at the crumpled pages covered with my pleading scrawl, my first instinct was to rip them up and start again, just like I had a dozen times before. I had meant to be so cool, so calm and collected—I had meant to set everything out so clearly and *make* you see. And instead I ended up crying onto the page in a mess of recrimination.

But then I reread what I'd written and I thought, *No. I can't start again. I just have to keep going.*

All this time I have been telling myself that if only someone would let me clear my head and get my side of the story straight, without interrupting, maybe this whole awful mess would get sorted out.

And here I am. This is my chance, right?

140 days, they can hold you in Scotland before a trial. Though there's a woman here who has been waiting almost ten months. Ten months! Do you know how long that is, Mr. Wrexham? You probably think you do, but let me tell you. In her case that's 297 days. She's missed Christmas with her kids. She's missed all their birthdays. She's missed Mother's Day and Easter and first days at school.

297 days. And they still keep pushing back the date of her trial.

Mr. Gates says he doesn't think mine will take that long because of all the publicity, but I don't see how he can be sure.

Either way, 100 days, 140 days, 297 days . . . that's a lot of writing time, Mr. Wrexham. A lot of time to think, and remember, and try to work out what really happened. Because there's so much I don't understand, but there's one thing I know. I did not kill that little girl. I *didn't.* However hard the police try to twist the facts and trip me up, they can't change that.

I didn't kill her. Which means someone else did. And they are out there.

While I am in here, rotting.

I will finish now, because I know I can't make this letter too long—you're a busy man; you'll just stop reading.

But please, you have to believe me. You're the only person who can help.

Please, come and see me, Mr. Wrexham. Let me explain the situation to you and how I got tangled into this nightmare. If anyone can make the jury understand, it's you.

I have put your name down for a visitor's pass—or you can write to me here if you have more questions. It's not like I'm going anywhere. Ha.

Sorry, I didn't mean to end on a joke. It's not a laughing matter, I know that. If I'm convicted, I'm facing—

But no. I can't think about that. Not right now. I won't be. I won't be convicted, because I'm innocent. I just have to make everyone understand that. Starting with you.

Please, Mr. Wrexham, please say you'll help. Please write back. I don't want to be melodramatic about this, but I feel like you're my only hope.

Mr. Gates doesn't believe me; I see it in his eyes.

But I think that you might.

12th September 2017
HMP Charnworth

Dear Mr. Wrexham,

It's been three days since I wrote to you, and I'm not going to lie, I've been waiting for a reply with my heart in my mouth. Every day the post comes round and I feel my pulse speed up, with a kind of painful hope, and every day (so far) you've let me down.

I'm sorry. That sounds like emotional blackmail. I don't mean it like that. I get it. You're a busy man, and it's been only three days since I sent my letter but . . . I guess I half hoped that if the publicity surrounding the case had done nothing else, it would have given me a certain twisted celebrity—made you pick out my letter from among all the others you presumably get from clients and would-be clients and nutters.

Don't you want to know what happened, Mr. Wrexham? I would.

Anyway, it's three days now (did I mention that already?) and . . . well, I'm beginning to worry. There's not much to do in here, and there's a lot of time to think and fret and start to build up catastrophes inside your head.

I've spent the last few days and nights doing that. Worrying that you didn't get the letter. Worrying that the prison authorities didn't pass it on (can they do that without telling me? I honestly don't know). Worrying that I didn't *explain* right.

It's the last one that has been keeping me awake. Because if it's that, then it's my fault.

I was trying to keep it short and snappy, but now I'm thinking, I shouldn't have stopped so quickly. I should have put in more of the facts, tried to show you *why* I'm innocent. Because you can't just take my word for it—I get that.

When I came here, the other women—I can be honest with you, Mr. Wrexham—they felt like another species. It's not that I think I'm better than them. But they all seemed . . . they all seemed to fit in here. Even the frightened ones, the self-harmers and the ones who screamed and banged their heads against their cell walls and cried at night, even the girls barely out of school. They looked . . . I don't know. They looked like they belonged here, with their pale, gaunt faces and their pulled-back hair and their blurred tattoos. They looked . . . well, they looked *guilty*.

But I was different.

I'm English, for a start, of course, which didn't help. I couldn't understand them when they got angry and started shouting and all up in my face. I had no idea what half the slang meant. And I was visibly middle-class, in a way that I can't put my finger on but which might as well have been written across my forehead as far as the other women were concerned.

But the main thing was, I had never been in prison. I don't think I'd ever even met someone who had, before I came here. There were secret codes I couldn't decipher, and currents I had no way of navigating. I didn't understand what was going on when one woman passed something to another in the corridor and all of a sudden the wardens came barreling out, shouting. I didn't see the fights coming; I didn't know who was off her meds, or who was coming down from a high and might lash out. I didn't know the ones to avoid or the ones with permanent PMS. I didn't know what to wear or what to do, or what would get you spat on or punched by the other inmates, or what would provoke the wardens to come down hard on you.

I sounded different. I looked different. I *felt* different.

And then one day I went into the bathroom and I caught a glimpse of a woman walking towards me from the far corner. She had her hair scraped back like all the others, her eyes were like chips of granite, and her face was set, hard and white. My first thought was, *Oh God, she looks pissed off; I wonder what she's in for.*

My second thought was, *Maybe I'd better use the other bathroom.*

And then I realized.

It was a mirror on the far wall. The woman was me.

It should have been a shock—the realization that I wasn't different at all but just another woman sucked into this soulless system. But in a strange way it helped.

I still don't fit in completely. I'm still the English girl—and they all know what I'm in for. In prison they don't like people who harm children, Mr. Wrexham; you probably know that. I've told them it's not true, of course—what I'm accused of. But they look at me and I know what they're thinking—*They all say that.*

And I know—I know that's what you'll be thinking too. That's what I wanted to say. I understand if you're skeptical. I didn't manage to convince the police, after all. I'm here. Without bail. I must be guilty.

But it's not true.

I have 140 days to convince you. All I have to do is tell the truth, right? I just have to start at the beginning and set it all out, clearly and calmly, until I get to the end.

And the beginning was the advert.

WANTED:

LARGE FAMILY SEEKS EXPERIENCED LIVE-IN NANNY

ABOUT US: *We are a busy family of four children, living in a beautiful (but remote!) house in the Highlands. Mum and Dad co-run the family architecture practice.*

ABOUT YOU: *We are seeking an experienced nanny, used to working with children of all ages, from babyhood to teens. You must be practical, unflappable, and comfortable looking after children on your own. Excellent references, background check, first aid certificate, and clean driving license are a must.*

ABOUT THE POST: *Mum and Dad work mainly from home, and during those periods you will have a simple eight-to-five post, with one night a week babysitting and weekends off. As far as possible we arrange our schedule so that one parent is always around. However, there are times when we may both need to be away (very occasionally for up to a fortnight), and when this occurs, you will be in loco parentis.*

In return we can offer a highly competitive remuneration package totaling £55,000 per annum (gross, including bonus), use of a car, and eight weeks' holiday a year.

Applications to Sandra and Bill Elincourt, Heatherbrae House, Carn Bridge.

I remember it nearly word for word. The funny thing was, I wasn't even looking for a job when it came up on my Google results—I was searching for . . . well, it doesn't really matter what I was looking for. But something completely different. And then there it was—like a gift thrown into my hands so unexpectedly I almost didn't catch it.

I read it through once, and then again, my heart beating faster the second time, because it was *perfect*. It was almost too perfect.

When I read it a third time I was scared to look at the closing date for applications—convinced I would have missed it.

But it was that very evening.

It was unbelievable. Not just the salary—though God knows, that was a pretty startling sum. Not just the post. But the luck of it. The whole package—just falling in my lap, right when I was in the perfect position to apply.

You see, my flatmate was away, traveling. We'd met at the Little Nippers nursery in Peckham, working side by side in the baby room, laughing about our terrible boss and the pushy, faddy parents, with their fucking fabric nappies and their homemade—

Sorry. I shouldn't have sworn. I've scribbled it out, but you can probably see the word through the paper and, God knows, maybe you've got kids, maybe you even put them in Little Plushy Bottoms or whatever the fashionable brand was at the time.

And I get it, I do. They're your babies. Nothing is too much trouble. I understand that. It's just that when you're the one having to stockpile a whole day's worth of pissy, shitty bits of cloth and hand them back to the parent at collection time with your eyes watering from the ammonia . . . it's not that I *mind* exactly, you know? It's part of the job. I get that. But we all deserve a moan, don't we? We all need to let off steam, or we'd explode with frustration.

Sorry. I'm rambling. Maybe this is why Mr. Gates is always trying to shut me up. Because I dig myself a hole with my words and instead of knowing when to stop, I keep digging. You're probably adding two and two together right now. *Doesn't seem to like kids much. Freely admits to frustration with role. What would happen when she was cooped up with four kids and no adults to "let off steam" with?*

That's exactly what the police did. All those little throwaway remarks—all those unedifying facts. I could see the triumph on their faces every time I dropped one, and I watched them picking them up like bread crumbs, adding them to the weight of arguments against me.

But that's the thing, Mr. Wrexham. I could spin you a web of bullshit about what a perfect, caring, saintly person I am—but it would be just that. Bullshit. And I am not here to bullshit you. I want you to believe that—I want it more than anything in the world.

I am telling you the *truth*. The unvarnished, ugly truth. And it is all that. It *is* unpolished and unpleasant, and I don't pretend I acted like an angel. But *I didn't kill anyone*. I just fucking didn't.

I'm sorry. I didn't mean to swear again.

God, I am messing this up so badly. I have to keep a clear head—get this all straight in my head. It's like Mr. Gates says—I should stick to the facts.

Okay then. Fact. The advert. The advert is a fact, right?

The advert . . . with its amazing, dizzying, fabulous salary.

That should have been my first warning signal, you know. The salary. Because it was *stupidly* generous. I mean it would have been generous even for London, even for a live-out nanny. But for a nanny in someone's house, with free accommodation provided and all bills paid, even down to the car, it was ridiculous.

It was so ridiculous, in fact, that I half wondered if there had been a typo. Or something that they weren't saying—a child with significant behavioral needs maybe? But wouldn't they have mentioned that in the ad?

Six months ago I probably would have paused, frowned a little, and then passed on without thinking too much more about it. But then, six months ago I wouldn't have been looking at that web page in the first place. Six months ago I had a flatmate and a job I liked, and even the prospect of promotion. Six months ago I was in a pretty good place. But now . . . well, things were a bit different now.

My friend, the girl at Little Nippers I mentioned, had left to go traveling a couple of months ago. It hadn't seemed like the end of the world when she told me—to be honest, I found her quite annoying, her habit of loading the dishwasher but never actually switching it on, her endless Euro-pop disco hits, hissing through my bedroom wall when I was trying to sleep. I mean, I knew I'd miss her, but I didn't realize how much.

She had left her stuff in her room, and we'd agreed she'd pay half rent and I'd keep the room open for her. It seemed like a good compromise—I'd had a series of terrible flatmates before we found each other, and I wasn't keen to return to posting on Facebook Local and trying to weed out weirdos by text message and email, and it felt, in some small way, like an anchor—like a guarantee that she would come back.

But when the first flush of freedom wore off, and the novelty of having the whole place to myself and watching whatever I liked on the shared TV in the living room had started to fade a little, I found I was lonely. I missed the way she'd say "Wine o'clock, darling?" when we rolled in together from work. I missed sounding off to her about Val, the owner of Little Nippers, and sharing anecdotes about the worst of the parents. When I applied for a promotion and didn't get it, I went to the pub alone to drown my sorrows and ended up crying into my beer, thinking how different it would have been if she had still been here. We could have laughed about it together, she would have flipped Val the bird behind her back at work, and given her earthy belly laugh when Val turned around to almost catch her in the act.

I am not very good at failing, Mr. Wrexham, that's the thing. Exams. Dating. Jobs. Any kind of test, really. My instinct is always to aim low, save myself some pain. Or, in the case of dating, just don't aim at all, rather than risk being rejected. It's why I didn't go to university in the end. I had the grades, but I couldn't bear the idea of being turned down, the thought of them reading my applications with a scornful snigger. "Who does she think she is?"

Better to achieve perfect marks on an easy test than flunk a hard one, that was my motto. I've always known that about myself. But what I didn't know, until my flatmate left, was that I am also not very good at being alone. And I think it was that, more than anything, that pushed me out of my comfort zone and made me scroll down that advert, holding my breath, imagining what lay at the other end of it.

The police made a lot out of the salary when they first questioned me. But the truth is, the money wasn't the reason I applied for the post. It wasn't even really about my flatmate, though I can't deny, if she hadn't left, none of it would have happened. No, the real reason . . . well, you probably know what the real reason was. It was all over the papers, after all.

I called in sick to Little Nippers and spent the entire day working on a CV and getting together everything that I knew I would need to convince the Elincourts that I was the person they were looking for. Background check—check. First aid certificate—check. Spotless references—check, check, and check.

The only problem was the driving license. But I pushed the issue aside for the moment. I could cross that bridge when I came to it—if I got that far. Right now, I wasn't thinking past the interview.

I added a note to the cover letter, asking the Elincourts not to contact Little Nippers for a reference—I told them that I didn't want my current employers knowing that I was casting about for another job, which was true—and then I emailed it off to the address provided and held my breath and waited.

I had given myself the best possible chance of meeting them face-to-face. There was nothing else I could do now.

Those next few days were hard, Mr. Wrexham. Not as hard as the time I've spent in here, but hard enough. Because—God—I wanted that interview *so much*. I was only just beginning to realize how much. With every day that passed, my hopes ebbed a little more, and I had to fight off the urge to contact them again and beg for an answer. The only thing that stopped me was the knowledge that looking so desperate would certainly not help my case if they were still deciding.

But six days later it came, pinging into my email inbox.

To: supernanny1990@ymail.com

From: sandra.elincourt@elincourtandelincourt.com

Subject: Nanny position.

Elincourt. The surname alone was enough to make my stomach start churning like a washing machine. My fingers were shaking almost too much to open it, and my heart was hammering in my throat. Surely, surely they didn't often contact unsuccessful applicants. Surely an email must mean . . . ?

I clicked.

Hi, Rowan! Thank you so much for your application, and apologies for taking so long to get back to you. I have to admit, we were slightly taken by surprise at the volume of applications. Your CV was very impressive, and we would like to invite you to interview. Our house is rather remote, so we are happy to pay your train fare and can offer you a room in our house overnight, as you will not be able to make the trip from London in one day.

However, there is one thing I must make you aware of up front, in case it affects your enthusiasm for the post.

Since we bought Heatherbrae we have become aware of various superstitions surrounding the house's history. It is an old building and has had no more than the usual number of deaths and tragedies in its past, but for some reason these have resulted in some local tales of hauntings, etc. Unfortunately, this fact has upset some of our recent nannies, to the extent that four have resigned in the past fourteen months.

As you can imagine, this has been very disruptive for the children, not to mention extremely awkward for myself and my husband professionally.

For that reason we wanted to be completely honest about our predicament, and we are offering a generous salary in the hopes of attracting someone who can really commit to staying with our family for the long term—at least a year.

If you do not feel that is you, or if you feel at all concerned about the history of the house, please say so now, as we are very keen to minimize further disruption to the children. With that in mind, the salary will be made up of a basic stipend, paid monthly, and then a generous year-end bonus on the anniversary of employment.

If you are still keen to attend the interview, please let me know your availability for the forthcoming week.

Best wishes, and I look forward to meeting you.

Sandra Elincourt

I closed down the email and for a moment just sat there staring at the screen. Then I got up and did a little silent scream, punching the air in jubilation.

I had done it. I had *done* it.

I should have known it was too good to be true.

I had done it, Mr. Wrexham. I had cleared the first hurdle. But it *was* only the first hurdle. I had to get through the interview next—and without slipping up.

Almost exactly one week after I had opened the email from Sandra Elincourt, I was on a train up to Scotland, doing my very best impression of Rowan the Perfect Nanny. My normally bushy hair was brushed to a shine and tamed into a neat, jaunty ponytail, my nails were buffed, and my makeup unobtrusively on point, and I was wearing my best "approachable yet responsible, fun yet hardworking, professional yet not too proud to get down on my knees and clear up vomit" outfit—a neat tweed skirt and a white cotton fitted shirt with a cashmere cardigan over the top. Not quite a Norland nanny, but definitely a nod in that direction.

My stomach was flipping with butterflies. I had never done anything like this before. Not the nannying, I mean. Obviously. I had done that for nearly ten years, though mostly in nurseries rather than private homes.

But . . . *this*. Putting myself on the line. Setting myself up for rejection like this.

I wanted this *so* much. So much that I was almost scared of what I was going to find.

Much to my annoyance, the train was delayed, so it took nearly six hours to get to Edinburgh instead of the time-tabled four and a half, and when I got off the train at Waverley, stiffly flexing my legs, I found it was past five o'clock, and I had missed my connection by a good hour. Fortunately there was another train due, and while I waited, I texted Mrs. Elincourt, apologizing profusely and warning her that I would be late into Carn Bridge.

At last the train arrived—much smaller than the big intercity, and older too. I settled myself in a window seat, and as the train headed north I watched the countryside change from rolling green fields to the smoke-blue and purples of heathered moors, mountains rising behind, darker and bleaker with every station we passed. It was so beautiful it made me forget my irritation at being late. The sight of the huge hills rising inexorably around us somehow put everything else into perspective. I felt the hard lump of trepidation lodged in my gut start to soften. And something inside me began . . . I don't know, Mr. Wrexham. It was like I began to *hope.* To hope that this could truly be real.

I felt, in some twisted kind of way, like I was coming home.

We passed through stations with half-familiar names, Perth, Pitlochry, Aviemore, the sky growing darker all the time. At last I heard "Carn Bridge, next stop Carn Bridge," and the train pulled into a little Victorian station, and I got out. I stood on the platform, jumpy with nerves, wondering what to do.

Someone will meet you, Mrs. Elincourt's email had said. What did that mean? A taxi? Someone holding up a sign with my name?

I followed the small straggle of travelers to the exit and stood awkwardly while the other passengers dispersed to cars and waiting friends and relatives. My case was heavy, and I set it down by my feet as I looked up and down the dusky platform. The shadows were lengthening into evening, and the fleeting optimism I had felt on the train was starting to fade. What if Mrs. Elincourt hadn't got my text? She hadn't replied. Perhaps a prebooked taxi had come and gone hours ago and I'd been marked up as a no-show.

Suddenly the butterflies were back—and badly.

It was early June, but we were pretty far north, and the night air was surprisingly cold after the fuggy summer warmth of London. I found I was shivering as I pulled my coat around me, a cool wind whipping down from the hills. The platform had emptied, and I was all alone.

I felt a strong urge for a cigarette, but I knew from experience that turning up to an interview stinking of fags was not a great start. Instead, I looked at my phone. The train had arrived exactly on time—at least, exactly at the revised time I had told Mrs. Elincourt in my text. I would give it five minutes and then call her.

Five minutes passed, but I told myself I'd give it just five minutes more. I didn't want to start off on the wrong foot, badgering them if they were stuck in traffic.

Five more minutes ticked away, and I was just digging in my bag, looking for the printout of Mrs. Elincourt's email, when I saw a man walking down the platform, hands in pockets.

For a moment something seemed to stutter in my chest, but then he got closer and he looked up, his eyes meeting mine, and I realized, it couldn't possibly be *him*. He was much too young. Thirty, thirty-five at the outside. He was also—and even in my nervousness I couldn't help but clock it—extremely good-looking, in a scrubby unshaven kind of way, with tangled dark hair and a tall, lean frame.

He was wearing overalls, and as he came up to me he took his hands out of his pockets and I saw they were grained with something—soil, or engine oil, though he'd made an attempt to clean them. For a moment I thought perhaps he was an employee of the railway, but as he drew level with me he spoke.

"Rowan Caine?"

I nodded.

"I'm Jack Grant." He grinned, his mouth curling disarmingly at the edges, as though appreciating a private joke. His accent was Scottish but softer and more distinct than the Glaswegian girl I'd worked with after school. He pronounced his surname with a lilt, to rhyme with *ant,* not the longer English *aunt.* "I work up at Heatherbrae House. Sandra asked me to pick you up. Sorry I'm late."

"Hi," I said, suddenly shy for no reason I could pin down. I coughed, trying to think of something to say. "Um, it's fine. No problem."

"It's why I'm in such a state." He looked ruefully down at his hands. "She didn't tell me you'd be wanting a lift until half an hour ago. I was halfway through fixing the mower, but I was worried I'd miss your train, so I just set out, dirt and all. Can I take your case?"

"Honestly, it's fine." I picked up my case. "It's not heavy. Thank you for coming out."

He shrugged.

"No need to thank me; it's my job."

"You work for the Elincourts?"

"For Bill and Sandra, aye. I'm . . . well I don't know quite what my job title would be. I think Bill's got me on his company payroll as a driver, but odd-job man would cover it better. I do the gardening, fix the cars, run them in and out of Carn Bridge. You'll be the nanny?"

"Not yet," I said nervously, but he grinned sideways at me, and I smiled in spite of myself. There was something infectious about his expression. "I mean, that's the position I'm going for, yes. Have they had many other interviewees?"

"Two or three. You're doing better than the first one. She didn't speak much English; I don't know who she got to write her application, but from what Sandra said it wasnae her."

"Oh." Somehow his words made me feel better. I'd been imagining a parade of starched and fiercely competent Mary Poppins types. I stood straighter, smoothing the wrinkles out of my tweed skirt. "Good. I mean, not good for her, I suppose. Good for me."

We were outside the station now, walking across the little sparsely populated car park, towards a long black car on the opposite side of the road. Jack clicked something on a fob in his pocket and the lights flashed and the doors opened, shooting up like bat wings, making my jaw drop involuntarily. I thought of my stepfather's bland gray Volvo, his pride and joy, and gave a short laugh. Jack grinned again.

"It's a bit conspicuous, isn't it? It's a Tesla. Electric. I don't know if it would have been my choice of vehicle, but Bill . . . well, you'll see. He's into technology."

"Is he?" The words were meaningless as a response, but somehow . . . just the knowledge of this small thing was a little nugget, a connection to this faceless man.

Jack stood back as I put my case into the rear of the car.

"Do you want to ride in the back, or up front?" he asked, and I felt my face color up.

"Oh, in front, please!"

The thought of sitting regally in the back, treating him like a chauffeur, was enough to make me squirm.

"The views are better anyway" was all he said, but he clicked something that made the batwing doors at the rear of the car swing closed, and then held open the front passenger door.

"After you, Rowan."

For a moment I didn't move, almost forgetting who he was speaking to. Then, with a start, I pulled myself together and climbed into the car.

I had known, on some level, I suppose, that the Elincourts were rich. I mean, they had a driver slash odd-job man, and they were offering fifty-five grand for a nanny position, so they must have had cash to spare, but it wasn't until we reached Heatherbrae House that I began to realize quite *how* rich they were.

The knowledge gave me a strange feeling.

I don't care about the money, I wanted to tell Jack as we stopped at a high steel gate, which swung slowly inwards, clearly sensing some sort of transmitter in the car. But it wasn't completely true.

How much do Sandra and Bill make? I found myself wondering.

The Tesla was eerily silent as we drove up the long winding drive, the sound of the gravel beneath the wheels louder by far than the hushed electric engine.

"Jesus," I muttered under my breath as we rounded yet another bend and still no house was in sight. Jack shot me a sideways look.

"Big place, isn't it?"

"Just a bit."

Land must be cheaper round here than down south, of course, but it couldn't be *that* cheap. We bumped across a bridge over a quick-running burn, the waters dark with peat, and then drove through a cluster of pines. I thought I saw a flash of something scarlet through the trees and craned to look, but it was getting dark, and I wasn't completely sure if I had imagined the movement.

At last we came out of the shelter of the trees and into a clearing, and I saw Heatherbrae House for the first time.

I had been expecting something ostentatious, a McMansion, maybe, or a sprawling log-built ranch. But that wasn't what greeted me at all. The house in front of me was a modest Victorian lodge, foursquare, like a child's drawing of a house, with a glossy black door in the center and windows on each side. It was not big but solidly built of granite blocks, with lush Virginia creeper rambling up one side of it, and I could not have put my finger on exactly why, but it exuded warmth and luxury and *comfort.*

Dusk had fallen, and as Jack turned off the engine of the Tesla and extinguished the headlights, the only illumination from all around was the stars, and the lamps from inside the house itself, shining out across the gravel. It looked like something from a sentimental illustration, those nostalgia-soaked twinkly photographs on the front of the jigsaws that my grandmother had loved.

Soft gray stone, lichened and weathered, golden lamps shining out through the clean rippled glass of the windows, overblown roses scattering their petals in the dusk—it was almost too perfect, unbearably perfect, in some strange way.

As I stepped out of the car and the cool evening air settled around me, pine-scented and sharp and clear as mineral water, I felt suddenly choked with longing for this life and all that it represented. The contrast with my own upbringing—the cheerless boxy suburbia of my parents' 1950s identikit bungalow, every room except my own neat as a pin, yet all utterly devoid of any character or comfort—was almost too bitter to bear, and it was more to banish the thought than because I was ready to meet Sandra that I stepped forward into the shelter of the covered porch.

Instantly something felt off-kilter. But what was it? The door in front of me was traditional enough, paneled wood painted a rich glossy black, but something seemed wrong, *missing,* even. It took me a second to notice what it was. There was no keyhole.

The realization was somehow unsettling. Such a small detail, and yet without it I was left wondering—was the door a fake? Should I go round the other side of the house?

There was no knocker either, and I looked over my shoulder, seeking Jack's guidance as to how I should announce myself. But he was still inside the car, checking something on the big illuminated touch screen that served as the dashboard controls.

I turned back and put out my hand, ready to rap on the wood with my knuckles, but as I did so, something embedded in the wall to the left of the door caught my eye. A ghostly illuminated icon in the shape of a bell had appeared from nowhere, shining out of what had seemed to be solid stone, and I saw that what I had taken for simply part of the wall was actually a cleverly inlaid panel. I went to press it, but it must have been motion sensitive, for I had not even made contact when a chime sounded from inside the house.

I blinked, suddenly thinking of Jack's comment in the car. *Bill . . . well, you'll see. He's into technology.* Was this what he had meant?

"Rowan! Hello!" The female voice seemed to come out of nowhere, and I jumped, looking around for a camera, a microphone, a grille to speak into. There was none. Or none that I could see.

"Um . . . y-yes," I said, speaking to the air in general, feeling like a complete fool. "Hi. Is that . . . Sandra?"

"Yes! I'm just getting changed. I'll be down in ten seconds. Sorry to keep you standing around."

There was no *click* to tell me that a receiver had been replaced, or any other indication that the conversation was over, but the panel faded back to blank and I stood waiting, feeling curiously both watched and ignored.

Finally, after what felt like a long time but was probably less than thirty seconds, there was a sudden cacophony of barking and the front door opened. Two black Labradors shot out, followed by a slim honey-blond woman of perhaps forty, laughing and snatching ineffectually at their collars as they ran rings around her, yelping joyfully.

"Hero! Claude! Get back here!"

But the dogs paid no attention, leaping up at me as I took a couple of steps backwards. One of them shoved its nose into my crotch, painfully hard, and I found myself laughing nervously, trying to push its muzzle away, thinking of my one spare pair of tights in my bag and gritting my teeth in case the dog ripped the ones I was wearing. It jumped up at me again, and I sneezed, feeling an itching begin in the back of my skull. Shit. Had I brought my inhaler?

"Hero!" the woman said again. "Hero, *stop* it." She stepped out of the shelter of the porch and towards me, holding out her hand. "You must be Rowan. Calm *down*, Hero, honestly!" She managed to clip the lead she was holding on to the dog's collar and dragged it back beside her. "Sorry, sorry, she's so friendly. Do you mind dogs?"

"Not at all," I said, though it was only partly true. I didn't mind dogs exactly, but they triggered my asthma if I didn't take my antihistamines. Besides, asthma or no asthma, I didn't want their noses shoved between my legs in a professional situation. I felt my chest tighten, though out here it couldn't be anything other than psychosomatic. "Good boy," I said, with all the enthusiasm I could muster, patting it on the head.

"Good girl, actually. Hero's a bitch; Claude is the boy. They're brother and sister."

"Good girl," I amended half-heartedly. Hero licked my hand enthusiastically, and I stifled the impulse to wipe my palm on my skirt. Behind me I heard a door slam, followed by Jack's feet crunching across the gravel, and it was with some relief that I watched the dogs turn their attention to him, woofing happily as he retrieved my case from the back of the car.

"Here's your case, Rowan. Pleasure meeting you," he said as he set it down beside me, and then, turning to Mrs. Elincourt, "I'll be getting back to fixing the mower, if it's all right, Sandra. Unless you need me for anything else?"

"What's that?" Mrs. Elincourt said distractedly, and then she nodded. "Oh, the mower. Yes, please do. Can you get it working again?"

"I hope so. If not, I'll call Aleckie Brown in the morning."

"Thank you, Jack," Sandra said, and shook her head as he walked away round the side of the building, his silhouette tall and square-shouldered against the evening sky. "Honestly, that man is *such* a treasure. I don't know what we'd do without him. He and Jean have been absolute rocks—it's what makes the whole nanny business all the more inexplicable."

The whole nanny business. There it was then. The first reference to the odd fact that had been at the back of my mind all the way up here: four women had already walked out of this post.

In the initial flush of exultation I hadn't really worried very much about that part of Sandra's letter. In the context of getting an interview it hadn't seemed very important, but as I reread the emails and travel instructions on the way up to Carn Bridge, I had stumbled over it again, and this time the remark had stuck out—its strangeness and faint absurdity. I had spent some time thinking about it during the long, boring hours on the train, turning her words over in my mind, torn between a desire to laugh and something more puzzled and uneasy.

I *didn't* believe in the supernatural—I should say that up front, Mr. Wrexham. And so the legends of the house didn't bother me at all; in fact the whole idea of nannies and servants driven out by mysterious spooky happenings seemed more than a little ridiculous—almost Victorian.

But the fact was that four women had left the Elincourts' employment in the last year. Having the bad luck to engage one nervous, superstitious employee seemed quite likely. Getting four in a row seemed . . . less so.

Which meant that there was a strong chance that something else was going on, and all sorts of possibilities had run through my mind on the long journey up to Scotland. I had been half expecting to find that Heatherbrae was a draughty ruin of a house, or that Mrs. Elincourt was a very difficult employer. So far, at least, that didn't seem to be the case. But I was reserving judgment.

Inside Heatherbrae the dogs were, if anything, more boisterous and excited to find a stranger admitted into the house, and at last Mrs. Elincourt gave up trying to control them and dragged them both by their collars through to a room at the back to shut them up.

As she disappeared, I hastily fumbled my inhaler out of my pocket and took a surreptitious puff, then waited for her just inside the front door, feeling the atmosphere of the house settle around me.

It wasn't a big house, just a family home. And the furnishings weren't ostentatious, just incredibly comfortable and well-built. But there was a sense of . . . of *money*. That's the only way I can put it. From the polished wooden banister and deep peat-colored carpet runner that curved around the long, elegant flight, to the squashy bronze velvet armchair squeezed beneath the stairs and the frayed Persian rug spread across the worn flagstones in the hall. From the slow, sure tick of a beautiful grandfather clock standing beside the long window, to the deep patina of age on the refectory table against the wall, everything conspired into an almost overwhelming sense of luxury. It wasn't that it was neat exactly—there were piles of newspapers scattered by the sofa, and a child's Wellington boot left abandoned by the front door. But there was not a single thing that felt wrong. The sofa cushions were plump with feathers, there were no drifts of dog hairs in the corners of the room, or muddy scuffs on the stairs. Even the *smell* was right—not a trace of wet dog or stale cooking, just beeswax polish, woodsmoke, and the faintest hint of dried rose petals.

It was . . . it was *perfect*, Mr. Wrexham. It was the house I would have made for myself if I had the money and the taste and the time to create something so deeply, infinitely welcoming and warm.

I was just thinking all this when I heard a door shut and saw Sandra coming back from the far side of the hallway, shaking her heavy, honey-colored hair out of her face and smiling.

"Oh dear, sorry, they don't see many strangers, so they do get terribly excited when new faces appear. They aren't like this all the time, I do assure you. Let's start again. Hello, Rowan, I'm Sandra."

She held out her hand for the second time, slim and strong and tanned, and studded with three or four expensive-looking rings. I shook it, feeling her fingers grip mine with unusual firmness, and returned her smile.

"Right, well, you must be famished and rather tired after such a long trip. You came up from London, is that right?"

I nodded.

"Let me show you to your room and then when you've changed and made yourself comfortable, come down and we'll have something to eat. I can't believe it's so late. Past nine already. Was your journey awful?"

"Not awful, no," I said. "Just slow. There was some kind of points failure at York, so I missed my connection. I'm really sorry; I'm usually very punctual."

That at least was true. Whatever my other flaws and failings, I'm very rarely late.

"I got your text. So sorry I didn't reply. I didn't see it at first; I was up to my elbows in the kids' bath time when it came through, and I only just managed to rush out and tell Jack to collect you. I hope you weren't waiting at the station for ages."

It wasn't a question exactly—more of a remark, but I answered anyway.

"Not too long. Are the children in bed then?"

"The three youngest, yes. Maddie is eight, Ellie is five, and the baby, Petra, is just eighteen months, so they're all in bed."

"And your other child?" I asked, thinking of the flash of red I'd seen between the trees on the drive up. "You said in the advert you had four?"

"Rhiannon is fourteen going on twenty-four. She's at boarding school—not really our choice; I'd prefer to have her at home, but there's no secondaries close enough. The nearest day school is more than an hour's drive, and it would just be too much every day. So she boards over near Inverness and comes home most weekends. It breaks my heart a little bit every time she goes, but she seems to enjoy it."

If you want her at home that badly, why don't you move? I thought.

"So I won't meet her?" I asked. Sandra shook her head.

"No, unfortunately not, but to be honest your time would be spent mostly with the little ones. Anyway—it means we can have a lovely chat now, and you can get to know the kids tomorrow. Oh, and I'm afraid my husband—Bill—can't be here either."

"Oh?" It was a surprise—a shock even. I wasn't going to meet him, then. I had been so sure that someone would want to meet the person they were considering hiring to look after their children . . . but I tried to keep my face neutral. Nonjudgmental. "Oh, that's a shame."

"Yes, he's away, working. It's been a pretty horrendous struggle, I have to say, with so many nannies leaving this year. The children are understandably very destabilized, and the business has really suffered. We're both architects in a two-man firm. Well, one man, one woman!" She flashed a smile, showing very white, perfectly even teeth. "It's just me and him, and it means that in busy periods when we've got more than one project going on, we can get terribly stretched. We try to juggle it so that there's always one of us around, but with Katya leaving—she was our last nanny—it's just been chaos. I've had to pick up all the slack here, and Bill's been trying to hold the business together—I need to be completely honest and say that whoever does get the post isn't going to get a very smooth introductory period. Normally I try to work from home for the first month or so to make sure everything is going okay, but that just won't be possible this time. Bill can't be in two places at once, and we have projects that desperately need me to be there and on the ground. We need someone very experienced who isn't going to be fazed by being left with the kids early on, and they need to be able to start ASAP." She looked at me, a little anxiously, a furrow between her strongly marked brows. "Do you think that describes you?"

I swallowed. Time to shed my doubts and step into the role of Rowan the Perfect Nanny.

"Definitely," I said, and the confidence in my voice almost convinced myself. "I mean, you've seen my CV—"

"We were very impressed with your CV," Sandra said, and I gave a little blushing nod of acknowledgment. "Quite frankly, it's one of the most impressive ones we've had. You tick all the boxes we need in terms of experience with the various age groups. But what's your notice period like? I mean obviously"—she was talking quickly now, as if slightly uncomfortable—"*obviously* getting the *right* nanny is the most important thing, that goes without saying. But actually we do need someone who can start pretty much . . . well, pretty much now, if I'm being completely honest. So it would be disingenuous of me to pretend that's not a factor."

"My notice period is four weeks." I saw Sandra's mouth twist in a little worried moue—and added hastily, "But I think I could probably negotiate an earlier finish. I have quite a bit of annual leave left . . . and I'd have to sit down with a calendar and do the sums, but I think there's a good chance I could get it down to two weeks. Maybe less."

If Little Nippers were prepared to be flexible, that was. God knows, they hadn't given me much reason for loyalty.

I didn't miss the flash of hope and relief that crossed Sandra's face. But then she seemed to realize where we were.

"Look at me, keeping you talking in the hallway. It's hardly fair for me to be interviewing you before you've even got your coat off! Let me show you to your room, and then we can retreat to the kitchen and have a proper talk while you get some food inside you."

She turned and began to make her way up the long curving flight of stairs, her feet silent on the thick, velvet-soft carpet. At the first landing she stopped and put her finger to her lips. I paused, taking in the wide sweep of space, the little table with a vase of blush peonies just beginning to shed their petals. A corridor disappeared off into semidarkness, lit only by a rose-tinted night-light plugged into a wall socket. Half a dozen doors led off from it. The one at the far end had wonky wooden letters stuck on it, and as my eyes got used to the low lighting, I made out the words. *Princess Ellie* and *Queen Maddie.* The door closest to the stairwell was slightly open, a night-light shining dimly in the recesses of the room. I could hear a baby's soft snorting breath coming through.

"The kids are asleep," Sandra whispered. "At least, I hope so. I heard some pattering earlier, but it all seems to be quiet now! Maddie in particular is a very light sleeper, so I do have to tiptoe around a bit. Bill and I sleep on this floor, but Rhi sleeps upstairs. This way."

At the top of the second flight, three more doors led off a slightly smaller landing. The middle one was open, and inside I saw a small cupboard housing a jumble of mops and brooms and a cordless Hoover charging on the wall. Sandra shut it hastily.

The door to the left of it was closed and had *FUCK OFF, KEEP OUT OR YOU DIE* written across the paneled wood in what looked like smeared red lipstick.

"That's Rhiannon's room," Sandra said with a slight lift of her eyebrows that might have indicated anything from amusement to resignation. "This one"—she put her hand on the knob of the door to the far right of the stairs—"is yours. Well, I mean—" She stopped, looking a little flustered. "I mean, it's where we always put the nanny, and it's where you'll be sleeping tonight. Sorry, don't want to be too presumptuous!"

I gave a slightly nervous attempt at a laugh as she opened the door. It was dark inside, but instead of groping for a switch Sandra pulled out her phone. I was expecting her to turn on the torch, but instead she pressed something, and the lights inside the room flickered into life.

It wasn't just the main overhead light—in fact that was turned down very low, giving off nothing but a kind of faint golden glow. The reading light by the bed had come on too, as well as a standing lamp next to a little table by the window and some fairy lights twined around the bedhead.

My surprise must have shown on my face, because Sandra gave a delighted laugh.

"Pretty cool, isn't it! We do have switches, obviously—well, panels, but this is a smart house. All the heating and lights and so on can be controlled from our phones." She swiped at something, and the main light grew suddenly much brighter, and then dimmer again, and across the room a light turned on in the en suite bathroom and then flicked off again.

"It's not just lighting . . . ," Sandra said, and she pulled across another screen and tapped an icon, and music started playing softly out of an invisible speaker. Miles Davis, I thought, though I wasn't very well up on jazz.

"There's also a voice option, but I find that a bit creepy, so I don't often use it. Still, I can show you." She coughed, and then said in a slightly artificial raised tone, "Music off!"

There was a pause, and then the Miles Davis shut off abruptly.

"Obviously you can also control the settings from the panel." She pressed something on the wall to demonstrate, and a white panel lit up briefly as the curtains on the window opposite swished closed and then opened again.

"Wow," I said. I really wasn't sure what to say. On the one hand it was impressive. On the other hand . . . I found myself coming back to Sandra's word. *Creepy.*

"I know," Sandra said with a little laugh. "It's a bit ridiculous, I do realize. But being architects it's a professional duty to try out all the cool gadgets. Anyway . . ." She looked at her phone again, checking the clock this time. "I *must* stop talking and get the supper out of the oven, and you must take off your coat and unpack. Shall I see you downstairs in . . . fifteen minutes?"

"Sounds good," I said, a little faintly, and she gave me a grin and disappeared, closing the door behind her.

After she had gone I set my case on the floor and crossed the room to the window. Outside it was completely dark, but by pressing my face to the glass and cupping my hands to my temples I could just make out a star-spattered sky and the dark shapes of mountains against the horizon. There were almost no lights.

The realization of how isolated this place really was made me shiver, just for a moment, and I turned my back on the window and set about surveying the room.

What struck me instantly was that it was an odd mixture of traditional and modern. The window was pure Victorian, right down to the brass latch and the slightly rippled glass panes. But the lights were twenty-first century—no boring bulb in the center of the ceiling. Instead, there was a plethora of spotlights, lamps, and uplighters, each focused on a different part of the room, and tuned to a different warmth and brightness. There were no radiators either; in fact I couldn't see where the heat was coming from, but clearly there must have been some source—the night was cool enough for my breath to have left white mist on the windowpane. Underfloor heating? Some kind of concealed vent?

The furniture was more conservative, with a strong air of an expensive country-house hotel. Opposite me, facing the window, was a king-size bed covered with the ubiquitous array of brocade cushions, and beneath the window was a small plumply stuffed sofa, with a little table beside it—the perfect space for entertaining a friend, or having a drink. There were chests of drawers, a desk, two upright chairs, and an upholstered blanket chest at the foot of the bed that could have done duty either as storage or additional seating. Doors led off to each side, and opening one at random I found a walk-in closet filled with empty racks and shelves, spotlights flickering into life above the bare shelves automatically as I pulled open the door. I tried the second one, but it seemed to be locked.

The third was ajar, and I remembered it was the one that Sandra had lit up to show the bathroom inside. Venturing in, I saw there was a panel on the wall, like the one Sandra had pressed by the main door to the room. I touched it, not entirely expecting it to work, but it glowed into life, displaying a confusing configuration of icons and squares. I pressed one at random, not completely sure what was going to happen, and the lights became slowly brighter, revealing a state-of-the-art wet room with a huge rainwater shower and a concrete vanity unit the size of my kitchen counter. There was nothing faux Victorian about this room at all. It was space-age in its complexity, sleek and modern in its styling, and had more glamour in one metro tile than most bathrooms possessed in their entirety.

I thought of my bathroom at home—hair in the rusting plughole, dirty towels kicked into the corner, makeup stains on the mirror.

God, I wanted this.

Before . . . I don't know what I had wanted before. I had focused on nothing except getting here and meeting the Elincourts and finding out what was at the end of this advert. That was it. I honestly hadn't even thought about actually getting the job.

Now . . . now I *wanted* it. Not just the fifty-five thousand a year, but everything. I wanted this beautiful house and this gorgeous room, right down to the sumptuous, marble-tiled shower, with its sparkling limescale-free glass and polished chrome fittings.

More than that, I wanted to be part of this family.

If I had had any doubts about what I was doing here, this room had crushed them.

For a long, long moment, I just stood at the vanity unit, my hands splayed on the counter, staring at myself in the mirror. The face that stared back at me was somehow unsettling. Not the expression exactly, but something in my eyes. There was something there—a kind of hunger. I must not look too desperate in front of Sandra. Keen, yes. But desperation—the kind of hungry desperation I saw staring back at me now—that was nothing but off-putting.

Slowly, I smoothed down my hair, licked a finger, wetted an unruly brow back into place. Then my hand went to my necklace.

I wore it every day—had done so ever since I had left school and jewelry was no longer banned by uniform codes. Even as a child I'd worn it at weekends and whenever I could get away with it, ignoring my mother's sighs and her comments about cheap nasty rubbish that turned your skin green. It had been a present for my first birthday, and now, after more than two decades, it felt like part of myself, something I barely even noticed, even when I reached to play with it in moments of stress or boredom.

Now I noticed it.

An ornate silver *R* on the end of a dangling chain. Or rather, as my mother had so frequently reminded me, not silver, but silver plate, something that was becoming more and more apparent, as the brassy metal beneath shone through where I had rubbed the pendant absentmindedly with my fingers.

There was no reason to take it off. It wasn't inappropriate. The chances of anyone even noticing it were very low. And yet . . .

Slowly, I reached round to the back of my neck and undid the clasp.

Then I put on a slick of lip gloss, straightened my skirt, tightened my ponytail, and prepared to go back downstairs to Sandra Elincourt and give the interview of my life.

When I got downstairs, Sandra was nowhere to be seen, but I could smell some kind of delicious, savory scent coming from the far side of the hallway. Remembering that that was where Sandra had ushered the dogs, I moved forward, cautiously. But when I pushed open the door I found I had stepped into another world.

It was like the back of the house had been sliced off brutally and grafted onto a startling modernist box, almost aggressively twenty-first century. Soaring metal beams went up to a glass roof, and beneath my feet the Victorian encaustic tiles of the hall had abruptly stopped, replaced by a poured concrete floor, polished to a dull sheen. It looked like a combination of a brutalist cathedral and an industrial kitchen. In the center was a shiny metal breakfast bar, surrounded by chrome stools, dividing the room into the bright kitchen area, and beyond it the dimly lit dining space, where a long concrete-topped table ran the length of the room.

In the middle was Sandra, standing in front of a monstrous free-standing stove, the largest I had ever seen, and ladling some kind of casserole into two bowls. She looked up as I came in.

"Rowan! Listen, I'm so sorry, but I forgot to ask, you're not veggie, are you?"

"No," I said. "No, I eat pretty much anything."

"Oh phew, that's a relief, because we've got beef casserole and not a lot else! I was just frantically wondering if I had time to do a baked potato. Which reminds me." She walked across to the huge steel fridge, tapped an invisible button on the fridge door with the knuckle of one hand, and said, enunciating her words clearly, "Happy, order potatoes, please."

"Adding potatoes to your shopping list," replied a robotic voice, and a screen lit up, showing a typed list of groceries. "Eat happy, Sandra!"

The shock of it made me want to laugh, but I pushed down the urge and instead watched as Sandra put both bowls on the long table, along with a crusty loaf on a board and a little dish of something like sour cream. The bowls were bone china and looked as if they were probably Victorian, hand-painted with delicate little flowers and embellished with gold leaf details. Somehow the contrast between the mathematically severe modernist lines of the glass room and the fragile antique bowls was almost absurd, and I felt slightly off-balance. It was like the rest of the house in reverse—Victorian stuffiness punctuated by splashes of space-age modernity. Here, the modernism had taken over, but the bowls and the heavy floral whirls of the silver cutlery were a reminder of what lay behind the closed door.

"There we go," Sandra said unnecessarily as she sat down and waved me to the seat opposite her. "Beef stew. Help yourself to bread to soak up the juices, and that's horseradish crème fraîche, which is very nice stirred in."

"It smells amazing," I said truthfully, and Sandra shook back her hair and gave a little smile that tried to look modest but really said, *I know.*

"Well, it's the stove, you know. A La Cornue. It's almost impossible to screw up—you just pop the ingredients in and forget about it! I do miss a gas range sometimes, but we're not on the mains here, so it's all electric. The burners are induction."

"I've never used an induction burner," I said, eyeing the stove rather doubtfully. It was a beast of a thing, six feet of metal doors, knobs, drawers, and handles, and on top a smooth cooking surface that seemed to be zoned in ways I couldn't even begin to guess at.

"They take a bit of getting used to," Sandra said. "But I promise you, they're really very intuitive to use. The flat plate in the middle is a teppanyaki. I was rather skeptical about the cost, but Bill was insistent, and I have to admit, it was worth every penny and then some."

"Oh," I said. "I see," though I didn't really. What on earth was a teppanyaki? I took a mouthful of the stew—which was thick and rich and delicious, the kind of meal I never had the time or organization to cook for myself at home—and let Sandra plop a blob of crème fraîche on top and ply me with a crusty chunk of bread. There was a bottle of red wine already open on the table, and she poured us out two glasses in beautifully etched Victorian goblets and pushed one across to me.

"Now, would you rather eat first and then talk, or shall we get started?"

"I . . ." I looked down at my plate, and then gave a mental shrug. No point in putting it off. I tugged my skirt down and sat up a little straighter on the metal stool. "Get started I suppose. What would you like to know?"

"Well, your CV was very comprehensive, and *very* impressive. I already contacted your previous employer—what was her name? Grace Devonshire?"

"Er . . . yes, that's right," I said.

"And she couldn't say enough good things about you. I hope you don't mind me taking up references before the interview, but I've been bitten a few times with unsuitable candidates, and I think there's no point in wasting everyone's time dragging you up here only to fail at the last fence. But Grace was positively gushing about you. The Harcourts seem to have moved, but I also spoke to Mrs. Grainger, and she was very complimentary as well."

"You didn't contact Little Nippers, did you?" I said slightly uneasily, but she shook her head.

"No, I completely understand. It's not always easy job hunting in an existing post. But perhaps you could tell me about your employment there?"

"Well, it's pretty much like I explained on the CV really—I've been there for two years, in charge of the baby room. I wanted a change from one-family nannying, and a nursery seemed like a good option. It's been excellent experience having a bit more managerial responsibility and having to organize staff schedules and stuff, but quite honestly I've found I miss the family feel of nannying. I love the children, but you don't get to spend as much one-on-one time with them as you do with a private position. What was stopping me making a change was the idea of taking a step backwards in terms of pay and responsibility, but your post seems like it might be the challenge I'm looking for."

I had rehearsed the speech inside my head, on the train on the way up, and now the words rattled out with a practiced authenticity. I had been to enough interviews to know that this was the key—to explain why you wanted to leave your current post without running down your existing employer and looking like a disloyal employee. But my—slightly massaged—version of events seemed to have done the trick, for Mrs. Elincourt was nodding sympathetically.

"I can quite imagine."

"Plus, of course," I added, this on the spur of the moment, for I had not thought this particular line through, "I'm keen to get out of London. It's so busy and polluted, I guess I'm just looking for a change of scenery."

"That I can *quite* understand," Mrs. Elincourt said with a smile. "Bill and I had the same long night of the soul a few years back. Rhiannon was about eight or nine and we were beginning to think about secondaries. Maddie was a toddler, and I was so sick of pushing her around dirty parks and having to check for needles in the sandpit before I let her play. This just seemed like the perfect chance to break away completely—build a new life, find a really super independent school for Rhi."

"And are you glad you made the move?"

"Oh, totally. It was tough on the children at the time, of course, but it was definitely the right thing. We adore Scotland—and we never wanted to be that kind of family who buys a second home and then puts it on Airbnb for nine months of the year. We wanted to really *live* here, become part of the community, you know?"

I nodded, as though second-home dilemmas were part of my everyday existence.

"Heatherbrae House was a real project," Sandra continued. "It had been totally neglected for decades, lived in by a very eccentric old man who went into a care home and then allowed it to fall into disrepair until his death. Dry rot everywhere, burst pipes, dodgy electrics—it was a case of really stripping it back to the bones and completely revamping it. Two years of absolute grind, reconfiguring the rooms and doing everything from rewiring to putting in a new cesspit. But it was worth it—and of course it made a wonderful case study for the business. We have a whole folder of before and after, and it really shows that good architecture can be as much about bringing out the spirit of an existing house as creating a new one from scratch. Though we do that too, of course. Our specialty is vernacular architecture."

I nodded as though I had a clue what this meant and took a gulp of wine.

"But that's enough about me and the house—what about yourself?" Sandra said, with the air of getting down to business. "Tell me a bit about what attracted you to nannying?"

Wow. That was a big question. About a dozen images flashed through my mind, all at once. My parents, shouting at me for getting Play-Doh in the carpet tiles at age six. Age nine, my mother, shaking her head over my report card, not bothering to hide her disappointment. At twelve, the school play no one bothered to come to. Age sixteen, "What a shame you didn't revise more for history," instead of congratulations on the As I got in maths, English, and science. Eighteen years of not being good enough, not being the daughter I was supposed to be, eighteen years of not measuring up.

"Well . . ." I felt myself flounder. This was not part of the story I had practiced, and now I cursed myself for it. It was an obvious question, one I should have prepared. "Well, I suppose . . . I mean . . . I just like kids." It was lame. Very lame. And also not completely true. But as the words left my mouth, I realized something else. Sandra was still smiling, but there was a certain neutrality in her expression that had not been there before, and suddenly I understood why. A woman on the cusp of her thirties, going on about how much she likes kids . . .

I hurried to repair my mistake.

"But I have to say, I'm in awe of anyone who wants to be a parent. I'm definitely not ready for that yet!"

Bingo. I could not miss the flash of relief that crossed Sandra's face, though it was quickly suppressed.

"Not that it's an option right now anyway," I said, feeling confident enough for a little joke, "since I'm firmly single."

"So . . . no ties to London then?"

"Not really. I have friends of course, but my parents retired abroad a few years back. In fact, once I've sorted things out with Little Nippers there's really nothing keeping me in London. I could take up a new post almost straightaway."

I carefully avoided saying *your post,* not wanting to seem like I was making assumptions that I would get the job, but Sandra was smiling and nodding enthusiastically.

"Yes, as you can probably tell from our talk earlier, I'd be lying if I said that wasn't a significant factor. We're coming up to the summer holidays, and we absolutely *must* get someone in the position before the schools break up or I'll be sunk. Plus there's a really, *really* important trade fair in a few weeks, and both Bill and I really need to be there."

"What's your deadline?"

"Rhi breaks up towards the end of June, which is what . . . about three or four weeks? But the trade fair begins the weekend before she breaks up. The truth is, the sooner the better. Two weeks is doable. Three weeks is . . . well, just about okay. Four weeks would be starting to get into disaster zone. You said your notice period is four weeks?"

I nodded. "Yes, but I was figuring it out while I unpacked, and I have at least eight days holiday owing, so I can definitely get it down to just over two weeks, if I factor in my leave, and maybe even less. I think they'll be prepared to negotiate."

In actual fact, I had no idea how helpful they would be, and my suspicion was, not very. Janine, my boss and current head of the baby room, wasn't my biggest fan. I didn't think she'd be particularly sorry to see me go, but I didn't think she'd bend over backwards to help me. However, there were ways and means—nursery workers weren't allowed to come into work for forty-eight hours after a vomiting bug. I was prepared to have a lot of vomiting bugs around the middle of June. Again, though, I didn't say that to Sandra. For some reason, no one wants a nanny with a flexible moral code, even when she's flexing it to help them out.

As we ate, Sandra ran through a few more interviewing-by-numbers questions of the kind I had come to expect—outline your strengths and weaknesses . . . give me an example of a difficult situation and how you handled it . . . all the usual suspects. I had answered these before in a dozen other interviews, so my responses were practiced, just slightly tweaked for what I thought Sandra in particular would want to hear. My standard answer to the question about a difficult situation concerned a little boy who had come to his settling-in day at Little Nippers covered in bruises—and the way I had dealt with the parents over the subsequent safeguarding concerns. It went down well with nurseries, but I didn't think Sandra would want to hear about me snitching on parents to the authorities. Instead, I gave a different story, about a little bullying four-year-old at a previous post, and the way I had managed to trace it back to her own fears over starting primary school.

As I talked she looked through the papers I had bought with me, the background check, the first aid certificates. They were all in order, of course; I knew that, but I still felt a little flutter of nerves beneath my ribs as she reviewed them. My chest tightened, though whether that was down to nerves or the dogs, I couldn't quite tell, and I pushed down the urge to pull out my inhaler and take a puff.

"And the driving license?" she asked as I finished my anecdote about the four-year-old. I put down my fork onto the smooth polished concrete top of the table and took a deep breath.

"Ah, right, yes. I'm afraid that's a problem. I do have a full UK driving license and it's clean, but the actual card was stolen last month when I lost my purse. I've ordered a new one, but they wanted an updated photo and it's taking an age to come through. But I promise you, I *can* drive."

That last part was true after all. I crossed my fingers, and to my relief she nodded and moved on to something about my professional ambitions. Did I want to get any additional qualifications. Where did I see myself in a year's time. It was the second question that really mattered; I could tell that from the way Sandra set down her wineglass and actually looked at me as I answered.

"In a year's time?" I said slowly, frantically trying to figure out what she wanted to hear from me. Did she want ambition? Commitment? Personal development? A year was a funny length of time to choose; most interviewers said five years, and the question had thrown me. What was she testing?

At last I made up my mind.

"Well . . . you know I want this job, Sandra, and to be honest, in a year's time I would hope to be here. If you were to offer me this position, I wouldn't want to uproot myself from London and all my friends just for a short-term post. When I work for a family, I want to think it's a long-term relationship, both for me and the kids. I want to really get to know them, see them grow up a little bit. If you'd asked me where I saw myself in five years . . . well, that's a different question. And I'd probably give you a different answer. I'm ambitious—I'd like to do a master's in childcare or child psychology at some point. But a year—any post I took now, I would definitely want to think of it lasting longer than a year, for all our sakes."

Sandra's face broke into a huge grin, and I knew—I just *knew* that I had given the right answer, the one she had been hoping for. But was it enough to get me the post? I didn't honestly know.

We chatted for about another hour or so, Sandra refilling my glass along with her own, though at some point after the second or third top-up I had the sense to put my hand over the goblet and shake my head.

"Better not. I'm not really much of a drinker; wine goes straight to my head."

It wasn't completely true. I could hold my wine as well as most of my friends, but I knew that another glass would probably see me throw caution to the wind, and then it would be harder to keep my answers diplomatic and on message. Stories would get tangled, I'd get names and dates in a muddle, and I'd wake up tomorrow with my head in my hands wondering what truths I'd let slip and what terrible faux pas I had made.

As it was, Sandra looked at the clock as she topped up her own glass and gave a little gulp of shock.

"Heavens, ten past eleven! I had no idea it was so late. You must be shattered, Rowan."

"I am a bit," I said truthfully. I'd been traveling all day, and the fact was starting to catch up with me.

"Well, look, I think we've covered everything I wanted to ask, but I was hoping you could meet the little ones tomorrow, see if you click, and then Jack will drive you back to Carn Bridge to catch your train, if that's okay? What time does it leave?"

"Eleven twenty-five, so that works fine for me."

"Great." She stood up and swept all the crockery into a stack, which she put beside the sink. "Let's leave that for Jean and call it a night."

I nodded, wondering again who this mysterious Jean was, but not quite wanting to ask.

"I'll just go and let the dogs out. Good night, Rowan."

"Good night," I said back. "Thank you so much for a delicious supper, Sandra."

"My pleasure. Sleep well. The children are usually up at six but there's no need for you to get up that early—unless you want to!"

She gave a little tinkly laugh, and I made a mental note to set my alarm for six, even while my eyes felt heavy at the thought.

As Sandra shooed the dogs into the garden, I made my way back into the old part of the house, with the same strange sense of jolting dislocation I had felt before, going the other way. The soaring glass ceiling abruptly lowered to wedding-cake-style frosting. The echoing sound of my kitten heels on the concrete floor changed to the soft click of parquet, and then the hush of carpet as I began to make my way up the staircase. At the first landing I stopped. The door closest to me, the baby's room, was still ajar, and I couldn't resist—I pushed it open and stepped inside, smelling the good, warm smells of clean, contented baby.

Petra was lying on her back, her arms and legs thrown out froggy-style. She had kicked off her blanket and, very gently, I drew it back over her, feeling her soft breath stirring the fine hairs on the back of my hand.

As I tucked it around her, she startled, flinging up one arm, and for a moment I froze, thinking that she was about to wake and cry. But she only sighed and settled back down, and I padded quietly from the room and up to my luxurious, waiting bedroom.

* * *

I tiptoed around cautiously as I washed and brushed my teeth, listening to the floorboards beneath my feet quietly creaking and not wanting to disturb Sandra below. But at last I was ready for bed, my alarm set, my clothes for tomorrow neatly set out on the plump little sofa.

Then I realized, I had not drawn the curtains.

Wrapping my dressing gown around myself, I walked across the room and tugged gently at their fabric. They didn't move.

Puzzled, I tried harder, then stopped, peering behind them in case they were somehow fake, ornamental drapes, and I was really supposed to use a blind. But no, they were real curtains, they had real runners. Then I remembered—Sandra pressing something on the wall, and the curtains swishing closed, then open again. They were automatic.

Shit. I walked across to the panel beside the door and waved a hand in front of it. Instantly it lit up with that confusing configuration of squares and icons. None looked like curtains. There was one that might have been a window, but when I pressed it, cautiously, a blast of jazz trumpet split the silence, and I hastily stabbed it with a finger.

Thank God it cut off immediately, and I stood for a moment, waiting, poised for a wail from Petra, or for Sandra to come pounding up the stairs demanding to know why I was waking the children, but nothing happened.

I returned to studying the panel, but this time I didn't press anything. I tried to remember what Sandra had done earlier. The big square in the center was the main light, I was fairly sure of that. And the mishmash of squares to the right presumably controlled the other lights in the room. But what was that spiral thing, and the slider to the left? Music volume? Heat?

Then I remembered Sandra's comment about the voice settings.

"Shut curtains," I said in a low voice, and somewhat to my shock, the curtains whisked across with a barely audible swoosh.

Great. Okay. That only left the lights to figure out.

The bedside light had a switch, so I knew I'd be able to handle that one, and the others I managed to figure out by trial and error, but there was one lamp by the armchair that I could not manage to extinguish.

"Turn off lights," I tried, but nothing happened. "Turn off lamp."

The bedside lamp extinguished.

"Turn off armchair lamp." Nothing happened. Bloody hell.

In the end I traced the cord back to an oddly shaped plug socket on the wall, not like a normal appliance socket, and pulled it out. The room was plunged instantly into darkness so thick, I could almost feel it.

Slowly I groped my way back across the room to the foot of the bed and crawled into it. I was just snuggling down when I remembered, with a sigh, that I hadn't plugged my phone in to charge. Shit.

I couldn't face contending with the lights again, so instead I switched on the torch on my phone, got out of bed, and began to rummage through my case.

The charger wasn't there. Had I taken it out already? I was sure I'd packed it.

I tipped the bag upside down, letting my possessions tumble out onto the thick carpet, but no electrical wire came snaking out with the other belongings. Shit. *Shit.* If I couldn't charge my phone, I'd have the world's most boring journey tomorrow. I hadn't even brought a book—all my reading matter was on the Kindle app. Had I forgotten it? Left it on the train? Either way, it clearly wasn't in my case. I stood there for a moment, chewing my lip, and then opened up one of the drawers in the bedside table, hoping against expectation that a previous guest might have left a charger behind.

And . . . bingo. Not a charger, but a charging lead. That was all I needed—there was a USB port built into the socket.

With a sigh of relief I untangled the lead from the leaflets and papers in the drawer, plugged it in, and attached my phone. The little charging icon illuminated, and I got thankfully back into bed. I was about to turn off the torch and lie back down when I noticed that something had fallen out of the drawer onto my pillow. It was a piece of paper, and I was about to screw it up and throw it onto the floor, but before I did, I glanced at it, just to check it was nothing important.

It wasn't. Just a child's drawing. At least . . .

I picked up the phone again, angling the torch at the page, looking more closely at the picture.

It was hardly a work of art, just stick figures and thick crayoned lines. It showed a house with four windows and a shiny black front door, not unlike Heatherbrae. The windows were colored in black, all except for one, which showed a tiny pale face peeping out of the darkness.

It was oddly disconcerting, but there was no name signed to it, and no way of knowing why it was in the bedside drawer. I turned it over, looking for clues. There was writing on the other side. It wasn't a child's but an adult's—sloped and looping and somehow non-English in a way I couldn't quite define.

To the new nanny, it read in neat, regular italics. *My name is Katya. I am writing you this note because I wanted to tell you to please be*

And then it stopped.

I frowned. Who was Katya? The name rang a bell, and then I remembered Sandra's voice at dinner saying *but with Katya leaving—she was our last nanny . . .*

So Katya had lived here. Slept here even. But what had she wanted to say to her successor? And had she run out of time, or thought better of what she was about to say?

Please be . . . *kind to the children*? Please be . . . *happy here*? Please be . . . *sure to tell Sandra you like dogs*?

It could have been anything. So why was the phrase that kept hovering on the tip of my tongue *please be careful*?

The two taken together, the eerie little drawing and the unfinished note, gave me a strange feeling that I could not put my finger on. Something like uneasiness, though I could not have said why.

Well, whatever it was she had wanted to say, it was too late now.

I folded the drawing and slipped it back into the drawer. Then I switched off my phone, pulled the covers up to my chin, and tried to forget everything that hung in the balance and sleep.

When I woke, it was to the insistent shrill beep of my alarm, and for a moment I could not think where I was, or why I was so tired. Then I remembered. I was in Scotland. And it was 6:00 a.m.—a full hour and a half earlier than I was accustomed to waking up.

I sat up, smoothing my rumpled hair and rubbing the sleep from my eyes. Downstairs I could hear thumps and shrill sounds of excitement. It sounded as though the children were probably up. . . .

The curtains were blackout, but the sunshine was already streaming through the gaps around the edges, and, forcing my legs out of bed, I walked across and tried to pull them open, before remembering the previous night.

"Curtains open," I said aloud, feeling more than slightly stupid, and they swooshed apart like a magician's trick. I don't know what I was expecting, but whatever it was, I was not prepared for the reality.

The beauty of the scene in front of me took my breath away.

The house had been perfectly sited by some long-dead Victorian architect to gaze out across an uninterrupted vista of blue hills, green valleys, and deep-verdant pine forests. On and on it stretched, the rolling foothills punctuated by little dark burns that rambled here and there, and the corrugated roofs of faraway crofts, and a few miles away a loch, reflecting the morning sun so brightly it looked like a patch of snow. In the distance, presiding above it all, were the Cairngorms—Gaelic for the blue mountains, according to Google.

When I had looked up the origin of their name, the translation had seemed faintly absurd. The photos online showed all the colors you might expect—green grass, brown bracken, reddish earth with the occasional purple splotch of heather, and in winter a covering of crisp white. The idea that they were blue seemed fanciful in the extreme.

But here, with the mist rising from their slopes in the morning sun, and the dawn pink still tingeing the sky behind them, they *did* look blue. Not the brackeny foothills, but the unforgiving granite slopes themselves, all jagged crags and peaks, far above the tree line. The highest peak looked like it was tipped with snow, even in June.

I felt my heart lift, and then I heard a noise in the garden below and looked down.

It was Jack Grant. He was walking across from a huddle of outbuildings tucked just around the corner of the house. His hair was wet, as if he had just showered, and he was holding a bag of tools in his hand. For a minute I watched him, staring down at the top of his dark head, before it began to feel more than a little voyeuristic, and I turned away from the window to head to the bathroom for my own shower.

Inside it was dark, and I automatically felt around for a switch, before I remembered the damn panel. At my touch it leapt into life, presenting me again with that confusing mosaic of squares, sliders, and dots. I pressed one at random, hoping I wasn't going to get more Miles Davis. I had been aiming for the same one I'd pressed yesterday, but evidently I'd missed my mark, because low blue lights suddenly illuminated the baseboards. Some sort of night setting, for if you wanted to go to the loo while your partner was asleep? Not bright enough to shower by, at all events.

The next button I tried made the blue lights disappear, and two low, golden lamps came on over the bath, suffusing my skin with a warm, flattering glow. It was exactly what I would have wanted if

I was soaking in a long bubble bath, but the shower enclosure was still dark, and I needed something brighter and more . . . well, more morningish.

I found it on the fourth or fifth try—a setting that was bright, but not agonizingly so, with an illuminated rim around the mirror perfect for doing my makeup. With a sigh of relief I dropped my robe to the floor and stepped into the shower, only to be faced with a different challenge. There was a dazzling array of nozzles, spouts, and showerheads. The question was, how did you operate them? The answer seemed to be yet another panel, a waterproof one this time, set in among the shower tiles. When I touched it, letters appeared. *Good morning, Katya.*

The name gave me a funny little jolt, and I remembered again that unfinished note on the child's drawing, from the night before. There was a smiley face and little down button. Well, I wasn't Katya. I pressed the down button, and the letters changed. *Good morning, Jo.* I pressed again. *Good morning, Lauren. Good morning, Holly. Good morning, guest.*

There were no more options. Guest it was, then. I pressed the smiley face. Nothing happened. Instead, the display changed to those cryptic dots, squares, and sliders. I pressed one at random and screeched when about twenty forceful jets of ice-cold water blasted my stomach and thighs. Hastily I mashed the off switch to the left of the panel and the jets turned off, leaving me panting and shivering, and more than a little annoyed.

Okay. Fine. Maybe I should try a preset option, until I had figured out how to work this thing. I touched the panel and *Good morning, Katya* flashed up again. This time with a feeling of slight trepidation, I pressed the smiley face, and the message *We're preparing your favorite shower. Wash Happy!* appeared on the screen. As the message faded away, to my astonishment, one of the showerheads slid smoothly upwards to a preprogrammed height, tilted to an angle, and a jet of warm water began to gush out. I stood for a moment, gaping, and then tested the water with one hand. Whoever Katya was, she had been very tall, and she liked her showers a little bit hotter than I did. I could have put up with the heat, but unfortunately she was so tall that the jet missed the top of my head completely and bounced off the glass screen opposite, which was going to make washing my hair very tricky.

I pressed the off button and tried again. This time I selected *Good morning, Holly* at random and waited, teeth gritted, for the result.

Bingo. Holly's setting turned out to be set to a kind of hot drenching rain from the grid overhead, which was . . . well, it was glorious. There was no other word for it. The water gushed out with an almost absurd abundance, soaking me with warmth. I felt the hot water drumming on the top of my skull, driving out the last remnants of my sleepiness and last night's red wine. Holly, whoever she was, had clearly been a woman after my own heart. I shampooed my hair, conditioned, and then rinsed, and then stood, my eyes closed, simply enjoying the feel of the water on my naked skin.

The temptation to stay there, reveling in the luxury, was very strong, but it had taken me probably ten minutes to even figure out the bathroom. If I wasted any more time, I would render that early alarm pointless. There was no point in forcing myself out of bed at the crack of dawn if I didn't make an appearance and ram my enthusiasm home to Sandra.

With a sense of resignation, I pressed the off button on the panel, reached out for the fluffy white towel warming on the heated rail, and reminded myself that if I pulled this off, it wouldn't be the last time I got to enjoy that shower. Very far from it.

* * *

Venturing downstairs, the first thing that greeted me was the smell of toast and the sound of children laughing. When I rounded the corner of the bottom of the stairs, I was met by a very small tartan dressing gown abandoned on the bottom step and a single slipper in the middle of the hall. Picking both up, I made my way through to the kitchen, where Sandra was standing in front of a huge gleaming chrome toaster, holding a piece of brown bread and waving it at the two little girls in bright red pajamas sitting at the metal breakfast bar. Their curly heads, one dark, the other white-blond, were tousled with sleep, and they were both giggling helplessly.

"Don't encourage her! She'll only do it again."

"Do what again?" I said, and Sandra turned.

"Oh, Rowan! Gosh, you're up early. I hope the girls didn't wake you. We're still trying to train certain members of the family to stay in bed past six a.m. . . ." She nodded pointedly at the younger of the two girls, the one with white-blond hair.

"It's fine," I said truthfully, adding, slightly less accurately, "I'm a naturally early riser."

"Well, that's certainly a good talent to have in this house," Sandra said with a sigh. She was wearing a dressing gown and looked more than a little harassed.

"Petra threw her porridge," said the girl, with a gurgling laugh, pointing at the pink-cheeked baby sitting in the high chair at the corner, and I saw that she was right. There was a dollop of porridge the size of an egg sliding down the front of the stove to plop onto the concrete floor, and Petra was crowing with delight and scooping up another spoonful, ready to throw it again.

"Peta frow!" she said, and took aim.

"Uh-uh," I said with a smile, and held out my hand for the spoon. "Petra, give it here, please!"

The baby looked at me uncertainly for a moment, sizing me up, her faint blond brows drawn into an adorable frown, and then her chubby face split in a grin and she repeated, "Peta frow!" and launched the porridge towards me.

I dodged, but not quick enough, and it hit me full in the chest.

At first I just gasped, and then a wave of absolute fury rose up inside me when I realized what she had done. Stupidly I hadn't brought a spare outfit, and yesterday's top was crumpled and had a red-wine stain on the top that I didn't remember making but must have done so.

I had literally no clean clothes left. I was going to be covered in porridge for the rest of the day. The little *shit.*

It was the younger of the two girls who saved me. She burst out giggling and then clapped her hands over her mouth, as if horrified.

I remembered who I was, where I was, why I was here.

I forced a smile.

"It's okay," I said to the little girl. "Ellie, isn't it? You can laugh. It *is* pretty funny."

She took her hands away and gave a cautious grin.

"Oh my God," Sandra said with a kind of weary resignation. "Rowan, I am *so* sorry. They talk about the terrible twos, but I swear, Petra's been auditioning for them for six months. Is your top okay?"

"Sandra, don't give it a second thought," I said. The top was not going to be okay, at least not until I could wash it, and possibly not even then. It was a silk blouse, dry-clean only, a stupid choice for a nannying interview, but I hadn't thought about the fact that I would be interacting with the kids. Maybe I could get a small moral advantage from the situation. "Honestly, these things happen when you have kids, right? It's only porridge! However—" I leaned over and took the bowl of porridge away from Petra before she realized what was happening and put it out of her reach. "I think you've had enough, little Miss Petra, so maybe I'll take charge of that while I clean up. Where's your mop, Sandra, and I'll clean up that blob on the floor before one of the girls slips on it."

"It's in the utility room, that door there," Sandra said, with a grateful smile. "Thank you so much, Rowan. I honestly wasn't expecting you to start pitching in unpaid, this is beyond the call of duty."

"I'm glad to help," I said firmly. I ruffled Petra's hair as I passed with an affection I didn't entirely feel, and gave Ellie a little wink. Maddie was not looking at me; she was staring down at her plate as though the whole thing had passed her by. Maybe she was ashamed at her earlier role, egging Petra on.

The utility room turned out to be in the older part of the house—probably the original scullery judging by the Victorian sink and stone-flagged floor—but I wasn't in the mood to appreciate architectural details. Instead, I shut the door behind me and took a couple of deep breaths, trying to rid myself of the last of my irritation, and then set to work trying to rescue my top. The worst of the porridge flicked off into the sink, but I was going to have to sponge the rest. After several tries that only succeeded in getting porridgy water onto my skirt, I pushed a mop against the handle of the kitchen door and peeled off my top.

I was standing there in my bra and skirt, dabbing at the porridgy patch under the tap and trying not to get the rest of the shirt wetter than necessary, when I heard a sound from the other side of the utility room and turned to see the door to the yard open and Jack Grant come in, wiping his hands on his overall trousers.

"Mower's going, San—" he called, and then broke off, his eyes widening in shock. A vivid blush spread across his broad cheekbones.

I gave a yelp of surprise and clutched my wet top to my breasts, trying my best to preserve my modesty.

"Oh my God, I'm so sorry," Jack said. He was covering his eyes, looking at the ceiling, the floor, anywhere but me. His cheeks were flaming. "I'll—I'll be—so sorry—"

And then he turned and fled, slamming the yard door behind him, leaving me gasping and not sure whether to laugh or cry.

There was not much point in either, so I hastily dried my wet top with a towel hanging over the radiator, filled up the mop bucket, and then made my way back to the kitchen with my cheeks almost as pink as Jack's.

"Shirt fixed?" Sandra said over her shoulder as I came in. "Let me get you a coffee."

"Yes." I was not sure whether to tell her what had just happened. Had she heard my squeak of surprise? Would Jack say something? "Sandra, I—"

But then my nerve failed me. I couldn't think of a way of saying, *Sandra, I just boob-flashed your handyman*, without sounding hopelessly unprofessional. I felt the blush on my face deepen in shame at the thought of it. I could *not* bring it up. I would just have to hope that Jack was enough of a gentleman not to refer to it himself.

"Milk and sugar?" Sandra said absently, and I set the conversation aside.

"Milk, thanks," I said, and put down the mop bucket and began clearing up Petra's missiles from the stove and floor, feeling my cheeks cool as I worked.

At last, when the coffee had come through and I was seated at the table, eating a piece of excellent toast and marmalade, I was almost able to pretend it had never happened.

"So," Sandra said, wiping her hands on a cloth. "Girls. I didn't get a chance to introduce you to Rowan. She's come to have a look around our house and meet you. Say hello."

"Hi," Maddie muttered, though she said it more to her plate than me. She looked younger than her eight years, with her dark hair and a sallow little face. Beneath the countertop I could see two skinny knees, covered in scabs.

"Hello, Maddie," I said, with what I hoped was a winning smile, but she kept her eyes firmly down. Ellie was easier; she was looking at me with frank curiosity from beneath her white-blond fringe. "Hello, Ellie. How old are you?"

"I'm five," Ellie said. Her blue eyes were round as buttons. "Are you going to be our new nanny?"

"I—" I stopped short, not sure what to say. Would *I hope so* come across as too nakedly pleading?

"Maybe," Sandra cut in, firmly. "Rowan hasn't decided yet whether she wants to work here, so we must be very well behaved to impress her!"

She gave me a little sideways wink.

"I tell you what, run upstairs and get dressed, and then we can show Rowan around."

"What about Petra?" Ellie asked.

"I'll sort her out. Go on—chop-chop."

The two girls slid obediently off the tall stools and pattered away across the hallway and up the stairs. Sandra watched them go, fondly.

"Gosh, they're very good!" I said, genuinely impressed. I had nannied enough children to know that five-year-olds getting dressed on command definitely wasn't a given. Even eight-year-olds tended to need supervision. Sandra rolled her eyes.

"They know not to play up in front of visitors. But let's see if they're actually doing as they're told . . ."

She pressed a button on an iPad lying on the counter, and a picture flickered into view. It was a children's bedroom, the camera obviously sited up near the ceiling, pointing downwards at two little beds. There was no sound, but the noise of a door slamming was loud enough to filter down the stairs, and a teddy bear on the mantelpiece rocked and fell. As we watched, Maddie stamped angrily into view at the bottom of the screen and sat crossly on the left-hand bed, her arms folded. Sandra pressed something else and the camera zoomed in on Maddie's face, or rather the top of her head, for she was looking down at her lap. There was a faint crackle coming from the iPad now, as if a microphone had been switched on.

"Maddie," Sandra said, "what have I told you about slamming doors?"

"I didn't." The voice came small and tinny from the iPad speaker.

"You did, and I saw you. You could have hurt Ellie. Now get your clothes on and you can watch some TV. They're all laid out on your chair, I put them out this morning."

Maddie said nothing, but she got up and pulled off her pajama top, and Sandra shut down the screen.

"Wow," I said, slightly taken aback. "Impressive!"

It was not the word I was thinking. *Stalkerish* was closer to the mark, though I wasn't completely sure why. Plenty of places I'd worked had nanny cams, or baby monitors with built-in speakers and cameras. Perhaps it was the fact that I hadn't known about it until now. I hadn't noticed any cameras last night, so wherever they were, they must be well hidden. Had Sandra watched me go up to bed last night? Had she seen me look into Petra's bedroom? The thought made my cheeks flame.

"The whole house is wired up," Sandra said casually, dropping the iPad back onto the counter. "It's very handy, especially in a place with several floors. It means I don't have to always be running up and down to check on the girls."

"Very handy," I echoed faintly, suppressing my unease. The *whole* house? What did that mean? The children's rooms, clearly. But the reception rooms? The bedrooms? The *bath*rooms? But no, that was beyond possibility. And illegal, surely. I put the remaining bit of toast back on the plate, my appetite suddenly gone.

"Finished?" Sandra said brightly, and when I nodded she swept the bit of toast into a waste-disposal unit and put the plate with the girls' porridge bowls by the sink. The ones from last night had disappeared, I noticed. Had the mysterious Jean come and gone already?

"Well, if you've had enough, let me give you the grand tour while the girls get dressed." She scooped Petra out of her high chair, scrubbed her face with a damp washcloth, hitched her onto her hip, and together we reentered the old part of the house and crossed the stone-flagged entrance hall to the two doors on each side of the front door.

"Right, so just to give you the layout—the hall is the center of the house—out the back is the kitchen, and leading off that is the utility room, which you've already seen, of course. That was part of the old servants' quarters, the only bit that survived, actually. The rest we had to pull down. At the front of the house we have the grander rooms—that's the old dining room"—Sandra waved a hand at an opening to the right of the front door—"but we found we were always eating in the kitchen, so we've converted it into a study slash library. Have a peek."

I put my head around the door and saw a smallish room with paneled walls painted a beautiful rich teal color. Ranged at one end were bookshelves from floor to ceiling covered in a mix of fiction paperbacks and hardback books on architecture. It could have been a small but perfectly formed library in a National Trust historic property—except that in the middle of the room was an enormous glass desk with a huge double-screen iMac sprawling across it, and a kind of aeronautical ergonomic chair facing the screens.

I blinked. There was something disconcerting about the way the old and new combined in this house. It wasn't like most homes, where modern additions rubbed up alongside original features and somehow combined into a friendly, eclectic whole. Here there was a strange impression of oil and water—everything was either self-consciously original or glaringly modern, with no attempt to integrate the two.

"What a beautiful room," I said at last, since Sandra seemed to be waiting for some kind of response. "The colors are just . . . they're fabulous."

Sandra smiled, jiggling Petra on her hip in a pleased sort of way. "Thank you! Bill does all the technical layout stuff, but the interior design is mostly me. I do love that shade of teal. This particular room is really Bill's domain, so I reined myself in, but you'll see I've gone a bit to town on it in the living room. I figure, it's my house, I don't have to please anyone else! Come through and have a look."

The room she led me into next was the living room she had mentioned, a cluster of deep button-backed sofas arranged in a square around a beautiful tiled fireplace. The ceiling and woodwork were the same shade of teal as the paneling in the study, but the walls themselves were startling—covered in a rich, intricate wallpaper with a design almost too convoluted to make out in deep blues, emeralds, and aquamarines. As I peered closer I saw that it was a mix of brambles and peacocks—both stylized and intertwined to the point of being practically unrecognizable. The brambles were dark green and indigo black, the peacocks iridescent blue and amethyst, their tails curling and spreading and tangling with the brambles into a kind of nightmarish labyrinth—half aviary, half briar thicket.

The design echoed the tiles around the fireplace, which were two peacocks standing tall on each side of the grate, their bodies on the bottommost tile, their tails spreading upwards. The fire itself was dead, but the room was not cold, far from it. Wrought iron Victorian radiators around the walls gave it a cozy warmth, and the sun slanted across another of the artfully faded Persian rugs. More books were strewn across a brass coffee table along with another arrangement of peonies, these ones drooping in a dry vase, but Sandra ignored them and led the way to a door on the left side of the fireplace, leading back in the direction of the kitchen.

Behind it was a much smaller oak-paneled room with a scuffed leather sofa and a TV on the far wall. It was easy to see what this room was used for—the floor was covered with discarded toys, scattered Duplo, decapitated Barbie dolls, and a partly collapsed play tent slumped in one corner. The rather dark paneled walls had been decorated with stickers and children's drawings, even the odd crayoned scribble on the paneling itself.

"This was the old breakfast room," Sandra said, "and it was rather gloomy, as it faces north and that pine tree blocks out a lot of the light, so we made it into a media room, but obviously the children ended up completely taking over!"

She gave a laugh and picked up a stuffed yellow banana, handing it to Petra.

"And now, to complete the circuit . . ."

She led the way through towards a second door concealed in the paneling—and again I had the feeling of tripping and finding myself in a different house entirely. We were again in the glass vault at the back of the house, but we had entered it from the opposite side. Without the big stove and the cupboards and appliances blocking the view, there was literally nothing in front of us but glass—and beyond that the landscape falling away, patched with forest and the faraway glimmer of lochs and burns. It was like there was nothing between us and the wilderness beyond. I felt that at any moment an osprey could have swooped down into our midst.

In one corner was a playpen, carpeted with jigsaw-shaped rubber mats, and I watched as Sandra plopped Petra inside with her banana and waved her hand around the walls. "This side was the old servants' hall, back in the day, but it was riddled with dry rot and the views were much too good to be confined to narrow little sash windows, so we made the decision to just"—she made a slitting gesture at her throat, and then laughed—"I think some people are a bit shocked, but trust me, if you'd seen it before, you'd understand."

I thought of my tiny flat in London, the way it could have fitted into even just this one room.

Something inside me seemed to twist and break, just a little, and suddenly I was not sure if I should have come here after all. But I knew one thing. I could not go back. Not now.

You're probably wondering why I'm telling you all this, Mr. Wrexham. Because I know you're busy, and I know that on the surface, at least, it seems as if this is nothing to do with my case. And yet . . . it's everything. I need you to *see* Heatherbrae House, to feel the warmth from the heating striking up through the floor, the sun on your face. I need to you to be able to reach out and stroke the soft cat's-tongue roughness of the velvet sofas and the silky smoothness of the polished concrete surfaces.

I need you to understand why I did what I did.

The rest of the morning seemed to pass in a blur. I spent the time making homemade Play-Doh with the children and then helping them fashion it into a variety of lumpy, lopsided creations, most of which Petra mashed into shapelessness again with crows of laughter and howls of annoyance from Ellie. Maddie was the one who puzzled me most—she was stiff and unyielding, as if determined not to smile for me, but I persisted, finding little ways of praising her, and at last, in spite of herself, she seemed to unbend a little, even going as far as laughing, a little unwillingly, when Petra unwisely shoved a handful of the pink dough into her mouth and spat it out, retching and gagging at the salty taste, with a comical expression of disgust on her chubby little face.

At last Sandra tapped me on the shoulder and told me that Jack was waiting to take me to the station, if I was ready, and I stood up and washed my hands and gave Petra a little chuck under the chin.

My bag was beside the door. I had packed before I came downstairs for breakfast, knowing that I might not have much time later, but I had no idea who had brought it down from the spare room. Not the unseen Jean, I fervently hoped, though I did not know why the thought made me uncomfortable.

Jack was waiting outside with the silently idling car, his hands in his pockets, the sunshine finding specks of deep auburn and red in his dark hair.

"Well, it was a *total* pleasure to meet you," Sandra said, and there was a genuine warmth in her eyes as she held out her hand. "I'll need to discuss things with Bill, but I think I can say . . . well, let's just say, you'll be hearing from us very soon with a final decision. *Very* soon. Thank you, Rowan, you were fabulous."

"It was lovely to meet you too, Sandra," I said. "Your girls are lovely." *Ugh, stop saying lovely.* "I hope I get the chance to meet Rhiannon sometime." *I hope I get the job*, that meant, in code. "Goodbye, Ellie." I stuck out my hand, and she shook it gravely, like a five-year-old businesswoman. "Goodbye, Maddie."

But Maddie, to my dismay, did not take my hand. Instead, she turned and buried her face in her mother's midriff, refusing to meet my eyes. It was a curiously childish gesture, one that made her seem much younger than her age. Over the top of her head, Sandra gave a little shrug as if to say, *What can you do?*

I shrugged back, ruffled the back of Maddie's hair, and turned towards the car.

I had stowed my luggage in the back seat, and was just walking around the opposite side of the car to climb into the front passenger seat when something hit me like a small, dark hurricane. Arms wrapped around my waist, a hard little skull digging into my lower ribs.

Wriggling round in the fierce embrace I saw, to my surprise, that it was Maddie. Maybe I had won her over after all?

"Maddie!" I said, but she did not answer. I was unsure of what to do, but in the end I bent down to give her a little hug back. "Thank you for showing me your lovely house. Goodbye."

I hoped that the last word might make her let go, but she only tightened her grip, squeezing me uncomfortably tight, making my breath come short.

"Don't—" I heard her whimper into my still-damp top, though I couldn't make out the second word. *Don't go*?

"I have to," I whispered back. "But I hope I'll be able to come back very soon."

That was the truth, all right. God, I hoped so.

But Maddie was shaking her head, her dark hair swishing against her knobbly spine. I felt the heat of her breath through my top. There was something strangely intimate and uncomfortable about the whole thing, something I could not put my finger on, and all of a sudden I very much wanted her to let go, but mindful of Sandra's presence, I did not prize Maddie's fingers away. Instead, I smiled and tightened my arms around her momentarily, returning her hug. As I did, she made a little sound, almost a whimper.

"Maddie? Is something wrong?"

"Don't come here," she whispered, still refusing to look at me. "It's not safe."

"It's not safe?" I gave a little laugh. "Maddie, what do you mean?"

"It's not *safe*," she repeated, with a little angry sob, shaking her head harder so that her words were almost lost. "They wouldn't like it."

"Who wouldn't like it?"

But with that, she tore herself away, and then she was running barefoot across the grass, shouting something over her shoulder.

"Maddie!" I called after her. "Maddie, wait!"

"Don't worry," Sandra said with a laugh. She came round to my side of the car. It was plain that she had not seen anything apart from Maddie's sudden hug and her subsequent flight. "That's Maddie, I'm afraid. Just let her go, she'll be back for lunch. But she must have liked you—I'm not sure she's ever voluntarily hugged a stranger before!"

"Thank you," I said, rather unsettled, and I let Sandra see me into the car and slam the door shut.

It was only as we began to wind slowly down the drive, while I kept one eye out for a fleeting child among the trees, that I found myself replaying Maddie's final remark, wondering if she had really said what I thought I'd heard.

For the thing she had called over her shoulder seemed almost too preposterous to be true—and yet the more I brooded over it, the more I was sure of what I'd heard.

The ghosts, she had sobbed. *The ghosts wouldn't like it.*

"Well, seems it's goodbye for now," Jack said. He stood at the barrier to the station, holding my bag in one hand, his other outstretched. I took it and shook it. There was oil deeply ground in around the nails from yesterday, but his skin was clean and warm, and the odd intimacy of the contact gave me a little shiver I couldn't explain.

"Nice to meet you," I said, a little awkwardly, and then, with a feeling that I might as well because I'd regret it if I didn't, I added, a little rashly, "Sorry I didn't get to meet Bill. Or . . . or Jean."

"Jean?" Jack said, looking a little puzzled. "She's not about much in the day. Goes home to her dad."

"Is she . . . is she young, then?"

"No!" He gave that grin again, the sides of his mouth curving into an expression of such beguiling amusement that I felt my own mouth curve in helpless sympathy, even though I didn't really understand the joke. "She's fifty if she's a day, maybe more, though I'd never dare ask her age. No, she's a—what's the word. A carer. Her father lives down in the village; he has Alzheimer's, I think. He can't be left alone for more than an hour or two. She comes up in the morning before he's awake and then again first thing in the afternoon. Does the dishes and that."

"Oh!" I felt my face flush, and I smiled, absurdly, and gave a little laugh. "Oh, I see. I thought . . . never mind. It doesn't matter."

I did not have time to analyze the relief I felt, but it gave me a strange sense of being off-balance, struck by something I had not expected to encounter.

"Well, good to meet you, Rowan."

"Good to meet you too—Jack." The name came off my tongue a little awkwardly, and I blushed again. Up the valley I heard the sound of the approaching train. "Goodbye."

"Goodbye." He held out the case, and I took it, still echoing his curving, beguiling smile, and began to walk to the platform, giving myself a stern injunction *not* to look back. When at last the train had drawn in and I had climbed aboard and settled myself in a carriage, I did risk one last glance out the window, to where he had been standing. But he was gone. And so, as the train pulled out of the station, my last glimpse of Carn Bridge was of an empty platform, crisply clean and sun-soaked, awaiting my return.

Back in London, I prepared myself for an agonizing wait. *Very soon,* Sandra had said. But what did that mean? She'd clearly liked me—unless I was deluding myself. But I'd done enough interviews to be able to pinpoint the feeling in the air as I left. In recent months I'd experienced both the triumph of having done myself justice and the furious disappointment of having let myself down. I'd felt much closer to the first one on the train back down to London.

Did they have other people to interview? She had seemed so very desperate to have someone start soon, and she must know that every day that ticked past without me giving notice was a day I couldn't work for her. But what if one of the other candidates could start immediately . . . ?

Given Sandra's emphasis on *very* soon, I had dared to hope for something on my phone by the time I got home, but there was nothing that evening, nor the next day when I left for work. We had to leave our phones turned off in our lockers at Little Nippers, so I resigned myself to a long morning, listening to Janine rattling on about her boring boyfriend and bossing Hayley and me about, while all the time my head was elsewhere.

My lunch shift wasn't until one, but when the clock ticked over I hastily finished the nappy I was changing and stood up, handing the baby to Hayley.

"Sorry, Hales, can you take him? I've got an emergency I need to sort out."

I pulled off the plastic disposable apron and virtually ran to the staff room. There, I grabbed my bag from my locker and escaped out the back entrance, into the little concrete yard—far away from the gaze of the children and parents—that we used for smoking, phone calls, and other activities that we weren't supposed to do on clock. It seemed to take an age for the phone to switch on and go through the endless start-up screen—but at last the lock screen came up, and I typed in my passcode with shaking fingers and pressed refresh on my emails, reaching as I did for my necklace, my fingers tracing the loops and ridges as the messages downloaded.

One . . . two . . . three came through . . . all either spam or completely unimportant, and I felt my heart sink—until I noticed the little icon in the corner of the screen. I had a message.

My stomach was turning over and over, and I felt a kind of fluttering nausea as I dialed into voice mail and waited impatiently through the automated prompts. If this didn't work out . . . If this didn't work out . . .

The truth was, I didn't know what I'd do if it didn't work out. And before I could finish the thought there was a beep and I heard Sandra's clipped plummy accent, sounding tinny through the little speaker.

"Oh, hello, Rowan. Sorry not to speak to you in person—I expect you're at work. Well, I'm delighted to say that I've discussed it with

Bill and we'd be happy to offer you the job *if* you can start on June seventeenth at the absolute latest, earlier if you can. I realize that we didn't discuss the exact terms and the bonus I mentioned in the letter. The plan would be for us to issue you with an allowance of a thousand pounds a month, with the remainder of the salary to come at year-end in the form of a completion bonus. I hope that's acceptable—I realize it's a little unconventional, but given you'll be living with us you won't have many day-to-day expenses. If you could let me know as soon as possible if you'd like to accept, and oh, yes, lovely to meet you the other day. I was very impressed with how the children warmed to you, particularly Maddie. She's not always the easiest child, and—well, I'm rambling, so I'd better cut this short, but we'd be happy to have you on board. Looking forward to hearing back from you."

There was a click, and the message ended.

For a minute I couldn't move. I just stood there, the phone in my hand, gaping at the screen. And then a huge rush of exhilaration raced through me, and I found I was dancing, hopping in circles, punching the air and grinning like a lunatic.

"Bloody hell, what's got into you?" a smoke-roughened voice said over my shoulder, and I turned, still grinning, to see Janine leaning against the door, a cigarette in one hand, lighter in the other.

"What's got into me?" I said, hugging myself, full of a glee I couldn't even try to suppress. "I'll tell you what's got into me, Janine. I've got a new job."

"Well . . ." Janine's expression as she flicked open the lighter was a little sour. "You needn't look so triumphant about it."

"Oh, come on, you're as fed up with Val as I am. She's screwing us all, and you know it. Ten percent she put up fees last year, and us assistants are barely getting minimum wage. She can't keep blaming the recession forever."

"You're just pissed off that I got made head of the baby room," Janine said. She took a drag of her cigarette, and then offered me the packet. I was trying to give up to improve my asthma (well, officially I *had* given up) but her words had hit home, and so I took one and lit it slowly, more as a way of giving myself time to rearrange my expression than because I actually wanted to smoke. I *had* been pissed off that she'd got promoted, when honestly I thought I had the better shot. I'd applied thinking I was a shoo-in—and the shock when the position had gone to Janine had been like a punch to the gut. But as Val had said at the time, there were two candidates and only one job. There was nothing she could do about that. Still, it had rankled, particularly when Janine had begun throwing her weight around and issuing orders in that grating drawl.

"Well, it doesn't matter now," I said, handing the lighter back with a sweet smile and exhaling the smoke. "Onwards and upwards, eh?" The slightly patronizing smile she gave made me add, a little maliciously, "Very much upwards, in fact."

"What do you mean?" Janine said. She narrowed her eyes. "Are we talking more than thirty K?"

I made a rising movement with my hand, and her eyes widened.

"Forty? *Fifty grand?*"

"*And* it's residential," I said smugly, watching her jaw drop. She shook her head.

"You're having me on."

"I'm not." Suddenly I didn't need the cigarette anymore. I took a final drag, then dropped it to join the mush of dead butts in the yard and ground it out under my heel. "Thanks for the fag. And now, if you'll excuse me, I need to phone up and accept a job."

I dialed Sandra's number, listening as it rang, and then clicked through to voice mail. In a way I was relieved, I didn't want to get grilled about my start date in front of Janine. If she knew it was a make-or-break condition, she might well tell Val, who could deliberately make life difficult for me.

"Oh, hi, Sandra," I said, when the beep had sounded. "Thanks so much for your message, I'm thrilled, and I'd be delighted to accept. I need to sort a few things out this end but I'll email you about the start date. I'm sure it won't be a problem. And . . . well, thanks, I guess! I'll be in touch. Let me know if there's anything you need from me to get the ball rolling."

And then I hung up.

I handed in my notice to Val that same day. She tried to act pleased for me, but in truth, she looked mostly pissed off, particularly when I informed her that the amount of leave I had stacked up meant that I would be finishing on the sixteenth of June, rather than the first of July, as she had assumed. She tried to tell me that I needed to work my notice and take the leave as pay, but when I more or less invited her to see me in court, she caved.

The next few days passed in a whirl of activity and practicalities. Sandra did all her payroll remotely through a company in Manchester and wanted me to contact them direct with payment details and ID rather than sending all the paperwork up to Scotland. I had expected the process to be a major stumbling block, maybe even requiring me to travel to Manchester for an interview in person, but in the end it was surprisingly, almost disconcertingly simple—I forwarded them Sandra's email with a reference number, and then when they replied, I sent the passport scan, utility bills, and bank details they requested. It went through without a hitch. Like it was meant to be.

The ghosts wouldn't like it.

The phrase floated through my head, spoken in Maddie's reedy little voice, its childlike quaver lending the words an eeriness I would normally have shrugged off.

But that was bollocks. Utter bollocks. I hadn't seen a whiff of the supernatural the whole time I was in Carn Bridge. More likely it was just a cover story seized on by homesick au pairs, girls barely out of their teens with poor English, unable to cope with the isolation and remote location. I'd seen enough of them working at places in London to know the drill—I'd even picked up some emergency work when they scarpered in the night with the return half of their plane ticket, leaving the parents to pick up the pieces. It wasn't uncommon.

I was considerably older and wiser than that, and I had very good reasons for wanting to make this work. No amount of alleged "haunting" was going to make me turn this chance down.

I look back, and I want to shake that smug young woman, sitting in her London flat, thinking she knew it all, had seen it all.

I want to slap her face and tell her she doesn't know what she's talking about.

Because I was wrong, Mr. Wrexham. I was very, very wrong.

Less than three weeks later, I was standing on Carn Bridge station platform, surrounded by more cases and boxes than it seemed possible for one person to carry.

When Jack came striding up the platform, car keys jangling in his hand, he actually broke into a laugh.

"Christ, how did you get all that across London?"

"Slowly," I said honestly. "And painfully. I took a taxi, but it was a bloody nightmare."

"Aye, well, you're here now," he said, and took my largest two cases, giving me a friendly shove when I tried to take the smaller one back off him. "No, no, you take those others."

"*Please* be careful," I said anxiously. "They're really heavy. I don't want you to put your back out."

He grinned, as if the possibility was so remote as to be laughable. "Come on, car's this way."

It had been another glorious day—hot and sunny—and although the sun was beginning to sink towards the horizon and the shadows were growing longer, the gorse was still popping audibly as we drove silently through the wooded lanes and moorland roads towards Heatherbrae. The house, as we drove up the drive, was even more beautiful than I had remembered, basking in evening sunshine, the doors flung open and the dogs running everywhere, barking their heads off. It suddenly occurred to me, with a little jolt, that I would presumably be in charge of the dogs as well as the kids, when Sandra and Bill were away. Or maybe that was Jack's job too? I would have to find out. Two children and a baby were in my comfort zone. A teen as well, I could just about manage. At least, I hoped I could. But add in two boisterous dogs, and I was starting to feel a little overwhelmed.

"Rowan!" Sandra came running out the front door, her arms outstretched, and before I was fully out of the car she had enveloped me in a maternal hug. Then, she stood back and waved her hand at a figure standing in the shadows of the porch—a tall man, balding slightly, with close-shaven hair.

"Rowan, this is my husband, Bill. Bill—meet Rowan Caine."

So this—*this* was Bill Elincourt. For a moment I couldn't think of what to say; I just stood there, awkwardly conscious of Sandra's arm around me, not sure of whether I should break away from her grip to go and greet him or—

I was still frozen in indecision when he solved the issue by striding towards me, sticking out his hand and giving me a quick, businesslike smile.

"Rowan. Good to meet you at last. Sandra's told me all about you. You have a very impressive résumé."

You don't know the half of it, Bill, I thought, as he picked up one of the cases from the boot and made his way back to the house. I took a deep breath and prepared to follow, and as I did, my hand went nervously to my necklace. But this time, instead of tracing its familiar grooves, I slipped the pendant inside the neck of my shirt, and hurried after them.

Inside the kitchen we had coffee, and I sat nervously on the edge of one of the metal breakfast stools while Bill quizzed me about my qualifications, feeling on edge in a way that I never had when Sandra had interviewed me. I wanted . . . I don't know. I wanted to impress him, I suppose. But at the same time, as he droned on about his punishing schedule and the difficulties of recruiting staff in the Highlands, and the inadequacies of his previous nannies, I increasingly wanted to shake him.

I don't know what I had imagined. Someone successful, I guess. I had known that from the advert and the house. Someone fortunate—with his beautiful kids and accomplished wife and interesting job. All that, I had taken for granted. But he was so . . . so *comfortable*. He was padded—every inch of him. I don't mean he was fat, but he was cushioned, physically, emotionally, financially, in a way that he just didn't seem to grasp, and it was his very ignorance of the fact that made it even more infuriating.

Do you know what it's like? I wanted to shout at him, as he complained about their gardener who had left to take up a full-time teaching job in Edinburgh, and the home help who had broken the £800 waste disposal unit in the sink and then run away because she couldn't face telling them what she'd done. *Do you understand what it's like for people who don't have your money, and your protection, and your privilege?*

As he sat there, holding forth as if there was nothing in the world so important as his inconsequential problems, Sandra gazing adoringly into his face like she was happy to listen to him drone on forever, the realization came to me, painfully. He was *selfish*. A selfish, self-centered man who had barely asked me a single personal question—not even how my journey had been. He just didn't care.

I don't know what I had expected to feel when I met him—this man who hadn't bothered to interview a woman he was planning to leave his children with for weeks at a time—but I hadn't expected to feel this level of hostility. I knew I had to get a grip on myself, or it would show in my face.

Perhaps Sandra saw something of my discomfort, for she gave a little laugh and broke in.

"Darling, Rowan doesn't want to hear about our domestic travails. Just make sure you don't go putting cutlery down the grinder, Rowan! Anyway, quite seriously, all the instructions are here"—she patted a fat red binder at her elbow. "It's a physical copy of the document I emailed you last week, and if you've not had a chance to sit down and read it yet, it's got everything from how to work the washing machine, right through to the children's bedtimes and what they do and don't like to eat. If you've got any concerns at all, you'll find the answers here, although of course you can always ring me. Did you download Happy?"

"I'm sorry?"

"Happy—the home-management app. I emailed you the authorization code?"

"Oh, I'm sorry, the app, yes, I downloaded it."

She looked relieved.

"Well that's the main thing. I've set up your Happy profile with all the permissions you'll need, and of course it stands in as a baby monitor, though we've got a regular one for Petra's room as well. Just in case, you know, but the app is very good. What else . . . oh, food! I've done you a menu planner here"—she pulled out a loose sheet from a plastic wallet on the first page of the binder—"which is full of stuff they'll eat fairly reliably, and bought all the ingredients, so you're absolutely set for the first week. Plus all the passwords are in there for Waitrose online and so on, and here is a credit card for any household expenses. The statement comes direct to me and Bill, but obviously do keep receipts—a quick snap on your phone is fine, you don't need to keep the physical bit of paper. Um . . . what else . . . I expect you're full of questions?"

She said the last in a slightly hopeful tone, though I wasn't completely certain whether she was hoping I would prompt her or hoping I'd say no.

"I did read the email," I said, though in truth, since the document was about fifty dense pages, I'd only skimmed through the pages. "But it'll be brilliantly helpful to have a printout of course—it's always so much easier to flick through a physical copy. It was impressively comprehensive. I think I've got a handle on everything—Petra's routine, Ellie's allergies, Maddie's . . . um—" I stopped, unsure how to phrase what Sandra had called her daughter's *explosive personality*. It sounded as though Maddie was quite the handful, or could be.

Sandra caught my eye and saw my predicament, and gave a little rueful smile that said, *Yup*.

"Well, yes, Maddie really! Rhiannon is staying at school this weekend for end-of-term celebrations. She'll be coming home next week, and I've sorted out her lift and everything so you've nothing to worry about there. What else . . . what else . . ."

"I don't think we completely sorted out when you're leaving," I said tentatively. "I know you said in your email that you had the trade show coming up next week—when does it start, exactly? Is it next Saturday?"

"Oh." Sandra looked taken aback. "Did I not say? Gosh, that was a bit of an oversight. That's the . . . um . . . well, that's the only issue really. It is Saturday, but not next Saturday, this one. We leave tomorrow."

"What?" For a moment I thought I hadn't heard properly. "Did you say you're leaving *tomorrow*?"

"Yeess . . . ," Sandra said, her face suddenly uncertain. "We're on the twelve thirty train, so we'll be leaving just before lunch. I . . . is that a problem? If you're not confident about coping straight out of the box, I can try to reschedule my early meetings . . ."

She trailed off, and I swallowed.

"It's fine," I said, with a confidence I didn't completely feel. "I mean, I'd have to hit the ground sometime; I really don't think it'll make much difference whether it's this weekend or next."

Are you mad? a voice was screaming inside my head. *Are you crazy? You barely know these children.*

But another part of me was whispering something very different—*Good*. Because in a way, this made things considerably easier.

"We can play it by ear," Sandra was saying. "I'll keep in touch by phone—if the children are too unsettled, then I can fly back mid-week perhaps? You'll only have the little ones for the first few days, so hopefully that'll make the transition a little bit easier . . ."

She stopped again, a little awkwardly this time, but I was nodding. I was actually nodding, my face stiff with the effort of holding in my real feelings.

"Well," Sandra said at last. She put down her coffee cup. "Petra's already in bed, but the girls are through in the TV room watching *Peppa Pig*. I don't want to delegate my last bedtime with them to you completely, but shall we do it together, so you can get a feel for their routine?"

I nodded and followed her as she led the way through the darkened glass cathedral towards the concealed door to the TV room.

Inside the blinds were drawn, the floor was still carpeted with scattered Duplo and battered dolls, and two little girls were curled up together on the sofa, wearing flannel pajamas and clutching soft, worn teddy bears. Maddie was sucking her thumb, though she took it swiftly out of her mouth as her mother came in, with a slightly guilty jump. I resolved to look that one up in the binder.

We perched on the arms of the sofa, Sandra fondly ruffling her fingers through Ellie's silky curls while the episode wound its way to the close, and then she picked up the remote control and shut down the screen.

"Oh, Mummeeeee!" The chorus was immediate, though slightly half-hearted, as if they didn't really expect Sandra to acquiesce. "Just one more!"

"No, darlings," Sandra said. She scooped up Ellie, who wrapped her legs around her waist and buried her face in her mother's shoulder. "It's super late. Come on, let's go up. If you're *very* lucky, Rowan will read you a story tonight!"

"I don't want Rowan," Ellie whispered into the crook of her mother's neck. "I want you."

"Well . . . we'll see when we get up there," Sandra said. She hitched Ellie into a more comfortable position and held out her hand to Maddie. "Come on, sweetie. Up we go."

"I want *you*," Ellie said doggedly as Sandra began to climb the stairs, me trailing after her. Sandra gave me a little eye roll and a smile over her shoulder.

"I tell you what," she whispered to Ellie, though deliberately loud enough for me to hear. "Maybe you'll get a story from me *and* a story from Rowan. How does that sound?"

Ellie made no reply to this, only dug her face further into Sandra's shoulder.

Upstairs the curtains on the landing were drawn, and I could see the dim pink light of Petra's night-light filtering across the carpet. Sandra supervised tooth brushing and the loo while I made my way down the softly carpeted hallway to Maddie and Ellie's doorway.

There they were—two little beds, each bathed in the soft glow of a bedside light—one pink, the other a kind of dusky peach. Above each one was a collection of framed prints—a baby footprint, a scribble just recognizable as a cat, a butterfly made out of two chubby handprints—and tangled around the frames were strings of fairy lights, giving off their gentle illumination.

It was picture-perfect—like an illustration from a nursery catalog.

I sat gingerly on the foot of one of the little beds, and at last I heard feet and whining voices, swiftly hushed by Sandra.

"Shh, Maddie, you'll wake Petra. Come on now, dressing gowns off and into bed."

Ellie jumped into hers, but Maddie stood stonily for a moment, regarding me, and I realized it must be her bed I was sitting on.

"Do you want me to move?" I asked, but she said nothing, only folded her arms mutinously, got into bed, and turned her face towards the wall, as if pretending I wasn't there.

"Shall I sit on the bean bag?" I asked Sandra, who gave a laugh and shook her head.

"You're fine. Stay there. Maddie takes a bit of time to warm up to people sometimes, don't you, sweetie?"

Maddie said nothing, and I wasn't sure I blamed her. It must be uncomfortable hearing herself discussed with a stranger like this.

Sandra began to read a Winnie the Pooh story, her voice low and soporific, and when at last she finished the final sentence, she leaned over, checking Ellie's face. Her eyes were closed, and she was snoring very gently. Sandra kissed her cheek, clicked off the lights, and then stood and came across to me.

"Maddie," she said very quietly, "Maddie, do you want a story from Rowan?"

Maddie said nothing, and Sandra leaned over and peered at her face, still turned to the wall. Her eyes were shut tight.

"Out like a light!" Sandra whispered, a touch of triumph in her voice. "Oh well, your rendition will have to wait until tomorrow. I'm sorry I didn't hear it."

She kissed Maddie's cheek too, drew her covers up a little, and tucked some kind of soft toy under her chin—I couldn't see what exactly—and then clicked off her light as well, leaving just the glow of the night-light. Then she gave a last glance at her sleeping daughters and made her way to the door, with me following behind.

"Can you close the door after you?" she said, and I turned, ready to do so, glancing back at the little white beds and their occupants, both in shadow now.

The night-light was very soft and too close to the floor to show much except for shadows around the girls' beds, but for a moment, deep in the blackness, I thought I saw the glint of two little eyes, glaring at me.

Then they snapped shut, and I pulled the door closed behind me.

I couldn't sleep that night. It wasn't the bed, which was as sumptuously comfortable as before. It wasn't the heat. The room had been oppressively warm when I first entered, but I had managed to persuade the system to switch to cooling mode, and now the air was pleasantly temperate. It wasn't even my worries over being left alone with the children the next day. If anything I was feeling relieved at the thought of getting rid of Bill and Sandra. Well . . . not Sandra . . . mostly Bill, if truth were told.

The uncomfortable end to the evening flashed though my head once more. We had been sitting in the kitchen, talking and chatting, and then at last Sandra had stretched and yawned and announced her intention to make an early night of it.

She'd kissed Bill and headed for the stairs, and just as I was thinking about following her, Bill had refilled both our glasses without asking me.

"Oh," I said, half-heartedly. "I was . . . I mean I shouldn't . . ."

"Come on." He pushed the glass towards me. "Just one more. This is my only chance to get to know you before I entrust my kids to your care, after all! You could be anyone for all I know."

He gave me a grin, his tanned cheeks wrinkling, and I wondered how old he was. He could have been anything from forty to sixty; it was hard to tell. He wore rimless glasses and had one of those tanned, slightly weather-beaten faces, and his cropped hair gave him an almost ageless quality, slightly Bruce Willis–esque.

I was very tired—the long journey and the stress of packing had finally hit me like a ton of bricks. But there was enough truth in his remark for me to sigh inwardly and draw the glass towards me. He was right, after all. This was our one chance to get to know each other before he left. It would seem strange and evasive to refuse him that.

He rested his chin on one hand and watched as I picked up the glass and put it to my lips—his head tilted, his eyes following the movement of the wine to my lips and staying there.

"So, who are you, Rowan Caine?" he asked. His voice was a little slurred, and I wondered how much he'd had to drink.

Something, something in his tone, in the directness of the question, in the uncomfortably intense intimacy of his gaze, made my stomach shift uneasily.

"What do you want to know?" I said, with an attempt at lightness.

"You remind me of someone . . . but I can't think who. A film star, maybe. You don't have any famous relatives, do you? A sister in Hollywood?"

I gave a smile at this rather tired line.

"No, definitely not. I'm an only child, and anyway, my family's about as ordinary as you can get."

"Maybe it's work . . . anyone in the family work in architecture?"

I thought of my stepfather's insurance sales business and only just stopped myself from rolling my eyes. Instead, I shook my head, firmly, and he looked at me over his wineglass, frowning so that a deep furrow appeared at the bridge of his nose.

"Maybe it's that . . . what's her name. That *Devil Wears Prada* woman."

"What, Meryl Streep?" I said, startled out of my nervousness enough to give a short laugh. He shook his head impatiently.

"No, the other one. The young one. Anne Hathaway, that's it. You've got a look of her."

"Anne Hathaway?" I tried not to look as skeptical as I felt. Anne

Hathaway maybe if she gained forty to sixty pounds and had acne scars and a haircut by the salon trainee. "I have to say, Bill, you're very kind, but that's the first time I've ever heard that comparison."

"It's not that though." He got up and came around the breakfast bar to my side of it, sitting on the gleaming chrome stool facing me, his legs spread wide so that I couldn't easily move without rubbing his thigh. "No, it's not that. I definitely feel like we've met. Who did you say you worked for before this?"

I rattled off the list again, and he shook his head, dissatisfied.

"I don't know any of them. Maybe I'm imagining it. I feel like I'd remember a face . . . well, a face like yours."

Fuck. Something twisted in the pit of my stomach. I had been in this situation too often not to recognize where this was heading. My first job out of school, a young waitress with a boss who dangled a pay raise and complimented me on my fuchsia-pink bra. Countless creeps on countless nights out, putting themselves between me and the door. Randy dads at the nursery, angling for sympathy about their postpartum wives who didn't understand them . . .

Bill was one of *them*.

He was my employer. He was my boss's husband. And worst of all, he was . . .

Jesus. I can't bring myself to say it.

My hands had begun to shake, and I clenched my fingers more tightly around the stem of my wineglass to try to hide it.

I cleared my throat and tried to push my stool back, but it was wedged against the edge of the breakfast bar. Bill's meaty denim-clad thighs blocked my way, effectively preventing me from getting down.

"Well, I'd better be heading up." My voice fluted slightly with nerves. "Early start tomorrow, right?"

"There's no hurry," he said, and he reached out and took the wineglass from my fingers, filled it up, and then put out his hand towards my face. "You've just . . . you've got a little bit . . ."

His smooth, slightly sweaty thumb stroked the corner of my bottom lip, and I felt one knee nudge, very gently, between mine.

For a second I froze, and a fluttering panicked nausea rose up, choking me. Then something inside me seemed to snap, and I slid abruptly down off the stool, barging past him so fast that the wine slopped and spilled onto the concrete.

"Sorry," I stammered. "So sorry, let me, I'll get a cloth—"

"It's fine," he said. He was not one iota discomfited, only amused at my reaction. He stayed in place, half sitting, half leaning comfortably against the barstool, as I grabbed a dishcloth and mopped at the floor between his legs.

For one second I looked up at him, and he looked down, and the quip I'd heard a thousand times, always accompanied by ribald laughter, flashed through the back of my mind. *While you're down there, love . . .*

I stood up, my face burning, and dumped the wine-stained cloth into the sink.

"Good night, Bill," I said abruptly, and I turned on my heel.

"Good night, Rowan."

And I walked up the two flights of stairs to bed, not looking back.

As I shut the door of my new room behind me, I felt a sense of overwhelming relief. I'd unpacked earlier, and even though the room didn't feel like home yet, it did have a sense of being a little corner of the house that was my own territory, somewhere I could spread out, stop acting a part, stop being Rowan the Perfect Nanny and just be . . . me.

I pulled the elastic band out of my tight, perky ponytail and felt my thick wiry hair spring out into a crown around my head and the polite, people-pleasing smile that I'd had plastered on my face since I'd arrived relax into a weary neutrality. As I stripped off the buttoned-up cardigan, blouse, and tweed skirt I felt like I was shedding layers of pretense, back to the girl I was behind the facade—the one who wore pajamas until bedtime at the weekends, who lay on the sofa not reading a self-help book, but mainlining *Judge Judy.* The one who would have called Bill a fucking pig instead of standing there, paralyzed into politeness, before offering to wipe up after herself.

The intricacies of the control panels were a welcome distraction from having to think about that part of things, and by the time I'd wrested control of the temperature down to something more reasonable and remembered how to work the shower, my heart was thumping less and I was talking myself round into an acceptance of the situation.

Okay, so Bill was a creep. He wasn't the first I'd encountered. Why was I so disappointed to find him here?

I knew the answer, of course. But it wasn't just who he was. It was everything he represented—all the hard work and careful planning that had brought me here, all the hopes and dreams bound up with my decision to apply. That feeling that for once in my life something was going *right,* falling into place. The whole situation had seemed perfect—too perfect, perhaps. There had to be a fly in the ointment, and maybe Bill was it.

Suddenly the supernatural stuff didn't seem so mysterious after all. Not a poltergeist. Just your average fiftysomething man who couldn't keep his dick in his pants. The same old, boring, depressing story.

Still, it felt like a kick in the guts.

It wasn't until I had finished showering and had done my teeth, and was lying in bed, that I looked up at the ceiling. At the recessed light fittings, and the little blinking smoke alarm by the door, and . . . something else in the corner over there. What *was* that? A burglar alarm sensor? A second smoke detector?

Or was it . . .

I thought of Sandra's remark at my interview: *The whole house is wired up . . .*

It *couldn't* be a camera . . . could it?

But no. That would be more than creepy. That would be illegal surveillance. I was an employee—and I had a reasonable expectation of privacy, or whatever the legal terminology was.

All the same, I got up, wrapped my dressing gown around myself, and dragged a chair over to the carpet beneath the egg-shaped thing in the corner. One of my socks was lying on the floor where I'd stripped it off before getting in the shower, and I picked it up, climbed onto the chair, and stood on tiptoes to fit it over the sensor. I could *just* reach. It fit perfectly, and the empty toe of the sock hung there, flaccid and slightly disconsolate.

Only then, comforted, though with a feeling of slight ridiculousness, did I get back into bed and finally let myself fall asleep.

I awoke in the night with a start, and the vague feeling of something wrong—without being able to put my finger on it. I lay there, my heart pounding, wondering what it was that had woken me. I had no memory of having been dreaming—only a sudden jerk into consciousness.

It took a minute, and then it came again—a noise. Footsteps. *Creak . . . creak . . . creak . . .* slow and measured, as though someone was pacing on a wooden floor, which made no sense at all, since all the floors up here were thickly carpeted.

Creak . . . creak . . . creeeeak . . . The sound was hollow, heavy, resonant . . . a slow tread like a man's, not the scamper of a child. It sounded as though it was coming from above, which was ridiculous, as I was on the top floor.

Slowly I sat up and groped for the light, but when I turned the switch, nothing happened. I flicked it again and then realized with a curse that I must have overridden the lamp at the main panel. I couldn't face grappling with the control panel in the middle of the night and risking turning on the sound system or something, so I grabbed my phone from where it was charging and switched on the torch.

My chest was tight, and as I took a pull at my inhaler I realized suddenly that the room was extremely cold. No doubt when I had changed the temperature settings I had overdone it. Now, outside of the warm cocoon of bedclothes, the chill was uncomfortable. But my dressing gown was on the foot of the bed, so I pulled it on and stood there, trying not to let my teeth chatter, the thin beam of torchlight illuminating a narrow sliver of wheat-colored carpet and not much else.

The footsteps had stopped, and I hesitated for a moment, holding my breath, listening, wondering if they would start up again. Nothing. I took another puff at my inhaler, waiting, considering. Still nothing.

The bed was warm, and it was tempting to crawl back under the duvet and pretend I hadn't heard anything, but I knew that I wouldn't sleep well unless I at least *tried* to check out the source. Pulling my dressing gown belt tighter, I opened the door of my room a crack.

There was no one outside, but nevertheless I peered into the broom cupboard. It was, of course, totally empty except for the brushes, and the winking charge light of the Hoover. No possibility of anything bigger than a mouse hiding in here.

I shut the cupboard and then, feeling a little like a trespasser, I tried Rhiannon's door, resolutely ignoring the scrawled *KEEP OUT OR YOU DIE.* I had thought it might be locked, but the handle turned without resistance, and the heavy door swung wide, shushing across the thick carpet.

Inside it was pitch-black, the blackout curtains firmly drawn, but it had the indefinable feel of an empty room. Still, I held up my phone and swung the narrow torch beam from wall to wall. There was no one there.

That was it. There were no other rooms on this floor. And the ceiling above was smooth and unbroken by so much as an attic hatch. For although my memory of the sounds was fading fast, my impression had been that the sounds were coming from above. Something on the roof maybe? A bird? It wasn't a person prowling around at any rate, that much was clear.

Shivering again, I returned to my own room, where I stood for a moment, irresolute, in the middle of the carpet, listening and waiting for the sounds to come again, but they did not.

I turned off the torch, climbed back into bed, and drew the covers up. But it was a long time before I slept.

"Mummy!"

The Tesla wound its way along the driveway and towards the main road, with Ellie running in its wake, the tears streaming down her face as Jack's driving speed outpaced her short legs.

"Mummy, come back!"

"Bye, darlings!" Sandra's head leaned out the rear window, her honey-colored hair whipping in the breeze as the car picked up speed. There was a cheerful smile on her face, but I could see the distress in her eyes, and I knew that she was keeping up a happy facade for the sake of the children. Bill did not turn around. He was bent over his phone in the back seat beside her.

"Mummy!" Ellie shouted, desperation in her voice. "Mummy, please don't go!"

"Bye, sweeties! You'll have a wonderful time with Rowan, and I'll be back very soon. Goodbye! I love you all!"

And then the car rounded the bend in the drive and disappeared from sight among the trees.

Ellie's legs slowed, and she stumbled to a halt, letting out a wail of grief before she threw herself dramatically to the ground.

"Oh, Ellie!" I hitched Petra higher on my hip and jogged down the drive to where Ellie lay, face-first on the gravel. "Ellie, darling, come on, let's go and get some ice cream."

I knew from Sandra's instructions that this was a big treat, something not allowed every day, because it made both girls rather hyper, but Ellie only shook her head and wailed louder.

"Come on, sweetheart." I bent down, with some difficulty—as I was holding Petra—and took her wrist, trying to pull her up, but she only let out a scream and wrenched her arm out of my hand, slamming her little fist onto the gravel.

"Ow!" she screamed, redoubling her sobs and looking up at me with angry, red, tear-filled eyes. "You *hurt* me!"

"I was just trying—"

"Go *away*, you *hurt* me, I'm going to tell my mummy!"

I stood for a moment, irresolute over her angry, prone form, unsure what to do.

"Go *away*!" she screamed again.

At last, I gave a sigh and began to walk back up the drive towards the house. It felt wrong leaving her there, in the middle of what was, basically, a road, but the gate at the foot of the drive was shut, and it would be at least half an hour before Jack returned. Hopefully she would have calmed down long before then and I could coax her back into the house.

On my hip Petra had begun grousing, and I suppressed another sigh. Please, not a meltdown from her as well. And where the hell was Maddie? She had disappeared before her parents left, flitting off into the woods to the east of the house, refusing to say goodbye.

"Oh, let her go," Bill had said, as Sandra flapped around trying to find her to kiss her goodbye. "You know what she's like; she prefers to lick her wounds in private."

Lick her wounds. Just a silly cliché, right? At the time I hadn't dwelt on it, but now I wondered. Was Maddie wounded? If so, how?

Up in the house I sat Petra in her high chair, strapped her in, and checked the red binder in case it gave instructions for what to do if the children disappeared off the face of the earth. The whole thing must have been at least three inches thick, and a cursory flick-through after breakfast had told me that it contained information on everything from how much Calpol to give and when, through to bedtime routines, favorite books, nappy-rash protocol, homework schedules, and which washing capsules to use for the girls' ballet uniforms. Virtually every moment of the day was accounted for, with notes ranging from what snacks to serve, right through to which TV programs to choose, and how much they were allowed to watch.

The one thing it didn't cover was total disappearance—or at least, if it did, I couldn't find the page where it was mentioned, but as I skimmed down the carefully annotated "typical weekend day," I saw that Petra was overdue for lunch, which might explain her irritability. I didn't really want to start preparing food before I'd tracked down Maddie and Ellie, but at least I could give Petra a snack to tide her over and stop her grumbling.

6:00, the page began. *All the younger ones (but particularly Ellie) are prone to early wakings. To that end, we have installed the sleep-training "Happy bunny clock" in the girls' room. It's a digital clock with a screen image of a sleeping bunny that soundlessly switches over to an image of a wide-awake "Happy bunny" at 6:00 a.m. If Ellie wakes before this, please gently (!) encourage her to check the clock and get back into bed if the bunny is still asleep. Obviously use your judgment regarding nightmares and toilet accidents.*

Jesus. Was there nothing in this house that wasn't controlled by the bloody app? I scanned the page, skipping past suggested outfits and wet-weather clothes, and acceptable breakfast menus, down to midmorning.

10:30–11:15—snack, e.g., some fruit (bananas, blueberries, grapes—QUARTERED for Petra, please), raisins (sparingly only—teeth!), breadsticks, rice cakes, or cucumber sticks. No strawberries

(Ellie is allergic), no whole nuts (nut butters are okay, but we only buy the sugar-/salt-free kind), and finally Petra is not allowed snacks containing refined sugar or excess salt (older girls are allowed sugar in moderation). This can be hard to police if you are out, so in that scenario I suggest taking a snack box.

Well, at least the app didn't prepare the snacks. Still, I'd never encountered anything like this level of detail at any other nannying job—at Little Nippers the staff handbook was a slim pamphlet that concentrated mostly on how to report staff sickness. Rules, yes. Screen time, sanctions, red lines, allergies—all of that was normal. But this—did she think I had spent nearly ten years in childcare without knowing you had to cut up grapes?

As I closed the scarlet folder and pushed it away from me across the table, I wondered. Was it the unsettling changes of staff that had made Sandra so controlling? Or was she just a woman desperately trying to be there for her family, even when she couldn't be physically present? Bill, it was clear, felt no compunction about leaving his children alone with a comparative stranger, however well qualified. But Sandra's binder spoke of a very different type of parent—one very conflicted about the situation she was in. Which begged the question of why, in that case, she was so determined to be with Bill rather than at home. Was it really just professional pride? Or was there something else going on?

There was a huge marble fruit bowl in the center of the concrete table, freshly stocked with oranges, apples, satsumas, and bananas, and with a sigh, I ripped a banana off the bunch, peeled it, and placed a few chunks on Petra's tray. Then I went into the playroom to see if Maddie had returned. She wasn't there, nor was she in the living room, or anywhere in the house, as far as I could tell. At last I went to the utility room door, the one she had left by, and called out into the woods.

"Maddie! Ellie! Petra and I are having ice cream." I paused, listening for the sound of running feet, cracking branches. Nothing came. "With sprinkles." I had no actual idea if there were sprinkles but at this point I didn't care about false advertising, I just wanted to know where they both were.

More silence, just the sound of birds. The sun had gone in, leaving the air surprisingly chilly, and I shivered, feeling the goose bumps rise on my bare arms. Suddenly hot chocolate seemed more appropriate than ice cream, in spite of the fact that it was June.

"Okay!" I called again, more loudly this time. "More sprinkles for me!"

And I walked back into the house, leaving the side door open a crack.

In the kitchen I did a double take.

Petra was standing up in her high chair on the far side of the breakfast bar, triumphantly waving a chunk of banana at me.

"Fuck!"

For a moment all feeling drained out of me, and I stood, frozen to the spot, looking at her precarious stance, the unforgiving concrete beneath her, her small wobbly feet on the slippery wood.

And then, regaining my senses, I ran, stumbling over a stray teddy, staggering around the corner of the breakfast bar to snatch her up, my heart in my mouth.

"Oh my God, Petra, you bad, bad girl. You *mustn't* do that. Jesus. Oh, Jesus Christ."

She could have died—that was the long and short of it. If she'd fallen and struck her head on the concrete floor, she would have been concussed before I could reach her.

How could I have been so stupid?

I'd supervised toddlers a million times before—I'd done all the right things, pulled her chair away from the counter so she couldn't push herself backwards with her feet, and I was sure, *certain* in fact, that I'd done up those clips. They were far too stiff for little fingers.

So how had she got free?

Had she wriggled out?

I examined the clips. One side was still fastened. The other was open. Shit. I must have not pushed one home quite hard enough, and Petra had worked it loose and then managed to squirm out of the other side of the restraint.

So it was my fault after all. The thought made my hands feel cold with fear, and my cheeks feel hot with shame. Thank *God* it hadn't happened when Sandra was here. That kind of safeguarding stuff was pretty much nannying 101. She would have been within her rights to sack me there and then.

Though, of course . . . she still could, if she was watching over the cameras. In spite of myself, my eyes flicked up to the ceiling, and sure enough there was one of those little white egg-shaped domes in the far corner of the room. I felt my face flush and looked away hastily, imagining Sandra seeing my guilty reaction.

Fuck. *Fuck.*

Well, there was nothing I could do, apart from hope that Sandra and Bill had better things to do than pore over the footage of their security cameras every hour of the day and night. I was pretty confident that Bill hadn't so much as glanced at the app since leaving, but Sandra . . . somehow that binder spoke of a level of intensity that I had not quite anticipated from her relaxed, cheerful manner at the interview.

But with any luck they would be in a mobile black spot, or even in the air by now. Did the footage record? How long was it stored for? I didn't know, and somehow I doubted whether that information was in the binder.

The realization was unsettling. I could be being watched, right now.

It was with a strange performative feeling that I hugged Petra tightly to my chest and dropped a shaky kiss on the top of her head. Beneath my lips I felt the gentle flex of her fontanelle, the fragility of a baby-soft skull almost, but not quite, closed over.

"Don't do that again," I told her, firmly, feeling the adrenaline still pulsing through me, and then, with an effort at restoring normality, I lifted her up and took her over to the sink, where I wiped her face. Then I looked at my watch, trying to breathe slowly and normally, and remember what I had been doing before Petra scared the life out of me.

It was just gone one. The binder had said Petra ate lunch twelve thirty to one and then went down for a nap at two. But in spite of that, she was grousing and rubbing her eyes crossly, and I found myself mentally adding up timings and trying to figure out how to handle this. At the nursery they'd gone down straight after lunch more or less, around one.

I didn't want to mess with her routine so early in the day, but on the other hand, stretching out a tired, cranky baby until the specified time wasn't a great idea either, and would probably result in a bad night's sleep if she was the type of child who got more wired the more exhausted she became. I stared doubtfully down at the top of her head, trying to decide. Suddenly, the idea of a quiet hour or so to round up Maddie and Ellie was very appealing. It would definitely be easier without a fussy toddler in tow.

Fretfully Petra scrubbed a balled-up fist at her eyes and gave a tired sob, and I made up my mind.

"Come on, you," I said aloud, and took her upstairs to her room.

Inside, the blackout blinds were already drawn, and I switched on the illuminated mobile as the binder had instructed and put her gently down on her back. She rolled over onto her tummy and rubbed her face into the mattress, but I sat quietly beside her, one hand on her wriggling spine, while the soft light show played over the ceiling and walls. Petra was grumbling to herself, but her cries were getting farther apart, and I could tell she was ready to go under at any moment.

At last, she seemed to be completely asleep, and I stood carefully and laid her rabbit comforter gently over one hand, where she could find it if she woke. For a moment she stirred and I froze, but her fingers only tightened onto the material as she let out a soft little snore. With a sigh of relief, I picked up the monitor that was hooked over the end of the cot, tucked it into my belt, and tiptoed out of the room.

The house was completely silent as I stood on the landing, listening for the sound of running feet or childish laughter.

Where the hell were they?

I hadn't been in Sandra and Bill's room, but I knew from the layout of the house that the window must overlook the drive, and holding my breath slightly, I turned the handle and opened the door.

The sight made my breath catch in my throat for a moment. The room was huge. They must have knocked together at least two other bedrooms to make it—maybe even three. There was an enormous bed piled high with plump cushions and white bed linen, and facing it a huge carved stone fireplace. Three long windows overlooked the front of the house. One was open a few inches, and muslin curtains fluttered a little in the breeze.

There were drawers left slightly open, and a closet ajar, and I felt a sharp tug of curiosity as I crossed the silver-gray carpet to the central window, but I pushed it down. For all I knew, Sandra and Bill could be watching me right now, and while I had an alibi for wanting to look out the window over the drive, I certainly had no excuse for rummaging in their cupboards.

When I reached the window, Ellie was nowhere in sight; the curve of drive where she had been lying was empty. I was not sure whether that was a relief. At least Jack wouldn't run her over when he brought the Tesla back. But where on earth was she? Sandra had seemed remarkably relaxed about the children running off into the woods, but every bone in my body was screeching discomfort with the situation—at the nursery we'd had to risk assess everything, from a trip to the park through to messy play with porridge oats, and there were a billion risks I had absolutely no way of knowing. What if there was a pond within the grounds? Or a steep fall? What if they climbed a tree and couldn't get down? What if the fencing wasn't secure and they wandered out into the road? What if a dog—

I broke off my mental litany of worst-case scenarios.

The dogs. I'd forgotten to ask Sandra whether their routine was down to me, but presumably an extra walk couldn't hurt, and surely they would be able to find the children. If nothing else, their presence would give me an excuse to go hunting in the woods without looking to the children like they were running rings around me. I had to establish myself as someone firmly in charge right from the outset, otherwise my authority was going to be shot to pieces, and I would never recover.

I pushed aside the unsettling thought of what would happen when Rhiannon returned and a teenager was added to the mix. Hopefully Sandra would be home by then to back me up. . . .

Downstairs the dogs were lying in their baskets in the kitchen, though they both looked up hopefully as I walked in carrying their leads.

"Walkies!" I said brightly, and they bounded over. "Good girl . . . er . . . Claude," I said as I struggled to find the right attachment on the collar, though in truth I wasn't sure if I had the girl or the boy. Claude bounded around me excitedly as I wrestled with Hero, but at last I had them both on leads and a handful of dog biscuits in my pocket in case of problems, and I set off, out of the utility room door, across the graveled yard, past the stable block, and into the woods.

It was a beautiful day. In spite of my growing anxiety about the children, I couldn't help but notice this as I walked down a winding, faintly marked path through the trees, the dogs straining at their leashes. The sun filtered through the canopy above, and our movements sent golden dust motes spinning and whirling up from the rich loam underneath our feet, the sun gleaming off the tiny particles of pollen and old man's beard that floated in the still air beneath the trees.

The dogs seemed to have a definite idea of where they were going, and I let them lead, conscious of the fact that they were probably puzzled about being kept on leashes in their own garden. They'd have to put up with it though. I had no idea if they'd come when I called, and I couldn't risk losing them as well.

We were heading downhill, towards the bottom of the drive, though I couldn't see it through the trees. Behind me I heard the crack of a twig and turned sharply, but there was no one there. It must have been an animal, a fox perhaps.

At last we broke out of the cover of the trees into a little clearing, and my stomach gave an uncomfortable lurch, for there it was—the thing I'd been fearing ever since the girls had disappeared—a pond. Not very deep, but plenty deep enough for a small child to drown. The water was peat-colored and brackish, an oily scum floating on the surface from the decomposing pine needles. I poked it doubtfully with a stick, and bubbles of stagnant air floated lazily to the surface, but to my relief the rest of the pond looked undisturbed, the water clear except for the swirls of mud my stick had stirred up. Or . . .

nearly undisturbed. Walking around the far side I saw the imprints of small shoes on the bank, skidding as if two little girls had been messing around by the water's edge. There was no way of knowing when they had been made, but they looked fairly fresh. The prints led down the bank, becoming deeper and deeper as the mud softened, and then turned and went away again, back into the forest. I followed them for a few meters until the ground became too hard to take a print, but there were two sets of shoes, and at least I knew now that they were probably together, and almost certainly safe.

The dogs were whining and straining against their leads, desperate to get into the muddy pond and splash about, but there was no way I was having that. I wasn't bathing a pair of filthy dogs on my first day on top of everything else.

There was no path up through the woods in the direction the footsteps had been leading, but I followed in as near an approximation as I could, when suddenly a crackling scream split the air. I stopped dead, my heart thumping erratically in my chest for the second time that day, the dogs barking hysterically and leaping at the end of their leashes.

For a second I didn't know what to do. I stood, looking wildly around. The scream had sounded close at hand, but I could see no one, and I couldn't hear any footsteps over the noise the dogs were making. Then it came again, long and almost unbearably high-pitched, and with a stomach-lurching realization, I understood.

I pulled the baby monitor out of my pocket, and watched as the lights flared and dipped in time with the long, bubbling shriek of pure fear.

For a moment I just stood there paralyzed, holding the monitor in my hand, the dogs' leads looped around my wrist. Should I try to access the cameras?

With shaking hands, I pulled out my phone and pressed the icon of the home-management app.

Welcome to Happy, Rowan, the screen said, with agonizing slowness. *Home is where the Happy is!* And then, to my despair, *Updating user permissions. Please be patient. Home is where the Happy is!*

I swore, stuffed both the phone and the monitor back into my pocket, and began to run.

I was a long way from the house, down a slope, and my breath was tearing in my throat by the time I left the cover of the trees and saw the house in front of me. The dogs had broken away from me some way back, tugging their leads out of my numb fingers, and now they were leaping and gamboling in front and behind me, barking joyfully, convinced that this was all some kind of game.

When I reached the front door, it was standing ajar, in spite of the fact that I knew it had been closed when I left—I had used the utility-room door, leaving it open for Maddie and Ellie in case they returned, and for a second I thought I might be sick. What had I done? What had happened to poor little Petra?

I was almost too frightened to stumble the last few steps up the flight of stairs to the nursery, but I forced myself, leaving the dogs in the hallway, tangled up in their own leads, and at last I was outside Petra's door, sick with fear about what I was about to find.

It was closed, just as I'd left it, and I pushed down a sob in my throat as I turned the knob—but what I found there made me stop short on the threshold, blinking and trying to fight down my gasping breath.

Petra was asleep, in her cot, arms flung out to either side, sooty lashes sweeping her pink cheeks. Her bunny was clutched in her left hand, and she had plainly not stirred since I had put her down.

It didn't make sense.

I had just enough self-control left to back out of the room, closing the door quietly behind me, before I sank to the floor in the hallway outside, my back hard against the knobbly banisters, my face in my hands, trying not to sob with shock and relief, feeling the wheeze in my chest as my lungs labored to take in enough oxygen to stabilize my pounding pulse.

With shaky hands, I pulled my inhaler out of my pocket and took a puff, then tried to make sense of it all. What had happened?

Had the sound *not* come from the monitor? But that was impossible—it was equipped with lights that illuminated to show when the baby was crying, in case you had the volume turned low for some reason. I had *seen* the lights. And the noise had been coming from the speaker, I was certain of it.

Had Petra had a nightmare and cried out? But when I thought back, that didn't make sense either. It was not a baby's cry. That was part of what had frightened me so much. The sound I'd heard was not the fretful wail I knew so well from the nursery but a long, throbbing shriek of terror, one made by a much older child, or even an adult.

"Hello?"

The voice came from downstairs, making me jump again, convulsively this time, and I stood, my pulse racing, and leaned over the bannisters.

"Hello? Who is it?" My voice came out not sharp and authoritative, as I had intended, but quavering and squeaky with fear. "Who's there?" It had been an adult voice, a woman, and now I heard footsteps in the hall and saw a face below, peering up at me.

"You'll be the new nanny, I dare say?"

It was a woman, perhaps fifty or sixty years old, her face ruddy and her body foreshortened by my perspective. She looked plump and motherly, but there was something in her voice and her expression that I couldn't quite pin down. It wasn't welcoming, that was for sure. A sort of . . . pinched disapproval?

There were leaves in my hair, and as I began to make my way down the flight of steps towards the ground floor, I saw that I'd left a trail of spattered mud on the thick carpet, in my headlong flight to Petra.

Two buttons had come adrift on my blouse and I fastened them and coughed, feeling my face still hot with exertion and fright.

"Um, hello. Yes. Yes, I'm Rowan. And you must be . . ."

"I'm Jean. Jean McKenzie." She looked me up and down, not troubling to conceal her disapproval, and then shook her head. "It's up to you, miss, but I don't approve of keeping children locked out, and I dare say Mrs. Elincourt wouldna like it either."

"Locked out?" I was puzzled for a moment. "What do you mean?"

"I found the poor bairns shivering on the step in their sundresses when I came to clean."

"But wait"—I put out a hand—"hang on a second. I didn't lock anyone out. They ran away from *me*. I was out looking for them. I left the back door open for them."

"It was locked when I arrived," Jean said stiffly. I shook my head. "It must have blown shut but I didn't lock it. I wouldn't."

"It was *locked* when I arrived," was all she said, with a touch of stubbornness this time.

Anger flared inside me, replacing the fear I'd felt for Petra. Was she accusing me of lying?

"Well . . . maybe it came off the latch or something," I said at last. "Are the girls okay?"

"Aye, they're having a bite in the kitchen wi' me."

"Were you—" I stopped, trying to figure out how to phrase this without placing myself even lower in her estimation. Plainly, for whatever reason, this woman didn't like me, and I mustn't give her any ammunition to report to Sandra. "I came back because I heard a sound from Petra on the baby monitor. Did you hear her?"

"She's not let out a peep," Jean said firmly. "I've been keeping my eye on them all"—*Unlike you*, was the unspoken subtext—"and I'd have heard her if she was greeting."

"Greeting?"

"Crying," Jean said impatiently.

"Maddie then? Or Ellie? Did either of them come up?"

"They've been down in the kitchen with me, miss," Jean said, a touch of real crossness in her voice. "Now, if you'll excuse me, I need to be getting back to them. They're too wee to be left alone wi' the stove."

"Of course." I felt my cheeks flush with the implied criticism. "But please, that's my job. I'll give them lunch."

"I've given it to them already. The poor wee mites were ravenous, they needed something hot in them."

I felt my temper, already frayed by the stress of the morning, begin to break.

"Look, Mrs. . . ." I groped for the name, and then found it, "McKenzie, I've already explained, the girls ran away from me; I didn't lock them out. Maybe if they got a bit cold and scared waiting for someone to let them in, that'll make them think twice about running off next time. Now, if you don't mind, I've got work to do."

I pushed past her and stalked into the kitchen, feeling her eyes boring into my back.

In the kitchen Maddie and Ellie were sitting at the breakfast bar eating chocolate chip cookies and drinking juice, with what looked like the remains of a pizza on a plate by the sink. I felt my jaw tighten. All those foods were strictly on Sandra's "occasional treat" list. I'd been planning to settle them down for a film in the afternoon with some cookies in the TV room. Now that was off the menu, Mrs. McKenzie was in their good books, and I would be the bitch nanny who locked them out and had to enforce a healthy supper.

I pushed down my irritation and made myself smile pleasantly.

"Hello, girls, were you playing hide-and-seek?"

"Yes," Ellie said with a giggle, but then she remembered our earlier quarrel, and frowned. "You hurt my wrist."

She held it out, and there, to my chagrin, was a ring of bruises on the pale skin of her stick-thin wrist.

I felt my cheeks color.

I thought about arguing with her, but I didn't want to raise the issue in front of Mrs. McKenzie, and besides, it seemed like I'd done enough to antagonize them both today. Better to swallow my pride.

"I'm ever so sorry, Ellie." I bent down beside her at the breakfast bar so that our heads were on a level, speaking softly so that Mrs. McKenzie wouldn't hear. "I truly didn't mean to. I was just worried you'd hurt yourself on the drive, but I really apologize if I was holding your arm too hard. It was an accident, I promise, and I feel terrible about it. Can we be friends?"

For a second, I thought I saw Ellie wavering, then she jerked and gave a little whimper.

Beneath the breakfast bar I saw Maddie's hand whip back into her lap.

"Maddie," I said quietly, "what just happened?"

"Nothing," Maddie said, almost inaudibly, speaking to her plate more than me.

"Ellie?"

"N-nothing," Ellie said, but she was rubbing her arm, and there were tears in her bright blue eyes.

"I don't believe you. Let me see your arm."

"Nothing!" Ellie said, more fiercely. She pulled down her cardigan and gave me a look of angry betrayal. "I said nothing, go away!"

"Okay."

I stood up. Whatever chance I had had there with Ellie, I'd blown it for the moment. Or rather Maddie had.

Mrs. McKenzie was standing against the counter, her arms crossed, watching us. Then she folded the tea towel and hung it over the stove rail.

"Well, I'll be away now, girls," she said. Her voice, when she spoke to the children, was softer and far more friendly than the terse, clipped tone she'd used with me. She bent and dropped a kiss on top of each head, first Ellie's blond curls, then Maddie's wispy dark locks. "You give your wee sister a kiss from me, now, mind."

"Yes, Mrs. M," Ellie said obediently. Maddie said nothing, but she squeezed Mrs. McKenzie's waist with one arm, and I thought I saw a wistful look in her eye as her gaze followed the woman to the door.

"Goodbye now, girls," Mrs. McKenzie said, and then she was gone. Outside I heard a car start up and bump down the drive to the road.

Alone in the kitchen with the two little girls I felt suddenly drained, and I sank down on the armchair in the corner of the room, wanting nothing more than to put my face in my hands and bawl. What had I taken on with these two hostile little creatures? And yet, I couldn't blame them. I could only imagine how I would have reacted if I'd been left for a week with a total stranger.

The last thing I could cope with was losing the children in the grounds again, so while they finished up their cookies, I crossed into the hallway and examined the inside of the big front door. There was no key—no keyhole even, as I'd observed the very first time I had arrived. Instead, the white panel I had noticed contained a thumb sensor—Sandra had programmed my thumbprint into her phone app earlier that morning, before she left, and shown me how to operate it.

There was a matching panel on the inside, and I gingerly touched it, watching as a series of illuminated icons sprang into life. One of them was a big key, and remembering Sandra's instructions, I tapped it cautiously, and heard a grinding click as the deadlocks inside the door slid home. There was something rather dramatic, even ominous about the sound, almost like a prison-cell lock grinding into place. But at least the door was secure now. There was no way Maddie or Ellie could even reach the panel without a set of steps, let alone activate the lock, since I very much doubted Sandra would have programmed their fingerprints into the system.

Then I went into the utility room. The door there operated with just a regular lock and key—as if Sandra and Bill's budget had run out, or as if they didn't care about the servants' entrance. Or maybe there was some practical reason one door needed to be traditionally operated. Something to do with power cuts or building regulations, perhaps. Either way, it was a relief to be faced with technology an average person could figure out, and it was with a feeling of satisfaction that I twisted the key firmly in the lock and then tucked it away on the doorframe above, just as the binder had instructed. *We keep all keys for the doors operated by traditional locks on the doorframe above the corresponding door, so that they are handy in case of emergency but out of reach of the children*, the paragraph had read. There was something comforting about seeing it up there, far away from little fingers.

Mission accomplished, I went back into the kitchen, my best and brightest smile firmly plastered on.

"Right, girls, what do you say we go through to the TV room and watch a movie. *Frozen*? *Moana*?"

"Yay, *Frozen*!" Ellie said, but Maddie butted in.

"We hate *Frozen*."

"Really?" I made my voice skeptical. "*Really?* Because do you know, I love *Frozen*. In fact I know a sing-along version of *Frozen* where they have the words on the screen and I'm really good at joining in on all the songs."

Behind Maddie I could see Ellie looking desperate but too scared to contradict her sister.

"We *hate Frozen*," Maddie repeated stubbornly. "Come on, Ellie, let's go play in our room."

I watched as she slid down from her stool and stomped into the hallway, the dogs' eyes following her with puzzlement as she went. In the doorway she paused and jerked her head meaningfully at her sister. Ellie's bottom lip quivered.

"We can still watch it if you want, Ellie," I said, keeping my voice as light as I could. "We could watch it together, just you and me. I could make popcorn."

For a minute I thought I saw Ellie hesitate. But then something in her face seemed to harden, and she shook her head, slid from her stool, and turned to follow her sister.

As the sound of their footsteps faded away up the stairs, I sighed and then turned to put on the kettle, to make myself a pot of tea. At least I would have half an hour to myself, to try to figure out the situation.

But before I had even finished filling the kettle, the baby monitor in my pocket gave a crackle and then broke into a fretful coughing cry, telling me that Petra had woken up, and I was back on duty.

No rest for the wicked then.

What had I taken on?

I know I'm going on. And I know you must be wondering when the hell I'm going to get to the point—to the reason I'm here, in this prison cell, and the reason I shouldn't be.

And I promise you, it's coming. But I can't—I can't seem to explain the situation quickly. That was the problem with Mr. Gates. He never let me explain properly—to show how it all built up, all the little things, all the sleepless nights and the loneliness and the isolation, and the craziness of the house and the cameras and everything else. To explain properly, I have to tell you how it happened. Day by day. Night by night. Piece by piece.

Only that sounds as if I'm building something—a house perhaps. Or a picture in a jigsaw. Piece by piece. And the truth is, it was the other way around. Piece by piece, I was being torn apart.

And the first piece was that night.

That first evening . . . well, it wasn't the worst, but it wasn't the best either, not by a long stretch.

Petra woke up from her nap cranky and fretful, and Maddie and Ellie refused to come out of their room all afternoon, even for supper, no matter how much I pleaded, no matter what ultimatums I laid down. *No pudding unless you are downstairs by the time I count from five . . . four . . . three . . .* no sound of feet on the stairs . . . *two . . . one and a half . . .*

It was when I said one and a half that I knew I had lost.

They weren't coming.

For a moment I thought about dragging them out. Ellie was small enough for me to grab her round the waist and carry her forcibly downstairs—but I had just enough sanity left to know that if I started that way, I would never be able to dial it back, and besides, it wasn't Ellie who was the problem, it was Maddie, and she was eight and solidly built, and there was no way I could carry a kicking, screaming, fighting child down that long, curving staircase all by myself, still less, force her to sit down and eat something once I got her into the kitchen.

In the end I capitulated and, after checking Sandra's suggested menu plan in the binder, I took pasta and pesto up to their bedroom—though the memory of those meek little heads bent over Jean McKenzie's chocolate chip cookies was bitter in the back of my head as I knocked on the door and heard Maddie's fierce *Go away!*

"It's me," I said meekly. "I've got your pasta. I'll leave it here outside the door. But me and Petra will be downstairs having ice cream if you want some pudding."

And then I left. It was all I could do.

Downstairs in the kitchen, I tried to stop Petra from throwing her pasta on the floor, and I watched Maddie and Ellie on the iPad. My personalized log-in gave me permission to view the cameras in the children's room, playroom, kitchen, and outside, and to control the lights and the music in some of the other rooms, but there was a whole menu of settings on the left that was grayed out and unavailable. I guessed I would have needed Sandra's log-in to control those.

Although I still found it a little creepy to be able to spy on the children from afar like this, I began to appreciate how useful it was. I was able to watch from my seat by the breakfast bar as Maddie moved towards the bedroom door and then came back into view of the cameras, dragging the tray of food across the carpet.

There was a little table in the middle of the room, and I watched as she directed Ellie to one seat and put out their bowls and cutlery, and sat opposite her sister. I didn't have the sound on, but it was plain from her actions that she was bossing Ellie around and telling her to eat up . . . probably making her try the peas I had mixed into the pesto, judging by Ellie's gestures as she protested. My heart gave a funny little clench, of angry pity mixed with a kind of affection. *Oh, Maddie,* I wanted to say. *It doesn't have to be like this. We don't have to be enemies.*

But for the moment at least, it seemed like we did.

After supper I bathed Petra, listening with half an ear to the sounds of some kind of audio book coming from Maddie and Ellie's room, muffled by the splashing of water, and then I put her to bed, or rather tried to.

I did exactly as the binder said, following the instructions to the letter, just as I had at lunchtime, but this time it wasn't working. Petra groused and thrashed and ripped off her nappy, and then when I put her firmly back into it and buttoned her sleep suit up the back, so she couldn't take it off, she began to wail, loudly and persistently.

For more than an hour I followed the binder's instructions and sat there, with my hand patiently on her back, listening to the soothingly repetitive jingle of the mobile and watching the lights circle on the ceiling, but it wasn't helping. Petra was getting more and more upset, and her cries were raising in pitch from irritated to angry, and from there to borderline hysterical.

As I sat there, stroking and trying not to let the tension in my wrist and hand convey itself to Petra, I glanced nervously up at the camera in the corner of the room. Maybe I was being watched right now. I could imagine Sandra at some corporate event, tensely sipping champagne as she followed the nursery feed on her phone. Was I about to get a call asking me what the hell I was doing?

The binder said to avoid taking Petra out of her cot after the lights were out, but the alternative, just leaving her there, didn't seem to be working either. In the end I picked her up and put her over my shoulder, walking her up and down the room, but she wailed angrily in my arms, arching her back as though trying to tip herself out of my grasp. So I put her back in the cot and she hauled herself to her feet and stood, sobbing furiously, her little red face pressed against the bars.

It seemed like there was nothing I could do, and my presence was only making her more furious.

At last, with a final, guilty glance at the camera, I gave up.

"Good night, Petra," I said aloud, and then stood and left the room, closing the door firmly behind me, and listening as the sound of her cries diminished as I walked down the corridor.

It was past 9:00 p.m., and I felt wrung out, exhausted by the effort of battling with the children all evening. I thought about going straight downstairs for a glass of wine, but in reality I *had* to check on Maddie and Ellie.

I could hear nothing coming from behind their bedroom door, and when I peered through the keyhole, everything inside seemed to be dark. Had they turned off the lights? I thought about knocking, but decided against it. If they were falling asleep the sound of a knock would probably undo all that.

Instead, I turned the knob very quietly, and pushed. The door opened a crack, but then met resistance.

Puzzled, I pushed harder, and there was a toppling crash, as a pile of something—I wasn't sure what—stacked up against the inside of the door fell with a clatter to the floor. I held my breath, waiting for wails and cries, but none came—apparently the children had slept through it.

Gingerly now, I slid through the gap I had created and switched on the torch of my phone to survey the damage. I wasn't sure whether to laugh or cry. They had piled up nearly all their movable furniture—cushions, teddies, books, chairs, the little table from the center of the room—into a barricade on the inside of the bedroom door. It was comic, and yet at the same time more than a little pathetic. What were they trying to protect themselves against? Me?

I swung the torch around the room and saw one of the bedside lamps, which they had unplugged and stacked on top of the pile of stuff. It had fallen to the floor when I toppled the stack, and the shade was wonky, but fortunately the bulb was not broken. Carefully, I straightened the shade, and then plugged it back in and set it on Ellie's bedside table. As the soft pink glow suffused the room, I saw them, curled together in Maddie's bed, looking for all the world like two little cherubs. Maddie's arms were firmly around her sister, almost constrictively, and I thought about trying to loosen her grip but then decided against it. I'd dodged a bullet once with that huge crash, no point in rocking the boat further.

In the end, I moved just enough stuff away from the door to make it possible to slip in and out without causing an avalanche, and then left them, turning on Happy's listening function on my phone so I could hear if they woke up.

Petra was still sobbing as I tiptoed quietly past her room, but the volume had decreased, and I hardened my heart and didn't look in. I told myself she would settle faster if I left her to it. And besides, I'd had nothing to eat or drink since noon—too busy trying to feed and bathe the girls to make supper for myself. I was suddenly ravenous, light-headed, and desperate for food.

Downstairs, in the kitchen, I walked over to the fridge. "You are low on milk," said the robot voice as I touched the door, making me jump convulsively. "Shall I add it to the shopping list?"

"Er . . . yes," I managed. Was I going insane, talking aloud to a household appliance?

"Adding milk to your shopping list," said the voice brightly, and again the screen on the door lit up, showing a list of groceries. "Eat happy, Rowan!"

I tried not to think about how it figured out who was standing in front of it. Face recognition? Proximity of my phone? Either way, it felt distinctly unsettling.

At first sight the fridge contents looked distressingly healthy—a huge drawer full of green veg, tubs of fresh pasta, various pots of things like kimchi and harissa, and a large jar of something that looked like pond water but which I thought might be kombucha. However right at the back, behind some organic yogurts, I saw a cardboard pizza box, and with some difficulty I inveigled it out and opened it up. I was just sliding the baking tray into the oven when there was a sharp rap from the glass wall on the far side of the kitchen table.

I jumped and swung around, scanning the room. It was getting dark, rain spattering the glass, and although the far side of the room was in shadow, I could see very little outside except the jeweled droplets running down the enormous glass pane. I was just beginning to think I might have imagined it, or that perhaps a bird had flown into the glass, when a dark shape moved against the gloaming, black against gray. Something—some*one*—was out there.

"Who is it?" I called out, a little more sharply than I had intended. There was no answer, and I marched past the breakfast bar, around the kitchen table, and towards the glass wall, shrouded in darkness.

There was no panel over here—or none that I could see—but then I remembered the voice commands.

"Lights on," I said sharply, and somewhat to my surprise, it worked—the huge brutalist chandelier above my head illuminating suddenly into a blaze of LED bulbs. The blast of brilliance left me blinking and astonished. But as soon as my eyes adjusted, I realized my mistake. With the lights on, I could see absolutely nothing outside now apart from my own reflection in the glass. Whereas whoever was out there could see me very plainly.

"Lights off," I said. Every light in the entire room went out immediately, plunging the kitchen into inky darkness.

"Shit," I said under my breath, and began to feel my way back across the kitchen, towards the panel by the door, to try to restore the settings to something halfway between retina-burning brilliance and total darkness. My eyes were still dazzled and hurting from the blast of light from the chandelier, but as my fingers finally sought out the control panel, I looked back toward the window, and thought, though I could not be sure, that I saw something whisk away around the side of the house.

I spent the rest of the time while the pizza was cooking glancing nervously over my shoulder into the dark shadows at the far side of the room, and chewing my nails. I had turned the baby monitor off, the better to hear any more sounds from outside, but Petra's sobs still filtered faintly down the stairs, not helping my stress levels.

I was tempted to put on some music, but there was something unnerving about the idea of drowning out the sound of a potential intruder. As it was, I hadn't seen or heard anything definite enough to call the police. A shape in the darkness and a knock that could have been anything from an acorn to a bird . . . it wasn't exactly *Friday the 13th*.

It was maybe ten or fifteen minutes later—though it felt like much more—that I heard another sound, this time from the side of the house, a knock that set the dogs barking from their baskets in the utility room.

The noise made me jump, though there was something more homely and ordinary about it than the hollow bang of before, and when I went through to the utility room, I could see a dark shape silhouetted outside the rain-spattered glass panes in the door. The figure spoke, his voice almost drowned by the hiss of the rain.

"It's me. Jack."

Relief flooded through me.

"Jack!" I wrenched the door open, and there he was, standing just under the threshold, hunched in a raincoat, hands in pockets. The water was streaming down his fringe and dripping from his nose.

"Jack, was that you, before?"

"Before when?" he asked, looking puzzled, and I opened my mouth to explain—and then thought better of it.

"Never mind, it doesn't matter. What can I help with?"

"I won't keep you," he said, "I just wanted to check you were all right, with it being your first day and all."

"Thanks," I said awkwardly, thinking of the awful afternoon and the fact that Petra was probably still sobbing into the baby monitor. Then, on an impulse I added, "Will you—I mean, do you want to come in? The kids are in bed. I was just getting myself some supper."

"Are you sure?" He looked at his watch. "It's pretty late."

"I'm sure," I said, standing back to let him inside the utility room. He stood, dripping onto the mat, and then stepped gingerly out of his boots.

"I'm sorry it's so late," he said, as he followed me into the kitchen. "I was meaning to come over before, but I had to take that bloody mower over to Inverness to be serviced."

"You couldn't fix it?"

"Oh, aye, I got it running. But it clapped out again yesterday. Whatever's the matter, I can't seem to get to the bottom of it. But never mind about that. I didn't come to moan at you about my troubles. How was it with the kids?"

"It was—" I stopped, feeling, with horror, my bottom lip quiver treacherously. I wanted to put on a brave face—what if he reported back to Sandra and Bill? But I just couldn't do it. And besides, if they looked at the security footage they would know the truth soon enough. As if to set the seal on it, Petra gave a long, bubbling wail of grief from upstairs that was loud enough to make Jack's head turn towards the stairs.

"Oh God, who am I kidding?" I said wretchedly. "It was awful. The girls ran away from me after Bill and Sandra left, and I went to look for them in the woods and then that woman—what's her name? Mrs. McKinty?"

"Jean McKenzie," Jack said. He pulled his raincoat off and sat at the long table, and I found myself sinking into a chair opposite. I wanted to put my head in my hands and cry, but I forced myself to give a shaky laugh.

"Well she turned up to clean and found the girls sitting on the doorstep claiming I'd locked them out, which I absolutely *didn't*, I'd deliberately left the door open for them. They hate me, Jack, and Petra's been screaming for like an hour and—"

The wail came again, and I felt my stress level rise in tandem with its pitch.

"Sit down," Jack said firmly, as I made to rise. He pushed me back into the chair opposite his. "I'll see if I can settle her. She's probably just not used to your face, it'll be better tomorrow."

It was in defiance of every safeguarding rule I'd ever been taught, but I was too tired and desperate to care—and besides, I told myself, Sandra and Bill would hardly have kept him on the premises if they thought he was a danger to their kids.

As the sound of his steps receded up the stairs, I switched on the baby monitor and listened to the door of Petra's room swish gently open and her choking, gasping cries subside as her body was lifted from the crib.

"There, there, my little love," I heard, a low, intimate croon that made my cheeks flush as if I were eavesdropping, though Jack must surely know the baby monitor was plugged in. "There, there, ma poor wee lassie." Upstairs, away from me, his accent was somehow stronger. "Shh . . . shh now, Petra . . . there, there . . . what a fuss over nothing."

Petra's cries were lower now, more hiccups and grumbling than real distress, and I could hear the creak of the boards as Jack paced softly up and down, holding her, soothing and gentling the fretful baby with a surprisingly practiced touch.

At last she fell silent, and I heard his feet stop, and the rattle of the cot bars as he leaned over, lowering her gently to the mattress.

There was a long pause, and then the shush of the door against the carpet, and Jack's feet on the stairs again.

"Success?" I said, hardly daring to believe it, as he entered the kitchen, and he nodded and gave a little wry smile.

"Aye, I think the poor wee thing was knackered, she was just looking for an excuse to put her head down. She fell asleep almost as soon as I picked her up."

"God, Jack, you must think I'm a complete—" I stopped, not sure what to say. "I mean, *I'm* the nanny. I'm supposed to be good at this kind of stuff."

"Don't be silly." He sat again at the table, opposite me. "They'll be fine when they get to know you. You're a stranger to them; that's all. And they're testing you. They've had enough nannies this past year to make them a bit mistrustful of a new one waltzing in and taking over. You know what kids are like—once they see you're here to stay and won't be off abandoning them again, it'll get better."

"Jack . . ." It was the opening I'd been waiting for, and yet now that it was here, I wasn't sure how to phrase my question. "Jack, what *did* happen with those other nannies? Sandra said they left because they thought the house was haunted, but I can't believe . . . I don't know, it just seems preposterous. Have you ever seen anything?"

As I said it I thought of the shadow I'd seen outside the glass wall of the kitchen and pushed the image away. It was probably just a fox, or a tree moving in the wind.

"Well . . . ," Jack said, rather slowly. He reached out one of his big, work-roughened hands—the nails still a little gray with oil in spite of what must have been repeated scrubbing—and picked up the baby monitor I had laid down on the table, turning it thoughtfully. "Well . . . I wouldn't say—"

But whatever he had been about to say was cut short by a loud, rather peremptory voice saying, "Rowan?"

Jack broke off, but I jumped so hard I bit my tongue and swung round, looking wildly for the source of the voice. It was that of an adult female, not one of the children, and it was very human, quite distinct from the robotic drone of the Happy app. Was someone in the *house*?

"Rowan," the voice repeated, "are you there?"

"He-hello?" I managed.

"Ah, hi, Rowan! It's Sandra."

With a rush of mingled relief and fury, I realized—the voice was coming out of the speakers. Sandra had somehow dialed in to the house system and was using the app to talk to us. The sense of intrusion was indescribable. Why the hell couldn't she have just phoned?

"Sandra." I swallowed back my anger, trying to restore my voice to the cheerful, upbeat tone I'd mastered at the interview. "Hi. Gosh, how are you?"

"Good!" Her voice echoed around the kitchen, magnified by the surround-sound system, bouncing off the high glass ceiling. "Tired! But more to the point, how are *you*? How's everything on the home front?"

I felt my eyes flicker to Jack, sitting at the table, thinking of how he had been the one to get Petra down. Had Sandra seen? Should I say something? I willed him not to cut in, and he didn't.

"Well . . . calm, right now," I said at last. "They're all in bed and safely asleep. Though I have to admit, Petra was a bit of a struggle. She went down like a lamb at lunchtime but maybe I let her sleep too long, I don't know. She was really hard to get down this evening."

"But she's asleep now? Well done."

"Yes, she's asleep now. And the other two went down quiet as mice."

Scared, defensive, angry mice—but they had at least been quiet. And they were asleep.

"I let them have supper in their room as they seemed really tired. I hope that was okay."

"Fine, fine," Sandra said, as though dismissing the question. "And they behaved okay the rest of the day?"

"They—" I pursed my lips, wondering how truthful to be. "They were a bit upset after you left, to be honest, especially Ellie. But they calmed down in the afternoon. I offered to let them watch *Frozen*, but they didn't want to. They ended up playing in their room." Well, that part was true enough. The problem was that they hadn't come *out* of their room. "Listen, Sandra, are there rules about the grounds?"

"How do you mean?"

"I mean, are they really allowed to just roam around, or should I be keeping them in? I know you and Bill are relaxed about it, but there's that pond—I'm just—it's making me a bit nervous."

"Oh that," Sandra said. She laughed, the sound echoing around the space in a way that made me wish I knew how to control the volume on the speakers. "It's barely six inches deep. Honestly, it's the reason Bill and I bought a place with big grounds, to give the children a bit of freedom to run wild. You don't need to helicopter them every second. They know they're not allowed to do anything silly."

"I—I'm—" I stopped, struggling with how to put my concerns

without sounding like I was criticizing her parenting. I was horribly conscious of Jack sitting across the table from me, his eyes politely averted, trying to pretend he wasn't listening. "Look, you know them better than I do, of course, Sandra, and if you're happy that they're okay with that I'll take your word on it, but I'm just—I'm used to a closer level of supervision, if you know what I mean. Particularly around water. I know the water isn't that deep, but the mud—"

"Well, look," Sandra said. She sounded a little defensive now, and I cursed myself. I had tried so hard not to sound critical . . . "Look, you must use your common sense, of course you must. If you see them doing something stupid, step in. It's your job to supervise them, that goes without saying. But I don't see the point of having children stuck in front of the TV all afternoon when there's a big beautiful sunny garden outside."

I was taken aback. Was this a dig about the fact that I had tried to bribe them with a film?

There was a long, uncomfortable pause while I tried to figure out what to say. I wanted to snap the truth—the fact that it was impossible for one person to adequately supervise a five-year-old, an eight-year-old, and a baby who could barely toddle when they were scattered across several acres of wooded grounds. But I had a feeling that doing so would get me fired. It was plain that Sandra didn't want to discuss the risks involved in letting the girls roam.

"Well," I said at last. "I totally take that point, Sandra, and obviously I'm very keen to take advantage of the beautiful grounds for myself as well. I'll—" I stopped, groping for what to say. "I'll use my common sense, as you suggest. Anyway, we had a pretty good day, considering, and the girls seem—they seem to have settled well. Would you like me to check in with you tomorrow?"

"I'll be in meetings all day, but I'll call before bedtime," Sandra said, her voice slightly softer now. "I'm sorry I didn't manage to speak to the girls before bed, but we were having dinner with a client. And anyway, it probably would have unsettled them. I find it's better to be out of sight, out of mind at first."

"Yes," I said. "Sure. I can appreciate that."

"Well, good night, Rowan. Sleep tight. I'm sure you will; you'll have an early start tomorrow, I'm afraid!"

She gave another laugh. I made myself echo it, though in truth I was feeling anything but amused. The idea of starting all this all over again at 6:00 a.m. was giving me a kind of sick feeling. *How* had I ever thought I could do this?

Remember why you're here, I thought grimly.

"Yes, I'm sure I will," I said, trying to infuse a smile into my voice. "Good night, Sandra."

I waited—but there was no click, or any sign that she had hung up, or closed the app.

"S-Sandra?" I said uncertainly, but she seemed to be gone. I slumped back in my chair, and ran my hand over my face. I felt exhausted.

"I should be going," Jack said awkwardly, evidently taking my gesture as a hint. He stood, pushing back his chair. "It's late, and you've an early start, I'd imagine, with the girls tomorrow."

"No, stay," I looked up at him, suddenly desperate not to be left alone in this house of hidden eyes and ears and speakers. The company of a person—a real, flesh-and-blood person, not a disembodied voice, was irresistible. "Please. I'd rather have someone to eat with." A whiff of something burning came from the oven, and I suddenly remembered the pizza. "Have you eaten?"

"No, but I won't take your supper."

"Of course you will. I put a pizza in the oven just before you arrived. It's probably burnt by now, but it's huge. I won't manage it all myself. Please, give me a hand, honestly, I want you to."

"Well . . ." He glanced at the utility room door, towards the garage, and, I assumed, his little flat above, its windows dark. "Well . . . if you insist."

"I do." I put on oven gloves and opened the door of the hot oven. The pizza was done. Overdone, in fact, the cheese crisping and charred around the edges, but I was too hungry to care. "Sorry, it's a bit blackened. I completely forgot about it. Do you mind?"

"Not at all. I'm hungry enough to eat a horse, let alone a slightly burnt pizza." He grinned, the tanned skin of his cheeks crinkling.

"And I don't know about you," I said, "but I need a glass of wine. You?"

"I wouldn't say no."

He watched as I chopped the pizza into slices and found two glasses in the cupboard.

"Are you okay with eating off the board?" I asked, and he gave another of his wide grins.

"I'm more than okay. It's you who's taking the risk. I'll gobble all your dinner if it's not safely ring-fenced, but if you're fine with that, it's not my lookout."

"I'm more than okay too," I said, and to my surprise, I found myself returning his grin with a slightly shy smile of my own, but a real one, not the forced, watery attempt of earlier tonight.

There was silence for a few minutes as we both worked our way through a greasy, delicious slice each, and then another. At last Jack picked up his third and spoke, balancing it on his fingertips, angling the slice so that the grease dripped back onto the board.

"So . . . about what you were asking earlier."

"The . . . the supernatural thing?"

"Aye. Well, the truth is, I've not seen anything myself, but Jean, she's . . . well, not superstitious exactly. But she loves a good yarn. She's always filling the kids' heads with folk tales—you know, selkies and kelpies, that sort of thing. And this house is very old, or parts of it are, anyway. There's been the usual amount of deaths and violence, I suppose."

"So . . . you think Jean's been telling the girls stuff and they've been passing it on to the nannies?"

"Maybe. I wouldn't want to say for sure either way. But, look, those other nannies were very young, most of them, at least. It's not everyone who's cut out to live in a place like this, miles away from a town or a bar or a pub. Au pairs, they don't want to be here, they want to be in Edinburgh or Glasgow, where there's nightclubs and other people who speak their own language, you ken?"

"Yeah." I looked out of the window. It was too dark to see anything, but in my mind's eye I saw the road, stretching away into darkness, the miles and miles of rolling hills, the mountains in the distance. There was silence apart from the rain. Not a car, not a passerby, nothing. "Yeah, I can understand that."

We sat in silence for a moment. I don't know what Jack was thinking, but I was filled with a mix of strange emotions—stress, tiredness, trepidation at the thought of the days stretched out ahead of me, and something else, even more unsettling. Something that was more about Jack, and his presence, and the scatter of freckles across his broad cheekbones, and the way his muscles moved beneath the skin of his forearm as he folded the final pizza slice into a neat parcel and finished it off in two quick bites.

"Well, I'd best be away to my bed." He stood, stretching so that I heard his joints click. "Thanks for the meal, it was nice to have someone to talk to."

"Same."

I stood, suddenly self-conscious, as if he had been reading my thoughts.

"You'll be all right?" he asked.

I nodded.

"Well, I'm just over the garage, in the old stable block if you need anything. It's the door around the side, the one painted green with a swallow on the plate. If anything happens in the night—"

"What would happen?" I broke in, surprised, and he gave a laugh.

"That came out wrong. I just meant, if you need me for anything, you know where I am. Did Sandra give you my mobile?"

"No."

He pulled a leaflet off the fridge and scribbled his number in the margin, then handed it to me.

"There you go. Just in case, like."

Just in case, what? I wanted to ask again, but I knew he would only laugh it off.

His gesture had been meant as a reassuring one, I was sure of it. But somehow it had left me feeling anything but.

"Well, thanks Jack," I said, feeling a little awkward, and he grinned again, shrugged himself into his wet coat, and then opened the utility room door and ducked out into the rain.

After he had gone I made my way into the utility room myself to lock up. The house felt very still and quiet somehow, without his presence, and I sighed as I reached above the top of the doorframe for the key. But it wasn't there.

I patted my way along the doorframe, feeling with my fingertips among the dust and little crunching lumps of dead insect, but there was nothing there.

It wasn't on the floor either.

Could Jean have moved it? Or knocked it down while dusting?

Except, I had a crystal clear memory of putting the key up there after Jean left, just as Sandra had instructed, to keep it handy in case of an emergency but out of reach of the children. Could it have fallen down? But if so, what had happened to it? It was large and brass. Too big to go unnoticed on the floor, or to fit up a Hoover pipe. Had it got kicked under something?

I got down on my hands and knees and shone my phone's torch under the washing machine and tumble dryer, but could see nothing under either, just flat white tiles and a few dust bunnies that quivered when I blew them aside. It wasn't behind the mop bucket either. Then, in spite of my doubts, I went to the cupboard where the downstairs Hoover lived—but the dust chamber had been emptied. There was nothing in there. It was the bagless kind with a clear plastic cylinder that you could see the dust circulating in—even setting aside the question of whether the key could have got inside, there was no way anyone could have tipped out a big brass key without noticing it.

After that I scoured the kitchen, and even checked the bin—but there was nothing there.

At last I opened the utility room door and stared out into the rain towards the stable block, where a light had come on in the upstairs window. Should I call Jack? Would he have a spare key? But if he did, could I really bear for him to think me so disorganized and helpless that I had waited only ten minutes before taking up his offer of help?

As I was wavering, the light in his window went out, and I realized he had probably gone to bed.

It was too late. I wasn't going to drag him out in his nightclothes.

After a last glance around at the yard directly outside the door, in case the key had got kicked outside somehow, I shut the door.

I'd ask Jack in the morning.

In the meantime, oh God, what would I do? I'd . . . I'd have to barricade the door with something. It was absurd—we were miles away from anywhere, behind locked gates, but I knew I wouldn't sleep well if I felt the place was insecure.

The handle was a knob, not the kind you could put a chair under to stop it from turning, and there was no bolt, but at last, after a lot of searching, I found a wedge-shaped door stopper in the Hoover cupboard. I rammed it firmly into the gap beneath the door and then turned the doorknob to test it.

Somewhat to my surprise, it held. It wouldn't stop a determined burglar—but then very little would. If someone was really set on breaking in they could just smash a window. But at the very least, it did give the impression that the door was locked, and I knew I would sleep more soundly because of it.

When I went back into the kitchen to clear away the pizza box and our plates, the clock above the stove read 11:36, and I could not suppress a groan. The girls would be up at six. I should have been in bed hours ago.

Well, it was too late to undo that. I'd just have to forgo a shower and get to sleep as quickly as possible. I was so tired, I was pretty sure that wouldn't be a problem, anyway.

"Lights off," I said aloud.

The room was instantly plunged into blackness, just the faint glow from the hallway illuminating the concrete floor. Smothering a yawn, I made my way up the stairs to bed, and was asleep almost before I had undressed.

When I woke, it was with a start, to complete darkness, and a sense of total disorientation. Where was I? What had woken me?

It took a minute for the memory to come back—Heatherbrae House. The Elincourts. The children. Jack.

My phone on the bedside table said it was 3:16 a.m., and I groaned and let it fall back to the wood with a clunk. No wonder it was still dark, it was the middle of the fucking night.

Stupid brain.

But what the hell had woken me? Was it Petra? Had one of the girls cried out in their sleep?

I lay for a moment, listening. I could hear nothing, but I was a floor away, and there were two closed doors between me and the children.

At last, suppressing a sigh, I got up, wrapped my dressing gown around myself, and went out onto the landing.

The house was quiet. But something felt . . . wrong, though I couldn't put my finger on it. The rain had stopped, and I could hear nothing at all, not even the far-off roar of a car, or the whisper of wind in the trees.

When the realization came, it was in the shape of two things. The first was the shadow on the wall in front of me, the shadow cast by the wilting peonies on the table downstairs.

Someone had turned the hall lights on downstairs. Lights that I was sure I had *not* left on when I went to bed.

The second came as I began to tiptoe down the stairs, and it made my heart almost stop and then begin beating hard enough to leap out of my chest.

It was the sound of footsteps on a wooden floor, slow and deliberate, exactly like the other night.

Creak. Creak. Creak.

My chest felt like it was constricted by an iron band. I froze, two steps down, looking at the light on the landing below, and then up at where the noise seemed to be coming from. Jesus Christ. Was someone in the house?

The light I could have understood. Perhaps Maddie or Ellie had got up to use the loo and left it on—there were dim little night-lights plugged into the wall at intervals, but they would probably have switched on the main hallway light anyway.

But the footsteps . . . ?

I thought of Sandra's voice, suddenly coming without warning over the sound system in the kitchen. Could *that* be the answer? The bloody Happy app? But how? More important, *why*? It didn't make sense. The only people with access to the app were Sandra and Bill, and they had no possible motivation to scare me like this. Quite the reverse, in fact. They had just gone to enormous trouble and expense to recruit me.

Besides, it just didn't sound like it was coming from the speakers. There was no sense of a disembodied noise, the way there had been with Sandra's voice in the kitchen. There, I'd had no impression of someone standing behind me, talking to me. It had sounded exactly like what it was—someone being broadcast through speakers. This, though, was different. I could hear the footsteps start on one side of the ceiling and move slowly and implacably to the other. Then they paused, and reversed. It sounded . . . well . . . as if there was someone pacing in the room above my head. But that made no sense either. Because there *was* no room up there. There was not so much as a loft hatch.

An image suddenly flashed into my head—something I hadn't thought of since the day I arrived. The locked door in my room. Where did it lead to? *Was* there an attic? It seemed improbable that someone could have entered through my room, but I could *hear* the footsteps from above.

Shivering, I tiptoed back into my own room and flicked the switch on the lamp by my bed. It didn't turn on.

I swore, Mr. Wrexham. I'm not too proud to admit it. I swore, long and loud. I had turned that light off by the switch, so why the fuck wouldn't it turn back *on* by the switch? What kind of sense did this stupid lighting system make anyway?

Furiously, not caring about the music or the heating system or anything else, I mashed my hand against the featureless panel on the wall, bashing randomly at the squares and dials as they illuminated beneath my palm. Lights flickered on and off in closets, the bathroom fan came on, a brief burst of classical music filled the air and then fell silent as I jabbed at the panel again, and some unseen vent in the ceiling suddenly began to blow out cold air. But finally, the main overhead light came on.

I let my hand fall to my side, breathing heavily but triumphant. Then I set about trying to open the locked door.

First I tried the key to my bedroom door, which Sandra had shown me, tucked away on the doorframe above the door, like the others. It didn't fit.

Then, I tried the key to the wardrobe on the other side. It didn't fit either.

There was nothing above the doorframe except a little dust.

Finally, I resorted to kneeling down and peering through the keyhole, my heart like a drum in my breast, beating so hard I thought I might be sick.

I could see nothing at all—just unending blackness. But I could *feel* something. A cool breeze that made me blink and draw back from the keyhole, my eye watering.

It was not just a cupboard inside that space. *Something* else was there. An attic, perhaps. At the very least, a space big enough to have a draft and a source of air.

The footsteps had stopped, but I knew that I would not sleep again tonight, and at last I wrapped my duvet around myself and sat, my phone in my hand, the overhead light blazing down on me, watching the locked door.

I don't know what I was expecting. To see the handle turn? For someone—some*thing*—to emerge?

Whatever it was, it didn't happen. I just sat there, as the sky outside my window began to lighten and a thin lemon-yellow streak of dawn crept across the carpet, mixing with the artificial light from above.

I felt nauseous with a mix of fear and tiredness, and dread of the day ahead.

At last, when I heard a low fractious wail come from downstairs, I loosened my grip on my phone, flexed my stiff fingers, and saw that the display said 5:57 a.m.

It was morning. The children were waking up.

As I crawled from my bed, my hand went up involuntarily to touch my necklace—but my fingers grazed only my collarbone, and I remembered that I had taken it off that first night, spooling it on the bedside table, just as I had done before the interview.

Now, I turned to pick it up, and it wasn't there. I frowned and looked down the back of the little nightstand. Nothing. Had Jean McKenzie tidied it away?

The wail from downstairs came again, louder this time, and I sighed and abandoned the hunt. I would look for it later.

But first I had to get through another day.

Coffeemaker—preloaded with beans and connected to mains water. Operated via the app, select "Appliances" from the menu, then "Baristo" and then choose from the preprogrammed selections or customize your own. If beans logo shows, the hopper needs to be refilled. If the ! error logo shows then there is either a Wi-Fi issue, or a problem with the water pressure. You can program it to dispense at a particular time every day, which is great for mornings, but of course you must not forget to put a cup underneath it the night before! The preprogrammed selections are as follows—

Jesus. I had confined myself mostly to tea since getting here, mainly because the coffeemaker was so extremely intimidating—a chrome beast of a thing covered with buttons and knobs and dials. Sandra had explained when I arrived that it was Wi-Fi enabled, and app-operated—but Happy was proving to be the least intuitive system I had ever encountered. However, after my sleepless night, I had decided that a cup of coffee was the only thing that was going to make me feel halfway normal, and while Petra chewed her way through a dish of mini rice cakes, I had resolved to try to figure it out.

I hadn't even switched it on when a voice behind me said, "Knock, knock . . ."

I jumped and swung round, my nerves still jangling with the traces of last night's stale fear.

It was Jack, standing in the open doorway to the utility room, jacket on and dog leashes in hand. I had not heard him come in, and evidently my shock and ambivalence must have shown in my face.

"Sorry, I didn't mean to make you jump. I did knock, but you didn't hear, so I let myself in. I've come to collect the dogs for their walk."

"No problem," I said, as I turned to take away Petra's rice cakes. She had stopped eating them and was mashing one into her ear. Jack's unexpected presence at least answered my question about whether I was also responsible for the dogs, and was one thing I could tick off my list. Claude and Hero were gamboling around, excited to get going, and Jack hushed them sharply. They fell silent at once, noticeably more quickly than they had obeyed Sandra, and he grabbed the collar of the largest one and began clipping on its lead.

"Sleep well?" he asked casually, as the lead slipped into place.

I turned, my hand frozen in the act of wiping Petra's face. *Sleep well?* What did that mean? Did he . . . did he . . . know?

For a minute I just stood there, gaping at him, while Petra took advantage of my momentary lapse of attention to grab a particularly soggy rice cake and mash it into my sleeve.

Then I shook myself. He was just asking in the way people do, to be polite.

"Not particularly well, actually," I said, rather shortly, wiping my sleeve on the dishcloth and taking Petra's rice cake away from her. "I couldn't find the key to the back door last night, so I couldn't lock up properly. Do you know where it's gone?"

"This door?" He jerked his head towards the utility room, one eyebrow raised, and I nodded.

"There's no bolt on it either. In the end I wedged it with a bit of wood." Though much good it had done. Presumably Jack had simply shoved the wedge aside without even noticing when he opened the door. "I know we're in the middle of nowhere, but it didn't make for a very comfortable night."

That and the sound of footsteps, I thought, but I couldn't quite bring myself to tell him about that. In the cold light of day it sounded crazy, and there were too many alternative explanations. Central heating pipes expanding. Joists shrinking as the roof cooled from the heat of the day. Old houses shifting. In my heart of hearts, I knew that none of those fully explained the sounds I had heard. But I didn't know how to convince Jack of that. The key, however, was different. It was something clear . . . and concrete.

Jack was frowning now.

"Sandra usually keeps the key on the doorframe above. She doesn't like to keep it in the lock in case the kids mess around with it."

"I know that." There was an edge of impatience in my voice that I tried to dampen down. It was not Jack's fault that this had happened. "I mean, she told me that. It was in the binder. And I put it up there yesterday, but it's not there now. Do you think Jean could have taken it?"

"Jean?" He looked surprised, and then gave a short laugh and shook his head. "No, I don't think so. I mean, why would she? She has her own keys."

"Someone else then?"

But he was shaking his head.

"No one comes up here without me knowing about it. They couldn't get through the gate for a start."

I didn't remind him that Jean had found the door locked when I came back from looking for Maddie and Ellie. I hadn't locked it. So who had?

"Maybe it fell down somewhere," he said, and went back through to the utility room to look, the dogs following like faithful shadows, sniffing around as he pushed aside the dryer and peered under the washing machine.

"I already looked," I said, trying to keep irritation out of my tone. And then, when he didn't straighten up or deviate from his search, "Jack? Did you hear me? I checked everywhere, even the bin."

But he was shifting the washing machine aside, grunting a little with the effort, the castors screeching on the tiled floor.

"Jack? Did you hear me? I said I *already*—"

He ignored me, leaning over the counter, one long arm stretched down the back of unit.

"*Jack*—" There was real irritation in my voice now, but he interrupted me.

"Got it."

He straightened, triumphantly, a dusty brass key in his fingers. I let my mouth snap shut.

I had looked. I had *looked*. I had a clear memory of peering under that washing machine and seeing nothing but dust.

"But—"

He came across, dropped it into my palm.

"But . . . I looked."

"It was tucked behind the wheel. I expect you wouldn't have seen. Probably fell out when the door slammed shut and skidded under there. All's well that ends well, isn't that what they say?"

I let my hand close around the key, feeling the brass ridges bite into my palm. I had *looked*. I had looked *carefully*. Wheel or no wheel, how could I have missed a three-inch brass key, when that was exactly what I was looking for?

There was no way I could have missed seeing that key if it was there. Which meant that maybe . . . it *wasn't* there. Until someone dropped it down there.

I looked up and met Jack's guileless hazel eyes, smiling down at me. But it couldn't be. He was so *nice.*

Maybe . . . a bit too nice?

You went straight to the washing machine, I wanted to say. *How did you know?*

But I could not bring myself to voice my suspicions aloud.

What I actually said was, "Thank you." But my voice in my own ears sounded subdued.

Jack didn't reply; he was already dusting off his hands and turning for the door, the dogs wheeling and yelping around his feet.

"See you in an hour or so?" he said, but this time, when he smiled, it no longer made my heart leap a little. Instead, I noticed the tendons in the back of his hands, the way he kept the dogs leashes very short, pulled in against his heel, dominating them.

"Sure," I said quietly.

"Oh, and I nearly forgot—today's Jean's day off. She won't be coming up, so no point in leaving the dishes for her."

"No problem," I said.

As he turned and made his way across the courtyard, dogs firmly at heel, I watched him go, turning the sequence of events over in my mind, trying to figure out what had happened.

Although I'd suggested Jean's name to Jack, I didn't honestly believe she was responsible. I remembered putting the key on the frame after she had gone. So unless she'd come back—which didn't seem likely—then she couldn't be to blame.

What had happened after that . . . Jack had come in by that door, I recalled, but had I unlocked it? No . . . I was pretty sure I'd just opened it—presumably Jack must have unlocked it with his own set of keys. Or had I unlocked it then? It was hard to remember.

Either way, it was technically possible that he had pocketed the key at some point during his visit, and dropped it down there just now. But why? To freak me out? It seemed unlikely. What could he possibly gain by engineering another nanny's departure?

Jean, I could have believed more easily. She had plainly disliked me. But even there—setting aside the likelihood of her creeping back to the house after she'd departed, which seemed more and more implausible the more I thought about it, she seemed to have a genuine affection for the children, and I couldn't believe she would deliberately leave the house unsafe and unsecured while they were asleep.

Because that was the final, unnerving possibility. That someone had taken it to ensure access to the house in the night. Not Jean or Jack, who had their own sets of keys but . . . someone else.

But no—that was crazy, I was beginning to talk myself into hysteria. Maybe it *had* been there all along. Tucked behind the wheel, Jack had said. Was it possible I just hadn't looked hard enough?

I was still thinking myself round in circles when there was an impatient noise from the kitchen, and I turned to see Petra kicking irritably against her high chair. I hurried back into the room, undid her straps, and dumped her into the playpen in the corner of the kitchen. Then I pulled my ponytail tighter, plastered on my best smile, and began looking for Maddie and Ellie.

They were in the playroom, huddled in a corner, whispering something, but both heads turned when I clapped my hands.

"Right! Come on, girls, we're going to go for a picnic. We can take sandwiches, crisps, rice cakes . . ."

I had more than half expected them to refuse, but to my surprise Maddie got up, dusting down her leggings.

"Where are we going?"

"Just the grounds. Will you show me around? I heard from Jack you have a secret den." That was completely untrue—he hadn't said anything at all, but I'd never met a child who didn't have some kind of hidey-hole or cache.

"You can't see our den," Ellie said instantly. "It's secret. I mean—" She stopped at a glaring, furious look from Maddie. "I mean, we don't have one," she added miserably.

"Oh, what a shame," I said breezily. "Well, never mind, I'm sure there's lots of other interesting places. Put your Wellies on. I'm going to put Petra in the pushchair so she doesn't wander off, but then let's set off. You can show me all the best picnic spots."

"Okay," Maddie said. Her voice was calm and level, even a little triumphant, and I found myself glancing at her suspiciously.

Even with Maddie's cooperation, it took a surprisingly long time to make the picnic and get everyone out of the house, but at last we were done and heading off round the back of the house, along a bumpy pebbled path that crested a small hill and then led down the other side. The views from this side of the grounds were just as spectacular, but, if anything, even bleaker. Instead of the little crofts and small villages scattered between us and the distant mountains, here there was nothing but rolling forest. In the far distance some kind of bird of prey circled lazily over the trees, looking for its kill.

We wound our way through a rather overgrown vegetable garden, where Maddie helpfully showed me the raspberry canes and herb beds, and past a fountain, full of a slightly brackish scum. It was not working, and the statue on top was cracked and gray with lichen, and it occurred to me then what a strange contrast the house made with this rather wild, unkempt garden. I would have expected outdoor seating areas and decking and elaborate planting schemes, not this slightly sad, crumbling neglect. Perhaps Sandra wasn't an outdoor person? Or maybe they had spent so long working on the house, they hadn't had time to tend to the grounds yet.

There was a set of swings tucked behind a dilapidated kitchen greenhouse, and Ellie and Maddie leapt on them and began competing to go higher. For a moment I just stood and watched them, and then something in my pocket gave a buzzing, jangling leap, and I realized my phone was ringing.

When I pulled it out, my heart gave a funny little jolt as I read the caller ID. It was the last person I'd been expecting, and I had to take a deep breath before I swiped the screen to accept the call.

"Hello?"

"Heeeeey!" she shrieked, her familiar voice so loud I had to hold the phone away from my ear. "It's me, Rowan! How are you? Oh my God, long time no speak!"

"I'm good! Where are you? This must be costing you a fortune."

"It is. I'm in a commune in India. Mate, it's amazing here. And sooo cheap! You should totally resign and come and join me."

"I—I did resign," I said, with a slightly awkward laugh. "Didn't I tell you?"

"*What?*"

I held the phone away from my ear again. It had been so long since we'd had an actual phone conversation, I'd forgotten how loud she could be.

"Yup," I said, still holding the phone a few inches from my ear. "Handed my notice in at Little Nippers. I left a few days ago. The look on Janine's face when I told her she could stick her stupid job was almost worth all the hours there."

"I bet. God, she was such a cow. I still can't believe Val didn't give you that job when I left."

"Me too. Listen, I meant to call you, I wanted to tell you—I've moved out of the flat."

"What?" The line was crackly, her voice echoing across the long miles from India. "I didn't hear you. I thought you said you'd left the flat."

"Yeah, I did. The post I've taken up, it's a residential one. But listen, don't worry, I'm still paying the rent, the pay here is really good. So your stuff is still there, and you'll have a place to come back to when you finish traveling."

"You can afford that?" Her tinny faraway voice was impressed. "Wow! This post must pay *really* well. How did you swing that?"

I skated round that one.

"They really needed someone," I said. It was the truth, at least. "But anyway, how are you? Any plans to come back?"

I tried to keep my voice casual, not letting on how important her answer was to me.

"Yeah, of course." Her laugh echoed. "But not yet. I've still got seven months left on my ticket. But oh, mate, it's good to hear your voice. I miss you!"

"I miss you too."

Ellie and Maddie had got down off the swing and were walking away from me now, down a winding brick path between overgrown heathers. I tucked the phone under my ear and began pushing the buggy across the rough ground, following.

"Listen, I'm working right now actually, so . . . I should probably . . ."

"Yeah, sure. And I should go too, before this bankrupts me. But you're okay, yeah?"

"Yeah, I'm okay."

There was an awkward pause.

"Well, bye, Rowan."

"Bye, Rach."

And then she hung up.

"Who was that?" said a little voice at my elbow, and I jumped and looked down to see Maddie scowling up at me.

"Oh . . . just a friend I used to work with. We were flatmates, back in London, but then she went traveling."

"Did you like her?"

It was such a funny question I laughed.

"What? Yes, yes, of course I liked her."

"You sounded like you didn't want to talk to her."

"I don't know where you got that idea." We walked a bit farther, the buggy bumping over a loose brick in the path, while I considered her remark. Was there a grain of truth in it? "She was calling from abroad," I said at last. "It's very expensive. I just didn't want to cost her too much money."

Maddie looked up at me for a moment, and I had the strangest feeling of her black button eyes boring into mine, and then she turned and scampered after Ellie, crying out, "Follow me! Follow me!"

The path led down and down, away from the house, growing more uneven by the second. Once it had been herringbone brick, but now the bricks had cracked in the frost and grown loose, some of them missing altogether. In the distance I could see a brick wall, about six feet high, with a wrought iron metal gate, which seemed to be where the children were heading.

"Is that the edge of the grounds?" I called after them. "Hold up, I don't want you going out onto the moors."

They stopped and waited for me; Ellie had her hands on her hips and was panting, her little face flushed.

"It's a garden," she said. "It's got a wall around it, like a room but no roof."

"That sounds exciting," I said. "Like the Secret Garden. Have you ever read that?"

"Of course she hasn't, she's not old enough to read chapter books," Maddie said, repressively. "But we watched it on TV."

We had drawn level with the wall now, and I could see what Ellie meant. It was a crumbling redbrick wall, slightly taller than I was, that seemed to be enclosing one corner of the grounds, forming a rectangular section quite separate from the rest of the landscaping. It was the kind of structure that might easily have enclosed a kitchen garden—protecting delicate herbs and fruit trees from frost—but the trees and creepers I could see emerging above the high walls didn't look at all edible.

I tried the handle of the gate.

"It's locked." Through the twining metalwork I could see a wild, overgrown mass of bushes and creepers, some kind of statue partly obscured by greenery. "What a shame, it looks very exciting in there."

"It *looks* locked," Ellie said eagerly, "but Maddie and I know a secret way of getting inside."

"I'm not sure—" I began, but before I could finish, she wound her little hand through the intricate metal fretwork, through a space far too narrow to admit even a fine-boned adult's hand, and did something I could not see to the far side of the lock. The gate sprang open.

"Wow!" I said, genuinely impressed. "How did you do that?"

"It's not very hard." Ellie was flushed with pride. "There's a catch on the inside."

Gently I pushed the gate open, listening to the hinges squeal, and pushed Petra inside, thrusting aside the trailing fronds of some creeper that was hanging overhead. The leaves brushed my face, tickling my skin with an almost nettlish sensation. Maddie ducked in behind me, trying not to let the leaves trail in her face, and Ellie came in too. There was something mischievous about her expression, and I wondered why Bill and Sandra kept this place locked.

Inside, the walls protected the plants from the exposed position of the rest of the grounds, and the contrast to the muted heathers and trees outside, and the austerity of the moors beyond, was startling. There were lush evergreen bushes studded with berries of all types, overgrown tangled creepers, and a few flowers struggling to survive beneath the onslaught. I recognized a few—hellebores and snowberries springing up from between dark-leaved laurels, and what I thought might be a laburnum up ahead. As we turned a corner, we passed underneath an ancient-looking yew so old it formed a tunnel over the path, its strange, tubular berries crunching underfoot. Its leaves had poisoned the ground, and nothing grew underneath its spread. There were more greenhouses in here, I saw, though they were smaller, still with enough glass in their broken frames to have built up an impressive amount of condensation. The inside of the glass was blotched with green lichen and mold, so thickly that I could barely see the remains of the plants inside, though some struggled up through the broken panes of the roof.

Four brick paths quartered the garden, meeting in a small circle in the center, where the statue stood. It was so covered in ivy and other creepers that it was hard to make out, but as I drew nearer, brushing aside some of the foliage, I saw that it was a woman, thin and emaciated and broken down, her clothes ragged, her face skull-like, her blank stone eyes fixing mine with an accusing stare. Her cheeks were scored with what looked like scratches, and when I peered closer I saw that the nails on her skeletal hands were long and pointed.

"God," I said, taken back. "What a horrible statue. Who on earth would put up something like that?" But there was no answer. The two little girls had disappeared into the thicket of greenery, and I could not see them. Peering closer I saw that there was a name on the pedestal she crouched on. *Achlys.* Was it some kind of memorial?

All of a sudden I felt a violent desire to get out of this overgrown nightmarish tangle of plants, out to the open air of the mountains and grounds.

"Maddie!" I called sharply. "Ellie, where are you?"

No answer came, and I suppressed a momentary unease.

"Maddie! We're going to have lunch now. Let's go and find a spot."

They waited, just long enough for me to start feeling serious panic, and then there was a burst of giggles and both children broke cover and pelted down the path in front of me, towards the gate and the cool, clean air outside.

"Come on," Maddie shouted over her shoulder. "We'll show you the burn."

The rest of the morning passed without incident. We had a quiet—even a nice—lunch on the shores of the peat-dark burn that cut through the corner of the grounds, and then afterwards the girls took off their shoes and socks and paddled in the tea-colored waters, screeching at the cold, and flicking me and Petra with ice-cold droplets that made me shriek, and Petra babble with excited glee. Only two things marred the general contentment—the first, Ellie's shoe falling in the burn. I managed to retrieve it, but she was tearful, and sobbed when we had to go and she had to put the soggy shoe back on.

The other was the prickling of my forehead, where the creeper had brushed me. From an initial tingle, it was now properly itching, like a nettle sting, but more painful. I splashed the cold water from the burn onto it, but the itching continued, hard to ignore. Was it some kind of allergic reaction? I'd never experienced a plant allergy before, but perhaps this was something native to Scotland I would not have encountered down south. Either way, the thought of the reaction getting worse while I was alone with the children was not comforting—nor was the realization that I had left my inhaler back at the house.

All in all I was glad when the sky clouded over and I could suggest packing up and starting home. Petra fell asleep on the way back to the house, and I parked her buggy in the utility room. To my surprise, both Maddie and Ellie fell in with my suggestion of a film, and we were cuddled up in the media room, me with a growing sense of superiority, when there was a crackle and Sandra's voice came over the speakers.

"Rowan? Is now a good time to chat?"

"Oh, hi, Sandra." It was less unnerving the second time around but still unsettling. I found myself glancing up at the cameras, wondering how she knew which room I was in. The girls were both absorbed in the film and didn't seem to have noticed their mother's voice coming over the speakers. "Hang on, I'll go through to the kitchen, so we can chat without disturbing the girls."

"You can divert the call to your phone if that's easier," Sandra's disembodied voice followed me as I eased myself out from beneath Ellie and walked through to the kitchen. "Just open the Happy app and click on the phone icon, then the divert arrow."

I did as she said, ignoring the bloody *Home is where the Happy is!*, and pressed the icons she had instructed, then lifted the phone to my ear. To my relief, her voice sounded again, this time from the phone speaker.

"Done?"

"Yes, I'm on the phone now. Thanks for showing me how to do that." If she could only have mentioned it last night rather than having that awkward conversation in front of Jack . . . but never mind. The rash on my forehead prickled, and I tried to ignore the desire to scratch it.

"No problem," Sandra was saying briskly. "Happy is amazing when you get used to it, but I have to admit, it takes a while to figure out all the intricacies! How's today going, anyway?"

"Oh, really good." I perched on the edge of a stool, resisting the urge to look up at the camera in the corner. "It's going great, thanks. We had a really good morning exploring the grounds. Petra's asleep, and the girls are—" I hesitated, thinking of her remark yesterday, but then forged on. No point in second-guessing myself all the time, and besides, she would presumably know what the girls were up to if she had checked the cameras before calling. "The girls are watching a film. I thought you wouldn't mind as they were out in the fresh air this morning. I think they needed some down time."

"Mind?" Sandra gave a little laugh. "Heavens, no. I'm not one of those helicopter parents."

"Would you like to speak to them?"

"Absolutely—it's why I called, really. Well, and to check you were coping of course. Do you want to put Ellie on first?"

I went back through to the den and handed Ellie the phone.

"It's Mummy."

Her face was a little uncertain as she picked up the phone, but she broke into smiles as she heard her mother's voice, and I went back into the kitchen, not wanting to hover too obviously, but listening with half an ear to Ellie's end of the conversation. At some point Sandra must have asked to be put across to Maddie, for there was a short whining complaint from Ellie, and then I heard Maddie's voice, and Ellie came padding disconsolately through to me.

"I miss Mummy." Her bottom lip was wobbling.

"Of course you do." I crouched down, not wanting to risk a hug that might be rejected, but trying to make myself available on her level if she wanted comforting. "And she misses you too. But we'll have lots of—"

But my remark was cut off by Maddie, coming through with the phone held out and a strange expression in her black eyes. I was not sure what it was—a mix of trepidation and glee, it looked like.

"Mummy wants to talk to you," she said. I took the phone.

"Rowan," Sandra's voice was clipped and annoyed. "What's this I hear about you taking them into the locked garden?"

"I— Well—" I was taken aback. What the hell? Sandra hadn't said anything about the garden being out of bounds. "Well, I did, but—"

"How dare you force your way into an area of the grounds that we expressly keep locked for the children's safety, I can't believe how irresponsible—"

"Hang on a minute, I'm very sorry if I've made a mistake, Sandra, but I had no idea the walled garden was out of bounds. And I didn't force my way in anywhere. Ellie and Maddie—"

Ellie and Maddie seemed to know how to open the gate, was what I had been going to say, but Sandra didn't let me finish. Instead, she interrupted with an angry sigh of exasperation and I fell silent, reluctant to talk over her and increase her annoyance.

"I told you to use your common sense, Rowan. If breaking into a poison garden is your idea of common—"

"*What?*" I butted in, not caring about rudeness now. "What did you say?"

"It is a *poison* garden," Sandra spat. "As you would know if you'd bothered to read the binder I provided. Which you clearly did not."

"A poison—" I reached for the binder, beginning to frantically flick through the pages. The injustice stung. I *had* read the fucking thing, but it was 250 pages long. If there was critical information she should have put it up front, rather than burying it in pages and pages about acceptable types of crisps and the right type of shoes to wear for PE. "Just— What even is that?"

"The previous owner of Heatherbrae was an analytical chemist with a specialty in biological toxins, and this was his personal"—she stopped, clearly too pissed off with the whole situation even to find words—"his personal testing ground, I suppose. Every single plant in that garden is toxic in some degree—some of them *extremely* toxic.

And many of them you don't need to ingest, brushing past them or touching the leaves is enough."

Oh. My hand went up to the blistering rash on my forehead, which made a sudden kind of sense.

"We're trying to find the best way to deal with it, but the bloody thing has heritage status or something. In the meantime we keep it firmly locked up, and I must say, it never occurred to me that you would take the children for a stroll—"

It was my turn to butt in now.

"Sandra." I made my voice level, and calmer, and more reasonable than I really felt. "I apologize unreservedly for not paying sufficient attention to that page in the binder. That is one hundred percent on me, and I'll rectify that immediately. But you should know, it wasn't my idea to go in there. Maddie and Ellie suggested it, and they know how to open the lock without a key—there's some kind of override on the inside, and Ellie can reach it. They've clearly been in there before."

That shut Sandra up. There was silence on the other end of the phone while I waited for her response. I could hear her breathing, and I wondered for a minute if I had made a bad strategic mistake in bringing up the fact that she clearly had no idea where her children had been roaming. Then she coughed.

"Well. We'll say no more about it for the moment. Can you put me back on to Maddie, please?"

And that was it. No, "thanks for bringing it to my attention." No admission that she herself wasn't exactly winning parenting golds. But perhaps that would have been too much to hope for.

I passed the phone back to Maddie, who gave me a little smile as I handed it over, her dark eyes full of malice.

She took it back through to the media room, Ellie padding after her, hoping for another turn, and as Maddie's end of the conversation grew fainter, I picked up the tablet that was lying on the kitchen counter and opened Google. Then I typed in *Achlys*.

A series of terrifying images popped up across the top of the screen—a variety of white, skull-like female faces in different states of decomposition, some pale and beautiful, with ravaged cheeks, others rotting and putrefying, with a stench of death coming from their rictus mouths.

Beneath them were various search entries, and I clicked one at random.

"Achlys—(pronounced *ACK-liss*)—Greek goddess of death, misery, and poison," it read.

I shut the screen down. Well, binder or no binder, I couldn't say I hadn't been warned. It had been right there, written on the base of the statue in the center of the garden. I just hadn't understood the message.

"I'm done." Maddie's voice came from the media room, and, pushing down my irritation, I walked back through to where the girls were crouched on the sofa, plainly waiting for me with some trepidation. I said nothing as Maddie handed me back the phone, just unpaused the film, and sat down on the far end of the sofa to continue watching, though their eyes kept flicking across to me, very different emotions on each face. Ellie's was anxious . . . waiting to be told off. She had known that they were not supposed to go into that garden, and she had allowed herself to be tempted—to show her cleverness in opening the gate and letting us in. Maddie's expression was very different, and harder to read, but I thought I could tell what it was. Triumph.

She had wanted me to get into trouble, and I had.

It was much later, over supper, as I wiped tomato sauce from Petra's cheek, and swallowed my own mouthful of Alphabetti Spaghetti, that

I said, casually, "Girls, did you know that the plants in that garden were dangerous?"

Ellie's eyes flicked to Maddie, who seemed to be wavering.

"What garden," Maddie said at last, though her tone didn't hold a question mark. She was buying herself more time, I thought. I gave her my sweetest smile and shot her a look that said, *Don't fuck with me, dear.*

"The poison garden," I said. "The one with the statue. Your mum said we weren't supposed to go in there. Did you know?"

"We're not allowed in without a grown-up," Maddie said evasively.

"Ellie, did you know?" I turned to her, but she refused to meet my eyes, and at last I took her chin, forcing her to look at me.

"Ow!"

"Ellie, look at me, did you know those plants were dangerous?"

She said nothing, just tried to twist her chin away.

"Did you know?"

"Yes," she whispered at last. "Another girl died."

It was not the answer I had been expecting, and I stopped, letting her chin go in my surprise.

"What did you say?"

"There was another little girl," Ellie repeated, still not meeting my eyes. "She died. Jean told us."

"Jesus!" The word slipped out without my realizing, and I saw from Maddie's smirk that that too would be stored up to repeat to Sandra next time she called.

"What happened? When?"

"A long time ago," Maddie said. It was plain that, unlike Ellie, she did not mind talking about the subject. In fact there was even a kind of relish in her tone. "Before we were born. She was the little girl of the man who lived here before us. It's why he went saft."

For a moment I didn't understand the last word, but then it came to me. She was saying the word *soft* but with a Scottish accent, repeating whatever Jean McKenzie had said to her.

"He went soft? Soft in the head you mean?"

"Yes, he had to be put away. Not straightaway, but after a while. Living here with her ghost," Maddie said, matter-of-factly. "She used to wake him in the middle of the night with her crying. After she was gone. Jean told us. So after a while he stopped sleeping. He just used to pace backwards and forward all night long. Then he went mad. People do go mad, you know, if you stop them from sleeping for long enough. They go mad, and then they *die*."

Pacing. The word gave me a sharp jolt, and for a second I didn't know what to say. Then I remembered something else.

"Maddie." I swallowed, trying to figure out how to phrase my question. "Maddie . . . is . . . is that what you meant? Before? When you said, the ghosts wouldn't like it?"

"I don't know what you mean." Her face was stiff and expressionless, and she had pushed her plate away.

"When you hugged me, that day I first came. You said *the ghosts wouldn't like it*."

"No, I didn't," she said stonily. "I didn't hug you. I don't hug people." But she had overreached herself with that last remark. I might have believed that she hadn't said what I thought I'd heard, but there was no way I could forget that stiff, desperate little hug. She *had* hugged me. And the knowledge suddenly made me sure of what I'd heard too. I shook my head.

"You know there's no such thing as ghosts, right? No matter what Jean has told you—it's just rubbish, Maddie, it's just people who are sad about other people who have died, and wish they could see them again, so they make up stories, and they imagine they see them. But it's all nonsense."

"I don't know what you're talking about," Maddie said, and she shook her head so that her straight dark hair flapped against her cheeks.

"There *aren't* any ghosts, Maddie. I promise you that. They're just make-believe. They can't hurt you—or me—or any of us."

"Can I get down now?" she asked flatly, and I sighed.

"Don't you want pudding?"

"I'm not hungry."

"Go on then."

She slid from her chair, and Ellie followed, her obedient little shadow.

I put a yogurt in front of Petra and then went round to clear the girls' plates. Ellie's was just the usual mess of toast crusts and spaghetti sauce, with as many peas as possible hidden under her spoon. But Maddie's . . . I was about to scrape it into the compost bin when I stopped, turning the plate.

She had eaten most of her supper, but a dozen or so alphabet letters had been left, and now I saw, just as I was about to throw them away, that the letters seemed to be arranged into words. The phrase was sliding diagonally across the plate where I had tipped it towards the compost bin, but it was still just readable.

WEH

AT

EU

We hate you.

Somehow, seeing it there in the innocence of Alphabetti Spaghetti was more upsetting than almost anything else. I scraped the plate with a violence that made the spaghetti ricochet off the inside of the compost bin lid, and then threw it into the sink, where it hit a glass, and they both shattered, sending shards of glass and spatters of tomato sauce flying.

Fuck.

Fuck fuck fuck fuck *fuck.*

I hate you too! I wanted to scream after their retreating backs, as they padded quietly away into the media room to fire up Netflix. *I hate you too, you vile, creepy little shits!*

But it wasn't true. Not completely.

I did hate them—in that moment. But I saw myself too. A prickly little girl, full of emotions too big for her small frame, emotions she could not understand or contain.

I hate you, I remembered sobbing into my pillow, after my mother threw away my favorite teddy bear, too old, too shabby, too babyish for a big girl like me, according to her. *I hate you so much!*

But it wasn't true then either. I loved my mother. I loved her so much that it suffocated her—or that was the impression she gave. All those years of small hands being disentangled from sleeves and skirts, and untwined from around necks. *That's enough now, you'll mess up my hair,* and, *Oh, for goodness' sake, your hands are filthy,* and *Stop being a baby now, a big girl like you.* All those years of being too needy, and too grabby, and too grubby-handed—of trying to be better and neater, and just more lovable.

She didn't want me. Or that's what it felt like, at times.

But she was all I had.

Maddie had so much more than me—a father, three sisters, a beautiful house, two dogs . . . but I recognized her sadness and her anger and her frustration—an angry little dark changeling among her blond sisters.

We even looked alike.

When she looked at me, with that touch of triumph in her dark, boot-button eyes, I had recognized something else too, and now I knew what it was. It was a flash of myself in those eyes. A flicker of my own dark brown eyes, and my own determination. Maddie was a woman with a plan, just like I was. The question was, what was it?

I was so tired after my near sleepless night the night before that I bundled the girls upstairs to bed ridiculously early. To my surprise they didn't protest, and I found myself wondering if they were as tired as I was.

Petra went down with no more than a token protest, and when I went to check on Maddie and Ellie they were both in their pajamas—or almost there, in the case of Ellie. I helped her figure out which way her top went and then shepherded them into the bathroom, where they did their teeth obediently as I stood over them.

"Do you want a story?" I asked as I tucked them into their little beds, and I saw Ellie's eyes flicker to Maddie, looking for permission to speak. But Maddie shook her head.

"No. We're too big for stories."

"I know that's not true," I said, with a little laugh. "Everyone likes bedtime stories."

Any other night I might have sat myself down, cracked open a book, and begun anyway, in defiance of Maddie's refusals. But I was tired. I was *so* tired. Being with the girls all day from sunup to sunset was exhausting in a completely different way to the nursery, a way I hadn't fully anticipated or understood until now. I thought of all the mums who had dropped their children off talking about how exhausted they were, and the slight contempt I'd felt for them when all they had to deal with was one or two at the most, but now I realized what they'd been talking about. It wasn't as physical as the work at the nursery, or as intense, but it was the way it stretched, endlessly, the way the needing never stopped, and there was never a moment when you could hand them over to your colleague and run away for a quick fag break to just be yourself.

I was never off duty here. Or at least, not for the foreseeable future.

"I tell you what," I said at last, seeing Ellie's chin wobble. "How about I put on an audiobook?"

Pulling out my phone, I managed to navigate to the Happy media system, and then to the audio files, where I scrolled through the list of titles. The organization was confusing—there didn't seem to be any distinction between the different file types, and Mozart was listed alongside *Moana*, Thelonious Monk, and L. M. Montgomery—but as I scrolled, I felt a little warm head thrust up under my arm, and Ellie's small hand took the phone.

"I can show you," she said, and pressed an icon that looked like a stylized panda bear, and then another icon that looked like a flattened out *v*, but which I realized, as Ellie pressed it, must be supposed to indicate books.

A list of children's audiobooks flashed up.

"Do you know which one you want?" I asked, but she shook her head, and scanning the list, I selected one at random—*The Sheep Pig* by Dick King-Smith, which seemed perfect. Long, calming, and nice and wholesome. I pressed play, selected "Girls' bedroom" from the list of speakers, and waited for the first notes of the introductory music to come out of the speakers. Then I tucked Ellie in.

"Do you want a kiss?" I said. She didn't reply, but I thought I saw a little nod, and I bent and swiftly kissed her baby-soft cheek before she could change her mind.

Next, I went across to Maddie. She was lying there with her eyes tightly shut, though I could see her pupils moving beneath the paper thinness of her lids, and I could tell from her breathing she was nowhere near asleep.

"Do you want a good-night kiss, Maddie?" I asked, knowing what the answer would be, but wanting to be fair.

She said nothing. I stood for a moment, listening to her breathing, and then said, "Good night, girls. Sweet dreams, and sleep well for school tomorrow," and then I left, shutting the door behind me.

Out in the hallway I breathed a tremulous, almost incredulous sigh of relief.

Could it be true? Were they really all safely in bed, washed, brushed, and no one screaming? It seemed, compared to last night, anyway, deceptively easy.

But perhaps . . . perhaps I had turned a corner with them. Perhaps that first angry protest was just shock at being away from their mum, with a comparative stranger in charge. Maybe a nice day together and a phone call from Sandra was all it had taken?

My heart softened as I checked the lock on the utility room door, did battle with the front-door panel and the lights in the hall, and then climbed the flights of stairs to my own room with a weariness I was having increasing trouble overcoming.

I was passing Bill and Sandra's room when I thought I heard something. Or perhaps saw it—it was hard to know. A little flicker of movement in the sliver of darkness between the door and the frame. Was it just my imagination? I was so tired. It could be my mind playing tricks on me.

Very, very quietly, not wanting to disturb the girls, I pushed the door with the flat of my hand, listening to it shushing across the thick silver carpet.

Inside, the room was quite empty and still. The curtains were undrawn, and though in London it would have been getting dark, here we were so far north that the sun was only just sliding behind the mountains. Livid squares of reddish light slanted obliquely across the floor, turning the carpet into a kind of fiery chessboard, though the corners of the room were in deep, impenetrable shadow. I let my hand slip over the thick, crisp cotton of their duvet cover as I passed their bed, glancing into the shadows, feeling my pulse quicken with the audacity of this intrusion. If Sandra were watching through the monitor now, what would she see? Someone prowling around her bedroom, fingering her bed linen. *I thought I heard a noise . . .* I practiced the excuse in my head, but I knew it was no longer true. I had been looking for an excuse.

There was a pair of earrings on the bedside table closest to the door. This must be Sandra's side. Which meant that Bill slept . . .

I tiptoed around the bed, keeping to the shadows as far as I could. I knew from peering at Maddie and Ellie's bedroom monitor that the resolution of the images in darkness was not good. It was very hard to make out anything beyond the little pool of warm light cast by the night-light, and in here the contrast between the squares of sunset and the deep shadow in the rest of the room was even greater.

Very, very quietly, I slid open Bill's bedside table drawer, and looked down at the tumble of personal possessions inside. A watch with a broken strap. A slew of loose change. A few tickets, a hay-fever spray, a comb. I'm not sure what I had been hoping for—but if it was to get a sense of the person who lived here, slept here, laid his head on the crisp white pillow, I was disappointed. It was strikingly impersonal.

I thought of that meeting in the kitchen, of his denimed leg slipping between my thighs with a confident intrusiveness born of long practice, and I felt sick. *Who are you?*

Suddenly I had to get out, and I hurried across the checkered carpet, no longer caring about keeping to the shadows, or whether Sandra or Bill saw me. Let them see. Both of them.

Up in my room, I closed the door with a feeling of barricading myself away from the rest of the house. As the curtains drew themselves robotically over the windowpane, my last glimpse of the outside world was of the bloody streaks of sunset fading behind the far-off peaks of the Cairngorms, and of a light in Jack's window shining steadfastly across the darkening courtyard.

I thought of him, as I let my head sink into the goose-feather softness of the pillow. I thought of his hands that morning, the ease with which he restrained the two excited dogs, the way he dominated them, keeping them at heel. And I thought of the key, and how he had gone unerringly to the place where it had been hidden, a place I had already checked.

But then I remembered other things—his kindness that first night, in coming to check on me. And his voice over the baby monitor, putting Petra to sleep, crooning to her with a gentleness that made my stomach clench in a strange way I could not pin down. There had been no deception there. No pretense. That gentleness was real, I was certain of it.

And I wondered, if it had been him in the kitchen that night, instead of Bill, would I have lurched queasily from the room with panicked disgust? Or would I have reacted very differently? Opened my legs to his, perhaps. Leaned forward. Blushed.

But even as the thought came to me, making my cheeks flush in the darkness, I remembered again, kneeling on the floor of the utility room, sweeping my phone torch beneath that washing machine. That key had *not* been there. The intervening hours had not made me doubt that fact anymore—quite the reverse. I was totally sure now.

Which meant . . .

I rubbed my hands over my face, resisting the urge to scratch the fading itch left by the creeper. I was being absurd. There was no earthly reason why he would steal that key simply to unnerve me. He had his own set, after all, and his thumbprint was authorized for use on the front door. (Though . . . there was probably a record every time someone used that lock, my subconscious whispered. A record that wouldn't exist with an old-fashioned lock and key.)

But no. *No.* It made no sense. Why would he go to the trouble of making a key disappear for a few hours? What would he gain from it? Nothing, except to put me on my guard. And there was my necklace too—my necklace, which I had still not found, though I'd not had time to look properly. That could not have been Jack, surely. This was paranoia, all of it. Things get lost all the time. Keys fall down. Necklaces get tidied away into pockets and drawers, and unearthed days later. There would be a perfectly reasonable explanation for all of this—one that did not require a conspiracy theory.

I pushed the thought down as I rolled over and let sleep cover me like a heavy blanket.

My last thought, as sleep claimed me, was not of Jack, nor of the key, nor even of Bill. It was of the footsteps in the attic.

And the old man who had lost his daughter to his poison garden.

There was another little girl.

My hand went vainly to my throat, trying to hold a necklace that wasn't there. And then at last I slept.

I woke to the sound of screams and a confusion so loud that my first instinct was to clap my hands over my ears, even as I bolted upright in my bed, staring wildly around, shivering with cold.

The lights were on—all of them, turned up to their brightest, most eye-searing maximum. And the room was icy-cold. But the noise—Jesus, the *noise.*

It was music, or at least I supposed so. But so loud and distorted that the tune was unrecognizable, the howling and squealing coming from the speakers in the ceiling turning it into a formless din.

For a minute I couldn't think what the hell to do. Then I ran to the panel on the wall and began pushing buttons, my pulse pounding in my ears, the screeching misshapen music like a howl in my head. Nothing happened except that the lights in the closets turned on to join the rest.

"Music off!" I shouted. "Speakers off! Volume down!"

Nothing, nothing.

From downstairs I could hear furious barking, and terrified steam-train shrieks coming from Petra's room, and at last, abandoning my attempts with the panel, I grabbed my dressing gown and fled.

The music was just as loud outside the children's rooms—louder even, for the narrow walls of the hallway seemed to funnel it. And the lights were on down here too, showing me a glimpse of Petra through the nursery doorway, standing up in her cot, her hair tousled on end, screaming in fear.

I snatched her up and ran to the girls' room at the end of the corridor, shoving the door open to find Maddie curled in a fetal position in her bed, her hands over her ears, and Ellie nowhere to be seen.

"Where's Ellie?" I bellowed, above the noise of the music, and Petra's fire-engine wails. Maddie looked up, her face blank with fear, her hands still clapped over her ears, and I grabbed her wrist and hauled her to her feet.

"*Where's Ellie?*" I yelled, directly into her face, and she pulled away and fled down the stairs, with me following.

In the entrance hall the noise was just as bad, and there, in the middle of the Persian rug at the foot of the stairs, was Ellie. She was crouched into a little ball, her arms wrapped around her head. All about her leapt the terrified dogs, released from their beds in the utility room, adding their frantic barks to the cacophony.

"Ellie!" I shouted. "What happened? Did you press something?"

She looked up at me, blank and uncomprehending, and I shook my head and then ran over to the tablet sitting on the metal breakfast bar. I opened up the home-management app, but when I tapped in my access code, nothing happened. Had I misremembered it? I tapped it in again, the dogs' furious woofs like a jackhammer of sound against my skull. Still nothing. *You are locked—* I had time to read, before the screen lit up momentarily and then died—a red battery warning flashing for an instant before it went black. *Fuck.*

I slammed my hand onto the wall panel and the lights above the cooker turned on and a screen on the fridge began blasting out YouTube, but the music volume didn't reduce. I could feel my heart thumping wildly in my chest, growing more and more panicked as I realized I had no way of turning this thing off. What a stupid fucking idea—a smart house? This was the least smart thing I could imagine.

The children were shivering now, Petra still letting out earsplitting shrieks of distress next to my ear as the dogs ran in circles around us, and I tried the power button on the tablet, more helplessly, not expecting the thing to work, and it didn't. The screen was completely dark. My phone was upstairs—but could I leave the terrified children long enough to fetch it?

I was staring round, wondering what on earth I was going to do, when I felt a touch on my shoulder. I jumped so wildly I almost dropped Petra, and swung round accusingly to find Jack Grant, standing so close behind me that my shoulder touched his bare chest as I turned. We both took an involuntary step back, me nearly tripping over a stool.

He was naked from the waist up and had plainly been asleep, judging by his rumpled hair, and he bellowed something, pointing at the door, but I shook my head, and he came close, cupping his hands around my ear.

"What's happening? I could hear the din from the stables."

"I have no idea!" I yelled back. "I was asleep—maybe one of the girls touched something—I can't get it to turn off."

"Can I try?" he shouted, and I felt like laughing in his face. Could he? I would kiss him if he succeeded. I shoved the tablet at him, almost aggressively.

"Be my guest!"

He tried to turn the tablet on and then realized, as I had, that it was out of power. Then he went to the utility room and opened up a cupboard there, the one where the Wi-Fi router was kept, along with the electricity meter. I'm not completely sure what he did in there, I was too busy comforting an increasingly distraught Petra, but all of a sudden everything went pitch-black, and the sound stopped with an abruptness that was disorienting. I found my ears were ringing with the aftermath.

In the silence, I could hear Ellie's panicked gasping sobs and Maddie rocking back and forth.

Petra, in my arms, stopped crying, and I felt her little body go stiff with surprise. Then she let out a gurgling laugh.

"Night night!" she said.

Then there was a click, and the lights came back on—less brightly this time, and fewer of them.

"There," Jack said. He came back through, wiping his forehead, the dogs padding in his wake, suddenly calm again. "It's gone back to default settings now. Bloody hell. Okay."

There was sweat on his forehead in spite of the chill in the air, and when he sat down at the kitchen counter, the tablet in his hands, I could see his hands were shaking.

Mine, as I set Petra beside Maddie, were trembling too.

Jack plugged the tablet in and now he put it down to wait until it had enough charge to turn on.

"Th-thank you," I said shakily. Ellie was still sobbing in the hallway. "Ellie, there's no need to cry, sweetie. It's okay now. Look . . . um . . ." I crossed the kitchen and began rummaging in the cupboards. "Look . . . here we are, have a jammie dodger. You too, Maddie."

"We've brushed our teeth," Maddie said blankly, and I suppressed a hysterical laugh. *Fuck teeth*, was what I wanted to say, but I managed to bite it back.

"I think just this once, it'll be okay. We've all had a shock. Sugar is good for shock."

"Aye, it's true," Jack said, rather solemnly. "Back in the old day they'd make you drink sweet tea, but since I don't really like sugar in my tea, I'll have a jammie dodger too, thanks, Rowan."

"See?" I handed one to Jack and bit into one myself. "It's fine." I spoke around the crumbs. "Here you go, Maddie."

She took it, warily, and then shoved it in her own mouth as if I were about to take it away again.

Ellie ate hers more slowly.

"Mine!" Petra shouted, holding up her arms. I gave a mental shrug. I wasn't going to win any prizes for child nutrition, but I no longer gave a fuck about that. Breaking one in half, I gave her a piece of biscuit too, and then threw a chunk to each of the dogs for good measure.

"Okay, we're up and running again," Jack said, as Petra began joyfully stuffing the biscuit into her mouth. For a minute I didn't realize what he meant, and then I saw that he was holding the tablet, the screen casting a glow onto his face. "I've got the app open. Try your PIN first."

I took the tablet from him, selected my username from the little drop-down menu, and put in the PIN Sandra had given me for the home-management app.

You are locked out, flashed up on the screen, and then when I tapped the little *i* button next to the message, *Sorry, you have entered your Happy number incorrectly too many times and are now locked out. Please enter an admin password to override this, or wait 4 hours.*

"Ah," Jack said ruefully. "Easy mistake to make in the circumstances."

"But wait," I said, annoyed. "Hang on, that makes no sense. I only entered my pass code once. How can it lock me out for that?"

"It doesn't," Jack said. "You get three goes, and it warns you. But I suppose with all the noise—"

"I only entered it once," I repeated, and then, when he didn't reply, I said, more forcefully, "Once!"

"Okay, okay," Jack said mildly, but he looked at me sideways beneath his fringe, something a little appraising in his eyes. "Let me try." I handed him the tablet, feeling irrationally annoyed. It was clear that he didn't believe me. So what had happened then? Had someone been trying to log in under my username?

As I watched, Jack switched users and entered his own PIN. The screen lit up briefly, and then he was inside the app.

His screen was laid out differently to mine, I saw. He had some permissions that I didn't—access to the cameras in the garage, and outside—but not to those in the children's bedroom and playroom, as I did. The icons for those rooms were grayed out and unavailable. But when he clicked on the kitchen, he was able to dim the lights by tapping on the controls on the app.

The realization was like a little shock.

"Hang on." The words blurted out before I had thought through how to phrase it. "You can control the lights in here from the app?"

"Only if I'm here," he said, clicking through to another screen. "If you're a master user—that's Sandra and Bill, basically—you can control everything remotely, but the rest of us can only control the rooms we're in. It's some sort of geolocation thing. If you're close enough to the panel in the room, you get access to that system."

It made sense, I supposed. If you were close enough to reach a light switch, why not give you access to the rest of the room's controls. But on the other hand . . . how close was close? We were directly beneath Maddie and Ellie's room here. Could he control the lights in there from his phone down here? What about outside in the yard?

But I caught myself. This was pointless. He didn't need to access the controls from the yard. He had a set of keys.

Except . . . what better way to make someone think you weren't involved . . . when really you were?

I shook my head. I had to stop this. It could have been Ellie, fiddling with the iPad in the middle of the night. Perhaps she had come down to play Candy Crush or watch a movie, and accidentally pressed something she shouldn't have. It could have been some kind of preprogrammed setting that I'd switched on without realizing, the app version of a butt dial. It could have been Bill and Sandra, if it came to that. If I was going to be paranoid, I might as well go the whole hog, after all. Why stop at random handymen? Why not extend the suspicion to everyone? The fact that they had only just recruited me and had least reason of anyone to drive me away was neither here nor there. Or, for that matter, there were other users. Who knew what permissions Rhiannon might have?

I became suddenly aware that Jack was watching me, his arms folded across his very naked chest. I caught a glimpse of myself reflected in the glass wall of the kitchen—braless in my skimpy top, with my face still pillow-crumpled, and my hair like I'd been dragged through a bush backwards—so far from the neat, buttoned-up professional image I tried to project during the day that the contrast was laughable. I felt my cheeks grow hot.

"God, I'm so sorry Jack. You didn't have to—" I ground to a halt.

He looked down at himself in turn, seeming to realize his own state of half dress, and gave an awkward laugh, a flush of red staining his cheekbones.

"I should have put something on. I thought you were all being murdered in your beds, so I didn't really stop to dress . . . Listen, you get the girls to sleep, I'll put a shirt on, settle the dogs, and then I'll run some antivirus software on the app."

"You don't have to do that tonight," I protested, but he shook his head.

"No, I want to. I can't for the life of me see why it's playing up, and I'll not have you all out of your beds a second time in one night. But you don't need to wait up for me. I can lock up after myself. Or I can sleep here if you're worried." He gestured to the couch. "I can bring over a blanket."

"No!" It came out sharper and more emphatic than I had meant, and I struggled to cover my overreaction. "No, I mean . . . you don't have to do that. Honestly. I'll—"

Shut up, you stupid girl.

I swallowed.

"I'll get the girls to bed, and come back down. I won't be long."

At least, I hoped I wouldn't. Petra was looking worryingly wide awake.

It was maybe an hour later, after I'd tucked the girls back into bed for the second time that night, and soothed Petra into a state of not quite sleeping but at least almost there, that I made my way back down to the kitchen. I was half expecting Jack to have packed up and gone, but he was waiting for me, a checked flannel shirt on this time, and a cup of tea in his hand.

"Do you want one?" he asked. For a minute I wasn't sure what he was talking about, then he raised his cup, and I shook my head.

"No, thanks. I won't sleep if I have anything caffeinated now."

"Fair enough. Are you okay?"

I don't know why it was that simple question that did it. Maybe it was the genuine concern in his voice, or the enormous relief of being with another adult after so many hours spent alone with the children. Maybe it was just the shock of what happened, finally setting in. But I burst into tears.

"Hey." He stood awkwardly, shoving his hands in his pockets and then taking them out again, and then, as if making up his mind, he crossed the kitchen quickly and put an arm around me. I turned—I couldn't help it—and buried my face against his shoulder, feeling my whole body shake with the sobs. "Hey, hey there . . . ," he said again, but this time his voice came to me through his chest wall, deeper and softer, and somehow slower. His hand hovered above my shoulder, and then settled, very gently, on my hair. "Rowan, it's going to be okay."

It was that one word, *Rowan*, that brought me back to my senses, reminded me of who I was, and who *he* was, and what I was doing here. I gulped furiously and took a step back, wiping my eyes on my sleeve.

"Oh my God, Jack, I'm so s-sorry."

My voice was still shaky and rough from crying, and he put out his hand. For a minute I thought he was going to touch my cheek, and I wasn't sure whether I wanted to pull away, or lean into his caress. Then I realized—he was offering me a tissue. I took it and blew my nose.

"God," I managed at last, and then I moved across to the kitchen sofa and sat down, feeling my legs about to give way. "Jack, you must think I'm a complete idiot."

"I think you're a woman who's had a bad scare and was keeping it together for the bairns. And I also think—"

He stopped, biting his lip at that. I frowned.

"What?"

"No, it doesn't matter."

"It does." Suddenly I wanted him to say whatever it was he had been about to say very badly indeed, even though I was more than a little afraid of what it might be. "Tell me," I pressed, and he sighed.

"I shouldn't say it. I don't bad-mouth my employers."

Oh. So not what I had been half fearing then. Now I was just plain curious.

"But?"

"But . . ." He broke off, chewing his lip, and then seemed to make up his mind. "Ah, fuck it. I've said too much already. I think that Sandra and Bill should never have put you in this position. It's not fair on you, and it's not fair on the children, if it comes to that."

Oh.

Now it was my turn to feel awkward. What could I say to that?

"I knew what I signed up for," I said at last.

"Aye, but did you?" He sat down beside me, making the sofa cushions squeak. "I bet they weren't one hundred percent honest about yon one, eh?"

"Who, Maddie?"

He nodded, and I sighed.

"Okay, no, you're right, they weren't. Or not totally. But I'm a childcare professional, Jack. It's nothing I haven't encountered before."

"Really?"

"Okay. I maybe haven't encountered anyone quite like Maddie, but she's just a little girl, Jack. We're getting to know each other, that's all. We had a good day today."

It wasn't quite true though, was it? She had tried to get me sacked, first by luring me into that bloody poison garden, and second by tattling on me to her mother in a way designed to make me look as bad as possible.

"Jack, is there any way it could have been . . ." I stopped myself, and amended what I had been going to say, "one of the kids who set all that stuff off? They were playing with the tablet earlier, is there any way they could have . . . I don't know . . . preprogrammed it by accident?"

Or deliberately, I thought, but did not say.

But he shook his head.

"I don't think so. There'd be a record of a log-in. And anyway, from what you said, it overrode every single speaker and lighting system in the house. None of the users on this tablet have access rights to do that. You'd need an admin password for that."

"So . . . you'd have to be Bill or Sandra, basically? Is that what you're saying?" The thought was very odd, and my doubts must have shown on my face. "Could the kids have got hold of their PIN somehow?"

"Maybe, but they're not even down as users on this tablet. Look." He clicked the little drop-down menu on the home-management app that listed the possible users for this device. Me, Jack, Jean, and a final one marked "Guest." That was it.

"So what you're saying is . . . ," I spoke slowly, trying to think it through, "to get an admin level of access, you wouldn't just need Sandra's PIN, you'd need her phone?"

"Pretty much, yeah." He pulled out his own phone, and showed me his access panel. "See? I'm the only user set up on my phone. It's the way it's configured."

"And to set up new users on a device . . ."

"You need a specific code. Sandra would have given you one when you came here, no?"

I nodded.

"And let me guess, the code can only be generated by . . ."

"By an admin user, yup. That's about the size of it."

It made no sense. Had Sandra or Bill done this somehow? It wasn't beyond the bounds of possibility—I had read up on the app when Sandra had first told me about it, and from what I could make out, the whole point of the system was that you could control it from anywhere with internet access—check the CCTV when you were on holiday in Verbier, turn on the lights when you were upstairs and wanted to come down, lower the heating when you were stuck in a traffic jam in Inverness. But why would they?

I remembered what Jack had said when I went to take the girls up to bed, and though I knew I was clutching at straws, I still had to ask the question.

"And the virus scans . . . ?"

He shook his head.

"Nothing on the tablet, at any rate. It's clean as a whistle."

"Shit." I ran my hands through my hair, and he put his hand on my shoulder, touching me again, lightly, but I felt a kind of static charge run between us, making the hairs on my arm prickle, and I shivered lightly.

Jack made a rueful face, misinterpreting my reaction.

"Look at me, blathering away. You must be cold and tired—I'll let you get to bed."

It wasn't true. Not anymore. I wasn't cold, and suddenly I was very far from tired too. What I wanted was a drink, with him—and preferably one as strong as possible. I didn't usually drink spirits, but it was on the tip of my tongue to mention the bottle of Scotch in the cupboard in the kitchen. But I knew that if I did, I would be starting something very stupid indeed, something I might not be able to stop.

"Okay," I said at last. "That's probably good advice. Thank you, Jack."

I stood up, and he did too, setting down his tea and stretching until I heard his joints crack, and a little sliver of flat stomach showed between the bottom of his shirt and his waistband.

And then, I did something that surprised even myself. Something I had not intended to do, until the instant I found myself doing it.

I stood on tiptoes, and, pulling his shoulder down towards me, I kissed his cheek. I felt the leanness of his skin, the roughness of a day-old beard beneath my lips, and the warmth of him. And I felt something at the core of me clench with wanting.

When I stepped back, his expression was blank surprise, and for a moment I thought I had made a horrible mistake, and the butterflies in my stomach intensified to the point of queasiness. But then his mouth widened into a broad grin, and he bent, and kissed me back, very gently, his lips warm and very soft against my cheek.

"Good night, Rowan. You're sure you'll be all right now? You don't need me to . . . stay?"

There was an infinitesimal pause before the last word.

"I'm sure."

He nodded. And then he turned and left by the utility room door.

I locked it after him, the key turning with a reassuring clunk, and then I tucked the key back into its resting place and stood, watching his silhouette against the light streaming from the stable windows as he walked back to his little flat. As he mounted the stairs to his front door he turned and lifted a hand in farewell, and even though I was not sure he would be able to see me in the darkness, I raised mine in return.

Then he was gone, the door closed behind him, and the outside light clicked off, leaving a shocking, inky darkness in its wake. And I was left standing in there, my skin shivering, and fighting the urge to touch the place on my cheek where his lips had been with the tips of my fingers.

I did not know what he had meant when he offered to stay. What he had been hoping, expecting.

But I knew what *I* had wanted. And I knew that I had come very close to saying yes.

I know what you're thinking, Mr. Wrexham. None of this is helping my case. And that's what Mr. Gates thought too.

Because we know where this leads, you and I, don't we?

To me, slipping out of the house on a rainy summer night, baby monitor in one hand, running across the courtyard and up the stairs to the stable-block flat.

And to a child's body, lying— But no. I can't think about that, or I'll start crying again. And if you lose it in here, you really lose it, I know that now. I never knew there were so many ways to deal with pain so unbearable that it cannot be endured, but in here I have seen them all. The women who cut their skin, and tear out their hair, and smear their cells with blood and shit and piss. The ones who snort and shoot and smoke their way to oblivion. The ones who sleep and sleep and sleep and never get out of bed, not even for meals, until they're nothing but bones and grayish skin and despair.

But I *have* to be honest with you, that's what Mr. Gates didn't—couldn't—understand. It was acting a part that got me here in the first place. Rowan the Perfect Nanny with her buttoned-up cardigans, her pasted-on smile, and her perfect CV—she never existed, and you know it. Behind that neat, cheerful facade was someone very different—a woman who smoked and drank and swore, and whose hand itched to slap on more than one occasion. I tried to cover her up—to neatly fold my T-shirts when my instinct was to throw them on the floor, to smile and nod when I wanted to tell the Elincourts to fuck off. And when the police took me in for questioning, Mr. Gates wanted me to keep on pretending, keep on hiding the real me. But where did that pretense get me? Here.

I have to tell the truth, the whole truth, and nothing but the truth. Because to leave out these parts would be less than the whole truth. To tell you only the parts that exonerate me would make me slip back into the old, old trap. Because it was the lies that got me here in the first place. And I have to believe that it's the truth that will get me out.

I had forgotten what day it was when I awoke. When my alarm went off I listened blearily for the sound of childish voices, and then, when only silence greeted me, I hit snooze and went back to sleep. It recurred ten minutes later, and this time I thought I could hear a noise coming from downstairs. After lying there for another ten minutes, gearing myself up for the day, I swung my legs out of bed and stood uncertainly, dizzy with lack of sleep. Then I went down into the kitchen to find not Maddie and Ellie but Jean McKenzie, scrubbing the dishes and looking disapproving.

"Are the bairns not up yet?" she said as I came into the room, rubbing my eyes and longing for a coffee. I shook my head.

"No, we had a . . ." What should I say? Suddenly I couldn't bring myself to go into the whole story. "A bit of a disturbed night," I finished at last. "I thought I'd let them sleep in."

"Well that's all very well on a weekend, but it's seven twenty-five and they need to be washed, dressed, and in that car by eight fifteen."

Eight fifteen? I did a mental double take, and then realized. Fuck.

"Oh God, it's Monday."

"Aye, and you'll need to be getting a move on if you're to make it in time."

* * *

"I'm not going." Maddie was lying facedown on her bed, with her hands over her ears. I began to feel desperate. It wasn't so much what I would tell Sandra if I couldn't get the girls to school, but the fact that I *needed* this break. I had had barely three hours' sleep last night. I could cope with a fractious baby. I couldn't cope with two primary school age–children as well, let alone one as stroppy and recalcitrant as Maddie.

"You're going, and that's that."

"I'm not, and you can't make me."

What could I say to that? It was true after all.

"If you get dressed now there'll still be time for Coco Pops."

It had come to that then. Basically bribing her with Sandra's list of forbidden foods at every single obstacle. But it had worked with Ellie, who was, I assumed, downstairs now, more or less dressed (though not washed or brushed) and eating cereal with Jean.

"I don't want Coco Pops. I don't *like* Coco Pops. They're for babies."

"Well, that seems about right, given you're behaving like a baby!" I snapped, and then regretted it when I heard her laugh.

Don't react, I thought. Don't give her that hold over you. You have to stay calm, or she'll know that she's got the power to get to you.

I thought about counting to ten, then I remembered the painful "one and a half" of a couple of nights before, and hastily revised my plans.

"Maddie, I'm getting very bored here. Unless you want me to take you to school in your nightie, then I suggest you get your uniform on."

She said nothing, and at last I sighed.

"Okay, well, if you want to behave like a baby, I'll have to treat you like one, and get you dressed the way I do with Petra."

I picked up the clothes and advanced slowly towards the bed, hoping that a bit of warning might induce her to scramble up and get her clothes on, but she just lay there, making herself as limp and heavy as she possibly could so that my back screamed in protest as I began manhandling her into her clothes. She was as floppy as a rag doll, but a hundred times as heavy, and I was breathing hard when at last I stepped back. Her skirt was askew, and her hair was rumpled from where I had dragged the T-shirt over her head, but she was more or less dressed within the meaning of the act.

Finally, figuring that I might as well take advantage of her passivity, I pulled a sock on each foot and then jammed her school shoes on.

"There," I said, trying to keep the triumph out of my voice. "You're dressed. Well done, Maddie. Now, I'll be downstairs eating Coco Pops with Ellie if you want to join us. Otherwise I'll see you in the car in fifteen minutes.

"I haven't done my teeth," she said woodenly, nothing moving apart from her mouth. I gave a laugh.

"I don't give a"—I stopped myself just in time, and then rephrased—"a monkey's. But if you're bothered . . ."

I went through to the bathroom in the hallway and put some toothpaste on the tip of the brush, intending to leave it up to her whether she brushed her teeth, but when I came back, holding the brush, she was sitting up on her bed.

"Will you brush for me?" she said, her voice almost normal after the sulky malice of a few minutes ago. I frowned. Wasn't eight a bit old to be having her teeth brushed? What had the binder said? I couldn't remember.

"Um . . . okay," I said at last.

She opened her mouth like an obedient little bird, and I popped the toothbrush in, but I hadn't been brushing for more than a few seconds when she twisted her head away from the brush and spat full in my face, a gob of minty white phlegm, sliding down my cheek and lips and onto my top.

For a minute I couldn't speak, couldn't say anything, and then, before I had time to think what I was doing, my hand shot out to slap her face.

She flinched, and with what felt like a superhuman effort, I stopped myself, my hand inches from her face, feeling my breath fast and ragged in my chest.

Her eyes met mine, and she began to laugh, totally without mirth, a kind of joyless, cackling glee that made me want to shake her.

My whole body was shuddering with adrenaline, and I knew how close I had come to really letting go—slapping the smirk off her knowing little face. If she had been my own child I would have done it, no questions. My rage had been white-hot and absolute.

But I had stopped myself. I *had* stopped.

Was that what it would look like on the monitor, though, if Sandra had been watching?

I couldn't trust myself to speak. Instead, I got up, leaving Maddie laughing that joyless, grinding laugh on the bed, and I walked shakily through to the bathroom, still holding the toothbrush, and with hands that trembled I wiped the toothpaste from my face and chest, and rinsed the flecks of spit out of my mouth.

Then I stood over the basin, letting the tap run, one hand on either side of the ceramic rim, feeling my whole body shake with pent-up sobs.

"Rowan?" The call came from downstairs, faint over the sound of running water and my own weeping gasps. It was Jean McKenzie. "Jack Grant's outside wi' the car."

"I'm—I'm coming," I managed back, hoping my voice didn't

betray my tears. Then I splashed water over my face, dried my eyes, and walked back into the bedroom, where Maddie was waiting.

"Okay, Maddie," I said, keeping my voice as level as I could. "Time for school. Jack's outside with the car, let's not keep him waiting."

And to my unending shock, she got up calmly, picked up her schoolbag, and headed for the stairs.

"Can I have a banana in the car?" she said over her shoulder, and I found myself nodding, as if nothing had happened.

"Yes," I said, hearing my own voice in my ears, flat and emotionless. Then I thought, *I have to say something, I can't let this go*. "Maddie, about what just happened—you *cannot* spit at people like that; it's disgusting."

"What?" She turned to look at me, her face a picture of injured innocence. "What? I sneezed. I couldn't help it."

And then she ran down the rest of the flight of stairs and out to the waiting car, as if the bitter struggle of the last twenty minutes had been nothing but a figment of my own imagination.

I found myself wondering who had won in that encounter, as I checked Petra's car seat and buckled myself in the front beside Jack. And then it struck me what a fucked-up dynamic this really was—that my relationship with this damaged little girl was not about caring and caregiving but about winning and dominance and war.

No. No matter what the outcome of that situation was, I hadn't won. I had lost the moment I let Maddie make it into a battle.

But I hadn't hit her. Which meant that, if nothing else, I had triumphed over my own worst instinct.

I hadn't let the demons win. Not this time.

As the school gate clanged shut, I felt a kind of weak relief come over me, so that I almost sank to the pavement, my back to the iron railings, my face in my hands.

I had done it. I had *done* it. And now my reward was five hours of something close to relaxation. I still had Petra of course—but five hours with her was nothing compared to Ellie's uncomfortable misery, and Maddie's bitter campaign of vengeance.

Somehow, though, I stayed upright and walked back round the corner to the side road, where Jack was waiting in the car, with Petra.

"Success?" he asked as I opened the car door and slid in beside him, and I felt a grin crack my face wide, unable to conceal my own relief.

"Yes. They're behind bars for the next few hours anyway."

"See? You're doing a great job," he said comfortably, pressing on the accelerator so that we slid away from the curb with the unnervingly silent hum I had come to expect from the car.

"I don't know about that," I said, a little bitterly. "It was touch-and-go getting Maddie out to the car, to be honest. But I've survived another morning, which is probably the main thing."

"Now, what do you want to do?" Jack asked practically, as we drove towards the center of the little town where the girls' primary school was. "We can go straight back to the house if you've stuff to be getting on with, or we can stop off for a coffee, if you like, and I can show you a wee bit of Carn Bridge."

"A little bit of a tour would be lovely. I've not really had a chance to see anything much apart from Heatherbrae yet, and Carn Bridge looked really pretty as we were coming through."

"Aye, it's a bonny little place. And it's got a good coffee shop too, the Parritch Pot. It's down at the other end of the village, but there's not much in the way of street parking there, so I'll park up by the kirk, and we can walk down along the high street. And I'll show you what there is to see."

Ten minutes later, I had wrestled Petra into her pram and we were walking down the main street of Carn Bridge, with Jack pointing out shops and pubs, and nodding at the occasional passerby. It was a quaint little place, somehow built on a smaller scale than you expected from afar, the granite buildings neater and narrower than they seemed from a distance. There were empty shops too; I saw one that had once been a butcher's and another that looked like it might have been a bookshop or a stationer's. Jack nodded when I pointed them out.

"There's plenty of big houses round about, but the little shops still find it hard going. The tourist ones are all right, but the small places can't compete with the supermarkets for price."

The Parritch Pot was a neat little Victorian tea shop right at the bottom of the high street, with a brass bell that jangled as Jack opened the door and held it for me to maneuver Petra across the threshold.

Inside, a motherly looking woman came out from behind the counter to welcome us.

"Jackie Grant! Well, and it's a good while since you were in here for a piece of cake. How are you doing, my dear?"

"I'm well, Mrs. Andrews, thank you. And how are you?"

"Och, well, I cannae complain. And who's your lady friend?" She gave me a look I couldn't quite decipher. There was something . . . well, *arch* was the closest word I could find to describe it, as if there was something more she could have said but was holding back. Perhaps it was just good old-fashioned curiosity. I wanted to roll my eyes. It wasn't the 1950s anymore. Surely men and women were allowed to have a cup of tea without setting tongues wagging, even in a little place like Carn Bridge.

"Oh, this is Rowan," Jack said easily. "Rowan, this is Mrs. Andrews, who runs the tea shop. Rowan is the new nanny up at Heatherbrae, Mrs. Andrews."

"Oh, so you are, my dear," Mrs. Andrews said, her brow clearing, and she smiled. "Jean McKenzie did tell me, and it slipped clean out my head. Well, it's a pleasure to meet you. Let's hope you've more staying power than the other lassies."

"I hear they didn't last long?" I ventured. Mrs. Andrews laughed and shook her head.

"No, indeed. But you don't look like the type to be easily scared."

I pondered her words as I unclipped Petra from her pram and slid her into the high chair Jack had fetched from the back of the tea shop. Was it true? A few days ago I would have said so. But now, as I remembered myself lying there stiff and trembling in bed, listening to the *creak . . . creak . . .* of footsteps above me, I was not so sure.

"Jack," I said at last, after we'd placed our order and were waiting for our drinks to appear. "Do you know what's above my bedroom?"

"Above your bedroom?" He looked surprised. "No, I didn't know there was another floor up there. Is it a storage loft, or a proper attic?"

"I don't know. I've never been up there. But there's a locked door in my room that I'm assuming leads up there, and, well . . ." I swallowed, unsure how to phrase this. "I thought . . . well, I heard some odd noises up there a couple of nights ago."

"Rats?" he asked, one eyebrow cocked, and I shrugged, too embarrassed to tell the truth.

"I don't know. Maybe. Maybe not though. It sounded . . ." I

swallowed again, trying not to say the word that hovered on the tip of my tongue—*human.* "Bigger."

"They make an awful racket in the night, or at least they can do. I've a bunch of keys somewhere, do you want me to have a try this afternoon?"

"Thanks." There was a kind of comfort in sharing my fear, however guardedly, though I felt like something of a fool now the words had left my lips. After all, what was I going to find up there, other than dust and old furniture? But it couldn't hurt, and maybe there was some simple explanation—a window left open, an old chair rocking in the draught, a lamp swinging in the breeze. "That's really kind."

"There you go, now." The voice came from behind us, and I turned to see Mrs. Andrews holding two coffees—proper cappuccinos, made by a human being, rather than a bloody app. I set mine to my lips and took a long, hot gulp, feeling it scald the inside of my throat, heating me from within, and for the first time in a few days, I felt my confidence return.

"This is great, thank you," I said to Mrs. Andrews, and she smiled comfortably.

"Och, you're welcome. I don't suppose it's a patch on Mr. and Mrs. Elincourt's fancy machine up at Heatherbrae, but we do our best."

"Not at all," I said with a laugh, thinking of my relief at dealing with a real person for once. "Actually, their coffeemaker is a bit *too* fancy for me, I can't get to grips with it."

"From what Jean McKenzie says, the whole house is a bit like that, no? She says that you take your life in your hands trying to turn on the light."

I smiled, exchanging a quick glance with Jack, but said nothing.

"Well, it wouldn't be my taste, what they've done to it, but it's nice that they took the place on at least," Mrs. Andrews said at last. She wiped her hands on her apron. "There's not many round here that would have, with that history."

"What history?" I looked up, startled, and she made a shooing motion with her hand.

"Och, don't listen to me. I'm just a gossipy auld woman. But there's something about that house, you know. It's claimed more than one child. The doctor's little girl wasn't the first, by all accounts."

"What do you mean?" I took another gulp of coffee, trying to quell the unease rising inside me.

"Back when it was Struan House," Mrs. Andrews said. She lowered her voice. "The Struans were a very old family and not quite"—she pursed her lips, primly—"well, not quite right in the head, by the end. One of them killed his wife and child, drowned them both in the bath, and another came back from the war and shot himself with his own rifle."

Jesus. I had a sudden flash of the luxuriously appointed family bathroom at Heatherbrae, with the outsize tub and Moroccan tiles. It couldn't be the same bathtub, but it might conceivably be the same room.

"I heard there was . . . a poisoning," I said uncomfortably, and she nodded.

"Aye, that was the doctor, Dr. Grant. He came to the house in the fifties, after the last Struan sold up and moved over the border. He poisoned his little girl, or so they say. Some'll tell you by accident, others—"

But she broke off. Another customer had come in, setting the bell above the door jangling, and Mrs. Andrews smoothed her apron and turned away with a smile.

"But listen to me rattling on. It's just idle gossip and superstition. You shouldn't pay any heed. Well, hello, Caroline. And what can I get for you this morning?"

As she moved away to serve her other customer, I watched her go, wondering what she had meant. But then I shook myself. She was right. It *was* just superstition. All houses above a certain age had experienced deaths and tragedies, and the fact that a child had died at Heatherbrae didn't mean anything.

Still though, Ellie's words rang in my head as I tied Petra's bib more firmly under her chin and dug out the pot of rice cakes.

There was another little girl.

We took the long way round back to Heatherbrae House, driving slowly along past peat-dark burns and through sun-dappled pine forests. Petra snoozed in the back as Jack pointed out local landmarks—a ruined castle, an abandoned fort, a Victorian station decommissioned long ago. In the distance the mountains loomed, and I tried to keep track of the peaks that Jack named.

"Do you like hill walking?" he asked, as we waited at a junction with the main road for a lorry to pass, and I realized that I didn't know the answer to his question.

"I— Well, I'm not really sure. I've never done it. I like walking, I guess. Why?"

"Oh . . . well . . ." There was a sudden hesitation in his voice, and when I looked sideways at him, there was a flush of red across his cheekbones. "I just thought . . . you know . . . when Sandra and Bill are back and your weekends are your own again, perhaps we might . . . I could take you up one of the Munros. If you liked the idea."

"I . . . do," I said, and then it was my turn to blush. "I do like the idea. I mean, if you don't mind me being slow . . . I suppose I'd have to get boots and stuff."

"You'd need good shoes. And waterproofs. The weather can turn very fast up on the mountain. But—"

His phone gave a little chirrup, and he glanced down at it, and then frowned, and handed it across to me.

"Sorry, Rowan, that's from Bill. D'you mind telling me what he says? I don't want to read it while I'm driving, but he doesn't normally text unless it's urgent."

I pressed the text on the home screen and a preview flashed up, all I could see without unlocking the phone, but it was enough.

"'Jack, urgently need the hard copies of the Pemberton files by tonight. Please drop everything and bring them—' And that's where it cuts off."

"Fuck," Jack said, and then glanced guiltily in the rearview mirror to where Petra was sleeping. "Sorry, I didn't mean to swear, but that's my afternoon and evening gone, and most of tomorrow too. I had plans."

I didn't ask what his plans were. I felt only a sudden swoop of . . . not quite loss . . . not quite fear either . . . but a sort of unease at the realization that he would be gone and I would be quite alone with the children for the best part of twenty-four hours, by the time Jack had driven down, rested, and then driven back.

It meant something else, too, I realized, as we came out of the dark tunnel of pine trees into the June sunlight: no possibility of trying the attic door until he got back.

Jack left almost as soon as we got back, and although I had gratefully accepted his offer to take the dogs with him, and relieve me of the responsibility to feed and walk them on top of everything else, the house had an unfamiliar, quiet feeling to it after they had all gone. I fed Petra and put her down for her nap, and then I sat for a while in the cavernous kitchen, drumming my fingers on the concrete tabletop and watching the changing sky out of the tall windows. It really was an incredible view, and in daylight like this, I could see why Sandra and Bill had hewn the house in half the way they had, sacrificing Victorian architecture for this all-encompassing expanse of hill and moor.

Still, though, it left an odd sensation of vulnerability—the way the foursquare front looked so neat and untouched, while at the back it had been ripped open, exposing all the house's insides. Like a patient who looked well enough above their clothes, but lift their shirt and you would find their wounds had been left unstitched, bleeding out. There was a strange feeling of split identity too—as though the house was trying hard to be one thing, while Sandra and Bill pulled it relentlessly in the other direction, chopping off limbs, performing open-heart surgery on its dignified old bones, trying to make it into something against its own will—something it was never meant to be, modern and stylish and slick, where it wanted to be solid and self-effacing.

The ghosts wouldn't like it... I heard it again in Maddie's reedy little voice and shook my head. Ghosts. How absurd. Just folktales and rumors, and a sad old man, living here after the death of his child.

It was more for want of anything else to do that I opened up my phone and typed in "Heatherbrae House, child's death, poison garden."

Most of the early results were irrelevant, but as I scrolled down and down, I came at last to a local-interest blog, written by some sort of amateur historian.

"STRUAN—Struan House (now renamed Heatherbrae), near Carn Bridge in Scotland, is another curiosity for garden historians, being one of the few remaining poison gardens in the United

Kingdom (another being the famous example at Alnwick Castle in Northumberland). Originally planted in the 1950s by the analytical chemist Kenwick Grant, it is thought to feature some of the rarest and most poisonous examples of domestic plants, with a particular focus on varieties native to Scotland. Sadly, the garden was allowed to fall into disrepair after the death of Grant's young daughter, Elspeth, who died in 1973, age eleven, having, according to local legend, accidentally ingested one of the plants in the garden. Although in its day occasionally open to researchers and members of the public, Dr. Grant closed the garden completely after his daughter's death, and after he himself passed away in 2009, the house was sold to a private buyer. Since the sale, Struan has been renamed Heatherbrae House, and it's believed that it has been the subject of extensive remodeling. It is unknown what remains of the poison garden, but it is to be hoped that the current owners appreciate the historical and botanical importance of this piece of Scottish history and maintain Dr. Grant's legacy with the respect it deserves."

There were no photographs, but I returned to Google and typed in "Dr. Kenwick Grant." It was an unusual name, and there were few results, but most of the pictures that came up seemed to be of the same man. The first was a black-and-white picture of a man aged perhaps forty, with a neatly clipped goatlike beard and small wire-framed spectacles, standing in front of what looked like the wrought iron gate of the walled garden where Maddie, Ellie, and I had entered the day before. He was not smiling, his face had the look of one that didn't smile easily, with an expression naturally serious in repose, but there was a kind of pride in his stance.

The next photograph made a sad contrast. It was another black-and-white shot, recognizably the same man, but this time Dr. Grant was likely in his fifties. His expression was totally different, a distorted mask of emotion that could have been grief, or fear, or anger, or a mix of all three. He seemed to be running towards an unseen photographer, his hand outstretched, either to push the camera away or shield his own face, it was not clear which. Behind the goatlike beard his mouth was twisted into a snarling grimace that made me flinch, even through the tiny screen, and the passage of decades.

The final photograph was in color, and it was a shot that seemed to have been taken through the bars of a gate. It showed an elderly man, stooped and bent, wearing a buff overall and a wide-brimmed hat that shaded his face. He was extremely thin, to the point of emaciation, and leaning on a stick, and his glasses were thick and fogged, but he was staring fiercely at the person taking the photo, his free hand upraised in a bony fist, as though threatening the viewer. I clicked on the picture, trying to find out the context for the shot, but there was none. It was just a Pinterest page, with no information on where the picture had been found. *Dr. Kenwick Grant*, the caption read, *2002.*

As I closed down the phone, my overwhelming emotion was a kind of desperate sadness—for Dr. Grant, for his daughter, and for this house, where it had all happened.

Unable to sit in silence with my thoughts any longer, I got up, put the baby monitor in my pocket, and, grabbing a ball of caterers' string from the drawer by the cooker, I left the house by the utility room door, tracing the path the girls had shown me the day before.

The sun of the morning had gone in, and I was cold by the time I reached the cobbled path that led to the poison garden. It was strange to think it was June—down in London I would have been sweating in short skirts and sleeveless tops, and cursing the shitty air-con at Little Nippers. Up here, almost halfway to the arctic circle, I was beginning to regret not taking my coat. The baby monitor was silent in my pocket as I reached the gate and slipped my hand through the metalwork to try to trip the catch, as Ellie had done.

It was more difficult than she had made it look. It was not just the fact that the hole in the wrought iron was too narrow for my hand to fit comfortably, it was also the angle. Even after I had forced my hand through, swearing as the rust ripped skin off my knuckles, I could not get my fingers to the catch.

I changed position, kneeling on the damp cobbles, feeling the chill strike up through the thin material of my sheer tights, and at last managed to get a fingertip to the tongue of the latch. I pressed, pressed harder . . . and then the gate opened with a clang and I almost fell forward onto the worn bricks.

It was hard to believe that I had ever mistaken it for a regular garden. Now that I knew its history, the warning signs were everywhere. Fat, black laurel berries, the thin needles of yew, straggling patches of self-seeded foxglove, clumps of nettles, which I had taken to be weeds when I first entered the garden but which I now saw bore a rusted metal tag dug deep into the earth labeled *Urtica dioica*. And others too that I did not recognize—a plant with flamboyant mauve flowers, another that brushed my leg with a sensation like tiny needles. A patch of something that looked like sage but must have been something very different. And, as I pushed open the door of a tumbledown shed, a profusion of mushrooms and toadstools, still sprouting gamely in the dark.

I could not suppress a shudder as I drew the door quietly shut, feeling the damp wood grate on the flags. So many poisons—some tempting, some decidedly not. Some familiar, and some I was certain I had never seen before. Some so beautiful I wanted to break off a branch and stick it in a jug in the kitchen—except that I did not dare. Even the familiar plants in these surroundings looked strange and ominous—no longer grown for their lovely flowers and colors, but for their deadliness.

I hugged my arms around my body as I walked, partly to protect myself, but the garden was so overgrown that it was impossible to avoid brushing up against the plants completely. The touch of the leaves felt like prickles on my skin, and I was unable to tell anymore which plants were toxic to touch, or whether it was pure paranoia on my part that sent my skin itching and tingling when I brushed past.

It was only when I turned to leave that I noticed something else—a set of pruning shears, sitting on the low brick wall holding back one of the beds. They were new and bright, not in the least rusted, and looking up, I saw that the bush above my head had been pruned—not much, but enough to clear the path. And further up, I saw that a piece of garden twine had been used to hold back a swag of creeper.

In fact, the more I looked, the more I was sure—this garden was not as neglected as it appeared. Someone had been tending to it—and not Maddie or Ellie. No child would have thought of neatly cutting back that hanging branch—they would have snapped it off, or just ducked under it, if they were even tall enough to notice.

So who then? Not Sandra. I was sure of that. Jean McKenzie? Jack Grant?

The name sounded in my head with a curious chime. Jack . . . Grant.

It wasn't an uncommon surname, particularly around here, but . . . still. Dr. Kenwick Grant. Could it really be coincidence?

As I stood, wondering, the baby monitor in my pocket gave a little grumbling squawk, recalling me to reality, and I remembered what I had come here to do.

Picking up the shears, I hurried back to the gate, and pulled it firmly shut behind myself. The clang as it closed set a flock of birds rising into the sky from pine trees up the slope, and seemed to echo back at me from the hills opposite, but I was in too much of a hurry now to care.

Taking the string out of my pocket, I clipped off a generous length and then I stood on tiptoes and began to wind it round and round the top of the gate, above the height of my own head, where no child could possibly reach, twining it in and out of the ornate fitting and round the brick lintel above, until at last the string was used up, and the gate was totally secure. Then I tied it in a granny knot, wrapping the ends around my fingers and pulling the string tight until my fingertips went white.

The baby monitor in my pocket wailed again, more determinedly this time, but I was sure now that the gate was secure, and that nothing short of a ladder would enable Maddie and Ellie to break in this time. Dropping the shears into my pocket, I picked up my phone and pressed the Happy app icon.

"Coming, Petra. There, there, sweetheart, no need to cry, I'm coming."

And I ran up the cobbled path to the house.

The next few hours were taken up with Petra, and then figuring out how to drive the Tesla to collect the girls from school. Jack had taken the Elincourts' second car, a Land Rover, with him to meet Bill, and had given me a quick crash course in driving the Tesla before he left, but it was an undeniably different style and it took me a few miles to get used to it—no clutch, no gears, and a strange slowing every time you took your foot off the accelerator.

The girls were both tired after their day at school. They said nothing as we drove home, and the afternoon and evening passed without incident. They ate supper, took turns playing on the tablet, and then got into their pajamas and climbed into bed with barely a peep. When I went up at eight to turn out their lights and tuck them in, I heard an adult's voice, coming over the speakers.

At first, I thought that they were listening to an audiobook, but then I heard Maddie say something, her small voice inaudible through the door, and the amplified voice on the speakers replied, "Oh darling, well done! Ten out of ten! I'm very proud of you. And what about you, Ellie? Have you been practicing your spellings too?"

It was Sandra. She had dialed into the children's room and was talking to them before they fell asleep.

For a moment I stood, hovering outside the door, my hand on the doorknob, listening to their conversation, half hoping—half fearing—to hear something about myself.

But instead, I heard Sandra tell the girls to snuggle down, the lights dimmed, and she began to sing a lullaby.

There was something so loving, so personal about the simple act, Sandra's voice wavering over the high notes, and tripping over an awkward lyric, that I was left feeling like an eavesdropper. I wanted, more than anything, to open the door, tiptoe in, and cuddle Maddie and Ellie, kiss their hot little foreheads, tell them how lucky they were to have a mother who at least *wanted* to be there, even if she couldn't.

But I knew that would break the illusion that their mother was really present, and I backed away. If Sandra wanted to speak to me, no doubt she would dial down to the kitchen after she had finished.

While I ate and tidied up, I waited, slightly nervously, for the sound of her voice, crackling over the intercom, but it didn't come. By 9:00 p.m. the house was silent and I locked up and went to bed with a feeling like walking on eggshells.

After I had done my teeth and turned out the lights, I lay down in bed, feeling my limbs ache with weariness. My phone was in my hand, but instead of plugging it in to charge and going straight to sleep, I found myself googling Dr. Grant again.

I stared at his photo for a long time, thinking of Mrs. Andrews's words in the café. There was something about the contrast between that first picture and the last that was almost shocking, something that spoke of long nights of grief and agony—perhaps even in this very room. What had it been like to live here all those years, with the local gossip swirling around him, and the memories of his daughter so stark and painful?

Returning to the search screen, I typed in "Elspeth Grant death Carn Bridge" and waited as the links came up.

There was no photo—at least none that I could find. And she had not had much of an obituary, just a passage in the *Carn Bridge Observer* (now defunct), stating that Elspeth Grant, much loved daughter of Dr. Kenwick Grant and the late Ailsa Grant, had died in St. Vincent's Cottage Hospital on 21st October 1973, aged eleven years.

Another brief piece a few weeks later, this time in the *Inverness Gazette*, recorded the results of a postmortem and inquest on Elspeth's death. It seemed she had died from eating *Prunus lauro-cerasus*, or cherry laurel berries, which had been accidentally made into jam. The berries were apparently easily mistaken for cherries or elderberries by inexperienced foragers, and it was thought that the child had gathered them herself and brought them to the house-keeper, who had simply tipped them into the pan without checking. Dr. Grant never ate jam himself, preferring porridge and salt, the housekeeper did not live in and took her meals at her own house in the village, and Elspeth's nanny had resigned her post almost two months before the incident, so Elspeth was the only person to ingest the poison. She had become unwell almost straightaway and had died of multiple organ failure, in spite of strenuous efforts to save her.

A verdict of misadventure was brought, and no charges were filed as a result of her death.

So. Elspeth had been the only person who was ever in danger of eating that jam. I could see why gossip had arisen—though quite why it had settled on Dr. Grant, and not the unnamed housekeeper, was unclear. Perhaps it had been a case of local people looking after their own. And what of the nanny? She had resigned "just two months before," according to the writer of the piece, who managed to put the simple phrase in such a way as to make it sound both innocent and suggestive, but presumably she could have had nothing to do with the incident, or it would have been raised at the inquest. Her absence had been noted purely in connection with the fact that Elspeth had been unsupervised at the time of picking the berries, and therefore, by inference, was more likely to make a slip concerning identification of the plants.

The more I pondered the idea, though, the more problems there seemed to be with the suggestion that Elspeth had gathered the berries by accident. I was a 1990s child of the suburbs, totally unused to fruit picking, and even I had a vague idea of what laurel looked like compared to elderberry. Would the daughter of a poisons expert with a locked garden explicitly dedicated to deadly plants really make such a slip?

Rereading the piece, I felt a sudden surge of sympathy for the nanny, the missing link in the case. She was not interviewed. Whatever had become of her was not stated. But she had missed, by just a few weeks, the possibility of being embroiled in scandal. What future was there for a nanny whose child had died in her care, after all? A very bleak one indeed.

* * *

I'm not sure when I finally drifted off, my phone still in my hand, but I know that it was very late when a sudden sound jerked me from sleep. It was a *ding-dong* noise, like a doorbell, not one of my usual alerts. I sat up, blinking and rubbing my eyes, and then realized the noise was coming from my phone. I stared at the screen. The Happy app was flashing. *Doorbell sounding,* read the screen. It came again, a low *bing-bong* that seemed to be able to override all my do-not-disturb settings. When I pressed the icon a message flashed up. *Open door? Confirm / Cancel.*

I hastily pressed cancel, and clicked through to the camera icon. The screen showed me a view of the front door, but the outside light was not on, and inside the shelter of the porch I could see nothing but grainy pixelated darkness. Had Jack come back? Had he forgotten his keys? Either way, as the doorbell sounded for the third time, I could hear the chimes filtering up the stairwell as well as coming out of my phone, and I knew I had to answer it before the noise woke the girls.

The room was unnaturally cold, and I pulled on my dressing gown before padding quietly downstairs, my feet soft on the thick carpet runner, picking my way in the semi darkness but not wanting to turn on the lights and risk waking the children. In the hallway I had a moment's struggle with the thumb panel, and then the door swung silently open to reveal . . . nothing.

It was quite dark. The Land Rover's parking space was still empty, and none of the motion-sensitive security lights around the yard were on, though the porch light flicked on as soon as I stepped over the threshold, detecting my presence. I shaded my eyes against its harsh glare and peered across the yard and down the drive, shivering slightly in the cool night air. Nothing. There were no lights on in Jack's flat either. Had something triggered it by mistake?

Closing the door, I made my way slowly back up towards my bedroom, but I was barely halfway up the second flight when the bell sounded again.

Damn it.

With a sigh, I belted my dressing gown tighter and made my way back downstairs, hurrying this time.

But when I wrenched open the door, again, there was no one there.

I slammed the door harder than I meant to this time, the tiredness making my frustration boil over for a second, and I stood in the dark of the hallway, holding my breath and listening for a sound from upstairs, the rising siren of Petra's wail perhaps. But none came.

Nevertheless, this time, instead of setting back upstairs to my own room, I stopped and peered in at Petra, sleeping peacefully, and then into Maddie and Ellie's room. In the soft glow of their night-light I could see both of them lying fast asleep, sweaty hair strewn across the pillows, their cherubic little mouths open, their soft snores barely disturbing the quiet. They looked so small and vulnerable in sleep, both of them, and my heart clenched at my anger towards Maddie that morning. I told myself that tomorrow I would do better—that I would remember how young she was, how disorienting it must be to be left with a woman she barely knew. Either way, it was clearly not one of them playing with the doorbell, and I shut the door softly and made my way back upstairs to my room.

It was still very cold, and as I closed the door behind me, the curtains billowed out, and I realized why. The window was open.

I frowned as I walked across to it.

It was open, and not just slightly, as if someone had wanted to air the room, but completely open, the bottom sash pushed up as high as it would go. Almost—the thought came unbidden—as if someone had been leaning out to smoke a cigarette, though that was absurd.

No wonder the room was cold. Well, it was easily solvable at least—easier than battling with the control panel at any rate. The curtains, doors, lights, gates, and even the coffee machine in this place might be automated, but the windows at least were still Victorian originals, blessedly operated by hand. Thank God.

I yanked the sash down, drew the brass catch across, and then scampered back into the still-warm sanctuary of the feather duvet, shivering pleasurably as I snuggled into its folds.

I was drifting back off to sleep when I heard it . . . not the doorbell this time, but a single, solitary *creeeeak.*

I sat up in bed, my phone clutched to my breast. Shit. Shit shit *shit.*

But the next sound did not come. Had I misheard? Was it not the footsteps that had woken me the night before, but something else . . . ? Just a branch in the wind, perhaps, or an expanding floorboard?

I could hear nothing apart from the whoosh of my own blood in my own ears, and at last I lay slowly back down, still clutching my phone in my hand, and shut my eyes against the darkness.

But my senses were on high alert, and sleep seemed impossible. For more than forty minutes I lay there, feeling my pulse thumping, feeling my thoughts race with a mixture of paranoia and wild superstitions.

And then, half as I'd feared, half as I'd been waiting for, it came again.

Creeeeak . . .

And then, after the smallest of pauses, *creak . . . creak . . . creak . . .*

This time there was no doubt—it was pacing.

My heart leapt into my throat with a kind of nauseating lurch, and my pulse sped up so fast that for a moment I thought I would faint, but then anger took over. I jumped out of bed and ran to the locked door in the corner of the room, where I knelt, peering through the keyhole, my heart like a drum in my chest.

I felt absurdly vulnerable, kneeling there in my nightclothes with one eye wide open and pressed to a dark hole, and for a moment I had a sick, jolting fantasy of someone shoving something through the hole, a toothpick perhaps, or a sharpened pencil, roughly piercing my cornea, and I fell back, blinking, my eye watering with the dusty draft.

But there was nothing there. No toothpick maliciously blinding me. Nothing to see either. Just the unending blackness, and the cool, dust-laden breeze of stale attic air. Even if there was a turn in the stair, or a closed door at the top, with a light on in the attic itself, *some* light would have escaped to pollute the inky dark of the stairs. But there was nothing. Not even the smallest glimmer. If there was someone up there, whatever they were doing, they were doing it in the dark.

Creak . . . creak . . . creak . . . it came again, unbearable in its regularity. Then a pause, and then again, *creak . . . creak . . . creak . . .*

"I can hear you!" I shouted at last, unable to sit there listening in silence and fear any longer. I put my mouth to the keyhole, my voice shaking with a mix of angry terror. "I can hear you! What the fuck are you doing up there, you sicko? How dare you? I'm calling the police so you'd better get the fuck out of there!"

But the steps didn't even falter. My voice died away as if I had shouted into an empty void. *Creak . . . creak . . . creak . . .* And then, just as before, a little pause, and they resumed without the slightest loss of rhythm. *Creak . . . creak . . . creak . . .* And I knew in truth that of course I wouldn't call the police. What the fuck could I say? "Oh, please, Constable, there's a creaking sound coming from my attic"?

There was no police station closer than Inverness, and they would hardly be taking routine calls in the middle of the night. My only option was 999—and even in my shaking state of fear, I had a pretty good idea what the operator would say if a hysterical woman rang the emergency number in the middle of the night claiming spooky sounds were coming from her attic.

If only Jack were here, if only *someone* were here, apart from three little girls I was paid to protect, not scare even further.

Oh God. Suddenly I could not bear it any longer, and I understood what dark terrors had driven those four previous nannies out of their post and away. To lie here, night after night, listening, waiting, staring into the darkness at that locked door, that open keyhole gaping into blackness . . .

There was nothing I could do. I could go and sleep in the living room, but if the noises started down there as well, I thought I might lose it completely, and there was something almost worse about the idea of those sounds continuing up in the attic while I, ignorant, slept down below. At least if I was here, watching, listening, whatever was up there could not . . .

I swallowed in the darkness, my throat dry. My palms were sweating, and I could not finish the thought.

I would not sleep again tonight, I knew that now.

Instead, I wrapped myself in the duvet, shivering hard, turned on the light, and sat, with my phone still in my hand, listening to the steady, rhythmic sound of the feet pacing above me. And I thought of Dr. Grant, the old man who had lived here before, the man Sandra and Bill had done their very best to get rid of, painting and scouring and remodeling until there was barely a trace of him left, except for that horrible poison garden, behind its locked gate.

And except, perhaps, whatever paced that attic in the night.

I heard the words again, in Maddie's cold little matter-of-fact voice, as if she were beside me, whispering in my ear. *After a while he stopped sleeping. He just used to pace backwards and forwards all night long. Then he went mad. People do go mad, you know, if you stop them from sleeping for long enough . . .*

Was I going mad? Was that what this was?

Jesus. This was ridiculous. People didn't go mad from two nights' lack of sleep. I was being completely melodramatic.

And yet, as the footsteps passed above me again, slow and relentless, I felt a kind of panic rise up inside me, possessing me, and I could not stop my eyes turning towards the locked door, imagining it opening, the slow tread, tread of old feet on the stairs inside, and then that cadaverous, hollow face coming towards me in the darkness, the bony arm outstretched.

Elspeth . . .

It was a sound not coming from above, but in my own mind—a death rattle cry of a grief-stricken father for his lost child. *Elspeth . . .*

But the door did not open. No one came. And yet still above me, hour after hour, those steps continued. *Creak . . . creak . . . creak . . .* the ceaseless pacing of someone unable to rest.

I could not bring myself to turn out the light. Not this time. Not with those ceaseless, restless footsteps above me.

Instead, I lay there, on my side, facing the locked door, my phone in my hand, watching, waiting, until the floor beneath the window opposite my bed began to lighten with the coming of dawn, and at last I got up, stiff-limbed and nauseous with tiredness, and made my way down to the warmth of the kitchen to make myself the strongest cup of coffee I could bear to drink, and try to face the day.

Downstairs was empty and echoing, eerily quiet without the snuffling, huffing presence of the dogs. I was surprised to find that a part of me missed the distraction of their questing noses and constant begging for treats.

As I made my way across the hall to the kitchen, I found I was picking up a treasure trail of the girls' possessions—a scatter of crayons on the hall rug, a My Little Pony abandoned beneath the breakfast bar, and then—oddly—a single purple flower, wilting, in the middle of the kitchen floor. I bent down, puzzled, wondering where it had come from. It was just a single bloom, and it looked as if it had fallen from a bouquet or dropped from a house plant, but there were no flowers in this room. Had one of the girls picked it? But if so, when?

It seemed a shame to let it die, so I filled a coffee mug with water and stuck the stem into it, and then put it on the kitchen table. Perhaps it would revive.

I was quietly nursing my second cup of coffee and watching the sun rise above the hills to the east of the house when the voice came, seemingly from nowhere.

"Rowan . . ."

It was a reedy quaver, barely audible, and yet somehow loud enough to echo around the silent kitchen, and it made me jump so that scalding coffee slopped over my wrist and the sleeve of my dressing gown.

"Shit." I began mopping up, twisting at the same time to see the source of the voice. There was no one there, at least, no one visible.

"Who's there?" I called, and this time I heard a creak from the direction of the stairs, a single creak, so eerily like those of the night before that my heart skipped a beat. "Who *is* it?" I called again, more aggressively than I had intended, and strode angrily out into the hallway.

Above me a small figure hesitated at the top of the stairs. Ellie. Her face was worried, her lip trembling.

"Oh, sweetheart . . ." I felt instantly contrite. "I'm sorry, you scared me. I didn't mean to snap. Come down."

"I'm not allowed," she said. She had a blanket in her hands, twisting the silky trim between her fingers, and with her bottom lip stuck out and wobbling dangerously close to tears, she looked suddenly much younger than her five years.

"Of course you are. Who says you're not allowed?"

"Mummy. We're not allowed out of our rooms until the bunny clock's ears go up."

Oh. Suddenly I remembered the paragraph in the binder about Ellie's early rising, and the rule about the Happy bunny clock, which clicked over to the wide-awake bunny at six. I looked back through the arch to the kitchen clock—5:47.

Well, I couldn't exactly contradict Sandra's rule . . . but here we were, and there was a large part of me that was relieved to see another human being. Somehow with Ellie around, the ghosts of the night before seemed to retreat back into absurdity.

"Well . . . ," I said slowly, trying to pick my way between backing up my employer, and compassion to a small child hovering on the verge of crying. "Well, you're up now. Just this once, I think we can pretend the bunny woke up early."

"But what will Mummy say?"

"I won't tell anyone if you don't," I said, and then bit my lip. It's one of the cardinal rules of childcare—don't ask a child to keep secrets from a parent. That's the path to all kinds of risky behavior and misunderstandings. But I'd said it now, and hopefully Ellie had read it as a lighthearted remark rather than an invitation to conspire against her mother. I couldn't help but glance up at the camera in the corner—but surely Sandra wouldn't be awake at 6:00 a.m. unless she had to be. "Come on down and we'll have a hot chocolate together and then when the bunny wakes up you can go up and get dressed."

Down in the kitchen, Ellie sat on one of the high stools, kicking her heels against the legs of the chair, while I heated up milk on the induction burner and stirred in hot chocolate powder. As Ellie drank, and I sipped my now-cooling coffee, we talked, about school, about her best friend Carry, about missing the dogs, and at last I ventured to ask about whether she missed her parents. Her face crumpled a little at that.

"Can we phone Mummy again tonight?"

"Yes, of course. We can try, anyway. She's been very busy, you know that."

Ellie nodded. Then, looking out of the window she said, "He's gone, hasn't he?"

"Who?" I was confused. Was she talking about her father, or Jack? Or perhaps . . . perhaps someone else? "Who's gone?"

She didn't answer, only kicked her legs against the stool.

"I like it better when he's gone. He makes them do things they don't want to do."

I don't know why, but the words gave me a sharp flashback to something I had barely thought about since my very first night here—

that crumpled, unfinished note from Katya. The words sounded inside my head, as though someone had whispered them urgently into my ear. *I wanted to tell you to please be—*

Suddenly it felt more like a warning than ever.

"Who?" I said, more urgently this time. "Who are you talking about, Ellie?"

But she misunderstood my question, or perhaps deliberately chose to misinterpret it.

"The girls." Her voice was matter of fact. And then she put down her hot chocolate and slid from the stool. "Can I go and watch some TV?"

"Ellie, wait," I said, standing too, feeling my heart suddenly pounding in my chest. "Who are you talking about? Who's gone? Who makes the girls do things?"

But I was too urgent, and as my hand closed on her wrist, she pulled away, suddenly frightened by my intensity.

"Nothing. I don't remember. I made it up. Maddie told me to say it. I didn't say it anyway." The excuses tumbled out, one after another, each as silly as the one before, and she twisted her small hand out of my grip. I had no idea what to say. I thought about following her as she slipped from the room, and the sound of the *Peppa Pig* theme tune filtered back into the play room, but I knew it wouldn't work. I had scared her and missed my chance. I should have asked more casually. Now she had closed down in that way that small children do when they realize they have said something more momentous than they meant to. It was the same panic I had seen in little children when they repeated an inappropriate word without understanding the reaction it would elicit—a startled attempt to pedal back from a response they had not anticipated, followed by total shut down, and a denial that they ever said it. If I pushed Ellie now, I would only be shooting myself in the foot, and preventing any further confidences.

The girls . . . He makes them do things they don't want to do . . .

My stomach turned over. It was the kind of thing every safeguarding manual warned about—the nightmare scenario you hoped never to encounter. But . . . was it? What girls was Ellie talking about? Herself and Maddie? Or some completely different girls? And who was the "he"? Bill? Jack? Or someone else entirely—a teacher or . . .

But no. I pushed away the image of the wild grief-stricken face staring out of my phone screen at me. That was pure fantasy. If I went to Sandra with something like that, she'd be entitled to laugh in my face.

But . . . *could* I go to Sandra with something like this? When Ellie would deny what she said, and when it might be nothing at all? There was nothing that I could pinpoint, after all, to say, "This is definitely worrying."

I was still staring after Ellie, biting at the edge of my nail, when a noise from the hallway made me jump, and I turned to see the door opening, and Jean McKenzie standing on the doorstep, taking off her coat.

"Mrs. McKenzie," I said. She was neatly dressed in a woolen skirt and a white cotton blouse, and I suddenly felt very conscious of my own state of undress, in a dressing gown, with not a great deal beneath.

"You're up early," was all she said, and I felt the prickle of her disapproval. Maybe it was the lack of sleep, or the leftover anxiety from Ellie's words, but my temper suddenly boiled up.

"Why don't you like me?" I demanded.

She turned to look back at me from stashing her coat in the hall cupboard.

"I beg your pardon?"

"You heard me. You've been completely off with me ever since I arrived. Why?"

"I think you're imagining things, miss."

"You know full well I'm not. If it's about that business on the first day, I didn't shut the damn door, and I *didn't* lock the children out. Why would I?"

"Kindness is as kindness does," Jean McKenzie said cryptically, and she turned to go into the utility room, but I ran after her, grabbing her arm.

"What the hell does that even mean?"

She pulled herself out of my grip, and suddenly her eyes blazed at me with what I could only call hatred.

"I'll thank you not to handle me like that, miss, and not to swear in front of the bairns, either."

"I was asking you a perfectly reasonable question," I retorted, but she ignored me, stalking away to the utility room, rubbing her arm with exaggerated care as if I'd given her a friction burn. "And stop calling me *miss*," I called after her. "We're not in bloody Downton Abbey."

"What would you prefer me to call you then?" she snapped over her shoulder.

I had turned on my heel, preparing to go and wake up Maddie, but her words stopped me in my tracks, and I swung round to stare at her expressionless back, bent over the utility room sink.

"Wh-what did you say?"

But she did not answer, only turned on the taps, drowning out my voice.

* * *

"Goodbye, girls!" I called, watching them through the school gate as they traipsed into their classrooms. Maddie said nothing, she just trudged onwards, head down, ignoring the chatter of the other little girls. But Ellie looked up from her conversation with a little red-headed girl and waved. Her smile was sweet and cheerful, and I felt myself smile back, and then down at Petra, jiggling and gurgling on my hip. The sun was shining, the birds were singing, and the warmth of a beautiful June day was filtering through the leaves of the trees. The fears and fantasies of last night—the memory of that twisted, grief-racked face peering out from the screen of my phone—all of that seemed suddenly preposterous in the light of day.

I was just strapping Petra back into her car seat when my phone pinged, and I glanced at it, wondering if it was something important. It was an email. From Sandra.

Oh shit.

Paranoid thoughts flitted through my mind—had she seen the camera footage of me almost hitting Maddie, or the endless stream of treats I had been bribing the girls with? Or was it something . . . else? Something Jean McKenzie had said?

My stomach was fluttering butterflies as I clicked to open, but the subject header was matter of fact enough: *Update.* Whatever that meant.

Hi, Rowan,

Sorry to email but I'm in a meeting and can't talk, and I wanted to send you a quick update with how things are going here. The trade fair has gone super well, but Bill has been called away to Dubai to do some troubleshooting out there, which means I'm going to have to take over on the Kensington project—not ideal as it means I will be away for a little longer than I had hoped, but it can't be helped. I should be back by next Tuesday (i.e., a week today). Are you managing okay? Does that sound doable?

In terms of the children, Rhiannon finishes school today. Elise's mum has kindly volunteered to collect both girls (they live down near Pitlochry so have to drive past anyway) and Rhi will be back at Heatherbrae any time from about twelve onwards. I have texted her, so she knows what's going on, and she's excited to meet you.

Jack spoke to Bill yesterday and mentioned that you are getting on very well with the girls; I'm very glad to hear it's all going okay. Do call if you have any concerns—I will try to ring tonight before the girls' bedtimes.

Sandra x

I shut down the email, unsure whether my overriding emotion was one of relief, or trepidation. I most definitely *was* relieved—not least about the fact that Jack had apparently put in a good word for me. But another week . . . I had not realized until I read Sandra's words how much I had been counting on her arrival back this Friday, ticking off the days in my head like a prison sentence.

And now . . . four more days added onto my term. And not just with the little ones, but with Rhiannon too. How did I feel about that?

The idea of having someone else in the house was undeniably comforting. There *was* something absurd about the memory of those slow, measured footsteps, but even in daylight, I could feel the hairs beginning to rise up on my arms as I recalled lying there, listening to them pacing back and forth. Having *someone*, even a stroppy fourteen-year-old, in the next bedroom would definitely take the edge off.

But as I started up the Tesla, the image that flashed through my head was a different one—that scarlet scrawl across the bedroom door: *FUCK OFF, KEEP OUT OR YOU DIE.* There was something there. Something very close to Maddie's furious, wordless anger.

Perhaps, whatever it was, I would be able to get to the bottom of it with Rhiannon.

The school run back to Heatherbrae took longer than the previous morning, because there was a van on the road ahead of me. I followed it slowly from Carn Bridge, tapping gingerly at the accelerator, sure that it would turn off at every junction we came to, but inexplicably it seemed to be going the same way, even as the road narrowed and grew more rural. It was with some relief that I realized we were nearly at the turn off to Heatherbrae House, and I was just about to signal left when the van signaled too, and drew up over the drive, forcing me to stamp on the brakes.

As I waited, the Tesla silently idling, the passenger door opened and a girl jumped out, a rucksack on her shoulder. She said something to the driver, and the back door of the van popped open. She dragged a huge case out, thumping it carelessly onto the gravel, and then slammed the door and stepped back as the driver pulled away from the curb. I was just about to lean out and ask her who she was and what she was doing in the middle of nowhere when she pulled her phone out of her pocket and held it up to the proximity sensor of the gates, and they swung open.

It couldn't be Rhiannon, surely—she wasn't due back until the afternoon, and that disreputable van certainly didn't look like it belonged to anyone's mother. Was it someone who worked here? But in that case, why the huge trunk?

I waited a few minutes for her to clear the gates, and then pressed on the accelerator. The Tesla slid smoothly up the drive, behind the girl, who turned, with a look of surprise on her face. However, instead of moving out of the way she stood her ground, hands on her hips, and the huge case at her feet. I braked again, feeling the gravel scrunch beneath the tires, and wound down the window.

"Can I help you?"

"I should be the one asking you that," the girl said. She had long blond hair, and a clipped expensive accent, without a trace of Scots in it. "Who the hell are you and what are you doing in my parents' car?"

So it *was* Rhiannon.

"Oh, hello, you must be Rhiannon. Sorry, I wasn't expecting you back for another few hours. I'm Rowan."

The girl was still looking at me blankly, and I added, beginning to feel a little impatient, "The new nanny? I thought your mum told you."

It seemed stupid to be carrying on this conversation through a car window, so I put the car into park and got out, holding out my hand.

"Nice to meet you. Sorry not to be expecting you, your mum said you wouldn't be here until twelve."

"Rowan? But you're—" the girl began, a furrow between her narrow brows; then something cleared and she shook her head. There was a smile on her lips, and it was not a very nice one. "Never mind."

"I'm what?" I dropped my hand.

"I said, never mind," Rhiannon said. "And don't pay any attention to what my mum told you, she hasn't got a fucking clue which way is up. As you may have already realized." She looked me up and down, and then said, "Well, what are you waiting for?"

"What?"

"Give me a hand with my case."

I was getting more and more irritated, but there was no point in starting off on the wrong foot, so I swallowed my anger and wheeled the case around to the back of the Tesla. It was even heavier than it looked. Rhiannon didn't wait for me to load it up, but climbed into the back seat, beside Petra.

"Hello, brat," she said, though there was an undertone of affection in her voice that had been notably absent when she spoke to me. And then, to me, as I slid into the driver's seat, "Well, let's not sit here all day admiring the view."

I gritted my teeth, swallowed my pride, and pressed down so hard on the accelerator that gravel spat from behind the wheels as we began to move up the drive towards Heatherbrae House.

Inside the house Rhiannon stalked into the kitchen, leaving me to unload both Petra and the huge heavy trunk. When I finally made it inside, Petra in tow, I saw that Rhiannon had already installed herself at the metal breakfast bar and was eating a giant sandwich she had clearly just put together.

"Sooooo," her voice came out like a drawl. "You're Rowan, are you? I must say, you don't look anything like what I was expecting."

I frowned. There was something a little malicious in her voice, and I wondered what exactly she meant.

"What were you expecting?"

"Oh . . . I don't know. Just someone . . . different. You don't look like a Rowan, somehow." She grinned, and then before I could react, took another bite of sandwich and said, thickly, through the mouthful, "You need to put more mayonnaise on the fridge order. Oh, and where the hell are the dogs?"

I blinked. I felt like it should be me asking the questions, grilling her. Why did I always seem to be on the wrong end of a power struggle? But it was a perfectly reasonable question, so I tried to keep my voice even as I answered it.

"Jack was called away to take some paperwork to your dad. He took the dogs with him—he thought they'd enjoy the trip."

That hadn't been what he'd said at all, but somehow I didn't want to admit to this haughty teenager that I hadn't felt equal to the task of wrangling three small children and two Labradors.

"When's he back?"

"Jack? I don't know. Today, I imagine."

Rhiannon nodded, chewing thoughtfully, and then said, around a mouthful of food, "By the way, it's Elise's birthday tonight and her mum's invited me over for a sleepover. Is that okay?"

There was something in her tone that made it clear that I was being asked only as a formality, but I nodded.

"I'd better text your mum and check, but of course, that's fine by me. Where does she live?"

"Pitlochry. It's about an hour's drive, but Elise's brother will give me a lift."

I nodded, pulled out my phone, and texted a quick message to Sandra.

Rhiannon safely back—wants to go to a sleepover with Elise tonight. Assume that's okay but please confirm.

The message pinged back almost straightaway.

No problem. Will call 6pm. Give my love to Rhi.

"Your mum sends love and says it's fine," I reported back to Rhiannon, who rolled her eyes as if to say, *Well, duh.* "What time are you getting picked up?"

"After lunch," Rhiannon said. She swung her legs over the side of the stool and shoved the dirty plate across the counter, towards me. "Laters."

I watched her as she made her way up the stairs, long legs in school uniform stalking up the graceful curve of the staircase, and then disappearing around the bend.

She did not come down for lunch. I wasn't particularly surprised, given the sandwich she'd eaten a couple of hours before, but since I was making lunch for me and Petra, I felt like should at least ask if she wanted to join us. I tried to speak to her using the intercom function, but it refused to connect. Instead, a message pinged back via the app. *NOT HUNGRY*. Huh. I hadn't even known it could do that.

OKAY, I messaged back. As I was putting my phone away, another thought occurred to me, and I pulled it back out of my pocket and reopened the Happy app. Feeling a little queasy, I clicked on the menu that showed the list of cameras available for me to access. As I scrolled down the list to *R*, I told myself I wouldn't look, but at least that way I would know . . . but when I got down there, *Rhiannon's room* was grayed out and unavailable, which was mostly a relief. There would have been something inexpressibly inappropriate about cameras in a fourteen-year-old girl's bedroom.

It was as I was spooning yogurt into Petra's eager mouth, dodging her "helping" fingers as she tried to grab the spoon, that I heard footsteps on the stairs and peered into the hallway to see Rhiannon, holding a small bag in one hand and her phone in the other.

"Elise's brother's here," she said abruptly.

"At the door?" I glanced automatically at my phone, puzzled. "I didn't hear the bell."

"Duh. At the gates."

"Okay." I resisted the urge to bite back a sarcastic retort. "I'll buzz him in."

My phone was on the counter, but I'd barely even opened up the app, let alone navigated the menu of the various gates, doors, and garages I had access too, before Rhiannon was already halfway to the door.

"No need." She pressed her thumb to the panel and then swung open the front door. "He's waiting for me down by the road."

"Wait." I moved the yogurt out of Petra's reach and then ran hastily after Rhiannon. "Hang on a sec, I need a number for Elise's mum."

"Uh . . . why?" Rhiannon said, heavy with sarcasm, and I shook my head, refusing to get drawn into her defiance.

"Because you're fourteen years old, and I've never met the woman, and I just do. Do you have it? If not I'll ask your mum."

"Yeah, I've got it." She rolled her eyes, but pulled out her phone and then cast around for a bit of paper. One of Maddie's drawings was lying on the stairs, and she picked it up and scribbled a number on the back. "There. Happy?"

"Yes," I said, though it was not entirely true. She slammed the door behind her, and I watched through the window as she disappeared around the curve in the drive, and then I looked down at the piece of paper. The number was scribbled across one corner along with the name Cass, and I tapped it into the messenger app on my phone.

Hi, Cass, it's Rowan here, I'm the Elincourts' new nanny. I just wanted to say thank you for having Rhiannon tonight and if there's any problems, please call or text this number. If you could let me know what time you'll be dropping her off, that would be great. Thanks. Rowan.

The reply came back reassuringly quickly, while I was spooning the last of the yogurt into Petra.

> **Hi! Nice to "meet" you. Pleasure, it's always nice to have Rhi over. I imagine we'll have her back by lunchtime tomorrow but let's play it by ear. Cass.**

It was only when I went to put Maddie's drawing back on the stairs that I finally looked at it. It reminded me of the drawing I'd found on the first night, of the house, and the pale little face staring out. But there was something distinctly darker and more disturbing about this one.

At the center of the page was a crude figure—a little girl, with curly hair and a sticking-out skirt—and she seemed to be locked inside some kind of prison cell. But when I peered at it more closely, I realized, it must be meant to represent the poison garden. The thick black bars of the iron gate were scored across her figure, and she was clutching at them with one hand, and holding something in the other—a branch, I thought, covered in green leaves and red berries. Tears were streaming down her face, her mouth was open in a despairing wail, and there were red scribbles of blood on her face and on her dress. The whole image was encircled in thick black spiraling lines, as if I were staring down the wrong end of a telescope, into some kind of nightmarish tunnel into the past.

On the one hand, it was just a little girl's drawing, no different from the sometimes violent scribbles I had seen at the nursery—superheroes gunning down baddies, policemen fighting robbers. But on the other . . . I don't know. It was hard to put my finger on what made me recoil, but there was something so indescribably nasty about it, so chilling and so full of satisfaction and glee in the macabre subject matter, that I let the paper drop from my fingers to the floor as if it had burned me.

I stood there, ignoring Petra's increasingly irritable cries of "Down. Down! Peta down NOW!" behind me, and stared at the picture. I wanted to screw it up and throw it away, but I knew what the child-protection advice at Little Nippers would have been. Put the drawing on file. Flag concerns with the safeguarding officer at the nursery. Discuss the issues raised in the drawing with parents/guardians if deemed appropriate.

Well, there was no safeguarding officer here except me. But if I were Sandra, I was pretty sure that I would want to know about this. Where Maddie was getting this stuff from, I wasn't sure, but it needed to be stopped.

Feeling more disturbed than I wanted to admit, I picked the drawing up from the floor, and slid it carefully into one of the drawers in the study. Then I returned to the kitchen and set about cleaning Petra up, and putting her down for her nap.

I hadn't meant to fall asleep in Petra's room, but I woke with a start, the armchair's gingham cover wet with drool beneath my cheek, and my heart pounding for reasons I could not put my finger on. Petra was still slumbering in her cot as I struggled upright, trying to figure out what had happened, and what had woken me so abruptly.

I must have drifted off while waiting for her to fall asleep. Had I—*Shit,* the thought came like a sudden punch to the solar plexus—had I slept through school pickup? But no. When I checked my phone it was only one thirty.

Then it came again, the noise that had woken me from sleep. The doorbell. *Doorbell sounding* flashed on my phone. And then *Open door? Confirm / Cancel.*

A Pavlovian jolt of dread flooded through me, and for a moment I sat there, paralyzed, half dreading, half expecting the *creak . . . creak* . . . to commence as it had last night, but it didn't, and at last I forced myself to move. I swung my feet to the floor and stood up, waiting for my blood pressure to settle and my heart to stop drumming with panic in my ears.

As I did so, I wiped the corner of my mouth and looked down at myself. It was only a few days since I'd turned up—note-perfect in my rendition of Rowan the Perfect Nanny, in her tweed skirt and neatly buttoned cardigan. I looked far from perfect now. I was wearing crumpled jeans, and my sweatshirt was stained with Petra's breakfast. I looked much closer to the person I really was, as if the real me was leaking out of the cracks in the facade, taking over.

Well, it was too late to change now. Instead, I left Petra sleeping peacefully in her cot, and made my way down the stairs to the hallway, where I pressed my thumb to the panel, and watched as the door swung silently open.

For a second it seemed like a continuation of last night—there was no one there. But then I saw the Land Rover parked across the driveway, heard the retreating crunch of gravel, and peering round the side of the house, I saw a tall, broad figure, disappearing towards the stables, two dogs bounding at his heels.

"Jack?" I called, my voice croaky with sleep. I cleared my throat and tried again. "Hey, Jack, was that you?"

"Rowan!" He turned at the sound of my voice and came striding back across the yard, grinning widely. "Yes, I rang the bell, I was going to ask if you fancied a cup of tea. But I thought you must have gone out."

"No . . . no, I was . . ." I paused, unsure what to say, then, in view of my sleep-crumpled face and draggled clothes, decided maybe the truth was best. "I'd fallen asleep actually. Petra's down for her nap and I must have drifted off. I— Well, I didn't get a very good night's rest last night."

"Oh . . . were the girls playing up?"

"No, no it's not that. It's . . ." I paused again, and then screwed up my courage. "It's those noises I was talking about. From the attic. I got woken up again. Jack, you know those keys you mentioned . . ."

He was nodding.

"Aye, sure, no problem. Want to try it now?"

Why not? The girls were at school, Petra would probably nap for at least an hour longer. It was as good a time as any.

"Yes, please."

"I'll have to hunt them out, give me ten minutes and I'll be with you."

"Okay," I said. I felt better already. The chances were, there was a simple explanation for the noise, and we were going to discover it. "I'll put the kettle on. See you in ten minutes."

In the event, he was back sooner than ten, a tangle of rusty keys in one hand and a tool kit in the other, a big bottle of WD-40 sticking out the top. The dogs followed him in, panting excitedly, and I found myself smiling as I watched them sniffing diligently around the kitchen, Hoovering up all the scraps the children had dropped. Then they flopped down on their beds in the utility room as though the whole trip had exhausted them beyond measure.

The kettle had just boiled, and I poured out two mugs and held one out to Jack. He shoved the keys in his back pocket, took it, and grinned.

"Just what I needed. D'you want to finish the teas down here or take them up?"

"Well, Petra's still asleep actually, so it might be a good idea to crack on before she wakes up."

"Suits me," he said. "I've been sitting in the car all morning. I'd rather drink on the go."

We carried everything carefully upstairs, tiptoeing past Petra's room, although when I peered in she looked like she was out for the count, sprawled like someone dropped from a great height onto a soft mattress.

Up in my bedroom, the curtains were still drawn, the bed rumpled, and my worn clothes were still scattered across the soft wheat-colored carpet. I felt my cheeks flush, and putting down my cup I hastily picked up my bra and knickers from the night before, along with a blouse, and shoved them into the laundry basket in the bathroom, before opening the curtains.

"Sorry," I said. "I'm not normally such a slob."

That was totally untrue. Back at my flat in London the majority of my underwear lived in a pile in the corner of the room, washed only when the clean pairs in my drawer ran out. But here, I'd been trying hard to keep up the image of meticulous neatness. Apparently it was slipping.

Jack, however, didn't seem bothered and was already trying the door in the corner of the room.

"It's this one, is it?"

"Yes, that's right."

"And you've tried all the other cupboard keys?"

"Yes, I tried all the ones I could find."

"Well, let's see if any of these match."

The ring he was holding held maybe twenty or thirty keys, all of varying sizes, from a huge black iron one, which I guessed must be the original key to the gate, before the electric lock had been installed, through to small brass ones that looked like they might be for desks or safes.

Jack tried a medium-size one that fit through the hole but rattled around loosely inside, plainly too small for the lock, and then a slightly larger one, which fit but did not turn all the way.

He squirted the can of lubricant inside the lock and tried again, but it still turned only a quarter of the way, and then stopped.

"Hmm . . . it could be jammed, but if it's the wrong key I don't want to risk forcing it and breaking the shank in the lock. I'll try a few more."

I watched as he tried maybe four or five others of the same size, but they were worse, either not fitting in at all, or jamming before he'd managed even a quarter turn. At last he seemed to make up his mind and returned to the second key he'd picked out.

"This is the only key on the bunch that has any give at all, so I'll try it again with a bit more force, and if it breaks, well, we'll just have to get the locksmith in. Wish me luck."

"Good luck," I said, and he began to force the key.

I found I was wincing preemptively as I watched him apply pressure, first gently, and then harder, and at last so hard that I could see the shaft of the key bending slightly, the round bow at the top twisting, twisting . . .

"Stop!" I cried, just as Jack gave an exclamation of satisfaction and there was a noisy scrape and click, and the key completed the full turn.

"Got it!" He stood, wiping the lubricant off his hands, and then turned to me with a mock courtly bow. "D'you wish to do the honors, milady?"

"No!" The word was out before I could think better of it, and then I forced a laugh. "I mean . . . I don't mind. It's up to you. But I warn you, if there's rats, I'll scream."

It was a lie. I'm not afraid of rats. I'm not afraid of very much, normally. And I felt like the worst kind of female cliché sheltering behind the big strong man. But Jack had not lain there, night after night, listening to that slow, stealthy *creak . . . creak . . .* above his head.

"I'll take one for the team, then," he said with a very small wink. And he twisted the handle, and the door opened.

I don't know what I expected. A staircase disappearing into the darkness. A corridor hung with cobwebs. I found I was holding my breath as the door swung back, peering over Jack's shoulder.

Whatever I expected, it wasn't what was there. It was just another closet. Very dusty, and badly finished so that you could see the gaps in the plasterboard, and much smaller and shallower than the one where I'd hung my clothes, but a closet nonetheless. An empty bar hung, slightly lopsided, about six inches down from the ceiling as if awaiting hangers and clothes.

"Huh," Jack said. He tossed the keys on the bed, looking thoughtful. "Well, that's weird."

"Weird? You mean, why lock up a perfectly usable closet?"

"Well, I suppose so, but what I really meant is, the draught."

"The draught?" I echoed stupidly, and he nodded.

"Look at the floor."

I looked where he pointed. Across the floorboards were streaks, where a breeze had plainly forced dust through the narrow gaps, and looking more closely at the stained and dusty plasterboard I could see the same thing. When I put my hand to the gap, there was a faint cool breeze, and the same dank smell that I had noticed coming from the keyhole last night when I had peered through, into the darkness.

"You mean . . ."

"There *is* something back there. But someone boarded it up."

He moved past me, and began rummaging in his tool kit, and suddenly, I was not at all sure that I wanted to do this.

"Jack, I don't think— I mean, Sandra might—"

"Ah, she won't mind. I'll board it back up more neatly if it comes to it, and she'll have a working closet instead of a locked door."

He took out a small crowbar. I opened my mouth to say something else—something about it being my bedroom, about the mess, about—

But it was too late. There was a crunching noise, and a slab of plasterboard toppled forward into the room so that Jack only just got out of the way. He picked it up, carefully avoiding the rusty nails that were sticking out of the edges, and propped it against the side of the closet, and I heard his voice, echoing now, as he let out a long, satisfied "Ah . . ."

"Ah, what?" I said anxiously, trying to peer past him, but his big frame filled the doorway, and all I could see was darkness.

"Have a look," he said, stepping back. "See for yourself. You were right."

And there it was. Just as I had imagined. The wooden treads. The swags of cobwebs. The staircase winding up into darkness.

I found my mouth was dry, and my throat clicked as I swallowed.

"Do you have a torch?" Jack asked, and I shook my head, feeling suddenly unable to speak. He shrugged.

"Nor me, we'll have to make do with phones. Mind your feet on those nails." And he stepped forward into the blackness.

For a moment I was completely frozen, watching him disappear up the narrow stairs, the beam of his phone a thin glimmer in the black, his footsteps echoing . . . *creak . . . creak . . .*

The sound was so close to the noise of last night, and yet, there was something different about it too. It was more . . . solid. More real, faster, and mixed with the crunch of plasterboard.

"Holy shit," I heard from above, and then, "Rowan, get up here, you've got to see this."

There was a lump in my throat as if I was about to cry, though I knew that I wasn't; it was pure fear that had lodged there, silencing me, making me unable to ask Jack what was up there, what he had found, what he needed me to see so urgently.

Instead, I switched on my phone torch with fingers that shook, and followed him into the darkness.

Jack was standing in the middle of the attic, staring openmouthed at his surroundings. He had switched off his phone, and there was light coming from somewhere, a thin, gray light that I couldn't immediately locate. There must be a window somewhere, but that wasn't what I was looking at. What I was looking at were the walls, the furniture, the *feathers*.

They were everywhere.

Strewn across the broken rocking chair in the corner, in the dusty, cobwebbed crib, over the rickety doll's house and the dusty chalkboard, across the pile of smashed china dolls piled up against the wall. Feathers, feathers, and not down from a burst pillow either. These were thick and black—flight feathers from a crow, or a raven I thought. And there was a stench of death too.

But that wasn't all of it. It wasn't even the worst of it.

The strangest thing was the walls—or rather, what was written on them.

Scribbled on all of them, in childish crayon letters, some small, some huge and scrawled, were words. It took me a minute or two to make them out, for the letters were misshapen and the words badly spelled. But the one right in front of me, the one staring me in the face over the small fireplace in the center of the room, was unmistakable. *WE HATE YOU.*

It was exactly the same as the phrase Maddie had spelled out in her Alphabetti Spaghetti, and seeing it here, in a locked, boarded-up room she could not possibly have entered, gave me a jolt to the stomach as if I had been punched. It was with a kind of sick dread that I held up my phone torch to some of the other phrases.

The goasts donet like you.

They hate yu.

We want you too go awa.

The gosts are angrie.

They haite you.

Get out.

There angry

Wee hate you.

We hite u.

GO AWAY.

We hate you.

Again and again, small and large, from tiny letters etched with concentrated hate in a corner by the door, to the giant sprawling scrawl above the fireplace that I had seen when I first entered.

We hate you. The words had been bad enough, sliding in slimy orange juice across a plate. But here, scrawled in a demented hand across every inch of plaster, they were nothing short of malevolent. And in my head I heard Maddie's little sobbing voice again, as though she had gasped the words in my ear—*the ghosts wouldn't like it.*

It was too close to be coincidence. But at the same time, it was totally impossible. This room was not just locked, it was boarded up, and the only entrance was through my own bedroom. And without question, *someone* else had been up here, and it had not been Maddie. I had heard those relentless, pacing footsteps just moments after staring down at Maddie's sleeping form.

Maddie had not written those words. But she had repeated them to me. Which meant . . . was she repeating what someone had whispered to *her* . . . ?

"Rowan." The voice seemed to be coming from a great distance, hard to hear beneath a shrill buzzing coming from inside my own skull. Through the ringing I felt a hand on my arm. "Rowan. *Rowan*, are you okay? You look a bit strange."

"I'm—I'm okay—" I managed, though my voice was strange in my ears. "I'm all right. It's just—oh God, who *wrote* that?"

"Kids messing about, don't you think? And, well, there's your explanation for the noise."

He nudged with his foot at something in the corner, and I looked to see a pile of moldering feathers and bones, held together by little more than dust.

"Poor wee bastard must have got in through that window and couldn't get out, battered himself half to death trying to escape."

He pointed to the opposite wall, to a minute window, only a little bigger than a sheet of paper. It was gray with dirt, and partway open. Letting go of my arm, Jack strode over and slammed it shut.

"Oh—oh my God," I found I couldn't catch my breath. The ringing in my ears intensified. Was I having some kind of panic attack? I groped for something to hold on to, and my fingers crunched against dead insects, and I let out a strangled sob.

"Look," Jack said practically, seeming to make up his mind, "let's get out of here, get you a drink. I'll come back in a bit, clear up the bird."

Taking my hand, he led me firmly towards the stairs. The feel of his large, warm hand in mine was unspeakably reassuring, and for a moment I let myself be pulled towards the door and the stairs, back towards the main house. But then something inside me rebelled. Whatever the truth of this attic, Jack was not my white knight. And I was not some terrified child who needed protecting from the reality of what lay behind this locked door.

As Jack turned sideways to edge between a pile of teetering chairs and a dried-up paint box, I took the opportunity to pull my hand out of his.

Part of me felt I was being ungrateful. He was only trying to be reassuring, after all. But the other part of me knew that if I fell into this role, I might never escape it, and I could *not* allow Jack to see me that way—as yet another hysterical, superstitious woman, hyperventilating over a pile of feathers and some childish scribbles.

And so, as Jack disappeared down the stairs towards the floor below, I made myself stop and turn, taking a last, long look back at that dust-shrouded room, filled with smashed dolls and toys, broken furniture and the spoiled debris of a lost childhood.

"Rowan?" Jack's voice came from down the stairs, hollow and echoing up the narrow corridor. "Are you coming?"

"Yes!" I said. My voice was cracked and I coughed, feeling my chest tighten. "I'm coming!"

I moved quickly to follow him, filled with a sudden dread of the door shutting, being trapped up here with the dust and the dolls and the stench of death. But my foot must have caught on something, for as I reached the top of the stairs, there was a sudden rushing clatter and the pile of dolls shifted and collapsed in on itself, china limbs cracking against one another with ominous chinks, dust rising up from threadbare moth-eaten dresses.

"Shit," I said, and watched, horrified, as the little avalanche subsided.

At last all was quiet, except for one single decapitated china head rolling slowly towards the center of the room. It was the way the warped floorboards bowed, I knew, but for a crazy second I had the illusion that it was pursuing me and would chase me down the stairs, its cherubic smile and empty eyes hunting me down.

It was just that, though, an illusion, and a few seconds later it came to a rocking halt, facing the door.

One eye had been punched out, and there was a crack across one pink cheek that gave its smile a curiously mocking appearance.

We hate you, I heard, in the corner of my mind, as if someone had whispered it in my ear.

And then I heard Jack's voice again, calling me from the bottom of the stairs, and I turned and followed him down the wooden steps.

Stepping out into the warmth and light of the rest of the house felt like returning from another world—after a trip into a particularly dark and nightmarish Narnia perhaps. Jack stood aside to let me out, and then shut the door behind us both and locked it. The key screeched in protest as he did so, then we both turned and made our way down to the bright, homely comfort of the kitchen.

I found my hands were shaking as I tried to rinse out the teacups and put the kettle on to boil, and at last, after a few minutes of watching me, Jack stood up and walked over to me.

"Sit down and let me make you a cup for a change. Or would you prefer something a wee bit stronger? A dram, maybe?"

"Whiskey, you mean?" I said, slightly startled, and he grinned and nodded. I gave a shaky laugh. "Bloody hell, Jack. It's barely lunch."

"All right then, just tea. But you sit there while I make it. You're always running around after those kids. Have a sit down for a change."

But I shook my head, stubborn. I would not be that woman. I would not be one of those other four nannies . . .

"No, I'll make the tea. But it would be great if you could—" I paused, trying to think of a job he could do, to soften the refusal of help. "If you could find some biscuits."

I remembered myself giving Maddie and Ellie jammie dodgers after the shock of the speakers going off in the middle of the night. *Sugar is good for shock*, I heard my own voice saying, as if I were a frightened child, able to be jollied back to cheerfulness with a forbidden treat.

I'm not normally like this, I wanted to say, and it was true. I wasn't superstitious, I wasn't nervy, I wasn't the kind of person who saw signs and portents around every corner and crossed themselves when they saw a black cat on Friday the thirteenth. That *wasn't* me.

But for three nights now I'd had little or no sleep, and no matter what I tried to tell myself I *had* heard those noises, loud and clear, and they were not a bird, whatever Jack thought. The senseless, panicked crashing of a trapped bird—that would have been scary enough, but it was nothing like the slow, measured *creak . . . creak . . .* that had kept me awake, night after night. And besides, that bird was dead—long dead. There was no way it could have been making noises last night, or any night for a while. In fact judging by the smell and the state of decomposition, it had probably been up there for several weeks.

The smell . . .

It had stayed with me, fusty and choking in my nostrils, and as I carried the tea across to the sofa, I found I could still smell it, even though I'd washed my hands. It clung to my clothes, and my hair, and glancing down I saw a long streak of gray on the sleeve of my jumper.

The sun had gone in, and in spite of the underfloor heating, the room was not particularly warm, but I shrugged the sweatshirt off and put it aside. I felt that I'd have frozen rather than put it back on.

"Here you go." Jack sat beside me, making the springs of the sofa squeak, and handed me a rich tea biscuit. I dipped it automatically into my tea, then took a bite, and shivered, I couldn't help myself. "Are you cold?"

"A bit. Not really. I mean, I have a jumper, it's just I didn't—I couldn't—"

I swallowed, then, feeling like a fool, I nodded at the streak of attic dust I'd noticed on the sleeve.

"I can't get the smell of that place out of my head. I thought maybe it was in my sweater."

"I understand," he said quietly, and then, as if reading my thoughts, he stripped off his own jacket, streaked with cobwebs, and laid it aside. He was only wearing a T-shirt underneath, but in contrast to my chill, his arms were warm, so warm that I could feel the heat from his skin as we sat, not quite touching, but uncomfortably close on the small two-seater sofa.

"You've goose pimples all up your arms," he said, and then, slowly, as if giving me time to move away, he put out a hand and rubbed the skin of my upper arm gently. I shivered again, but it was not with cold, and for a long moment I had an almost overwhelming urge to close my eyes and lean into him.

"Jack," I said, at the same time as he cleared his throat, and the baby monitor on the counter let out a crackling wail.

Petra.

"I'd better go and get her." I stood, setting the tea down on the counter, and then staggered as a sudden wash of dizziness came over me, from standing up too fast.

"Hey." Jack stood too, putting a hand on my arm, steadying me. "Hey, are you all right?"

"I'm fine." It was true, the moment of faintness had passed. "It's nothing. I get low blood pressure sometimes. And I'm just—I didn't sleep well last night."

Ugh. I had already told him that. He was going to think I was coming apart, adding amnesia to my list of frailties. I was better than this. Stronger than this. I had to be.

I badly wanted a cigarette, but the CV I had handed in to Sandra had said "nonsmoker" and I couldn't risk unpicking that particular thread. I might discover everything unraveled.

I found myself glancing up, towards the ever-watching egg-shaped eye in the corner of the room.

"Jack, what are we going to tell Sandra?" I asked, and then the baby monitor crackled into life again, this time a more determined cry that I could hear both through the speaker, and coming down the stairs. "Hold that thought," I said, and sprinted hastily for the stairs.

Ten minutes later I was back down with a freshly changed Petra, who was grumpy and blinking, and looking as tousled and confused as I felt. She glowered at Jack as I came back into the kitchen, her little hands gripping my top like a small marsupial, but when he chucked her under the chin she gave a little, reluctant smile, and then a proper one as he pulled a funny expression, laughing and then twisting her face away in that funny way children do when they know they're being charmed into good spirits in spite of themselves.

She let herself be settled in her high chair with some segments of satsuma, and then I turned back to Jack.

"I was just saying—Sandra and Bill. We have to tell them about the attic—right? Or do you think they know?"

"I'm not sure," Jack said thoughtfully. He rubbed his chin, his fingers rasping over dark auburn stubble. "They're sort of perfectionists, the way that cupboard was boarded up inside didn't look like their work. And I can't imagine they'd leave all that crap up there. Sorry, excuse my French, Petra," he said formally, giving her a little mock bow. "All that rubbish, is what I meant to say. They cleared the house when they moved in from what I understand—I didn't start work until a couple of years after they bought it, so I didn't see the renovations, but Bill'll bore the hind leg off a donkey if you give him an excuse to talk about the work. I can't imagine them just ignoring something like that. No, my best bet is that they'd never opened the cupboard and didn't know the attic was there. The key was pretty stiff, you'd be forgiven for thinking you had the wrong one. It's only because I'm a stubborn bastard I forced it."

"But . . . the poison garden," I said slowly. "They did just ignore that, right?"

"The poison garden?" He looked at me, startled. "How do you know about that?"

"The girls took me in," I said shortly. "I didn't know what it was at the time. But my point is they've done the same thing there, haven't they? Shut the door, forgotten about it?"

"Well," Jack said slowly, "I . . . well, I think that's a bit different. They've never been as hands-on in the grounds. There's nothing up there to harm anyone, though."

"What about the writing?"

"Aye, that's a bit weird, I'll give you that." He took a long gulp of tea and frowned. "It looked like a child, didn't you think? But according to Jean, there'd been no kids in the house for more than forty years, when the Elincourts moved in."

"It did look like a child." My thoughts flickered to Maddie, then Elspeth, and then to the heavy manlike tread I'd heard, night after night. That had not been the step of a child. "Or . . . like someone pretending to be a child," I added slowly, and he nodded.

"Could be vandals, I suppose, trying to creep people out. It's true the house was empty for a long time. But then . . . no, that doesn't make sense. Vandals would hardly have boarded up behind themselves. It must have been the previous owners who did that."

"Dr. Grant . . ." I paused, trying to think how to phrase the question that had been hovering at the edge of my mind ever since I had read the newspaper article. "Did you . . . I mean, are you . . . ?"

"Related?" Jack said. He gave a laugh, and shook his head. "God, no. Grants are ten a penny up here. I mean, I suppose we'd have all been part of the same clan back in the day, but there's no connection between our families nowadays. I'd never even heard of the man until I began working here. Poor bastard killed his daughter, isn't that the story?"

"I don't know." I looked down at Petra, at the soft vulnerable curve of her skull beneath the thistle-down hair. "I don't know what happened to her. She ate poison berries according to the inquest."

"I heard he fed her some experiment from his dabblings. That's what the folk in Carn Bridge'll tell you if you ask."

"Jesus." I shook my head, though whether in denial or disgust, I wasn't sure. There was something inexpressibly upsetting about hearing the suggestion in Jack's cheerful, matter-of-fact voice, and I wasn't sure what bothered me most—the idea that Dr. Grant might have killed his own child and got away with it, or the fact that local gossip had apparently tried and condemned him as a murderer in the absence of any concrete proof.

It seemed impossible though that anyone would poison their own child, and it hardly fitted with the wild, grief-stricken face I'd seen on the web. He looked like a man destroyed by his own pain and despair, and all of a sudden, I felt a fierce urge to defend him.

"The article I read said that Elspeth accidentally picked cherry laurel berries thinking they were elderberries or something, and the cook made them into jam, not realizing what they were. I can't see how that could be anything more than an accident."

"Well, the folks round here would have you believe that he was—" He stopped, looking at Petra, and seemed to think better of whatever he had been about to say, even though she was too little to understand any of it. I knew how he felt. There was something obscene about discussing such horrible things in front of her. "Well, never mind. Not a pretty story, either way." He drained his cup and put it neatly in the dishwasher, and then gave a little wry smile, very different from the warmth of his usual broad, expansive grin. "There's a reason the house was empty for a decade before Sandra and Bill brought it. There's not many from round here would have lived at Struan, even if they had the money to renovate it."

Struan. The name from the article gave me a little prickle, a reminder that whatever Sandra and Bill had done to erase it, this house had a past, and that people in Carn Bridge remembered it. But Jack was continuing on, untroubled.

"What d'you want me to do about it, then?"

"Me?" I asked, startled. "Why do I need to decide?"

"Well, it's your bedroom it opens onto. I'm not a superstitious man, but I wouldn't fancy sleeping next to that lot myself."

I shuddered, unable to help myself.

"Yup, me either. So . . . what are my options?"

"Well, I suppose I can board it up, leave it for Sandra and Bill to decide when they get back. Or I could try to . . . tidy the attic up a wee bit."

"Tidy it up?"

"Paint over some of that writing," he said. "But that would mean leaving it open. I mean, I could lock the door, but it wouldn't be worth boarding over the inside again, if we were planning to go back in. I don't know how you feel about that."

I nodded, biting my lip. Truth be told, I didn't want to sleep in this room again, and in fact I wasn't sure if I could. The thought of lying in that bed, listening to the *creak* . . . *creak* . . . of the boards, with that demented writing just feet away from me behind nothing more sturdy than a locked cupboard door . . . well, it creeped me out. But the idea of boarding the room back up didn't seem much better either.

"I think we should paint it," I said at last. "If Sandra and Bill agree, of course. We can't—we can't just *leave* it. It's too horrible."

Jack nodded. Then he pulled the bunch of keys out of his back pocket, where he had stashed them, and began winkling the long black attic key off the bunch.

"What are you doing?" I asked, just as it came clear with a little click. He held it out.

"Take it."

"Me? But I don't want—" I swallowed, trying not to show the depth of revulsion I felt. "I don't want to *go* up there."

"I know that. But if it were me, I'd feel better knowing that I had the key in my own hands."

I pressed my lips together, then took the key from him. It was heavy, and very cold, but to my surprise, he was right. There was something . . . not quite powerful, but at least an illusion of control in holding the key in my own hands. That door was locked. And only I had the power to unlock it.

I pushed it into my jeans pocket. I was just trying to work out what to say, when Jack nodded again, but this time at his watch.

"Have you seen the time?"

I looked down at my phone.

"Shit."

I was late to pick up the girls.

"I'd better go but—but thank you, Jack."

"What for?" He looked genuinely surprised. "The key?"

"Not that. Just—I don't know. Taking me seriously. Not making me feel like an idiot for being freaked out."

"Listen." His face softened. "That writing freaked me out too, and I'm all the way across the courtyard. But it's over, okay? No more mysterious noises, no more writing, no more wondering what's behind that door. We know now, and it's creepy and a little bit sad, but it's done, okay?"

"Okay," I said, and I nodded. I should have known it was too good to be true.

I have been scared a lot in prison, Mr. Wrexham. The first night as I lay there, listening to the laughs and shouts and shrieks of the other women, trying to get used to the feeling of the narrow concrete walls closing around me, and many, many nights following that. And later, after one of the other girls beat me up in the cafeteria and I was moved to another wing for my own protection, as I lay there trembling in a strange cell, remembering the hate on her face, and the way the guards had waited just that slight instant too long before intervening, counting down the hours until the next day when I'd have to face them all again. And the nights when the dreams come, and I see her face again, and I wake with the stench of blood in my nostrils, shaking and shaking.

Oh, God, I've been scared.

But I have never been quite as scared as I was that night in Heatherbrae House.

The girls flaked out early, thankfully, and all three of them were out for the count by half past eight.

And so, at quarter to nine, I climbed the stairs to the bedroom—I could no longer think of it as *my* bedroom—on the top floor.

I found I was holding my breath as I touched the door handle. I could not help imagining something horrible flying out and ambushing me—a bird, clawing at my face, or perhaps for the writing to have spread like a cancer out from behind the locked door and across the walls of the bedroom. But when at last I forced myself to turn the knob, shoving the door open with a violence that sent it banging against the wall, there was nothing there. The closet door was closed, and the room looked just as it had that first night I had seen it, apart from a few flecks of dust that Jack and I had trodden across the carpet in our haste to get out of the attic.

Still though, I knew I couldn't possibly sleep here, so I slid my hand under my pillow and grabbed my pajamas, quickly, as if I were expecting to find something nasty there, waiting. I changed into my pajamas in the bathroom, did my teeth, and then I rolled up my duvet and carried it downstairs to the media room.

I knew if I just lay down and waited for sleep I would be waiting a long time, maybe all night, while the images of the attic intruded and the words on the wall whispered themselves again and again in my ears. Drugging myself into oblivion with a familiar film seemed like a better option. At least if I had a loud laugh track ringing in my ears, I would not be wincing at every warped floorboard and sigh from the dogs. I was not sure if I could bear to lie there in silence, waiting for the *creak . . . creak . . .* to start up again.

Friends seemed about the right level of intensity, and I put it on the huge wide-screen TV, pulled the duvet up to my chin . . . and slept.

When I woke, it was with a sense of complete disorientation. The TV had gone onto standby in the night, and there was daylight streaming underneath the blackout blinds in the media room.

There was a hot, heavy weight on my legs . . . no . . . *two* heavy weights, and my chest was tight and wheezing. Hauling myself into a sitting position and pushing my hair out of my eyes I looked down, expecting to see the two dogs, but there was only one black hairy monster sprawled across the foot of the sofa. The other hot little body was Ellie.

"Ellie?" I said huskily, and then felt in the pocket of my dressing gown. My inhaler was in there, as always, but it knocked against something unfamiliar as I drew it out, and with an odd rush I remembered the key, and all the crazy events of yesterday. Then wiped the mouthpiece of the inhaler on my dressing gown, put it to my lips, and took a long hissing puff. The relief was instant, and I took a deeper breath, feeling the release in my chest, and then said again, more loudly, "Ellie. Sweetheart, what are you doing here?"

She woke up, blinking and confused, and then realized where she was and smiled up at me.

"Good morning, Rowan."

"Good morning to you too, but what are you doing down here?"

"I couldn't sleep. I had a bad dream."

"Well, okay, but—"

But . . . what? I wasn't sure what to say. Her presence had shaken me. How long had she been padding around the house last night by herself without me hearing her? She had evidently been able to get out of bed and come all the way downstairs and tuck herself in beside me without me hearing a thing.

There didn't seem much I could say at this point though, so I just rubbed the sleep out of my eyes and then pulled my legs out from under the dog and stood up.

As I did, something fell out of the folds of the duvet and hit the floor with a dull ceramic-sounding crack.

The sound made me jump. Had I knocked over a forgotten coffee mug or something? I'd had hot milk last night, but I could have sworn I'd left the cup safely on the coffee table. In fact, yes, there was the mug still sitting on its coaster. So what had made the noise?

It was only when I pulled up the blind and folded the duvet that I saw it. It had rolled halfway under the sofa before coming to a halt, facing me, so that its wicked little eyes and cracked grin seemed to be laughing at me.

It was the doll's head from the attic.

The feeling that washed over me was—it was like someone had poured a bucket of ice water over my head and shoulders, a drenching, paralyzing deluge of pure fear that left me unable to do anything but stand there, shaking and gasping and shivering.

I heard, as if from a long way away, Ellie's reedy little voice saying, "Rowan, are you all right? Are you okay, Rowan? You look funny."

It took a huge effort for me to drag myself back from the brink of panic and realize that she was talking to me, and that I needed to answer.

"Rowan!" There was a frightened whine in her voice now, and she tugged at my nightshirt, her little fingers cold against the skin of my waist. "*Rowan!*"

"I—I'm okay, honey," I managed. My voice was strange and croaky in my ears, and I wanted to grope my way to the couch and sit down, but I couldn't bring myself to go anywhere near that . . . that *thing*, with its mocking little grin.

But I had to. I couldn't leave it under there, like an obscene little grenade, waiting to explode.

How? How had it got there? Jack had locked the door, I had *seen* him do it. And he had preceded me down the stairs. And I had the key in my pocket. I could feel it, warm against my thigh with my own body heat. Had *I* . . . could I have possibly . . . ?

But no. That was absurd. Impossible.

And yet, there it was.

It was while I was standing there, trying to get a hold of myself, that Ellie bent down to see what I was staring at and gave a little squeal.

"A dolly!"

She crouched, bum jutting in the air like the toddler she still half was, and reached, and I heard a sudden roar in my ears, my own voice shouting, "Ellie, for God's sake, don't touch it!" and felt myself snatching her up, almost before I realized what I was going to do.

There was a long moment of silence, Ellie hanging limp and heavy in my arms, my own breath panting in my ears, and then her whole body stiffened and she let out a wail of indignant shock and began to cry, with all the desolate surprise of a child told off for something they had not realized was wrong.

"Ellie," I began, but she was struggling in my arms, her face red and contorted with upset and anger. "Ellie, wait, I didn't mean—"

"Let me go!" she howled. My instinct was to tighten my arms around her, but she was thrashing like a cat, digging her nails into my arms.

"Ellie—Ellie calm *down,* you're hurting me."

"I don't care! Let me go!"

Kneeling, painfully, trying to keep my face away from her thrashing hands, I let her slide to the floor, where she collapsed with a wail onto the rug.

"You're mean! You shouted!"

"Ellie, I didn't mean to scare you, but that doll—"

"Go away!" she wailed. "I hate you!"

And then she scrambled to her feet and ran from the room, leaving me ruefully rubbing the scratches on my arms. I heard her feet on the stairs, and then the slam of the door of her room.

Sighing, I went through to the kitchen and tapped on the tablet. When I clicked through to the camera, it was to see Ellie facedown in bed, plainly bawling, with Maddie sleepily rubbing her eyes in puzzled surprise at being woken up like this.

Shit. She had come to me last night for reassurance—and for a moment there I had thought we were making a breakthrough. And now I had screwed it up. Again.

And it was all because of that vile little doll's head.

I had to get rid of it, but somehow I could not bring myself to touch it, and in the end I went through to the utility room and got a plastic bin liner. I slid it over my hand, inside out, like a makeshift glove, and then knelt, and reached under the sofa.

I found I was holding my breath, absurdly, as I reached into the dark, slightly dusty space, my fingers groping for the hard little head. I touched hair first, just a few straggling strands, for the little porcelain skull was almost bald, and I used it to tug the head itself closer, and then closed my hand over it in one firm, swift movement, like scooping up a dead rat, or some insect you fear may still sting you, even dead.

I was gripping it hard—as if the force of my grip could stop it exploding or escaping from my grasp. It did neither. But as I stood, gingerly, I felt something twinge in my index finger, a shard of glass, so sharp I had barely felt it go in. It had pierced the bag itself and driven into my finger, drawing blood, which now dripped with a steady rhythm onto the wooden floor. The head was not china, I realized, but painted glass.

At the sink I pulled the glass out of my finger and then wound my hand in a piece of kitchen paper before wrapping the head in a tea towel, and then another bin bag. I tied the top and stuffed it deep, deep into the rubbish bin, feeling like I was burying a corpse. My finger throbbed as I pressed down on it, making myself wince.

"What happened to Ellie?"

The voice made me jump, as if I'd been caught hiding the evidence of something guilty, and swinging round I saw Maddie standing in the doorway. Her expression was slightly less truculent than usual, and with her hair standing on end she looked like what she was—just a little girl with a comical case of bed head, woken up too early.

"Oh . . . it's my fault," I said ruefully. "I'm afraid I shouted at her. She was about to touch some broken glass and I scared her, trying to stop her. I think she thought I was angry . . . I just didn't want her to hurt herself."

"She said you found a doll and you wouldn't let her play with it?"

"Just a head." I didn't want to go into the whys and wherefores with Maddie. "But it was made of glass, and sharp where it had got cracked. I cut myself clearing it up."

I held out my hand like evidence, and she nodded, somberly, seemingly satisfied with my incomplete explanation.

"Okay. Can I have Coco Pops for breakfast?"

"Maybe. But, Maddie—" I stopped, not quite sure how to phrase what I wanted to ask. Our rapprochement felt so fragile that I was scared of endangering it, but there were too many questions buzzing in my head to abandon the topic completely. "Maddie, have you ever . . . do you know where the doll came from?"

"What do you mean?" Her face was puzzled, guileless. "We've got lots of dolls."

"I know, but this is a special, old-fashioned doll."

I couldn't bring myself to fish the nightmarish broken head out of the bin, so instead I pulled out my phone and searched on Google Images for "Victorian doll," scrolling down until I found one that was a slightly less malevolent version of the doll from the attic. Maddie stared at it, frowning.

"There was one like that on TV one time. It was a program about selling ankeets."

"Ankeets?" I blinked.

"Yes, old things that are worth a lot of money. A lady wanted to sell an old doll for money but the person in charge of the show told her it wasn't worth anything."

"Oh . . . antiques. I know the show you mean. But you've never seen one in real life?"

"I don't think so," Maddie said. She turned away, and I tried to read her expression. Was she being *too* casual? Wouldn't a normal child ask more questions than this? But then I shook myself. This second-guessing of everything was starting to border on paranoia. Children were self-absorbed. I knew that well enough from the nursery. Hell, there were plenty of *adults* who were incurious enough not to question something like this.

I was just trying to formulate a way of bringing the conversation back to the writing on the wall and Maddie's Alphabetti Spaghetti, when she changed the subject abruptly, bringing it back to her original question with the single-mindedness typical of young children.

"So, *can* I have Coco Pops for breakfast?"

"Well . . ." I bit my lip. Sandra's list of "occasional" foods were being consumed more and more frequently by the day. But then again, she shouldn't have it in the house if she didn't want the children to eat it, should she? "Yes, I guess so, just for today. But it's the last time this week, okay? Back to Weetabix tomorrow. Go up and get your school uniform on, and I'll have it ready by the time you get down. Oh, and will you tell Ellie there's a bowl for her too, if she wants it?"

She nodded, and as she disappeared upstairs I reached for the kettle.

I was spooning some porridge into Petra's mouth with my uninjured hand when a little face appeared at the kitchen door and then just as quickly slipped away, leaving a piece of paper scudding across the floor.

"Ellie?" I called, but there was no answer, only the sound of feet disappearing. Sighing, I made sure that Petra's straps were secure and went to pick up the piece of paper.

To my surprise it was a typed letter, formatted like an email, though with no subject, and nothing in the "To" field. Under the Gmail header was a single line of text with no punctuation.

> Dave Owen I am very sorry for scratching and waning away from you and saying that I hate you please don't be angry and don't go away like the others I am sorry love Ellie p. S. I got dressed by myself

Dave Owen? The words made my brow furrow, but there was no mistaking the intent of the rest of the message, and I unclipped Petra, put her in the playpen in the corner, and picked up the letter again.

"Ellie?"

Silence.

"Ellie, I got your letter, I'm really sorry for shouting. Can I say sorry to you too?"

There was a long pause, then a little voice said, "I'm in here."

I made my way through the media room to the living room. At first sight it looked empty, but then a movement caught my eye, and I walked slowly to the far corner of the room, filled with shadow where the morning sun had not yet come round. She was wedged in between the end of the sofa and the wall, almost invisible apart from her blond hair, and the tips of her shoes peeping out.

"Ellie." I crouched down, holding out the letter. "Did you write this?"

She nodded.

"It's really good. How did you know all the spellings? Did Maddie help you?"

"I did it myself. Only . . . the acorn helped me."

"The acorn?" I was puzzled, and she nodded.

"You push the acorn and you tell it what you want to write and it writes it down for you."

"What acorn?" I was bewildered now. "Can you show me?" Ellie flushed with shy pleasure at demonstrating her own cleverness, and squeezed out of the little corner. There was dust on her school skirt, and her shoes were on the wrong feet, but I ignored both, and followed her through to the kitchen, where she picked up the tablet, opened up Gmail, and pressed the microphone symbol above the keyboard. Light dawned. It did look a little bit like a stylized acorn—particularly if you had no idea what an old-fashioned microphone looked like.

Now she spoke into the tablet.

"Dear Rowan, this is a letter to say I am very sorry, love Ellie," she said slowly, saying the words as distinctly as her childish palate would allow.

Dave Owen the letters unfurled on the screen, as if by magic, *this is a letter to say I am fairy—*

There was an infinitesimal pause and the app self-corrected.

very sorry love Ellie

"And then you press the dots here and it prints on the printer in Daddy's study," she said proudly.

"I see." I wasn't sure whether I wanted to laugh or cry. I compromised by crouching down and hugging her. "Well, you're very clever, and it's a lovely letter. And I'm very sorry too. I shouldn't have shouted, and I promise I'm not going anywhere."

She hung on to me, breathing heavily on my neck, her chubby cheek warm against mine.

"Ellie," I said softly, unsure if I was about to wreck our hard-won confidence, but unable not to ask. "Ellie, can I ask you something?"

She didn't say anything, but I felt her nod, her little pointy chin digging into the tendon that ran from my collar bone to my shoulder.

"Did you . . . did you put that dolly head on my lap?"

"No!" She pulled back, looking at me, a little upset but not as much as I'd feared. She shook her head vehemently, her hair flying like thistledown. Her eyes were wide, and I could see in them a kind of desperation to be believed. But why? Because she was telling the truth? Or because she was lying?

"Are you sure? I promise I won't be angry. I just . . . I wondered how it got there, that's all."

"It wasn't *me*," she said, stamping her foot.

"It's okay, it's okay," I backpedaled a little, not wanting to lose what ground I'd gained. "I believe you." There was a pause, and she slipped her hand in mine. "So . . ." I was treading carefully now, but this was too important not to press a little further. "Do you . . . do you know who did?"

She looked away at that, not meeting my eyes.

"Ellie?"

"It was another little girl," she said. And somehow I knew that was all I would ever get out of her.

"Maddie, Ellie, come on!" I was standing in the hallway, keys in hand as Maddie came flying down the stairs with her coat and shoes already on. "Oh, well done, sweetie. You did your shoes yourself!" She slipped past, avoiding my outstretched arms, but Ellie, coming out of the downstairs toilet, was less quick and I caught her up, growling like a bear, kissed her squashy little tummy, then set her squealing and laughing back onto the floor, and watched as she scampered out of the front door after her sister to clamber into the car.

I turned back, to pick up their schoolbags, and as I did, I almost collided with Mrs. McKenzie, standing with her arms folded in the archway that led to the kitchen.

"Shit!" The word slipped out without meaning to, and I flushed, annoyed with myself for giving her more ammunition for her dislike of me. "I mean, gosh, I didn't hear you come in, Mrs. McKenzie. Sorry, you startled me."

"I came in the back way, I had mucky shoes," was all she said, but there was something a little bit softer than usual in her face, as her eyes followed the girls out to the car. "You're . . . ," she stopped, and then shook her head. "Never mind."

"No, what?" I said, feeling annoyed. "Come on, if you've got something to say . . ."

She pursed her lips, and I folded my arms, waiting. Then, quite unexpectedly, she smiled, transforming her rather grim face, making her look years younger.

"I was just going to say, you're doing very well with those girls. Now, you'd best be getting a move on, or you'll be late."

As I drove back from Carn Bridge Primary School, Petra strapped into the car seat behind me, pointing out the window and babbling her half-talk, half-nonsense syllables to herself, I found myself remembering that first drive back from the station with Jack—the evening sunset gilding the hills, the quiet hum of the Tesla as we wound through the close-cropped fields, filled with grazing sheep and Highland cows, and over stone bridges. It was gray and drizzling today, and the landscape felt very different—bleak and raw and entirely un-summer-like. Even the cows in the fields looked depressed, their heads lowered, rain dripping off the tips of their horns.

When the gate swung inwards and we began to climb the winding drive up to the house, I had a sharp flash of déjà vu back to that first evening—the way I had sat there beside Jack, scarcely able to breathe with hope and wanting.

We swung around the final curve of the drive, and the squat gray facade of the house came into view, and I remembered too the rush of emotion I had felt on seeing it for the first time, golden and warm and full of possibilities.

It looked very different today. Not full of the potential for a new life, new opportunities, but as gray and forbidding as a Victorian prison—only I knew that was a kind of a lie as well, that the Victorian facade presented to the driveway was only half the story, and that if I walked around to the back, I would see a house that had been ripped apart and patched back together with glass and steel.

Last of all, my gaze went to the roof, the stone tiles wet and slick with rain. The window Jack had shut was not visible from here; it opened onto the inner slope of the roof, but I knew that it was there, and the thought made me shiver.

There was no sign of Jean McKenzie's car in the drive—she must have already left for the day—and both Jack and the dogs were nowhere to be seen, and somehow, what with everything that had happened, I could not bring myself to enter the house alone. It had come to something, I thought, as I parked the car and unclipped Petra from her seat, that even fending off the dogs from trying to put their noses up my skirt would have been a welcome distraction from the silent watchfulness of that house, with its glassy egg-shaped eyes observing me from every corner.

At least out here I could think and feel and speak without watching my every word, my every expression, my every mood.

I could be *me*, without fearing that I would slip up.

"Come on," I said to Petra. Her buggy was in the boot of the car, and I opened it up and slid her in, clipping the rain cover over her. "Let's go for a walk."

"Me walk!" Petra shouted, pushing her hands against the plastic, but I shook my head.

"No, honey, it's too wet, and you've not got your waterproofs on. You stay snug and dry in there."

"Puggle!" Petra said, pointing through the plastic. "Jumpin muggy puggle!" It took me a minute to realize what she was saying, but then I followed her gaze to the huge pool of water that had collected on the gravel in the old stable yard, and understanding clicked.

Muddy puddles. She wanted to jump in muddy puddles.

"Oh! Like Peppa Pig, you mean?"

She nodded vigorously.

"You haven't got your Wellies on, but look—"

I began to walk faster, and then jog, and then with an enormous splash, I ran, buggy and all, through the puddle, feeling the water spray up all around us and patter down on my anorak and the buggy's rain cover.

Petra screamed with laughter.

"Again! More puggle!"

There was another puddle farther around the side of the house and obligingly I ran through that too, and then another on the graveled path down towards the shrubbery.

By the time we reached the kitchen garden, I was soaked and laughing, but also getting surprisingly cold, and the house was beginning to seem a little bit more welcoming. Full of cameras and malfunctioning tech it might be, but at least it was warm and dry, and out here my fears of the night before seemed not just silly, but laughable.

"Puggle!" Petra shouted, bouncing up and down underneath her clips. "More puggle!"

But I shook my head, laughing too.

"No, that's enough, sweetie, I'm wet! Look!" I came round to stand in front of her, showing her my soaked jeans, and she laughed again, her little face scrunched up and distorted through the crumpled plastic.

"Woan wet!"

Woan. It was the first time she had made an attempt at my name, and I felt my heart contract with love, and a kind of sadness too—for everything I could not tell her.

"Yes!" I said, and there was a lump in my throat, but my smile was real. "Yes, Rowan is wet!"

It was as I was turning the buggy around to start the climb back up to the house that I realized how far we had come—almost all the way down the path that led to the poison garden. I glanced over my shoulder at the garden as I began to push the buggy up the steep brick path—and then stopped.

For something had changed since my last visit.

Something was missing.

It took me a minute to put my finger on it—and then I realized. The string tying up the gate had gone.

"Just a second, Petra," I said, and ignoring her protests of "More puggles!" I put the brake on the buggy and ran back down the path to the iron gate, the gate where Dr. Grant had been photographed, standing proudly before his research playground, so many years ago, the gate I had tied up securely, in a knot too high for little hands to reach.

The thick white catering string had gone. Not just untied, or snipped and thrown aside, but gone completely.

Someone had undone my careful precautions.

But who? And why?

The thought nagged at me as I walked slowly back up the hill to where Petra was still sitting, growing increasingly fretful, and it continued to nag as I pushed the buggy laboriously back up the hill, to where the house was waiting.

By the time I reached the front door, Petra was cross and grizzling, and looking at my watch I saw that it was long past her snack time, and in fact getting on for lunch. The buggy's wheels were caked with mud, but since I had left the key to the utility room on the inside, I had no option other than the front door, so at last I got her out of the buggy, folded it awkwardly with one hand, holding Petra against my hip with the other to stop her from running off in search of more puddles, and left it in the porch. Then I pressed my thumb to the white glowing panel, and stood back as the door swung silently open.

The smell of frying bacon hit me instantly.

"Hello?"

I put Petra down cautiously on the bottom stair, shut the door, and prized off my muddy boots.

"Hello? Who's there?"

"Oh, it's you." The voice was Rhiannon's, and as I picked up Petra and began to make my way through to the kitchen, she came out of the doorway, holding a dripping bacon sandwich in one hand. She looked terrible, green around the gills and with dark shadows under her eyes as if she'd slept even less than me.

"Oh, you're back," I said unnecessarily, and she rolled her eyes and stalked past me to the stairs, taking a great bite of sandwich as she did.

"Hey," I called after her as a blob of brown sauce hit the tiled floor with a splat. "Hey! Take a plate, can't you?"

But she was already gone, loping up the stairs towards her room.

As she passed though I caught a whiff of something else—low and masked by the scent of bacon, but so odd and out of place, and yet so familiar, that it stopped me in my tracks.

It was a sweet, slightly rotten smell that jerked me sharply back to my own teenage years, though it still took me a minute to pin down. When the association finally clicked into place, though, I was certain—it was the cherry-ripe reek of cheap alcohol, leaching out of someone's skin, the morning after it's been drunk.

Shit.

Shit.

Part of me wanted to mutter that it was none of my business—that I was a nanny and had been hired for my expertise with younger children—that I had no experience with teenagers, and no idea of what Sandra and Bill would consider appropriate. Did fourteen-year-olds drink now? Was that considered okay?

But the other part of me knew that I was in loco parentis here. Whether or not Sandra would be concerned, *I* had seen enough to worry me. And there were plenty of red flags about Rhiannon's behavior. But the question was, what should I do about it. What *could* I do about it?

The questions nagged at me as I made myself and Petra a sandwich and then put her down for her nap. I could go and question Rhiannon—but I was pretty sure she'd have a ready excuse, assuming she deigned to talk to me.

Then I remembered. Cass. If nothing else, she would be able to explain the exact sequence of the night's events to me, and maybe give me an idea of whether I was ascribing more to this than I should. A bunch of fourteen-year-old girls at a birthday party . . . it wasn't impossible Cass had supplied some alcopops herself, and Rhiannon had just drunk more than her fair share.

Cass's return text was still in my list of messages, and I scrolled down until I found it, and pulled out the number. Then I waited while it rang.

"Yup?" The voice was rough, and Scottish, and very male.

I blinked, looked at the phone to check I had dialed the right number, and then put it back to my ear.

"Hello?" I said, cautiously. "Who is this?"

"I'm Craig," said the voice. It didn't sound like a kid, the voice had to be someone at least twenty, maybe older. And it definitely didn't sound like anyone's mum, or dad for that matter. "More to the fucking point, who the fuck are you?"

I was too shocked to reply. For a second I simply sat there, mouth open, trying to figure out what to say.

"Hello?" Craig said, irritably. "Hellooo?" And then, beneath his breath, "Stupid cunts wi' their fucking wrong numbers."

And then he hung up.

I shut my mouth and walked slowly through to the kitchen, still trying to figure out what had just happened.

Plainly, whoever that number belonged to, it wasn't Elise's mum. Which meant . . . well it could have meant that Rhiannon had written it down wrong, except that I had texted that number and got back a confirmation, supposedly from "Cass."

Which meant that Rhiannon had been lying to me.

Which also meant that very probably, she hadn't been out with Elise at all. Instead, she had very likely been with Craig.

Fuck.

The tablet was lying on the kitchen island, and I picked it up and tried to compose an email to Sandra and Bill.

The problem was, I didn't know what to begin with. There was too much too say. Should I start with Rhiannon? Or Maddie's behavior? Or should I lead with my concerns about the attic? The noises, and the way Jack and I had broken in, and the crazy writing?

What I wanted to tell them was everything—from the dead, rotten smell that still hung in my nostrils, and the broken shards of the doll's head in the rubbish bin, right through to Maddie's scribbled prison-cell drawing, and my conversation with Craig.

Something is wrong, I wanted to write. *No, scrap that,* everything *is wrong.* But . . . how could I tell them about Rhiannon and Maddie without seeming like I was criticizing their parenting? Let alone, how could I say what I had seen and heard in this house without being dismissed as just another superstitious nanny? How could I expect to persuade someone who hadn't even seen the inside of that creepy, demented room?

The subject line first then. Anything I could think of seemed either hopelessly inadequate or ridiculously dramatic, and in the end I settled on *An update from Heatherbrae.*

Okay. Okay. Calm and factual. That was good. Now for the body of the email.

Dear Sandra and Bill, I wrote, and then sat back and nibbled at the fraying edge of the bandage on my finger, trying to think what to put next. *First of all, I should tell you that Rhiannon arrived back this morning safe and sound, but I have a few concerns about her account of her trip to Elise's.*

Okay, that was good. That was clear and factual and nonaccusatory. But then how to segue from that into

Stupid cunts wi' their fucking wrong numbers.

Let alone from that to

we hate you

There angry

GO AWAY

We hite you

Most of all, how to explain that I would not—could not—sleep in that room again, listen to those footsteps pacing above, breathe the same air as those rotted dusty feathers.

In the end I just sat there, staring at the screen, remembering the slow *creak . . . creak . . .* on the boards above me, and it was only when I heard Petra's cranky wail coming over the intercom and looked at the clock that I realized it was time to pick up Maddie and Ellie from school.

Gone to get the girls I tapped out on the messaging screen to Rhiannon, *we need to talk when I get back.* And then, leaving the email unsent on the tablet, I ran upstairs to change Petra and bundle her into the car.

* * *

I didn't think of the email again until nearly 9:00 p.m. The afternoon had been a good one—Maddie and Ellie had both been delighted to see Rhiannon, and she'd been touchingly sweet with them—a far cry from the glossy, entitled private school brat she played with me. She was visibly hungover, but she played Barbies with them in the playroom for a couple of hours, ate some pizza, and then disappeared upstairs while I did battle with baths and bed and then tucked the girls in with a kiss and turned out the lights.

When I came downstairs I was gearing myself up for the promised discussion, trying to imagine what Rowan the Perfect Nanny would have done. Firm but clear. Don't lead with sanctions and accusations, get her to talk.

But Rhiannon was waiting in the kitchen, tapping her nails on the counter, and I did a double take at what she was wearing. Full makeup, heels, miniskirt, and a midriff-baring top that showed off a pierced navel.

Oh shit.

"Um," I began, but Rhiannon forestalled me.

"I'm going out."

For a second I had no idea what to say. Then I pulled myself together.

"I don't think so."

"Well, I do."

I smiled. I could afford to smile. It was growing dark. I had the keys to the Tesla in my pocket, and the nearest station was the best part of ten miles.

"Are you planning to walk in those heels?" I asked. But Rhiannon smiled back.

"No, I've got a lift coming."

Double shit.

"Okay, look, Rhiannon, this is very funny and everything, but you do know there's absolutely no way I can let you do that. I'll have to call your parents. I have to tell them—" Oh fuck this, fuck *accusations,* I had to say something to make her realize she'd been rumbled. "I have to tell them you came home stinking of alcohol."

I expected the words to act like a punch to the gut, but she barely reacted.

"I don't think you should do that," was all she said.

But I had already picked up my phone.

I hadn't checked it since before supper, and to my surprise, there was an email icon flashing. It was from Sandra.

I pressed it, in case it was something I should know about before I spoke to her, and then blinked in puzzlement as the subject header came up.

Re: An update from Heatherbrae

What? Had I sent the email without meaning to? I had logged into my personal Gmail on the children's tablet, the one they used for playing games, and had a horrible feeling that I had forgotten to log out. Could Petra or one of the girls have accidentally pressed send?

Panic-stricken, I opened up Sandra's reply, expecting something along the lines of *?? What's going on?* but it was totally different.

Thanks for the update Rowan, sounds good. Glad Rhiannon had a fun time with Elise. Bill is off to Dubai tonight, and I'm at a client dinner, but do text if anything urgent and I'll try to FaceTime the girls tomorrow. X

It didn't make sense. At least, it didn't until I scrolled down a little further and looked at the email I had supposedly sent, at 2:48 p.m., a good twenty minutes after I'd left to collect Maddie and Ellie.

> Dear Bill and Sandra, just an update from home. All is good, Rhiannon is back safe and sound from Elise's house, and she seems to have had a great time.
>
> We've had a very nice afternoon and she's a credit to you both. Maddie and Ellie both send love.
>
> Rowan.

There was total silence and then I turned to Rhiannon.

"You little shit."

"Charming," she drawled. "Is that the kind of language they expected at Little Nippers?"

"Little—what?" How did she know where I'd worked? But then I pulled myself together, refusing to be derailed. "Look, don't try to change the subject. This is utterly unacceptable, and stupid to boot. First of all, I know about Craig." A look of shock flickered across Rhiannon's face at that. She recovered herself quickly, her expression back to bored indifference almost instantly. However, I had seen it and I couldn't stop a triumphant smile from spreading across my own face. "Oh yes, didn't he tell you that? I rang 'Cass.' Obviously the first thing I'm going to do is call your mum and explain that you sent that email, and the second thing I'm going to do is tell her about this Craig person and explain that you propose waltzing out with this guy I've never met, in a top that barely comes to your navel, and see what she has to say on that subject."

I don't know what I had expected—perhaps a show of temper, or even for Rhiannon to start crying and begging to be let off.

But her reaction was neither of those things. Instead, she smiled, rather sweetly, in a way that was totally unnerving, and said, "Oh, I don't think you'll do that."

"Give me one good reason why not!"

"I'll do better than that," she said. "I'll give you two. Rachel. Gerhardt."

Oh fuck.

The silence in the kitchen was absolute.

For a second, I thought my knees were about to give way, and I groped my way for a barstool and slumped down on it, feeling my breath catch in my throat.

I was cornered. I realized that now. I just didn't know quite how tight that corner was going to get.

Because this is where it gets very, very bad for me, doesn't it, Mr. Wrexham?

This is where the police case on me shifted from being someone in the wrong place at the wrong time, to someone with a motive.

Because she was right. I couldn't ring Sandra and Bill.

I couldn't do that, because Rhiannon knew the truth.

It will be no surprise to you, Mr. Wrexham, not if you've read the newspaper pieces.

Because you will have known right from the outset that the nanny arrested in the Elincourt case was not Rowan Caine but Rachel Gerhardt.

But to the police, it was like a bombshell. Or, no, not a bombshell. More like one of those exploding piñatas that showers you with gifts.

Because I had handed them their case on a plate.

Afterwards they focused very hard on how I managed to do it, as if I were some kind of criminal mastermind, who had plotted all this in exhaustive detail. But what they couldn't seem to understand was how temptingly, laughably simple it had been. There had been no forgery, no elaborate identity theft or manufactured papers. *How did you obtain the fake identity papers, Rachel?* they kept asking, but the truth was, there had been no fake papers. All I had done was pick up my friend Rowan's nannying paperwork from her bedroom in our shared flat, and show it to Sandra. Background check, first aid certificate, CV, none of it had any photographs. There was absolutely no need for me to fake anything, and no way of Sandra knowing that the woman standing in front of her was not the person named on the certificates she was holding out.

And, I tried to tell myself, it wasn't much of a deception. After all, I really did have those credentials—most of them, anyway. I had a background check and a first aid certificate. Like Rowan, I had worked in the baby room at Little Nippers, albeit not quite as long as she had, and not as supervisor. And I had done nannying beforehand, though not as much, and I wasn't sure that my references would have been quite as gushing. But the basics were all there. The name thing was just a . . . technicality. I even had a clean driving license, just as I had told Sandra. The only problem was that I couldn't show it to her because of the photo. But everything I had told her—every qualification I had claimed—it was all true.

Everything except for my name.

There was luck involved of course too. It had been lucky that Sandra had agreed to my request and hadn't contacted Little Nippers themselves for a reference. If she had, they would have told her that Rowan Caine had left a couple of months back. Lucky that she never pushed me on the driving license.

And it had been lucky too that she used a remote payroll service, so that I never had to present Rowan's passport in person and could simply forward the scan she had left on her computer desktop along with our shared bills.

The biggest piece of good fortune was that banks, slightly incredibly, didn't seem to care whose name was on a bank transfer, as long as the account number and sort code matched up. That had been something I'd never expected. I had lain awake wondering how to figure that part out. Claim that my account was in a different name? Ask for cash, or checks made out to R. Gerhardt and cross my fingers Sandra didn't ask why? I'd practically laughed when I found out that none of that mattered, that if you paid by transfer you could put Donald Duck in the payee box, and it would go through. It seemed unbelievably careless.

But the truth was, to begin with, I hadn't even looked past that first stage. All I had focused on was getting that interview, standing in Heatherbrae House, looking Sandra and Bill in the eye. That was all

I had wanted. That was the only reason I had answered the ad. And yet somehow, the opportunities had kept presenting themselves, like temptingly wrapped gifts on a plate, begging me to pick them up and make them mine.

I shouldn't have done it, I know that now, Mr. Wrexham. But can't you see—can't you see what it must have been like?

Now, standing in the kitchen with Rhiannon laughing in my face, I felt a great wave of panic break over me, followed by a strange sense of something else—almost of relief, as if I had known this moment was coming, and was relieved to have it over and done with.

For a moment I thought about bluffing, asking her what she meant, pretending I had never heard the name Rachel Gerhardt. But only for a moment. If she had got far enough to discover my real name, she was not going to be thrown off the scent by an indignant denial.

"How did you find out?" I asked instead.

"Because, unlike my dear parents, I bother to do a little digging when a new girl turns up out of the blue. You'd be surprised what you can find out online. They teach it in school now, you know, managing your digital footprint. I guess they didn't do that in your day?"

The barb was palpable, but I didn't bother to respond. It scarcely seemed important. What mattered was how far she had dug, and why—and what exactly she had found out.

"It didn't take me long to track down Rowan Caine," Rhiannon was saying. "She's pretty boring isn't she? Not much ammunition."

Ammunition. So that was what this was about. Rhiannon had been digging around online for any little indiscretion she could use as leverage. Only she had stumbled on something much, much bigger.

"I couldn't understand it," she said, a little smile tugging at the corner of her mouth. "It all matched up—the name, the date of birth, the time at that nursery with the stupid twee name—*Little Nippers*," she said mockingly. "Ugh. But then suddenly there were all these pictures from Thailand and Vietnam. And when I saw you on the driveway, I began to think I'd fucked up, that maybe I *did* have the wrong person. It took me a few hours to track down the real you. Must be losing my touch. Shame for you she doesn't keep her friend list private. Or that you didn't bother to delete your Facebook profile."

Fuck. So it had been as simple as that. As simple as scrolling down a list of Rowan's Facebook friends and picking out the face I had so obligingly posted up for all the world to see. How could I have been so stupid? But truthfully, it had never occurred to me that anyone would join the dots so assiduously. And I hadn't been setting out to deceive, that's the thing. That's what I tried to explain to the police. If I had really been setting up a fraudulent second life, wouldn't I have bothered to cover my tracks?

Because this *wasn't* fraud, not really. Not in the way the police meant. It was . . . it was just an accident, really. The equivalent of borrowing your friend's car while they're away. I never meant for all this to happen.

The problem was, the thing I couldn't tell the police, was *why* I had come to Heatherbrae under an assumed name. They kept asking me and asking me and digging and digging, and I kept floundering, and trying to come up with reasons—things like, Rowan's references were better than mine (which was true) and she had more experience than me (true again). I think at first they thought I must have some deep, dark professional secret—a lapsed registration, or a conviction as a sex offender or something. And of course none of that was the case, and as hard as they tried to find something, there was nothing wrong with my own papers.

It looked very, very bad for me, I knew that, even at the time. But I kept telling myself, if Rhiannon hadn't discovered why I had come here, then perhaps the police wouldn't either.

But that was stupid, of course. They are the police. It's their job to dig.

It took them some time. Days, maybe even weeks, I can't totally remember. The interrogation starts to run together after a while, the days blurring into one another, as they picked and picked and prodded and probed. But eventually they came into the room holding a piece of paper and they were smiling like Cheshire cats, while simultaneously somehow trying to look grave and professional.

And I knew. I knew that they knew.

And I knew that I was sunk.

But that was afterwards. And I'm getting ahead of myself.

I have to tell the other part. The hardest part. The part I can't quite believe even now.

And the part I can't fully explain, even to myself.

I have to tell you about that night.

After Rhiannon walked out, I stood for a long moment in the hallway, watching the lights of the van disappear down the drive, and trying to figure out what I should do. Should I phone Sandra? And say what? Confess? Brazen it out?

I looked at my watch. It was just half past nine. The line from Sandra's email floated into my head—*Bill is off to Dubai tonight, and I'm at a client dinner, but do text if anything urgent.*

There was no way I could ambush her with all this in the middle of a client dinner, still less, text it through.

Oh, hi, Sandra, hope all is good. FYI, Rhiannon has gone out with a strange bloke, and I applied for this job under a fake name. Speak soon!

The idea would have been laughable if the whole situation hadn't been so serious. Shit. *Shit.* Could I email her and explain the situation properly? Maybe. Though if I were going to do that, I should really have done it earlier, before Rhiannon sent that fake update. It would be even harder to explain myself now.

But as I pulled the tablet towards myself, I realized I couldn't really email. That was the coward's way out. I owed her a call—to explain myself, if not face-to-face, then at least in person. But what the hell could I say?

Shit.

The bottle of wine was there on the kitchen counter, like an invitation, and I poured out a glass, trying to steady my nerves, and then another, this time with a glance at the camera squatting in the corner. But I no longer cared. The shit was about to hit the fan, and soon whatever footage Sandra and Bill had on me would be the least of my worries.

It was deliberate self-sabotage, I knew that really, in my heart of hearts, as I filled the glass for the third time. By the time there was only one glass left in the bottle I knew the truth—I was too drunk to call Sandra now, too drunk to do anything sensible at all, except go to bed.

Up on the top landing, I stood for a long time, my hand on the rounded knob to my bedroom, summoning up the courage to enter. But I could not do it. There was a dark crack at the bottom of the door, and I had a sudden, unsettling image of something loathsome and shadowy slithering out from beneath it, following me down the stairs, enveloping me in its darkness . . .

Instead, I found myself letting my hand drop and then backing away, almost as if that dark something might indeed come after me if I turned my back. Then, at the top of the stairs, I turned resolutely and all but ran back downstairs to the warmth of the kitchen, ashamed of myself, of my own cowardice, of everything.

The kitchen was cozy and bright, but when I shut my eyes I could still smell the chilly breath of the attic air coursing out beneath my bedroom door—and as I stood, irresolute, wondering whether to make up a bed on the sofa or try to stay awake for Rhiannon's return, I could feel the throb of my finger where I had sliced it on that vile broken doll's head. I had put a bandage over it, but the skin beneath felt fat and swollen, as if infection was setting in.

Walking over to the sink, I pulled off the dressing, and then jumped, convulsively, as there was a thud at the back door.

"Wh-who is it?" I called out, trying not to let my voice shake.

"It's me, Jack." The voice came from outside, muffled by the wind. "I've got the dogs."

"Come in, I'm just—"

The door opened, letting in a gust of cold air, and I heard his footsteps in the utility room, and the thud of his boots as he pulled them off and let them drop onto the mat, and the barking of the dogs as they capered around him while he tried to hush them. At last they settled into their baskets, and he came into the kitchen.

"I don't normally walk them so late, but I got caught up. I'm surprised you're still awake. Good day?"

"Not really," I said. My head was swimming, and I realized afresh how drunk I was. Would Jack notice?

"No?" Jack raised an eyebrow. "What happened?"

"I had a . . ." Jesus, where to start. "I had a bit of a run-in with Rhiannon."

"What kind of a run-in?"

"She came back and we—" I stopped, unsure how to put this. It felt completely wrong to put the full picture to Jack before I confessed to Sandra, and I was pretty sure I would be breaking all sorts of confidentiality guidelines if I discussed Rhiannon's problems with someone who was not her parent. But on the other hand, I felt that I might go crazy if I didn't confide at least some of this in another adult. And perhaps there was history here, for it was becoming clearer and clearer that not everything had been included in that big red binder. "We argued," I said at last. "And I threatened to call Sandra and she—she just—" But I couldn't finish.

"What happened?" Jack pulled out a chair, and I sank into it, feeling despair wash over me again.

"She's gone. She's gone out by herself—with some awful unsuitable friend. I told her not to, but she went anyway, and I don't know what to do—what to tell Sandra."

"Look, don't worry about Rhiannon. She's a canny wee thing, pretty independent, and I highly doubt she'll come to any harm, much as Sandra and Bill might disapprove."

"But what if she does? What if something happens to her and it's on my watch?"

"You're a nanny, not a jailer. What were you supposed to do—chain her to her bed?"

"You're right," I said at last. "I know you're right, it's just— Oh God," the words burst out of me of their own accord. "I'm so *tired*, Jack. I can't think, and it doesn't help that my hand hurts like a bastard every time I touch anything."

"What happened to your hand?"

I looked down at it, cradled in my lap, feeling it throb in time with my pulse.

"I cut it." I didn't want to go into the hows and whys now, but the thought of that grinning, evil little face made me shudder, involuntarily.

Jack frowned.

"Can I take a look?"

I said nothing, just nodded, and held out my hand, and he took it very gently, angling it towards the light. Very lightly, he pressed the puffy skin either side of the cut, and made a face.

"It doesn't look too good, if you don't mind me saying. Did you put anything on it, when you cut it?"

"Just a bandage."

"I didn't mean that, I meant, antiseptic. Anything like that?"

"Do you think it really needs it?"

He nodded.

"It's deep, and I don't like the way it's puffed up like that, looks like it could be getting infected. Let me go and see what Sandra's got."

He stood, pushing back his chair with a screech, and walked through to the utility room, where there was a small medicine cabinet on the wall. I had found the bandages in there earlier, and hadn't noticed anything like antiseptic or rubbing alcohol, just a jumble of Peppa Pig bandages and bottles of children's liquid paracetamol.

"Nothing," Jack said, coming back through into the kitchen. "Or at least, nothing except six different flavors of Calpol. Come back to mine, I've got a proper first aid kit in the flat."

"I—I can't." I straightened up, pulled my hand away, curled my injured finger to my palm, feeling it throb with pain. "I can't leave the kids."

"You're not leaving anyone," Jack said patiently. "You're right across the courtyard, you can take the baby monitor. Sandra and Bill sit out in the garden all the time in the summer. It's no different. If you hear a peep you can be back there before they even wake up."

"Well . . ." I said slowly. Thoughts flickered through the back of my head, their edges softened and blurred by the amount of wine I'd drunk earlier. I could ask him to bring the first aid supplies back here, couldn't I? But a little part of me . . . okay, no, a big part of me . . . that part was curious. I wanted to go with Jack. I wanted to see inside his flat.

And, to be completely truthful, Mr. Wrexham, I wanted to get out of this house.

If you really thought there was a threat, how could you leave the kids to deal with it? It was the woman police officer who asked me that, barely trying to conceal her disgust as she asked the question.

And I tried to explain. I tried to tell her how the kids had seen nothing, heard nothing. How every little bit of malevolence had seemed to be directed solely at *me*. *I* had heard the footsteps. *I* was the one who had read those messages. *I* had been kept awake, night after night, by the noises and the doorbells and the cold.

None of the others, even Jack, had seen or heard what I had.

If there was something in that house, and even now I only half believed that there could be, in spite of everything that had happened, *if* there was, then it was out to get me. Me and the other four nannies who had packed up and left in a hurry.

And I just wanted five minutes out from its influence. Just five minutes, with the baby monitor in my pocket and the tablet with its surveillance cameras under my arm. Was that too much to ask?

The police officer didn't seem to buy it. She just stood, shaking her head in disbelief, her lip curled with contempt for the stupid, selfish, careless bitch sitting opposite her.

But do *you* buy it, Mr. Wrexham? Do you understand, how hard it was, shut up there, night after night with nothing but the sound of pacing footsteps? Do you understand why just those few yards across the courtyard seemed like both nothing at all, and everything?

I don't know. I'm not sure if I've managed to convince you, to explain what it was like, what it was *really* like.

All I can tell you is that I picked up the monitor, and the tablet, and I followed Jack as he crossed the kitchen and held open the back door for me, shutting it behind us both. I felt the warmth of his skin, as he shepherded me across the dark, uneven cobblestoned courtyard to the stairs up to his flat. And I mounted the stairs after him, watching the flex and shift of his muscles under his T-shirt as he climbed.

At the top he pulled a key out of his pocket, twisted it in the lock, and then stood back to let me pass inside.

Inside, I expected Jack to fumble for a panel or pull out his phone, but instead he reached out, flicked something, and as the lights came on, I saw a perfectly ordinary light switch made of white plastic. The relief was so absurd, and so great, that I almost laughed.

"Don't you have a control panel?"

"No, thank God! These were designed as staff accommodation. No point in wasting technology on the likes of us."

"I suppose so."

He flicked on another light, and I saw a small, bright sitting room, furnished with good basics and a faded cotton sofa. The remains of a log fire smoldered in the little stove in the corner, and I could see a kitchenette on the far side. Beyond was another door, that I supposed was his bedroom, but it didn't seem polite to ask.

"Right, sit here," he said, pointing at the sofa, "and I'll be back with a proper dressing for that cut."

I nodded, grateful for the sense of being taken care of, but mostly just content to sit there, feeling the warmth of the fire on my face and the reassuringly cheap and cheerful Ikea cushions at my back while Jack rummaged in the kitchen cupboards behind me. The sofa was exactly like the one Rowan and I had back in our flat in London. Ektorp, it was called, or something like that. It had been Rowan's mum's before she handed it down to us. Guaranteed to last for ten years, with a washable cotton cover that had once been red, in Jack's case, but had faded to a slightly streaky dark pink with sun and repeated launderings.

Sitting on it was like coming home.

After the luxurious split personality of Heatherbrae, there was something not just refreshing, but endearing about this place. It was solidly built, and all of a piece—no sudden disorienting switches from Victorian opulence to sleek futuristic technology. Everything was reassuringly homey, from the mug stains on the coffee table, to the medley of photos propped on the mantelpiece—friends and their kids, or maybe nieces and nephews. One little boy cropped up more than once, clearly a relative from the family resemblance.

I felt my eyes closing, two sleep-deprived nights catching up with me . . . and then I heard a cough and Jack was standing in front of me, a dressing and some disinfectant in one hand, and two glasses in the other.

"D'you want a drink?" he asked, and I looked up puzzled.

"A drink? No, I'm fine, thanks."

"Are you sure? You might need something to take the edge off when I put this stuff on. It's going to sting. And I think there's a wee bit of glass or something still in there."

I shook my head, but he was right. It did sting like fuck, first when he dabbed it with antiseptic, and then again when he pushed a pair of tweezers deep inside the cut, and I felt the sickening grind of metal against glass, and the sting of a forgotten shard sliding deeper into my finger.

"Fuck!" The groan slipped out without my meaning to voice it, but Jack was grinning, holding something bloodstained up at the end of his tweezers.

"Got it. Well done. That must have hurt like a bastard."

My hand was shaking as he sat down beside me.

"You know, you've stuck it out longer than the last few."

"What do you mean?"

"The last couple of nannies. Actually, I tell a lie, Katya made it to three weeks, I think. But since Holly, they've come and gone like butterflies."

"Who was Holly?"

"She was the first one, the one who stayed the longest. Looked after Maddie and Ellie when they were wee, and she stayed for nearly three years, until—" He stopped, seeming to think better of what he had been about to say. "Well, never mind that. And number two, Lauren, she stayed nearly eight months. But the one after her didn't last a week. And the one before Katya, Maja her name was, she left the first night."

"The first *night*? What happened?"

"She called a taxi, left in the middle of the night. Left half her things too; Sandra had to send them on."

"I don't mean that, I mean, what happened to make her leave?"

"Oh, well . . . that, I don't really know. I always thought—" He flushed, the back of his neck staining red as he looked down at his empty glass.

"Go on," I prompted, and he shook his head, as if angry at himself.

"Fuck it, I said I wouldna do this."

"Do what?"

"I don't bad-mouth my employers, Rowan, I told you that on the first day."

The name gave me a guilty jolt, a reminder of all that I was concealing from him, but I pushed the thought aside, too intent on what he had been about to say to worry about my own secrets. Suddenly I had to know what had driven them away, those other girls, my predecessors. What had set them running?

"Jack, listen," I said. I hesitated, then put a hand on his arm. "It's not disloyalty. I'm their employee too, remember? We're colleagues.

You're not shooting your mouth off to an outsider. You're allowed to talk about work stuff to a colleague. It's what keeps you sane."

"Aye?" He looked up from his contemplation of the whiskey glass, and gave me a little wry smile, rather bitter. "Is that so? Well . . . I've said half of it already, so I might as well tell you the whole lot. You've maybe a right to know anyway. I always thought what scared them off—" He took a breath, as if steeling himself to do something unpleasant. "I thought it was maybe . . . Bill."

"Bill?" It was not the answer I had been expecting. "In—in what way?"

But the words were no sooner out of my mouth than I knew. I remembered his behavior on my own first night, the spread thighs, the persistent offerings of wine, his knee insinuating itself, unwanted, between my own . . .

"Shit," I said. "No, you don't need to say. I can imagine."

"Maja . . . she was on the young side," Jack said reluctantly. "And very pretty. And it crossed my mind that maybe he'd . . . well . . . come on to her, and she'd not known what to do. I'd wondered before . . . Bill had a black eye one time, when Lauren was here, and I did think maybe she'd . . . you know . . ."

"Belted him one?"

"Aye. And if she did, he must have deserved it or she'd have been sacked, you know?"

"I guess. Jesus. Why didn't you tell me?"

"Bit hard to say, *Oh, aye, by the by, ma boss is a wee bit o' a perve,* you know? Difficult to bring it up on a first day."

"I can see that. Fuck." My cheeks felt as flushed as Jack's, though in my case it was more than half wine. "God. Ugh. Oh *yuck.*"

The sense of betrayal was all out of proportion, I knew that. It wasn't like I hadn't known. He'd tried it on me, after all. But somehow the idea that he'd been systematically preying on his daughters' carers, time after time, careless of the fact that he was helping to drive them away . . . I suddenly felt a desperate urge to wash myself, scrub all traces of him off my skin, even though I'd not seen him for days, and when I had, he'd barely touched me.

Ellie's voice filtered through my head, her reedy little treble. *I like it better when he's gone. He makes them do things they don't want to do.*

Was it possible she had been talking about her own father, predating the young women and girls his wife had picked out to look after his children?

"Jesus." I put my face in my hands. "The absolute fucker."

"Listen." Jack sounded uncomfortable. "I could be wrong, I don't have any proof of this, it's just—"

"You don't need proof," I said wretchedly. "He tried it on with me the first night."

"What?"

"Yup. Nothing—" I swallowed, gritting my teeth. "Nothing I'd get very far with at an employment tribunal. All vague remarks and 'accidentally' blocking my way. But I know when I'm being harassed."

"Jesus, God, Rowan, I'm so— I'm so sorry— I'm just—"

"It's not your fault, don't apologize."

"I should have bloody said something! No wonder you've been a bag of nerves, hearing blokes creeping about in—"

"No," I said forcefully. "That's nothing to do with it. Jack, I'm a grown woman, I've been hit on before; it's nothing I couldn't handle. The attic stuff is completely unrelated. This is—it's something else."

"It's fucking disgusting, is what it is." His cheeks were flushed, and he stood, as if unable to contain his anger while sitting still. He paced to the window, then back, his fists clenched. "I'd like to—"

"Jack, leave it," I said, urgently. I stood up too, and put my hand on his arms, pulling him round to face me, and then— God, I don't even know how it happened.

I don't have the words for it, without writing it like a trashy novel. Melting into each others' arms. Lips coming together like a crash of waves. All those stupid clichés.

Except there was no melting. No softness. It was hard, and fast, and urgent, and more than a little painful in its intensity. I was kissing and being kissed, and then I was biting, my own skin between his teeth too, and then my fingers were in his hair, and his hands were fumbling my buttons, and then it was skin against skin and lips against lips and—I can't write this to you. I can't write this but I can't stop remembering it. I don't know how to stop.

Afterwards, we lay in each others' arms in front of the wood fire, our skin slicked with sweat and stickiness, and he fell asleep, his head on my breast, rising and falling gently with every breath I took. For a while, I just watched him, the way his skin paled to milk white below his hips, the brush of freckles on the bridge of his nose, the dark sweep of his lashes on his cheeks, the curl of his hand around my shoulder. And then I looked up, to the mantelpiece above us both, where the baby monitor sat, silently waiting.

I could not go back. And yet I had to.

At last, when I could feel I was beginning to slip into sleep myself, I knew that I had to get up or risk lying here all night, and waking to find the girls making their own breakfast, while I conducted a chilly walk of shame back to the main house in the dawn light.

And there was Rhiannon too. I couldn't take the chance of her finding me here when she did come back from wherever she was. I had enough explaining to Sandra to do already, without adding nighttime walks to the agenda.

Because I had to fess up to her. That was the only possibility, I had realized that as I lay in Jack's arms . . . maybe I had even known before. I had to fess up to everything, and risk losing the job. If she sacked me—well, I couldn't blame her. And in spite of everything, in spite of the financial hole I would find myself in, with no job, and no money, and no references, in spite of all that, I would just have to suck it up, because I deserved it.

But if I explained, if I really explained *why* I had done what I'd done, then maybe, just maybe . . .

I had my jeans almost on when I heard the noise. It was not over the baby monitor but coming from somewhere outside the house, a noise halfway between a crack and a thud, as if a branch had fallen from a tree. I stopped, holding my breath, listening, but there were no more sounds, and no squawking wail from the baby monitor to indicate that whatever it was had woken Petra and the others.

Still, I pulled out my phone and checked the app. The camera icon marked *Petra's room* showed her flung on her back with her usual abandon; the picture was pixelated and ill-defined in the soft glow from the night-light, but the shape was clear. As I watched, she sighed and stuck her thumb in her mouth.

The camera in the girls' room showed nothing at all, I'd forgotten to switch their night-light on when I tucked them in, and the resolution was too poor to show anything except grainy black, punctuated by the occasional gray speckle of interference. But if they'd woken up they would have switched on the bedside light, so the absence was good news.

Shaking my head, I buttoned up my jeans, pulled my T-shirt over my head, and then bent and very softly kissed Jack on the cheek. He said nothing, just rolled over and murmured something indistinct that might have been, "'Night, Lynn."

For a moment my heart stilled, but then I shook myself. It could have been anything. *'Night, love. 'Night then*. And even if it was *'Night, Lynn* or *Liz*, or any other name, so what? I had a past. Maybe Jack did too. And God only knew, I had too many secrets of my own to hold someone else's up to the light to condemn them.

I should have just left.

I should have picked up the baby monitor, walked to the door, and let myself out.

But before I returned to the house, I could not resist one final look back at Jack, lying there, his skin golden in the firelight, his eyes closed, his lips parted in a way that made me want to kiss him one last time.

And as I glanced back, I saw something else.

It was a purple flower, lying on the countertop. For a minute I couldn't work out why it looked familiar, nor why my gaze had snagged on it. And then I realized—it was the same as the flower I had found the other morning in the kitchen and put into the coffee cup to revive. Had *Jack* left the flower on the kitchen floor? But no—he had been away that night, running errands for Bill . . . hadn't he? Or was that a different night? Lack of sleep was making the days blur, run into each other, and it was becoming hard to remember which of the long, nightmarish stretches of darkness belonged to which morning.

As I stood there, frowning, trying to remember, I noticed something else. Something even more mundane. But something that made me stop in my tracks, my stomach lurching with unease. It was a little coil of string. Totally innocuous—so why had it unnerved me so?

I walked back across the room and picked it up.

It was a hank of white caterers' string, doubled and tripled up, and tied with a granny knot that was suddenly horribly familiar. And it had been cleanly severed—snipped in half by a very sharp knife, or perhaps the very pair of pruning shears I had rescued from the poison garden.

Whichever it was, it didn't really matter now.

What mattered was that it was the hank of string I had wound around the poison garden gate, too high for little hands to reach—the string I had put there to keep the girls safe. But what was it doing in Jack's kitchen? And why was it lying next to that innocent-looking flower?

As I pulled out my phone and opened up Google, there was a sick fluttering feeling in my chest, as if I already knew what I was going to find. *Purple flower poisonous* I typed into the search bar, and then clicked on Google Images, and there it was, the second image, its strange drooping shape and bright purple color totally unmistakable. *Aconitum napellus (monkshood),* I read, the feeling of sickness growing inside me with every line. *One of the most toxic flowers native to the UK. Aconitine is a potent heart and nerve toxin, and any part of the plant, including stems, leaves, petals, or roots, can be deadly. Most deaths result from ingesting A. napellus, but gardeners are advised to use extreme caution in handling cuttings, as even skin contact can cause symptoms.*

Underneath it was a list of deaths and murders associated with the plant.

I shut down the phone, and turned to look at Jack, unable to believe it. Had it really been him, all along?

Him in the locked garden, pruning the poisonous plants, keeping that horrible place alive.

Him undoing the safety measures I had set up to try to protect the children.

Him, carefully selecting the most poisonous blossom he could find and leaving it lying in the middle of the kitchen floor. All I had done was handle it—but it could so easily have been found by the children, or even one of the dogs.

And I had just fucked him.

But why? Why would he do it? And what else was he responsible for?

Had he been the person who hacked into the system to jolt us all out of our beds in the middle of the night with deafening music and terrified screams?

Was he the one who had been setting off the doorbell, jerking me from sleep, and keeping me awake with the terrifying *creak, creak* of stealthy footsteps?

And worst of all, had he been the one who wrote those horrible things in the locked attic room, and then boarded up after himself, only to "rediscover" it when the time was right?

I found that my breath was coming quick and short, my hands shaking as I shoved the phone back into my pocket, and suddenly I had to get out, get away from him at all costs.

Not troubling now to be silent, I flung open the door to the flat, and stepped out into the night, slamming it behind me. It had started to rain again, and I ran, feeling the rain on my cheeks, the tightness in my throat, and the blurring of my eyes.

The utility room door was still unlocked, and I let myself in, leaning back against the door and using my T-shirt to wipe my eyes, trying to get a hold of myself.

Fuck. *Fuck.* What was it about me and the men in my life? Why were they such shits, all of them?

As I stood there, trying to calm my gulping breath, I remembered the faint sound I'd heard before, as I was dressing. The house was just as I'd left it: no sign of Rhiannon's high heels kicked off in the hallway, or handbag abandoned on the bottom step of the stairs. But I hadn't really expected that. I would have heard a car pulling up. It had probably been one of the dogs.

I wiped my eyes again, peeled off my shoes, and walked slowly through to the kitchen, feeling the faint warmth of the underfloor heating striking up through the concrete. Hero and Claude were curled sleepily in their baskets, snoring quietly. They looked up as I came in, and then laid their heads wearily back down as I sat at the breakfast bar, put my head in my hands, and tried to decide what to do.

I could not go to bed. No matter what Jack had said, Rhiannon was still missing, and I couldn't just forget that fact. What I should do—what I *needed* to do, in fact—was write an email to Sandra. A proper one, explaining everything that had happened.

But there was something else I had to do first.

For the more I thought about it, the more Jack's behavior did not add up. It wasn't just the poison garden—it was everything. The way he was always hanging around when things went wrong. The fact that he seemed to have keys to every room in the house and access to parts of the home-management system that he shouldn't. How had he known how to override the app that night when the music came screaming out of the speakers? How had he just happened to have a key to the locked attic door?

And whatever he said, he was, after all, a Grant. What if there was some connection I was missing? Could he be some long-lost relative of Dr. Kenwick Grant, come back to drive the Elincourts out from his ancestral home?

But no—that last what-if was too much. This wasn't some nineteenth-century peasant's revenge drama. What would Jack gain from driving the Elincourts out of their own home? Nothing. All he'd get would be another English couple in their place. And besides, it wasn't the Elincourts who seemed to be targeted. It was me.

Because the fact was that four nannies—five if you counted Holly—had left the Elincourts. No, not left; they had been systematically driven away, one by one. And I might have believed that Bill's roving hands were responsible, if it hadn't been for my own experiences in Heatherbrae House. Someone in this house, someone or some*thing*, was driving the nannies away, in a deliberate and sustained campaign of persecution.

I just didn't know who.

Somewhere behind my eyes, a dull throbbing ache had begun, echoing the pain in my hand—the light-headedness from the wine I'd drunk earlier was already morphing into the beginnings of a shocking hangover. But I couldn't give way to that now. Slowly, unsteadily, I slid from the breakfast barstool, walked over to the sink, and splashed my face, trying to wake myself up, clear my head for what I was about to do.

But as I stood, water dripping from my loose hair, hands braced either side of the sink, I saw something. Something that had not been there when I left, I was sure of it—or at least, as sure as I could be, for now nothing seemed certain anymore.

To the right of the sink was my almost-empty wine bottle. Only now it was totally empty. What should have had a glass left in it was now completely drained. And in the groove around the edge of the waste-disposal unit was a single crushed berry.

It could have been the remnants of a blueberry or a raspberry, mashed out of all recognition, but somehow, I knew it was not.

My heart was thumping as I reached, very slowly, into the waste-disposal unit.

Deep, deep into the metal mouth I reached, until my fingers touched something at the bottom. Something soft and hard by turns, into which my fingers sank as I clawed up the mass.

It was a mush of berries. Yew. Holly. Cherry laurel.

And in spite of the water I'd sluiced down the drain, I could smell, quite clearly, the dregs of wine still clinging to them.

It didn't make sense. *None* of it made sense. Those berries had not been in the wine when I left—how could they have been? I had opened the bottle myself.

Which meant someone had put them in there when I was not looking. Someone who had been in this kitchen tonight, after the children were in bed.

But then . . . but then someone else had tipped them out.

It was like there were two forces in the house, one fighting to drive me away, another to protect me. But who—*who* was doing this?

I didn't know. But if there were answers to be found, I knew where I had to look.

My chest was tight as I straightened up, and I groped in my jeans pocket for my inhaler and took a puff, but the tension didn't loosen, and I found my breath was coming quick and shallow as I made my way to the stairs, and began to climb into the darkness.

As I got closer and closer to the top landing, I couldn't help remembering the last time I had stood there, hand on the rounded knob, simply unable to go any further—unable to face whatever watchful darkness lay behind that door.

Now, though, I was beginning to suspect that whatever haunted Heatherbrae was very human. And I was determined that this time, I would turn the knob, open the door, and find evidence to that effect—

evidence that I could show Sandra when I told her about tonight's events.

But when I got to the landing, I found I didn't need to open it at all. For my door . . . the door to my room, was open. And I had left it closed.

I had a clear, a crystal clear memory of standing in front of it, looking at the crack beneath it, totally unable to turn the handle.

And now it stood open.

It was very cold again, even colder than it had been that time I woke in the night, shivering, to find the thermostat turned down and the air conditioning blasting out. But this time I could feel it was more than just the chill of the room; it was an actual breeze.

For a moment I felt every part of that firm resolution shrivel down like plastic in a flame, disappearing into the core of me, melting and curling into a hard blackened core.

Where was the breeze coming from? Was it the attic door? If it was open again—in spite of the lock and the key in my pocket, and in spite of Jack lying asleep in his flat across the courtyard—I thought I would scream.

Then I got a hold of myself.

This was insane. There was no such thing as ghosts. No such thing as haunting. There was nothing in that attic but dust and the relics of bored children, fifty years dead.

I walked into the room and pressed the button on the panel.

Nothing happened. I tried a different square, one I was sure had made the lamps come on last night. Still nothing, though an unseen fan began to hum. For a long moment I stood in the dark, trying to figure out what to do. I could smell the cold dusty air that blew through the attic keyhole, and I could hear something too—not the *creak, creak* of before, but a low, mechanical buzzing that puzzled me.

And then, out of nowhere, a sudden wave of anger washed over me.

Whatever it was, whatever was up there, I would *not* let myself be scared like this. Someone, some*thing*, was trying to drive me away from Heatherbrae, and I was not giving in to it.

I don't know if it was the remnants of the wine in my veins that gave me courage, or the knowledge that when I rang Sandra the next day, very likely I would be going home anyway, but I took my phone out of my pocket, switched on the torch, and strode across the bedroom to the attic door.

As I did so, the buzzing sounded again. It was coming from above my head. The sound was familiar, but I couldn't put my finger on why. It sounded like a furiously angry wasp, but there was something . . . something robotic about it, a quality that did not make me think it was a living thing.

I felt in my jeans pocket for the key, which was still there from yesterday, hard and unyielding against my leg, and I drew it out.

Softly, very softly, I put the key into the closet door, and turned it. It was stiff—but not as stiff as last time. The WD-40 had done its work, and although I felt resistance, it turned quietly, without the screech of metal on metal it had given when Jack forced the lock.

Then I set my hand to the door, and opened it.

The smell was just as I remembered from last time—dank, musty, the smell of death and abandonment.

But there *was* something up there, I could see that now, something casting a low white glow that illuminated the cobwebs the spiders had woven across the attic steps. Yet, no one had been up there since Jack and me, that was plain. It was not just the key in my pocket that told me that—but the thick unbroken webs across my path, painstakingly respun since my last passage. There was no way someone could have passed this way without disturbing them. As it was, I was forced to step cautiously, sweeping my hand in front of my face to try to keep the clinging strands out of my eyes and mouth.

What *was* the light? The moon, shining through that tiny window? Perhaps, though it was so covered with grot, I would have been surprised.

At the top of the stairs I drew a silent breath, steeling myself, and then I stepped into the attic.

I saw two things straightaway.

The first was that the attic was just as I had last seen it when I took a final glance back at the place before following Jack down the steps the day before. The only thing that was missing was the doll's head that had rolled out from the pile to rest in the center of the room. That was gone.

The second was that the moon *was* shining into the attic, and surprisingly brightly, for the window—the window that Jack had shut—was open again. He had evidently not latched it properly and it had blown open in the night. Striding angrily across the creaking boards, I slammed it, harder than he had, and fumbled in the darkness for a catch. At length I found one—a long tongue drilled with holes. It was covered in thick cobwebs, and I was forced to brush them aside with my hands, feeling the crunch of long-dead prey in the webs, as I wiggled it back into place, ensuring that there was no way the window could work itself open again.

At last it was secure, and I stepped back into the room, wiping my hands. The light had dimmed instantly as I shut the window, the mildewed glass shutting out everything but a thin trickle. But as I turned back to the stairs, the thin beam from my torch illuminating a narrow path across the floor boards, I noticed something else. There was another light. A fainter, bluer one this time, and it was coming from a corner of the attic opposite the window, a corner totally in shadow, a corner where no light had a right to be.

My heart was thudding as I crossed the floor. Was it an opening to one of the rooms downstairs? Something else? Whatever the source of the light was, it was hidden behind a trunk, and I pulled it roughly aside, no longer trying to be quiet, for I no longer cared who found me up here, I had only one instinct—to find out what was really going on.

What I saw made me draw back, astonished, and kneel down in the dust to look closer.

Hidden behind the old trunk was a small pile of belongings. A book. Some chocolate bar wrappers. A bracelet. A necklace. A handful of twigs and berries, wilting, yes, but by no means desiccated.

And a mobile phone.

It was the light from the phone that I had seen from across the attic, and as I picked it up, it buzzed again, and I realized that was the source of the odd noise I had heard earlier. It had evidently updated, and was stuck in a loop of trying to turn itself back on, failing, and restarting, buzzing each time.

It was an old model, similar to one I'd had myself a few years ago, and I tried a trick that had sometimes worked when my own phone was dying, holding the volume-up and power buttons simultaneously for a long press. It hung for a moment, the screen whirling, and then went black, and I pressed restart.

But as I waited for it to reload, something caught my eye. A silvery glint, coming from the little pile of rubbish I had pushed aside to pick up the phone.

And there it was, strewn innocently across the floorboards among the rest of that pathetic pile of detritus, the light from my phone torch glinting from one of its curves.

My necklace.

My heart was beating fast in my throat as I picked it up, unable to believe it. My necklace. *My* necklace. What was it doing here, in the darkness?

I don't know how long I sat in the kitchen, my fingers wrapped around a mug of tea, letting the thin links of my necklace chain trickle through my fingers, and trying to make sense of it all.

I had brought the phone down too, but without a PIN I couldn't open it to see who it belonged to. All I could tell was that it was old, and that it appeared to be connected to the Wi-Fi but didn't seem to have a SIM card in.

It wasn't the phone that bothered me though. That was strange, yes, but there was something personal about finding my necklace hidden up there, amid the darkness and the rotting feathers. I should have been thinking about Rhiannon, worrying about where she was, and the argument we were bound to have when she walked through the door. I should have been thinking about Sandra, considering my options and trying to work out what to say—how to tell her the truth.

I was thinking about both things. But above and below and around those thoughts were twined like the links of my necklace, as I tried to figure out chronologies and timings and work out how my necklace could have disappeared inside a locked room, behind a door to which the only key lay in my pocket, up a corridor sealed by a hundred unbroken spiderwebs. Had it been up there before, when Jack and I first broke in? But that explained nothing. That cupboard had been boarded up for months, *years*. The dust traces, the thick swags of cobwebs, no one had entered via the stairs for a long, long time. And the window was barely large enough for me to get my head and shoulders through, and it looked out onto sheer slates.

After I found the necklace I had scoured every inch of the room looking for trapdoors, loft hatches, hidden doors—but there was nothing. The Victorian floorboards ran from side to side in an unbroken line, the walls gave onto nothing except for the roof tiles, and I had moved every stick of furniture, looked at every inch of the ceiling from below. Whatever else I was unsure of, I was absolutely certain that there was no way in or out apart from the flight of stairs leading up from my room.

The moon was still high in the sky, but the clock above the stove had ticked through 3:00 and 4:00 a.m. when I at last heard tires on the gravel of the drive, whispered laughter outside the porch, and the sound of the front door swinging automatically open as someone activated the thumbpad lock. The door closed stealthily as the van drove off, and I heard cautious footsteps, and then a stumble.

My stomach flipped, but I forced myself to stay calm.

"Hello, Rhiannon." I kept my voice level, and I heard the footsteps on the hallway flags freeze, and then an exclamation of disgust as Rhiannon realized she had been busted.

"Fuck."

She walked unsteadily through to the kitchen. Her makeup was halfway down her face, and her tights were laddered, and she smelled strongly of some mix of sweet alcohol—there was Drambuie in there, I thought, and Malibu too, along with something else, Red Bull, perhaps?

"You're drunk," I said, and she gave a nasty laugh.

"Kettle, black. I can see the wine bottles in the recycling from here."

I shrugged.

"Fair point, but you know I can't let you get away with this, Rhiannon. I have to tell your parents. You can't just walk out like that.

You're fourteen. What if something happened and I didn't know where you were or who you were with?"

"Okay," she said, slumping down at the kitchen island and pulling the biscuit tin towards her. "You do that, *Rachel*. And good luck with the fallout."

"It doesn't matter," I said.

As she picked out a biscuit and pushed the tin away, I took a biscuit too, dunking it calmly in my tea, though my hands were shaking a little beneath my careful control. "I've made up my mind. I'm going to tell your mum. If I lose my job, so be it."

"*If* you lose your job?" She snorted derisively. "*If?* You're delusional. You're here under a fake name, probably with fake qualifications, for all I know. You'll be lucky if you don't end up getting sued."

"Maybe," I said, "but I'll take that risk. Now get upstairs and wipe that stuff off your face."

"Fuck you," she said, through a mouthful of biscuit, her words accompanied by an explosion of crumbs that spattered across my face, making me recoil, blinking and brushing fragments out of my eyes.

"You little bitch!" My temper, so carefully held, was suddenly fraying fast. "What is wrong with you?"

"What's wrong with *me*?"

"Yes, you. All of you, actually. Why do you hate me so much? What have I ever done to any of you? Do you actually want to be left here alone? Because that's what's going to happen if you keep being such a fucking bitch to the staff."

"What the fuck do you know about it?" she spat, and suddenly she was as angry as me, pushing back her metal stool so that it toppled and fell with a ringing clang onto the concrete floor. "You can fuck off as far as I'm concerned, we don't want you, we don't *need* you."

There was a biting retort on the tip of my tongue, but somehow, as she stood there, the kitchen spotlights making her tousled, tangled blond hair glow like fire, with her face twisted into a grimace of rage and pain, she looked so like Maddie, so like *me,* that my heart gave a little skip.

I remembered myself, age fifteen, coming in after curfew, standing in the kitchen with my hands on my hips, shouting at my mum, "I don't care if you were worried. I never asked you to stay up; I don't need you looking out for me!"

It was a lie, of course. A total lie.

Because everything I did, every test I aced, every curfew I broke, every time I tidied my room and every time I didn't—all of it was aimed at one thing. Making my mother notice me. Making her *care.*

For fourteen years, I had tried so hard to be the perfect daughter, but it was never enough. No matter how neat my handwriting, no matter how high I scored in the spelling test, or how good my art project was, it was never enough. I could spend a whole afternoon coloring a picture for her, and she would notice the one place I had sneezed and jerked my pen across the line.

I could spend my Saturday tidying my room to perfection—and she would grumble that I had left my shoes in the hall.

Whatever I did was wrong. I grew too fast, my clothes were too expensive, my friends were too noisy. I was too chubby, or conversely, I picked at my food. My hair was too messy—too thick, too hard to tame into the neat plaits and ponytails she favored.

And so as I crossed the line from child to teenager, I began to do the opposite. I had tried being perfect—so then I tried being imperfect. I stayed out. I drank. I let my grades slip. I went from total compliance to serial defiance.

It made no difference. No matter what I did, I was not the daughter I should have been. All I was doing now was confirming that fact to both of us.

I had ruined her life. That was always the unspoken message—the thing that hung between us, making me clutch at her even harder as she pulled away. And at last, I couldn't deal with seeing that truth in her face anymore.

I left home at eighteen, with nothing but a handful of mediocre A levels and the offer of an au pair job in Clapham. By that time I was old enough not to have a curfew, or someone sitting up for me past their bedtime, reproach in their eyes when I came home.

But I was very, very far from not needing anyone to look out for me.

Maybe Rhiannon was too.

"Rhiannon." I stepped forward, trying to keep the pity out of my voice. "Rhiannon, I know that since Holly—"

"Don't you dare say her name," she growled. She took a step backwards, stumbling on her high heels, and suddenly she looked like what she was—a little girl, teetering in clothes too old for her that she had barely learned how to wear. Her lips were curled in a way that could have been anger but I suspected meant she was trying not to cry. "Don't you *dare* talk about that slut-faced hell witch here."

"Who—Holly?" I was taken aback. There was something here, something different from the generalized world-hating hostility I had felt emanating from Rhiannon up until now. This was pointed, vicious, *personal*, and Rhiannon's voice shook with it.

"What—what happened?" I asked. "Is this because she abandoned you?"

"Abandoned us?" Rhiannon gave a kind of derisive, hooting laugh. "Fuck no. She didn't abandon us."

"Then what?"

"*Then what?*" she imitated, cruelly mocking my south London accent, blurring her cut-glass consonants, swallowing the final *t* into an estuary drawl. "She stole my fucking father, if you must know."

"*What?*"

"Yes, my dear darling daddy. Shagged him for the best part of two years and had Maddie and Ellie wound round her little finger covering up for them both, telling my mother lies. And do you know what the worst part of it was, I didn't even realize what was going on until my friend came to stay and pointed it out. I didn't believe her at first—so I set them up to find out the truth. My dad doesn't have cameras in his study—did you ever notice that?" She gave a bitter, staccato laugh. "Funny that. He can spy on the rest of us—but *his* privacy is sacrosanct. I got Petra's baby monitor, and I plugged it in under his desk and I *heard* them—I heard him telling Holly that he loved her, that he was going to leave my mum, that she just had to be patient, that they were going to be together in London, just like he'd promised."

Oh fuck. I wanted to put my arms around her, hug her, tell it was okay, that it was not her fault, but I couldn't move.

"And I heard her too, begging, wheedling, telling him she just couldn't wait, that she wanted them to be together—I *heard* it, all the stuff that she wanted to do to him—it was—" She stopped, choking with disgust for a moment, and then seemed to pull herself together, folding her arms, her face set in a mask of grief too old for her. "So, I framed the bitch."

"What—?" But I couldn't finish. I could barely even form the word.

Rhiannon smiled, but her face was twisted like she was holding back tears.

"I got her in front of the cameras, and I wound her up until she hit me."

Oh God. So this was where Maddie had learned it.

"And then I told her to get out, or I'd put the footage on YouTube and ensure she never worked in this country ever again, and ever since then—"

She stopped, gulping, and then tried again.

"And ever since—"

But she couldn't finish. She didn't need to. I knew the truth, what she was trying to say.

"Rhiannon." I stepped towards her, my hand outstretched like I was trying to tame and gentle a wild animal, my own voice shaking now. "Rhiannon, I swear to you, there is no way in a thousand—no, a *million* years, I'd ever have sex with your father."

"You can't promise that." Her face was swollen, there were tears running down her cheeks now. "That's what they all think, when they come here. But he keeps on, and on, and on, and they can't afford to lose their jobs, and he's got money, and he can even be kind of charming, when he wants to be, you know?"

"No." I was shaking my head. "No, no, no. Rhiannon, listen, I—I can't explain, but just—no. There's no way. There's just no way I'd ever do that."

"I don't believe you," she said. The words came out like sobs. "He's done it before, you know. Before Holly. And that time he *did* leave. He had another family. Another child, a *baby*. I heard my m-mother t-t-talking one day. And he l-*left* them—it's who he is, and if I hadn't stopped him—he j-just—"

But she couldn't finish. Her voice dissolved into sobs. I felt an awful kind of realization wash over me, and I put my hands on her arms, trying to steady us both, linking us both, trying to communicate everything I could not say with the certainty of my voice.

"Rhiannon, listen, I can promise you this—this is absolutely cast-iron. I swear on—on my *grave*, I am never, never going to sleep with your father."

Because.

It was on the tip of my tongue.

I am never, never going to sleep with your father because—

I wish I had finished the sentence, Mr. Wrexham. I wish I had just said it, told her, explained. But I was still clinging to the idea of explaining the reason for my deception to Sandra the next day, and I couldn't tell Rhiannon the truth before I confessed to her mother. I had to confess that I wasn't Rowan, and Sandra's pity and understanding about why I had come to her house under a false name was my only chance of making it out of the situation without being at minimum sacked, and very possibly sued.

But you don't need me to finish the sentence, do you, Mr. Wrexham? You know why. At least, I imagine you do, if you've read the papers. You know, because the police know. Because they found out. Because they put two and two together, as you are very possibly doing, even now.

You know that the reason I would never sleep with Bill Elincourt was because he was my father too.

I told you, Mr. Wrexham, didn't I, that I wasn't even looking for a job when I stumbled across the advert? In fact I was doing something totally different, something I'd done many times before.

I was googling my father's name.

I'd always known who he was, and for a while I'd even known *where* he was—a fancy semidetached house in Crouch End, with electric gates that slid automatically across the driveway, and a shiny BMW on the forecourt. I had been there once in my midteens, under the cover of a pretended shopping trip to Oxford Street with a friend. I remember the taste in my mouth, the way my hands shook when I showed the bus driver my travel card, every step of the walk from Crouch End Broadway.

I stood outside that gate for a long time, consumed with a strange mix of fear and anger, too afraid to ring the bell and face up to the man I'd never met, the man who had walked out when my mother was nine months pregnant.

He sent checks for a while, but he wasn't on my birth certificate, and I suppose my mother was too proud to pursue him and force him to pay.

Instead, she picked herself up, got a job in an insurer's firm, and met the man she eventually married. The man—the message was very clear—that she *should* have been with all along.

And so, when I was six, we moved into his boxy little house.

It was their home. Hers and his. It was never mine. Not from the day I moved into the little room above the stairs and was told sharply not to scuff my suitcase on the hall baseboards. Not until the day I packed a different, larger suitcase and moved out, twelve long years later.

It was their home, but I—I was always there to spoil it for them. This living, breathing, constant reminder of my mother's past. Of the man who had left her. And every day, she had to look at me staring at her over the breakfast cereal with *his* eyes. When she brushed my thick, wiry hair into a ponytail, it was *his* hair she brushed, not her own fine, flyaway stuff.

For that was all I had from him. That, and the necklace he had sent me on my first birthday, the last contact I had from him. A necklace with my initial on it—*R* for *Rachel.*

Cheap, nasty rubbish, my mother had called it, but that didn't stop me from wearing it all the hours I was allowed. At weekends, at first, and every day in the holidays, and then when I began work as an au pair, tucking it beneath my T-shirts and plastic aprons, so that it was always there, the worn metal warm between my breasts.

I was working as a nanny in Highgate when she rang me up and told me. She and my stepfather were selling the house and retiring to Spain. Just like that. It wasn't that I had any particular affection for that house—I had never been happy there.

But it had been . . . well, if not my home, at any rate, the only place I could call home. "Of course you're welcome to come and visit," she said, her voice high and slightly defensive, as if she knew what she was doing, and I think it was that, more than anything, that made me lose it. *You're welcome to come and visit.* It was the kind of thing you say to a distant relative, or a friend you don't particularly like, hoping they won't take you up on the offer.

I told her to fuck off. I'm not proud of that. I told her that I hated her, that I'd had four years of therapy to try to deal with my upbringing, and that I never wanted to hear from her again.

It wasn't true. Of course it wasn't true. Even now, even here, at Charnworth, she was the first person I put on my prison call list. But she's never called.

It was two days after her announcement that I went back to Crouch End.

I was twenty-two. And I wasn't angry this time. I was just . . . I was terribly, terribly sad. I had lost the only parent I'd ever known—and my need to replace her with *something*, however poor and inadequate, was consuming me.

"Hello . . . Bill." I had practiced the words in my bedroom the night before, standing in front of the mirror. My face was scrubbed clean of makeup, making me look younger and even more vulnerable, though that hadn't been my intention, and I found that my voice was unnaturally high, as if I wanted to make an appeal to his pity. I didn't know what kind of daughter he'd want—but I was prepared to try and be that person. "Hello, Bill. You don't know me, but I'm Rachel. I'm Catherine's daughter."

My heart was thudding in my chest as I walked up to the gate and rang the bell, waiting for the gate to slide back, or perhaps the crackle of voices to come over the intercom. But nothing happened.

I tried again, holding the buzzer long and hard, and eventually the front door opened and a small woman in an overall, holding a duster, came out across the shingled drive.

"Hello?" She was in her forties or fifties, and her voice was heavily accented—Polish, I thought, or perhaps Russian. Eastern Europe. "I can help you?"

"Oh . . . hello." My pulse rate had sped up, until I thought I might possibly faint from nerves. "Hello. I'm looking for Mr.—" I swallowed. "Mr. Elincourt. Bill Elincourt. Is he here?"

"He is not here."

"Oh, well, will he be back later?"

"He gone. New family now."

"Wh-what do you mean?"

"He and his wife moved last year. Different country. Scotland. New family is here now. Mr. and Mrs. Cartwright."

Oh. Fuck.

It was like a punch to the gut.

"Do you . . . do you have an address?" I asked, my voice faltering, and she shook her head. There was pity in her eyes.

"Sorry, I do not have, I am just cleaning."

"You—" I swallowed hard. "You mentioned a wife. Mrs. Elincourt. Can I ask—what's her name?"

I don't know why that was suddenly important to me. Only that I knew the trail had gone cold, and any scraps of information seemed better than nothing. The cleaner looked at me sadly. Who did she think I was? A spurned girlfriend? A former employee? Or maybe she had guessed the truth.

"She called Sandra," she said at last, very quietly. "I must go now." And then she turned and made her way back into the house.

I turned too and began the long walk back to Highgate, saving the bus fare. There was a hole in my shoe, and as I started up the hill, it began to rain, and I knew I had lost my chance.

After that I didn't try looking again in earnest for a few years. And then, one day, when I was idly typing *Bill Elincourt* into Google, there it was. The advert. With a house in Scotland. And a wife called Sandra.

And a family.

And suddenly, I couldn't *not*.

It was like the universe had set this up for me—to give me a chance.

I didn't want him to be my dad, not now, not after all these years. I just wanted to . . . well, just to *see*, I suppose. But obviously, I couldn't travel up to Scotland under my own name without telling him who I was, and setting up a whole weight of expectation and potential rejection. Even with nearly thirty years of water under the bridge, it was unlikely that Bill would have forgotten the name of his firstborn daughter, and Gerhardt was unusual enough as a surname for him to do a double take, and register it as that of the mother of his child.

But I didn't need to go under my own name. In fact, I had a better name, a better identity, just ready and waiting for me. One that would get me through the front door without any strings attached, at which point I could do whatever I wanted. And so I picked up the papers that Rowan had left so temptingly lying around in her bedroom—the papers that were, almost, going to waste. The papers so very, very close to my own that really, it didn't seem like much of a deception at all.

And I applied.

I didn't expect to get the job. I didn't even want it. I just wanted to meet the man who had abandoned me all those years before. But when I saw Heatherbrae, I knew, Mr. Wrexham. I knew that one visit was never going to be enough for me. I wanted to be a part of all this, to sleep in the softness of those feather beds, to sink into the velvet sofas, to bask under the rainwater showers—to be a part of this family, in short.

And I wanted, very, *very* badly, to meet Bill.

And when he didn't appear at the interview, I could see only one way to make that happen.

I had to get the job.

But when I did . . . and when I met Bill that first night, and realized the kind of man he was, God, it's like a metaphor for this whole thing, Mr. Wrexham. It's all connected. The beauty and luxury of this house, and the seeping poison underneath the high-tech facade. The solid Victorian wood of a closet door, with its polished brass escutcheon—and the cold, rank smell of death that breathes out of the hole.

There was something sick in that house, Mr. Wrexham. And whether Bill had been sick when he went there and brought it with him, or whether he had caught its sickness and become the man I met on that first night, that predatory, abusive man, I don't know.

All I know is that the two run hand in hand, and that if you scratched the walls of Heatherbrae House, scoring the hand-blocked peacock wallpaper with your nails, or gouging the polished granite tiles, that same darkness would seep out, the darkness that lay very close beneath Bill Elincourt's skin.

Don't look for him. That was one of the few things my mother had said to me about him, before she shut off the subject completely. *Don't look for him, Rachel. Nothing good will come of it.*

She was right. God, she was so right. And how I wish I'd listened to her.

"Come on," I said at last. "Up to bed, Rhiannon. You're tired, I'm tired, we've both had too much to drink . . . We'll talk about all this in the morning."

I'd ring Sandra and explain. Somehow. With my head aching from the beginnings of a hangover, and tiredness scratching at the back of my eyes, I could not quite think of the words, but they would come. They would have to. I couldn't carry on like this, being blackmailed by Rhiannon.

For a moment, as I climbed the stairs, Rhiannon in front of me, I had an absurd mental picture of Sandra welcoming me with open arms, telling me I completed their family, telling me— But no. That was ridiculous, and I knew it. Even the most generous of women would take time to adjust to a long-lost stepchild turning up, and to find out this way, in these circumstances . . . well. I had no illusions how the conversation was likely to pan out. Difficult would be the best-case scenario.

Well, I had made my bed, and I would have to lie on it. I would almost certainly be sacked—I couldn't really see any way around that. But I was fairly sure that Bill would not want to sue his estranged daughter, to whose mother he had paid just pennies in child support, before disappearing for good. It would not be a good look for Elincourt and Elincourt. No, it would be swept under the rug, and I'd be free to carry on. Alone.

And far away from Heatherbrae.

* * *

I hadn't really thought about my room and where I was going to sleep until we got to the second-floor landing, and Rhiannon turned the handle on her graffitied bedroom door and flung her shoes in, with total unconcern.

"Good night," she said, as if nothing had happened, as if the events of the night had been just another family row.

"Good night," I said, and I took a deep breath and opened the door to the bedroom. The strange phone was hard in my pocket, and my necklace—the necklace I had feared Bill Elincourt might recognize—lay warm around my neck.

Inside, the door to the attic was shut and locked, as I had left it. I was about to grab my night things and take them downstairs to the sofa to try to catch a few hours before dawn when there was a sudden gust of wind, making the trees outside groan. The curtains flapped suddenly and wildly in the breeze, and the fresh pine-laden scent of a Scottish night filled the room.

The room was still painfully cold, just as it had been earlier that night, and suddenly I realized. The cold had never come from the attic—it must have been the window, open all along. Only before I had been so fixated on finding out the truth of what was behind the locked door that I hadn't even glanced towards the curtains.

At least the chill was explained then. Nothing supernatural—just the cold night air.

But the problem was, I had not opened that window. I hadn't even touched it since I slammed it shut a few nights before. And now, suddenly, my stomach was turning over and over in a way that made me feel very, very sick.

Turning, I ran out of the room and down the stairs, ignoring Rhiannon's sleepy "What the fuck?" as I slammed the door behind me. Downstairs, my heart hammering in my chest, I opened Petra's bedroom door, the wood shushing on the thick carpet, and waited for my eyes to get adjusted to the dim light.

She was there, quite asleep, her arms and legs flung out, and I felt my pulse rate calm, just a little, but I had to check on the others before I could relax.

Down the corridor then, to the door marked Princess Ellie and Queen Maddie.

It was shut, and I turned the handle very softly, pushing gently. It was pitch-black inside without the night-light, the blackout curtains shutting out even the moonlight, and I cursed myself for forgetting to switch it on, but when my eyes got used to the darkness, I could hear the faint sound of snores, and I felt my breath coming a little more easily. Thank God. Thank God they were okay.

I tiptoed across the thick carpet and felt along the wall for the lead to the night-light, followed it back to the switch, and then I switched it on. And there they were, Ellie scrunched into a tight little ball as though trying to hide from something, Maddie scooched down under the duvet so that I could see nothing except her shape beneath the covers.

My panic calmed as I turned back to the door, laughing at myself for my paranoia.

And then . . . I stopped.

It was ridiculous, I knew that, but I just had to check, I had to *see* . . .

I tiptoed across the carpet and drew back the cover. To find . . .

. . . a pillow, pushed into the curved shape of a sleeping child.

My heart began to race sickeningly hard.

The first thing I did was check under the bed. Then all the cupboards in the room.

"Maddie," I whispered, as loud as I dared, not wanting to wake Ellie but hearing the panicked urgency in my own voice. "Maddie?"

But there was no answering sound, not even a stifled giggle. Just nothing. Nothing.

I ran out of the room.

"Maddie?" I called louder this time. I rattled the handle of the bathroom, but it was unlocked, and when the door swung open I saw its emptiness, the moonlight streaming across the bare tiles.

"Maddie?"

Nothing in Sandra and Bill's bedroom either, just the unruffled smoothness of the bed, the moonlit expanse of carpet, the white columns of the open curtains standing sentinel either side of the tall windows. I flung open the closets, but the faint illumination of the automatic lights showed nothing but neat rows of suits and racks of high heels.

"What is it?" Rhiannon's sleepy voice came from upstairs. "What the fuck's going on?"

"It's Maddie," I called up, trying to keep the panic out of my voice. "She's not in bed. Can you look upstairs? Maddie!"

Petra was stirring now, woken by my increasingly loud calls, and I heard her crotchety grumble, preparatory to a full-on wail, but I didn't stop to comfort her. I *had* to find Maddie. Had she come downstairs to find me when I was with Jack? The thought gave me an unpleasant lurch, followed by another, even more unpleasant.

Had she— Oh God. Had she possibly *followed* me? I had left the back door unlocked. Could she have gone looking for me in the grounds?

Horrible visions ran through my mind. The pond. The stream. Even the road.

Ignoring Petra, I ran down the stairs, shoved my feet into the first pair of Wellingtons I found at the back door, and ran out into the moonlight.

The cobbled yard was empty.

"Maddie!" I called, full-throated, desperate now, hearing my voice echo from the stone walls of the stables and back to the house. "Maaaddie? Where are you?"

There was no answer, and I had a sudden, even more horrible thought, worse than the forest clearing, with the treacherously muddy pond.

The poison garden.

The poison garden left unlocked and unguarded by Jack Grant.

It had already killed one little girl.

Dear God, I prayed, as I began to sprint towards the back of the house, towards the path down through the shrubbery, my feet slipping in the too-big Wellingtons. Please let it not claim another.

But as I rounded the corner of the house, I found her.

She was lying crumpled facedown below my bedroom window, sprawled across the cobblestones in her nightdress, the white cotton soaked through and through with blood, so much blood I would never have imagined her small body could hold it all.

It ran across the cobbles like treacle, thick and sticky, slicking my knees as I knelt in it, clinging to my fingers as I picked her up, cradling her, feeling the birdlike fragility of her little bones, begging her, pleading with her to be okay.

But of course it was impossible.

She would never be okay again. Nothing would.

She was quite, quite dead.

The next few hours are the ones that the police have made me go over again and again, like nails scratching and scratching at a wound, making it bleed afresh every time. And yet, even after all their questions, the memories only come in snatches, like a night illuminated by flashes of lightning, with darkness in between.

I remember screaming, holding Maddie's body for what felt like the longest time, until first Jack came, and then Rhiannon, holding a wailing Petra in her arms, almost dropping her when she saw the horror of what had happened.

I remember her wail, that awful sound, as she saw her sister's body. I don't think I will ever forget that.

I remember Jack taking Rhiannon inside and then trying to pull me away, saying she's dead, she's dead, we can't disturb the body, Rowan, we have to leave her for the police, and I couldn't let her go, I could only weep and cry.

I remember the flashing blue lights of the police at the gate, and Rhiannon's face, white and stricken as she tried to comprehend.

And I remember sitting there, covered in blood on the velvet sofa, as they asked me what happened, what happened, what happened.

And I still don't know.

I still don't know, Mr. Wrexham, and that's the truth.

I know what the police think, from the questions they asked, and the scenarios they put to me.

They think that Maddie went up to my room to find me missing, and that she saw something incriminating up there—perhaps she went to the window and saw me creeping back from Jack's flat. Or perhaps they think she found something in my belongings, something to do with my real name, my true identity.

I don't know. I had so much to hide, after all.

And they think that I came back to find her there, and realized what she had seen, and that I opened the window and that—

I can't say it. It's hard even to write it. But I have to.

They think that I threw her out. They think that I stood there, with the curtains blowing wide, and watched her bleed to death on the cobblestones, and then went back downstairs to drink tea, and wait calmly for Rhiannon to come home.

They think that I left the window open deliberately, to try to make it seem like she could have fallen. But they are sure that she didn't. I am not certain why—I think it's something to do with the position of where she landed—too far away from the building to be a slip, with an arc that could only have been caused by a push, or a jump.

Would Maddie have jumped? That's a question I have asked myself a thousand, maybe a million times.

And the truth is, I just don't know.

We may never know. Because the irony is, Mr. Wrexham, in a house filled with a dozen cameras, there are none that show what happened to Maddie that night. The camera in her room shows nothing but darkness. It points away from the door, at the girls' beds, so there is not even a silhouette in the doorway to show what time Maddie left.

And as for my room . . . oh God . . . as for my room, that is one of the bricks in the edifice of evidence the police built against me.

"Why did you cover the security camera in your room if you had nothing to hide?" they kept asking me again, and again, and again.

And I tried to tell them—to explain what it's like to be a young woman, alone, in a strange house, with strangers watching you. I tried to tell them how I was okay with a camera in the kitchen, the den, the living room, the corridors, even with cameras in the girls' rooms. But that I needed somewhere, just one place, where I could be myself, unwatched, unmonitored. Where I could be not Rowan but Rachel—just for a few hours.

"Would you want a camera in your bedroom?" I asked the detective, point-blank, but he just shrugged as if to say, *It's not me on trial, love.*

But the truth is, I did cover up that camera. And if I hadn't, we might know what happened to Maddie.

Because, I *didn't* kill her, Mr. Wrexham. I know I've said that already. I told you in the very first letter I sent you. I didn't kill her, and you have to believe me, because it's the truth. But I don't know, writing these words in my cramped cell, with the Scottish rain drizzling down the window outside . . . Have I convinced you? How I wish I could persuade you to come here. I've put you on my list of visitors. You could come tomorrow, even. And I could look into your eyes and tell you—I didn't kill her.

But I didn't convince the police of that. I didn't convince Mr. Gates either.

In the end, I'm not sure I even convince myself.

For if I hadn't left her that night, if I hadn't spent those hours with Jack, in his flat, in his arms, none of this would have happened.

I didn't kill her, but her death is on my hands. My little sister.

If you didn't kill her, who did? Help us out here, Rachel. Tell us what you think happened, the police asked, again and again, and I could only shake my head. Because the truth is, Mr. Wrexham, I don't know. I have constructed a thousand theories—each wilder than the other. Maddie, leaping like a bird into the night; Rhiannon, coming back early from her night out somehow; Jean McKenzie, hiding in the attic; Jack Grant, creeping past me while I was waiting downstairs for Rhiannon.

Because Jack turned out to have secrets too, did you know that? Nothing as grand or melodramatic as what I had imagined—he wasn't related to Dr. Kenwick Grant, or at least if he was, neither he nor the police managed to trace the link. And when I told the police about the hank of string in his kitchen and the *Aconitum napellus* blossom, he, unlike me, had a quick and reasonable explanation. Because Jack, it seemed, had recognized the purple flower sitting in the coffee cup on the kitchen table—or thought he had. And so he had taken it with him to compare it to the plants in the poison garden. When he discovered that what he had suspected was correct, that the flower in the kitchen was not just poisonous but deadly, he had removed my makeshift string barrier, and replaced it with a padlock and chain.

No, Jack's deep, dark secret was much more mundane than that. And instead of exonerating me, it only piled up the evidence against me—adding to the weight of reasons I might have wanted to cover up my liaison with him.

Jack was married.

When they realized I didn't know, the police took great delight in ramming the fact home, reminding me at every possible opportunity, as if they wanted to see me wince with pain afresh each time. But the truth was, I was beyond caring. What did it matter, if Jack already had a wife and a two-year-old back in Edinburgh? He had promised me nothing. And in the face of Maddie's death, none of it seemed important.

I would be lying though if I said that in the days and weeks and months since I've been in here I haven't thought of him and wondered why. Why hadn't he told me about her? About his little boy?

Why were they living apart? Was it financial—was he sending money back to them? If the Elincourts were paying him half as much as they'd offered me, it was more than plausible that he'd taken the job for money reasons.

But maybe not. Perhaps they were separated, estranged. Perhaps she'd thrown him out, and this offer of a job, with a flat attached, had been the perfect way to move on.

I don't know, because I never had the chance to ask him. I never saw him again, after I was taken down to the station for questioning, and then cautioned, and then remanded in custody. He never wrote. He never phoned. He never visited.

The last time I saw him was as I stumbled into the back of a police car, still covered in Maddie's blood, feeling his hands gripping mine, strong and steady.

"It'll be all right, Rowan." It was the last thing he said to me, the last words I heard as the car door slammed shut behind me and the engine started up.

It was a lie. A lie, from first to last. I was not Rowan. And nothing was ever going to be all right again.

But the thing I keep coming back to is what Maddie said to me that very first time I met her, her arms wrapped hard around me, her face buried in my top.

Don't come here, she had said. *It's not safe.*

And then, those last words, sobbed in parting, and later denied, words that I am still certain I heard, months later.

The ghosts wouldn't like it.

I don't believe in ghosts, Mr. Wrexham. I never have. I'm not a superstitious person.

But it was not superstition that I heard pacing the attic above me, night after night. It was not superstition that made me wake in the night, shivering, my breath white clouds in the moonlight, my room cold as an icebox. That doll's head, rolling across the Persian rug, that was real, Mr. Wrexham. Real as you and me. Real as the writing on the walls of the attic, real as my writing to you now.

Because I know, I know that's when I really sealed my fate with the police. It wasn't just the fake name, and the stolen documents. It wasn't just the fact that I was Bill's estranged daughter, come back to exact some sort of twisted revenge on his new family. It wasn't any of that.

It was what I told them on that first awful night, sitting there in my bloodstained clothes, shaking with shock and grief and terror. Because that first night, I broke down and told them everything that had happened. From the footsteps in the night, to the deep, seeping sense of evil I felt when I opened the attic door and stepped inside.

That, more than anything that came after, was the moment the key turned in the lock.

That was when they *knew*.

I've had a lot of time to think in here, Mr. Wrexham. A lot of time to think, and ponder, and figure things out since I started this letter to you. I told the police the truth, and the truth undid me. I know what they saw—a crazed woman, with a backstory more full of holes than a bullet-pocked signpost. They saw a woman with a motive. A woman so estranged from her family that she had come to their house under false pretenses, to enact some terrible, unhinged vengeance.

I know what I think happened. I have had a long time to put pieces together—the open window, the footsteps in the attic, the father who loved his daughter so much that it killed her, and the father who walked away from his children again and again and again.

And most of all, two pieces I never connected right up until the very end—the phone, and Maddie's white, pleading little face, that very first day as I drove away, and her whispered, anguished *the ghosts wouldn't like it.* And those two things were what did it for me with the police. My fingerprints on the phone, and my account of what Maddie had said to me, and the domino of effects her words began.

But at the end of the day, it doesn't matter what I think, or what my theories are. It's what the jury thinks that matters. Listen, Mr. Wrexham, I don't need you to believe everything that I've told you. And I know that presenting even half of what I've said here would get you laughed out of court, and risk alienating the jury forever. That's not why I told you all this.

But I tried to give just part of the story before—and it's what got me locked up here.

I believe that the truth is what will save me, Mr. Wrexham, and the truth is that I didn't, that I *couldn't* kill my sister.

I picked you, Mr. Wrexham, because when I asked the other women in here who I should get to represent me, your name came up more than any other lawyer. Apparently you've got a reputation for getting even no-hopers off the hook.

And I know that's what I am, Mr. Wrexham. I have no hope anymore.

A child is dead, and the police, and the public, and the press, they all want someone to pay. And that someone must be me.

But I didn't kill that little girl, Mr. Wrexham. I didn't kill Maddie.

I loved her. And I don't want to rot in jail for something I didn't do.

Please, *please* believe me.

Yours truly,

Rachel Gerhardt.

8th July 2019

Richard McAdams

Ashdown Construction Services, internal post.

Rich, bit of a funny one, one of the guys working on the Charnworth redevelopment found this pile of old papers when he was ripping out a wall. Looks like one of the prisoners hid them. He didn't know what to do with them, so he passed them to me and I said I'd ask around. I've only glanced at the top few, but looks to be a bunch of letters from an inmate to her solicitor before her trial—don't know why they were never posted. The guy who found them leafed through, and says it was quite a well-known case; he's a local from round here, and he remembered the headlines.

Anyway, he felt a bit awkward chucking them in the skip in case they were evidence or legally privileged or something and he ended up on the wrong side of the law by destroying them. TBH, I don't imagine it matters now—but to put his mind at rest, I said I'd see it was properly dealt with. Is there anyone in management you could sound out about it? Or do you think just ignore and bin? Don't want to get tied up in a load of paperwork.

The top part is her letters to the lawyer, but she'd also hidden a few letters written to her in the same place. They seem to be just family stuff, but I'm sticking them in the packet as well, just in case.

Anyway, be very grateful if I could leave it with you to decide what to do, if anything.

Cheers,

Phil

1st November 2017

Dear Rachel,

Well. It feels very strange addressing you by that name, but here we are.

I must start by saying how sorry I am about what happened. I imagine that's not what you expected me to say, but I am, and I'm not ashamed to say it.

What you must understand is that I have watched over those children for the best part of five years now—and I've watched more nannies come and go than I've had hot dinners. I was the one who had to sit and watch while that baggage Holly carried on with Mr. Elincourt under his wife's nose, and I was the one who patched everything up when she walked out and left the girls in bits. And since then, I've had to sit there and watch as nanny after nanny came and went, and broke those poor bairns' hearts a bit more every time.

And every time they came, and they were another pretty young lass, I felt it like a cold hand around my heart and I lay awake at night and I wondered—should I tell Mrs. Elincourt what kind of a man her husband was, and what kind of a woman that Holly was, and why she really left? And every time I found I couldn't do it, and I swallowed my anger, and I told myself it would be different next time.

So I confess, when I met you, and found out that Mrs. Elincourt had hired yet another pretty young girl, my heart sank. Because I knew what he would be up to, and whatever kind of girl you were, whether you were one to make the most of your opportunities, like Holly, or one who shrank from him, I knew either way those poor children would be the ones to suffer again when you upped and left, maybe taking him with you this time. And that made me very angry. Yes it did. I'm not ashamed to say that. But I am ashamed of how I treated you—I should not have taken my anger out on you like that, and I feel heart sorry when I think back on some of the things I said to you. Because whatever the police say, I know that you would have walked a mile over glass before you hurt one of those little lassies, and I told the officer who interviewed me so, I wanted you to know that. I said, I did not like that girl, and I made no secret of it, but she would not have hurt wee Maddie, and you are barking up the wrong tree, young man.

So anyway, that is partly why I am writing. To say all of that to you, and get it off my chest.

But the other reason is because Ellie has written you a letter. She put it in an envelope and sealed it up before she gave it to me, and she made me promise not to read it, and I said I would not. I have kept that promise, because I think you should keep your word, even to children, but I must ask you, if there is anything in that letter you think I should know, or anything that you think her mother should know, you must tell us.

There is no point in writing to the house, for it is shut up, and God knows Mrs. Elincourt has enough on her plate to worry about, poor woman. She has left her husband, did the police tell you that? She has taken the children and moved back down south to her own family. And Mr. Elincourt has moved away too—there is some sort of lawsuit against him connected with an intern at his firm, or so they are saying in the village, and the rumor is that the house will have to be sold to pay for the legal fees.

But I am putting my address at the bottom of this letter, and I ask that if you have any concerns, you write to me there, and I will do whatever needs to be done. I have faith that you will do that, for I believe that you loved those children, as I did and do. I don't believe you will let any harm come to Ellie, will you? I have prayed to God, and tried to listen to His answer, and I am trusting you on this, Rachel. I pray that you won't let me down.

Yours very sincerely,
Jean McKenzie
15a High Street
Carn Bridge

From:

To:

Subject:

Dave Owen only they said that your name is Rachel is that true

I miss you a lot and I am fairy very sorry about what happened especially because it's all my fault but I can't tell anyone especially not mummy or Daddy because they will be so angry and then daddy will go away like he tried to before like Maddie always said he would

it was me Rowan I pushed mad he because she was going to make you go away like the others she made all the others go away by playing tricks with Mummy's old phone she took their things and she kind into the Attic window up the roof from your room the Attic was her secret den where she always went but she said I was too little to climb up and the she made the happy wake them up in the night and she took a YouTube video and played it on the speakers on the happy to make it sound like there was people in the Attic walking around but it wasn't it was just the video and she took the dollies head out of the attic and she made me put the doggies head on your lap and I am so sorry because I said it wasn't true and it was it was me who did that

she woke up and you weren't there and mad he was going to poison you with you berries but I ran after her and I poured the wine down the sink and then Maddie was fairy angry and she said she said she was going to climb into the attic window again and get you into trouble with Mummy by setting off all the alarms because you had gone and I ran after her an eye asked not to do it and she said no I will do it or she will take Daddy away and I said no don't Rowan with nice and I don't want her to go she wouldn't do that and mad he said I'm going to a new can't stop me and she kind up and I pushed her I didn't mean for 2 happen and I am so sorry

please please please don't tell the police Rowan I don't want to go to prison and I am so sorry but it isn't fair for you to get told off for a thing I did so can you just say that it wasn't you and that you know who did it but you can't say who because it's a secret but it wasn't you

we are going away tomorrow to a new house daddy can't come right now but I hope you can I love you please come back soon love Ellie elancourt age 5 goodbye

Acknowledgments

Thank you so much to the tireless team of editors, publicists, marketers, designers, sales reps, rights people, production editors, and everyone who works behind the scenes. That the book you hold in your hands is beautiful, readable, and exists at all is largely down to their efforts.

To Alison, Liz, Jade, Sara, Jen, Aimée, Brita, Noor, Meagan, Bethan, Catherine, Nita, Kevin, Richard, Faye, Rachel, Sophie, Mackenzie, Christian, Chloe, Anabel, Abby, Mikaela, Tom, Christina, Monique, Jane, Jennifer, Chelsea, Kathy, Carolyn and everyone at Simon & Schuster and PRH, my heartfelt thanks.

Thanks also to Mason, Susi, and Stephanie for being the very best readers.

To Eve and Ludo, guardian ninjas, thank you for always having my back.

To my fabulous writer friends—online and off—thank you for keeping me sane and laughing.

And of course to my family—thank you for being there, and for not making me live in a smart house.

BOOK CLUB FAVORITES

READER'S GUIDE

THE TURN OF THE KEY

RUTH WARE

This reader's guide for The Turn of the Key *includes an introduction, discussion questions, and ideas for enhancing your book club. The suggested questions are intended to help your reading group find new and interesting angles and topics for your discussion. We hope that these ideas will enrich your conversation and increase your enjoyment of the book*

Introduction

When she stumbles across the ad, she's looking for something else completely. But it seems like too good an opportunity to miss—a live-in nanny post, with a staggeringly generous salary. And when Rowan Caine arrives at Heatherbrae House, she is smitten—by the luxurious "smart" home fitted out with all modern conveniences, by the beautiful Scottish Highlands, and by this picture-perfect family.

What she doesn't know is that she's stepping into a nightmare—one that will end with a child dead and herself in prison awaiting trial for murder.

Writing to her lawyer from prison, she struggles to explain the unraveling events that led to her incarceration. It wasn't just the constant surveillance from the cameras installed around the house, or the malfunctioning technology that woke the household with booming music, or turned the lights off at the worst possible time. It wasn't just the girls, who turned out to be a far cry from the immaculately behaved model children she met at her interview. It wasn't even the way she was left alone for weeks at a time, with no adults around apart from the enigmatic handyman, Jack Grant.

It was everything.

She knows she's made mistakes. She admits that she lied to obtain the post, and that her behavior toward the children wasn't always ideal. She's not innocent, by any means. But, she maintains, she's not guilty—at least not of murder. Which means someone else is.

Topics and Questions for Discussion

1. The book opens with Rowan Caine's desperate plea for help from prison. If you received this letter as Mr. Wrexham, would you keep reading? Is there anything she could say that would persuade you to represent her?

2. Rowan describes the Elincourt estate in detail when she visits for her interview. What is your first impression of the house? What aspects were appealing or unappealing to you?

3. The interview with Sandra is standard but revealing. What do we learn about Rowan as she tries to come up with the perfect answers? Would you say Rowan is trustworthy? What do you learn about Sandra during this initial interaction?

4. Maddie, the second oldest girl, has an unexpected reaction to Rowan's departure and makes a terrifying proclamation: "Don't come here. It's not safe" (p. 74). After everything Rowan saw and learned in the previous twenty-four hours, should she have heeded Maddie's warning? Would you have listened to Maddie?

5. Rowan has a very negative first impression of Bill Elincourt and their relationship only gets worse from there. Why is her initial reaction so strong? How would you handle the ensuing harassment by an employer?

6. Sandra and Bill leave Rowan on her first day with the kids and she struggles to reign them all in. Discuss the kids' behavior and

how Sandra's constant check-ins affect Rowan's authority in the house. Look specifically at the interactions on page 131 and 158.

7. Rowan believes she is finally building a relationship with Maddie and Ellie when they show her their secret garden. But when their malicious intent is exposed, Rowan, Maddie, and Ellie all react intensely. Describe each of their reactions and the emotions behind them.

8. After the house goes haywire in the middle of the night, Rowan is sleep-deprived, on edge, and paranoid, and she jumps to several rash conclusions. Are these thoughts reasonable possibilities or delusions based in fear? Imagine how you might respond in her situation.

9. The Elincourts' housekeeper, Jean McKenzie, immediately dislikes Rowan, but it seems to run deeper than their negative first encounter. Why? Could Jean be the one tormenting Rowan at night, as she suspects?

10. Rowan is deeply disturbed by the girl in Maddie's drawing. "Tears were streaming down her face, her mouth was open in a despairing wail, and there were red scribbles of blood on her face and on her dress" (p. 228). What do you think it represents? Do you think Rowan should have addressed this directly?

11. When Jack and Rowan break into the attic, it is much worse than they expected. Discuss their ensuing conversation. What answers does Rowan have now and what questions remain? How do you think the doll head came to be in Rowan's lap?

12. Rowan's opinion of Jack changes repeatedly in her short time at Heatherbrae. He began as her confidant, became her lead sus-

pect, and finally seemed to earn her trust. Do you think he is trustworthy? Why or why not?

13. We finally learn who Rachel Gerhardt is and of her personal connection to the family. Were there any clues that led you to suspect this before the big reveal? Do you believe Rachel's version of events as she explains them to Mr. Wrexham?

14. In the last chapter, the truth of what happened to Maddie is finally revealed. How does Ellie's letter align with Rachel's retelling of that night? What, if any, questions remain?

Enhance Your Book Club

1. The entire book is written as a letter to a defense attorney from prison. Discuss how this adds to or detracts from the story. How did you feel knowing a child would die from the beginning? Did it ruin the element of surprise or elevate the feeling of suspense?

2. We see Rachel in many high-pressure, stressful situations during her time at Heatherbrae House. How would you have described her character before learning the truth about her father? Did learning the truth change what you thought of her? Discuss.

3. Discuss Heatherbrae House and its many "amenities." What it would be like to live in a house dependent on technology? Could you live there?

4. The story jumps from 2017 to 2019, when the letters to Mr. Wrexham and those from Jean McKenzie and Ellie are discovered. The man who found them reveals two important details. First, that Rachel never sent her pleas for help and second, that the truth they reveal no longer matters. Discuss why the letters never posted and what happened to Rachel in those two years.

TURN THE PAGE FOR AN EXCLUSIVE SNEAK PEEK OF RUTH WARE'S HIGHLY ANTICIPATED SIXTH NOVEL,

ONE BY ONE

COMING SEPTEMBER 2020 FROM SCOUT PRESS

From the “About Us” page of the Snoop company website.

Hey. We’re snoop. Come meet us, message us, snoop on us—whatever. We’re pretty cool. Are you?

Topher St. Clair-Bridges

Who’s the daddy? Well, if anyone’s got a claim, it’s Toph. snoop cofounder (along with ex-girlfriend, model/artist/professional badass @evalution), it all started here. If he’s not at his desk, he’s probably riding the moguls in Chamonix, losing his mind in Berlin’s Berghain, or just hangin’. Come find him on snoop at @xtopher or hit him up via his PA, Inigo Ryder—the only dude who gets to tell Topher what to do.

Listening to: Oscar Mulero / Like a Wolf

Eva van den Berg

From Amsterdam to Sydney, New York to London, Eva’s career has taken her all over the world—but right now home is Shoreditch, London, where she lives with her husband, financier Arnaud Jankovitch, and their daughter, Radisson. In 2010 she cofounded snoop with her then life partner @xtopher—their idea born of a single desire: to maintain their connection across 5,000 kilometers of ocean. Topher and Eva have since uncoupled, but their connection remains: snoop. Make your own connection with Eva on @evalution, or via her personal assistant, Ani Cresswell.

Listening to: Nico / Janitor of Lunacy

Rik Adeyemi

head of beans

Rik's the money man, the bean counter, the keeper of the keys—you get the picture. He's been keepin' snoop real since the very first days, and he's known Toph for even longer. What can we say? snoop's a family affair. Rik lives with his wife, Veronique, in Highgate, London. You can snoop him at @rikshaw.

Listening to: Willie Bobo / La Descarga del Bobo

Elliot Cross

chief nerd

Music may be snoop's beating heart, but code is its DNA and Elliot is the maestro of code. Before snoop was a hot-pink logo on your phone, it was just lines of java in someone's head—and that someone was Elliot. Best friends with Toph since before they could shave, he's cooler than any techhead has a right to be. snoop him at @ex.

Listening to: Kraftwerk / Autobahn

Miranda Khan

friends czar

Miranda is into killer heels, sharp fashion, and really *great* coffee. Between savoring Guatemalan carbonic maceration and surfing Net-a-Porter, she's snoop's smile to the world. Wanna write us up, hit us up, haul us over the coals, or just say hi? Miranda's the place to start. snoop knows you can never have enough followers—or enough friends. Make Miranda one of yours at @mirandelicious.

Listening to: Madonna / 4 Minutes

Tiger-Blue Esposito

head of cool

The epitome of chill, Tiger keeps her trademark zen state with the help of daily yoga, mindfulness and—of course—a steady stream of snoop through her oversize headphones. When she's not pulling a bhujapidasana or relaxing into an anantasana (that's a side reclining leg lift to the uninitiated), she's polishing snoop's cogs to make sure we look our very best and getting the word out. Chill with her on @blueskythinking.

Listening to: Jai-Jagdeesh / Aad Guray Nameh

Carl Foster

lawman

There's no two ways about it—Carl keeps us on the straight and narrow, making sure that wherever we snoop, we're doing it on the right side of the law. Trained at University College London, Carl did his pupillage at Gray's Inn. Since then he's worked in a variety of international firms, mostly in the entertainment industry. He lives in Croydon. snoop him on @carlfoster1972.

Listening to: The Rolling Stones / Sympathy for the Devil

Taken from the BBC News website:

Thursday, 16th January

4 BRITONS DEAD IN SKI RESORT TRAGEDY

The exclusive French ski resort of St Antoine was rocked by news of a second tragedy this week, only days after an avalanche that killed six and left much of the region without power for days.

Now, reports are emerging that in one remote ski chalet, cut off by the avalanche, a "house of horror" situation was unfolding, leaving four Britons dead, and two hospitalised.

The alarm was only raised when survivors trekked more than three miles through the snow to radio for help, raising questions of why the French authorities did not work to re-establish power and mobile phone coverage more quickly following Sunday's avalanche.

Local police chief Etienne Dupont refused to comment, except to say that "an investigation is in progress," but a spokesperson at the British embassy in Paris said, "We can confirm that we have been informed of the deaths of four British citizens in the Savoie department of the French Alps and that the local police are treating these incidents as a linked murder enquiry at this stage. Our sympathies are with the friends and families of the victims."

The families of the deceased have been informed.

Eight survivors, also thought to be British, are said to be helping the police investigation.

This year has been marked by unusually heavy snowfalls. Sunday's avalanche is the sixth since the beginning of the ski season and brings the total of fatalities in the region to twelve.

Five Days Earlier

Liz

Snoop ID: ANON101
Listening to: James Blunt / You're Beautiful
Snoopers: 0
Snoopscribers: 0

I keep my earbuds shoved into my ears on the minibus from Geneva Airport. I ignore Topher's hopeful looks and Eva, glancing over her shoulder at me. It helps, somehow. It helps to shut out the voices in my head, their voices, pulling me this way and that, pummeling me with their loyalties and their arguments to and fro.

Instead, I let James Blunt drown them out, telling me I'm beautiful, over and over again. The irony of the statement makes me want to laugh, but I don't. There's something comforting in the lie.

It is 1:52 p.m. Outside the window the sky is iron gray, and the snowflakes swirl hypnotically past. It's strange. Snow is so white on the ground, but when it's falling, it looks gray against the sky. It might as well be ash.

We are starting to climb now. The snow gets thicker as we gain height, no longer melting into rain when it hits the window, but sticking, sliding along the glass, the windshield wipers swooshing it aside into rivulets of slush that run horizontally across the passenger window. I hope the bus has snow tires.

The driver changes gear; we are approaching yet another hairpin bend. As the bus swings around the narrow curve, the ground falls away, and I have a momentary feeling that we're going to fall—a lurch of vertigo that makes my stomach heave and my head spin. I shut my eyes, blocking them all out, losing myself in the music.

And then the song stops.

And I am alone, with only one voice left in my head, and I can't shut it out. It's my own. And it's whispering a question that I've been asking myself since the plane lifted off the runway at Gatwick.

Why did I come? *Why?*

But I know the answer.

I came because I couldn't afford not to.

Erin

Snoop ID: N/A
Listening to: N/A
Snoopers: N/A
Snoopscribers: N/A

The snow is *still* falling—fat white flakes drifting lazily down to lie softly over the peaks and pistes and valleys of St. Antoine.

Three meters have fallen in the last couple of weeks, and there's more forecast. A snowpocalypse, Danny called it. Snowmaggedon. Lifts have been closed, and then reopened, and then closed again. Currently almost every lift in the entire resort is closed, but the faithful little funicular that leads up to our tiny hamlet is still chugging away. It's glassed in, so even the heaviest dump doesn't affect it, the snow just lies like a blanket over the tunnel rather than clogging the rails. Which is good—because on the rare occasions it does shut, we're totally cut off. There's no road up to St. Antoine 2000, not in winter, anyway. Everything, from the guests in the chalet, right through to every scrap of food for breakfast, lunch, and dinner, has to come up in the funicular. Unless you've got the money for a helicopter transfer (which, believe me, is not unheard of in this place). But the helicopters won't fly in poor conditions. If a blizzard comes in, they stay safely down in the valley.

It gives me a strange feeling if I think about it too much—a kind of claustrophobia that's at odds with the wide-open vistas from the chalet. It's not just the snow; it's a hundredweight of unwelcome memories bearing down on me. If I stop for more than a minute or two, the images start to come unbidden, crowding into my mind—numb fingers scrabbling through hard-packed snow, the sheen of sunset on blue skin, the glint of frosted lashes. But fortunately I've got no time to stop today. It's past one o'clock and I'm still cleaning the second-to-last bedroom when I hear the shuddering sound of the gong from downstairs. It's Danny. He shouts my name and then something I can't make out.

"What?" I call down, and he shouts again, his voice clearer this time. He must have come out into the stairwell.

"I *said*, 'Grub's up.' Truffled parsnip soup. So get your lazy arse down here."

"Yes, chef," I shout back mockingly. I quickly dump the contents of the bathroom bin into my black sack, change the liner, and then jog down the spiral stairs to the lobby, where the delicious smell of Danny's soup greets me, along with the sound of "Venus in Furs" emanating from the kitchen.

Saturday is both the best day of the week and the worst. Best, because it's changeover day—there are no guests, and Danny and I have the chalet to ourselves, free to laze in the pool, steam in the outdoor hot tub, and play the music we like at the volume we want.

Worst, because it's changeover day, which means nine double beds to change, nine bathrooms to clean (eleven, if you count the loo downstairs and the shower room by the pool), eighteen ski lockers to sweep and Hoover, not to mention the living room, the dining room, the den, the snug and the outdoor smoking area, where I have to pick up all the disgusting butts the smokers always strew around in spite of the prominent bins and buckets. At least Danny takes care of the kitchen, though he has his own to-do list. Saturday night is always a big dinner. Got to put on a show for the new guests, don't you know.

Now, we sit down together at the big dining room table, and I read through the information Kate emailed this morning as I spoon Danny's delicious soup into my mouth. It's sweet and earthy, and there are tiny little crunchy bits scattered over the top—shaved parsnip roasted in truffle oil, I think.

"This soup is really good," I say. I know my role here. Danny rolls his eyes, in a *Well, duh* gesture. If there is one thing about Danny, he's not modest. But he is a good cook.

"Think they'll like it tonight?" He's fishing for more compliments of course, but I can't blame him. Danny's an unashamed diva about his food and, like any artiste, he enjoys appreciation.

"I'm sure they will. It's gorgeous, really warming and . . . um . . . complex." I am striving to pin down the particular savory quality that makes the soup so good. Danny likes compliments to be *specific.* "Like autumn in a bowl. What else are you doing?"

"I've got amuse-bouches." Danny ticks the courses off on his fingers. "Then the truffled soup for starter. Then venison haunch for the carnies and mushroom ravioli for the veggies. Then crème brûlée for dessert. And then the cheese."

Danny's crème brûlée is his showstopper, and it's to die for. I've literally seen guests come to blows over a spare portion.

"Sounds perfect," I say encouragingly.

"As long as there aren't any fucking stealth vegans this time," he says morosely. He's still reeling from last week, when one of the guests turned out to be not just vegan but gluten intolerant as well. I don't think he's forgiven Kate yet.

"Kate was *really* clear," I say, cajoling. "One lactose intolerant, one gluten-free, three veggies. No vegans. That's it."

"It won't be," Danny says, still enjoying his martyrdom. "One of them will be low-carbing or something. Or a fruitarian. Or a breatharian."

"Well, if they're a breatharian, they won't be bothering you, will they?" I say reasonably. "They've got all the air they could want up here."

I wave an arm at the huge window that dominates the south side of the room. It overlooks the peaks and ridges of the Alps, a panorama so breathtaking that even though I live here now, I still find myself stopping mid stride on certain days, almost winded by its beauty. Today the visibility is poor, the clouds are low, and there's too much snow in the air. But on a good day you can see almost to Lake Geneva. Behind us, to the northeast of the chalet, rises the Dame Blanche, the mountain that forms the highest peak of the St. Antoine valley, overshadowing everything.

"Read out the names," Danny says, around a mouthful of soup, only he says it more like *read aht the names*. His accent is pure sarf London, though I know in reality he grew up in Portsmouth. I'm never quite sure how much is all part of the act. Danny's a performer, and the more I get to know him, the more I'm fascinated by the complicated mix of identities beneath the surface. The cheeky Cockney geezer he puts on for the guests is just one of them. On nights out in St. Antoine I've seen him pivot from note-perfect Guy Ritchie to a gloriously flaming RuPaul, all in the space of five minutes.

Not that I can talk. I'm putting on my own act. We all are on some level, I suppose. That's one of the joys of coming here, to a place like this, where everyone is passing through. You get to have a fresh start.

"I need to get it right this time," he says, breaking into my thoughts. He puts a minuscule grind of fresh black pepper onto his soup and tastes it, then looks approving. "Can't afford another fucking Madeleine. Kate'll have my guts for garters."

Kate is the area rep, and is in charge of coordinating all the bookings and logistics for all six of the company's chalets. She likes us to greet the clients by their names right from day one. It's what marks us out from the big chain operators, she says. The personal touch. Only it's harder than it sounds, week in, week out. Last week Danny made friends with a woman called Madeleine, only when the feedback forms came in, it turned out there was no one called Madeleine in the group. Or any woman with a name beginning with *M*. He's still got no idea who he was talking to all week.

I run my finger down the list Kate sent through last night.

"So it's a corporate party this time. Tech company called Snoop. Nine people, all in separate rooms. Eva van den Berg, cofounder. Topher St. Clair-Bridges, cofounder. Rik Adeyemi, head of beans. Elliot Cross, chief nerd."

Danny snorts out his soup through his nose, but I carry on.

"Miranda Khan, friends czar. Inigo Ryder, Topher's "boss." Ani Cresswell, chief Eva-tamer. Tiger-Blue Esposito, head of cool. Carl Foster, lawman."

By the time I'm finished, Danny is actually crying with laughter and his soup has gone down the wrong way.

"Is that really what it says?" he manages, between coughs. "Head of beans? Tiger—what the fuck else? I didn't think Kate had a sense of humor. Where's the real list?"

"That *is* the real list," I say, trying not to laugh at the sight of Danny's screwed-up face, shining with tears. "Have a napkin."

"What? Are you shitting me?" he gasps, and then sits back, fanning himself. "Actually, I take that back. Snoop's that sort of place."

"You've heard of them?" I'm surprised. Danny isn't normally the sort of person with his finger on the button that way. We get all sorts here, lots of private parties, the odd wedding or anniversary, but a surprising number of corporate retreats too—I guess the price tag is easier to swallow if your company is paying. There's a lot of law firms, hedge funds, and Fortune 500 companies. This is the first time Danny's heard of one of the companies and I haven't. "What do they do?"

"Snoop?" Now it's Danny's turn to look surprised. "Have you been living in a fucking cave, Erin?"

"No, I'm just—I've never heard of them. Are they a media company?" I don't know why I chose that. Media seems like the kind of industry that would have a Tiger-Blue Esposito.

"No, they're an app." Danny looks at me suspiciously. "Have you *really* not heard of them? You know—Snoop—the music app. It lets you—well, snoop on people. That's kind of it."

"I have literally no idea what you're on about."

"Snoop, Erin," Danny says, more acidly this time, like if he keeps saying it, I'll smack my forehead and go, O*h yeah,* that *Snoop!* He pulls out his phone and scrolls down the apps to one that looks like two eyes on a hot-pink background. Or maybe two cogs, it's hard to see on the logo. He presses it, and the screen goes bright pink, then black, blazoned with *SNOOP. Real people, real time, real loud* in fuchsia letters.

This time the two *o*s of the name are the wheels of a cassette tape.

"You like hook it up to your Spotify account or whatever," Danny explains, scrolling through menus as he does, as if lists of random celebrities will make everything clear. "And it makes your listening public."

"Why would anyone want to do that?" I say blankly.

"It's a quid pro quo, innit," Danny says, sounding impatient. "The whole point is no one wants to listen to you, but if you join, you get to listen to other people. *Voyeurism for your ears* is what Snoop calls it."

"So . . . I can see what . . . I don't know . . . Beyoncé is listening to? If she were on there."

"Yup. And Madonna. And Jay-Z. And Justin Bieber. And whoever else. Celebs love it—it's the new Instagram. It's like, you can connect, yeah? But without actually giving away too much information."

I nod slowly. I can actually kind of see the attraction of that.

"So it's basically famous people's playlists?"

"Not playlists," Danny says. "Because the whole point is that it's real time. You get what they're listening to *right now*."

"What if they're asleep?"

"Then you don't get anything. They don't appear in the search bar if they're not online and listening, and if you're snooping on someone and they stop listening, their feed goes dead and you get the option to shunt along to someone else."

"So if you're snooping on someone and they pause a song to answer the phone—"

Danny nods. "Yeah, it just cuts off."

"That's a really terrible idea."

He laughs and shakes his head. "Nah, you're not getting it. The whole point is . . ." He stops, trying to formulate something unquantifiable into words. "The whole point is the connection. You're actually listening to the same thing at the same moment as they are—beat for beat. You know that wherever she is in the world, Lady Gaga is listening to the exact same thing you are. It's like"—inspiration strikes, and his face lights up—"it's like, you know when you're first going out with someone and you're sharing a set of headphones, one earpiece in their ear, one earpiece in yours?"

I nod.

"Well, it's like that. You and Lady Gaga, sharing her earphones. It's really powerful. When you're lying there in bed, and they switch off, and you know that somewhere they're probably doing the exact same thing as you, rolling over, falling asleep . . . it's pretty intimate, you know? But it's not just celebrities. If you're in a long-distance relationship, say, you can snoop your bloke and listen to the same song at the same time. Assuming you know his Snoop ID of course. I keep mine locked down."

"Okay . . ." I say slowly. "So . . . like . . . your feed is public, but no one knows it's you?"

"Yeah, so I have like two followers, because I've not bothered to hook up any of my contact list. Mind you, some of the most popular Snoopees are totally incognito. There's this one guy in Iran, HacT, he's called. He's in the top ten Snoopees pretty much every month. Well, I say in Iran, but there's no actual way of knowing. That's just what it says on his Snoop biog. He could be from Florida."

An alert pings on his phone, and he brings it up.

"Ah, yeah, see? This is someone I'm subscribed to, Msaggronistic. She's this French-Canadian chick in Montreal, she listens to some really cool punk stuff. That alert was telling me she's come online and she's playing . . ." He scrolls down the notification. "The Slits, apparently. Not sure that's my cup of tea, but that's the thing, it might be. I just don't know."

"Right." I'm not sure I'm any the wiser really, but it's sort of making sense.

"Anyway," Danny says. He gets up and starts clearing our plates. "That's what I meant, these tech start-ups, you could actually imagine them calling their head of finance Chief Bean Counter or whatever the fuck he was called. They'd think it was edgy or something. Coffee?"

I look at my watch—2:17.

"I can't. I've got a couple of rooms still to do, then the pool."

"I'll bring you one up."

I stand and stretch, working the kinks out of my neck and shoulders. It's physical work, cleaning. I never realized how much before I started this job. Heaving Hoovers up and down stairs, scrubbing toilets and tiles. Doing nine rooms on the trot is a workout.

I'm finishing the pool when Danny comes in with a cup of coffee. He's wearing his usual trunks—the smallest, tightest ones I've ever seen in real life. They are banana yellow, and when he turns around to put my coffee down on the lounger, you can see that he has *BAD BOI* written across his butt in scarlet letters.

"Don't make *any* splashes," I warn him, as he stands poised at the edge of the pool, his arms outstretched. "I'm not mopping again."

He says nothing, just sticks out his tongue and then does a perfect, splash-free dive into the shallow end of the pool. It's not really deep enough for diving, but he skims the bottom and comes up safely at the far end.

"Come on, the bloody place is clean enough. Get in."

I waver. I haven't Hoovered the dining room, but I don't know if anyone would be able to tell.

I look at my watch—3:15. The guests are supposed to arrive at 4:00 p.m. I'm cutting it fine.

"Oh, all right, then."

It's our weekly ritual. A ten-minute dip after all the chores are done, like a way of reclaiming our territory, reminding ourselves who's actually in charge in this place.

My bikini is on under my clothes, and I pull off my sweaty T-shirt and stained cleaning jeans and ready myself to dive. I'm just about to push off when I feel a hand grab my ankle and yank me forward, and with a shriek, I pitch into the pool.

I surface, spluttering, raking hair out of my eyes. There is water *everywhere.*

"You fucking imbecile! I said no splashes!"

"Chill," Danny is laughing uproariously, the water like jewels on his dark skin. "I'll mop it, I swear."

"I'll bloody kill you if you don't."

"I'll do it! I said so, didn't I? I'll do it while you dry your hair." He points to his buzz-cut scalp, reminding me that he's got a head start on me in that department.

I punch him on the shoulder, but I can't stay mad at him, and for the next few minutes we swim and wrestle, and fight like puppies, until at last we're both drenched and gasping for air and have to stop to catch our breath.

Danny pulls himself out of the water, grinning and panting, and pads off to the changing room to get dressed and greet the guests.

I should follow him, I know it. There is plenty still left to do, jobs to complete, tasks to finish. But for a moment, just a moment, I let myself float, spread-eagled on the clear blue water. I touch my fingers to the scar that runs across my cheek, tracing the dented line where the skin is thin and still tender, and I gaze up at the gray sky through the glass roof above, watching as the snowflakes come spiraling down.

The sky is the *exact* color of Will's eyes.

The clock is ticking down to the arrival of our guests, and I can hear Danny beginning to mop the changing rooms. I should get out, but I can't. I can't look away. I just lie there, my dark hair fanning out around me, floating, gazing up. Remembering.

PRAISE FOR RUTH WARE'S
INSTANT *NEW YORK TIMES, USA TODAY,* AND
LOS ANGELES TIMES BESTSELLER

THE WOMAN IN CABIN 10

Chosen by librarians as the #1 *LibraryReads* "Favorite of Favorites" for 2016 • A *Skimm Reads* Pick • A finalist in the 2016 Goodreads Choice Awards • Named by the *Washington Post* as one of "the best mysteries and thrillers of 2016" • An *Entertainment Weekly* "Summer Must List" Pick • A *New York Post* "Summer Must-Read" Pick • A finalist for the Book of the Month Club's "Book of the Year 2016" • Included in summer book guides from *Bustle,* Oprah.com, *PureWow,* and *BuzzFeed*

"An edge-of-your-seat thriller set on the most beautiful yacht in the world . . . Full of great characters and twists, y'all should check it out!"

—Reese Witherspoon

"A fantasy trip aboard a luxury liner turns nightmarish for a young journalist in *The Woman in Cabin 10,* the pulse-quickening new novel by Ruth Ware, author of *In a Dark, Dark Wood.*"

—*O, The Oprah Magazine*

"[*The Woman in Cabin 10*] generate[s] a dark, desperate tension that will appeal to Ware's and Gillian Flynn's many fans. This is the perfect summer read for those seeking a shadowy counter to the sunshine."

—*Booklist,* starred review

"Ruth Ware is back with her second hair-on-the-back-of-your-neck-tingling tale."

—*Marie Claire*

"Lots of twists and surprises in an old-fashioned mystery."

—R. L. Stine, *Thrillist*

"Ware's propulsive prose keeps readers on the hook and refuses to let anyone off until all has been revealed."

—*Shelf Awareness*

"[A] snappy thriller set on the high seas . . . The first chapter will grab your attention, force it against a wall, and hold it there until the end."

—Associated Press

"No one does spooky without the supernatural element better than Ruth Ware, and *The Woman in Cabin 10* is proof for any who doubt it."

—*New York Journal of Books*

"A gripping maritime psychological thriller that will keep readers spellbound. The intense final chapters just might induce heart palpitations."

—*Library Journal*, starred review

"[The Woman in Cabin 10] just may do to cruise vacations what *Jaws* did to ocean swimming."

—*StarTribune*

"The claustrophobic feeling of being on a ship and the twists and turns of who, and what, to believe keep you on the edge of your seat. Count on this being one of the hot reads this summer!"

—*LibraryReads*

"Ruth Ware's *The Woman in Cabin 10* is an atmospheric thriller as twisty and tension-filled as her 2015 debut, *In a Dark, Dark Wood*. . . . The novel's tone is dark and claustrophobic as Lo continues her search for the woman even though someone is trying to stop her—maybe even kill her."

—*The Washington Post*

"If you're a fan of Agatha Christie, get ready to curl up with this suspenseful mystery."

—*Bustle*

"A classic 'paranoid woman' story with a modern twist in this tense, claustrophobic mystery . . . The cast of characters, their conversations, and the luxurious but confining setting all echo classic Agatha Christie."

—*Kirkus Reviews*

"Haunting and absurdly suspenseful."

—*PureWow*

"A twisted and suspenseful mystery that entangles friendship, identity, and memory with a possible murder . . . Subtly tips its hat to authors such as Agatha Christie and Dorothy L. Sayers."

—*Metro*

"A great modern whodunit!"

—*New York Post*

"With a flawed but likeable heroine, and a fast moving plot, it makes for a stylish thriller."

—*Sunday Mirror*

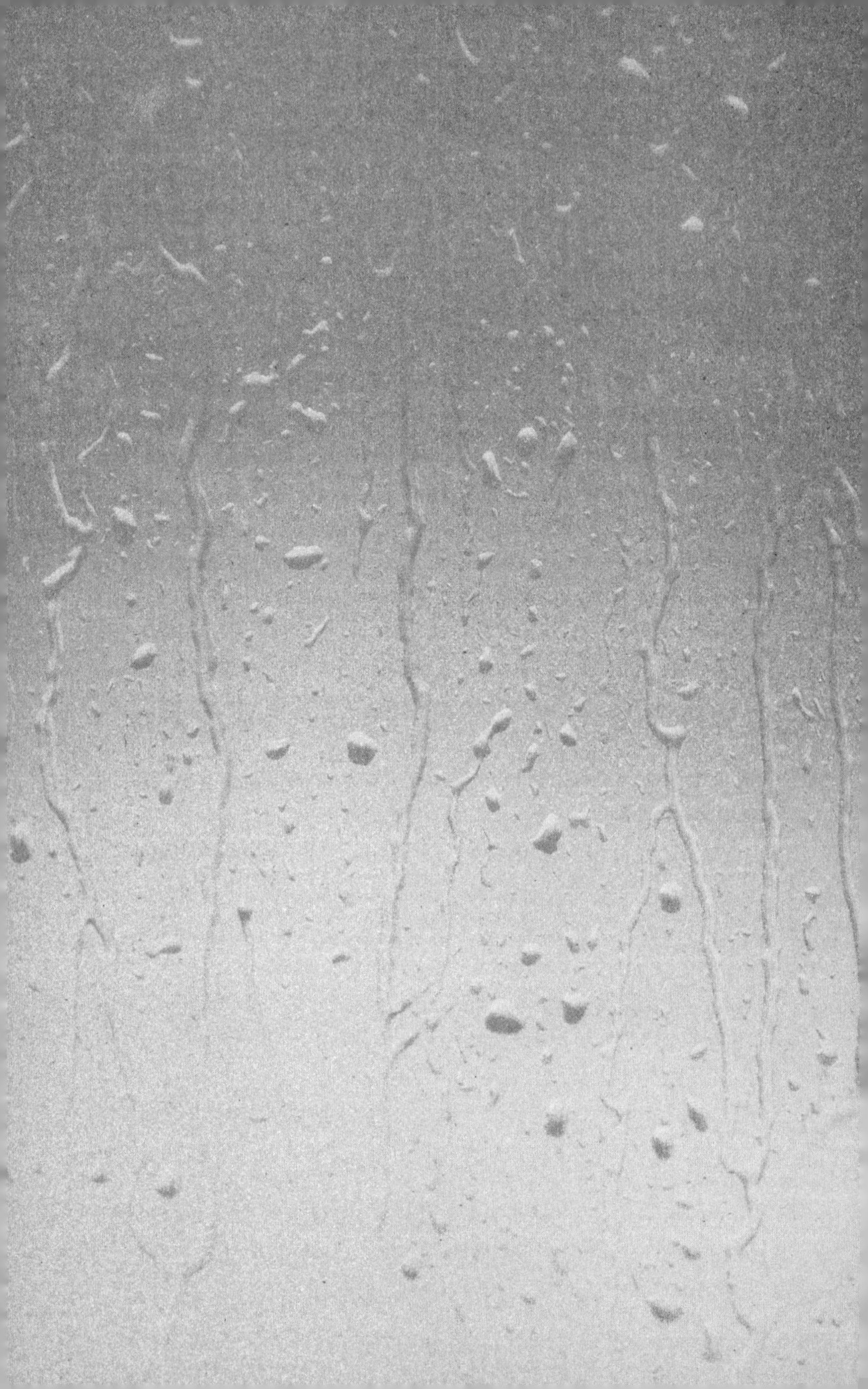

THE WOMAN IN CABIN 10

RUTH WARE

SCOUT PRESS

New York London Toronto Sydney New Delhi

Scout Press
An Imprint of Simon & Schuster, Inc.
1230 Avenue of the Americas
New York, NY 10020

This book is a work of fiction. Any references to historical events, real people, or real places are used fictitiously. Other names, characters, places, and events are products of the author's imagination, and any resemblance to actual events or places or persons, living or dead, is entirely coincidental.

Originally published in Great Britain in 2016 by Harvill Secker
Published by arrangement with The Random House Group Ltd.

First Scout Press trade paperback edition April 2017

Interior design by Jaime Putorti

Manufactured in the United States of America

40 39 38 37 36 35 34 33 32 31

The Library of Congress has cataloged the hardcover edition as follows:

Names: Ware, Ruth, author.
Title: The woman in cabin 10 / Ruth Ware.
Description: First Scout Press hardcover edition. | New York : Scout Press, 2016.
Identifiers: LCCN 2016007713| ISBN 9781501132933 (hardcover) | ISBN 9781501132957 (softcover) | ISBN 9781501132940 (ebook)
Subjects: LCSH: Women journalists—Fiction. | Cruise ships—Fiction. | Psychological fiction. | BISAC: FICTION / Suspense. | FICTION / Literary. | GSAFD: Suspense fiction. | Mystery fiction.
Classification: LCC PR6123.A745 W66 2016 | DDC 823/.92—dc23
LC record available at http://lccn.loc.gov/2016007713

ISBN 978-1-5011-3293-3
ISBN 978-1-5011-3295-7 (pbk)
ISBN 978-1-5011-3294-0 (ebook)

To Eleanor, with love

In my dream, the girl was drifting, far, far below the crashing waves and the cries of the gulls in the cold, sunless depths of the North Sea. Her laughing eyes were white and bloated with salt water; her pale skin was wrinkled; her clothes ripped by jagged rocks and disintegrating into rags.

Only her long black hair remained, floating through the water like fronds of dark seaweed, tangling in shells and fishing nets, washing up on the shore in hanks like frayed rope, where it lay, limp, the roar of the crashing waves against the shingle filling my ears.

I woke, heavy with dread. It took me a while to remember where I was, and still longer to realize that the roar in my ears was not part of the dream but real.

The room was dark, with the same damp mist I'd felt in my dream, and as I pulled myself to sitting I felt a cool breeze on my cheek. It sounded like the noise was coming from the bathroom.

I climbed off the bed, shivering slightly. The door was shut, but as I walked across to it, I could hear the roar building, the pitch of my heart rising alongside. Taking my courage in both hands, I flung open the door. The noise of the shower filled the small room as I groped for the switch. Light flooded the bathroom—and that's when I saw it.

Written across the steamy mirror, in letters maybe six inches high, were the words STOP DIGGING.

PART ONE

- CHAPTER 1 -

FRIDAY, SEPTEMBER 18

The first inkling that something was wrong was waking in darkness to find the cat pawing at my face. I must have forgotten to shut the kitchen door last night. Punishment for coming home drunk.

"Go away," I groaned. Delilah mewed and butted me with her head. I tried to bury my face in the pillow but she continued rubbing herself against my ear, and eventually I rolled over and heartlessly pushed her off the bed.

She thumped to the floor with an indignant little *meep* and I pulled the duvet over my head, but even through the covers I could hear her scratching at the bottom of the door, rattling it in its frame.

The door was closed.

I sat up, my heart suddenly thumping, and Delilah leaped onto my bed with a glad little chirrup, but I snatched her to my chest, stilling her movements, listening.

I might well have forgotten to shut the kitchen door, or I could even have knocked it to without closing it properly. But my bedroom door opened outward—a quirk of the weird layout of my flat. There was no way Delilah could have shut herself inside. *Someone* must have closed it.

I sat, frozen, holding Delilah's warm, panting body against my chest and trying to listen.

Nothing.

And then, with a gush of relief, it occurred to me—she'd probably been hiding under my bed and I'd shut her inside with me when I came home. I didn't remember closing my bedroom door, but I might have swung it absently shut behind me when I came in. To be honest, everything from the tube station onwards was a bit of a blur. The headache had started to set in on the journey home, and now that my panic was wearing off, I could feel it starting up again in the base of my skull. I *really* needed to stop drinking midweek. It had been okay in my twenties, but I just couldn't shake off the hangovers like I used to.

Delilah began squirming uneasily in my arms, digging her claws into my forearm, and I let her go while I reached for my dressing gown and belted it around myself. Then I scooped her up, ready to sling her out into the kitchen.

But when I opened the bedroom door, there was a man standing there.

There's no point in wondering what he looked like, because, believe me, I went over it about twenty-five times with the police. "Not even a bit of skin around his wrists?" they kept saying. No, no, and no. He had a hoodie on, and a bandanna around his nose and mouth, and everything else was in shadow. Except for his hands.

On these he was wearing latex gloves. It was that detail that scared the shit out of me. Those gloves said, "I know what I'm doing." They said, "I've come prepared." They said, "I might be after more than your money."

We stood there for a long second, facing each other, his shining eyes locked on to mine.

About a thousand thoughts raced through my mind: Where the hell is my phone? Why did I drink so much last night? I would have heard him come in if I'd been sober. Oh Christ, I wish Judah was here.

And most of all—those gloves. Oh my God, those gloves. They were so professional. So *clinical.*

I didn't speak. I didn't move. I just stood there, my ratty dressing gown gaping, and I shook. Delilah wriggled out of my unresisting hands and shot away up the hallway to the kitchen, and I just stood there, shaking.

Please, I thought. Please don't hurt me.

Oh God, where was my phone?

Then I saw something in the man's hands. My handbag—my new Burberry handbag, although that detail seemed monumentally unimportant. There was only one thing that mattered about that bag. My mobile was inside.

His eyes crinkled in a way that made me think he might be smiling beneath the bandanna, and I felt the blood drain from my head and my fingers, pooling in the core of my body, ready to fight or flee, whichever it had to be.

He took a step forwards.

"No . . ." I said. I wanted it to sound like a command, but it came out like a plea—my voice small and squeaky and quavering pathetically with fear. "N—"

But I didn't even get to finish. He slammed the bedroom door in my face, hitting my cheek.

For a long moment I stood, frozen, holding my hand to my face, speechless with the shock and pain. My fingers felt ice-cold, but there was something warm and wet on my face, and it took a moment for me to realize it was blood, that the molding on the door had cut my cheek.

I wanted to run back to bed, to shove my head under the pillows and cry and cry. But a small, ugly voice in my skull kept saying,

He's still out there. What if he comes back? What if he comes back for you?

There was a sound from out in the hall, something falling, and I felt a rush of fear that should have galvanized me but instead paralyzed me. *Don't come back. Don't come back.* I realized I was holding my breath, and I made myself exhale, long and shuddering, and then slowly, slowly, I forced my hand out towards the door.

There was another crash in the hallway outside, breaking glass, and with a rush I grabbed the knob and braced myself, my bare toes dug into the old, gappy floorboards, ready to hold the door closed as long as I could. I crouched there, against the door, hunched over with my knees to my chest, and I tried to muffle my sobs with my dressing gown while I listened to him ransacking the flat and hoped to God that Delilah had run out into the garden, out of harm's way.

At last, after a long time, I heard the front door open and shut, and I sat there, crying into my knees and unable to believe he'd really gone. That he wasn't coming back to hurt me. My hands felt numb and painfully stiff, but I didn't dare let go of the handle.

I saw again those strong hands in the pale latex gloves.

I don't know what would have happened next. Maybe I would have stayed there all night, unable to move. But then I heard Delilah outside, mewing and scratching at the other side of the door.

"Delilah," I said hoarsely. My voice was trembling so much I hardly sounded like myself. "Oh, Delilah."

Through the door I heard her purr, the familiar, deep, chainsaw rasp, and it was like a spell had been broken.

I let my cramped fingers loosen from the doorknob, flexing them painfully, and then stood up, trying to steady my trembling legs, and turned the door handle.

It turned. In fact it turned too easily, twisting without resistance under my hand, without moving the latch an inch. He'd removed the spindle from the other side.

Fuck.

Fuck, fuck, fuck.

I was trapped.

- CHAPTER 2 -

It took me two hours to prize my way out of my bedroom. I didn't have a landline, so I had no way of calling for help, and the window was covered by security bars. I broke my best nail file, hammering away at the latch, but at last I got the door open and I ventured out into the narrow hallway. There are only four rooms in my flat—kitchen, living room, bedroom, and tiny bathroom—and you can pretty much see the full extent of it from outside my bedroom, but I couldn't stop myself from peering into each doorway, even checking the cupboard in the hallway where I keep my hoover. Making sure he was really gone.

My head was pounding and my hands were shaking as I made my way outside and up the steps to my neighbor's front door, and I found myself looking over my shoulder into the dark street as I waited for her to answer. It was around four a.m., I guessed, and it took a long time and a lot of banging to wake her up. I heard grumbling, over the sound of Mrs. Johnson's feet clumping down her stairs, and her face when she cracked open the door was a mixture of bleary confusion and fright, but when she saw me huddled on the doorstep in my dressing gown, with blood on my face and on my hands, her expression changed in an instant and she took off the chain.

"Oh my days! Whatever's happened?"

"I got burgled." It was hard to talk. I don't know if it was the chilly autumn air, or the shock, but I had started shivering convulsively and my teeth chattered so hard I had a momentary horrible image of them shattering in my head. I pushed the thought away.

"You're bleedin'!" Her face was full of distress. "Oh, bless my soul, come in, come in!"

She led the way into the paisley-carpeted entrance to her maisonette, which was small and dark and grimly overheated, but right now felt like a sanctuary.

"Sit down, sit down." She pointed to a red plush sofa and then went creakily to her knees and began to fiddle with the gas fire. The gas popped and flared, and I felt the heat rise a degree as she got painfully to her feet again. "I'll make you some hot tea."

"I'm fine, honestly, Mrs. Johnson. Do you think—"

But she was shaking her head sternly.

"There's nothin' to beat hot sweet tea when you've had a shock."

So I sat, my shaky hands clasped around my knees, while she rattled around in the tiny kitchen and then came back with two mugs on a tray. I reached out for the closest and took a sip, wincing at the heat against the cut on my hand. It was so sweet I could barely taste the dissolving blood in my mouth, which I supposed was a blessing.

Mrs. Johnson didn't drink but just watched me, her forehead wrinkled in distress

"Did he . . ." Her voice faltered. "Did he *hurt* you?"

I knew what she meant. I shook my head, but I took another scalding sip before I could trust myself to speak.

"No. He didn't touch me. He slammed a door in my face—that's the cut on my cheek. And then I cut my hand trying to get out of the bedroom. He'd locked me in."

I had a jolting flash of myself battering at the lock with a nail file and a pair of scissors. Judah was always teasing about using the proper tools for the job—you know, not undoing a screw with the tip of a dinner knife, or prizing off a bike tire using a garden trowel.

Only last weekend he'd laughed at my attempt to fix my showerhead with duct tape, and spent a whole afternoon painstakingly mending it with epoxy resin. He was away in Ukraine and I couldn't think about him right now. If I did, I'd cry, and if I cried now, I might never stop.

"Oh, you poor love."

I swallowed.

"Mrs. Johnson, thank you for the tea—but I really came to ask, can I use your phone? He took my mobile, so I've got no way of calling the police."

"Of course, of course. Drink your tea, and then it's over there." She indicated a doily-covered side table, with what was probably the last turn-dial phone in London outside an Islington vintage-retro boutique. Obediently I finished my tea and then I picked up the phone. For a moment my finger hovered over the nine, but then I sighed. He was gone. What could they reasonably do now? It was no longer an emergency, after all.

Instead, I dialed 101 for nonemergency response and waited to be put through.

And I sat and thought about the insurance I didn't have, and the reinforced lock I hadn't installed, and the mess tonight had become.

I was still thinking about that, hours later, as I watched the emergency locksmith replace the crappy bolt-on latch of my front door with a proper deadlock, and listened to his lecture on home security and the joke that was my back door.

"That panel's nuffing but MDF, love. It'd take one kick to bash it in. Want me to show you?"

"No," I said hastily. "No, thanks. I'll get it fixed. You don't do doors, do you?"

"Nah, but I got a mate who does. I'll give you his number before I go. Meantime, you get your hubby to whack a good piece of eighteen-mil plywood over that panel. You don't want a repeat of last night."

"No," I agreed. Understatement of the century.

"Mate in the police says a quarter of all burglaries are repeats. Same guys come back for more."

"Great," I said thinly. Just what I needed to hear.

"Eighteen-mil. Want me to write it down for your husband?"

"No, thanks. I'm not married." And even in spite of my ovaries, I *can* remember a simple two-digit number.

"Aaaah, right, gotcha. Well, there you go, then," he said, as if that proved something. "This doorframe ain't nothing to write home about, neither. You want one of them London bars to reinforce it. Otherwise you can have the best lock in the business, but if they kick it out the frame you're back in the same place as before. I got one in the van that might fit. Do you know them things I'm talking about?"

"I know what they are," I said wearily. "A piece of metal that goes over the lock, right?" I suspected he was milking me for all the business he could get, but I didn't care at this point.

"Tell you what"—he stood up, shoving his chisel in his back pocket—"I'll do the London bar, and I'll chuck in a piece of ply over the back door for free. I got a bit in the van about the right size. Chin up, love. He ain't getting back in *this* way, at any rate."

For some reason the words weren't reassuring.

After he'd gone, I made myself a tea and paced the flat. I felt like Delilah after a tomcat broke in through the cat flap and pissed in the hallway—she had prowled every room for hours, rubbing herself up against bits of furniture, peeing into corners, reclaiming her space.

I didn't go as far as peeing on the bed, but I felt the same sense of space invaded, a need to reclaim what had been violated. *Violated?* said a sarcastic little voice in my head. *Puh-lease, you drama queen.*

But I did feel violated. My little flat felt ruined—soiled and unsafe. Even describing it to the police had felt like an ordeal—yes, I saw the intruder; no, I can't describe him. What was in the bag? Oh, just, you know, my life: money, mobile phone, driver's license, medication, pretty much everything of use from my mascara right through to my travel card.

The brisk impersonal tone of the police operator's voice still echoed in my head.

"What kind of phone?"

"Nothing valuable," I said wearily. "Just an old iPhone. I can't remember the model, but I can find out."

"Thanks. Anything you can remember in terms of the exact make and serial number might help. And you mentioned medication—what kind, if you don't mind me asking?"

I was instantly on the defensive.

"What's my medical history got to do with this?"

"Nothing." The operator was patient, irritatingly so. "It's just some pills have got a street value."

I knew the anger that flooded through me at his questions was unreasonable—he was only doing his job. But the burglar was the person who'd committed the crime. So why did I feel like I was the one being interrogated?

I was halfway to the living room with my tea when there was a banging at the door—so loud in the silent, echoing flat that I tripped and then froze, half standing, half crouching in the doorway.

I had a horrible jarring flash of a hooded face, of hands in latex gloves.

It was only when the door thudded again that I looked down and realized that my cup of tea was now lying smashed on the hallway tiles and that my feet were soaked in rapidly cooling liquid.

The door banged again.

"Just a minute!" I yelled, suddenly furious and close to tears. "I'm coming! Will you stop banging the bloody door!"

"Sorry, miss," the policeman said when I finally opened the door. "Wasn't sure if you'd heard." And then, seeing the puddle of tea and the smashed shards of my cup: "Crikey, what's been going on here then? Another break-in? Ha-ha!"

It was the afternoon by the time the policeman finished taking his report, and when he left, I opened up my laptop. It had been in the bedroom with me, and it was the only bit of tech the burglar hadn't taken. Aside from my work, which was mostly not backed up, it had all my passwords on it, including—and I cringed as I thought about it—a file helpfully named "Banking stuff." I didn't actually have my pin numbers listed. But pretty much everything else was there.

As the usual deluge of e-mails dropped into my in-box, I caught sight of one headed "Planning on showing up today ;)?" and I realized with a jolt that I'd completely forgotten to contact *Velocity*.

I thought about e-mailing, but in the end, I fetched out the twenty-pound note I kept in the tea caddy for emergency cab money and walked to the dodgy phone shop at the tube station. It took some haggling, but eventually the guy sold me a cheap pay-as-you-go plus SIM card for fifteen pounds and I sat in the café opposite and phoned the assistant features editor, Jenn, who has the desk opposite mine.

I told her what happened, making it sound funnier and more farcical than it really had been. I dwelled heavily on the image of me chipping away at the lock with a nail file and didn't tell her about the gloves, or the general sense of powerless terror, or the horribly vivid flashbacks that kept ambushing me just as I was rummaging for change, or stirring tea, or thinking of something else completely.

"Shit." Her voice at the end of the crackly line was full of horror. "Are you okay?"

"Yeah, more or less. But I won't be in today, I've got to clear up the flat." Although, in actual fact, it wasn't that bad. He'd been commendably neat. For, you know, a criminal.

"God, Lo, you poor thing. Listen, do you want me to get someone else to cover you on this northern lights thing?"

For a minute I had no idea what she was talking about—then I remembered. The *Aurora*. A boutique super-luxury cruise liner traveling around the Norwegian fjords, and somehow, I still wasn't quite sure how, I had been lucky enough to snag one of the handful of press passes on its maiden voyage.

It was a huge perk—in spite of working for a travel magazine, my normal beat was cutting and pasting press releases and finding images for articles sent back from luxury destinations by my boss, Rowan. It was Rowan who had been supposed to go, but unfortunately, after saying yes she had discovered that pregnancy didn't agree with her—hyperemesis, apparently—and the cruise had landed in my lap like a big present, fraught with responsibility and possibilities. It was a vote of confidence from her, giving it to me when there were more senior people she could have buttered up, and I knew if I played my cards right on this trip, it would be a big point in my favor when it came to jockeying for Rowan's maternity cover and maybe—just maybe—getting that promotion she'd been promising for the last few years.

It was also this weekend. Sunday, in fact. I'd be leaving in two days.

"*No*," I said, surprising myself with the firmness in my voice. "No, I definitely don't want to pull out. I'm fine."

"Are you sure? What about your passport?"

"It was in my bedroom; he didn't find it." Thank God.

"Are you *absolutely* sure?" she said again, and I could hear the concern in her voice. "This is a big deal—not just for you, for the mag I mean. If you don't feel up to it, Rowan wouldn't want you—"

"I am up to it," I said, cutting her off. There was no way I was letting this opportunity slip through my fingers. If I did, it might be the last one I had. "I promise. I really want to do this, Jenn."

"Okay . . ." she said, almost reluctantly. "Well, in that case, full steam ahead, eh? They sent through a press pack this morning, so I'll courier that across along with your train tickets. I've got Rowan's notes somewhere; I think the main thing is to do a really nice puff piece on the boat, because she's hoping to get them on board as advertisers, but there should be some interesting people among the other guests, so if you can get anything else done in the way of profiles, so much the better."

"Sure." I grabbed a pen from the counter of the café and began taking notes on a paper napkin. "And remind me what time it leaves?"

"You're catching the ten thirty train from King's Cross—but I'll put it all in the press pack."

"That's fine. And thanks, Jenn."

"No worries," she said. Her voice was a little wistful, and I wondered if she'd been planning to step into the breach herself. "Take care, Lo. And 'bye."

It was still just about light as I trudged slowly home. My feet hurt, my cheek ached, and I wanted to go home and sink into a long, hot bath.

The door of my basement flat was bathed in shadow as it always was, and I thought once again that I must get a security light, if only so that I could see my own keys in my handbag, but even in the dimness I could see the splintered wood where he'd forced the lock. The miracle was that I hadn't heard him. *Well, what do you expect, you were drunk, after all,* said the nasty little voice in my head.

But the new deadlock felt reassuringly solid as it clunked back, and inside I locked it shut again, kicked off my shoes, and walked wearily down the hall to the bathroom, stifling a yawn as I set the taps running and slumped onto the toilet to pull off my tights. Next I began to unbutton my top . . . but then I stopped.

Normally I leave the bathroom door open—it's only me and Delilah, and the walls are prone to damp, being under ground level. I'm also not great with enclosed spaces, and the room feels very small when the window blinds are down.

The front door was locked, and the new London bar was in place, but I still checked the window and closed and locked the bathroom door before I finished peeling off my clothes. I was tired—God, I was *so* tired. I had an image of falling asleep in the tub, slipping below the water, Judah finding my naked bloated body a week later . . . I shook myself. I needed to stop being so bloody dramatic. The tub was barely four feet long. I had trouble contorting myself so I could rinse my hair, let alone drown.

The bath was hot enough to make the cut on my cheek sting, and I shut my eyes and tried to imagine myself somewhere else, somewhere quite different from this chilly, claustrophobic little space, far away from sordid, crime-ridden London. Walking on a cool Nordic shore, perhaps, in my ears the soothing sound of the . . . er . . . would it be the Baltic? For a travel journalist I'm worryingly bad at geography.

But unwanted images kept intruding. The locksmith saying "a quarter of all burglaries are repeats." Me, cowering in my own bedroom, feet braced against the floorboards. The sight of strong hands encased in pale latex, the black hairs just showing through . . .

Shit. *Shit.*

I opened my eyes, but for once the reality check didn't help. Instead, I saw the damp bathroom walls looming over me, shutting me in. . . .

You're losing it again, my internal voice sniped. *You can feel it, can't you?*

Shut up. Shut up, shut up, shut up. I squeezed my eyes closed again and began to count, deliberately, trying to force the pictures out of my head. *One. Two. Three. Breathe in. Four. Five. Six. Breathe out. One. Two. Three. Breathe in. Four. Five. Six. Breathe out.*

At last the pictures receded, but the bath was spoiled, and the need to get out of the airless little room was suddenly overwhelming. I got up, wrapped a towel around myself and another around my hair, and went into the bedroom, where my laptop was still lying on the bed from earlier.

I opened it, fired up Google, and typed: *What % burglars return.*

A page of links came up and I clicked on one at random and scanned down it until I came to a paragraph that read:

WHEN BURGLARS RETURN . . .

> **A nationwide survey indicated that, over a twelve-month period, approximately 25 to 50 percent of burglaries are repeat incidents; and between 25 and 35 percent of victims are repeat victims. Figures gathered by UK police forces suggest that 28 to 51 percent of repeat burglaries occur within one month, 11 to 25 percent within a week.**

Great. So it seemed like my friendly doom-and-gloom merchant, the locksmith, had actually been *under*stating the problem, not winding me up. Although the maths involved in up to 50 percent repeat offenses but only 35 percent repeat victims made my head hurt. Either way, I didn't relish the idea of being among their number.

I had promised myself I wouldn't drink tonight, so after I had checked the front door, back door, window locks, and front door for the second—or maybe even the third—time, and put the pay-as-you-go phone on to charge beside my bed, I made myself a cup of chamomile tea.

I took it back through to the bedroom with my laptop, the press file for the trip, and a packet of chocolate cookies. It was only eight o'clock and I hadn't had any supper, but I was suddenly exhausted—too exhausted to cook, too exhausted even to phone for takeaway. I opened up the Nordic cruise press pack and huddled down into my duvet, and waited for sleep to claim me.

Except it didn't. I dunked my way through the whole packet of cookies and read page after page of facts and figures on the *Aurora*—just ten luxuriously appointed cabins . . . maximum of twenty passengers at any one time . . . handpicked staff from the world's top hotels and restaurants . . . Even the technical specifications of the boat's draft and tonnage weren't enough to lull me to sleep. I stayed awake, shattered yet somehow, at the same time, wired.

As I lay there in my cocoon I tried not to think about the burglar. I thought, very deliberately, about work, about all the practicalities I had to sort out before Sunday. Pick up my new bank cards. I had to pack and do my research for the trip. Would I see Jude before I left? He'd be trying my old phone.

I put down the press pack and pulled up my e-mails.

"Hi, love," I typed, and then I paused and bit the side of my nail. What to say? No point in telling him about the burglary, not yet. He'd just feel bad about not being here when I needed him. "I've lost my phone," I wrote instead. "Long story, I'll explain when you get back. But if you need me, e-mail, don't text. What's your ETA on Sunday?

I'm off to Hull early, for this Nordic thing. Hope we can see each other before I leave—otherwise, see you next week? Lo x"

I pressed send, hoping he didn't wonder what I was doing up and e-mailing at 12:45 a.m., and then shut down the computer, picked up my book, and tried to read myself to sleep.

It didn't work.

At 3:35 a.m. I staggered through to the kitchen, picked up the bottle of gin, and poured myself the stiffest gin and tonic I could bring myself to drink. I gulped it down like medicine, shuddering at the harsh taste, and then poured a second and drank that, too, more slowly this time. I stood for a moment, feeling the alcohol tingling through my veins, relaxing my muscles, damping down my jangled nerves.

I poured the dregs of the gin into the glass and took it back to the bedroom, where I lay down, stiff and anxious, my eyes on the glowing face of the clock, and waited for the alcohol to take effect.

One. Two. Three. Breathe in. Four. . . . Five. . . . Fi . . .

I don't remember falling asleep, but I must have. One minute I was looking at the clock with bleary, headachy eyes, waiting for it to click over onto 4:44, the next minute I was blinking into Delilah's furry face as she butted her whiskery nose against mine and tried to tell me it was time for breakfast. I groaned. My head ached worse than yesterday—although I wasn't sure if it was my cheek or another hangover. The last gin and tonic was half full on my bedside table, beside the clock. I sniffed it and almost choked. It must have been two-thirds gin. What had I been thinking?

The clock said 6:04 and I calculated that meant I'd had less than an hour and a half's sleep, but I was awake now, no point in trying to fight it. Instead, I got up, pulled back the curtain, and peered into the gray dawn and the thin fingers of sun that trickled into my basement window. The day felt cold and sour, and I shoved my feet into my slippers and shivered as I made my way down the hall to the thermostat, ready to override the automatic timer and start the heating for the day.

It was Saturday, so I didn't have to work, but somehow the work involved in getting my mobile number assigned to a new phone and my bank cards reissued took up most of the day, and by the evening I was drunk with tiredness.

It felt as bad as the time I'd flown back from Thailand via LA—a series of red-eyes that left me wild with sleep deprivation and hopelessly disoriented. Somewhere over the Atlantic, I realized that I had gone beyond sleep, that I might as well give up. Back home, I fell into bed like falling into a well, plunging headlong into oblivion, and I slept for twenty-two hours, coming up groggy and stiff-limbed to find Judah banging at my door with the Sunday papers. But this time, my bed was no longer a refuge.

I *had* to get myself together before I left for this trip. It was an unmissable, unrepeatable opportunity to prove myself after ten years at the coalface of boring cut-and-paste journalism. This was my chance to show I could hack it—that I, like Rowan, could network and schmooze and get *Velocity*'s name in there with the high fliers. And Lord Bullmer, the owner of the *Aurora Borealis*, was a very high flier indeed, from what I'd gathered. Even 1 percent of his advertising budget could keep *Velocity* afloat for months, not to mention all the well-known names in travel and photography who would doubtless have been invited along on this maiden voyage, and whose bylines on our cover would look very nice indeed.

I wasn't about to start hard selling Bullmer over dinner—nothing as crude and commercial as that. But if I could get his number on my contacts list and ensure that when I phoned him up, he took my call . . . well, it would go a long way to finally getting me that promotion.

As I ate supper, mechanically forking frozen pizza into my face until I felt too full to continue, I picked up where I'd left off with the press pack, but the words and pictures swam in front of my eyes, the adjectives blurring into one another: *boutique . . . glittering . . . luxury . . . handcrafted . . . artisan . . .*

I let the page drop with a yawn, then looked at my watch and realized it was past nine. I could go to bed, thank God. As I checked and rechecked the doors and locks, I reflected that the one silver lining to being so shattered was that it couldn't possibly be a repeat of last night.

I was so tired that even if a burglar *did* come, I'd probably sleep right through it.

At 10:47, I realized I was wrong.

At 11:23, I started to cry, weakly and stupidly.

Was this it, then? Was I never going to sleep again?

I had to sleep. I *had* to. I'd had . . . I counted on my fingers, unable to do the maths in my head. What . . . less than four hours of sleep in the last three days.

I could *taste* sleep. I could *feel* it, just out of my reach. I had to sleep. I had to. I was going to go crazy if I didn't sleep.

The tears were coming again—I didn't even know what they were. Tears of frustration? Rage, at myself, at the burglar? Or just exhaustion?

I only knew that I couldn't sleep—that it was dangling like an unkept promise just inches away from me. I felt like I was running towards a mirage that kept receding, slipping away faster and faster the more desperately I ran. Or that it was like a fish in water, something I had to catch and hold, that kept slipping through my fingers.

Oh God, I want to sleep. . . .

Delilah turned her head towards me, startled. Had I really said it aloud? I couldn't even tell anymore. Christ, I was losing it.

A flash of a face—gleaming liquid eyes in the darkness.

I sat up, my heart pounding so hard that I could feel it in the back of my skull.

I had to get away from here.

I got up, stumbling, trancelike with exhaustion, and pushed my feet into my shoes, and my sleeves into my coat, over the top of my pajamas. Then I picked up my bag. If I couldn't sleep, I'd walk. Somewhere. Anywhere. I'd try to exhaust myself into sleeping.

If sleep wouldn't come to me, then I'd damn well hunt it down myself.

- CHAPTER 3 -

The streets at midnight weren't empty, but they weren't the same ones I trod every day on my way to work, either.

Between the sulfur-yellow pools of streetlight, they were gray and shadowed, and a cold wind blew discarded papers against my legs, leaves and rubbish gusting in the gutters. I should have felt afraid—a thirty-two-year-old woman, clearly wearing pajamas, wandering the streets in the small hours. But I felt safer out here than I did in my flat. Out here, someone would hear you cry.

I had no plan, no route beyond walking the streets until I was too tired to stand. Somewhere around Highbury and Islington I realized that it had begun to rain, that it must have started some time back because I was wet through. I stood in my soggy shoes, my exhausted punch-drunk brain trying to formulate a plan, and almost by themselves my feet began to walk again, not homewards, but south, towards Angel.

I didn't realize where I was going until I was there. Until I was standing beneath the porch of his building, frowning dazedly at the bell panel, where his name was written in his own small, neat handwriting. LEWIS.

He wasn't here. He was away in Ukraine, not due back until tomorrow. But I had his spare keys in my coat pocket, and I couldn't face the walk back to my flat. *You could get a cab,* carped the small, snide voice in the back of my head. *It's not the walk you can't face. Coward.*

I shook my head, sending raindrops spattering across the stainless-steel bell panel, and I sorted through the bunch of keys until I found the one for the outside door and slipped inside, into the oppressive warmth of the communal hallway.

Up on the second floor, I let myself cautiously into the flat.

It was completely dark. All the doors were closed, and the entrance hall had no windows.

"Judah?" I called. I was certain he wasn't home, but it wasn't impossible that he'd let a mate crash there, and I didn't want to give anyone a middle-of-the-night heart attack. I knew, all too well, what that felt like. "Jude, it's just me, Lo."

But there was no answer. The flat was silent—completely and utterly silent. I opened the door to the left of me, the door to the eat-in kitchen, and tiptoed inside. I didn't switch on the light. I just peeled off my wet clothes—coat, pajamas, and all—and dumped them in the sink.

Then I walked, naked, through to the bedroom, where Judah's wide double bed lay empty in a shaft of moonlight, the gray sheets tumbled as if he'd just that moment got up. I crawled on my hands and knees into the middle of the bed, feeling the lived-in softness of the sheets, and smelling the scent of him, of sweat and aftershave and just—*him*.

I shut my eyes.

One. Two. . . .

Sleep crashed over me, claiming me like a wave.

I woke to the sound of a woman screaming, and the feeling of someone on top of me, holding me down, someone grappling with my hands even as I fought.

A hand grabbed at my wrist, the grip far stronger than mine. Blind, mad with panic, I groped in the pitch black with my free hand, searching for something, anything, to use as a weapon, and my hand closed over the bedside lamp.

The man's hand was over my mouth now, smothering me, the weight of him choking me, and with all my strength, I lifted up the heavy lamp and brought it crashing down.

There was a shout of pain, and through the fog of terror I heard a voice, the words slurred and broken.

"Lo, it's me. It's me for Christ's sake, stop!"

What?

Oh God.

My hands were shaking so much that when I tried to find the light, all I did was knock something over.

From beside me I could hear Judah, gasping, alongside a bubbling sound that terrified me. Where the hell was the lamp? Then I realized—the lamp was gone. I'd smashed it into Judah's face.

I stumbled out of bed, my legs shaking, and found the switch by the door, and the room was instantly flooded with the unforgivingly bright glare of a dozen halogen spots, each illuminating every detail of the horror show in front of me.

Judah was crouched on the bed, holding his face, with blood soaking his beard and his chest.

"Oh my God, Jude!" I scrambled across to him, my hands still trembling, and began to grab tissues from the box by the bed. He pressed them to his face. "Oh God, what happened? Who was screaming?"

"You!" he groaned. The paper was already sodden and red.

"What?" I was still flooded with adrenaline. I looked confusedly around the room for the woman and the attacker. "What do you mean?"

"I came home," he said painfully, his Brooklyn accent blurred through the paper. "You started screaming, half-asleep. So I tried to wake you up and—this."

"Oh, fuck." I put my hands to my mouth. "I'm so sorry."

That screaming—it had been so real. Was it really just me?

He took his hands cautiously away from his mouth. There was something in the wad of scarlet paper, something small and white. It was only when I looked at his face that I realized—one of his teeth was missing.

"Oh Jesus."

He looked at me, blood still dripping slowly from his mouth and his nose.

"What a welcome home," was all he said.

"I'm sorry." I felt tears prick at the back of my throat but I refused to cry in front of the taxi driver. Instead, I swallowed against the hard ache. "Judah?"

Judah said nothing; he just looked out of the window at the gray dawn that was starting to break over London. It had taken two hours at UCH accident and emergency, and then all they'd done was stitch Judah's lip and refer him to an emergency dentist who shoved the tooth back in place and told him, more or less, to cross his fingers. Apparently the tooth might be saved if it reimplanted. If not, it would be either a bridge or a dental implant. He shut his eyes wearily, and I felt my gut twist with remorse.

"I'm sorry," I said again, more desperately this time. "I don't know what else to say."

"No, I'm sorry," he said wearily. The word came out as *shorry,* like a drunken Sean Connery impression, the local anesthetic in his lip making it hard to talk.

"You? What are you sorry for?"

"I don't know. Fucking up. Not being there for you."

"The burglar, you mean?"

He nodded.

"That. But any time, really. I wish I wasn't away so much."

I leaned across and he put his arm around me. I rested my head on his shoulder and listened to the slow, steady thud of his heart, reassuringly unhurried in comparison to my own panicky drumming pulse. Beneath his jacket he was wearing a blood-spattered T-shirt, the fabric soft and worn beneath my cheek. When I breathed in, a long, shaky breath, it smelled of his sweat, and I felt my pulse slow in time with his.

"You couldn't have done anything," I said into his chest. He shook his head.

"I still should have been there."

It was growing light as we paid off the taxi driver and climbed wearily up the two flights of stairs to his flat, and when I looked at my watch I saw that it was nearly six. Shit. I had to be on a train to Hull in a few hours.

Inside, Judah stripped off his clothes and we fell into bed, skin against skin. He pulled me against him, inhaling the scent of my hair as he closed his eyes. I was so tired I could hardly think straight, but instead of lying back and letting sleep claim me, I found myself climbing on top of him, kissing his throat, his belly, the dark stripe of hair that arrowed to his groin.

"Lo . . ." He groaned, and he tried to pull me up towards him, to kiss me, but I shook my head.

"Don't, your mouth. Just lie back."

He let his head fall back, his throat arching in the pale strip of dawn that penetrated the curtains.

It was eight days since I'd last seen him. Now it would be another week until I saw him again. If we didn't do this now . . .

Afterwards, I lay in his arms, waiting for my breathing and heart to steady, and I felt his cheek against mine crinkle in a smile.

"That's more like it," he said.

"More like what?"

"More like the homecoming I was expecting."

I flinched and he touched my face.

"Lo, honey, it was a joke."

"I know."

We were both quiet for a long time. I thought he was slipping into sleep, and I shut my own eyes and let the tiredness wash over me, but then I felt his chest lift, and the muscles in his arm tense as he took a deep breath.

"Lo, I'm not going to ask again, but . . ."

He didn't finish, but he didn't have to. I could feel what he wanted to say. It was what he'd said on New Year's Eve—he wanted us to move forward. Move in together.

"Let me think about it," I said at last, in a voice that didn't seem to be mine, a voice that was unusually subdued.

"That's what you said months ago."

"I'm still thinking."

"Well, I've made up my mind." He touched my chin, pulling my face gently towards his. What I saw there made my heart flip-flop. I reached out for him, but he caught my hand and held it. "Lo, stop trying to make this go away. I've been really patient, you know I have, but I'm starting to feel like we're not on the same page."

I felt my insides flutter with a familiar panic—something between hope and terror.

"Not on the same page?" My smile felt forced. "Have you been watching *Oprah* again?"

He let go of my hand at that, and something in his face had closed off as he turned away. I bit my lip.

"Jude—"

"No," he said. "Just—no. I wanted to talk about this but you clearly don't, so— Look, I'm tired. It's nearly morning. Let's go to sleep."

"Jude," I said again, pleadingly this time, hating myself for being such a bitch, hating *him* for pushing me into this.

"I said no," he said wearily, into the pillow. I thought he was talking about our conversation, but then he continued. "To a job. Back in New York. I turned it down. For you."

Fuck.

- CHAPTER 4 -

I was sleeping a deep, stupefied sleep, as if I'd been drugged, when the alarm dragged me to consciousness a few hours later.

I didn't know how long it had been going off, but I suspected a long, long time. My head ached, and I lay for a long moment trying to orientate myself before I managed to reach out and silence the clock in case it woke Judah.

I rubbed the sleep out of my eyes and stretched, trying to work the kinks from my neck and shoulders, and then levered myself painfully up to vertical, climbed out of bed, and made my way through to Judah's kitchen. While the coffee percolated, I took my pills, and then hunted in the bathroom for painkillers. I found ibuprofen and paracetamol, as well as something in a brown plastic bottle that I vaguely remembered Judah being prescribed when he twisted his knee in a football match. I opened the childproof lid and inspected the pills inside. They were huge, half-red and half-white, and looked impressive.

In the end I chickened out of taking them, and instead pressed two ibuprofen and a fast-acting paracetamol into my palm from the assorted blister packs on the bathroom shelf. I gulped them down with a cup of coffee—black, there was no milk in the empty fridge—and then sipped the rest of the cup more slowly as I thought about last night, about my stupid actions, about Judah's announcement. . .

I was surprised. No, more than surprised—I was shocked. We'd never really discussed his plans long-term, but I knew he missed his friends in the US, and his mum and younger brother—neither of whom I'd met. What he'd done . . . had he done it for himself? Or for us?

There was half a cup of coffee left in the jug, and I poured it into a second mug and carried it carefully through to the bedroom.

Judah was lying sprawled across the mattress as if he'd fallen there. People in films always look peaceful in sleep, but Judah didn't. His battered mouth was hidden beneath his upflung arm, but with his angular nose and furrowed brow he looked like an angry hawk, shot down by a gamekeeper midflight and still pissed off about it.

I set the coffee cup very gently on his bedside table and, putting my face close on the pillow next to him, I kissed the back of his neck. It was warm, and surprisingly soft.

He stirred in his sleep, putting out one long tanned arm to loop over my shoulders, and his eyes opened, looking three shades darker than their usual hazel brown.

"Hey," I said softly.

"Hey." He scrunched up his face and yawned, and then pulled me down beside him. For a moment I resisted, thinking of the boat and the train and the car waiting for me at Hull. Then my limbs seemed to melt like plastic and I let myself fold into him, into his warmth. We lay there staring into each other's eyes, and I reached out and tentatively touched the Steri-Strip across his lip.

"Think it'll re-root?"

"I don't know," he said. "I hope so, I've got to go to Moscow tomorrow, and I don't want to be messing around with dentists while I'm out there."

I said nothing. He closed his eyes and stretched, and I heard his joints click as he did. Then he rolled onto his side and put his cupped hand gently over my bare breast.

"Judah . . ." I said. I could hear the mix of exasperation and longing in my voice.

"What?"

"I can't. I've got to go."

"So go."

"Don't. Stop that."

"Don't, stop? Or don't stop?" He gave a slow lopsided smile.

"Both. You know which one I mean." I pulled myself upright and shook my head. It hurt, and I regretted the movement instantly.

"Your cheek okay?" Judah asked.

"Yeah." I put a hand up to it. It was swollen, but not as much as before.

His face was troubled, and he put out a finger to stroke the bruise, but I flinched away in spite of myself.

"I should have been there," he said.

"Well, you weren't," I said snappishly, more snappishly than I'd meant to. "You never are."

He blinked and pulled himself up on his elbows to look at me, his face still soft with sleep, crumpled with marks from his pillow.

"What the . . . ?"

"You heard me." I knew I was being unreasonable, but the words came tumbling out. "What's the future, Jude? Even if I move in here—what's the plan? Do I sit here weaving my shroud like Penelope and keeping the home fires burning while you drink Scotch in some bar in Russia with the other foreign correspondents?"

"Where'd this come from?"

I just shook my head and swung my legs out of bed. I began pulling on the pile of spare clothes I'd left on the floor after the trip to A&E.

"I'm just tired, Jude." *Tired* was an understatement. I hadn't slept longer than two hours in the last three nights. "And I can't see where this is heading. It's hard enough now when it's just the two of us. I don't want to be your wife-in-every-port stuck at home with a kid and a raging case of postnatal depression while you're getting shot at in every hellhole this side of the equator."

"Recent events kind of imply I'm in more danger in my own apartment," Judah said, and then winced as he saw my face. "Sorry, that was an asshole thing to say. It was an accident, I know that."

I swung my still-damp coat round my shoulders and picked up my bag.

"'Bye, Judah."

"'Bye? What do you mean, 'bye?"

"Whatever you want."

"What I *want* is for you to stop acting like a goddamn drama queen and move into my flat. I love you, Lo!"

The words hit me like a slap. I stopped in the doorway, feeling the weight of my tiredness like something physical around my neck, pulling me down.

Hands in pale latex, the sound of a laugh . . .

"Lo?" Judah said uncertainly.

"I can't do this," I said, my face to the hallway. I was not sure what I was talking about—I can't leave, I can't stay, I can't have this conversation, this life, this everything. "I just— I have to go."

"So that job," he said, the beginnings of anger in his voice. "The one I turned down. Are you saying I was wrong?"

"I never asked you to do that," I said. My voice was shaking. "I never asked you. So don't you put that on me." I hoisted my bag up onto my shoulder and turned to the door.

He didn't say anything. He didn't try to stop me. I walked out of the flat reeling like I was half-drunk. It was only when I got on the tube that the reality of what had just happened hit me.

- CHAPTER 5 -

I love ports. I love the smell of tar and sea air, and the scream of the gulls. Maybe it's years of taking the ferry to France for summer holidays, but a harbor gives me a feeling of freedom in a way that an airport never does. Airports say *work* and *security checks* and *delays.* Ports say . . . I don't know. Something completely different. *Escape,* maybe.

I had spent the train journey avoiding thoughts of Judah and trying to distract myself with research on the trip ahead. Richard Bullmer was only a few years older than me, but his CV was enough to make me feel hopelessly inadequate—a list of businesses and directorships that made my eyes water, each a stepping-stone to an even higher level of money and influence.

When I brought up *Wikipedia* on my phone, it showed a bronzed, handsome man with very black hair, arm in arm with a stunningly beautiful blonde in her late twenties. *Richard Bullmer with his wife, the heiress Anne Lyngstad, at their wedding in Stavanger,* read the caption.

Given his title, I'd assumed that his wealth had been handed to him on a plate, but it looked, from *Wikipedia* at least, as if I'd been unfair. The early part of the picture was cushy enough—prep school, Eton and Balliol. However, in his first year at university his father had died—his mother seemed already to be out of the picture, it wasn't entirely clear—and the family estate had been swallowed up in death duty and debts, leaving him, at nineteen years of age, homeless and alone.

Under those circumstances, the fact that he got through Oxford with a degree would have been achievement enough, but he had also created a dot-com start-up in his third year. Its stock market flotation in 2003 was the first in his string of successes, culminating with this boutique ten-cabin cruise liner conceived as a super-luxury retreat for hopping the Scandinavian coastline.

Available for the wedding of your dreams, a dazzling corporate event to woo your clients with the "wow" factor, or simply for an exclusive holiday you and your family will never forget, I read from the press pack as the train hurtled north, before turning to a floor plan of the cabin deck. There were four large suites in the nose of the boat—the prow, I supposed you'd call it, and a separate section with six smaller cabins arranged in a horseshoe shape at the back. Each cabin was numbered, odd and even on either side of a central corridor, with cabin 1 right in the tip of the prow, and cabins 9 and 10 adjoining each other in the curved stern of the boat. I guessed I'd be in one of the smaller cabins—presumably the suites were reserved for VIPs. There were no measurements on the floor plan and I frowned, remembering some of the cross-channel ferries I'd been on, the claustrophobic, windowless little rooms. The thought of spending five days in one of those wasn't a comfortable one, but surely on a boat like this, we'd be talking something considerably more spacious?

I turned the page again, hoping to find a photo of one of the cabins to reassure myself, but instead I was confronted with a shot of a dazzling array of Scandinavian delicacies spread out on a white cloth. The chef on the *Aurora* had trained at Noma and elBulli, apparently. I yawned and pressed my hands into my eyes, feeling the grit of tiredness and the weight of everything from last night pressing down on me once again.

Judah's face as I'd left him, stitched up with the blow from the night before, came into my head and I flinched. I wasn't even sure what had happened. Had Judah and I broken up? Had I dumped him? Every time I tried to reconstruct the conversation, my exhausted brain took over, adding in stuff I hadn't said, the responses I wished I'd made, making Judah more clueless and more insulting, to justify my own position, or alternatively more unconditionally loving, to try to convince myself this was all going to be okay. I hadn't *asked* him to turn down the job. So why was I suddenly expected to be grateful for it?

I dozed off for about thirty painful minutes in the car from the station to the port, and when the car driver's cheerful announcement broke into my sleep it was like a splash of cold water to the face. I stumbled out of the car into the searing sunshine and the salt-sting of the breeze, feeling bleary and dazed.

The driver had dropped me off almost at the end of the gangway, but as I looked across the steel bridge to the boat, I couldn't quite believe we were in the right place. The pictures from the brochure were familiar—huge glass windows reflecting the sun without a single fingerprint or speck of salt water, and gleaming white paint so fresh that it could have been finished that morning. But what had been missing from the brochure photos was a sense of scale. The *Aurora* was so *small*—more like a large yacht than a small cruise liner. *Boutique* had been the phrase in the press pack—and now I saw what they meant. I'd seen bigger boats hopping around the Greek islands. It seemed impossible that everything mentioned in the brochure—library, sunroom, spa, sauna, cocktail lounge, and all the other things apparently indispensable to the *Aurora*'s pampered passengers—could fit into this miniature vessel. Its size, along with the perfection of its paintwork, gave it a curiously toylike quality, and as I stepped onto the narrow steel gangway I had a sudden disorienting image of the *Aurora* as a ship imprisoned in a bottle—tiny, perfect, isolated, and unreal—and of myself, shrinking down to match it with every step I took towards the boat. It was a strange feeling, as if I were looking down the wrong end of a telescope, and it gave me a dizzying sensation almost like vertigo.

The gangway shifted beneath my feet, the oily, inky waters of the harbor swirling and sucking beneath, and I had a momentary illusion that I was falling, the steel beneath my feet giving way. I shut my eyes and gripped the cold metal rail.

Then I heard a woman's voice from up ahead.

"It's a wonderful smell, isn't it!"

I blinked. A stewardess was standing in the entrance to the ship. She was bright, almost white blond, with tanned walnut-brown skin, and beaming as if I were her rich, long-lost relative from Australia. I took a breath, trying to steady myself, and then made my way across the rest of the gangway and onto the *Aurora Borealis*.

"Welcome, Miss Blacklock," the stewardess said as I entered. Her accent was slightly clipped in a way I couldn't place, and her words somehow managed to convey the impression that encountering me was a life experience on a par winning the lottery. "I am so *very* pleased to welcome you on board. Can one of our porters take your case?"

I looked around me, trying to work out how she knew who I was. My bag was gone before I could protest.

"Can I offer you a glass of champagne?"

"Um," I said, distinguishing myself with witty repartee. The stewardess took that for yes and I found myself accepting the dewy flute she put into my hand. "Uh, thanks."

The interior of the *Aurora* was gobsmacking. The boat might be small, but they had crammed in enough bling for a vessel ten times the size. The gangway doors opened up onto the landing of a long, curving staircase and literally every surface that could be French polished, encased in marble, or draped with raw silk had been so. The whole flight was illuminated by an eye-watering chandelier, suffusing the place with tiny splashes of light that reminded me of nothing so much as the sun glinting off the sea on a summer's day. It was slightly nauseating—not in a social-conscience sort of way, although if you thought about it too hard, that too. But more the disorientation—the way the crystals acted like a prism on every drop of light, dazzling you, throwing you off-balance with a sensation like peering into a child's kaleidoscope. The effect, combined with lack of sleep, was not completely pleasant.

The stewardess must have seen me gawping, because she gave a proud smile.

"The Great Stairway is really something, isn't it?" she said. "That one chandelier has more than two thousand Swarovski crystals."

"Gosh," I said faintly. My head throbbed and I tried to remember if I'd packed the ibuprofen. It was hard not to blink.

"We are *very* proud of the *Aurora*," the stewardess continued warmly. "My name is Camilla Lidman and I am in charge of hospitality on the vessel. My office is on the lower deck, and if there is *anything* I can do to make your stay with us more enjoyable *please* do not hesitate to ask. My colleague Josef"—she indicated a smiling blond man to her right—"will show you to your cabin and give you a tour of the facilities. Dinner is at eight, but we would invite you to join us at seven p.m. in the Lindgren Lounge for a presentation on the boat's facilities and the wonders you can expect to enjoy on this cruise of the famous Norwegian fjords and the Swedish archipelago islands. Ah! Mr. Lederer."

A tall dark man in his forties was coming up the gangway behind us, followed by a porter struggling with a huge suitcase.

"Please be careful," he said, wincing visibly as the porter bumped the trolley over a joint in the gangway. "That case has some very delicate equipment in it."

"Mr. Lederer," Camilla Lidman said, with the exact same amount of near-delirious enthusiasm she had injected into her welcome to me. I had to hand it to her; I was impressed at her acting skills, though in the case of Mr. Lederer it probably took less effort since he was kind of easy on the eye. "Let me welcome you aboard the *Aurora*. Can I offer you a glass of champagne? And Mrs. Lederer?"

"Mrs. Lederer won't be coming," Mr. Lederer said. He ran a hand through his hair and glanced up at the Swarovski chandelier with an air of slight bemusement.

"Oh, I am so sorry." Camilla Lidman's flawless brow puckered in a frown of concern. "I hope nothing is wrong."

"Well, she's in fine health," Mr. Lederer said. "In fact, she's fucking my best friend." He smiled and took the champagne.

Camilla blinked and then said smoothly, almost without pause, "Josef, please do take Miss Blacklock to her cabin."

Josef gave a little half bow and extended a hand towards the downward sweep of the staircase.

"This way, please?" he said.

I nodded dumbly and allowed myself to be ushered away, still clutching my glass of champagne. Over my shoulder I could hear Camilla telling Mr. Lederer about her office on the lower deck.

"You are in cabin nine, the Linnaeus Suite," Josef told me as I followed him down into the beige dimness of a thickly carpeted, windowless corridor. "All the cabins are named after notable Scandinavian scientists."

"Who gets the Nobel?" I cracked nervously. The corridor was giving me a strange, stifled feeling, a heavy weight of claustrophobia on the back of my neck. It wasn't just the size but the soporifically low lamps and lack of natural light.

Josef answered seriously.

"On this particular voyage, the Nobel Suite will be occupied by Lord and Lady Bullmer. Lord Bullmer is director of the Northern Lights Company, which owns the vessel. There are ten cabins," he told me as we descended a set of stairs. "Four forward and six aft, all on the middle deck. Each cabin consists of a suite of up to three rooms, with its own bathroom, featuring full-sized bath and separate shower, full-sized double bed, and private veranda. The Nobel Suite has a private hot tub."

Veranda? Somehow the idea of having a veranda on a cruise ship seemed completely wrong, but I supposed, thinking about it, it wasn't any weirder than having any other open-deck area. Hot tub—well, least said about that the better.

"Every cabin has a named steward to assist you, day or night. Your stewards will be myself and my colleague Karla, who you will be meeting later this evening. We will be delighted to help you in any way we can during your stay on the *Aurora*."

"So this is the middle deck, right?" I asked. Josef nodded.

"Yes, this deck is solely passenger suites. Upstairs you will find the dining room, spa, lounge, library, sundeck, and other public areas. All are named after Scandinavian writers—the Lindgren Lounge, the Jansson Dining Room, and so on."

"Jansson?"

"Tove," he supplied.

"Oh, of course. Moomins," I said stupidly. God my head was aching.

We had reached a paneled wooden door with a discreet plaque reading 9. LINNAEUS. Josef threw open the door and stood back to allow me to step inside.

The place was, by no stretch of exaggeration, about seven or eight times nicer than my flat at home, and not a great deal smaller, either. Mirrored wardrobes stretched away to my right, and in the center, flanked by a sofa to one side and a dressing table to the other, was a huge double bed, the white linen expanse invitingly smooth and crisp.

But the thing that made the biggest impression on me was not the space—which was impressive—but the light. Coming out of the narrow, artificially lit corridor, the light streaming in from the huge veranda doors opposite was blinding. Sheer white curtains waved in the breeze and I saw that the sliding door was open. I felt an instant sense of relief, as if a tightness in my chest had lifted.

"The doors can be latched back," Josef explained from behind me, "but the catch will automatically disengage in the event of adverse weather conditions."

"Oh, great," I said vaguely, but all I could think of was how much I wanted Josef to *go,* so I could flop down on the bed and sink into oblivion.

Instead, I stood awkwardly, suppressing my yawns, while Josef told me unnecessarily about the functions of the bathroom (yes, I had used one before, thank you), the fridge and minibar (all complimentary—unfortunately for my liver), and explained that the ice would be refreshed twice a day and I could ring for him or Karla at *any* time.

At last my drooping yawns were no longer ignorable, and he gave a little half bow and excused himself, leaving me to take in the cabin.

There's no point in pretending I wasn't impressed. I was. Mainly by the bed, which was practically shrieking an invitation to throw myself down and sleep for maybe thirty to forty hours.

I looked at the pristine white duvet and the gold and white scatter cushions, and longing washed through me like a physical substance in my veins, sending prickles from the nape of my neck to the tips of my fingers and toes. I *needed* sleep. I was beginning to crave it, like a drug addict, counting the hours until my next fix. The thirty uncomfortable minutes in the taxi had only made it worse. But I couldn't sleep now. If I did, I might not wake up, and I could not afford to miss dinner.

I might be able to skip some of the functions later in the week, but I absolutely *had* to go to tonight's dinner and presentation. It was the first night on board—everyone would be making contacts and networking furiously. If I missed that, it would be a huge black mark against me, and I would never catch up.

Forcing down a yawn, I went out to the balcony, hoping the fresh air would help me wake from the creeping fog of exhaustion that seemed to encroach every time I stopped moving or talking.

The veranda was as delightful as one would imagine a private balcony on a luxury cruise ship to be. The barrier was made of glass so that sitting inside the suite you could almost imagine there was nothing between you and the ocean at all, and there were two deck chairs and a tiny table so that one could sit there on an evening and enjoy the midnight sun or northern lights, depending on which cruise one had booked.

I spent a long, long time watching the little ships toiling in and out of Hull harbor and feeling the salty wind in my hair, and then suddenly something about the feel of the ship changed. For a minute I couldn't think what it was—and then I realized. The engine, which had been purring discreetly for the last half hour or so, had gone up a notch, and something about the boat had shifted. With a grinding roar, we began to inch round, away from the quayside, to point out towards the sea.

As I stood and watched, the boat edged out of the harbor, past the green and red lights showing the mouth of the safe passage, and

I felt the change in its movement as we left the shelter of the harbor wall and entered the North Sea, the smooth lapping waves giving way to the great, rolling swells of the deep ocean.

Slowly, the shoreline slipped away, and the buildings of Hull dwindled into ridges on the horizon, and then into a dark line that could have been anywhere. As I watched it disappear, I thought of Judah, and everything I'd left undone. My phone was heavy in my pocket, and I took it out, hoping for something from him before we left the range of the UK transmitters. *Good-bye. Good luck. Bon voyage.*

But there was nothing. The signal dipped by one bar, and then another, and the phone in my hand was silent. As the coast of England disappeared from view, the only noise was the crashing of the waves.

From: Judah Lewis

To: Laura Blacklock

Sent: Tuesday, 22 September

Subject: Are you ok?

Hey honey, I haven't heard from you since your e-mail on Sunday. Not sure if our messages are crossing. Did you get my reply, or the text I sent you yesterday?

Getting kind of worried, and hoping you don't think I'm off somewhere being an asshole and nursing my wounds. I'm not. I love you, I miss you, and I'm thinking about you.

Don't worry about what happened back home—and the tooth is okay. I think it'll re-root like the doc said. I'm self-medicating with vodka anyway.

Let me know how the cruise is going—or if you're busy, just drop me a line to say you're okay.

Love you, J

From: Rowan Lonsdale

To: Laura Blacklock

CC: Jennifer West

Sent: Wednesday, 23 September

Subject: Update?

Lo, could you please reply to my e-mail sent two days ago requesting an update on the cruise? Jenn tells me you've filed nothing, and we were hoping for some kind of copy by tomorrow—a sidebar piece at the least.

Please let Jenn know ASAP where you're at with this, and cc me to your reply.

Rowan

PART TWO

- CHAPTER 6 -

Even rich people's showers were better.

The jets buffeted and massaged from every angle, numbing in their ferocity, so after a while it was hard to tell where the water started and my body ended.

I soaped my hair, then shaved my legs, and finally I just stood underneath the stream, watching the sea and the sky and the circling gulls. I'd left the bathroom door open and I could see across the bed and out to the veranda and the sea beyond. And the effect was just . . . well, I'm not going to lie, it was pretty nice. I guess you had to get something for the eight grand or whatever it was they were charging for this place.

The amount was slightly obscene, in comparison to my salary or even Rowan's salary. I had spent years drooling over the reports she sent back from a villa in the Bahamas or a yacht in the Maldives and waiting for the day when I, too, would be senior enough to get those kinds of perks, but now I was actually getting a taste of it, I wondered—how did she stand it, these regular glimpses into a life no regular person would ever be able to afford?

I was idly trying to work out how many months I'd have to work to pay for a week on the *Aurora* as a passenger, when I heard something—an indistinct little noise—beneath the roar of the water, that I couldn't place, but it definitely sounded like it came from my room. My heart quickened a little, but I kept my breathing firm and steady as I opened my eyes to turn off the shower.

Instead, I saw the bathroom door swinging towards me, as though someone had shoved it with a swift, sure hand.

It banged shut, the solid, firm clunk of a heavy door that was made of the very best-quality material, and I was left in the hot, wet dark with the water pounding on the top of my skull and my heart beating hard enough to register on the boat's sonar.

I couldn't hear anything above the hiss of blood in my ears and the roar of the shower. And I couldn't see anything, apart from the red gleam of the digital controls to the shower. Fuck. *Fuck.* Why hadn't I double-locked the cabin door?

I felt the walls of the bathroom closing in on me, the blackness seeming to swallow me whole.

Stop. Panicking, I told myself. No one's hurt you. No one's broken in. Chances are it's just a maid come to turn down the bed, or the door shutting by itself. *Stop. Panicking.*

I forced myself to feel for the controls. The water went freezing, then agonizingly hot so that I yelped and staggered back, cracking my ankle against the wall, but then finally I found the right button, the stream stopped, and I groped my way to the lights.

They came on, flooding the little room with an unforgiving glare, and I stared at myself in the mirror—bone white, with wet hair plastered to my skull like the girl from *The Ring.*

Shit.

Was this going to be what it was like? Was I turning into someone who had panic attacks about walking home from the tube or staying the night alone in the house without their boyfriend?

No, fuck that. I would *not* be that person.

There was a bathrobe on the back of the bathroom door, and I swathed it hastily around myself and then took a deep, shaking breath.

I would not be that person.

I opened the bathroom door, my heart beating so hard and fast that I was seeing stars in my vision.

Do not panic, I thought fiercely.

The room was empty. Completely empty. And the door *was* double-locked, even the chain was across. There was no way anyone had got in. Maybe I'd just heard someone in the corridor. Either way, it was obviously just the tilting movement of the ship that had caused the door to swing shut, impelled by its own weight.

I checked the chain again, feeling the thick weight of it heavy in the palm of my hand, reassuringly solid, and then, on weak legs, I made my way to the bed and lay down, my heart still pounding with suppressed adrenaline, and waited for my pulse to return to something approaching normal.

I imagined burying my face in Judah's shoulder and for a second I nearly burst into tears, but I clenched my teeth and swallowed them back down. Judah was not the answer to all this. The problem was me and my weak-ass panic attacks.

Nothing happened. Nothing happened.

I repeated it in time with my rapid breaths, until I felt myself begin to calm down.

Nothing happened. Not now. Not then. Nobody hurt you.

Nothing happened.

Okay.

God, I needed a drink.

Inside the minibar was tonic, ice, and half a dozen miniatures of gin, whiskey, and vodka. I shook ice into a tumbler and then emptied in a couple of the miniature bottles, pouring with a hand that still shook slightly. I topped up with a splash of tonic water and gulped it down.

The gin was so strong it made me choke, but I felt the warmth of the alcohol spreading through my cells and blood vessels and felt instantly better.

When the glass was empty, I stood up, feeling the lightness in my head and limbs, and pulled my phone out of my bag. No reception, so clearly we were out of range of the UK transmitters, but there was Wi-Fi.

I clicked on mail and downloaded my e-mails, chewing my nails as they popped one by one into the in-box. It wasn't quite as bad as I'd been fearing—it was a Sunday after all—but as I scanned down the list, I realized I was tense as an elastic band about to snap, and at the same time, I understood what I was looking for, and why. There was nothing from Judah. I felt my shoulders slump.

I answered the few that were urgent, marked the others unread, and then pressed compose to start a new e-mail.

Dear Judah, I wrote, but the rest of the words wouldn't come. I wondered what he was doing right now. Was he packing his bag? Crammed onto some economy flight? Or was he lying on his bed in his room, tweeting, texting, thinking of me . . .

I relived again the moment I'd smashed the heavy metal lamp into his face. What had I been *thinking*?

You weren't thinking, I told myself. You were half-asleep. It's not your fault. It was an accident.

Freud says there are no accidents, said the voice in the back of my head. *Maybe it's you. . . .*

I shook my head, refusing to listen.

Dear Judah, I love you.

I miss you.

I'm sorry.

I deleted the one to Judah and started a new one.

To: Pamela Crew

From: Laura Blacklock

Sent: Sunday, 20 September

Subject: Safe and sound

Hi, Mum, safe on board the boat, which is seriously swanky. You'd love it! Just a quick reminder to pick up Delilah tonight. I've left her cat basket on the table, and the food is under the sink. I had to change the locks—Mrs. Johnson upstairs has the new key.

Lots of love and THANKS!

Lo xx

I pressed send, then pulled up Facebook and messaged my best friend, Lissie.

This place is insanely nice. There are UNLIMITED free drinks in the minibar in my cabin—sorry, I mean fucking enormous SUITE—which doesn't bode well for my professionalism, or my liver. See you on the other side, if I'm still standing. Lo xx

I poured myself another gin and then I went back to the Judah e-mail.

I had to write something. I couldn't leave things the way they were when I walked out.

Dear J. I'm sorry I was such a bitch before I left. What I said—it was incredibly unfair. I love you so much.

I had to stop at that, because tears were blurring the screen. I paused and took a couple of shaking breaths. Then I scrubbed crossly at my eyes and finished.

Text me when you get to Moscow. Safe journey.

Lo xxx

I refreshed my in-box, less hopefully this time, but nothing new downloaded. Instead, I sighed and drained my second gin. The clock by the bed read 6:30, which meant it was time for ball gown number one.

Rowan, after she'd informed me that the dress code for dining on board was "formal" (translation: insane), had recommended that I rent at least seven evening dresses, so that I wouldn't have to wear the same dress twice; but since she wasn't proposing to shell out the cost, I had rented three, which was three more than I'd have done if left to my own devices.

My favorite in the shop had been the most over-the-top one—a long silvery-white sheath studded with crystals that, the shop assistant had claimed without a glimmer of sarcasm, made me look like Liv Tyler in *The Lord of the Rings*. I'm not sure I kept my face sufficiently straight when she said that, because she kept shooting me suspicious looks as I tried on the others.

But I wasn't feeling quite brave enough to kick off with crystal studs, given there might well be people there wearing jeans, for all I knew, so I picked out the most modest choice—a long, narrow slip in dark gray satin. There was a little spritz of sequined leaves across the right shoulder because you didn't seem to be able to get away with none. Apparently the majority of ball gowns were designed by five-year-old girls armed with glitter guns, but at least this one didn't look entirely like an explosion in a Barbie factory.

I wriggled into it and zipped it up the side, then I shook out the full array of ammo from my makeup bag. It was going to take more than a swipe of lip gloss to get me looking even halfway human tonight. I was just smudging concealer across the cut on my cheekbone when I realized my mascara wasn't among the clutter.

I hunted through my handbag in the vain hope that it might be there, trying to remember where I'd last seen it. Then I realized. It had been in my handbag—pinched along with everything else. I don't always wear it, but without dark lashes, my smoky-eye makeup looked strange and out of proportion—like I'd given up halfway through. I thought briefly and ridiculously about improvising with liquid eyeliner, but instead I tried one last, vain hunt in my bag—tipping everything out onto the bed, just in case I'd misremembered, or had a spare one stuck in the lining. In my heart, though, I knew it wasn't there, and I was replacing everything back into the bag when I heard a noise from the cabin next door—the roar of the pressurized toilet flushing, recognizable even above the muted hum of the engine.

Taking my room key in my hand, I went out barefoot into the corridor.

The ash wood door to my right had a little plaque that read 10. PALMGREN, which made me think that the supply of eminent Scandinavian scientists must have worn a little thin by the time they finished fitting out this boat. I knocked, slightly hesitantly.

There was no answer. I waited. Maybe the occupant was in the shower.

I knocked again, three sharp knocks, and then, as an afterthought, a final loud whack in case they were hard of hearing.

The door flew open, as if the occupant had been standing on the other side.

"What?" she demanded, almost before the door had opened. "Is everything okay?" And then her face changed. "Shit. Who are you?"

"I'm your neighbor," I said. She was young and pretty with long dark hair, and she was wearing a ratty Pink Floyd T-shirt with holes, which somehow made me like her quite a lot. "Laura Blacklock. Lo. Sorry, I know this sounds really weird, but I wondered if I could borrow some mascara?"

There was a scatter of tubes and creams visible on the dressing table behind her, and she was wearing quite a bit of it herself, which made me fairly sure I was on safe ground.

"Oh." She looked flustered. "Right. Hang on."

She disappeared, closing the door behind her, and then came back with a tube of Maybelline and stuck it into my hand.

"Hey, thanks," I said. "I'll bring it right back."

"Keep it," she said. I protested, automatically, but she waved my words away. "Seriously, I don't want it back."

"I'll wash the brush," I offered, but she shook her head impatiently.

"I told you, I don't want it."

"Okay," I said, slightly puzzled. "Thanks."

"You're welcome." She shut the door in my face.

I went back to my cabin wondering about the odd little encounter. I felt out of place enough on this trip, but she looked even more of a fish out of water. Someone's daughter, maybe? I wondered if I'd see her at dinner.

I'd just finished applying the borrowed mascara when there was a knock at the door. Maybe she'd changed her mind.

"Hey," I said, opening the door, holding it out. But it was a different girl outside, one wearing a stewardess's uniform. Her eyebrows had been rather savagely overplucked, giving her an expression of permanent surprise.

"Hello," she said, with a singsong Scandinavian inflection. "My name is Karla and I'm your suite attendant along with Josef. This is just a courtesy call to remind you of the presentation at—"

"I remember," I said, rather more brusquely than I'd intended. "Seven p.m. in the Pippi Longstocking Room or whatever it's called."

"Ah, I see you know your Scandinavian writers!" She beamed.

"I'm not so hot on the scientists," I admitted. "I'll be right up."

"Wonderful. Lord Bullmer is looking forward to welcoming you all on board."

After she'd gone I rummaged in my case for the wrap that had come with the dress—a sort of gray silk shawl that made me feel like a long-lost Brontë sister—and draped it round my shoulders.

I locked the door behind me and dropped the key inside my bra, and then I made my way along the corridor, up to the Lindgren Lounge.

- CHAPTER 7 -

White. *White.*

Everything was white. The pale wood floor. The white velvet sofas. The long raw-silk curtains. The flawless walls. It was spectacularly impractical for a public vessel—deliberately so, I had to assume.

Another Swarovski chandelier hung from the ceiling and I couldn't help but pause in the doorway, more than a little dazed. It wasn't just the light, the way it glinted and refracted from the crystals on the ceiling, it was something about the scale. The room was like a perfect replica of a drawing room in a five-star hotel, or a reception room on the *QE2,* but it was *small.* There could not have been more than twelve or fifteen people in the room, and yet they filled the space, and even the chandelier was scaled down to fit. It gave the strangest impression—a little like looking in through the doorway of a doll's house, where everything is miniaturized and yet slightly off-kilter, the replica cushions a little too large and stiff for the tiny chairs, the wineglasses the same size as the fake champagne bottle.

I was scanning the room, looking for the girl in the Pink Floyd T-shirt, when a low, amused voice came from the corridor behind me.

"Blinding, isn't it?"

I turned to see the mysterious Mr. Lederer standing there.

"Just a touch," I said. He held out his hand.

"Cole Lederer."

The name was faintly familiar but I couldn't put my finger on it.

"Laura Blacklock." We shook, and I took him in. Even in jeans and a T-shirt struggling up the gangway, he was what Lissie would have called "eye candy." Now he was wearing a dinner jacket in a way that made me remember Lissie's rule of thumb: a dinner jacket added 33 percent to a man's attractiveness.

"So," he said, taking a glass off a tray proffered by yet another smiling Scandinavian stewardess. "What brings you to the *Aurora*, Miss Blacklock?"

"Oh, call me Lo. I'm a journalist, I work for *Velocity.*"

"Well, very happy to meet you, Lo. Can I offer you a drink?"

He picked up a second flute and held it out with a smile. The empty miniatures in the cabin floated up before my eyes, and I wavered for a moment, knowing I was on the cusp of drinking too much so early in the evening but not wanting to seem rude. My stomach was very, very empty and the gin hadn't quite worn off, but surely one more glass couldn't hurt?

"Thanks," I said at last. He handed it over, his fingers brushing mine in a way I wasn't sure was accidental, and I took a gulp, trying to drown my nerves. "How about you? What's your role here?"

"I'm a photographer," he said, and I suddenly realized where I'd heard the name before.

"Cole Lederer!" I exclaimed. I was ready to kick myself. Rowan would have been all over him, right from the gangway. "Of course—you did that amazing shoot for the *Guardian* of the melting ice caps."

"That's right." He grinned, unashamedly pleased at being recognized, though you would have thought the thrill would have worn off for him by now. The guy was only a couple of steps down from David Bailey. "I've been invited to cover this lot, you know, moody shots of the fjords and stuff."

"It's not usually your thing, is it?" I said doubtfully.

"No," he agreed. "I tend to do mainly endangered species or at-risk environments these days, and I don't think you could say this lot were at any particular risk of extinction. They all look particularly well-fed."

We gazed around the room together.

I had to agree with him when it came to the men. There was a little knot in the far corner who looked like they could survive for several weeks off their fat reserves, if we were ever shipwrecked. The women were a different story, though. They all had that lean, polished look that spoke of hot Bikram yoga and a macrobiotic diet, and they didn't look like they'd survive long if the ship went down. Maybe they could eat one of the men.

I recognized a few faces from other press shindigs—there was Tina West, whippet-thin and wearing jewelry weighing more than she did, who edited the *Vernean Times* (motto: *Eighty days is just the start*); the travel journalist Alexander Belhomme, who wrote features and foodie articles for a number of cross-channel and in-flight magazines and was sleek and rotund as a walrus; and Archer Fenlan, who was a well-known expert on "extreme travel."

Archer, who was maybe forty but looked older with his perma-tanned weathered face, was shifting from foot to foot, looking distinctly uncomfortable in his tie and dinner jacket. I couldn't quite imagine what he was doing here—his normal beat was eating witchetty grubs up the Amazon, but maybe he was having a bit of time off.

I couldn't see the girl from the next-door cabin anywhere.

"Boo!" said a voice from behind me.

I whipped round.

Ben Howard. What the hell was he doing here? He was grinning at me through a thick hipster beard that was new since I'd last seen him.

"Ben," I said thinly, trying to suppress my shock. "How are you? Have you met Cole Lederer? Ben and I used to be at *Velocity* together. Now he writes for the . . . what is it at the moment? *Indie*? *Times*?"

"Me and Cole know each other," Ben said easily. "We covered that Greenpeace thing together. How's it going, man?"

"All right," Cole said. They did that sort of manly half-hug thing, where you're too metrosexual for a handshake and not hip enough for a fist bump.

"Lookin' good, Blacklock," Ben said, turning to me and giving me the once-over in a way that made me want to knee him in the balls, except that the sodding dress was too tight. "Although . . . have you, er, been cage fighting again?"

For a minute I couldn't work out what he was on about. Then I realized: the bruise on my cheek. Obviously my expertise with the concealer wasn't as good as I'd thought.

The flashing memory of the door slamming into my cheek and the man in my flat—about Ben's height, with the same liquid dark eyes—was so vivid that my heart had begun thumping and my chest felt tight, and for a long moment I couldn't find the words to reply. I just stared at him, not trying to keep the ice out of my expression.

"Sorry, sorry." He held up a hand. "My own beeswax, I know. Christ, this collar's tight." He yanked at his bow tie. "How did you land this gig, then? Going up in the world?"

"Rowan's ill," I said shortly.

"Cole!" A voice broke into the awkward pause and we all turned to look. It was Tina, sashaying smoothly across the pristine white-oak floor, her silver dress rustling like snakeskin. She gave Lederer a lingering kiss on both cheeks, ignoring me and Ben. "Sweetie, it's been *far* too long." Her voice was throaty with emotion. "And *when* are you going to do that shoot you promised for the *Vernean*?"

"Hi, Tina," Cole said, with just a touch of weariness in his tone.

"Let me introduce you to Richard and Lars," she purred, and, slipping her arm through his, she bore him off to the knot of men I'd noticed at the beginning. He allowed himself to be carried away, with just a little rueful smile over his shoulder as he went. Ben watched him go and then turned back to me, cocking an eyebrow with such perfect comic timing that I let out a snort.

"I think we know who the belle of the ball is, right?" he said dryly, and I had to nod. "So how are you, anyway?" he continued. "Still with the Yank?"

What could I say? I don't know? There's a strong possibility I might have screwed things up enough to have lost him?

"Still very much unavailable," I said at last, sourly.

"Shame. But you know, what happens in the fjords stays in the fjords. . . ."

"Oh, piss off, Howard," I snapped. He put up his hands.

"Can't blame a guy for trying."

Yes, I can, I thought, but I didn't say it. Instead, I grabbed another glass from a passing waitress and looked round for something to change the subject.

"Who are the others, then?" I asked. "I've got you, me, Cole, Tina, and Archer ticked off. Oh, and Alexander Belhomme. What about that crowd over there?" I nodded at the little group Tina was chatting to. There were three men and two women, one of them about my age but about fifty thousand pounds better dressed, and the other . . . well, the other was sort of a surprise.

"That's Lord Bullmer and his cronies. You know, he's the owner of the boat and the . . . I guess you'd call it the company figurehead?"

I stared at the little knot in the corner, trying to make out Lord Bullmer from the snap on *Wikipedia*. At first I couldn't work out which one he was, and then one of the men gave a full-throated laugh, throwing back his head, and I knew at once it was him. He was tall, wirily slim, and dressed in a suit so well cut that I was certain it must be tailored. He was fiercely tanned, as if he spent a lot of time outdoors, his bright blue eyes narrowed into slits as he laughed, and there was a streak of premature gray at each temple, but it was the grayness that comes sometimes with extremely black hair, not old age.

"He's so young," I said wonderingly. "Seems kind of weird for someone our age to be a peer, don't you think?"

"He's Viscount Something as well, I think. The money's mainly down to his wife, of course. She's the Lyngstad heiress, her family owned that huge car manufacturer. You know the ones I mean?"

I nodded. My business knowledge might be shaky, and the family might be famously private, but even I'd heard of the Lyngstad Foundation. Every time I saw footage of an international disaster zone, their logo was on the trucks and aid parcels. I had a sudden memory of a shot I'd seen all over the papers last year—it might even have been one of Cole's—of a Syrian mother standing in front of a Lyngstad-branded truck with a baby in her arms, holding the child up towards the driver like a talisman to make the vehicle stop.

"And is that her?" I nodded at the willowy white-blonde with her back to me, who was laughing at something one of the other men had said. She was dressed in a devastatingly simple gown of rose-colored wild silk that made me feel like I'd cobbled mine together from my childhood dressing-up box. Ben shook his head.

"No, she's Chloe Jenssen. Ex-model and married to that chap with the blond hair, Lars Jenssen. He's a big noise in finance, head of a Swedish investment group. I imagine Bullmer's got him here as a potential investor. No, that's Bullmer's wife, next to him, in the headscarf."

Oh . . . She was the surprise. In contrast to the other women in the group, the woman in the headscarf looked . . . well, she looked ill. She was wearing a kind of shapeless gray silk kimono wrap that matched her eyes, and looked halfway between an evening dress and a dressing gown, but even from here I could see she was wearing a silk scarf wound around her scalp, and her skin was waxily pale. Her gray pallor stood out in sharp contrast to the rest of the group, who looked almost obscenely healthy in contrast. I realized I was staring and dropped my eyes.

"She's been ill," Ben said unnecessarily. "Breast cancer. I think it was pretty serious."

"How old is she?"

"Barely thirty, I think. Younger than him, anyway."

As Ben drained his glass and turned to look for a waiter to fill up, I found my gaze drawn back. I would never in a million years have recognized her from the photograph I'd seen on *Wikipedia*. Perhaps it was the gray skin, or the loose-fitting silks, but she seemed years older, and with that glorious mane of golden hair gone, she looked like a completely different woman.

Why was she here and not at home lying on a sofa? But then again, why *shouldn't* she be here? Maybe she didn't have long to live. Maybe she was trying to make the most of her time. Or maybe—here was a thought—just maybe, she wished that the woman in the gray dress would stop staring at her with pitying eyes and leave her alone.

I looked away again and cast around for someone less vulnerable to speculate about. There was only one person left in the group unaccounted for, a tall older man with a neatly clipped graying beard and a gut that could only be the product of a lot of long lunches.

"Who's the Donald Sutherland look-alike?" I said to Ben. He turned back round.

"Who? Oh, that's Owen White. UK investor. Richard Branson type—just on a slightly smaller scale."

"Jesus, Ben. How do you *know* all this? Have you got an encyclopedic knowledge of high society or something?"

"Er, no." Ben looked at me, a touch of disbelief in his expression. "I rang up the press office for a list of guests and then googled them. It's not exactly Sherlock Holmes stuff."

Fuck. *Fuck.* Why hadn't I done that? It was what any good reporter would have done—and I'd not even thought of it. But then, Ben probably hadn't spent the last few days in a haze of sleep deprivation and PTSD.

"How about—"

But whatever Ben had been about to say, it was drowned out by the *ting ting ting!* of metal against champagne flute, and Lord Bullmer moved into the center of the room. Camilla Lidman put down the flute and teaspoon she was holding and made as if to step forward and introduce him, but he waved a hand and she melted into the background with a self-effacing smile.

The room fell into a respectful, faintly anticipatory silence, and Lord Bullmer began to speak.

"Thank you, everyone, for coming to join us here on the *Aurora* on this, its maiden voyage," he began. His voice was warm, and had that curiously classless tone that people from public school seemed to strive for, and his blue eyes had a kind of magnetic quality that was hard to look away from. "My name is Richard Bullmer, and my wife, Anne, and I would like to welcome you aboard the *Aurora*. What we have sought to do with this ship is make it nothing less than a home away from home."

"Home away from home?" Ben whispered. "Maybe his home has a sea-view balcony and a free minibar. Mine sure as hell doesn't."

"We do not believe that travel has to mean compromise," Richard Bullmer continued. "On the *Aurora*, everything should be as you would wish, and if it's not, my staff and I want to hear." He paused and gave a little wink at Camilla, including her in the remark as an acknowledgment that she would likely be on the sharp end of any complaints.

"Those of you who know me will know of my passion for Scandinavia—for the warmth of its people"—he shot a quick smile at Lars and Anne—"for the excellence of its food"—he nodded at the tray of dill and prawn canapés traveling past—"and the spectacular glory of the region itself: from the rolling forests of Finland, to the scattered islands of the Swedish archipelago, to the majesty of the fjords in my wife's native Norway. But I think that, for me, the defining quality of the Scandinavian landscape is—perhaps paradoxically—not the land at all, but the skies—wide, and almost preternaturally clear. And it is those skies that provide what for many is the crowning glory of the Scandinavian winter experience—the northern lights, the aurora borealis. With nature nothing is certain, but I very much hope to share the spectacular majesty of the northern lights with you on this trip. The aurora borealis is something that everyone should see before they die. And now, please raise your glasses, ladies and gentlemen, to the maiden voyage of the *Aurora Borealis*—and may the beauty of her namesake never fade."

"To the *Aurora Borealis*," we chorused obediently, and downed our glasses. I felt the alcohol trickle through me, taking the edge off everything, even my still-aching cheek.

"Come on, Blacklock," Ben said, setting down his empty glass. "Let's go do our bit and schmooze."

I felt a twinge of reluctance to approach the group with him. The thought of being taken for a couple was awkward, given our past, but I wasn't about to let Ben start making connections while I hung back. As we started across the room, I saw Anne Bullmer touch her husband's arm and whisper something in his ear. He nodded, and she gathered up her wrap and the two of them began to make their way towards the doorway, Richard holding Anne's arm solicitously. We passed in the center of the room, and she smiled, a sweet smile that illuminated her drawn, fine-boned face with a shadow of what must have been her former beauty, and I saw that she had no eyebrows at all. The lack of them, together with her jutting cheekbones, gave her face a curious, skull-like appearance.

"You'll excuse me, I'm sure," she said. Her voice was pure BBC English, no trace of accent that I could detect. "I'm very tired—I'm afraid I'm ducking out of dinner tonight. But I look forward to meeting you tomorrow."

"Of course," I said awkwardly, and then tried to smile. "I—I look forward to it, too."

"I'm just going to see my wife to her cabin," Richard Bullmer said. "I'll be back before dinner is served."

I looked at them as they walked slowly away and then said to Ben, "Her English is amazing. You'd never know she was Norwegian."

"I don't think she actually lived there much when she was younger. She spent most of her childhood at boarding schools in Switzerland, as far as I know. Right, cover me, Blacklock, I'm going in."

He strode across the room, scooping up a handful of canapés as he went, and inserted himself into the little group with the practiced ease of a born journalist.

"Belhomme," I heard him say, his tone full of a sort of Old Etonian faux bonhomie, which I knew to be completely out of keeping with his actual background, growing up on an Essex council estate. "Great to see you again. And you must be Lars Jenssen, sir, I read that profile of you in the *FT*. I very much admire your stance on the environment—mixing principles with business isn't as easy as you make it look."

Ugh, look at him, networking like a bastard. No wonder he was working at the *Times* doing proper investigative stuff, while I was stuck in Rowan's shadow at *Velocity.* I should get over there. I should inveigle myself into conversation with them just as Ben had. This was my chance and I knew it. So why was I standing here, holding my glass with cold fingers, unable to make myself move?

The waitress came past with a bottle of champagne and, slightly against my better judgment, I let her fill up my glass. As she moved away, I took a reckless gulp.

"Penny?" said a low voice in my ear, and I whipped round to see Cole Lederer standing behind me.

"Sorry, Penny who?" I managed, though my palms were prickling with sweat. I had *got* to get over this.

He grinned, and I realized my mistake.

"Oh, of course, for my thoughts," I said, cross with myself, and with him for being so coy.

"Sorry," he said, still smiling. "Stupid cliché. I don't know why I said it. You just looked particularly pensive standing there, biting your lip like that."

I was biting my lip? Well, hell, why not trail the tips of my Mary Janes in the dirt as well and maybe flutter my eyelashes?

I tried to remember what I had been thinking about, other than Ben and my lack of networking skills. The only thing that came to mind was the bastard who broke into my flat, but I was damned if I'd bring that up here. I wanted Cole Lederer to respect me as a journalist, not feel sorry for me.

"Oh . . . uh . . . politics?" I brought out, at last. The champagne and the tiredness were starting to hit. My brain didn't seem to be working properly, and my head was starting to ache. I realized that I was halfway to being drunk, and not the good kind of drunk, either.

Cole looked at me skeptically.

"Well, what were *you* thinking, then?" I said crossly. There's a reason why we keep thoughts inside our heads for the most part—they're not safe to be let out in public.

"Other than looking at your lips, you mean?"

I resisted the urge to roll my eyes and tried to channel my inner Rowan, who would have flirted with him until she got his business card.

"If you must know," Cole continued, propping himself against the wall as the ship heaved over a wave and the ice in the champagne buckets rattled, "I was thinking about my soon-to-be ex-wife."

"Oh. Sorry," I said. He was drunk, too, I saw, just hiding it well.

"She's screwing my best man, from our wedding. I was thinking how much I'd like to return the favor."

"Screw her bridesmaid?"

"Or just . . . anyone, really."

Huh. As propositions went, it was certainly direct. He grinned again, somehow managing to make the line sound fairly charming, like he was trying his luck, rather than acting like a sleazy pickup artist.

"Well, I think you shouldn't have too much trouble," I said lightly. "I'm pretty sure Tina would oblige."

Cole gave a snort of laughter, and I felt a sudden twinge of guilt, thinking about how I would feel if Ben and Tina were over on the other side of the room making jokes about me throwing myself at Cole for the sake of my career. So Tina had turned on the charm. Big deal. It was hardly the crime of the century.

"Sorry," I said, wishing I could take back the remark. "That was a pretty cheap dig."

"But accurate," Cole said dryly. "Tina would skin her own grandmother for the sake of a story. My only worry"—he took another slug of champagne and grinned—"would be coming out of the encounter alive."

"Ladies and gentlemen . . ." A steward's voice broke into our conversations. "If you would like to make your way through to the Jansson room, dinner will shortly be served."

As we started to file through, I felt someone's eyes on my back, and I turned to see who it was. The person standing behind me was Tina, and she was looking at me very speculatively indeed.

- CHAPTER 8 -

It took a surprisingly long time for the staff to usher us through into the miniature dining room next door. Somehow I'd been expecting something practical, like the ferries I had been on with rows of tables and a long lunch counter. Of course, the reality was quite different—a room about the size of a private dining room in a restaurant. We could have been in someone's home, if I knew anyone whose home had raw-silk curtains and cut-glass goblets.

By the time we sat down, my head was throbbing painfully, and I was desperate for some food—or better still some coffee, though I presumed I'd have to wait until dessert for that. It felt like a long way off.

The guests had been arranged into two tables of six each, but there was an empty place at each. Was one where the girl in cabin 10 had been supposed to sit? I did a quick head count under my breath.

Table one had Richard Bullmer, Tina, Alexander, Owen, and Ben. The spare place was opposite Richard Bullmer.

Table two had me, Lars and Chloe, Archer, Cole, and a spare place beside Cole.

"You can clear this," Cole said to the waitress who arrived with a bottle of wine. He waved a hand at the unused setting. "My wife wasn't able to attend the trip."

"Oh, my apologies, sir." She gave a little half bow, said something to her colleague, and the place setting was whisked away.

Well that explained that. The empty place at the first table remained, though.

"Chablis?" the waitress asked.

"Yes, please." He held out his glass. As he did, Chloe Jenssen leaned across the table with her hand extended towards me.

"I don't think we've been introduced." She had a low, husky voice, quite unexpected for her tiny frame, and the hint of an Essex accent. "I'm Chloe—Chloe Jenssen, although my professional name's Wylde."

Of course. Now that she'd said it, I recognized her, the famous wide cheekbones and slightly Slavic tilt to her eyes, the white-blond hair. Even without stagy makeup and lighting, she looked slightly otherworldly, like she'd been plucked from a tiny Icelandic fishing village, or a Siberian dacha. Her looks made the story of her being discovered by a modeling scout in an out-of-town supermarket all the more incongruous.

"Pleased to meet you," I said, and took her hand. Her fingers were cold, and her grip was almost painfully strong, made more so by the chunky rings she wore, which cut into my knuckles. Up close she was even more stunning, the austere beauty of her dress so obviously outclassing mine, I felt like we might as well have come from different planets. I resisted the urge to tug at the neckline. "I'm Lo Blacklock."

"Lo Blacklock!" She gave a gurgling laugh. "I like it. Sounds like a fifties film star, the sort with a wasp waist and tits up to her chin."

"I wish." In spite of the growing ache in my head, I grinned. There was something about her amusement that was infectious. "And this must be your husband . . . ?"

"This is Lars, yes." She looked across at him, ready to bring him into the conversation and introduce him, but he was deep in conversation with Cole and Archer, and she just rolled her eyes and turned back to me.

"Have they got someone else joining them?" I nodded at the spare place at the first table. Chloe shook her head.

"I think that was for Anne—you know, Richard's wife? She's not well. Decided to have supper in her cabin, I think."

"Of course." I should have thought of that. "Do you know her well?" I asked. Chloe shook her head.

"No, I know Richard quite well, via Lars, but Anne doesn't often leave Norway." She lowered her voice and spoke confidentially. "She's supposed to be kind of a recluse, actually, so I was surprised to find she was on board—but I'd imagine that having cancer might make you—"

But whatever she had been about to say was interrupted by the arrival of five dark square plates, scattered across with small rainbow-colored squares and clumps of foam arranged on what looked like grass clippings. I realized I had no idea what I was about to eat.

"Beet-pickled razor clam," announced the head server, "with a bison grass foam and air-dried samphire shards."

The waiters retreated and Archer picked up his fork and poked at the most neon-colored of the squares.

"Razor clam?" he said dubiously. His Yorkshire accent was somehow stronger than it sounded on TV. "Never been that keen on raw shellfish, somehow. It gives me the willies."

"Really?" Chloe said. She gave a curving, catlike smile that indicated something between flirting and disbelief. "I thought bush tucker was your thing—you know, bugs and lizards and stuff."

"If you got paid to eat droppings for your day job, maybe you'd fancy a nice steak on your day off, too," he said, and grinned. He turned to me and stuck out his hand. "Archer Fenland. Not sure if we've been introduced."

"Lo Blacklock," I said through a mouthful of something that I was *hoping* was not cuckoo spit, though it was hard to be sure. "We've met, actually, but you won't remember. I work for *Velocity*."

"Oh, aye. Do you work for Rowan Lonsdale, then?"

"That's right."

"She like that piece I did for her?"

"Yes, it was very popular. Got a lot of tweets."

Twelve Surprisingly Delicious Foods You Didn't Know Were Edible, or something along those lines. It had been illustrated with a picture of Archer roasting something unspeakable over a fire and grinning up at the camera.

"Aren't you going to eat it?" Chloe said, nodding at Archer's plate. Her own plate was nearly clear and she swiped her finger across a slick of foam and licked it up.

Archer hesitated and then pushed his plate away.

"I think I'll sit this one out," he said. "Wait for the next course."

"Fair play," Chloe said. She gave another slow, curving smile. A movement in her lap caught my eye and I saw that beneath the level of the table, not quite hidden by the cloth, she and Lars were holding hands, his thumb rhythmically stroking across her knuckles. The sight was somehow so intimate, yet so public, that I felt a little shock run over me. Maybe her flirtatious persona wasn't all it seemed?

I realized Archer was talking to me, and I turned my attention back to the table and focused on him with an effort.

"I'm sorry," I said. "I was somewhere else. What did you say?"

"I said, can I refill you? Your glass is empty."

I looked down at it. The Chablis had gone—though I barely remembered drinking it.

"Yes, please," I said. As he poured, I stared into the glass, trying to work out how much I had drunk already. I took a sip. As I did, Chloe leaned over and said quietly, "I hope you don't mind me asking, but what happened to your cheek?"

Maybe my surprise showed in my face, because she flapped a hand in a *forget about it* gesture.

"Sorry, ignore me, none of my business. I just . . . well, I've been in bad relationships, that's all."

"Oh, no . . ." For some reason the misunderstanding made me feel ashamed, like it was my fault or I'd been criticizing Judah behind his back, although neither was true. "No, it's nothing like that. I got burgled."

"Really?" She looked shocked. "While you were in?"

"Yup. Getting more common, apparently, or so the police said."

"And he attacked you? Jesus."

"Not quite." I felt an odd reluctance to go into details, not just because talking about it brought back unpleasant flashes of what had happened but also out of a kind of pride. I wanted to sit at this table as a professional, the smooth, capable journalist able to take on all comers. I didn't relish the portrait of myself as a frightened victim, cowering in my own bedroom.

But the story was out now—at least 90 percent of it was—and not explaining felt like getting sympathy under false pretenses.

"It—it was an accident really. He slammed a door in my face; it hit my cheek. I don't think he meant to hurt me."

I should have just stayed in my room, head beneath the duvet, was the truth. Stupid Lo, sticking your neck out.

"You should learn self defence," Archer said. "That's how I started, you know. Royal Marines. It's not about size, even a girl like you can overpower a man if you get the leverage right. Look, I'll show you." He pushed back his chair. "Stand up."

I stood, feeling slightly awkward, and with extraordinary swiftness he grabbed my arm and twisted it up behind my back, tilting me off-balance. I grabbed for the table with my free hand, but the twisting motion in my shoulder continued, pulling me backwards, the muscles screaming in protest.

I made a noise, half of pain and half of fright, and out of the corner of my eye I saw Chloe's shocked face.

"Archer," she said, and then more urgently, "Archer—you're scaring her!"

He let go, and I sank back into my chair, my legs trembling, trying not to show how much my shoulder was protesting.

"Sorry," Archer said with a grin as he pulled his chair back to the table. "Hope I didn't hurt you. Don't know my own strength. But you see what I mean—very tricky to get out of, even if your attacker's bigger than you. Anytime you want a lesson . . ."

I tried for a laugh, but it came out sounding fake and shaky.

"You look like you need a drink," Chloe said bluntly, and she topped up my glass. Then, as Archer turned away to speak to a waiter, she added in a lower voice, "Ignore Archer. I'm starting to believe the rumors about his first wife were true. And look, if you want something to cover up that bruise, come over to my cabin sometime. I've got a whole array of stuff and I'm a pretty mean makeup artist. You need it in the trade."

"I'll do that," I said, and attempted a smile. It felt false and strained and I picked up my glass and took a sip to hide it. "Thanks."

After the first course, the places switched around and I found myself, somewhat to my relief, at the other table from Archer, sitting between Tina and Alexander, who were having a very knowledgeable conversation about foods of the world over the top of my head.

"Of course the one type of sashimi you really *must* try is fugu," Alexander said expansively, smoothing his napkin across his straining cummerbund. "It's simply the most exquisite taste."

"Fugu?" I said, trying to insert myself into the conversation. "Isn't that the horribly poisonous one?"

"Absolutely, and that's what *makes* the experience. I've never been a drug taker—I know my own weaknesses, and I am very aware of being one of life's lotus-eaters, so I've never trusted myself to dabble in that sort of thing—but I can only assume that the high one experiences after eating fugu triggers a similar neuron response. The diner has diced with death, and won."

"Don't they say," Tina drawled, sipping at her wine, "that the art of the really superlative chef is to slice as closely as possible to the poisonous parts of the fish and leave just a sliver of the toxins on the flesh to heighten the experience?"

"I have heard that," Alexander conceded. "It is supposed to act as a stimulant in very small quantities, although that particular slicing technique may be more to do with the expense of the fish and the chef's disinclination to waste even a morsel."

"So how poisonous is it?" I asked. "In terms of quantity, I mean? How much would you have to eat?"

"*Well,* that's the question, isn't it?" Alexander said. He leaned across the table, a rather unpleasant gleam in his eye as he warmed to his topic. "Different parts of the fish have a different toxic load, but in terms of the most poisonous parts—which is to say, the liver, the eyes, and the ovaries—we're talking very, very little. Grams, if that. They say it's around a thousand times more deadly than cyanide." He pushed a forkful of fish carpaccio into his mouth and spoke through the delicate flesh. "It must be a quite horrible way to die—the chef who prepared it for us in Tokyo took great delight in describing the process of the poison—it paralyzes the muscles, you know, but the mind of the victim is quite unaffected, and they stay fully conscious throughout the experience as their muscles atrophy and they become unable to breathe." He swallowed, licked his moist lips, and smiled. "Eventually they quite simply suffocate."

I looked down at the slivers of raw fish on my own plate, and whether it was the wine, or Alexander's vivid description, or whether the sea had picked up, I felt rather less hungry than I had before dinner. I put a piece reluctantly in my mouth and chewed.

"Tell us about yourself, darling," Tina said suddenly, surprising me by flicking her attention abruptly from Alexander to me. "You work with Rowan, I hear?"

Tina had started at *Velocity* in the late eighties and had briefly crossed paths with Rowan, who still talked about her and her legendary ferocity.

"That's right." I swallowed my mouthful with uncomfortable haste. "I've been there about ten years."

"She must think very highly of you to send you on a trip like this. Quite the coup, I would have thought."

I shifted in my chair. What could I say in answer to that? *Actually, I don't think there's any way she would have trusted me with this if she weren't on a hospital drip?*

"I'm very lucky," I said at last. "It's a real privilege to be here, and Rowan knows how keen I am to prove myself."

"Well, enjoy it is my advice." Tina patted my arm, her rings cool against my skin. "You only live once. Isn't that what they say?"

- CHAPTER 9 -

We swapped seats twice more, but somehow I never found myself next to Bullmer, and it was not until the coffee was served, and we were free to leave our seats and return to the Lindgren Lounge, that I had the chance to accost him. I was just walking across the room, a cup of coffee in my hand, balancing myself precariously against the shifting of the boat, when a flash went off in my face, and I stumbled, narrowly avoiding drenching myself in coffee. As it was, a few drops spattered the hem of the rented gown and the white sofa next to me.

"Smile," said a voice in my ear, and I realized the photographer was Cole.

"Shit, you *idiot*," I said crossly, and then instantly wanted to kick myself. The last thing I wanted was him reporting my rudeness back to Rowan. I must be drunker than I thought. "Not you," I said awkwardly, trying to cover my slip. "Me, I meant. The sofa."

He saw my discomfort and laughed.

"Nice recovery. Don't worry, I'm not going to tell tales on you to your boss. My ego's not that fragile."

"I didn't . . ." I floundered, but it was so uncannily close to what I *had* been thinking that I couldn't think how to finish. "I just—"

"Forget about it. Where were you off to in such a hurry anyway? You were striding across the room like a marksman hunting down a lame antelope."

"I . . ." It felt slightly pathetic to admit it, but my head was throbbing with a mix of tiredness and alcohol, and somehow it seemed easier to tell the truth. "I was hoping to talk to Richard Bullmer. I've been trying to speak to him all evening, I just never had the chance."

"And you were making your move when I wrecked it," Cole said with a gleam in his eye. He smiled again, and I realized it was his incisors that gave him a slightly wolfish, predatory air. "Well, I can sort that out anyway. Bullmer!"

I cringed as Richard Bullmer turned from his conversation with Lars and looked across.

"Did I hear my name?"

"You did indeed," Cole said. "Come and speak to this nice girl, make amends for my ambushing her."

Bullmer laughed, picked up his cup from the arm of the chair next to him, and strolled across. He moved easily, in spite of the slight roll of the ship, and I had the impression of someone who was very physically fit, and probably hard as nails beneath the well-cut suit.

"Richard," Cole said with a wave of his hand, "this is Lo—Lo, Richard. I surprised her with a candid shot as she was making her move on you, and she spilled her coffee."

My cheeks flamed red, but Bullmer was shaking his head at Cole.

"You know what I said about being discreet with that thing." He nodded at the heavy camera slung around Cole's neck. "Not everyone wants paparazzi shots of themselves at inopportune moments."

"Ah, they love it," Cole said easily, showing his teeth in a wide grin. "Gives 'em the proper celebrity experience along with the swanky venue."

"I mean it," Richard said, and although he was smiling, his voice no longer sounded amused. "Anne, especially." He lowered his voice. "You know she's self-conscious since . . ."

Cole nodded, the laugh dying out of his face.

"Yeah, sure, man. That's different. But Lo here doesn't mind, do you, Lo?" He slung an arm around my shoulders, crushing me into him so that my shoulder crunched against his camera, and I tried to smile.

"No," I said awkwardly. "No, of course not."

"That's the spirit," Bullmer said, and he gave a little wink. It was an odd gesture—the same one I'd noticed before when he spoke to Camilla Lidman—not avuncular, as it might have been, but more as if he were trying to level what he knew to be an intimidatingly uneven playing field. *Don't think of me as an international millionaire,* that wink said. *I'm just an ordinary approachable guy.*

I was just trying to think how to reply, when Owen White tapped him on the shoulder and he turned.

"What can I do for you, Owen?" he said, and before I had a chance to open my mouth, the opportunity was gone.

"I—" I managed as he turned away, and he looked back over his shoulder at me.

"Hey, look, it's always hard to talk at these things. Why don't you swing past my cabin tomorrow after the planned activities, and we can chat properly?"

"Thanks," I said, trying not to sound too pathetically grateful.

"Great. It's number one. Looking forward to it."

"Sorry," Cole said in a low voice, his breath tickling the hair tucked behind my ear. "Did my best. What can I say? He's a wanted man. How can I make it up to you?"

"Never mind," I said awkwardly. He was standing uncomfortably close and I wanted to take a step back, but Rowan's voice was nagging in the back of my head: *Network, Lo!* "Tell me . . . tell me something about yourself instead. What made you come? You said it's not your usual thing."

"Richard's kind of an old friend," Cole said. He grabbed a coffee from a passing stewardess's tray and took a gulp. "We were at

Balliol together. So when he asked me to come, I felt I couldn't say no."

"Are you close?"

"I wouldn't say close. We don't really move in the same circles—it's hard when one of you is a struggling photographer and the other one's married to one of the wealthiest women in Europe." He gave a grin. "But he's a good guy. He might look like he was born with a silver spoon in his mouth, but that's not the full picture. He's had some tough times and I guess that's what makes him hold on all the harder to . . . well, all this." He waved a hand at our surroundings—at the silk and crystals and burnished fittings. "He knows what it's like to lose things. And people."

I thought of Anne Bullmer, and the way Richard had walked her to her cabin in spite of the roomful of guests waiting to talk to him. And I thought perhaps I knew what Cole meant.

It was around eleven that I finally made my way back to my room. I was drunk. Very, very drunk. Although it was hard to tell exactly *how* drunk, as we were now midocean, and the shifting movement of the sea mixed queasily with the champagne . . . and the wine . . . oh, and the frozen shots of aquavit. Christ. What had I been thinking?

There was a moment of clarity when I got to my door and stood for a moment, steadying myself on the frame. I knew why I'd got drunk. I knew exactly why. Because if I was drunk enough, I would sleep the sleep of the dead. I couldn't cope with another broken night—not here.

But I pushed the thought away and began the task of retrieving my room key from where I'd stashed it inside my bra.

"Need a hand, Blacklock?" slurred a voice behind me, and Ben Howard's shadow fell across the doorframe.

"I'm fine," I said, turning my back so that he couldn't see me struggling. A wave hit the boat and I lurched and staggered. *Go away, Ben.*

"Sure?" He leaned over me, deliberately peering over my shoulder.

"Yes"—my teeth were gritted with fury—"I'm sure."

"Because I could help." He gave a lascivious grin and nodded towards the top of my dress, which I was gripping with one hand to stop it from peeling down. "You look like you could use an extra hand. Or two."

"Fuck *off,*" I said shortly. There was something wedged beneath my left shoulder blade, something warm and hard that felt a lot like a key. If I could only get my fingers far enough round . . .

He moved closer, and before I'd realized what he was about to do, he shoved his hand roughly down the front of my dress. I felt a streak of pain as his cuff links dragged over my skin, and then his fingers closed over my bare breast and squeezed, hard, in a way that was presumably meant to be erotic.

It wasn't.

I didn't even think about it. There was a ripping noise like a snarling cat, and my knee connected with his groin so hard that he didn't even cry out, he just toppled slowly to the floor, making a kind of weak, gasping whimper.

And I burst into tears.

Some twenty minutes later I was sitting on the bed in my cabin, still sobbing and wiping borrowed mascara off my cheeks, and Ben was crouched next to me, one arm around my shoulders and the other holding a tumbler of ice against his crotch.

"I'm sorry," he said again, his voice still croaky with suppressed pain. "Please, Lo, please, stop crying. I'm really sorry. I was a dick, a complete arsehole. I deserved it."

"It's not you," I sobbed, though I wasn't sure he could understand the words. "I can't cope anymore, Ben, ever since the burglar I've just been— I think I'm going mad."

"What burglar?"

I told him—between sobs. Everything I hadn't told Jude. What it had been like, waking up, realizing there was someone in my flat, realizing that no one would hear if I cried out, realizing that I had no way of getting help, no chance of fighting the intruder off, that I was vulnerable in a way I'd never thought I was before that night.

"I'm sorry," Ben kept repeating, like a mantra. He rubbed my back with his free hand. "I'm so sorry."

His awkward sympathy only made me sob harder.

"Look, sweetheart—"

Oh no.

"Don't call me that." I sat up, shaking my hair away from my face, and pulled out of his hold.

"Sorry, it just— It slipped out."

"I don't care, you can't say that anymore, Ben."

"I know," he said distractedly. "But, Lo, if I'm honest, I never—"

"Don't," I said urgently.

"Lo, what I did, I was a shit, I know I was—"

"I said *don't.* It's over."

He shook his head, but his words, somehow, had stopped my crying. Maybe it was the sight of him, stricken, hunched, and so very miserable.

"But, Lo." He looked up at me, his brown eyes puppy-dog soft in the soft bedside light. "Lo, I—"

"No!" It came out harsher and louder than I meant, but I had to shut him up. I wasn't sure what he was about to say, but whatever it was, I was certain I couldn't afford for him to say it. I was stuck on this boat with Ben for the next five days. I couldn't let him embarrass himself more than he already had done, or this trip would become unendurable when we had to rub shoulders in the cold light of day. "Ben, no," I said more gently. "It was over a long time ago. Anyway, *you* were the one who wanted out, remember?"

"I know," he said wretchedly. "I know. I was a twat."

"You weren't," I said. And then, feeling dishonest: "Okay, you were. But I know I wasn't the easiest— Look, that's not the point now. We're friends, right?" That was overstating it, but he nodded. "Okay, then don't screw this up."

"All right," he said. He stood up painfully and swiped at his face with the arm of his dinner jacket, then looked at it ruefully. "Hope they've got an onboard dry cleaner."

"Hope they've got an onboard dress mender." I nodded at the rip all the way up the side of the gray silk dress.

"Will you be all right?" Ben said. "I could stay. I don't mean that in a sleazy way. I could sleep on the couch."

"You totally could," I agreed, looking at the length of it, and then shook my head as I realized how my words sounded. "No, you couldn't. It's big enough, but you can't; I don't need you to. Go back to your cabin. For Christ's sake, we're on board a ship in the middle of the ocean—it's about the safest place I could possibly be."

"All right." He walked, hobbling slightly, to the door and half opened it, but he didn't actually go. "I—I'm sorry. I mean it."

I knew what he was waiting for, hoping for. Not just forgiveness, but something more, something that would tell him that squeeze wasn't completely unwanted.

I was damned if I'd give it to him.

"Go to bed, Ben," I said, very weary, and very sober. He stood in the doorway a moment longer, just a millisecond *too* long, long enough for me to wonder, with a shift in my stomach that echoed the shifting sea, what I would do if he didn't go. What I'd do if he shut the door and turned around and came back into the room. But then he turned and went, and I locked the door after him and then collapsed onto the sofa with my head in my hands.

At long last, I don't know how much later, I got up, poured myself a whiskey from the minibar, and drank it down in three long gulps like medicine. I shuddered, wiped my mouth, and peeled off my dress, leaving it coiled on the floor like a sloughed-off skin.

I stripped off my bra, stepped out of the sad little pile of clothes, and then fell into bed and into a sleep so deep, it felt like drowning.

I don't know what woke me up—only that I shot into consciousness as if someone had stabbed me in the heart with a syringe of adrenaline. I lay there rigid with fear, my heart thumping at about two hundred beats per minute, and I scrabbled for the soothing phrases I'd repeated to Ben just a few hours before.

You're fine, I told myself. *You're completely safe. We're on a boat in the middle of the ocean—no one can get in or away. It's about the safest place you could possibly be.*

I was clutching the sheets with a rigor mortis–like grip, and I forced my stiff fingers to relax and flexed them slowly, feeling the pain in my knuckles subside. I concentrated on breathing in . . . and out. In . . . and out. Slow and steady, until at last my heart followed suit, and I could no longer feel its frantic pounding in my chest.

The drumming in my ears subsided. Apart from the rhythmic shush of the waves, and the low engine hum that permeated every part of the vessel, I couldn't hear anything.

Shit. *Shit.* I had to get a grip.

I couldn't self-medicate with booze every night for the rest of this trip, not without sabotaging my career and flushing any chance of advancement at *Velocity* down the drain. So that left—what? Sleeping pills? Meditation? None of that seemed much better.

I rolled over and switched on the light and checked my phone: 3:04 a.m. Then I refreshed my e-mail. There was nothing from Judah, but I was too wide-awake now to go back to sleep. I sighed and picked up my book instead, lying splayed like a broken-backed bird on the bedside table, and opened it to the last page I'd read.

But although I tried to concentrate on the words, something niggled at the corner of my mind. It wasn't just paranoia. *Something* had woken me up. Something that left me jumpy and strung out as a meth addict. Why did I keep thinking of a scream?

I was turning the page when I heard something else, something that barely registered above the sound of the engine and the slap of the waves, a sound so soft that the scrape of paper against paper almost drowned it out.

It was the noise of the veranda door in the next cabin sliding gently open.

I held my breath, straining to hear.

And then there was a splash.

Not a small splash.

No, this was a big splash.

The kind of splash made by a body hitting water.

JUDAH LEWIS

24 September at 8.50am

Hey, guys, bit concerned about Lo. She hasn't checked in for a few days since she left on a press trip. Anyone heard from her? Getting kinda worried. Cheers.

Like Comment Share

LISSIE WIGHT Hi Jude! She messaged me on Sunday—20th I guess it must have been? Said the boat was amazing!

Like · Reply 24 September at 9.02am

JUDAH LEWIS Yeah, I heard from her then, too, but she didn't reply to my e-mail or my text on Monday. And she hasn't updated facebook or twitter, either.

Like · Reply 24 September at 9.03am

JUDAH LEWIS Anyone? Pamela Crew? Jennifer West? Carl Fox? Emma Stanton? Sorry if I'm tagging random people, I'm just—this is kind of out of character to be honest.

Like · Reply 24 September at 10.44am

PAMELA CREW She emailed me on Sunday, Jude love. Said the boat was lovely. Do you want me to ask her dad?

Like · Reply 24 September at 11.13am

JUDAH LEWIS Yes, please, Pam. I don't want to worry you both, but I feel like she'd have made contact by now, normally. But I'm stuck here in Moscow, so I don't know if she's been trying to phone and not getting through.

Like · Reply 24 September at 11.21am

JUDAH LEWIS Pam, did she tell you the name of the boat? I can't find it.

Like · Reply 24 September at 11.33am

PAMELA CREW Hi, Judah, sorry, I was on the phone to her dad. He's not heard anything, either. The boat was the Aurora, apparently. Let me know if you hear anything. Bye love.

Like · Reply 24 September at 11.48am

JUDAH LEWIS Thanks, Pam. I'll try the boat. But if anyone hears anything, please message me.

Like · Reply 24 September at 11.49am

JUDAH LEWIS Anything?

Like · Reply 24 September at 3.47pm

JUDAH LEWIS Please, guys, anything?

Like · Reply 24 September at 6.09pm

PART THREE

- CHAPTER 10 -

I didn't even think about what to do next.

I ran to the veranda, threw open the French windows, and hung out over the rail, desperately searching for a glimpse of something—or someone—in the shifting waves. The dark surface was spattered with bright refracted light from the ship's windows, making it almost impossible to make out the shape of anything in the swell, but I thought I saw something beneath the crest of a black wave—a swirling white shape that trailed beneath the surface as it sank, like a woman's hand.

Then I turned to look at the balcony next to mine.

There was a privacy screen between the two cabins, so I couldn't see very much, but as I peered over, I saw two things.

The first was that there was a smear on the glass safety barrier of the next-door veranda. A smear of something dark and oily. A smear that looked a lot like blood.

The second was a realization, and one that made my stomach clench and shift. Whoever had been standing there—whoever had thrown that body overboard—could not have missed my stupid, headlong dash to the balcony. In all likelihood they'd been standing on the next-door veranda as I dashed onto mine. They would have heard my door crash back. They would probably even have seen my face.

I darted back into the room, slamming the French windows behind me, and checked the cabin door was double-locked. Then I put the chain across. My heart was thumping in my chest, but I felt calm, calmer than I had in ages.

This was it. This was real danger, and I was coping.

With the cabin door secure, I ran back and checked the veranda windows. There was no deadlock on this—just the normal latch—but it was as secure as I could make it.

Then I picked up the bedside phone with fingers that shook only slightly and dialed 0 for the operator.

"Hello?" said a singsong voice. "How can I help you, Miss Blacklock?"

For a minute I was so disconcerted that she knew it was me that I completely lost my train of thought. Then I realized—my room number would probably come up on the desk phone. Of course it would be me. Who else would be phoning from my room in the middle of the night?

"H-hello!" I managed. In spite of the tremor, my voice sounded surprisingly calm. "Hello. Who is this, please?"

"It's your cabin stewardess, Karla, Miss Blacklock. Can I help you?" Beneath her perky phone manner a touch of concern had crept in. "Are you all right?"

"No, no, I'm not all right. I—" I stopped, aware how ridiculous this might sound.

"Miss Blacklock?"

"I think—" I swallowed. "I think I've just seen a murder."

"Oh my goodness." Karla's voice was shocked, and she said something in a language I didn't understand—Swedish perhaps, or maybe Danish. Then she seemed to control herself and spoke in English again. "Are you safe, Miss Blacklock?"

Was I safe? I looked across at the cabin door. It was double-locked and with the chain across, I was as certain as I could be that no one could get in.

"Yes, yes, I think I am. It was in the next-door cabin—number ten. Palmgren. I—I think someone threw a body overboard."

My voice cracked as I said it, and I suddenly felt like laughing—or maybe crying. I took a deep breath and pinched the bridge of my nose, trying to get ahold of myself.

"I will send someone right away, Miss Blacklock. Don't move. I will call you when they are at the door so you know who it is. Hold on, please, and I will call you right back."

There was a click, and she hung up.

I was still holding the receiver, and I put it gently back on the cradle, feeling oddly dissociated, almost like I was having an out-of-body experience. My head was throbbing, and I realized I needed to get dressed before they arrived.

I picked up the bathrobe from where it hung on the back of the bathroom door—and did a double take. When I went down to dinner I had left it on the floor, along with the clothes I'd worn on the train. I remembered looking back over my shoulder at the bomb site I'd made in the bathroom—clothes on the floor, makeup scattered across the counter, lipstick-smeared tissues in the sink—and thinking, *I'll deal with that later.*

It was all gone. The bathrobe had been hung up, my dirty clothes and underwear had disappeared, whisked off to God knows where.

On the vanity counter, my cosmetics had been neatly set out in rows, along with my toothbrush and toothpaste. Only my tampons and pills were left inside my toiletry bag, a weirdly coy touch that was somehow worse than everything being out in the open, and made me shudder. Someone had been inside my room. Of course they had. That was what maid service *meant*, for heaven's sake. But someone had been inside my room, messing with my things, touching my wrinkled tights and my half-used eyeliner pencil.

Why did the thought make me want to cry?

I was sitting on the bed, head in my hands and thinking about the contents of the minibar, when the phone rang, and a couple of seconds later, as I crawled across the duvet to pick up the receiver, there was a knock on the door.

I picked up the phone.

"Hello?"

"Hello, Miss Blacklock?" It was Karla.

"Yes. There's someone at the door. Should I answer it?"

"Yes, yes, please do. It is our head of security, Johann Nilsson. I will leave you now with him, Miss Blacklock, but please do call me at any time if you need any further assistance."

There was a click and the line went dead, and the knock on the door came again. I belted my bathrobe more securely and went to open it.

Outside was a man I hadn't seen before, dressed in some kind of uniform. I don't know what I was expecting—something pseudo-policeman-like. This was more like a nautical uniform—closer to a purser or something. He was about forty or thereabouts, and tall enough to have to stoop as he took a step forward into the doorway, with rumpled hair that looked like he'd only just got out of bed, and eyes so startlingly blue that it looked almost as if he were wearing colored contacts. I was staring at them when I realized, suddenly, that he was holding out a hand.

"Hello, you must be Miss Blacklock, I presume?" His English was very, very good. Just a faint trace of a Scandinavian accent, so slight he might almost have been Scottish or Canadian. "My name is Johann Nilsson. I am head of security on the *Aurora*. I understand you've seen something that disturbed you."

"Yes," I said firmly, suddenly painfully aware of the fact that I was in a dressing gown with my mascara halfway down my cheeks while he was fully and professionally dressed. I tightened the belt again, nervously this time. “Yes. I saw—heard—something thrown overboard. I—I think it was, it must have been . . . a body.”

“You saw, or heard?” Nilsson said, cocking his head to one side.

“I heard a splash—a very loud splash. It was quite clearly something very big falling overboard—or being pushed. And then I ran to the balcony and I saw something—a body, it looked like—disappearing under the waves.” Nilsson’s expression was grave but guarded, and as I spoke his frown deepened. “And there was blood on the glass wall of the balcony,” I added.

His lips tightened at that, and he gave a short nod towards the veranda door.

“Your balcony?”

“The blood? No. Next door.”

“Can you show me?”

I nodded, pulled the belt again, and watched as he undid the latch of the veranda door. Outside, the wind had picked up, and it was very cold. I led the way to the narrow space, which felt painfully small now with Nilsson’s bulk beside me. He seemed to take up all the room there was and more, but part of me was very glad he was there. I didn’t think I could have brought myself to go out there on my own.

“There.” I pointed over the privacy barrier that separated my veranda from that of cabin 10. “Look over there. You’ll see what I mean.”

Nilsson peered over the barrier and then looked back at me, frowning slightly.

“I don’t see where you mean. Could you show me?”

“What do you mean? It was a big smear all down the glass.”

He edged backwards, extending a hand towards the barrier by way of invitation, and I pushed past him to peer over. My heart was pounding in spite of myself. I didn’t expect to see the murderer still there, or to get a fist in my face, or feel a bullet fly past my ear. But it felt horribly vulnerable to peer over the wall not knowing what I might find on the other side.

But what I found was . . . nothing.

No murderer, crouched to spring. No smear of blood. The glass barrier shone in the moonlight, clean, innocent of so much as a fingerprint.

I turned back to Nilsson, knowing that my face must be stiff with shock. I shook my head, tried to find the words. He watched me, something sympathetic in his blue eyes.

It was the sympathy that stung more than anything else.

"It was there," I said angrily. "He's obviously wiped it off."

"He?"

"The murderer! The fucking murderer, of course!"

"There's no need to swear, Miss Blacklock," he said mildly, and went back inside the cabin. I followed him, and he carefully shut and latched the door behind me and then stood, his hands by his sides, as if waiting for me to say something. I could smell his cologne—not an unpleasant smell, faintly woody. But suddenly the spacious room felt oppressively small.

"What?" I said at last, trying and failing not to make the word sound aggressive. "I told you what I saw. Are you saying I'm lying?"

"Let's go next door," he said diplomatically.

I yanked the bathrobe belt tighter still, so tight now I could feel it digging into my stomach, and followed him, barefoot, into the corridor. He gave one short knock at the door of cabin 10, and then, when there was no answer, produced a passkey from his pocket and opened the door.

We stood in the doorway. Nilsson said nothing, but I could feel his presence at my back as I gazed, openmouthed, at the room.

It was utterly empty. Not just of people—but of everything. There were no suitcases. No clothes. No cosmetics in the bathroom. Even the bed was stripped back to the mattress.

"There was a girl," I said at last, my voice unsteady. I shoved my hands in the pockets of the bathrobe so that he wouldn't see how my fingers were clenched into fists. "There was a girl. In this room. I *talked* to her. I spoke to her. She was here!"

Nilsson said nothing. He walked through the silent moonlit suite and opened the door of the veranda, then looked outside, inspecting the glass barrier with almost insulting conscientiousness. But I could see from here there was nothing. The glass gleamed in the moonlight, misted faintly with ocean spray but otherwise quite untouched.

"She was here!" I repeated, hearing and hating the edge of hysteria in my voice. "Why won't you believe me?"

"I didn't say that I didn't believe you." Nilsson came back into the room and latched the veranda window. Then he walked me to the cabin door, and closed and locked it behind us.

"You don't have to," I said bitterly. My own door was still open and he escorted me inside. "But I tell you, she was there. She lent me— Oh!" Something suddenly struck me, and I ran to the bathroom. "She lent me a mascara. God damn it, where is it?"

I was rummaging through the carefully set-out cosmetics, but it wasn't there. Where had it gone?

"It's here," I said desperately. "I know it is." I looked around wildly, and something caught my eye, a flash of shocking pink behind the retractable shaving mirror at the side of the basin. I pulled it out—and there it was—an innocent little pink tube with a green cap.

"There!" I brandished it triumphantly at him, like a weapon. Nilsson took a step back, and then took the mascara gently from my hand.

"I see," he said, "but with respect, Miss Blacklock, I'm not sure what this proves, apart from the fact that you borrowed a mascara from someone today—"

"What does it prove? It proves she was really there! It proves she existed!"

"It proves you saw a girl, yes, but—"

"What do you *want*?" I interrupted, desperately. "What more do you want from me? I've told you what I heard—what I saw. I've told you there was a girl in that cabin, and now she's gone. Look on the manifest—there's a guest missing. Why aren't you more concerned?"

"That cabin is empty," he said gently.

"I know!" I shouted, and then, seeing Nilsson's face, I made a huge, concentrated effort to get myself under control. "I know—that's what I've been trying to tell you, for God's sake."

"No," he said, still with that same quiet gentleness, the gentleness of a big man with nothing to prove. "This is what I'm trying to explain, Miss Blacklock. It has *always* been empty. There was no guest in that cabin. There never has been."

- CHAPTER 11 -

I stared at him, openmouthed.

"What do you mean?" I managed at last. "What do you mean, no guest?"

"The cabin is empty," he said. "It was reserved for another guest, an investor named Ernst Solberg. But he pulled out at the last minute—personal reasons, I understand."

"So the girl I saw—she wasn't supposed to be there?"

"Perhaps she was a member of the staff, or a cleaner."

"She *wasn't*. She was getting dressed. She was *staying* there."

He said nothing. He didn't have to—the question was obvious. If she was staying there, where was all her stuff?

"Someone could have taken it out," I said weakly. "Between seeing me and your coming."

"Really?" Nilsson's voice was quiet, his question not skeptical, not mocking, just . . . uncomprehending. He sat down on the sofa, the springs squeaking beneath his bulk, and I sank onto the bed and put my face in my hands.

Because he was right. There was no way someone could have cleared the room. I didn't know exactly how much time had elapsed between me calling Karla and Nilsson appearing at my door, but there was no way it was more than a few minutes. Five, seven at the outside. Probably not even that.

Whoever was in there *might* have had time to wipe the blood off the glass, but that was it. There was no way they could have emptied the entire cabin. What could they have done with the stuff? I would have heard if they had tipped it over the side. And there simply hadn't been time for them to pack it up and take it down the corridor.

"Shit," I said at last, into my hands. *"Shit."*

"Miss Blacklock," Nilsson said slowly, and I had a sudden premonition that I was not going to like his next question. "Miss Blacklock, how much did you have to drink last night?"

I looked up, letting him see my ravaged makeup and the fury in my sleep-bleared eyes.

"I *beg* your pardon?"

"I simply asked—"

There was no point in denying it. There were enough people who'd seen me at the dinner last night, knocking back champagne, then wine, then after-dinner shots, to blow a hole a mile wide in any claim that I was completely sober.

"Yes, I was drinking," I said nastily. "But if you think that half a glass of wine turns me into some hysterical drunk who can't tell reality from fantasy, you've got another think coming."

He said nothing to that, but his gaze traveled to the bin beside the minibar, where a number of whiskey and gin miniatures and a considerably smaller quantity of tonic cans were stacked up.

There was a silence. Nilsson didn't ram home his point, but he didn't need to. Bastard room cleaners.

"I may have been drinking," I said through clenched teeth, "but I *wasn't* drunk. Not like that. I know what I saw. Why would I make it up?"

He seemed to accept that and nodded wearily.

"Very well, Miss Blacklock." He rubbed a hand over his face, and I heard his blond stubble rasp against his palm. He was tired, and

I noticed, suddenly and incongruously, that his uniform jacket was buttoned up askew, with an orphan buttonhole at the bottom. "Look, it is late, you are tired."

"*You're* tired," I shot back with more than a touch of malice, but he only nodded, without rancor.

"Yes, I am tired. I think there is nothing we can do now until the morning."

"A woman has been thrown—"

"There is no proof!" he said louder, his voice cutting over mine, and for the first time there was exasperation in his tone. "I'm sorry, Miss Blacklock," he said more quietly. "I should not have contradicted you. But I don't feel there is sufficient evidence to wake the other passengers at this point. Let us both get some sleep"—*and you can sober up* was the unspoken translation—"and we will try to resolve this in the morning. Perhaps if I take you to meet the ship's staff we can track down this girl that you saw in the cabin. It is evident that she was not a passenger, correct?"

"She wasn't at the dinner last night," I admitted. "But what if she was a staff member? What if someone's missing, and we're wasting time in raising the alarm?"

"I'll speak to the captain and the purser now, let them know the situation. But there are no staff members unaccounted for that I am aware of; if there were, someone would have noticed. This is a very small ship with a tight-knit crew. It would be hard for someone to go missing undetected, even for a few hours."

"I just think—" I began, but he cut me off, politely and firmly this time.

"Miss Blacklock, I will not wake up sleeping staff and passengers for no good reason. I'm sorry. I will inform the captain and the purser and they will take whatever action they see fit. In the meantime, perhaps you could give me a description of the girl you saw, and I can double-check the passenger manifest and arrange that all the off-duty staff members who match the description are in the staff restaurant for you to meet tomorrow after breakfast."

"All right," I said sulkily. I was beaten. I *knew* what I had seen, what I'd heard, but Nilsson was not budging, that much was plain. And what could I do, out here in the middle of the ocean?

"So," he prompted. "She was how old, how tall? Was she Caucasian, Asian, black . . . ?"

"Late twenties," I said. "About my height. White—very pale skin, in fact. She spoke English."

"With an accent?" Nilsson put in. I shook my head.

"No, she was English—or if she wasn't, she was completely bilingual. She had long, dark hair . . . I can't remember what color eyes. Dark brown, I think. I'm not certain. Slimmish build . . . she was just—pretty. That's all I remember."

"Pretty?"

"Yes, pretty. You know? Nice features. Clear skin. She was wearing makeup. Lots of eye makeup. Oh—and she was wearing a Pink Floyd T-shirt."

Nilsson wrote it all down solemnly and then rose, the springs squeaking in protest, or perhaps relief.

"Thank you, Miss Blacklock. And now I think we should both get some sleep." He rubbed his face, looking for all the world like a big blond bear dragged out of hibernation.

"What time should I expect you tomorrow?"

"What time would suit you? Ten? Ten thirty?"

"Earlier," I said. "I won't sleep, not now." I was buzzing, and I knew I would never get back to sleep.

"Well, my shift starts at eight. Is that too early?"

"That's perfect," I said firmly. He walked to the door, suppressing a yawn as he did, and I watched as he lumbered off along the corridor towards the stairs. Then I shut and double-locked the door, and went and lay on the bed, staring at the sea. The waves were dark and slick in the moonlight, heaving themselves up like the backs of whales, and then slipping back down, and I lay and felt the boat rise and fall with the swell.

I would never sleep. I knew that. Not with my blood ringing in my ears, and my heart beating in angry staccato thumps in my chest, I would never relax.

I was furious—but I was not sure why. Because a woman's body was even now floating down into the black darkness of the North Sea, probably never to be found? Or was part of it something smaller, baser—the fact that Nilsson had not believed me?

Maybe he's right, the nasty little voice in my head whispered. Pictures flitted across my mind's eye—me, cowering in the shower because of a door blowing shut in the wind. Defending myself against a nonexistent intruder by attacking Judah. *Are you completely sure? You're not exactly the most reliable witness. And at the end of the day, what did you actually* see?

I saw the blood, I told myself firmly. And a girl is missing. Explain that.

I switched the light out and drew the cover across myself, but I didn't sleep. Instead, I lay on my side watching the sea, rising and falling with strange hypnotic silence outside the thick, stormproof panes. And I thought, *There is a murderer on this boat. And no one knows but me.*

- CHAPTER 12 -

"Miss Blacklock!" The knock came again, and I heard a passkey in the door, and the bang as the door itself opened a centimeter and the security chain pulled taut.

"Miss Blacklock, it's Johann Nilsson. Are you okay? It's eight o'clock. You asked me to call you?"

What? I struggled up onto my elbows, my head pounding with the effort. Why the hell had I asked to be called at eight o'clock?

"One sec!" I managed. My mouth was dry, as if I'd swallowed ashes, and I reached for the glass of water by my bed and choked some down. As I did, the memory of last night came flooding back.

The noise that had woken me in the night.

The blood on the veranda glass.

The body.

The splash . . .

I swung my legs out of bed and felt the boat shift and lurch beneath me, and I felt suddenly and violently nauseous.

I ran to the bathroom and just managed to get myself positioned over the bowl in time for the retching heave of last night's dinner against clean white porcelain.

"Miss Blacklock?"

Go. Away.

The words didn't make it out of my mouth, but maybe the sound of splashing vomit conveyed the sentiment, because the door shut, very quietly, and I was able to stand up and examine myself without an audience.

I looked awful. The dregs of my eye makeup were smudged across my cheeks, and I had vomit in my hair, and my eyes were bloodshot and red-rimmed. The bruise on my cheek just added to the whole impression.

The boat heaved itself up onto a wave and down the other side, and everything around the sink shifted and clinked. I pulled my dressing gown around myself and went back into the cabin, where I pulled the door open the tiniest, tiniest crack—barely enough to see through.

"I've got to take a shower," I said tersely. "Do you mind waiting?" And then I shut the door.

Inside the bathroom I flushed the toilet and wiped around the rim, trying to destroy all traces of my vomit. But when I straightened, it was not my own pale, ravaged face that caught my eye, but the tube of Maybelline, standing sentinel by the sink. As I stood, clutching the vanity table, my breath coming short and sharp, the ship gave another roll, and everything on the countertop shifted and wobbled, and the tube fell, with a tiny crack, and rolled into the bin. I reached in bare-handed and pulled it out, holding it in my fist.

It was the only tangible evidence that that girl *had* existed, that I wasn't going mad.

Ten minutes later I was dressed in jeans and a crisp white shirt, pressed by whoever unpacked my case, and my face was pale but clean. I pulled back the security chain and opened the door to find Nilsson waiting patiently in the corridor, talking on a radio. He looked up when he saw me and shut it off.

"I'm very sorry, Miss Blacklock," he said. "Perhaps I should not have woken you, but you were so insistent last night . . ."

"It's fine," I said through gritted teeth. I didn't mean to sound quite so curt, but if I opened my mouth too much I might be sick again. Thank God the movement of the boat provided an alibi for my queasy stomach. Being a bad sailor was not exactly chic, but it was less unprofessional than being considered an alcoholic.

"I have spoken to the staff," Nilsson said. "No one has been reported missing, but I suggest you come down to the staff quarters and you can see if the woman you spoke to is there. It may put your mind at rest."

I was about to protest that she *wasn't* staff, not unless the cleaners valeted rooms wearing Pink Floyd T-shirts and not much else. But then I shut my mouth. I wanted to see below decks for myself.

I followed him along the lurching corridor to a small service door by the stairwell. It was fitted with a keypad lock, into which he tapped a quick six-digit code, and the door swung outwards. From the outside I would have assumed the door hid a cleaning cupboard, but in fact there was a small, dimly lit landing and a flight of narrow stairs led down into the depths of the ship. As we descended I realized, unsettlingly, that we must now be below the waterline, or very near it.

We emerged into a cramped corridor that had a completely different feel to the passenger part of the ship. Everything was different—the ceiling was lower, the air was several degrees hotter, and the walls were closer together and painted a dingy shade of beige, but it was the lights that made me feel instantly claustrophobic—dim and fluorescent, with a strange high-frequency flicker that made your eyes tire almost at once.

Doors opened off to the left and the right, eight or ten cabins crammed into the same space as two above. We passed one door that was ajar and I saw a windowless shared bunk room lit by the same graying fluorescent light, and an Asian woman sitting on a bunk inside, pulling on her tights, her head and shoulders cramped in the narrow space beneath the bunk above. She looked nervously up as Nilsson passed, and then at the sight of me her face froze, like a panicked rabbit in the headlights. For a moment she just sat, motionless, and then with a convulsive start she reached out with her foot and kicked the door shut, the sound as loud as a gunshot in the confined space.

I felt myself blush like a Peeping Tom caught in the act, and hurried after Nilsson's retreating back.

"This way," Nilsson said over his shoulder, and we turned into a door marked STAFF MESS.

This room was larger at least, and I felt the growing sense of claustrophobia lift slightly. The ceiling was still low, and there were still no windows, but the room opened out into a small dining room, a lot like a miniature version of a hospital canteen. There were only three tables, each seating maybe half a dozen people, but the Formica surfaces, the steel grab rails, and the powerful smell of institutional cooking all combined to underline the difference between this deck and the one above.

Camilla Lidman was seated alone at one of the tables, drinking coffee and going through some kind of spreadsheet on a laptop, and across the room, five girls were sitting around another, eating breakfast pastries. They looked up as Nilsson entered.

"*Hej*, Johann," one of them said, and followed with something in singsong Swedish, or maybe Danish, I wasn't sure.

"Let's speak in English, please," Nilsson said, "as we have a guest present. Miss Blacklock is trying to trace a woman she saw in the next-door cabin—number ten, Palmgren. The woman she saw was white, with long dark hair, in her late twenties or early thirties, and she spoke good English."

"Well, there's me and Birgitta," said one of the girls with a smile, nodding at her friend opposite. "My name is Hanni. But I don't think I've been in Palmgren. I work behind the bar mainly. Birgitta?"

But I was shaking my head. Hanni and Birgitta both had pale skin and dark hair but neither was the girl from the cabin, and even though Hanni's English was excellent, she had a noticeable Scandinavian accent.

"I'm Karla, Miss Blacklock," said one of the two blond girls. "We met yesterday, if you recall. And we spoke on the phone last night."

"Of course," I said absently, but I was too busy scanning the faces of the other girls to pay proper attention. Karla and the fourth girl at the table were both blond, and the fifth had Mediterranean coloring and very short hair, almost a pixie cut. More important, none of them looked like my memory of that vivid, impatient face.

"It's not any of you," I said. "Is there anyone else who fits the description? What about the cleaners? Or the sailing crew?"

Birgitta frowned and said something to Hanni in Swedish. Hanni shook her head and spoke in English.

"The crew are mainly men. There's one woman, but she's red-headed and perhaps forty or fifty, I think. But Iwona, one of the cleaners, has dark hair. She's Polish, I'm not sure how old she is."

"I'll get her," Karla said. She got up with a smile and squeezed out from behind the table.

"There's Eva," Nilsson said thoughtfully, as Karla left the room in search of the absent Iwona. "She's one of the spa therapists," he added to me.

"She's up in the spa, I think," said Hanni. "Setting up for the day. But she's in her late thirties at least, maybe forties."

"We'll go and speak to her after this," Nilsson said.

"Don't forget Ulla." The pixie-haired girl spoke up for the first time.

"Ah, yes," Nilsson said. "Is she on duty? Ulla is one of the stewardesses for the forward cabins and the Nobel Suite," he added to me.

The girl nodded.

"Yes, but I think she'll be coming off shortly."

"Miss Blacklock," said a voice from behind me, and I turned to see Karla presenting a colleague, a small, dumpy woman in her forties with dyed-black hair showing threads of gray at the roots. "This is Iwona."

"I can to help?" Iwona said, in a heavy Polish accent. "There is a problem?"

I shook my head.

"I'm so sorry." I wasn't sure whether to address the answer to Iwona, Nilsson, or Karla. "She's— You're not the woman I saw. But I just want to say: there's no question of this woman being in trouble. It's not that she's stolen anything or anything like that. I'm worried about her—I heard a scream."

"A scream?" Hanni's narrow eyebrows nearly disappeared into her fringe, and she exchanged a look with Karla, who opened her mouth to say something, but behind us, Camilla Lidman rose, and spoke for the first time.

"I am sure none of the crew is the woman you're looking for, Miss Blacklock." She came across the room to stand by the table, putting her hand on Hanni's shoulder. "They would have said if they had any cause for alarm. We are a very—what's the expression—very tightly knitted."

"Very close," Karla said. Her gaze flickered to Camilla Lidman and back to me, and she smiled, although her raised, overplucked brows gave the expression an oddly unconvincing, anxious air. "We are a very happy crew."

"Never mind," I said. I could see I wasn't going to get anything out of these girls. The mention of the scream had been a mistake; they had closed ranks now. And maybe speaking to them with Camilla and Nilsson present had been an error, too. "Don't worry. I'll go and speak to . . . Eva, was it? And Ulla. Thank you for talking to me. But if you hear anything, anything at all—I'm in cabin nine, Linnaeus. Please do come and see me, anytime."

"We heard nothing," said Hanni firmly. "But of course we will let you know if that changes. Have a wonderful day, Miss Blacklock."

"Thanks," I said. As I turned, the ship lurched, making the girls at the table give little laughing shrieks of alarm, and clutch hold of their coffees. I stumbled, and would have fallen if Nilsson hadn't grabbed my arm.

"Are you all right, Miss Blacklock?"

I nodded, but actually his grip had hurt, leaving my arm aching. The shock of the movement had sent a stabbing pain through my head and I wished I'd taken an aspirin before heading out.

"I enjoy that the *Aurora* is a smaller ship, not one of these Caribbean monsters, but it does mean that you can feel the impact of a big wave more than you might on a larger vessel. Are you sure you're okay?"

"I'm fine," I said shortly, rubbing my arm. "Let's go and speak to Eva."

"First, let us take a detour via the kitchen," Nilsson said. "Then we can head up to the spa to speak to Eva, and finally we can finish in the breakfast room." He had a list of staff in his hand and was crossing off names. "That should be everyone apart perhaps from two members of the sailing crew, and a few cabin stewards we can find at the end."

"Fine," I said tersely. In truth I wanted to get out—out from the narrow, claustrophobic walls and the airless corridors, away from the gray lighting and the feeling of being hemmed in, trapped below the waterline. I had a brief, horrible image of the ship striking something, water flooding the confined space, mouths gasping for the fleeing scraps of air.

But I could not give up now. To do that would be to admit defeat, to admit that Nilsson was right. Instead, pushing the thoughts away, back into my subconscious, I followed him down a corridor towards the nose of the ship, feeling the floor shift and lurch beneath me, while the smell of cooking became stronger. There was bacon and hot fat, and the distinctive buttery tang of baking croissants, but also boiled fish, and gravy, and something sweet. The combination brought a rush of saliva to my mouth, not in a good way, and I gritted my teeth again and grabbed hold of the rail as the ship heaved up another wave and dropped into the trough, leaving my stomach behind.

I was just wondering whether it was too late to turn back and ask Nilsson if we could do this another time, when he stopped at a steel door with two small glass windows and pushed it open. White-hatted heads turned, their faces registering polite surprise as they saw me standing behind Nilsson.

"*Hej, alla!*" Nilsson said, followed by something else in Swedish. He turned to me. "I'm sorry, all of the deck and hospitality staff speak English but not all the cooks do. I'm just explaining why we're here."

There were smiles and nods from the staff, and one of the chefs came forward, his hand stuck out.

"Hello, Miss Blacklock," he said, in excellent English. "My name is Otto Jansson. Any of my staff will be pleased to help, although they do not all speak good English. I can translate. What do you need to know?"

But I couldn't speak. I could only gulp, staring down at his outstretched hand, in the pale latex catering glove, while the blood hissed in my ears.

I looked up, into his friendly blue eyes, and then back down at the latex glove, with dark hairs showing through, pressed against the rubber, and thought, *I must not scream. I must not scream.*

Please God, don't let me scream.

Jansson looked down at his hand, as if to see what I was gaping at, and then laughed, and pulled the glove off with his other hand.

"So sorry, I forget I am wearing these. They are for catering, you know?"

He threw the pale flaccid glove into the bin and then shook my limp, unresisting hand; his grip was firm, his fingers warm and slightly dusty from the latex coating.

"I'm looking for a girl," I said, knowing I was being abrupt, but too shaken to be more polite. "Dark-haired, about my age or a bit younger. Pretty, with pale skin. She didn't have an accent—she was either English or completely bilingual."

"I'm sorry," Jansson said regretfully, and he did look sorry. "I don't think any of my staff fit that description, though you are welcome to take a walk around and see if any of them are the girl you are looking for. I have only two female staff members and neither speak very good English. Jameela is over by the serving hatch, and Ingrid is on salads, behind the grill station there. But neither of them fit your description. Perhaps one of the stewards or waiting staff?"

I craned my head to see the two women he indicated, and saw that he was right. Neither was remotely like the girl I'd seen. Although she had her head bowed and her body hunched away from me, I was certain that Jameela was the Asian woman I'd seen in the cabin as we came down. She was Pakistani or Bangladeshi, I thought—and absolutely tiny, probably not even five feet tall. Ingrid, on the other hand, was Scandinavian and at least two hundred pounds, plus she had a good six inches on me. As I looked at her she put her hands on her hips, squaring up to me almost aggressively, although I knew it was unfair to think that—it was her height that made the gesture seem threatening.

"Never mind," I said. "Sorry for disturbing you."

"*Tack*, Otto," Nilsson said, and then made a joke in Swedish that set Otto laughing. He patted Nilsson on the back and said something that made Nilsson guffaw in return, a great belly laugh that set his stomach shaking. He raised his hand to the rest of the crew. "*Hejdå!*" he called, and then ushered me out into the corridor.

"I'm sorry about that," he said over his shoulder, as he led the way towards the stairs. "The official language of the boat is English and it's policy that we don't speak other languages in front of our English guests, but I thought under the circumstances . . ." He trailed off and I nodded.

"It's fine. Better that everyone was comfortable and understood what they were being asked properly."

We were passing the crew's cabins again, and as we passed the few open doors I glanced in, shocked afresh at the dinginess of the cramped quarters. I couldn't imagine spending week after week, month after month, in the windowless confines. Perhaps Nilsson felt my silence at his back, for he spoke again.

"They're a little small, aren't they? But there's only a dozen or so staff on the boat, excluding the sailing crew, so we don't need much space. And I can tell you, they are better than much of the accommodation on rival ships."

I didn't say what I was thinking, which was not that it was the space itself that shocked but the contrast with the light, airy rooms above. In truth the rooms were no worse than plenty of cross-channel ferries I'd traveled on; in fact they were more spacious than some. But it was the graphic illustration of the gap between the haves and have-nots that was upsetting, a modern upstairs-downstairs in action.

"Does everyone share?" I asked, as we passed a darkened cabin where someone was getting dressed with the door ajar, while their bunkmate snored. Nilsson shook his head.

"The junior staff share cabins, the cleaners and the younger stewards and so on, but all the senior staff have their own."

We had reached the staircase that led to the upper deck and I made my way slowly up, following Nilsson's wide back, and holding on to the grab rails as the ship heaved and tipped. Nilsson opened the dividing door that separated the guest part of the ship from the workers and then turned to me, as he shut the door behind us both.

"I'm sorry that did not work out so well," he said. "I had hoped that one of the girls would be the woman you saw, and put your mind at rest."

"Look . . ." I rubbed my face, feeling the roughness of the healing scar on my cheek, and the pressure headache that was beginning to build. "Look, I'm not sure—"

"Let's press on and speak to Eva," Nilsson said firmly. And he turned and led the way along the corridor towards yet another set of stairs.

The ship heaved itself up another crest, and down in the trough, and I swallowed against the gush of spit in my mouth and felt the cold clamminess of sweat on my spine, beneath my shirt. For a moment I almost considered ducking back to my cabin. It wasn't only my head—I had work to do—I still had to finish reading the press pack, and I needed to make a start on the piece Rowan would be expecting when I got back. I was horribly conscious that Ben, Tina, Alexander, and all the others were probably already making notes, filing pieces, googling Bullmer, and sorting out press shots.

But then I steeled myself. If I wanted Nilsson to take me seriously I had to go through with this. And as much as I wanted to climb the ladder at *Velocity*, some things were more important.

We found Eva in the spa reception, which was a beautiful, tranquil room on the upper deck, almost all glass, with long curtains that floated in the cool breeze from the open door. The glass walls looked out onto the deck, the light almost searingly bright after the beige warren of dimly lit rooms below decks.

A striking dark-haired woman in her forties with wide gold hoops in her ears looked up as Nilsson and I entered.

"Johann!" she said pleasantly. "What can I do for you? And this must be . . . ?"

"Lo Blacklock," I said, holding out my hand. I felt instantly better out of the claustrophobic confines of the staff quarters, the clammy nausea retreating in the sea breeze.

"Good morning, Ms. Blacklock," she said, smiling. I shook her hand, her grip firm, her fingers bony but strong. Her English was astonishingly good—almost as good as the girl in the cabin's had been, but it wasn't her. She was much too old, her carefully moisturized skin still betraying that slight weathering of a complexion that had seen a little too much sun. "What can I do for you?"

"I'm sorry," I said. "I was looking for someone, and the girls below decks suggested it might be you, but it's not."

"Miss Blacklock saw a woman last night," Nilsson put in. "In the cabin next to hers. She was in her twenties, with long dark hair and pale skin. Miss Blacklock heard some noises that made her concerned, and we were trying to ascertain if it was a member of staff."

"I'm afraid it wasn't me," Eva said, but quite kindly. There was no trace of the slightly tribal defensiveness the girls downstairs had betrayed. She gave a little laugh. "If I'm being honest, it's a long time since I was in my twenties. Have you spoken to the stewardesses? Hanni and Birgitta both have dark hair and are around that age. And so does Ulla."

"Yes, we've spoken to them," Nilsson said. "And we're on our way to see Ulla now."

"She's not in any trouble," I said. "The woman, I mean. I'm worried for her. If you can think of anyone it might be . . ."

"I'm sorry not to be able to help," Eva said. She spoke directly to me, and she did look sorry, the most genuinely concerned of any of the people I had spoken to so far. There was a little frown between her beautifully plucked brows. "I really am. If I hear anything . . ."

"Thank you," I said.

"Thanks, Eva," Nilsson repeated, and turned to go.

"You're welcome," Eva said. She walked us to the door. "I look forward to seeing you later, Ms. Blacklock."

"Later?"

"At eleven a.m. It is the ladies' spa experience—in your press schedule?"

"Thanks," I said. "See you then." And as I turned to leave I thought, guiltily, of the unread pages of the press pack back in my cabin, and wondered what else I might have missed.

We left the spa via the exit to the deck, and as the door swung back, it was wrenched out of my hand by the strong breeze, banging sharply against a rubber stand put there for the purpose. Nilsson closed it behind me, and I moved to the ship's rail, shivering in the wind.

"Are you cold?" Nilsson shouted, above the roar of the wind and the noise of the engines. I shook my head.

"No, I mean, yes, I am, but I need the fresh air."

"Are you still feeling unwell?"

"Not out here. But my head's aching."

I stood, holding on to the cold painted iron of the railing, and leaned out, looking down, past the glass-walled balconies of the cabins aft, down at the creaming waves at the ship's wake, and the great dark expanse farther out, unimaginably deep and cold. I thought of the fathoms and fathoms of swirling blackness beneath us, of the darkness and silence below, and how something—someone—might fall for days through those black depths, to rest at last on a lightless seabed.

I thought of the girl the night before, how easy it would be for someone—Nilsson, Eva, anyone—to just walk up behind me, give me a gentle push . . .

I shuddered.

What *had* happened? I couldn't have imagined it. The scream, and the splash maybe. But not the blood. I couldn't have imagined that.

I took a huge lungful of the clean North Sea air, turned around, and smiled determinedly at Nilsson, shaking my hair back, where the wind had whipped it across my face.

"So whereabouts are we?"

"International waters," Nilsson said. "On our way to Trondheim, I believe."

"Trondheim?" I tried to think back to the bits of the press pack I'd actually read. "I thought we were going to Bergen first."

"A change of plan, perhaps. I know that Lord Bullmer is very much hoping that you will all get a glimpse of the northern lights. Perhaps there are particularly good conditions tonight so he wanted to hasten north. Or it might have been a suggestion of the captain; there may be climatic reasons why it's better to do the trip that way round. We have no fixed itinerary. We are very much able to cater to the whims of our passengers. It may be that someone at dinner last night was particularly anxious to see Trondheim."

"What's in Trondheim?"

"Trondheim itself? Well, there is a famous cathedral. And parts of the city are very attractive. But it's mainly the fjords. That and the fact that the city is of course much farther north than Bergen, so there's a better chance of seeing the aurora. But it might be that we have to go farther north still, to Bodø or even Tromsø. At this time of year, it's still uncertain."

"I see." For some reason his words unsettled me. It was one thing to feel yourself part of an organized, itinerized trip. It was quite another to realize you were a helpless passenger with someone else at the wheel.

"Miss Blacklock—"

"Call me Lo," I interrupted. "Please."

"Lo, then." Nilsson's broad, comfortable face looked pained, something troubled in his teddy-bear expression. "I don't want you to think that I don't believe you, Lo, but in the cold light of day—"

"Am I still sure?" I finished. He nodded. I sighed, a little unhappily, thinking back to my doubts of the night before and the way Nilsson's unspoken question echoed the unpleasant little nagging voice at the back of my skull. I twisted my fingers in the cloth of my top before I spoke. "The truth is, I don't know. It was late, and you're right, I had been drinking—I could have been mistaken about the scream and the splash. Even the blood—I guess it *could* have been a trick of the light, although I'm pretty sure of what I saw. But the woman in the cabin—there's no way I could have imagined her. I just couldn't. I *saw* her, I *spoke* to her. If she's not here—not on the ship, I mean—then where is she?"

There was a long silence.

"Well, we haven't spoken to Ulla," he said at last. "From your description, I'm not sure it's her, but we should rule it out at least." He drew out his staff radio and began tapping at the buttons. "I don't know about you, but I could do with a coffee, so perhaps we could ask her to meet us in the passenger dining room."

The breakfast room was the same room we had eaten dinner in last night, but the two large tables had been broken up into half a dozen smaller ones, and when Nilsson pushed open the door, no one was there apart from a young waiter with corn-colored hair swept into a side parting. He came forward to greet me with a smile.

"Miss Blacklock? Are you ready for breakfast?"

"Yes, please," I said vaguely, looking around the room. "Where should I sit?"

"Anywhere you like." He waved a hand at the empty tables. "Most of the other guests have chosen to breakfast in their cabins. Perhaps by the window? Can I bring you tea, coffee?"

"Coffee, please," I said. "Milk, no sugar."

"And a cup for me, please, Bjorn," Nilsson said. And then, over Bjorn's shoulder, "Ah, hello, Ulla."

I turned to see a stunningly beautiful girl with a heavy black bun walking across the dining room to our table.

"Hello, Johann," she said. Her singsong accent clinched the matter, but I was sure, even before she spoke, that she wasn't the girl in the cabin. She was singularly beautiful, her skin against her black hair as white and clear as porcelain. The girl in the cabin had been vividly good-looking, but not that delicate, classical loveliness, like a Renaissance painting. Also Ulla must have been nearly six feet. The girl in the cabin had been around my height, nowhere near Ulla's. Nilsson gave me a questioning look, but I shook my head.

Bjorn returned with two cups on a tray and a menu for me, and Nilsson cleared his throat.

"Won't you have a cup with us, Ulla?"

"Thank you," she said, shaking her head so that her heavy bun swayed at the nape of her neck. "I've had breakfast already today, but I'll sit for a moment."

She slipped onto a chair opposite and looked at us both, smiling expectantly. Nilsson coughed again.

"Miss Blacklock, this is Ulla. She's the stewardess for the forward cabins, so the Bullmers, the Jenssens, Cole Lederer, and Owen White. Ulla, Miss Blacklock is looking for a girl who she saw yesterday and is anxious to trace. She's not on the passenger list, so we are thinking she may be a member of staff, but we have had no luck in finding her. Miss Blacklock, do you want to describe the girl you saw?"

"She had long dark hair," I said. "She was about your age—late twenties, maybe—really pretty, and she spoke English like someone born in Britain. She was about my height. Can you think of anyone"—I was aware my voice had started to sound pleading—"*anyone* who would fit that description?"

"Well, I have dark hair, obviously," Ulla said with a laugh. "But it was not me, so after that I am not so sure. There is Hanni, she has dark hair, and Birgitta—"

"I've met them," I interrupted. "It's not them. Anyone else? Cleaners? Sailing crew?"

"N-no . . . there's no one on the sailing crew who could fit that description," Ulla said slowly. "On the staff there is also Eva, but she is too old. Have you spoken to the kitchen staff?"

"Never mind." I was beginning to despair. This was starting to feel like a recurring nightmare, interviewing person after person after person, while all the while the memory of the dark-haired girl began to dissolve and shimmer, slipping through my fingers like water. The more faces I saw, each corresponding slightly but not completely to my memory, the harder I was finding it to hold on to the image in my head.

And yet, there was something defining about that girl, something I was sure I'd recognize if I saw her again. It wasn't the features—they were pretty, but ordinary enough. It wasn't the hair, or the Pink Floyd T-shirt. It was something about *her*, the sheer liveliness and vivacity of her expression as she peered sharply out into the corridor, her surprise as she had seen my face.

Was it really possible she was dead?

But the alternative was not much better. Because if she wasn't, the only other possibility—and suddenly I wasn't sure if it was better or worse—was that I was going mad.

- CHAPTER 13 -

Ulla and Nilsson both excused themselves when my breakfast arrived, leaving me to stare out the window as I ate. Up here, with a view of the sea and the deck, I didn't feel quite so sick, and I managed a respectable amount of breakfast, feeling the energy come back into my limbs and the nagging nausea abate. It struck me that at least half the reason I had been feeling so crappy was probably low blood sugar. I always get strange and shaky on an empty stomach.

But though the food and the sight of the ocean made me feel physically better, I could not stop running over last night's events in my head, replaying the conversation with the girl, the surprise on her face, the touch of irritation as she shoved the mascara into my hand. Something had been going on—I was sure of it. It felt like coming into a film halfway through, struggling to work out who the characters were. I had interrupted the girl *doing* something. But what?

Whatever it was, it was probably linked to her disappearance. And whatever Nilsson thought, I could not believe she had been cleaning the room. No one cleaned a room in a thigh-skimming Pink Floyd T-shirt. And besides—she just hadn't *looked* like a cleaner. You didn't get hair and nails like that on a cleaner's wage. The gloss on that thick dark mane had spoken of years of conditioning wraps and expensive low lights. Industrial espionage? A stowaway? An affair? I remembered the cold glint in Cole's eyes as he spoke about his ex-wife, and Camilla Lidman's bland reassurances downstairs. I thought of Nilsson's lumbering strength, of Alexander unpleasantly dwelling on the topic of poison and unnatural death last night at dinner—but each possibility seemed more unlikely than the last.

It was her face that troubled me. The more I struggled to remember it, the more it blurred. The concrete bits—her height, the color of her hair, the state of her nails—all that I could picture clearly. But her features . . . a neat nose . . . narrow dark brows carefully plucked. That was about it. I could say what she was *not*: plump, old, acne-spotted. Saying what she *was* was far harder. Her nose had been . . . normal. Her mouth . . . normal. Not wide, not rosebud, not pouting, not bee-stung. Just . . . normal. There was nothing distinctive that I could put my finger on.

She could have been me.

I knew what Nilsson wanted. He wanted me to forget what I'd heard, the scream, the stealthy slide of the screen door, and that horrible, huge slithering splash.

He wanted me to start doubting my own account of things. He was taking me seriously, only to make me start undermining myself. He was letting me ask all the questions I wanted—enough to convince myself of my own fallibility.

And part of me couldn't blame him—this was the *Aurora*'s maiden voyage, and the boat was stuffed with journalists and photographers and influential people. There was hardly a worse time for something to go wrong. I could imagine the headlines now: "Voyage to Death—Passenger on Luxury Press Trip Drowned." As head of security, Nilsson's neck would be on the line. He'd lose his job, at the very least, if something went wrong on the *Aurora*, on the very first voyage he was involved in.

But more than that—the kind of publicity that an unexplained death would generate could sink the whole enterprise. Something like this could scupper the *Aurora* before she was even launched, and if that happened, everyone on board could lose their jobs, from the captain down to Iwona, the cleaner.

I knew that.

But I had heard *something*. Something that had made me start from my sleep with my heart pounding two hundred beats per minute, and my palms wet with sweat, and the conviction that somewhere very close by, another woman was in grave trouble. I *knew* what it was like to be that girl—to realize, in an instant, how incredibly fragile your hold on life could be, how paper-thin the walls of security really were.

And whatever Nilsson might say, if nothing had happened to that girl, then where was she? The scream, the blood—all those I could have imagined. But the girl—I definitely hadn't imagined the girl. And she could not have vanished into thin air without help.

I rubbed my eyes, feeling the gritty residue of last night's eye makeup, and I realized—I had just one single thing to prove she had not been a figment of my imagination: that Maybelline mascara.

Wild thoughts tripped through my head, one after the other. I would take it back to England in a plastic bag and get it fingerprinted. No, better yet, I'd get it DNA tested. There was DNA on makeup brushes, wasn't there? On *CSI: Miami* they would have based an entire prosecution case on a trapped eyelash. There must be *something* they could do.

I pushed aside the mental image of myself marching up to Crouch End police station with a mascara in a bag and demanding advanced forensic analysis from a police officer only barely restraining his amused smile. *Someone* would believe me. They had to. And if they didn't I'd—I'd pay to get it done myself.

I pulled out my phone, ready to google "private DNA testing cost," but even before I had unlocked the home screen, I realized how crazy it was. I wasn't going to get police-grade DNA testing from an Internet company specializing in cheating spouses. And what would the results tell me anyway, without anything to compare it to?

Instead, I found myself checking my e-mail. Nothing from Judah. In fact, nothing at all. There was no phone reception, but I seemed to be connected to the boat's Wi-Fi network and I forced a refresh. But nothing happened. The little "updating" icon whirred and whirred, and then NO NETWORK CONNECTION popped up.

With a sigh, I put the phone away in my pocket and surveyed the blueberries on my plate. The pancakes had been delicious, but my appetite was gone. It seemed impossible, surreal: I'd witnessed a murder—or had heard one at least—and yet here I was, trying to force down pancakes and coffee, while all the time there was a murderer walking free and there was nothing I could do.

Did they know they'd been heard and reported? With the noise I'd been making, and the questions I'd been asking all round the boat, if they didn't last night, they did now.

The boat took another wave, broadside on, and I pushed the plate away and stood up.

"Is there anything else, Miss Blacklock?" Bjorn asked, and I jumped violently and swung around. He had appeared as if by magic from a door set into the paneling at the back of the room. It was almost impossible to see unless you knew it was there. Had he been there all that time, watching me? Was there some kind of *spy hole*?

I shook my head and did my best to smile as I walked across the slowly tilting floor.

"No, thank you, Bjorn. Thanks for all your help."

"Have a wonderful morning. Do you have plans? If you haven't tried it, the view from the deck-top hot tub is stunning."

I had a sudden vision of myself, alone in the hot tub, a hand in latex gloves pushing me beneath the water . . .

I shook my head again.

"I'm supposed to be going to the spa, I think. But I might go for a lie-down in my cabin first. I'm very tired. I didn't sleep well last night."

"Of course." He pronounced it like *off course.* "I completely understand. A little ara and ara is prescribed, perhaps!"

"Ara and ara?" I was puzzled.

"Is that not the expression? Ara and ara, rest and relaxion?"

"Oh!" I blushed. "Rest and relaxation. Yes, of course. Sorry—like I said, I'm só tired . . ." I was edging towards the door, my skin suddenly crawling at the thought of the unseen eyes that could be watching our conversation. At least in my cabin I could be sure of being alone.

"Enjoy your rest!"

"I will," I said. I turned to go—and walked slap into a bleary-eyed Ben Howard.

"Blacklock!"

"Howard."

"Last night . . ." he said awkwardly. I shook my head. I wasn't about to have this conversation in front of the softly spoken Bjorn, who was smiling at the opposite side of the room.

"Let's not go there," I said curtly. "We were both drunk. Have you only just woken up?"

"Yeah." He stifled a huge yawn. "After I left your cabin I bumped into Archer and we ended up playing poker with Lars and Richard Bullmer until stupid o'clock."

"Oh." I chewed my lip. "What time did you get to bed?"

"Christ knows. Four-ish, I think."

"Only because . . ." I started. And then stopped. Nilsson did not believe me. I was getting to the point where I barely believed myself. But Ben . . . He would believe me—right?

I thought back to our time together, to how it ended . . . Suddenly I wasn't so sure.

"Never mind," I said shortly. "I'll tell you later. Have your breakfast."

"Are you all right?" he said as I turned to go. "You look terrible."

"Great. Thanks."

"No, I just mean—you look like you've barely slept."

"I didn't." I was trying not to snap, but anxiety and exhaustion were making me more abrupt than I meant. Then, as the boat lurched over another wave, "I'm finding this sea a bit rough."

"Yeah? I'm lucky, I never get seasick." There was an irritating touch of smugness in his voice and I resisted the urge to snap back something short and sharp. "Never mind, we'll be in Trondheim early tomorrow."

"Tomorrow?" My voice must have betrayed my dismay, for he looked at me sharply.

"Yes. Why, what's the matter?"

"I thought—I imagined, today . . ." I trailed off. He shrugged.

"It's a long way, you know."

"Never mind." I needed to get back to my room, think this through—try to work out what I had and hadn't seen. "I'm going to go back to my room—have a lie-down."

"Sure. See you later, Blacklock," Ben said. His tone was light. But his eyes, as he watched me walk away, were worried.

I thought I was heading for the stairs to the lower deck, but I must have taken a wrong turn because I ended up in the library—a tiny paneled version of a country-house library, complete with green-shaded reading lamps and tiered shelving, re-created on a miniature scale.

I sighed, and tried to work out where I'd gone wrong, and if there was a quicker route back than retracing my steps and facing Ben again. It seemed impossible to get lost on such a small boat, but there was something very confusing about the way the rooms were fitted together, like a locking puzzle designed to squeeze out every inch of empty space, and navigating the maze was made more complicated by the way the boat's movement messed with my sense of direction.

It didn't help that, unlike a ferry, there were no floor plans or maps, and minimal signage—I supposed to help the impression that this was a private home that you just happened to share with a load of rich people.

There were two exits, and more or less at random, I opened the door to the deck. At least outside I could be certain which way I was facing, relative to the direction of travel. As I stepped outside, feeling the wind buffet my face, I heard a hoarse, nicotine-soaked voice from behind me.

"Darling, it's a miracle you're standing! How are you this morning?"

I turned. It was Tina, standing beneath a curved glass smoking shelter, a cigarette between her fingers. She took a long drag.

"Little bit the worse for wear?"

I suppressed the urge to turn and flee. I was supposed to be networking. I couldn't let a self-inflicted hangover get in the way of that. I attempted a smile, hoping it was convincing.

"A bit. I shouldn't have drunk so much."

"Well, I was rather impressed by the amount you put away," she said, with a slightly mocking smile. "As my old boss told me when I started at the *Express* back in the days of the *really* long lunch, if you can outdrink your interviewee, you're on your way to your first scoop."

I looked at her through the haze of smoke. Office gossip was that she had made her way up the corporate ladder by treading on the backs of more young women than you could count, and then, once she was through the glass ceiling, pulling the ladder up behind her. I remembered Rowan once saying, *Tina is one of those women who thinks every bit of estrogen in the boardroom is a threat to her own existence.*

But somehow, I couldn't quite square her remarks with the woman standing in front of me. I knew at least one ex-colleague who said she owed Tina her career, and as I looked at her now, her heavily made-up eyes laughing at me, I thought about what it must have been like to be a female journalist in that generation, clawing your way up through the ranks of the old-boys' network. It was hard enough now. Maybe it wasn't Tina's fault she couldn't take every other woman in the office with her.

"Come here, darling, I'll let you into a little secret," she said, and beckoned me over, her rings chinking on her skeletal fingers. "Hair of the dog, followed by a long, slow screw."

There was only one possible response that didn't start with *eeeeeeww*, and that was a noncommittal silence. Tina gave her throaty, nicotine-soaked laugh again.

"I've shocked you."

"Not really. It's just—you know—we're a little short on candidates."

"I thought you and that sexy little Ben Howard were looking rather friendly last night . . ." she drawled. I repressed a shudder.

"Ben and I were together, years back," I said firmly. "And I've got no desire to go back there."

"Very sensible, darling." She patted my arm, her rings clinking against my skin. "As the Afghans say, a man may never bathe in the same lake twice."

I wasn't sure what to say to this.

"What's your name again?" she said abruptly. "Louise, was it?"

"Lo. It's short for Laura, actually."

"Nice to meet you, Lo. And you're with Rowan at *Velocity*, is that right?"

"Yes, that's right," I said. "I'm a features writer." And then, surprising myself, "But I'm hoping to cover her maternity leave while she's off. It's partly why I got this trip, I think. They wanted to test the waters. See how I did."

Although if this was a test, I was well on my way to failing it. Accusing my hosts of covering up a death was definitely not what *Velocity* had had in mind.

Tina drew on her cigarette again, and then spat out a thread of tobacco and looked at me appraisingly.

"Lot of responsibility, that role. But it's good that you want a step up. And what will you do when she gets back?"

I opened my mouth to reply—and then stopped. What *would* I do? Go back to my old job? I was just wondering how to answer when she spoke.

"Give me a call sometime, when we're back in the office. I'm always on the lookout for freelancers, particularly savvy little things with a bit of ambition."

"I'm on a staff contract," I said regretfully. I appreciated it was a compliment, and I didn't want to throw it back at her, but I was pretty sure my noncompete clause wouldn't let me moonlight.

"Suit yourself," Tina said with a shrug. The boat lurched as she spoke, and she staggered against the metal rail. "Blast, my ciggie's gone out. You don't have a light, do you, sweetie? I left mine in the lounge."

"I don't smoke," I said.

"Damn it." She flicked the end over the rail and we both watched as it was snatched by the wind and whisked out of sight, gone before it even hit the churning water. I really should have given her my card, or at the very least started subtly pumping her about the *Vernean*'s plans for future issues and how far she'd got in buttering up Lord Bullmer. It was what Rowan would have done. Ben would probably have scored a freelance contract by now, and sod the noncompete stuff.

But right at this moment—with Nilsson probably even now shooting holes in my story to the captain—my career didn't seem as important. If anything, I should be quizzing her, working out her whereabouts last night. After all, Ben had been playing poker with Lars, Archer, and Bullmer, which left a comparatively small pool of people who could have been in the cabin next to mine. Was Tina strong enough to push a woman overboard? I eyed her covertly as she began to hobble across the salt-sprayed deck toward the door, her narrow heels skidding slightly on the painted metal deck. She was greyhound thin, more sinew than muscle, but I could imagine there would be a wiry strength in her arms, and the picture Rowan had painted was of a woman whose ruthlessness more than compensated for her physical size.

"So how about you?" I said as I followed her towards the door. "Did you have a good time last night?"

She stopped abruptly at that, the heavy door held in one hand, her fingers clenched on the metal, the tendons on the back of her hand standing out like iron cables. She turned to stare at me.

"What did you say?" Her neck was thrust forward like a velociraptor's, her eyes boring into me.

"I—" I stopped, taken aback by the ferocity of her response. "I didn't—I was just wondering . . ."

"Well, I suggest you stop wondering, and keep your insinuations to yourself. A clever girl like you knows better than to make enemies in this business."

Then she let go of the door and let it slam shut behind her.

I stood on deck, staring blankly after her retreating back through the salt-misted door, and wondering what on earth had just happened.

I shook my head and pulled myself together. There was no point in trying to figure it out now. I should be back in the cabin, preserving the one bit of evidence I had left.

I had locked the door before I left with Nilsson but I realized, as I made my way carefully down the stairs to the cabin deck and saw the cleaners pulling their vacuums after them, their trolleys piled with towels and linens, that I had forgotten to put out the DO NOT DISTURB sign.

Inside, the suite had been valeted to within an inch of its life. The sink had been polished. The windows cleaned of salt spray. Even my dirty clothes had magically disappeared. The torn evening dress was also gone.

But I wasn't interested in any of it. Instead, I went straight to the bathroom, to the neat ranks of makeup and cleansers on the vanity surface.

Where was it?

I pushed aside the lipstick and gloss, the toothpaste, moisturizer, eye makeup remover, half-used blister pack of pills . . . but it wasn't there. No flash of pink and green leaped out at me. Under the counter, then—in the bin.

I went through to the main bedroom, opening drawers one after another, hunting under chairs. Where was it? Where *was* it?

But I knew the answer, even as I sank to the bed, head in my hands. It was gone. The tube of mascara—my one link to the missing girl—was gone.

Saturday, 26 September

Harringay Echo website

LONDON TOURIST MISSING FROM NORWEGIAN CRUISE VESSEL

Friends and relatives of missing Londoner Laura Blacklock are said to be growing "increasingly concerned" about her safety. Blacklock (32), who resides in West Grove in Harringay, was reported missing by her partner, Judah Lewis (35), during a holiday aboard the exclusive tourist ship the *Aurora Borealis*.

Mr. Lewis, who was not with Miss Blacklock on board, reported that he had become concerned after Miss Blacklock did not return messages on board the cruise liner, and when attempts to contact her failed.

A spokesperson for the *Aurora Borealis*, whose maiden voyage left Hull last Sunday, confirmed that Blacklock had not been seen since a planned trip to Trondheim on Tuesday, 22 September, but the company said that it had been initially assumed that she had decided to curtail her trip. It was only when Miss Blacklock failed to return to the UK on Friday and her partner raised the alarm that they became aware that her departure had not been planned.

Pamela Crew, the missing woman's mother, said that it was extremely out of character for her daughter not to have made contact, and appealed for anyone who might have seen Miss Blacklock, also known as Lo, to come forward.

PART FOUR

- CHAPTER 14 -

I tried not to let the panic overwhelm me.

Someone had been in my room.

Someone who *knew*.

Someone who knew what I'd seen, and what I'd heard, and what I'd said.

The minibar had been restocked, and I longed with a sudden visceral sharpness for a drink, but I shoved the thought aside and began to pace the cabin, which had seemed so large yesterday and now seemed to be closing in on me.

Someone had been in here. But who?

The urge to scream, to run away, to hide under the bed and never come out, was almost overwhelming, but there was no escape—not until we reached Trondheim.

The realization jolted my thoughts out of their rat-run and I stood, my hands on the dressing table, my shoulders bowed, looking at my white, gaunt face in the mirror. It wasn't just the lack of sleep. There were deep circles of exhaustion under my eyes, but it was something in my eyes themselves that made me pause—a look of fear, like an animal run to ground.

A whining roar came from the corridor, and I remembered, with a jolt, the cleaners valeting the rooms. I took a deep breath and stood straighter, shaking my hair back over my shoulder. Then I opened the door and put my head out into the corridor, where the hum of the vacuum cleaner still buzzed. Iwona, the Polish woman I had been introduced to downstairs, was cleaning Ben's cabin just up the corridor, the door wide-open.

"Excuse me!" I called, but she didn't hear. I ventured closer. "Excuse me!"

She jumped and turned around, her hand on her heart.

"Excuse!" she said, breathlessly, putting her foot down on the switch to silence the hoover. She was wearing the dark blue uniform all the rest of the cleaners wore, her heavy features pink with exertion. "I am startle."

"I'm sorry," I said penitently. "I didn't mean to shock you. I wanted to ask—did you clean my room?"

"Yes, I did already. Something is not clean?"

"It's not that. It's very clean—beautiful, in fact. It's just that I wondered—did you see a mascara?"

"Mass—?" She shook her head, but not meaning no, her expression was uncomprehending. "What it is?"

"Mascara. For your eyes—like this." I mimed putting it on, and her face cleared.

"Ah! Yes, I know," she said, and said something that sounded like *toosh do resh*. I had no idea if this was Polish for *mascara* or *I put it in the bin*, but I nodded vigorously.

"Yes, yes, in a pink-and-green tube. Like—" I pulled out my phone, meaning to google Maybelline, but the Wi-Fi still wasn't working. "Oh, damn, never mind. But it's pink and green. Have you seen it?"

"Yes, I see last night when I clean."

Shit.

"But not this morning?"

"No." She shook her head, her face troubled. "Is not in bathroom?"

"No."

"I am sorry. I did not see. I can to ask Karla, stewardess, if possible to, um . . . how say . . . to buy new—"

Her floundering words and worried expression made me realize, suddenly, what this must seem like—a madwoman half-accusing a cleaner of stealing a used mascara. I shook my head, put out my hand to her arm.

"I'm sorry. It doesn't matter. Please don't worry."

"But yes, it matter!"

"No, honestly. It was probably me. I expect I left it in a pocket."

But I knew the truth. The mascara was gone.

Back in the cabin I double-locked the door and put the chain across, then I picked up the phone, pressed 0, and asked to be put through to Nilsson. There was a long piped-music delay, and a woman who sounded like Camilla Lidman came back on the line.

"Miss Blacklock? Thank you for holding. I'll put you through."

There was a click and a crackle, and then a man's deep voice came on the line.

"Hello?" It was Nilsson. "Johann Nilsson speaking. Can I help you?"

"The mascara is gone," I said without preamble. There was a pause; I could feel him sorting through his mental filing cabinet of notes. "The mascara," I said impatiently. "The one I told you about last night—that the woman in cabin ten gave to me. This *proves* my point, can't you see?"

"I don't see—"

"Someone came into my cabin and took it." I spoke slowly, trying to keep ahold of myself. I had the strange feeling that if I didn't speak calmly and clearly, I might start screaming down the phone. "Why would they do that, if they didn't have anything to hide?"

There was a long pause.

"Nilsson?"

"I'll come and see you," he said at last. "Are you in your cabin?"

"Yes."

"I'll be about ten minutes. I'm with the captain, I must finish here, but I will come as soon as possible."

"Good-bye," I said, and banged the phone down, more angry than afraid, though I wasn't sure if it was with myself, or with Nilsson.

I paced the small cabin again, running through the events of last night, the pictures, sounds, fears, crowding my head. The feeling I could not get over was one of violation—someone had been in my *room*. Someone had taken advantage of the fact that I was busy with Nilsson to come and pick through my belongings and pull out the one piece of evidence that supported my story.

But who had access to a key? Iwona? Karla? Josef?

There was a knock at the door and I turned sharply and went to unlock it. Nilsson stood outside, an uneasy mixture of truculent, ursine, and tired. The dark circles under his eyes were not as big as mine, but they were getting there.

"Someone took the mascara," I said.

He nodded.

"May I come in?"

I stood back, and he edged past me into the room.

"Can I sit?"

"Please."

He sat, the sofa protesting gently, and I perched opposite him on the chair from the dressing table. Neither of us spoke. I was waiting for him to begin—perhaps he was doing the same, or simply trying to find the words. He pinched at the bridge of his nose, a delicate gesture that looked oddly comic in such a big man.

"Miss Blacklock—"

"Lo," I said, firmly. He sighed and began again.

"Lo, then. I have spoken to the captain. None of the staff are missing, we are quite certain of that now. We've also spoken to all the staff and none of them saw anything suspicious about that cabin, all of which leads us to the conclusion—"

"Hey," I interrupted hotly, as if somehow preventing him from saying the words would affect the conclusion he and the captain had come to.

"Miss Blacklock—"

"No. No, you don't get to do this."

"Don't get to do what?"

"Call me 'Miss Blacklock' one minute, tell me you respect my concerns and I'm a valued passenger blah blah blah, and then the next minute brush me off like a hysterical female who didn't see what she saw."

"I don't—" he started, but I cut him off, too angry to listen.

"You can't have it both ways. Either you believe me or— Oh, no, wait!" I stopped in my tracks, unable to believe I hadn't thought of it before. "What about CCTV? Don't you have some kind of security system?"

"Miss Blacklock—"

"You could check the tapes of the corridor. The girl will be on there—she must be!"

"Miss Blacklock," he said more loudly, "I have spoken to Mr. Howard."

"What?"

"I have spoken to Mr. Howard," he said, more wearily. "Ben Howard."

"So?" I said, but my heart was thumping fast. "What can Ben possibly know about this?"

"His cabin is on the other side of the empty one. I went to see him, to find out if he could have heard anything, if he could corroborate your account of a splash."

"He wasn't there," I said. "He was playing poker."

"I know that. But he told me . . ." Nilsson trailed off.

Oh, Ben, I thought, and there was a sinking sensation in my stomach. Ben, you traitor. What have you done?

I knew what he'd said. I knew it from Nilsson's face, but I wasn't going to let him off the hook that easily.

"Yes?" I said through gritted teeth. I was going to force him to do this properly. He was going to have to spell this out, one excruciating syllable at a time.

"He told me about the man in your flat. The burglar."

"That has nothing to do with this."

"It, um—" He coughed and folded first his arms, then his legs. The picture of a man his size, perched uncomfortably on a sofa, trying to efface himself into nothing, was almost ludicrously comic. I said nothing. The sensation of watching him squirm was almost exquisite. *You know,* I thought viciously, *you know what a shit you're being.*

"Mr. Howard tells me that you, er, you haven't been sleeping well, since the, er, the break-in," he managed.

I said nothing. I sat there cold and hard with rage against Nilsson, but mostly against Ben Howard. That was the last time I confided in him. Would I never learn?

"And then there is the alcohol," he said. His fair, crumpled face was unhappy. "It, um . . . it doesn't mix well with . . ."

He trailed off. His head turned towards the bathroom door, to the pathetic pile of personal belongings.

"With what?" I said, my voice low and hard and totally unlike my own. Nilsson raised his eyes to the ceiling, his discomfort radiating through the room.

"With . . . antidepressants," he said, his voice almost a whisper, and his gaze flicked again to the crumpled half-used packet of pills beside the sink, and then back to me, every inch of him apologetic.

But the words were said. They could not be unsaid, and we both knew it.

I sat, saying nothing, but my cheeks were burning as if I'd been slapped. So this was it. Ben Howard really had told him everything, the little shit. A few minutes, he'd talked to Nilsson. One conversation, and in that time he'd not only failed to support my story—he'd spilled every detail of my biography that he had at hand, and made me look like an unreliable, chemically imbalanced neurotic in the process.

Yes. Yes, I take antidepressants. So what?

No matter that I've been taking—and drinking on—those pills for years. No matter that I had anxiety attacks, not delusions.

But even if I'd had full-blown psychosis, that didn't detract from the fact that, pills or no pills, *I saw what I saw.*

"So that's it, then," I spoke, finally, the words clipped and flat. "You think, just because of a handful of pills, I'm a paranoid nutjob who can't tell fact from fiction? You do know that there are hundreds of thousands of people on the same medication I take?"

"That is absolutely not what I was trying to say," Nilsson said awkwardly. "But it is a fact that we have no evidence to support your account and, Miss Blacklock, with respect, what you believe happened is very close to your own exper—"

"NO!" I shouted, standing up, towering over his unhappily crouched body, in spite of the fact that he must have half a foot on me ordinarily. "I told you, you do *not* get to do this. You don't get to call me obsequious names and then dismiss what I've told you. Yes, I haven't been sleeping. Yes, I'd been drinking. Yes, someone broke into my flat. It has *nothing to do with what I saw*."

"But that is the problem, isn't it?" He stood, too, now, nettled, a flush across his broad cheeks. "You didn't *see* anything. You saw a girl, of which there are many on this boat, and then much later you heard a splash. From that you have jumped to conclusions which are very close to the traumatic event you yourself experienced a few nights ago—a case of two and two making five. This does not warrant a murder investigation, Miss Blacklock."

"Get out," I said. The ice around my heart seemed to be melting. I could feel that I was about to give way to something very stupid.

"Miss—"

"Get. Out!"

I stalked to the door and wrenched it open. My hands were trembling.

"Get out!" I repeated. "Now. Unless you want me to call the captain and tell him that a lone female traveler asked you repeatedly to leave her cabin and you refused. GET THE FUCK OUT OF MY CABIN."

Nilsson hunched his head into his neck and walked stiffly to the door. He paused in the doorway for a moment, as if he was about to say something, but perhaps it was my face, or something in my eyes, because when he looked up and met my gaze, he seemed to flinch and turn away.

"Good-bye," he said. "Miss—"

But I didn't wait to hear any more. I slammed the door in his face and then flung myself on the bed to sob my heart out.

- CHAPTER 15 -

There's no reason, on paper at least, why I need these pills to get through life. I had a great childhood, loving parents, the whole package. I wasn't beaten, abused, or expected to get nothing but As. I had nothing but love and support, but that wasn't enough somehow.

My friend Erin says we all have demons inside us, voices that whisper we're no good, that if we don't make this promotion or ace that exam we'll reveal to the world exactly what kind of worthless sacks of skin and sinew we really are. Maybe that's true. Maybe mine just have louder voices.

But I don't think it's as simple as that. The depression I fell into after university wasn't about exams and self-worth, it was something stranger, more chemical, something that no talking cure was going to fix.

Cognitive behavioral therapy, counseling, psychotherapy—none of it really worked in the way that the pills did. Lissie says she finds the notion of chemically rebalancing your mood scary, she says it's the idea of taking something that could alter how she really is. But I don't see it that way; for me it's like wearing makeup—not a disguise, but a way of making myself *more* how I really am, less raw. The best me I can be.

Ben has seen me without makeup. And he walked away. I was angry for a long time, but in the end, I realized, I don't blame him.

The year I turned twenty-five was pretty bloody awful. If *I* could have walked away from myself, I would have.

But that didn't excuse what he'd done now.

"Open up!"

The sound of laptop keys stopped, and I heard a chair scrape back. Then the cabin door opened cautiously.

"Yes?" Ben's face filled the gap, his expression turning to surprise as he saw me. "Lo! What are you doing here?"

"What do you think?"

He had the grace to look slightly abashed at that.

"Oh, that."

"Yes, *that*. You spoke to Nilsson," I said tightly.

"Look—" He put up a hand, placating, but I wasn't to be soothed.

"Don't *look* me. How could you, Ben? How long did it take you to spill all the beans—the breakdown, the meds, the fact that I almost lost my job—did you tell him all that? Did you tell him about the days I couldn't get dressed, couldn't leave the house?"

"No! Of course not. Christ, how could you think that?"

"Just the pills, then? And the fact that I was broken into, and a few other spicy details to give the idea that I'm definitely not to be trusted?"

"No! It wasn't like that!" He walked to the veranda door and then turned to face me, running his hands through his hair so it stood on end. "I just— Shit, it all came out. I don't know how. He's good at his job."

"You're the journalist! What the hell happened to 'No comment'?"

"No comment," he groaned.

"You have no idea what you've done," I said. My hands were clenched into fists, my nails biting into my palms, and I forced myself to unclench them, rubbing my aching palms on my jeans.

"What d'you mean? Look, hang on, I need a coffee. Want one?"

I wanted to tell him to sod off. But the truth was, I did want a coffee. I nodded curtly.

"Milk, no sugar, right?"

"Right."

"Some things haven't changed," he said, as he filled the espresso machine with mineral water and slotted in a foil pod. I shot him a look.

"A hell of a lot has changed, and you know it. How *could* you tell him that stuff?"

"I'm— I don't know." He shoved his hands into his unruly hair again, gripping the roots as if he could somehow grasp an excuse out of his head if he pulled hard enough. "He ran into me on the way back from breakfast, stopped me in the corridor, and started saying he was concerned about you—stuff about noises in the night—I was hungover, I actually couldn't really work out what he was on about. I thought he was talking about the break-in at first. Then he starts on about you being in a fragile state— Jesus, Lo, I'm sorry, it's not like I went and knocked his door down desperate for a chat. What was he on about?"

"It doesn't matter." I took the coffee he held out. It was too hot to drink, and I held it in my lap.

"It does. It's clearly knocked you for six. Did something happen last night?"

About 95 percent of me wanted to tell Ben Howard to piss off, and that he had forfeited the right to my trust by blabbing about my private life and reliability as a witness to Nilsson. Unfortunately the remaining 5 percent seemed to be particularly forceful.

"I . . ." I swallowed against the ache in my throat, and the desire to tell *someone* what had happened. Maybe if I told Ben he could suggest something I'd not thought of? He *was* a reporter, after all. And, though it hurt to admit it, a pretty respected one.

I took a deep breath and then relayed the story I'd told Nilsson the night before, gabbling this time, desperate to make my case convincing.

"And the thing is she *was* there, Ben," I finished. "You have to believe me!"

"Whoa, whoa," Ben said. He blinked. "Of course I believe you."

"You do?" I was so surprised, I put down the cup of coffee with a crack on the glass tabletop. "Really?"

"Of course I do. I've never known you to imagine anything."

"Nilsson doesn't."

"I can see why Nilsson doesn't *want* to believe you," Ben said. "I mean, we all know that crime on cruise ships is a pretty murky area."

I nodded. I knew as well as he did—as well as any travel journalist did—the rumors that abounded about cruise ships. It's not that the owners are any more criminal than any other area of the travel industry, it's just that there's an inherent gray area surrounding crime committed at sea.

The *Aurora* wasn't like some ships I'd written about, which were more like floating cities than boats, but it had the same contradictory legal status in international waters. Even in cases of well-documented disappearances, things get brushed under the carpet. Without a clear police jurisdiction to take control, the investigation is too often left to the onboard security services, who're employed by the cruise liner and can't afford to ruffle feathers, even if they wanted to.

I rubbed my arms, feeling suddenly cold, in spite of the fuggy warmth of the cabin. I'd gone in to Ben to bawl him out with the aim of making myself feel better. The last thing I expected was for him to back up my unease.

"The thing that worries me most . . ." I said slowly, then stopped.

"What?" Ben prompted.

"She . . . she lent me a mascara. That was how I met her—I didn't know the cabin was empty, and I banged on the door to ask if I could borrow one."

"Right . . ." Ben took another gulp of coffee. His face over the top of the cup was puzzled, clearly not seeing where this was leading. "And?"

"And . . . it's gone."

"What—the mascara? What d'you mean, gone?"

"It's gone. It was taken out of my cabin while I was with Nilsson. Everything else I could almost write off—but if there's nothing going on, why take the mascara? It was the only concrete thing I had to show that there *was* someone in that cabin, and now it's gone."

Ben got up and went to the veranda, pulling the gauze curtains shut, although it seemed an odd, unnecessary gesture. I had the strange, fleeting impression that he didn't want to face me and was thinking about what to say.

Then he turned and sat back down on the end of the bed, his expression pure businesslike determination.

"Who else knew about it?"

"About the mascara?" It was a good question, and one, I realized with a touch of chagrin, that I had not thought to ask myself. "Um . . . I guess . . . no one apart from . . . Nilsson."

It was not a reassuring thought. We looked at each other for a long time, Ben's eyes reflecting the uncomfortable questions that were suddenly churning inside me.

"But he was with me," I said at last. "When it was taken."

"The whole time?"

"Well . . . more or less . . . No, wait, there was a gap. I ate breakfast. And I spoke to Tina."

"So he could have taken it."

"Yes," I said slowly. "He could." Had *he* been the one in my cabin? Was *that* how he had known about my medication, and the advice not to mix them with alcohol?

"Look," Ben said at last. "I think you should go and see Richard Bullmer."

"Lord Bullmer?"

"Yes. Like I said, I played poker with him last night and he seems like a decent bloke. And there's no sense in messing around with Nilsson—Bullmer is where the buck stops. My dad always used to say, if you've got a complaint, go straight to the top."

"This is hardly a customer services issue, Ben."

"Regardless. But this Nilsson guy—it doesn't look good for him, does it? And if there's anyone on this boat who can hold Nilsson accountable, it's Bullmer."

"But will he? Hold him accountable, I mean? He's got as much motive as Nilsson for hushing this up. More, in fact. Like you say, this has got the potential to play out very badly for him, Ben. If this gets out, the *Aurora*'s future will be very shaky. Who the hell wants to pay tens of thousands of pounds for a luxury trip on a boat where a girl died?"

"I bet there's a niche market," Ben said, with a slightly twisted smile. I shuddered. "Look, it can't hurt to go and see him," he persisted. "At least we know where he was all last night, which is more than we can say for Nilsson."

"You're sure none of the people you were with left the cabin?"

"Absolutely sure. We were in the Jenssens' suite—there's only one door and I was sat facing it all night. People got up and went to the loo and stuff, but they all used the bathroom in the cabin suite. Chloe sat and read for a while and then went into the bedroom next door—there's no exit from that except through the main room of the suite. No one left until four at the earliest. You can rule out all four men, plus Chloe."

I frowned, ticking off passengers on my fingers.

"So that's . . . you, Bullmer . . . Archer . . . Lars, and Chloe. Which leaves Cole, Tina, Alexander, Owen White, and Lady Bullmer. Plus the staff."

"Lady Bullmer?" Ben raised an eyebrow. "I think that's stretching it."

"What?" I said defensively. "Maybe she's not as ill as she looks."

"Yup, that's right, she's faked four years of recurrent cancer and grueling chemo and radiotherapy just to provide an alibi for the murder of a strange girl."

"There's no need to be sarcastic. I was just making the point."

"I think the passengers are a red herring, though," Ben said. "You can't get away from the fact that you and Nilsson were the only people who knew about that mascara. If he didn't take it, he must have told the person who did."

"Well . . ." I said, and then stopped. An uneasy feeling, not unlike guilt, was trickling down the back of my neck.

"What?"

"I—I was trying to think. When Nilsson took me round the staff. I can't absolutely remember . . . I could have mentioned it."

"Jesus, Lo," Ben said. He stared at me. "Did you? Or didn't you? It kind of matters."

"I know that," I said peevishly. The boat heaved up and down a wave, and the feeling of nausea swept over me again, the half-digested pancakes shifting uneasily in my gut. I tried to think back to the conversations below decks, but it was hard to remember, I'd been so hungover, so distracted by the claustrophobic artificial light of those narrow, windowless cabins. I shut my eyes, feeling the sofa lurch and tilt beneath me, and tried to think back to the staff canteen and the pleasant, scrubbed faces of the girls tipped up towards me. What the *hell* had I said?

"I can't remember," I said at last. "I really can't. But I could have mentioned it. I don't *think* I did, but I can't absolutely say that I didn't."

"Bollocks. Well, that widens things out considerably."

I nodded soberly.

"Look," Ben said at last. "Maybe one of the other passengers saw something. Someone going in and out of the empty cabin, or whoever stole the mascara going into yours. Who's in the aft cabins?"

"Um . . ." I counted them out on my fingers. "Well, there's me in nine, you in eight. Alexander is in . . . I think it might be six?"

"Tina's in five," Ben said thoughtfully. "I saw her go in last night. Which means Archer must be in seven. Okay. Want to go and do some door stepping?"

"All right," I said. For some reason, maybe it was the surge of anger, or the feeling of being believed, or maybe just the effect of having a plan, I was feeling better already. But then I caught sight of the clock on Ben's laptop. "Shit, I can't, not now. I've got this bloody ladies' spa thing."

"What time does it finish?" Ben asked.

"No idea. But I shouldn't think it will run over lunchtime. What are the men supposed to be doing?"

Ben stood up and flicked through a brochure on the desk.

"Tour of the bridge. Nice and sexist—blokes get technology, women get aromatherapy. Oh, no, wait, there's a men's spa morning tomorrow. Maybe it's just to do with space." He picked up a pad and pen from the dressing table. "I need to be going, too, but let's see what we can dig up this morning, and then we can rendezvous back here after lunch and door step the remaining passengers. After that we can take the whole lot to Bullmer. Maybe he can get the boat to divert—get the local police on board."

I nodded. Nilsson hadn't taken me seriously, but if we could find out something to corroborate my story—even just someone else who'd heard the splash, it would be a lot harder for Bullmer to ignore.

"I keep thinking about her," I blurted as we reached the door. Ben stopped, his hand on the latch.

"What do you mean?"

"About the girl—the girl in Palmgren. What she must have felt when he went for her—whether she was alive when she went over. I keep thinking what it must have been like, the shock of the cold water, the sight of the boat pulling away . . ."

Had she screamed as the waves closed over her? Had she tried to call out, as the salt water flooded her lungs, her chest laboring as the cold bit harder and the oxygen leached from her blood, and she sank deeper and deeper . . . ?

And her body, drifting through the cold silent blackness of the deep ocean, white as bone, the fishes nibbling at her eyes, her hair floating in the current like a stream of dark smoke . . . All that I was thinking of, too, though I didn't say it.

"Don't," Ben said. "Don't let your imagination run away with you, Lo."

"I know what it's like," I said, as he opened the door. "Don't you see? I know what she must have felt like, when someone came for her in the middle of the night. That's why I have to find out who did this to her."

And because if I didn't find out, they might come for me next.

- CHAPTER 16 -

Chloe and Tina were waiting in the spa when I arrived. Tina was leaning over the counter, reading something on the laptop Eva had left open behind the desk, and Chloe was ensconced deep in a luxuriously upholstered vintage leather chair, playing on her phone. I was surprised to see that without her makeup on, she looked completely different—the huge smoky eyes and jutting cheekbones of last night looking somehow faded and flat by the light of day.

She caught me looking at her in the mirror and grinned.

"Apparently I'm down for a facial, so I took it off. I told you, I'm quite the makeup artist."

"Oh, I didn't . . ." I trailed off, feeling myself blush.

"Contouring," Chloe said. She swung the chair around to face me and winked. "Honestly, it'll change your life. I could turn you into anyone from Kim Kardashian to Natalie Portman with what I've got in my cabin."

I was just about to make a joking reply, when I caught a movement out of the corner of my eye, and I saw with a shock that one of the full-length mirrors behind the desk was moving, swinging inwards. Another door? Seriously, how many concealed entrances did this boat have?

Tina's head jerked up from the laptop as Eva came through the gap, smiling politely.

"Can I help you, Miss West?" she asked. "We keep our client lists and confidential information on that computer, so I'm afraid we don't allow guests to use it. If you wish to use a computer, Camilla Lidman will be delighted to arrange one for your cabin."

Tina straightened awkwardly and turned the laptop to face the desk again.

"Sorry, darling." She had the grace to look slightly shamefaced. "I, ah . . . was just looking for the list of treatments."

Since there was a full list in the press pack, it was a slightly lame excuse.

"I would be delighted to give you a printout," Eva said. There was no hint of coolness in her tone, but she looked at Tina rather appraisingly. "We have the usual types of massage and therapies, facials, pedicures, and so on. The manicures and hair treatments take place in this room." She indicated the chair that Chloe was perching on.

I was just wondering where the other treatments took place, as there was only one chair in the spa, and no more room on the upper deck as far as I could make out—the hot tub and the sauna took up most of the rest of the space—when the deck door swung open and, somewhat to my surprise, Anne Bullmer came in. She looked a little better than last night, her skin less sallow, her face somehow slightly less drawn, but her dark eyes were circled with deep shadows as though she hadn't slept.

"I'm sorry," she said, breathlessly, trying to smile. "It takes me so long on the stairs at the moment."

"Here." Chloe stood up hastily and tried to edge out of the way into an unoccupied corner of the room. "Have my seat."

"There's no need," Anne said. Chloe began to insist, but Eva cut across their polite exchange with a smile.

"We're heading to the treatment rooms now, in any case, ladies. Lady Bullmer, if you would like to take a seat here. Miss West, Ms. Blacklock, and Mrs. Jenssen, shall we make our way down?"

Down? Before I could wonder what that meant, she opened the mirrored door behind the desk—a touch at the frame sent it swinging inwards—and we began to descend a set of narrow, dark stairs, one after the other.

The contrast, after the light and air of the reception room, was extreme, and I found myself blinking, my eyes trying to get used to the low light. Small electric tea lights were placed in holders at intervals along the staircase, but the flickering yellow glow they cast merely intensified the darkness around them, and as the boat tilted slightly over a big wave, I had a momentary wash of vertigo. Perhaps it was the staircase disappearing into darkness below us—or perhaps it was the realization that the lightest of touches from Chloe—who was directly behind me—would send me tumbling into the back of Tina and Eva in front. If I broke my neck, there would be no way of knowing that I hadn't simply tripped in the dark.

At last, after what seemed like an interminable descent, we stopped in a small lobby. There was the sound of water from a small electric water feature in a niche on the wall, the kind that trickled endlessly recycled water over a stone globe into a bowl below. The noise should have been soothing, and probably would have been on dry land, but the effect on a boat was somehow different. I began to think about leaks, and emergency exits. Were we below the waterline here? There were no windows at all.

My chest started to feel tight and I clenched my fists. *Don't panic. Do not, for God's sake, have a panic attack down here.*

One. Two. Three. . . .

I realized that Eva was speaking, and tried to concentrate on her words, not on the low ceiling and cramped airless space. Perhaps when we got into the treatment rooms, and were less crowded, it would be better.

"... three treatment rooms down here," Eva was saying. "Plus the chair upstairs, so I have taken the liberty of selecting therapies that we can run concurrently."

Please, please, please let mine be an upstairs one. My fingernails were digging into my palms.

"Miss West, I have you down for an aromatherapy session in treatment room one with Hanni," Eva said, consulting her list. "Miss Jenssen, you are having a facial in treatment room two with Klaus. I hope you don't mind a male therapist? Miss Blacklock, I have booked you a mud wrap in room three with Ulla."

I felt my breath quicken.

"What about Lady Bullmer?" Chloe said, looking around. "Where's she?"

"She is having a manicure upstairs."

"Um . . ." I spoke diffidently. "I don't suppose . . . could I have a manicure upstairs, too?"

"I'm sorry," Eva said, and she did sound sorry. "But there's only one chair upstairs. I'd be delighted to book you in for a manicure this afternoon, after your wrap. Or is there another treatment you'd prefer? We can offer Reiki, Swedish massage, Thai massage, reflexology. . . . We also have a flotation tank—if you've never tried one, they're incredibly soothing."

"No!" I said reflexively. Tina and Chloe turned their heads, and I realized suddenly how loudly I'd spoken, and consciously lowered my voice. "No, no, thank you. Flotation's not . . . not really my thing."

Just the thought of lying down here in a sealed plastic coffin full of water . . .

"No problem," Eva said with a smile. "Well, if you're all ready to begin? The treatment rooms are down the corridor. Each has its own en suite shower. Robes and towels are provided."

I nodded, hardly hearing her instructions, and then as she turned to go back upstairs, I followed Chloe and Tina down the corridor, hoping that my growing fear didn't show in my face. I could do this. I could *not* let my phobias get in the way of doing a good job. *Hi, Rowan, no, I didn't try the spa because it was two floors down and had no windows. Sorry.*

No. No way. It would be better once we were out of this narrow corridor and in our own treatment rooms.

I'd been hoping that the spa treatment time would give me a chance to talk to Tina, Anne, and Chloe, and sound them out about their movements last night, but as Chloe disappeared into her treatment room, the door closing behind her, I realized that wasn't going to be the case.

On the other side of the corridor, Tina had stopped at a door marked "Treatment Room 1," and I waited for her to enter so I could pass on down the corridor, but she turned back to face me, her hand on the doorknob.

"Darling," she said awkwardly, "I, um . . . I may have been a little abrupt, when we last spoke."

For a moment I couldn't think what she was talking about, and then it came back—our encounter on the deck, her spitting fury at my questions. Why *had* she been so touchy about her movements last night?

"What can I say . . . hangover . . . lack of cigs. But that's no excuse for snapping at you." Her whole bearing and manner screamed a woman more used to demanding apologies than giving them.

"It's fine," I said stiffly. "I completely understand, I'm not a morning person, either. I— Honestly, consider it forgotten." But I felt my face flush with the lie.

Tina put her hand out and squeezed my arm, with what I assumed was meant to be a friendly gesture of farewell, but her rings were cold against my skin, and as the door swung shut behind her, I let the shudder I had been repressing roll over me.

Then I took a deep breath and tapped at the door of treatment room three.

"Come in, Miss Blacklock!" said a voice from inside, and the door swung open and Ulla was standing there smiling, wearing a white spa uniform. I stepped inside the little room, looking around me. It was small—but not as narrow as the corridor, and with only Ulla and myself, it felt considerably less crowded. I felt the tightness in my chest ease slightly.

The room was lit with the same flickering electric candles as the stairwell, and there was a raised bed in the center, covered with clear plastic film. A white sheet was folded at the foot.

"Welcome to the spa, Miss Blacklock," Ulla said. "Today you will be experiencing a mud wrap. Have you had one before?"

I shook my head, mutely.

"It is very pleasurable and very good for detoxing the skin. The first step is to please remove your clothes and lie upon the bed, covering with the sheet."

"Should I keep my underwear on?" I said, trying to sound as if I went to spas every day.

"No, the mud will stain," Ulla said firmly. My face must have expressed my feelings, because she bent and took what looked like a piece of crumpled hand towel from a cupboard.

"If you prefer, we provide disposable panties. Some of our guests use them, some do not; it is entirely how you feel comfortable. And now I will leave you to undress. The shower, if you wish it, is through here."

She indicated a door to the left of the bed, and then backed out of the room with a smile, closing the door softly, and I began to strip off my clothes layer by layer, feeling more and more uncomfortable. I piled them on the chair along with my shoes and then, when I was completely naked, I stepped into the flimsy paper knickers and climbed onto the bed, my bare skin sticking uncomfortably to the plastic, and pulled the white sheet up to my chin.

Almost as soon as I'd done so—quickly enough to make me wonder queasily whether there was some kind of camera in the room—there was a soft knock on the door and I heard Ulla's voice.

"May I come in, Miss Blacklock?"

"Yes," I said croakily, and she entered, holding a bowl of what looked like, and presumably was, warm mud.

"If you would like to lie on your front," Ulla said softly, and I wriggled around. It was surprisingly difficult, with the sticky film clinging to my skin, and I felt the sheet slip, but Ulla deftly tweaked it back into place. She touched something to the side of the door and the room was filled with soft whale sounds and the crash of waves. I had the unsettling image again of the weight of water just the other side of the thin metal hull . . .

"Could you . . ." I said awkwardly, speaking into the bed. "Is there another track?"

"Of course," Ulla said. She pressed something and the music changed to Tibetan metal bells and wind chimes. "Is that better?"

I nodded, and she said, "Now, if you're quite ready . . . ?"

The treatment was surprisingly soothing, once I had forced myself to relax a little. I even got used to the feeling of having a complete stranger massaging mud into my mostly naked body. Halfway through I realized, with a jolt, that Ulla was speaking to me.

"Sorry," I managed sleepily. "What did you say?"

"If you could turn over," she murmured, and I turned onto my back, the mud slipping and sliding against the plastic. Ulla draped the sheet over my upper body once again and began to massage the fronts of my legs.

She worked her way methodically up my body, and at last smoothed the mud over my forehead, cheeks, and closed eyes, before speaking again, in her low, soothing voice.

"I will wrap you up now, Miss Blacklock, to allow the mud to work, and I will return in about half an hour to help you unwrap and shower. If you need anything, there's a call button to your right." She pressed my hand to a button set into the side of the bed. "Is everything quite all right?"

"Quite all right," I said drowsily. The warmth of the room and the soft chimes of the music were extraordinarily soporific. I was finding it hard to remember everything that had happened the night before. Harder to care. I just wanted to sleep. . . .

I felt the plastic film close around me, and then something heavy and warm on top of that—a towel, I thought. Behind my closed lids, I was aware that the lights of the room had been dimmed.

"I will be just outside," she said, and I heard the soft click of the door. I stopped fighting the tiredness, and I let the warmth and the darkness close over my head.

I dreamed of the girl, drifting miles below us in the cold, sunless depths of the North Sea. I dreamed of her laughing eyes white and bloated with salt water, of her soft skin, wrinkled and sloughing, of her T-shirt ripped by jagged rocks and disintegrating into rags.

Only her long black hair remained, floating through the water like fronds of dark seaweed, tangling in shells and fishing nets, washing up on the shore in hanks like frayed rope, where it lay, limp, the roar of the crashing waves against the shingle filling my ears.

I woke uneasy and heavy with dread. It took me a while to remember where I was, and still longer to realize that the roar in my ears was not part of the dream but real.

I climbed off the bed, shivering slightly, and wondering how long I'd been lying here. The warm towel had cooled off and the mud on my skin had dried and cracked. The noise sounded like it was coming from the en suite shower room.

My heart was thumping in my chest as I approached the closed door, but taking my courage in both hands, I turned the bathroom door handle and flung open the door, a wave of hot steam engulfing me. I coughed as I fought my way across the misty bathroom to turn off the shower, getting half drenched in the process. Had Ulla come in and turned it on? But why hadn't she woken me?

As the shower trickled and gurgled to a halt, I groped my way back to the door, my dripping hair plastered to my face, and felt for the light, which would activate the extractor fan and clear some of the steam.

I hit the switch and light flooded the shower room—and that's when I saw it.

Written across the steamy mirror, in letters maybe six inches high, were the words *STOP DIGGING.*

Monday, 28 September

BBC News Website
Monday 28th September

MISSING BRITON LAURA BLACKLOCK: BODY FOUND BY DANISH FISHERMEN

Danish fishermen dredging in the North Sea off the coast of Norway have found the body of a woman.

Scotland Yard have been called in to assist the Norwegian police investigation into the discovery of a body, dredged up in the early hours of Monday morning by Danish fishermen, lending weight to speculation that the deceased may be missing British journalist Laura Blacklock (32), who disappeared last week while holidaying in Norway. A spokesperson for Scotland Yard confirmed that they have been called in to help with the investigation, but declined to comment on possible links to Ms. Blacklock's disappearance.

Norwegian police said that the body was that of a young Caucasian woman, and that the process of confirming the woman's identity was under way.

Laura Blacklock's partner, Judah Lewis, when telephoned at his home in North London, refused to respond to the speculation, except to say that he was and is "devastated by Laura's continued disappearance."

PART FIVE

- CHAPTER 17 -

For a second I couldn't do anything. I just stood, staring at the dripping letters, my heart beating until I thought I would be sick. There was a strange roaring in my ears, and I could hear sobbing sounds, like a frightened animal—it was a horrible noise halfway between terror and pain and an odd, detached part of myself knew that the person making the sounds was me.

Then the room seemed to shift and the walls started to close in, and I realized I was having a panic attack, and was going to pass out unless I got myself somewhere safe. Half crawling, I lurched to the bed, where I lay, curled in the fetal position, trying to slow my breathing. I remembered what my CBT coach used to say: *Calm conscious breathing. In, and progressive relaxation, one muscle at a time. Calm breathing . . . conscious relaxation. Calm . . . and conscious. Conscious . . . and . . . calm . . .*

I hated him even then. It barely took the edge off the panic attack at the time, let alone now, when there really was something to panic about.

Calm . . . and conscious . . . I heard his light, smug tenor in my head and somehow the well-remembered fury anchored me, made me strong enough to slow my shallow, panicked breaths and, at last, to sit up, dragging my hands through my damp hair and look about me for a phone.

Sure enough, there was one on the counter, beside an empty pack of spa mud. My hands were shaking, and crusted with dried mud so that I could barely pick up the phone, let alone dial 0, but when I did, and I heard a Scandinavian-accented voice say, "Hallo, may I help you?" I did not speak, I just sat, my finger poised over the dial.

Then I put the phone down with a click.

The message was gone.

I could see the shower-room mirror from where I sat on the bed, and now that the shower was turned off and the extractor fan was running, the steam had all but disappeared. All you could see were a couple of runnels of water where the bottom of the two *I*s in *DIGGING* had been, and that was it.

Nilsson would never believe me.

When I had showered and dressed, I walked back along the corridor. I looked in as I passed the other two rooms, but they were quite empty, their doors open, showing neatly cleared couches ready for the next clients. How long had I been asleep for?

When I made my way up the stairs to the spa reception, it, too, was empty, apart from Eva, who was sitting at the desk and typing something on a laptop. She looked up as I emerged from the concealed door and smiled.

"Ah! Miss Blacklock. Did you enjoy your treatment? Ulla went down to remove the wraps a little while ago but you were deeply asleep; she was planning to return in quarter of an hour. I hope you weren't disorientated to wake up alone."

"It's fine," I said tightly. "When did Chloe and Tina leave?"

"About twenty minutes ago, I think."

I nodded at the door behind me, the one I'd just come through—now closed again and invisible unless you knew the mirror's secret.

"Is this the only entrance to the spa?"

"It depends what you mean by *entrance*," she said slowly, obviously confused by the question. "It is the only entrance but it is not the only exit. There is a fire exit downstairs that leads into the staff quarters, but it is . . . what's the word. Single way? It opens outwards only. Also it is alarmed, so I don't recommend you use it or there will be an evacuation! Why do you ask?"

"No reason."

I had made a mistake in blabbing to Nilsson this morning. I wasn't going to make that mistake again. I was keeping my cards close to my chest this time.

"They are serving lunch in the Lindgren Lounge," Eva said, "but don't worry, you haven't missed anything—it is a buffet lunch, so people are free to come and go. Oh, and I almost forgot," she said as I turned to go. "Did Mr. Howard find you?"

"No." I stopped dead, my hand on the door. "Why?"

"He came here looking for you. I explained that you were undergoing a treatment so he could not speak to you personally, but he went downstairs to leave a message with Ulla. Would you like me to try to find it?"

"No," I said shortly. "I'll find him myself. Did anyone else go down?"

She shook her head.

"No. I have been here the whole time. Miss Blacklock, are you *sure* nothing is wrong?"

I didn't answer. I just turned and left the spa, feeling the chill damp of my skin beneath my clothes, and a cold dread that had spread far deeper.

• • •

The Lindgren Lounge was empty except for Cole, who was sitting at a table with his camera in front of him, and Chloe, who was across from him, staring out of the window and forking salad absentmindedly into her mouth. She looked up when I came in and nodded at the chair next to her.

"Hey! Wasn't the spa amazing?"

"I guess," I said as I pulled up a chair, and then, realizing how strange and ungracious I must be sounding, I tried again. "I mean, yes, it was. My treatment was very good. I'm just—I'm not good with enclosed spaces. I'm kind of claustrophobic."

"Oh!" Her face cleared. "I wondered why you looked so tense downstairs. I thought you were hungover."

"Well." I gave a false-sounding laugh. "That too, probably."

Could it have been her, down in the spa? It was definitely possible. But Ben had been so clear about last night—she had never left the room.

What about Tina, then? I thought of her wiry strength, and her fierce reaction to my question about where she had been last night, and I absolutely could believe she would push someone overboard.

Could it have been *Ben*? He had come down into the spa, and I only had his own word for his alibi last night, after all.

I wanted to scream. This was sending me mad.

"Listen," I said casually to Chloe, "you were playing poker last night, weren't you?"

"I wasn't playing. But I was there, yes. Poor Lars got fleeced, but then, he can afford it." She gave a short, rather heartless laugh, and Cole looked up from the other table and flashed her a grin.

"This is going to sound like an odd question . . . but did any of the others leave the cabin?"

"I couldn't honestly say," Chloe said. "I went through to the bedroom after a while. Poker's the most boring game to watch. Cole was there for a bit of it, weren't you, Cole?"

"Only for about half an hour," Cole said. "Like Chloe says, poker's not really a spectator sport. I do remember Howard leaving. He went to get his wallet." My mouth was suddenly dry as he continued, "Why d'you want to know?"

"Doesn't matter." I tried to force a smile, and changed the subject before he could pin me down for an answer. "How are the photos?"

"Take a look if you like," he said, tossing the camera across with such casualness that I gasped, and nearly dropped it. "Press the play button on the back and you can scroll through them. I'll send you a print of any you like."

I began to work my way through the pictures, going back in time through the voyage, past moody shots of clouds and wheeling gulls, past the poker game last night, pictures of Bullmer laughing and scooping Ben's chips towards him, and Lars groaning as he laid down a pair of twos to Ben's three fives. One, from last night, almost took my breath away. It was a photo of Chloe, taken from very close. Her eyes had just flicked towards the camera. You could see the tiny hairs on her cheek, golden in the lamplight, and the smile that just tugged at the corner of her mouth, and there was something so intimate and so tender about the shot that I felt like an intruder even looking at it. My gaze went to Chloe, almost inadvertently, wondering about her and Cole, and she looked up.

"What is it? Found one of me?"

I shook my head and hastily flicked on to the next picture before she had time to look over my shoulder at the little screen. The next one was of myself, the shot that Cole had taken last night that had caught me unawares and caused me to spill my coffee. He had snapped me as I flung my head up in alarm, and the look in my eyes made me flinch.

I pressed the button to continue.

The others were just more of the ship . . . one of Tina on deck looking piercingly at the camera, her eyes like a raptor's, one of Ben carrying an oversize rucksack up the gangway. I was reminded again of Cole's enormous trunk. What *was* in it? Photographic equipment, he'd said, but all I'd seen him use so far was this one point-and-click.

And then I was past the pictures of the ship and into some society party. I was about to hand the camera back when my heart seemed to stutter in my chest and I froze. The screen was displaying a picture of a man eating a canapé.

"Who's he?" Chloe said over my shoulder. And then, "Wait, isn't that Alexander Belhomme in the background, talking to Archer?"

It was. But it wasn't Alexander or Archer I was looking at.

It was the waitress holding the tray of canapés.

She had her face turned half away from the camera and her dark hair was falling out of its clip, across her cheek.

But I was almost certain—almost completely certain—that she was the woman in cabin 10.

- CHAPTER 18 -

I handed the camera back carefully, my heart thumping, wondering whether to say anything. This was proof—irrefutable proof—that Cole, Archer, and Alexander had been in the same room as the woman I'd seen. Should I ask Cole if he knew her?

I sat in an agony of indecision as he switched off his camera and began packing it away.

Fuck. *Fuck.* Should I say something?

I had no idea what to do. It was possible Cole didn't realize the significance of the picture he'd taken. The girl was half out of the shot, the focus was on some other person completely, a man I'd never met.

If Cole had something to hide, I'd be incredibly foolish to flag what I'd just seen. He'd deny it, and then he'd probably delete the picture.

On the other hand, it was very likely he had no idea who the girl was and might be willing to let me have the image. But if I raised the issue now, in front of Chloe, and with who knew who else possibly listening . . .

I thought of the way Bjorn had appeared from behind the paneling at breakfast and I involuntarily looked over my shoulder. The last thing I wanted was for this picture to go the way of the mascara. I wasn't going to make the same mistake twice. If I did decide to confront Cole, I should do it in private. The photo had been safe on Cole's camera up until now; it would be safe a little longer.

I stood up, my knees suddenly shaky.

"I'm—I'm actually not very hungry," I said to Chloe. "And I'm supposed to be meeting Ben Howard."

"Oh, I forgot," she said casually. "He was in here looking for you. I met him coming up out of the spa. He said he had something important to tell you."

"Did he say where he was going?"

"Back to his cabin to do some work, I think."

"Thanks."

Bjorn appeared again like a genie from behind the concealed screen.

"May I get you a drink, Miss Blacklock?"

I shook my head.

"No, I've remembered I'm supposed to be meeting someone. Could you please send a sandwich to my suite?"

"Certainly." He nodded, and I slipped out of the room with an apologetic nod to Cole and Chloe.

I was hurrying along the corridor that led towards the aft cabins when I rounded a corner and ran slap into Ben himself—literally. We collided with a crash that knocked the breath out of me.

"Lo!" He grabbed my arm. "I've been looking for you everywhere."

"I know. What were you doing down in the spa?"

"Didn't you just hear me? Looking for you."

I stared at him, at his face, the picture of innocence, his eyes above his dark beard round and full of urgency. Could I trust him? I had absolutely no idea. A few years ago I would have said I knew Ben inside out—right up until the moment he walked out. Now I had learned that I couldn't even totally trust myself, let alone another person.

"Did you come into my treatment room?" I asked abruptly.

"What?" He looked momentarily confused. "No, of course not. They said you were getting a mud wrap. I didn't think you'd want me barging in. I was told to look for some girl called Ulla, but she wasn't there, so I pushed a note under your door and came back up."

"I didn't see any note."

"Well, I left one. What's this about?"

Something in my chest felt like bursting—a mixture of fear and frustration. How could I possibly know if Ben were telling the truth? The note would be a stupid thing to lie about anyway—even if he'd written the message in the steam, why fib about leaving me a note? Perhaps it *had* been there, and I'd just overlooked it in my panic.

"Someone else left me a message," I said at last. "Written in steam on the mirror of the shower next door while I was having the treatment. It said *Stop digging.*"

"What?" His pink face went slack with shock, his mouth hanging open. If he was acting, it was the best performance I'd ever seen him give. "Are you serious?"

"One hundred percent."

"But—but didn't you see them go in? Is there another entrance to the bathroom?"

"No. They must have come through the room. I . . ." I felt oddly ashamed saying it, but I put my chin up, refusing to be apologetic. "I fell asleep. There's only one entrance to the spa, and Eva says no one went down except for Tina and Chloe . . . and you."

"And the spa staff," Ben reminded me. "Plus, surely there must be a fire exit down there?"

"There's an exit, but it's one-way. It leads into the staff quarters, but you can't open it from the other side. I asked."

Ben looked unconvinced.

"Not that hard for someone to wedge it open, though, right?"

"No, but it's alarmed. There would have been sirens going off all over the place."

"Well, I guess it's possible if you knew enough about the system you could fiddle with the alarm settings. But Eva wasn't there the whole time, you know."

"What do you mean?"

"She wasn't there when I came back up. Anne Bullmer was—she was waiting for her nail varnish to dry. But Eva was gone. So if she says she was there for the whole time, she's not telling the truth."

Oh God. I thought about myself, lying there, half-naked beneath the thin film wraps and towels, and how someone—anyone—could have come in and placed a hand over my mouth, wound a sheet of plastic around my head . . .

"So what did you want to see me about?" I said, trying to sound normal. Ben looked uneasy.

"Oh . . . that. Well, you know we were on a tour of the bridge and so on?"

I nodded.

"Archer was trying to text someone, I think, and he dropped his phone. I picked it up, and it was open on the contacts page."

"And?"

"The name just said *Jess,* but the preview picture was a girl, a lot like the one you described. Late twenties, long dark hair, dark eyes . . . and this is the thing—she was wearing a Pink Floyd T-shirt."

Something cold trickled down my spine. I remembered Archer last night, his laughing face as he twisted my arm up behind my back, Chloe's disapproving *maybe the rumors about his first wife are true. . . .*

"Was she the person he was trying to text?" I asked. Ben shook his head.

"I don't know. He might have pressed a few buttons when he fumbled the phone."

Automatically, I pulled out my own phone, ready to google "Jess Fenlan"—but the search bar whirred fruitlessly. The Internet was still down, and my e-mails were still not loading.

"Is your Internet working?" I asked Ben. He shook his head.

"No, there's some issue with the router, apparently. I suppose teething problems are par for the course with maiden voyages, but it's a right pain. Archer was sounding off about it over lunch; he kicked up quite a stink to poor Hanni. I thought she was about to burst into tears at one point. Anyway, she went and spoke to Camilla Wotserface, and it'll be fixed shortly, apparently. At least, I bloody hope it will be, I've got a piece to file."

I frowned as I pushed the phone back in my pocket.

Could Archer have been the person who wrote the message in the steam? I thought of his strength, the hint of cruelty in his smile last night, and I felt sick at the idea of him tiptoeing past me while I slept.

"We went down to the engine room," Ben said, almost as if reading my thoughts. "It's three decks down, we probably passed fairly close to that exit from the spa you were talking about."

"Would you have noticed if someone had peeled off from the group?" I asked. Ben shook his head.

"I doubt it. The engine deck was very cramped, we were all kind of strung out, slotting in and out of small spaces, the group only got back together when we got upstairs."

I felt suddenly and nauseously claustrophobic, as if the stifling opulence of the boat were closing around me.

"I've got to get out," I said. "Anywhere."

"Lo." Ben put a hand out towards my shoulder, but I pulled myself away from his grasping fingers and staggered towards the deck door, forcing it open against the wind.

On deck, the wind hit me in the face like a punch, and I stumbled to the rail, hanging over it, feeling the pitch of the boat. The dark gray waves stretched out like a desert—mile upon mile, stretching to the horizon, no sign of land of any kind, nor even a ship. I shut my eyes, seeing the fruitless whirling of the Internet search engine icon. There was literally no way of calling for help.

"Are you all right?" I heard over my shoulder, the words snatched by the wind. Ben had followed me. I screwed my eyes shut against the salt spray that smacked the side of the ship and shook my head.

"Lo . . ."

"Don't touch me," I said through gritted teeth, and then the boat went up and over a particularly big wave and I felt my stomach clench and I threw up over the rail, my stomach heaving and heaving until my eyes watered and there was nothing left but acid. I saw, with a kind of vicious pleasure, that my vomit was spattered across the hull and porthole below. *Paintwork not so perfect now*, I thought as I wiped my mouth with my sleeve.

"Are you okay?" Ben said again from behind me, and I clenched my fists on the rail. *Be nice, Lo . . .*

I turned round and forced myself to nod.

"I actually feel a bit better. I've never been a great sailor."

"Oh, Lo." He put an arm around me and squeezed, and I let myself be pulled into his hug, suppressing the urge to pull away. I needed Ben on my side. I needed him to trust me, to think I trusted him. . . .

A whiff of cigarette smoke caught my nostrils and I heard the *tap, tap* of high heels coming along the port side of the boat.

"Oh God." I stood up straighter, moving away from Ben almost as if it were accidental. "It's Tina, can we go in? I can't face her at the moment."

Not now. Not with tears drying on my cheeks and vomit on my sleeve. It was hardly the professional, ambitious image I was trying to project.

"Sure," Ben said solicitously, and he held open the door as we hurried inside, just as Tina rounded the corner of the deck.

After the roar of the wind the corridor was suddenly quiet, and stiflingly hot, and we watched in silence as Tina strolled to the rail and leaned over, just a few paces upwind of where I had vomited moments before.

"If you want to know the truth," Ben said, looking out through the glass at Tina's unconscious back, "my money would be on her. She's a stone-cold bitch."

I looked at him in shock. Ben had sometimes been hostile about the women he worked with, but I'd never heard such naked dislike in his voice.

"*Excuse* me? Because she's an ambitious woman?"

"Not just that. You haven't worked with her, I have. I've met a few careerists in my time, but she's in another league. I swear she'd kill for a story or a promotion, and it's women she seems to pick on. I can't stand women like that. They're their own worst enemy."

I kept silent. There was something close to misogyny in his words and tone, but at the same time, it was so uncomfortably close to what Rowan had said that I wasn't sure if I could dismiss it as just that.

But Tina *had* been downstairs in the spa with me when the message appeared. And then there was her defensiveness earlier this morning. . . .

"I asked her where she was last night," I said, half reluctantly. "She was really odd. Very aggressive. She said I shouldn't go about making enemies."

"Oh *that*," Ben said. He smiled, but it wasn't a pleasant smile, there was something rather unkind about it. "You won't get her to admit it, but I happen to know she was with Josef."

"*Josef*? As in, cabin attendant Josef? Are you kidding me?"

"Nope. I got it from Alexander during the tour. He saw Josef tiptoeing out of Tina's cabin in the early hours in a state of—let's just say *déshabillé*."

"Blimey."

"Blimey indeed. Who'd have thought Josef's devotion to passenger comfort would extend so far. He's not really my type, but I wonder if I could persuade Ulla to do the same. . . ."

I didn't laugh. Not with the narrow, sunless rooms just a couple of decks beneath where we were standing right now.

How far might someone go to escape their confines?

But then Tina turned from where she was smoking at the rail and caught sight of me and Ben inside the boat. She flicked her cigarette over the rail and gave me a little wink before making her way back along the deck, and I felt suddenly vile at the thought of all the men chuckling about her little adventure behind her back.

"What about Alexander, then, if it comes to that?" I said accusingly. "His cabin's aft, along with ours. And what was he doing spying on Tina in the middle of the night?"

Ben snorted.

"Are you kidding me? He must be three hundred and fifty pounds. I can't see him lifting an adult woman over a rail."

"He wasn't playing poker, so we've no idea where he was, apart from the fact that he was prowling around in the early hours of the morning." I remembered, too, with a sudden chill, that he had been in the photo on Cole's camera.

"He's the size of a walrus. Plus he's got a heart condition. Have you ever seen him take the stairs? Or, more to the point, heard him?

He sounds like a steam train, and you start to worry when he gets to the top that he'll kark it and fall back on you. I can't imagine him overcoming anyone in a struggle."

"She could have been very drunk. Or drugged. I bet anyone could tip an unconscious woman overboard—it would be just a matter of leverage."

"If she was unconscious, then what about the scream?" Ben said, and I felt a sudden pulse of fury run through me.

"God, do you know what, I'm so fed up with everyone picking at and questioning me as if I should have the answers to all this. I don't *know*, Ben. I don't know what to think anymore. All right?"

"All right," he said mildly. "I'm sorry—I didn't mean it like that. I was just thinking aloud. Alexander—"

"Taking my name in vain?" came a voice from up the corridor, and we both swung around. I felt my cheeks go scarlet. How long had Alexander been there? Had he heard my speculations?

"Oh, hello, Belhomme," Ben said smoothly. He didn't seem at all put out. "We were just talking about you."

"So I heard." Alexander drew level with us, panting slightly. Ben was right, I realized. The smallest exertion set him gasping breathlessly. "All good, I hope?"

"Of course," Ben said. "We were just discussing dinner tonight. Lo was saying how knowledgeable you were about food."

For a minute I couldn't think of anything to say, stunned by how good a liar Ben had become since we were together. Or had he always been such a slick deceiver and I'd just never noticed?

Then I realized both Ben and Alexander were waiting for me to speak, and I stammered, "Oh, yes, remember, Alexander? You were telling me about fugu."

"Of course. *Such* a thrill. I do think it's one's responsibility to wring every *ounce* of sensation out of life, don't you? Otherwise, without that, it's just a short, nasty, and brutal interlude until death."

He gave a broad, slightly crocodile-like smile, and hoisted something beneath his arm. It was a book; a volume of Patricia Highsmith, I saw.

"Where are you off to?" Ben asked casually. "We've got a few hours free until dinner now, I think."

"Don't tell anyone," Alexander said confidentially. "But this color isn't *entirely* natural." He touched his—now that he mentioned it—rather walnut-colored cheek. "So I'm off to the spa for a little touch-up. My wife always says I look better with a color."

"I didn't know you were married," I said, hoping my surprise wasn't too evident in my voice. Alexander nodded.

"For my sins. Thirty-eight years this year. You get less for murder, I'm led to believe!"

He gave a slightly grating laugh, and I inwardly cringed. If he hadn't heard what we were saying earlier, it was an odd remark. If he *had* heard, then it was in very poor taste indeed.

"Have a nice time in the spa," I said at last, lamely. He smiled again.

"I will. See you at dinner!"

He was turning to go when I spoke, suddenly, compelled by an impetus I couldn't quite dissect.

"Wait, Alexander—"

He turned, one eyebrow raised. I felt my courage falter, but I carried on.

"I—this is going to sound a little strange, but I heard some noises last night, coming from cabin ten, the one at the end of the ship. It's supposed to be empty but there was a woman in it yesterday—only now we can't track her down. Did you see or hear anything last night? A splash? Any other noise? Ben said you were up."

"I was *indeed* up," Alexander said dryly. "I have trouble sleeping—you do, you know, when you get to my age, and a new bed always makes the matter worse. So I slipped up on deck for a little midnight walkies. And on my way there and back I saw quite a few comings and goings. Our dear friend Tina had a little visit from our *very* attentive cabin crew. And that dishy Mr. Lederer was prowling round here at one stage. I don't know *what* he was doing out of bounds. His cabin is at quite the other end of the ship. I did wonder if he might have been coming to see you . . . ?"

He cocked an eyebrow at me and I blushed furiously.

"No, definitely not. Could he have been going into cabin ten?"

"I didn't see," Alexander said regretfully. "I just caught a glimpse of him rounding the corner. On his way back to his cabin to establish an alibi for his crimes, perhaps?"

"What time did you see all this?" Ben asked. Alexander pursed his lips, thinking.

"Hmm . . . it must have been around four or four thirty, I think."

I exchanged a glance with Ben. I had been woken up at 3:04. That meant that the sighting of Josef at four a.m. probably ruled out Tina—presumably he had been in her cabin all night. But Cole . . . what reason could he possibly have for being down at this end of the ship?

I thought again of his huge case of equipment being bumped up the gangway.

"And who was the woman I saw coming out of *your* cabin?" Alexander said, rather slyly, looking at Ben. Ben blinked.

"Sorry? Are you sure you have the right cabin?"

"Number eight, isn't that right?"

"That's mine"—Ben gave an uneasy laugh—"but I can assure you no one was in my cabin apart from me."

"Is that so?" Alexander raised his eyebrow again, and then chuckled. "Well, if you say so. It *was* dark. Perhaps I mistook the cabin." He hoisted his book under his arm again. "Well, if you have no further questions, my dears?"

"N-no . . ." I said, slightly reluctantly. "At least, not now. May I come and find you if I think of anything else?"

"Of course. In that case, adieu until dinner, when I shall emerge bronzed as a young Adonis, and basted as a Christmas turkey. Toodle pip . . ."

He puffed away, up the corridor. Ben and I watched as he rounded the corner.

"He's the full package, isn't he?" Ben said when he'd disappeared.

"He's—he's just so full-on. Do you think that character is all an act? Or is he really like that twenty-four/seven?"

"I have no idea. I suspect it started out as a bit of a pose, but it's become second nature now."

"And his wife—have you ever met her?"

"No. But apparently she really exists. She's supposedly something of a dragon—daughter of a German count, and apparently quite the beauty in her day. They've got this incredible house in South Kensington, it's full of original artworks—Rubens and Titians, utterly unbelievable stuff. It was featured in *Hello!* a while back and there were all these rumors that they were actually looted Nazi stuff and they got a tap on the shoulder from the IFAR, but I think that's bollocks."

"I can't work out whether he said anything useful." I rubbed my hands over my face, trying to scrub away the weariness that was starting to settle over me like a black cloud. "That stuff about Cole, that was weird, right?"

"Y-yes . . . I guess. But if it was around four, does that really help? And, to be honest, I'm starting to think that he's maybe just making stuff up for effect. That thing about me having a girl in my cabin was pure bollocks. You *do* believe that, right?"

"I—" I felt a lump rise in my throat. I was so tired. I was *so* tired. But I couldn't rest. Jesus, so much for this trip being the making of my career. If I carried on causing trouble like this I could end up with an address book full of enemies, not contacts. "Yes, of course," I managed. Ben looked at me, as if trying to gauge whether I was telling the truth.

"Good," he said at last. "Because, I swear, there was no one in my cabin. Unless someone got in while I was out, of course."

"Do you think he heard us?" I asked, more to change the subject than because I wanted to know. "Before, I mean. The way he came round that corner—you wouldn't think someone so big could creep up on you like that."

Ben shrugged.

"I doubt it. I don't think he's the type to hold a grudge, anyway."

I said nothing, but inwardly I wasn't sure I agreed. Alexander struck me as *exactly* the type to hold a grudge, and enjoy holding it, too.

"What do you want to do now?" Ben asked. "Want me to come with you to find Bullmer?"

I shook my head. I needed to go back to my cabin, get some food inside me. And besides, I wasn't at all sure I wanted Ben to come with me to see Lord Bullmer.

- CHAPTER 19 -

The door to my cabin was locked, but inside an open sandwich was resting on a room service tray on the dressing table, alongside a bottle of mineral water. It had been there some time, judging by the runnels of condensation on the side.

I wasn't hungry, but I'd had nothing since breakfast, and most of that I'd thrown up, so I sat and forced myself to eat it. It was prawn and hard-boiled egg on heavy rye bread, and as I chewed it, I watched the sea rise and fall outside the window, its ceaseless movement echoing the restless thoughts that were running around inside my head.

Cole, Alexander, and Archer had actually been in the same room as that girl—I was almost sure of it. Her face had been turned away from the camera, and it was hard for me to remember the brief flash of features I'd seen through the open cabin door yesterday, but the jolt of recognition I had felt when I saw the picture had been like an electric shock—I *had* to hang on to that certainty.

Archer at least had an alibi—but I was beginning to realize that it was one that rested entirely on Ben's evidence, and that he had his own reasons for wanting that room to be secure. And no matter how you spun it, he had deliberately lied to me. If it hadn't been for Cole's chance remark, I would never have known that Ben himself had left the cabin.

But Ben. *Ben?* Surely not. If I could trust anyone on board this boat it *had* to be him, right?

I wasn't sure anymore.

I swallowed the final crust of bread, wiped my fingers on the napkin, and stood, feeling the rock and sway of the boat beneath me. While I'd eaten, a sea mist had crept in, and the room had become darker, so I switched on the light before checking my phone. There was nothing there—nothing from Judah, either. I refreshed, hoping without hope for an e-mail from someone, anyone. I didn't dare think about Judah—about what his silence meant.

When the CONNECTION FAILED notification came up, I felt a shift in my stomach that was mingled fear and relief. Relief because it meant that perhaps, just perhaps, Judah had been trying to contact me. That his silence didn't mean what I feared it might.

But fear because the longer the Internet was down, the more I was starting to think that someone was deliberately trying to stop me from accessing the Web. And that was starting to make me feel very worried indeed.

The door to suite 1, Nobel, was the same anonymous white wood as the rest of the cabin doors, but you could tell from the fact that it was by itself in the prow of the boat, with a blank expanse of corridor stretching away behind us, that it must be something pretty special.

I knocked, cautiously. I'm not sure what I expected—Richard Bullmer, or perhaps even a maid, neither would have surprised me. But I was thrown completely when the door opened and Anne Bullmer was standing there.

She had clearly been crying, her dark eyes rimmed with red and circled with deep shadows, and there were traces still on her gaunt cheeks.

I blinked, completely losing the thread of the carefully prepared request I'd rehearsed in my head. Phrases skittered through my mind, each more inappropriate and impossible than the other: *Are you okay? What's wrong? Is there anything I can do?*

I said none of them, just gulped.

"Yes?" she said, with a touch of defiance. She brought up a corner of her silk robe and wiped at her eyes, and then put her chin up. "Can I help you?"

I swallowed again, and then said, "I, yes, I hope so. I'm sorry for intruding, you must be tired after the spa morning."

"Not particularly," she said, rather shortly. I bit my lip. Maybe referring to her illness hadn't been tactful.

"I was actually hoping to speak to your husband."

"Richard? He's busy, I'm afraid. Is it something I can help with?"

"I—I don't think so," I said awkwardly, and then wondered whether to make my excuses and leave, or stay and explain. I felt bad disturbing her, but it seemed equally wrong to knock and then leave so abruptly. Part of my discomfort was the tears—pulling me in two directions, to go and leave her to her private grief, to stay and offer comfort. But it was also because I found her gaunt, smooth face so unsettling. She seemed so unassailable in every other way. To see someone like Anne Bullmer, so privileged, with every advantage that money could buy—the latest medicine, the best doctors and treatments available—to see her fighting for her life like this, before our very eyes, was almost unbearable.

I wanted to run away, but that knowledge forced me to stand my ground.

"Well, I'm sorry," she said. "Perhaps it can wait until later? Can I tell him what it's about?"

"I . . ." I twisted my fingers together. What could I possibly say? There was no way I was spilling my suspicions to this frail, haunted-looking woman. "I— He promised me an interview," I said, remembering his throwaway words after dinner. It was kind of half-true, after all. "He told me to come to the cabin this afternoon."

"Oh." Her face cleared. "I am sorry. He must have forgotten. I think he's gone to the hot tub with Lars and a few others. Hopefully you can catch him at dinner."

I had no intention of waiting that long, but I didn't say that, just nodded.

"Am I— Will we see you at dinner?" I asked, and cringed at the way I was stumbling over my words. *For God's sake. She's ill, not a leper.* She nodded.

"I hope so. I'm feeling a little better today. I get very tired, but it seems like a capitulation to let my body win too often."

"Are you still undergoing treatment?" I asked. She shook her head, the soft silk scarf around her skull rustling as she did.

"Not at the moment. I've finished my last round of chemotherapy, for the moment, anyway. I'll undergo radiotherapy when we get back, and then I suppose we'll see."

"Well, best of luck," I said, and then winced at the way the innocent remark seemed to make her survival into a kind of game of chance. "And, um, thanks," I finished.

"No problem at all."

She shut the door and I turned to walk back towards the stairs to the upper deck, feeling my face burn with a kind of shame.

I had never been to the hot tub, but I knew where it should be—on the top deck above the Lindgren Lounge, just outside the spa. I made my way up the thickly carpeted stairs towards the restaurant deck, expecting that feeling of light and space that I'd had before—but I'd forgotten the sea mist. When I got to the door that opened onto the deck, a wall of gray greeted me behind the glass, blanketing the ship in its folds so you could barely see from one end of the deck to the other, giving a strange, muffled feeling.

The mist had brought a chill to the air, fogging the hairs on my arms with drizzle, and as I stood uncertainly in the lee of the doorway, shivering and trying to get my bearings, I heard the long, mournful boom of a fog horn.

The whiteness made everything seem unfamiliar, and it took me a few minutes to work out where the stairs to the top deck were, but eventually I realized they must be to my right, further up towards the prow of the boat. I couldn't imagine anyone enjoying a Jacuzzi in this weather, and for a moment I wondered if Anne Bullmer had been mistaken. But as I rounded the glassed-in tip of the restaurant I heard laughter and looked up to see lights glowing in the mist above my head, coming from the deck above. Seemingly there were people mad enough to strip down, even in this cold.

I wished I'd brought a coat, but there was no sense going back for one, so I wrapped my arms around myself and climbed the slippery vertiginous steps to the upper deck, following the sound of voices and laughter.

There was a glass screen halfway along the deck, and when I slipped round it, there they were—Lars, Chloe, Richard Bullmer, and Cole, seated around the edge of the most enormous Jacuzzi I'd ever seen. It must have been eight or ten feet across, and they were leaning back against the sides, with just their shoulders and heads showing, the steam rising so densely from the bubbling water that it was hard for a moment to see who was in there.

"Miss Blacklock!" Richard Bullmer called heartily, his voice carrying easily above the roaring of the jets. "Have you recovered from last night?"

He stuck out a tanned, muscular arm, steaming and goose-bumped in the cold air, and I shook his dripping hand and then wrapped my arms back around myself, feeling the warmth of his grip fade immediately and the chill of the wind on my now-damp hands.

“Come for a dip?” Chloe asked with a laugh, waving an inviting hand at the rolling cauldron of bubbles.

“Thanks”—I shook my head, trying not to shudder—“but it’s a bit cold.”

“It’s warmer in here, I can tell you!” Bullmer gave a wink. “Hot Jacuzzi, cold shower”—he indicated an open-sided shower to one side of the Jacuzzi, a vast rainwater shower rose poised above the tray. There was no temperature control, just a steel push button with a blue center, and the sight made me shudder involuntarily—“and then straight into the sauna,” he finished, jerking a thumb at a wooden cabin tucked behind the glass screen. Craning my head round I could see a glass door streaming with condensation, and through the trickling runnels, the red glow of a brazier. “Then rinse and repeat as many times as your heart can stand it.”

“It’s not really my cup of tea,” I said awkwardly.

“Don’t knock it till you’ve tried it,” Cole said. He grinned, showing his pointed incisors. “I have to say, jumping out of the sauna into the cold shower was a pretty incredible experience. What doesn’t kill you makes you stronger, right?”

I flinched.

“Thanks, but I think I won’t.”

“Suit yourself.” Chloe smiled. She stretched out a languorous arm, dripping water onto Cole’s camera, which was resting on the floor below, and picked up a frosted glass of champagne from a little table placed alongside the tub.

“Look . . .” I took my courage in both hands and spoke directly to Lord Bullmer, trying to ignore the watching, interested faces of the others. “Lord Bullmer—”

"Call me Richard," he interrupted. I bit my lip and nodded, trying to keep my thoughts in order.

"Richard, I was hoping to talk to you about something, but I'm not sure if now is the right time. Could I come and see you later, in your cabin?"

"Why wait?" Bullmer shrugged. "One thing I've learned in business—now almost always *is* the right time. What feels like prudence is almost invariably cowardice—and someone else gets in there before you."

"Well . . ." I said, and then stopped, unsure what to do. I really didn't want to speak in front of the others. The "someone gets there before you" part certainly wasn't reassuring.

"Have a glass of something," Bullmer said. He pressed a button on the rim of the Jacuzzi and a girl appeared silently out of nowhere. It was Ulla.

"Yes, sir?" she said politely.

"Champagne, for Miss Blacklock."

"Certainly, sir." She melted away.

I took a deep breath. There was no alternative. No one could divert the boat except Bullmer, and if I didn't do this now, I might never get the chance. Better to speak up, even with an audience, than risk . . . I pushed that thought away.

I opened my mouth. *Stop digging* hissed the voice inside my head, but I forced myself to speak.

"Lord Bullmer—"

"Richard."

"Richard, I don't know if you've spoken to your head of security, Johann Nilsson. Have you seen him today?"

"Nilsson? No." Richard Bullmer frowned. "He reports to the captain, not to me. Why do you ask?"

"Well . . ." I began. But I was interrupted by Ulla appearing at my elbow with a tray, on which was a champagne glass and a bottle in a holder full of ice.

"Um, thanks," I said uncertainly. I wasn't sure I wanted to drink right now—not after Nilsson's biting comments earlier, and on top of the hangover from last night—and it seemed an incongruous accompaniment to what I was about to say. But I felt again the impossibility of my position—I was Bullmer's guest, and *Velocity*'s representative, and I was supposed to be impressing all these people with my professionalism and dazzling them with my charm, and instead I was about to hurl the very worst of all possible accusations at his staff and guests. The least I could do was to accept his champagne with good grace.

I took the glass, sipping tentatively at it as I tried to get my thoughts in order. It was sour and made me shiver, and I almost pulled a face before realizing how rude that would appear to Bullmer.

"I— This is difficult."

"Nilsson," Bullmer prompted. "You were asking if I'd spoken to him."

"Yes. Well, last night I had to phone him. I . . . I heard noises, coming from the cabin next to mine. Number ten," I said, and then stopped.

Richard was listening, but so were the other three, rather avidly in Lars's case. Well, since I didn't have a choice, maybe I could turn that to my advantage. I cast a quick look round the circle of faces, trying to gauge their reactions, check for any trace of guilt or anxiety. Out of the three, Lars's moist red lips were curled in a disbelieving skepticism, and Chloe's green eyes were wide with frank curiosity. Only Cole was looking worried.

"Palmgren, yes," Bullmer said. He was frowning, puzzled as to where this was leading. "I thought that one was empty. Solberg canceled, didn't he?"

"I went to the veranda," I said, gaining momentum. I glanced around the listeners again. "And when I looked out there was no one there, but there was blood on the glass safety barrier."

"Good Lord," Lars said. He was openly grinning now, not even trying to hide his disbelief. "It's like something out of a novel." Was he deliberately trying to undermine my account, throw me off-balance? Or was this just his normal manner? I couldn't tell. "Go on," he said, with something close to sarcasm. "I'm on tenterhooks to find how this turns out."

"Your security guard let me in," I said, my voice harder now, and speaking fast. "But the cabin was empty. And the blood on the glass had been—"

There was a chink and a splash, and I stopped.

We all turned and looked at Cole, who was holding something over the side of the Jacuzzi. His hand was dripping blood, running down his fingers onto the pale wooden decking.

"I'm okay, I think," he said unsteadily. "I'm sorry, Richard, I don't know how, but I knocked my champagne over and I broke it, trying to save the glass. I don't think there's any glass in the water."

He held out a palmful of bloodstained shards, and Chloe gulped and squeezed her eyes shut.

"Ugh!" Her face was greenish white. "Oh God, Lars . . ."

Richard put down his glass, heaved himself out of the Jacuzzi, his near-naked body steaming in the cold air, and grabbed a white robe from a pile left on the bench. For a moment he said nothing, just looked dispassionately at Cole's hand, streaming blood onto the deck, and glanced at Chloe, who appeared close to fainting. Then he issued a series of orders like a surgeon barking out commands in an operating theater.

"Cole, for God's sake put down that pile of glass. I'll ring for Ulla to get you cleaned up. Lars, take Chloe off to lie down, she's gone white as chalk. Give her a Valium if that's what it takes. Eva has access to the medical supplies. And Miss Blacklock . . ." He turned to me and then paused, seeming to weigh his words very carefully as he belted the robe around himself. "Miss Blacklock, please take a seat in the restaurant, and when I've sorted this mess out, we'll run through what you actually saw and heard."

- CHAPTER 20 -

By the end of the next hour, I could see why Richard Bullmer had got to where he had in life.

He didn't just take me through my story—he grilled me on every single word, pinning me down on times, specifics, winkling out details I thought I didn't even know—like the exact shape of the blood spatter on the glass screen, and the way it was smeared, rather than sprayed, across the surface.

He didn't fill in any gaps with speculation, didn't try to lead me on, or persuade me on details I wasn't sure of. He just sat and fired questions at me between sips of scalding black coffee, his blue eyes very bright: What time? How long? When was that? How loud? What did she look like? As he spoke the slightly mockney overlay to his speech vanished, and the intonation became pure Old Etonian and 100 percent business. He was utterly focused, his attention on my story absolute, and without a trace of emotion in his face.

If someone had been walking along the deck outside and had glanced in the window, they would never have known that I had just told him something that could deal a sucker punch to his business, and revealed the presence of a possible psychopath on board a small ship. As my story unfolded I was expecting echoes of Nilsson's distress, or the clannish denial of the stewardesses, but although I watched Bullmer's face carefully, I saw neither of those, no hint of accusation or censure. We might have been trying to solve a crossword, for all the emotion he displayed, and I couldn't help being a little impressed by his stoicism, though it felt strange to be on the receiving end of it. It had not been pleasant dealing with Nilsson's skepticism and upset, but it did at least feel a very human reaction. With Bullmer, I couldn't tell what he was feeling. Was he furious, or panicked, and simply hiding it well? Or was he really as cool and calm as he seemed?

Perhaps, I thought, as he ran me through the conversation I'd had with the girl again, this sangfroid was simply what it took to have accomplished what he had—pulling himself up by his bootstraps to a position dealing with hundreds of jobs and millions of pounds of investment.

At last we had gone through my account backwards, forwards, and sideways, and I had no more details to contribute. Bullmer sat for a moment, his head bowed, his brows knitted, thinking. Then he looked briefly at the Rolex on his tanned wrist and spoke.

"Thank you, Miss Blacklock. I think we've got as far as we can, and I can see the staff will want to start laying the table for dinner in a moment. I'm sorry, this has clearly been a very distressing and frightening experience for you. If you'll give me permission, I'd like to discuss it with Nilsson, and Captain Larsen, to make sure that everything is being done that possibly can be, and perhaps we could meet first thing tomorrow to discuss the next steps. In the meantime, I very much hope you will be able to relax enough to enjoy the dinner that's coming and the rest of the evening, in spite of what's happened."

"What will the next step be?" I asked. "I understand we're heading to Trondheim—but is there anywhere closer we could stop? I feel like I should report this to the police as soon as possible."

"It's possible there might be somewhere closer than Trondheim, yes," Bullmer said, getting to his feet. "But we'll be in Trondheim early tomorrow morning, so it might be that it's still the best place to head for. If we stop somewhere in the middle of the night I think our chances of finding an on-duty police station might be slim. But I'll have to speak to the captain to find out what the most appropriate course of action would be. The Norwegian police may not be able to act if the incident took place in British or international waters—it's a question of legal jurisdiction, you understand, not their willingness to investigate. It will all depend."

"And if it did? What if we were in international waters?"

"I believe the boat is registered in the Cayman Islands. I'll have to speak to the captain about how that might affect the situation."

I felt a sinking in my stomach. I'd read accounts of investigations on boats registered to the Bahamas and so on—one solitary policeman dispatched from the island to do a cursory report and get the issue off his desk as quickly as possible—and that, only where there was a clear sign of someone gone missing. What would happen in this case, where the only evidence that the girl had even existed was long gone?

Still, I felt better for having spoken to Richard Bullmer. At least he seemed to believe me, to take my story seriously, unlike Nilsson.

He held out his hand, taking his leave, and as his piercing blue eyes met mine, he smiled, almost for the first time. It was a curiously asymmetric smile that pulled up one side of his face more than the other, but it suited him, and there was something wryly sympathetic about it.

"There's one other thing you should know," I said abruptly. Bullmer's eyebrows went up, and he dropped his hand.

"Yes?"

"I . . ." I swallowed. I didn't want to say this, but if he was going to speak to Nilsson, it would come out anyway. It would be better coming from me. "I was drinking, the night before . . . before it happened. And I also take antidepressants. I have done so for several years, since I was about twenty-five. I—I had a breakdown. And Nilsson—I think he felt . . ." I swallowed again. Bullmer's eyebrows rose even higher.

"Are you saying that Nilsson threw doubt on your story because you take medication for depression?"

The bluntness of his words made me cringe, but I nodded.

"Not in so many words—but yes. He made a comment about medication not mixing well with alcohol and I think he thought . . ."

Bullmer said nothing, he just regarded me impassively, and I found my words tumbling out, almost as if I were trying to defend Nilsson.

"It's just that I was burgled, before I came on board the ship. There was a man—he came into my flat and attacked me. Nilsson found out about it and I think that he felt, well, not that I'd made it up, but that I . . . might have overreacted."

"I'm deeply ashamed that a member of this boat's staff made you feel that way," Bullmer said. He took my hand, holding it in a viselike grip. "Please believe me, Miss Blacklock, I take your account with the utmost seriousness."

"Thanks," I said, but that one small word didn't do justice to the relief that someone, *someone* finally believed me. And not just someone—Richard Bullmer, the *Aurora*'s owner. If anyone had the power to get this sorted, it was him.

As I walked back to my cabin, I pressed my hands to my eyes, feeling them sting with tiredness, and then I felt in my pocket for my mobile to check the time. Almost five. Where had the time gone?

Automatically I opened up my e-mails and forced a refresh—but there was still no connection and I felt a pang of unease. Surely, *surely* this outage had gone on too long? I should have mentioned it to Bullmer, but it was too late now. He had gone—slipping into one of those unsettling concealed exits behind a screen, presumably to talk to the captain or radio land.

What if Jude had e-mailed? Rung, even, though I doubted we'd be close enough to land yet for a signal. Was he still ignoring me? For a minute I had a sharp flash of his hands on my back, my face against his chest, the feel of his warm T-shirt beneath my cheek, and it hit me with such force that I almost staggered beneath the weight of longing for his presence.

We would be in Trondheim tomorrow, at least. No one could prevent me from accessing the Internet then.

"Lo!" said a voice from behind me, and I turned to see Ben walking along the narrow corridor. He wasn't a big man, but he seemed to fill it entirely, an *Alice in Wonderland* trick of the perspective that made the corridor seem to shrink down to nothing and Ben grow bigger and bigger as he came nearer.

"Ben," I said, trying to make my voice convincingly cheerful.

"How did it go?" He began to walk alongside me towards our cabins. "Did you see Bullmer?"

"Yes . . . I think it went okay. He seemed to believe me, anyway." I didn't say what I had started thinking after Richard left, which was that he had not got as far as he had by showing all the cards in his hand. I'd come out of the meeting feeling confident and appeased, but as I ran back through his words, I realized he hadn't *promised* anything; in fact, he hadn't really said anything that could be quoted out of context as unqualified support for my story. There had been a lot of *if this is true* . . . and *if what you say* . . . nothing very concrete, when you came down to it.

"Great news," Ben said. "Is he diverting the boat?"

"I don't know. He seemed to think it wouldn't make any difference to divert now, that we'd do better to push on to Trondheim and get there as early as possible tomorrow."

We had reached our cabins, and I pulled my room key out of my pocket.

"God, I hope this dinner isn't another eight-course one tonight," I said wearily as I unlocked and opened my door. "I want to get enough sleep to be coherent for the police in Trondheim tomorrow."

"That's still your plan, then?" Ben asked. He leaned his hand on the doorframe, effectively preventing me from either leaving or closing the door, though I assumed it wasn't that calculated.

"Yes. As soon as the boat docks I'm going there."

"Doesn't it depend on what the captain says about the boat's position?"

"Probably. I think Bullmer's speaking to him about it now. But regardless, I want to get this on record with someone official, even if they can't investigate." The sooner my words were down in some official file, the safer I'd feel.

"Fair enough," Ben said easily. "Well, whatever happens tomorrow, you've got a clean slate with the police. Stick to the facts—be clear and unemotional, like you sound like you were with Bullmer. They'll believe you. You've got no reason to lie." He dropped his arm and took a step back. "You know where I am if you need me, yeah?"

"Yeah." I gave him a tired smile and was about to shut the door when he put his hand back on the frame so that I couldn't shut it without trapping his fingers.

"Oh, I nearly forgot," he said casually. "Did you hear about Cole?"

"His hand?" I'd almost forgotten, but it came back to me now with shocking vividness, the slow drip of blood on to the decking, Chloe's greenish face. "Poor guy. Will he need stitches?"

"I don't know, but it's not just that. He managed to knock his camera into the hot tub at the same time—he's beside himself, says he can't understand how he came to leave it so close to the edge."

"You're kidding me."

"Nope. He reckons the lens will be okay, but says the body and the SD card's fucked."

I felt the room shift and move a little, as if everything were going in and out of perspective, and I had a prickling flash of the photo of the girl on the little screen—a photo that was most likely gone forever now.

"Hey," Ben said with a laugh, "no need to look so doom-laden! He'll have insurance, I'm sure. It's just a shame about the shots. He was showing them to us over lunch. He had some great pics, there was a lovely one of you from last night." He stopped and put out a hand to touch my chin. "Are you okay?"

"I'm fine." I jerked my head away from him and then tried to force a convincing smile. "I'm just—I don't think I'd go on a cruise again, it's really not suiting me . . . you know . . . the sea . . . the kind of hemmed-in-ness of it all. I really just want to get to Trondheim now."

My heart was hammering, and I couldn't wait for Ben to get his hand off the door and leave. I needed to get my head together—needed to work this out.

"Do you . . . mind?" I nodded at Ben's hand, still resting on the doorframe, and he gave an easy laugh and straightened up.

"Sure! Sorry, I shouldn't be gabbing. You probably want to dress for dinner . . . right?"

"Right," I said. My voice sounded high and false. Ben moved his hand, and I closed the door with an apologetic smile.

When he was gone, I slid the dead bolt across and then I slumped down with my back against the wood, drew my knees up to my chest, and rested my forehead on my knees, a picture, stark in front of my closed lids. It was Chloe, reaching out for her glass of champagne, her arm dripping onto Cole's camera on the deck below.

There was no way Cole or anyone else could have knocked that camera in. It wasn't on the rim of the tub. Someone had taken advantage of the kerfuffle surrounding my announcement and the broken glass and had picked it up from the floor and thrown it in. And I had absolutely no way of knowing who that was. It could have happened at any time—even after we'd all left the deck. It could have been almost any of the guests or staff—or even Cole himself.

The room seemed to close around me, stiflingly warm and airless, and I knew I had to get out.

On the veranda the sea mist was still close around the boat, but I took great gulping breaths of the cold air, feeling the freshness fill my lungs, jolting me out of my stupor. I had to *think.* I felt like I had all the pieces of the puzzle in front of me, that I must be able to put them together if I only tried hard enough. If only my head wasn't aching so much.

I leaned over the balcony, just as I had the night before, remembering that moment—the sound of the veranda door sliding stealthily back, the huge smacking splash, shocking in the quiet, and the smear of blood across glass, and suddenly I was absolutely and completely certain that I had *not* imagined it. None of it. Not the mascara. Not the blood. Not the face of the woman in cabin 10. Most of all, I had not imagined her. And for her sake, I could not let this drop. Because I knew what it was like to *be* her—to wake in the night with someone in your room, to feel that utter helpless certainty that something awful was going to happen, with nothing you could do to prevent it.

The September night air felt suddenly cold, very cold, reminding me how far north we were—almost to the Arctic Circle now. I shivered convulsively and, drawing my phone out of my pocket, I checked the reception one more time, holding it up high as if that would somehow magically improve the signal, but there were no bars.

Tomorrow, though. Tomorrow we would be in Trondheim, and no matter what, I was going to get myself off this boat and straight to the nearest police station.

- CHAPTER 21 -

Making myself up for dinner that night, I felt like I was applying war paint—lacquering on, layer by layer, the calm, professional mask that would enable me to get through this.

Part of me, a big part, wanted to go and huddle beneath my duvet—the idea of making small talk with a group of people containing a potential murderer, eating food served by someone who might have killed a woman last night—that thought was terrifying, and utterly surreal.

But another, more stubborn part refused to give in. As I applied mascara borrowed from Chloe in the bathroom mirror, I found myself searching in my reflection for the angry, idealistic girl who'd started her journalism course at uni fifteen years ago, thinking of the dreams I'd had of becoming an investigative reporter and changing the world. Instead, I had fallen into travel writing at *Velocity* to pay the bills and, almost in spite of myself, I'd begun to enjoy it—had even started to relish the perks, and to dream of a role like Rowan's, running my own magazine. And that was fine—I wasn't ashamed of the writer I'd become; like most people, I'd taken work where I could find it and tried to do the best I could in that job. But how could I look that girl in the mirror in the eye, if I didn't have the courage to get out there and investigate a story that was staring me in the face?

I thought of all the women I'd admired reporting from war zones around the world, of people who'd exposed corrupt regimes, gone to prison to protect their sources, risked their lives to get at the truth. I couldn't imagine Martha Gellhorn obeying an instruction to *Stop digging*, or Kate Adie hiding in her hotel room because she was scared of what she might find.

STOP DIGGING. The letters on the mirror were etched in my memory. Now, as I finished my makeup with a swipe of lip gloss, I huffed on the mirror, and wrote in the steam obscuring my reflection one word: *NO*.

Besides, as I shut the bathroom door behind me and put on my evening shoes, a smaller, more selfish part of me was whispering that I was safest in company. No one could harm me in front of a room full of witnesses.

I was just straightening my gown when there was a knock on the door.

"Who is it?" I called.

"It's Karla, Miss Blacklock."

I opened the door. Karla was outside, smiling with that permanent air of slightly anxious surprise.

"Good evening, Miss Blacklock. I just wanted to remind you that dinner is in ten minutes, and drinks are being served in the Lindgren Lounge, whenever you wish to join us."

"Thank you," I said, and then, on impulse as she turned to go, "Karla?"

"Yes?" She turned back, her eyebrows raised so that her round face looked almost alarmed. "Is there something else with which I can help?"

"I—I don't know. It's just . . ." I took a deep breath, trying to think how to phrase it. "When I came and talked to you earlier today in the staff quarters, I felt like . . . I felt like maybe there was something else you could have told me. That perhaps you didn't want to speak in front of Miss Lidman. And I just wanted to say—I'm going into Trondheim tomorrow, to talk to the police about what I saw, and if there's anything—anything at all—that you wanted to say, now would be a really good time to tell me. I could make sure it was anonymous." I thought again of Martha Gellhorn and Kate Adie, of the kind of reporter I'd once wanted to be. "I'm a journalist," I said as convincingly as I could. "You know that. We protect our sources—it's part of the deal."

Karla said nothing, only twisted her fingers together.

"Karla?" I prompted. For a moment I thought that there might be tears in her blue eyes, but she blinked them away.

"I don't . . ." she said, and then muttered something under her breath in her own language.

"It's okay," I said. "You can tell me. I promise it won't go any further. Are you frightened of someone?"

"It is not that," she said miserably. "I am sad because I am sorry for you. Johann is saying that you make it up, that you are . . . what's the word? *Paranoid,* and that you . . . you seek the attention by making up stories. And I don't believe this. I believe you are a good person and that you believe what you say is true. But, Miss Blacklock, we need our jobs. If the police say that something bad happened on this boat, no one will want to travel with us, and it may not be so easy to find another job. I need this money, I have a little boy, Erik, at home with my mother; she needs the money that I send back. And just because perhaps someone let a friend use an empty cabin, that doesn't mean she was killed, you know?"

She turned away.

"Hang on." I put out a hand towards her arm, trying to stop her going. "What are you saying? There *was* a girl in there? Did someone smuggle her in?"

"I am saying nothing." She pulled her arm out of my grip. "I am saying, please, Miss Blacklock, don't make trouble if nothing happened."

And then she ran up the corridor, punched the code into the staff door, and was gone.

On the way up to the Lindgren Lounge, I found myself replaying the conversation in my head, trying to work out what it meant. *Had* she seen someone in the cabin, or suspected someone was there? Or was she just torn between her sympathy for me and her fear of what might happen if what I was saying was true?

Outside the lounge I checked my phone surreptitiously, hoping against hope that we might be close enough to land for a signal, but there was still nothing. As I was putting it away in my evening bag, Camilla Lidman glided up.

"May I take that for you, Miss Blacklock?" She indicated the bag. I shook my head.

"No, thank you." My phone was set to beep when it connected to roaming networks. If a signal did come, I wanted it by my side so I could act immediately.

"Very well. May I offer you a glass of champagne?" She indicated a tray on a small table by the entrance, and I nodded and took a frosted flute. I knew I should keep a clear head for tomorrow, but one glass for Dutch courage couldn't hurt.

"Just to let you know, Miss Blacklock," she said, "that the talk on the northern lights has been canceled tonight."

I looked at her blankly, realizing that I'd forgotten, yet again, to check the itinerary.

"There was to have been a presentation on the northern lights after dinner," she explained, seeing my expression. "A talk from

Lord Bullmer accompanied by photographs from Mr. Lederer, but unfortunately, Lord Bullmer has been called away to deal with an emergency and Mr. Lederer has hurt his hand, so it has been rescheduled for tomorrow, after the group returns from Trondheim."

I nodded again and turned to the rest of the room to see who else was missing.

Bullmer and Cole were both absent, as Camilla had said. Chloe was not there, either, and when I asked Lars, he said she was feeling ill and lying down in her room. Anne was present, although she looked pale, and as she raised her glass to her lips, her robe slipped, showing a deep purple bruise on her collarbone. She saw me glance, and look hastily away, and gave a self-conscious laugh.

"I know, it looks terrible, doesn't it? I tripped in the shower, but I bruise so easily now, it looks worse than it is. It's a side effect of the chemotherapy, unfortunately."

As we took our seats at dinner, I saw Ben motion invitingly at the seat next to his, opposite Archer, but I pretended not to see, and instead took the chair closest to where I was standing, next to Owen White. He was giving Tina a long talk on his financial interests and his role at the investment company he worked for.

As I listened, half an ear on their conversation, half an ear on the rest of the table, I realized that the talk had shifted, and he was speaking in a low voice, as if unwilling to be overheard.

". . . quite honestly, no," he was confiding to Tina. "I'm just not one hundred percent convinced that the setup is sustainable—it's such a niche investment area. But I don't imagine Bullmer will have trouble getting interest from elsewhere. And of course he has pretty deep pockets of his own, or rather Anne does, so he can afford to wait for the right person to come on board. It's a shame Solberg wasn't able to come, this is much more his bailiwick."

Tina nodded wisely, and then the conversation passed on to other topics—holiday destinations they had in common, the identity of the neon green cube of jelly that had just appeared on a plate in front of us, flanked by a little pile of something I thought might be seaweed. I let my gaze pass over the room, Archer was saying something to Ben and laughing uproariously. He looked drunk, his bow tie already askew. Anne, at the same table, was talking to Lars. There was no trace of the tears I'd seen earlier that afternoon, but there was something haunted about her expression, and her smile, as she nodded at something Lars was saying, was strained.

"Pondering our hostess?" said a low voice from across the table, and I turned to see Alexander sipping at a glass. "She's quite the enigma, isn't she? Looks so fragile, and yet they say she's the power behind Richard's throne. The iron fist in the silk glove, you could say. I suppose that having that kind of money from the age when most children are still drooling into their cornflakes has a steeling effect on one's character."

"Do you know her well?" I asked. Alexander shook his head.

"Never met her. Richard spends half his life on a plane, but *she* almost never leaves Norway. It's totally alien to me—as you know, I *live* for travel; I can't imagine confining yourself to a petty little country like Norway when the restaurants and capitals of the world await. Never to taste suckling pig at elBulli, or sample the glorious fusion of cultures that is Gaggan in Bangkok! But I suppose it's a reaction against her upbringing—I believe she lost her parents in a plane crash at the age of eight or nine, and spent the rest of her life being shuttled around the boarding schools of Europe by her grandparents. I imagine you might choose to go the other way as an adult."

He picked up his fork, and we were just starting to eat when there was a noise at the door, and I looked up to see Cole walking unsteadily across to the table.

"Mr. Lederer!" A stewardess hurried to take an extra chair from the ones at the side of the room. "Miss Blacklock, might I ask you to just . . ."

I moved my plate and chair slightly and she put a seat at the head of the table for Cole, who slumped heavily down. His hand was bandaged, and he looked as if he'd been drinking.

"No, I won't have champagne," he said in answer to Hanni gliding up with a tray. "I'll have a Scotch."

Hanni nodded and hurried away, and Cole sat back in his chair and passed a hand over his unshaven face.

"Sorry about your camera," I said cautiously. He scowled, and I saw that he was very drunk already.

"It's a fucking nightmare," he said. "And the worst of it is, it's my own bloody fault. I should have backed it up."

"Are all the shots gone?" I asked. Cole shrugged.

"No idea, but probably, yes. Got a guy back in London who might be able to get some of the data off, but it's showing fuck all when I put it in my computer, it's not even reading the card."

"I'm really sorry," I said. My heart was beating fast. I wasn't sure if this was sensible, but I figured I had nothing to lose now. "Was it just stuff from the voyage? I thought I saw one shot from somewhere else . . . ?"

"Oh, yeah, I was swapping the cards over, it had a few shots from a shoot I did a couple of weeks back at the Magellan."

I knew the Magellan—it was a very exclusive all-male members club in Piccadilly, founded as a meeting place for diplomats and what the club described as "gentlemen travelers." No women were allowed as members, but female guests were permitted, and I had attended functions there once or twice in Rowan's stead.

"Are you a member?" I asked. He gave a snort.

"Not bloody likely. Not my style, even if they'd let me in, which is doubtful. Too crusty for my taste—anywhere that won't let you wear jeans isn't for me. The Frontline is more my cup of tea. Alexander's a member, though. So is Bullmer, I think. You know the drill, you have to be either too posh to function or rich as shit, and fortunately I'm not either."

His last remark fell into a lull in conversation from the rest of the table, the words painfully loud and noticeably slurred in the silence, and I saw a few heads turn, and Anne glance at the steward with a nod that I interpreted as *Get his food over there before the whiskey.*

"What were you doing there, then?" I said, keeping my voice low, as if I could persuade him to moderate his tone by osmosis.

"Pictures for *Harper's*." His plate arrived and he began spearing foodstuffs at random, shoving the fragile architectural morsels into his mouth seemingly without even tasting them. "Some launch, I think. Can't remember. Christ." He looked down at his hand, the fork awkwardly balanced against the bandage. "This is sodding painful. There's no way I'm trailing round Trondheim cathedral tomorrow, I'm going to the doctor to get this checked out and get some decent painkillers."

After dinner finished, we took our coffee through to the lounge, and I found myself standing next to Owen White, both of us staring out the long window, into the fog. He nodded politely but seemed in no hurry to open the conversation. I tried to think what Rowan would do. Charm him? Or brush him off and go and talk to someone of more immediate use to *Velocity*? Archer, perhaps?

I glanced over my shoulder at Archer and saw that he was very, very drunk and had pinned Hanni into a corner of the room, her back to the window, his broad frame effectively blocking her exit. Hanni was holding a jug of coffee in one hand and was smiling politely but with a trace of wariness. She said something and gestured to the coffeepot, obviously as a way of taking her leave, but he laughed and put one heavy arm around her shoulders in a gesture of avuncular possession that made my flesh creep a little.

Hanni said something else that I didn't catch, and then slipped out from under his grip with what looked like practiced dexterity. For a moment Archer's face looked a mixture of foolishness and fury, but then he seemed to shrug it off and moved across to talk to Ben.

I turned back to Owen White with a sigh, though I was not sure whether it was a sigh of relief for Hanni, or resignation at my own reluctance to deal with unpleasant people, even for the sake of my career.

Owen, by contrast, seemed reassuringly harmless, though I realized, as I looked covertly at his profile in the reflection of the darkened, foggy window, that I had no real idea whether he would be of use to *Velocity* or not. Ben had said he was an investor, but White had kept himself to himself so much this voyage that I had no clear impression of what he actually did. Perhaps he would be the perfect angel investor for the group, if *Velocity*'s owner ever decided to go into some more profitable area. In any case, I had no desire to go across to the other side of the room.

"So, um," I began awkwardly, "I feel slightly like we haven't been properly introduced. My name is Laura Blacklock. I'm a travel journalist."

"Owen White," he said simply, but there was no sense of dismissal in his tone, I got the impression that he was just a man of few words. He held out his hand, and I shook it clumsily with my left, which was holding a petit four, but seemed better than my right, which was holding a hot cup of coffee.

"So what brings you to the *Aurora*, Mr. White?"

"I work for an investment group," he said, and took a long sip of his coffee. "Bullmer was, I think, hoping I'd recommend the *Aurora* as an investment opportunity."

"But . . . from what you were saying to Tina, that won't be the case?" I said cautiously, wondering if it was bad manners to admit overhearing, though I could hardly have helped it. He nodded, not seeming offended.

"That's so. I must admit, it's not really my area, but I was flattered to be asked and too venal to pass up the chance of a free trip. As I was saying to Tina, it's a shame Solberg couldn't make it."

"He was supposed to have cabin ten, wasn't he?" I asked. Owen White nodded. It occurred to me suddenly that I had no real idea of who the missing Solberg was, or why he hadn't come. "Did you—I mean, do you know him? Solberg, I mean?"

"Yes, fairly well. We're in the same area. He's based in Norway, while my head office is back in London, but it's a small world that we operate in. One gets to know all one's competitors. It must be the same in travel journalism, I imagine." He smiled as he popped a petit four in his mouth, and I smiled back, acknowledging the truth of his remark.

"So, if this is more his cup of tea, why didn't he come?" I asked.

Owen White said nothing, and for a moment I wondered if I'd gone too far, been too bold with my questioning, but then he swallowed and I realised he was simply having trouble with his petit four.

"There was a break-in," he said around a mouthful of bits of nut, and swallowed again, trying to clear his mouth. "At his house, I believe. His passport was taken, but I think that was only part of the reason he didn't come—his wife and children were home, from what I understand, and were rather shaken up. And say what you will about Scandinavian businesses . . ." He paused again and swallowed, heroically this time. "They do understand the importance of putting family first. Dear me, I advise you not to try this nougat unless you have very good teeth, I think I may have loosened a filling."

"*Not* the nougat!" I heard over my shoulder, as I was trying to process what I had just heard and piece this revelation together with my own break-in. I turned to see Alexander bearing down on us both. "Owen, *please* tell me you haven't."

"I did." Owen took a gulp of coffee and swilled it around his mouth, wincing slightly. "To my regret."

"The stuff should carry a dental health warning at the *very* least. You"—he pointed at me—"an investigative report is what's needed. *Velocity*'s no-punches-pulled exposé of Richard Bullmer's shady links with the cosmetic dentistry industry. What with that and the other *incident*, I should think future guests of this cruise liner will find it *very* hard to get health insurance, don't you?"

"Other incident?" I said sharply, trying to remember what I'd told Alexander. I was sure I hadn't mentioned the full story of the accident to him. Had Lars related the conversation in the hot tub? "What other incident are you talking about?"

"Why," Alexander said, his eyes opened almost theatrically wide, "Cole's hand. Of course. What were you thinking of?"

After coffee, the group began to break up—Owen disappearing quietly without a good-bye, and Lars taking a loud leave with a joke about Chloe. Bullmer was still nowhere to be seen, nor was Anne.

"Come for a snifter of something in the bar?" Tina said to me as I placed my empty cup on a side table. "Alexander's going to have a tinkle on the baby grand in there."

"I—I'm not sure," I said. I was still pondering what Owen White had told me over coffee about Solberg's break-in. What did it mean? "I might turn in."

"Ben?" Tina purred. He looked at me.

"Lo? Want me to walk you back to your cabin?"

"No need, I'm fine," I said, and turned to go. I was almost at the door when I felt a hand catch at my wrist and turned. It was Ben.

"Hey," he said quietly. "What's going on?"

"Ben." I glanced behind him at the other guests, laughing and chatting obliviously as the stewards cleared up around them. "Let's not do this here. Nothing's going on."

"Then why were you acting so weird all through dinner? You saw me saving you a chair and you deliberately ignored me."

"Nothing's going on." There was a painful pressure in my temples, as if the anger I'd been suppressing all night was taking its toll.

"I don't believe you. Come on, Lo, spit it out."

"You lied to me." It burst out in a furious whisper, before I could consider the wisdom of the accusation. Ben looked taken aback.

"What? No, I didn't!"

"Really?" I hissed. "So you never left the cabin when everyone was playing poker?"

"No!" It was his turn to glance over his shoulder now at the other guests. Tina was looking across at us, and he turned back, lowering his voice. "No, I didn't— Oh, no, wait, I did go and get my wallet. But that wasn't a lie—not really."

"Not a lie! You told me categorically no one left that cabin. And then I find out from Cole not only that you *did* leave, but anyone else could have left, too, while you weren't there."

"But that's different," he muttered. "I left, God, I don't know when, but it was early in the evening. It wasn't round the time you were talking about."

"So why lie about it?"

"It wasn't a lie! I just didn't think. Jesus, Lo—"

But I didn't let him finish. I pulled my wrist out of his grip and hurried away, through the doors and into the corridor, leaving him gaping after me.

I was so busy thinking about Ben that as I rounded the corner near the upper-deck toilet, I almost tripped over Anne Bullmer. She was leaning back against the wall as if steeling herself for something, although whether to return to the party, or make her way back to her cabin, I wasn't sure. She looked extremely tired, her face gray, the shadows around her eyes darker than ever.

"Oh, I'm so sorry!" I gasped, and then, thinking of the bruise on her collarbone, "I didn't hurt you, did I?"

She smiled, the fine skin around her mouth crinkling, but the expression didn't reach her eyes.

"I'm fine, I'm just very tired. Sometimes . . ." She swallowed, and her voice cracked for a moment, something in the cut-glass English accent slipping. "Sometimes it all just seems too much—d'you know what I mean? Such a *performance*."

"I do," I said sympathetically.

"If you'll excuse me, I am going to bed," she said, and I nodded and turned to make my own way back aft, down the flight of stairs that led to the rear set of cabins.

I was almost at the door of my suite when I heard an angry voice from behind me.

"Lo. Lo, wait, you can't make those kind of accusations and walk away."

Shit. Ben. I felt a strong urge to slip inside my cabin and slam the door, but I made myself turn to face him, my back against the door.

"I didn't make any accusations. I just said what I'd been told."

"You pretty much implied you're suspecting me now! We've known each other more than ten years! Do you realize how that makes me feel—that you could accuse me of lying like that?"

There was genuine hurt in his voice, but I refused to let myself soften. It had been Ben's favorite tactic in arguments, when we were together, to divert the discussion away from whatever was annoying me to the fact that I'd hurt his feelings and was acting irrationally. Time and again I'd ended up apologizing for the fact that *I'd* upset *him*—my own feelings completely ignored, and always, in the process, we'd somehow wound up losing sight of the issue that had provoked the disagreement in the first place. I wasn't falling for it now.

"I'm not making you feel anything," I said, trying to keep my voice even. "I'm stating facts."

"Facts? Don't be ridiculous!"

"Ridiculous?" I folded my arms. "What does that mean?"

"I mean," he said hotly, "that you're acting completely paranoid. You're seeing bogeymen behind every corner! Maybe Nilsson—"

He stopped. I clenched my fist around my delicate evening bag, feeling the solid bulk of my phone beneath the slippery sequins.

"Go on? Maybe Nilsson . . . what?"

"Nothing."

"Maybe Nilsson was right? Maybe I am imagining things?"

"I didn't say that."

"But it was what you were implying, right?"

"I'm just asking you to take a step back and *look* at yourself, Lo. Look at this rationally, I mean."

I forced myself to keep a hold on my temper and smiled.

"I am rational. But I'm very happy to take a step back." And with that, I opened my suite door, stepped inside, and slammed it in his face.

"Lo!" I heard from outside, and a thump on the door. Then a pause. *"Lo."*

I said nothing, just slid the bolt and the chain across. No one was getting through that door without a battering ram. Least of all Ben Howard.

"Lo!" He banged again. "Look, will you just *talk* to me? This is really getting out of hand. Will you at least tell me what you're going to say to the police tomorrow?" He paused, waiting for me to reply. "Are you even listening?"

Ignoring him, I threw my bag on the bed, stripped off my evening gown, and walked into the bathroom, shutting the door and turning on the taps to drown out the sounds from outside. When at last I stepped into the scaldingly hot water and turned off the taps, the only sound I could hear was the gentle hum of the extractor fan. Thank God. He must have given up at last.

I had left my phone in the bedroom, so I wasn't sure what time it was when I climbed out of the bath, but my fingers were waterlogged and wrinkled, and I felt heavy with sleep, but in a good way, quite unlike the nervous, edgy exhaustion of the last day or two. As I cleaned my teeth, dried my hair, and belted the white bathrobe around myself, I thought of the good night's sleep I would have, and the logical, carefully rehearsed story I would give to the police tomorrow.

And then . . . Christ. I felt almost weak with relief thinking about it. Then I would get a bus or a train or whatever bloody transport Trondheim possessed and get myself to the nearest airport and *home*.

When I opened the door to the cabin, I held my breath, half expecting Ben's hammering and shouting to start up again, but there was no sound. I walked cautiously to the door, my feet silent on the thick pale carpet, and, lifting the cover to the spy hole, I looked out into the corridor. There was no one there. At least no one I could make out—in spite of the fisheye lens, I could only see part of the corridor, but unless Ben were lying on the floor beneath my door, he was gone.

I let out a sigh and picked up my abandoned evening bag to check the time on my phone and set the alarm for tomorrow. I wasn't waiting for a call from Karla—I wanted to be up and off the boat as soon as possible.

But my phone wasn't inside.

I turned the bag upside down, shaking it out but knowing it was fruitless—the bag was small and light, and there was no way anything heavier than a postcard could have been concealed inside. It wasn't on the bed. Could it have slipped onto the floor?

I tried to think clearly.

I could have left it at the dinner table—but I hadn't taken it out of my bag, and in any case, I had a clear memory of feeling it inside my evening bag during the argument with Ben. And I would have noticed its weight missing when I threw the bag on the bed.

I checked the bathroom in case I'd taken it in there on autopilot, but it wasn't there, either.

I began to search harder, throwing the duvet onto the floor, pushing the bed to one side—and that's when I saw it.

There was a footprint, a wet footprint, on the white carpet, very close to the veranda door.

I froze.

Could it have been me? Getting out of the bath?

But I knew that was impossible. I'd dried my feet in the bathroom, and I hadn't walked anywhere near that window. I moved closer, touching the cold, damp shape with my fingertips, and I realized this was the print of a shoe. You could see the shape of the heel.

There was only one possibility.

I stood up, slid back the veranda door, and went out onto the balcony. There, I hung out over the rail, looking across to the empty veranda on the left of mine. The white glass privacy screen to either side was very high, and very sheer, but if you were daring and had a head for heights, and didn't mind the possibility of slipping to a watery grave, you could *just* get over it.

I was shivering convulsively, my thin dressing gown no protection from the cold North Sea wind, but there was one more thing I had to try, though I was going to be very sorry and feel very stupid if it turned out I was wrong.

Carefully, I dragged the sliding glass door closed and let it click into position.

Then I tried to pull it back.

It worked—smooth as silk.

I went inside and did the same thing, and then checked the lock. As I had thought, there was no way of securing the veranda door to prevent someone entering from the outside. It was logical, really, now that I thought about it. The only person who should be on the veranda was an occupant of the room. You couldn't risk someone accidentally locking themselves out there in bad weather, unable to get back inside and raise the alarm, or a child shutting a parent out there in a moment of rebellion, and then being unable to work the lock.

And really—what was there to fear? The veranda faced the sea—there was no possibility of someone accessing it from the outside.

Except there was. If you were very bold, and very stupid.

Now I understood. All the locks and bolts and DO NOT DISTURB signs in the world wouldn't do any good on my cabin door, not when the balcony offered a clear route to anyone with access to the empty room, and enough upper-body strength to pull themselves over.

My room was not safe, and never had been.

Back inside the suite, I got into my jeans and boots, and my favorite hoodie. Then I checked the lock on the cabin door and huddled on the sofa with a cushion hugged to my chest.

There was no possibility of sleep now.

Anyone could have access to the empty suite. And from there, it was just a short climb across the glass divider into mine. The truth was, I could draw the bolt across my cabin door as much as I liked, but any member of the staff could open the empty cabin with their passkey. As for the guests . . .

I thought again of the layout of the cabins. To the right of mine was Archer's, ex-marine, with an upper-body strength that made me wince when I remembered it. And to the left . . . to the left was the empty cabin, and beyond that, curving round the ship to the other side of the corridor, was Ben Howard's.

Ben. Who had deliberately cast doubt on my story with Nilsson.

Ben, who had lied about his alibi.

And he had known about the photos on Cole's camera before I did. His words came back to me as if in a dream: *He was showing them to us over lunch. He had some great pics . . .*

Ben Howard. The one person on board I had thought I could trust.

But I pushed that thought away—focusing on the phone, and the stupidity and daring of coming in to steal it while I was in the bath. He had risked a lot to take it, and the question was why. Why now? But I thought I knew.

The answer was Trondheim. As long as the boat's Internet was down, the perpetrator had nothing to worry about. I couldn't make a call to land without going through Camilla Lidman. But once we started to draw closer to land . . .

I hugged the cushion harder to my chest, and I thought of Trondheim, and Judah, and the police.

All I had to do was make it until dawn.

WHODUNNIT WEB FORUM—

A DISCUSSION PLACE FOR ARMCHAIR DETECTIVES

Please read the forum rules *before* starting a thread, and exercise caution in posting anything potentially prejudicial and/or libelous to live cases. Posts that violate these guidelines will be taken down.

Monday 28 September

iamsherlocked: Hey guys, anyone else been following this Lorna Blacklock case? Looks like theyve found a body.

TheNamesMarpleJaneMarple: I think you'll find it's Laura Blacklock actually. Yes, I've been following it. Really tragic and sadly not that unusual. I read somewhere that more than 160 people have gone missing off cruise ships in the past few years, and almost none of those have been solved.

iamsherlocked: Yeah I think I've heard that too. Saw in the Daily Fail that her ex was on board the ship. Theres a big sobby interview wiv him saying how worried he is. He reckons she got off on her own accord. Is it me or is that a bit suss? Don't they say that a third of women are killed by ex's or partners or something?

TheNamesMarpleJaneMarple: *"a third of women are killed by ex's or partners or something?"* I presume that must be in the case of women who are murdered, a third of them are killed by a partner or ex, not a third of all women! But yes, that kind of proportion sounds plausible. And of course there's the boyfriend. Something about his statement's not quite ringing true, and apparently he was out of the country at the time . . . hmm . . . very convenient. Not that hard to get a plane to Norway, right?

AnonInsider: I'm a regular on WD (although I've name-changed as

I don't want to out myself) and actually I know something about this case, I'm a family friend. I don't want to say too much for fear of making myself identifiable or impinging on the family's privacy, but I can tell you Judah is completely devastated about Lo's disappearance, and I'd be very careful about implying anything to the contrary or you'll probably find this thread gets taken down.

TheNamesMarpleJaneMarple: Anon, I'd find your claims more convincing if you dropped the mask, and in any case none of what I said above was libelous. I said I didn't personally find his statement convincing. Show me the libel in that?

AnonInsider: Look, MJM, I'm not interested in debating this with you, but I do know the family very well. I was at school with Laura, and I can tell you, you're barking up the wrong tree. If you must know, Lo's got serious problems—she's taken medication for depression for years and she's always been . . . well, I think unstable would be the kind way of putting it. I imagine that's the line the police will be looking at.

iamsherlocked: what suicide you reckon?

AnonInsider: Not really my place to speculate on the police investigation—but yes, that's my reading of it between the lines. If you notice, they're being very careful not to describe it as a murder investigation in the press.

JudahLewis01: A friend told me about this thread and I've registered to post this, and unlike Anon this is my real name. Anon, I have no idea who you are and to be honest you can fuck off. Yes, Lo takes medication (although FYI it's for anxiety, not depression and if you were really a friend of hers you'd know that) but so do literally hundreds of thousands of people, and the idea that that automatically makes her either "unstable" as you put it, or suicidal, is fucking offensive. Yes, I was out of the country. I was in Russia, working. And yes, they've found a body, but it's not been identified as Lo, so at this stage it's still a missing person's investigation, which is why you've not seen any suggestion it's a murder investigation. Can you people remember this is a real person you're talking about and not just your personal episode of *Murder, She Wrote*? I don't know who the admins of this shitshow are, but I'm reporting this thread.

iamsherlocked: *"unlike Anon this is my real name"* not being funny but we've only got you're word for that mate.

MrsRaisin (admin): Hi all, sorry to say we agree with Mr. Lewis, this thread is straying into some rather unpleasant speculation so we'll be deleting it. We obviously don't want to stop you discussing what's in the news, so feel free to take it elsewhere, but please stick to the reported facts.

InspektörWallander: So what about this Norwegian polis scanner blog that is reporting a positiv identification of Laura's body?

MrsRaisin (admin): We are now closing this thread.

PART SIX

- CHAPTER 22 -

I was trapped. I was not certain where, or how, but I had a pretty good idea.

The windowless room was small and stifling, and I lay on the bunk with my eyes shut and my arms wrapped around my head, trying not to give way to the feelings of panic rising up inside me.

I must have replayed the events a thousand times in my head, through the rising fog of fear—hearing, again and again, the knock at the door as I sat on the edge of the sofa, waiting for Trondheim and dawn.

The sound, though not particularly loud, had been shocking as a gunshot in the silent cabin. My head jerked up, the cushion falling from my hands onto the floor, my heart going a mile a minute. Jesus. I found I was holding my breath and I forced myself to exhale, long and slow, and then inhale, counting the seconds.

It came again, not a rough banging, just a *tap tap tap*, then a long pause and a final *tap* as if an afterthought, slightly louder than the rest. At that last *tap*, I scrambled to my feet and made my way, as quietly as I could, to the door.

Cupping my hand over the opening so no telltale flash of light could betray my presence, I slid the little steel cover of the peephole open. Then when my face was close enough to the glass to shield any gray dawn light from my window, I withdrew my fingers and peered through the fisheye.

I don't know who I was expecting to see. Nilsson, maybe. Ben Howard. I wouldn't even have been surprised to see Bullmer.

But not even for one minute did I imagine the person actually standing outside. *Her.*

It was the woman from cabin 10. The missing girl. Standing outside like nothing had ever happened.

For a minute I just stood there, gasping like I'd been punched in the stomach. She was *alive.* I'd been wrong. Nilsson was right—and I'd been wrong all this time.

And then she turned on her heel and began to walk down the corridor, towards the door to the staff quarters. I had to get to her. I had to get to her before she disappeared behind that locked door.

Slamming back the chain and the bolt, I wrenched open the door.

"Hey!" I shouted. "Hey, you, wait! I need to talk to you!"

She didn't pause, didn't even glance back over her shoulder, and now she was at the door to the lower deck, punching in the code. I didn't stop to think. I just knew that *this time* I wasn't going to let her disappear without a trace. I ran.

She was already through the staff door by the time I was halfway down the corridor, but I caught the edge of the door as it was just closing, pinching my fingers painfully, and then I wrenched it open and flung myself into the gap.

Inside it was darkness, the bulb at the top of the steps burned out. Or taken out, as I later thought.

As the door swung shut behind me, I stopped for a second, trying to get my bearings, see where the top step was. And that's when it happened—a hand grabbing my hair from behind, another twisting my arm behind me, limbs grappling mine in the darkness. There was a short interval of panting, scrabbling terror, my nails in someone's skin, my free hand trying to reach behind me to get a grip on the thin, strong hand laced in my hair—and then the hand pulled harder, twisting my head painfully back, and rammed my head forwards against the locked door. I heard the crack of my skull against the metal doorframe—and nothing.

I came to alone, lying on a bunk with a thin blanket over me. The pain in my head was agonizing, throbbing with a low pulse that made the dim lights in the room warp and shimmer, with a strange halo effect around them. There was a curtain on the wall opposite and with trembling limbs I slithered off the bed and half stumbled, half crawled across the floor towards it. But when I dragged myself upright, using the top bunk for support, and pulled back the thin orange cloth, there was no window there—just a blank wall of creamy plastic, lightly patterned as if in imitation of textured wallpaper.

The walls seemed to close in, the room narrowing around me, and I felt my breath come faster. *One. Two. Three. Breathe in.*

Shit. I felt the sobs rising up inside me, threatening to choke me from the inside.

Four. Five. Six. Breathe out.

I was trapped. Oh God, oh God, oh God . . .

One. Two. Three. Breathe in.

Propping myself against the wall with one hand, I made my way unsteadily back towards the door, but I knew before I tried it that it was useless. It was locked.

Refusing to think about what that meant, I tried the other door, set into the wall at an angle, but it opened into a minuscule en suite, empty except for a single dead spider curled in the washbasin.

I stumbled back to the first door and tried again, pulling harder this time, straining every muscle, rattling the door in its frame, yanking so hard at the handle that the effort left me panting, stars exploding in my vision as I slumped to the floor. No. No, this was not possible—was I really trapped?

I got to my feet and looked around me for something to lever into the door, but there was nothing, everything in the room was bolted or screwed down, or made of fabric. I tried forcing the handle again, trying not to think about the fact that I was in a windowless cell maybe four foot by six, and well below sea level, a thousand tons of water just inches away behind a skin of steel. But the door didn't move, the only thing that changed was the pain in my head, jabbing with neon intensity until at last I stumbled back to the bunk and crawled onto it, trying not to think about the weight of water pressing in on me, focusing instead on my aching skull. It was pounding now so much that I could feel my pulse in my temples. Oh God, I had been so stupid, running out of that room straight into the trap. . . .

I tried to think. I had to stay calm, had to keep my head above the rising tide of fear. Stay logical. Stay in control. Think. *I had to.* What day was it? It was impossible to tell how much time had passed. My limbs felt stiff, as if I'd been lying in that position on the bunk for a while, but although I was thirsty I wasn't completely parched. If I'd been unconscious for more than a few hours I would have woken up seriously dehydrated. Which meant it was probably still Tuesday, the twenty-second.

In which case . . . Ben knew that I'd been intending to go ashore at Trondheim. He would come looking for me—wouldn't he? He wouldn't let the boat leave without me.

But then I realized that the engine was running and I could feel the rise and fall of waves beneath the hull. Either we hadn't stopped at all, or else we'd already left the port.

Oh God. We were heading out to sea—and everyone would assume I was still in Trondheim. If they looked for me at all, it would be in completely the wrong place.

If only my head didn't hurt and my thoughts didn't keep stumbling over each other . . . if only the walls weren't closing in on me like a coffin, making it hard to breathe, hard to *think*.

Passports. I didn't know how big Trondheim port was, but they must have some kind of customs check, or passport control. And there would be someone from the ship on duty at the gangway, surely, checking passengers in and out. They couldn't risk leaving without someone. Somewhere, there would be a record of the fact that I hadn't left the boat. Someone would realize I was still here.

I had to hang on to that.

But it was hard—hard when the only light was a dim bulb that flickered and dipped every so often, and the air seemed to be running out with every breath. Oh God, it was so hard.

I closed my eyes, shutting out the looming walls and the claustrophobic warping light, and pulled the thin cover over myself. I tried to focus on something. The feel of the flat, limp pillow beneath my cheek. The sound of my own breathing.

But the image I kept coming back to was that of the girl, standing nonchalantly outside my door in the corridor, her hand on her hip, and then the swing of her gait as she walked towards the staff door.

How. *How?*

Had she been hiding on the boat all along? In this room, maybe? But I knew, even without opening my eyes to look around, that no one had been living here. It had no sense of being inhabited, there were no stains on the carpet, no coffee marks on the plastic shelf, no fading scent of food and sweat and human breath. Even that spider curled in the sink spoke of disuse. There was no way that girl, full of snapping life and vivacity, could have been in this room without leaving some impression. Wherever she'd been staying, it wasn't here.

This place felt like a tomb. Maybe it was already mine.

- CHAPTER 23 -

I was not sure when I fell asleep, but I must have, exhausted by the ache in my head and the roar of the ship's motor, because I awoke, to the sound of a click.

I sat up sharply, cracking my scalp against the bunk above, and then fell back, groaning and clutching my head as the blood pounded in my ears, a shrill ringing in the back of my skull.

I lay there, my eyes squeezed tightly shut against the pain, but at last it receded enough for me to roll onto my side and open my eyes again, squinting against the dim fluorescent light.

There was a plate on the floor, and a glass of something—juice, I thought. I picked it up and sniffed it. It looked and smelled like orange juice, but I couldn't bring myself to drink it. Instead, I got painfully to my feet and opened the door to the little en suite, where I emptied the juice down the sink and refilled the glass with water from the tap. The water was warm and stale, but I was so thirsty now that I would have drunk worse. I gulped down the glass, refilled, and began to sip the next more slowly as I made my way back from the sink and onto the bunk.

My head ached powerfully, and I wished I had some painkillers, but more than that I felt awful—shivery and weak, as if I were coming down with the flu. It was probably hunger—it was hours since I'd eaten and my blood sugar must be at rock bottom.

Part of me wanted to lie down and rest my throbbing head, but my stomach growled, and I made myself examine the plate of food that was on the floor. It looked completely normal—meatballs in some kind of sauce, mashed potato and peas, and a bread roll on the side. I knew I should eat—but the same gut revulsion that had made me pour away the juice was kicking in. It just felt so wrong—eating food provided by someone who'd locked me into an underwater dungeon. There could be anything in there. Rat poison. Sleeping pills. *Worse.* And I'd have no choice but to eat it.

Suddenly, the thought of putting even a spoonful of that sauce in my mouth made me feel panicked and ill, and I felt like flushing the whole lot down the loo along with the juice, but even as I half stood, ready to pick up the plate, I realized something, and I sat back down again on slow, shaky legs.

They didn't need to poison me. Why would they? If they wanted to kill me they could just starve me.

I tried to think clearly.

If whoever had brought me here had wanted to kill me, they'd have done it. Right?

Right. They could have hit me again, harder, or put a pillow over my face when I was passed out, or a plastic bag around my neck. And they hadn't. They'd dragged me here at some inconvenience to themselves.

So they didn't want me dead. Not right now, at any rate.

One pea. You couldn't die from one poisoned pea, surely?

I picked it up on the end of a fork, looking at it. It looked completely normal. No trace of any powder. No odd color.

I put it in my mouth and rolled it slowly round, trying to detect any strange taste. There was none.

I swallowed.

Nothing much happened. Not that I'd expected it to—I didn't know much about poison, but I imagined that the ones that killed you within seconds were few and far between, and not easy to obtain.

But something did happen. And that was that I started to feel hungry.

I scooped up a few more peas and ate them, cautiously at first, and then picking up speed as the food made me feel better. I skewered a meatball with my fork. It smelled and tasted completely normal—with that slightly institutional air of food prepared for a large number of people.

At last the plate was empty and I sat and waited for someone to come and collect it.

And waited.

And waited.

Time is very elastic—that's the first thing you realize in a situation without light, without a clock, without any way of measuring the length of one second over the length of another. I tried counting—counting seconds, counting my pulse—but I got to two thousand and something and lost count.

My head ached, but it was the weak shiveriness in my limbs that worried me more. At first I thought it was low blood sugar, and then, after I'd eaten, I started to worry that perhaps there *had* been something in the food, but now I began to count back, to try to work out when the last time was that I'd taken my pills.

I remembered popping one out of the packet right after seeing Nilsson on Monday morning. But I hadn't actually taken it. Something—some stupid need to prove that I *wasn't* chemically dependent on these innocent little white dots—had stopped me. Instead, I'd left it on the countertop, not quite able to bring myself to down it, not quite wanting to throw it away.

I hadn't been intending to stop. Just to show . . . I don't know what. That I was in charge I guess. A little, pointless "fuck you" to Nilsson.

But then the argument with Ben had driven it from my mind. I'd gone off to the spa without taking it, and then the episode with the shower . . .

That made it . . . I couldn't quite work it out. At least forty-eight hours since I'd had a dose. Maybe more like sixty hours. The thought was uncomfortable. Actually, more than uncomfortable. It was terrifying.

I had my first panic attack when I was . . . I don't know. Thirteen maybe? Fourteen? I was a teenager. It came . . . and went, leaving me frightened and freaked-out, but I never told anyone. It seemed like something only a weirdo would get. Everyone else walked through life without shaking and finding themselves unable to breathe, right?

For a while it was okay. I did my GCSEs. Started my A levels. It was around then that things started to get really shaky. The panic attacks came back. First, one. Then a couple. After a while, it seemed like coping with anxiety had become a full-time business, and the walls began to close around me.

I saw a therapist, several in fact. There was the "talking cure" person my mum picked out of the phone book, a serious-faced woman with glasses and long hair who wanted me to reveal some dark secret that would be the key to unlocking all this, except I didn't have one. For a while I thought about making one up—just to see if it would make me feel better. But my mum got annoyed with her (and with her bills) before I could come up with a really good story.

There was the hip young community support leader, with his group of young girls who ran the gamut of problems, from anorexia to self-harm. And finally there was Barry, the cognitive behavioral therapist that my GP provided, who taught me to breathe, and count, and left me with a lifelong allergy to balding men with soft, supportive tenor voices.

None of them worked for me, though. Or none of them worked completely. But I kept it together enough to get through my exams, and then I went away to university and I felt a bit better, and it seemed like maybe all that—that *stuff*—was something I'd grow out of, like *NSYNC, and cherry lip gloss. That I'd leave behind, in my old bedroom at my parents' house, along with all my other childhood baggage. Uni was pretty great. When I left, with my shiny new degree, I felt ready to take on the world. I met Ben, and I got a job at *Velocity* and my own place in London, and everything seemed to be falling into place.

And that was when I fell apart.

I tried to come off the pills once. I was at a good place in my life, I was over Ben (oh my God, I was *so* over Ben). My GP lowered the dose to twenty milligrams a day, then ten, and then, since I was coping pretty well, to ten milligrams every other day, and finally I stopped.

I lasted two months before I cracked, and by that time I had lost thirty pounds and was in danger of losing my job at *Velocity*, although they didn't know why I'd stopped coming into the office. At last, Lissie called my mum, and she marched me back to the GP, who shrugged and said that maybe it was withdrawal, and maybe it just wasn't the right time for me to come off. He put me back on forty milligrams a day—my original dose—and I felt better almost within days. We agreed to try again another time—and somehow that time never came.

Now was not the right time. Not here. Not shut in a steel box six feet below sea level.

I tried to remember how long it had taken last time—how long it had been before I started to feel really, *really* shitty. It hadn't been that long, from what I could recall. Four days? Maybe less.

In fact I could feel the panic begin to prickle over my skin in little cold electric shocks.

You'll die here.

No one will know.

Oh God. Oh God oh God oh God oh God oh—

There was a sound at the door and I stopped. Stopped everything—stopped breathing, thinking, panicking—I sat, frozen, my back against the bunk. Should I pounce? Attack?

The door handle began to turn.

My heart was pounding in my throat. I stood up and backed away against the far wall. I knew I should fight—but I couldn't, not without knowing who was coming through that door.

Pictures flashed through my head. Nilsson. The chef in his latex gloves. The girl in the Pink Floyd T-shirt, a knife in her hand.

I swallowed.

And then a hand snaked through the gap and grabbed the plate, quick as blinking, and the door slammed shut. The light went out, plunging the cabin into inky blackness so thick I could taste it.

Fuck.

There was nothing I could do. I lay there in the impenetrable darkness for what felt like hours but might have been days, or minutes, drifting in and out of consciousness, hoping each time I opened my eyes to see *something,* even just a thin line of light in the corridor, something that would prove I was really here, that I really existed and wasn't just lost in some hell of my own imagining.

At last I must have fallen properly asleep, for I awoke with a jump, and my heart thumping and fluttering erratically in my chest. The cabin was still in complete darkness, and I lay there, shaking and sweating, holding on to the bunk like a life raft as I clawed my way back from the most horrible dream I could remember in a long time.

In the dream, the girl in the Pink Floyd T-shirt was in my cabin. It was dark, but somehow in the darkness I could . . . not exactly see her, but sense her. I just knew that she was there, standing in the middle of the cabin, and I couldn't move, the darkness pressing me down, like a living thing, squatting on my chest. She came closer, and closer, until she was standing just inches away, the T-shirt skimming the tops of her long, slim thighs.

She smiled, and then with one sinuous movement she pulled off the shirt. Beneath it she was skinny as a whippet, all ribs and collarbone and jutting pelvis, her elbow joints wider than her forearms, her wrists knobbly as a child's. She looked down at herself, and then she pulled off her bra, slow as a striptease, except there was nothing erotic about it, nothing sexy about her small, shallow breasts and the hollow of her stomach.

But as I lay on the bunk, panting, paralyzed with fear, she didn't stop there. She kept stripping. Her knickers slipped from her narrow hips to form a puddle at her feet. And then her hair, yanking it out by the roots. Then she pulled off her eyebrows, first one, and then the other, and her lips. She let her nose drop to her feet. She drew out her fingernails, one by one, slowly, like a woman loosening her evening gloves, and let them fall with a slight clatter to the floor, followed by her teeth, *click* . . . *click* . . . *click*, one after another. And finally—and most horribly—she began to peel away her skin, as if she were stepping out of a tight-fitting evening dress, until she was just a bloody streak, muscle and bone and sinew, like a skinned rabbit.

She went down on all fours and began to crawl towards me, her lipless mouth spread wide in a horrible parody of a smile.

Closer and closer she crawled, until at last, though I backed away, I came up against the rear wall of the bunk and could retreat no farther.

I felt my breath whimper in my throat. I tried to speak, but I was dumb. I tried to move, but I was frozen with fear.

She opened her mouth, and I knew that she was about to speak—but then she reached inside, and pulled out her own tongue.

I awoke, gasping and crawling with the horror of it, the blackness like a clenched fist around me.

I wanted to scream. The panic built inside me like a volcano, pressing up through the layers of closed throat and clenched teeth. And then I thought, in a kind of delirium—if I scream, what's the worst that can happen? Someone might hear? Let them hear. Let them hear, and maybe they'll come and get me.

So I let it out, the scream that had been rising up inside me, growing and swelling and pressing to get out.

And I screamed and I screamed and I screamed.

I don't know how long I screamed for, how long I lay there, shaking, my fists curled around the thin, limp pillow, my nails digging into the bare mattress beneath.

I only know that at last it was quiet in the little cabin, except for the low roar of the engine, and my own breath, rasping in a throat scoured raw and hoarse.

No one had come.

No one had banged on the door to ask what was going on, or threatened to kill me unless I shut up. No one had done anything. I might as well have been in outer space, screaming into a soundless vacuum.

My hands were trembling, and I could not get the girl from my dream out of my head, the idea of her raw, moist form crawling towards me, clutching, *needing.*

What had I done? Oh God, why had I done this, kept pushing, kept refusing to shut up. I had *made* myself a target, by my refusal to be silenced about what happened in that cabin. And yet . . . and yet what *had* happened?

I lay there, my hands pressed to my eyes in the suffocating darkness, trying to make sense of it. The girl was alive—whatever I had heard, whatever I *thought* I had seen, it wasn't murder. Had she been on the ship all along?

She must have. We hadn't stopped. We hadn't even got near enough to land to see it. But who was she, and why was she hiding on the ship?

I tried to ignore my aching head, to think logically. Was she a member of the crew? She had access to the staff door, after all. But then I remembered Nilsson punching in the code, me standing behind him as he did. He'd made no effort to shield the keypad. If I'd wanted to, it would have been child's play to note down the numbers as he entered them. And after that, once you were below decks, there were not many further locked doors.

She'd had access to the empty cabin, though—and that *did* require a passkey, either a guest one, programmed to that door specifically, or a staff one that opened all the cabin doors. I thought of the cleaners I'd seen in their little hutches below decks, their scared faces looking out at me before the door swung shut. How much would one of them sell a passkey for? A hundred kroner? A thousand? They wouldn't even need to sell it—I was certain there were places you could get key cards copied. They would just have had to loan it out for an hour or two, no questions asked. I thought of Karla—she had practically *told* me that it went on, that someone might have lent the cabin to a friend.

But it didn't have to be that. The passkey could have been stolen, for all I knew, or bought off the Internet—I had no idea how those electronic locks worked. There might have been no one else involved at all.

Was it possible that all this time I had been looking for an accomplice—a perpetrator among the crew or passengers—and they'd been innocent all along? I thought of the accusations I'd hurled at Ben, the suspicions I'd had of Cole, of Nilsson, of everyone, and I felt sick.

But the fact that this girl existed and was alive, that didn't automatically rule out someone else's involvement. The more I thought about it, the more I was sure that *someone* had been helping her above decks—someone had written that message on the spa wall, had tipped Cole's camera into the hot tub, had stolen my phone. They couldn't *all* have been her. Someone would have seen and recognized the girl I had been shouting about for two days if she'd been wandering around the ship.

Ugh, this was making my head hurt. Why? That was the question I couldn't answer. Why go to such lengths to hide on board the ship, to stop me from asking questions? If the girl had died, the cover-up made sense. But she was alive and well. It must be *who* she was that was important. Someone's wife? Someone's daughter? Lover? Someone trying to get out of the country with no questions asked?

I thought of Cole and his ex-wife, Archer and his mysterious "Jess." I thought of the way the photograph had disappeared from the camera.

None of it made sense.

I rolled over, feeling the weight of the darkness all around. Wherever we were, it was very deep beneath the ship, I was sure of that now. The engine was loud, much louder than on the passenger deck, louder even than I remembered it being on the staff deck. I was somewhere else, on an engine deck, perhaps, far below the waterline, deep in the hull.

At that thought, I felt again the horror begin to creep over me, the tons and tons of water weighing on my head and shoulders, pressing against the hull, the air in the cabin circulating, circulating, and me here suffocating in my own panic. . . .

My legs shaking, I climbed cautiously off the bunk and made my way slowly across the floor, my arms stretched out in front of me, cringing from what might be in here with me in the absolute darkness. My imagination conjured up horrors from my childhood nightmares—giant spiderwebs across my face, men with clutching arms, even the girl herself, lidless, lipless, tongueless. But another part of me knew that there was no one here but myself—that I would have been able to hear, smell, *sense* another human being in such a confined space.

After a few moments of cautious inching, my fingers encountered the door, and I felt my way across it. The first thing I tried was the handle, but it was still locked—I hadn't expected anything else. I felt for a spy hole, but there was none, or none that I could find on the blank expanse of plastic. I didn't remember seeing one earlier, anyway. What I did remember, and what I felt for next, was the flat beige light switch to the left of the door. My fingers found it in the darkness, and I pressed it, my heart beating hard in my chest.

Nothing happened.

I flicked it back, but without hope this time, because I knew what they'd done. There must be some kind of override in the passage outside, some sort of master switch or fuse. The door was already shut when the light went out, and in any case, in any cabin I'd been in before there was always some kind of security light—you were never in *complete* darkness, even when the lights were turned out. This was something else—this was an utter, total darkness that could only come from the electricity being completely cut.

I crawled back to the bunk and beneath the covers, my muscles shaking with a mixture of panic and that sick flu-like feeling I'd had before. My head felt filled with a spreading blankness, as if the dark of the cabin had seeped inside my skull and was filtering through my synapses, deadening and muffling everything apart from the panic that was building in my gut.

Oh God. Don't. Don't give way, not now.

I couldn't. I *wouldn't.* I wouldn't let her win.

The anger that flooded over me suddenly was something that I could hang on to, something concrete in the silent blackness of this little box. That bitch. What a traitor. So much for the fucking sisterhood. I had fought for her, put my credibility on the line, endured Nilsson's doubt and Ben's probing—and all for what? So that she could betray me, bash my head into a steel frame post, and lock me into this fucking coffin.

Whatever the plot was—she was in on it.

She had definitely been the person who had ambushed me in the corridor. And the more I thought about it, the more I was sure that the hand that had come snaking in to snatch my food tray was hers, too, a skinny, lithe, strong hand. A hand that could scratch and slap and smack a person's head against the wall.

There must be *some* reason for all this—no one would go through this elaborate charade for nothing. Had she been faking her own death? Had I been *meant* to see what happened? But if so, why go to such lengths to pretend she was never there? Why clear the cabin, wipe away the blood, destroy the mascara, and deliberately discredit everything about my account of that night?

No. She hadn't wanted to be seen. Something had happened in that cabin, and whatever it was, I was not supposed to have witnessed it.

I lay there, cudgeling my battered brain to try to work it out, but the more I tried to ram the bits of information together, the more it felt like a jigsaw with too many pieces to fit the frame.

I tried to think through the possibilities that would mesh with the scream and the blood and the cover-up. A fight? A blow to the nose, a yell of pain, a gush of blood as the person ran to the veranda to try to bleed into the sea, leaving that smear on the glass . . . no deaths. And if the girl was some kind of stowaway, that could explain why they had covered it up—moved her to a different location, cleaned away the blood.

But other parts of the picture didn't fit. If the fight had been unintended and unpremeditated, how had they cleared the cabin so fast? I had seen the girl in situ earlier that day, the room behind her cluttered with clothes and belongings. If the fight had been unplanned, there was no way they could have stripped and cleaned that suite in the few minutes it had taken me to ring Nilsson.

No—whatever had happened in there had been *planned*. They had cleared it beforehand, meticulously cleaned it. And I was beginning to suspect it was not chance that it was number ten that had been empty. No, one cabin had been left empty deliberately, and it *had* to be ten. Palmgren was the very last one on the ship. Its veranda was not overlooked, and there were no other cabins to see something floating past, disappearing in the foam of the ship's wake.

Someone *had* died. I was sure of it. Just not that girl. But then who?

I tossed and turned in the darkness, listening for any sounds above the roar of the engine and trying to answer the questions churning uneasily inside. My brain felt fogged and thick, but I kept coming back to that question. Who? *Who had died?*

- CHAPTER 24 -

When I woke next it was to the same metallic click I'd heard before, and the lights flickered on. They strobed for a moment, the warming hum of the low-energy bulbs audible above the engine sound and mingling with the whining in my ears. I jumped up, my heart going a mile a minute, knocking over something on the floor beside the bed as I gazed wildly around.

I had missed my chance.

God *damn* it, I had missed my chance again.

I *had* to find out what was going on here, what they intended to do with me, why they were keeping me shut up here. How long had I been here? Was it daytime now? Or was this just the time that it suited the girl—or whoever my captor was—to turn the electricity back on?

I tried to count back. I had been hit in the early hours of Tuesday morning. At the very least it was Wednesday morning now, possibly later. It felt as if I'd been here longer than twenty-four hours—much longer.

I went to the bathroom to splash water on my face. It was as I was drying myself that a wave of vertigo washed over me, making my head reel and the whole room shift and shudder. I had the sudden sensation of falling, and I put out my hand to steady myself against the doorframe, shutting my eyes against the sensation of plummeting very far and very fast into black water.

At last the sensation receded, and I made my way back to the bunk, where I sat and put my head between my knees, feeling my skin shiver with cold and hot. *Had* the ship moved? It was hard to know what was dizziness and what was the movement of the waves, so far down beneath the decks. The movement of the ship felt very different down here—not so much a rhythmic rise and fall, but a sluggish roll that mingled with the constant roar of the engine to give a strange, hypnotic feeling.

There was a tray beside the bed, with a Danish pastry and a bowl of slopped muesli. That must have been what I knocked when I jumped up out of sleep. I picked it up and forced myself to take a spoonful. I wasn't hungry, but I'd eaten nothing but a few meatballs since Monday night. If I were going to get out of here, I would need to fight, and to fight, I needed to eat.

What I really wanted, though, was not food. It was my pills. I *wanted* them, with a fierce, physical longing that I remembered from the last time I tried to stop taking them. Only this time I knew that things wouldn't get better without them, as I had kept telling myself last time. They were going to get worse.

If you're around to see it, said a nasty little voice in my head. The muesli stuck in my throat, and suddenly I couldn't swallow.

I longed for the girl from the cabin to come back. A vivid, luxuriantly violent image flashed across my brain: me, grabbing her hair the way she'd grabbed mine, smashing her cheekbone against the sharp metal edge of the bunk, watching the blood flow, the way it would smell sharp and raw in the confined, airless cabin. I remembered again the blood on the veranda, the way it had smeared across the glass, and I wished with a powerful, vicious longing that it *had* been hers.

I hate you, I thought. I swallowed against the pain in my throat, forcing the soggy half-chewed muesli down. I took another spoonful, my fingers shaking as I conveyed it to my mouth. *I hate you so much. I hope you* do *drown.* The muesli felt like cement, choking me as I tried to swallow it, but I forced it down again and again, until the bowl was half empty.

I did not know if I could do this, but I had to try.

I picked up the tray, the thin melamine tray, and I smacked it on the metal edge of the bunk. It bounced back and I only just flinched out of the way in time. I had a sudden, sharp flashback to the burglary—to the door smacking into my cheekbone, and I had to shut my eyes for a moment and steady myself on the bunk.

I didn't try that again. Instead, I leaned the tray on the metal edge and put my knee on the nearest side, and all my weight on my hands on the far edge. Then I pushed down. The tray did nothing at first, and I pressed harder. Then it snapped in half with a noise like a gunshot, sending me sprawling onto the bed. But I had what I'd been aiming for—two pieces of plastic, not quite razor-sharp, but each with an edge formidable enough to do some damage.

I picked up each piece, weighing them in my hand for the best way to hold them, and then, holding the one that felt like the most intimidating weapon, I walked across to the door and crouched against the wall next to the frame.

And I waited.

It seemed to last for hours, that day. Once or twice I felt my eyes sliding shut, my body trying to shut down amid the exhausting flood of adrenaline and fear, but I jerked them back open. *Stay with it, Lo!*

I began to count. Not from panic this time but just to keep myself awake. One. Two. Three. Four. When I got to a thousand I changed and began to count in French. *Un. Deux. Trois. . . .* Then in twos. I played games in my own head—fizz-buzz, that children's game where you say "fizz" for every five or multiple of five, and "buzz" for every seven.

One. Two. Three. Four. Fizz. (My hands were shaking.) Six. Buzz. Eight. Nine. Ten— No wait, that should have been fizz.

I shook my head impatiently, rubbed my aching arms, and started again. One. Two. . . .

And then I heard it—a noise in the corridor. A door slamming. I caught my breath.

They were coming closer. My heart began to race. The pit of my stomach clenched.

A key in the lock . . .

And then the door cracked cautiously open and I pounced.

Her.

She saw me leap towards the gap and tried to close it, but I was too quick for her. I thrust my arm in the gap, and it slammed onto my forearm—hard. I screamed with pain, but the door bounced back, and I was able to wedge half my body into the gap, stabbing at her grappling arm with the jagged edge of the broken tray, but instead of falling backwards as I'd anticipated, she rushed forwards into the room, thumping me back against the plastic wall, the tray cutting painfully into my arm. I pulled myself up, blood dripping down the back of my hand, but she was faster. She lunged at the door, locked it, and then stood with her back to it, the key clenched in her fist.

"Let me go." It came out like the growl of an animal—not quite human. She shook her head. Her back was to the door, and she had my blood on her face, and she was scared, but kind of exhilarated, too, I could see it in her eyes. She had the upper hand, and she knew it.

"I'll kill you," I said. I meant it. I held up the tray, stained with my own blood. "I'll cut your throat."

"You couldn't kill me," she said, and her voice was just as I remembered it, with a kind of scornful defiance behind her words. "Look at you, you can barely stand up, you poor bitch."

"Why?" I said, and there was a note in my voice that sounded like a whining little child. "Why are you doing this?"

"Because you *made* us," she hissed, suddenly furious. "You wouldn't stop digging, would you? No matter how much I tried to warn you off. If you'd just kept your mouth shut about what you saw in that bloody cabin—"

"What did I see?" I said, but she shook her head, her lip curling.

"God, you must think I'm even dumber than I look. Do you actually *want* to die?"

I shook my head.

"Good. What do you want, then?"

"I want to get out of here," I said. I sat down on the bunk abruptly, not sure if my legs would hold me much longer.

She shook her head once more, vehemently this time, and I saw that flicker of fear in her eyes again.

"He'd never let me."

He? The word sent a prickle through me, the first concrete evidence that someone upstairs had been helping her. Who was *he*? But I didn't dare ask, not now. There was something more important I needed first.

"My pills, then. Let me have my pills."

She looked at me appraisingly.

"The ones you had by the sink? I might be able to do that. Why d'you want them?"

"They're antidepressants," I said bitterly. "They have— You shouldn't withdraw from them too fast."

"Oh . . ." There was sudden comprehension on her face. "That's why you look so bad. I couldn't work it out. I thought I'd hit your head too hard. Okay. I can do that. But you have to promise me something in return."

"What?"

"No more trying to attack me. These are for good behavior, right?"

"All right."

She straightened, picked up the plate and bowl, and held out her hand for the shards of tray. I hesitated for a moment and then handed them over.

"I'm going to unlock the door now," she said. "But don't do anything stupid. There's another door outside this one, operated by a code. You won't get very far. So no silly buggers, all right?"

"All right," I said reluctantly.

After she'd gone I sat on the bench staring into space, thinking about what she'd said.

He.

She *did* have an accomplice on board. And that one word meant I could rule out Tina, Chloe, Anne, and two-thirds of the staff.

Who was *he*? I ticked them off in my head.

Nilsson.

Bullmer.

Cole.

Ben.

And Archer.

In the less-likely column I put Owen White, Alexander, and the crew and stewards.

My mind circled the possibilities, but the one factor I kept coming back to was the spa and the *STOP DIGGING* message. There was only one man who had been down there, one man who could have written that sign. Ben.

I had to stop focusing on motives. *Why* was an unsolvable question that I just didn't have enough information to answer.

But the *how*—there were very few people on board with the opportunity to write that note. There was one functional entrance into the spa, and Ben was the only male who I was certain had used it.

So many things made sense. His quickness to undermine my story to Nilsson. The fact that he—alone of everyone on board—had tried to get into my cabin on that last night, and knew that I was locked in the bathroom, making it possible to steal my phone.

The fact that his cabin was on the other side of the empty one, yet he'd heard nothing and seen nothing.

The fact that he'd lied about his alibi, playing poker.

And the fact that he had tried so hard to stop me from pushing on with the investigation.

The clicking of the puzzle pieces into place should have given me satisfaction, but they didn't. Because what use were answers to me down here? I needed to get out.

- CHAPTER 25 -

I was lying on my side, staring at the cream melamine wall when the knock came.

"Come in," I said dully, and then almost laughed at myself for the stupidity of social niceties in a situation like this. What did it matter if I said "Come in" when they would do as they liked regardless?

"It's me," said the voice outside the door. "No more shit with the trays, okay? Or this'll be the last pill you get off me, right?"

"Okay," I said. I was trying not to sound too eager, but I sat up, pulling the thin blanket around myself. I hadn't used the shower since I got here and I smelled of sweat and fear.

The door cracked open cautiously, and the girl pushed a tray of food through the bottom with her foot and then slipped through the gap, locking it behind herself.

"Here you go," she said. She held out her hand, and on the palm was a single white tablet.

"One?" I said incredulously.

"One. Maybe I can bring you a couple more tomorrow, if you behave."

I had just given her the best blackmail weapon ever. But I nodded and took the pill from her palm. From her pocket she pulled a book—one of mine, in fact, from my room. *The Bell Jar.* Not what I'd have chosen under the circumstances, but it was better than nothing, I guessed.

"I thought you might like something to read, you might be going a bit nuts with nothing to do." Her eyes strayed to the pill, and then she added, "No offense."

"Thanks," I said. She turned to go and I said, "Wait."

"Yeah?"

"I—" Suddenly I wasn't sure how to ask what I wanted to ask. I clenched my hand around the pill in my palm. Shit. "What—what's going to happen to me?"

Her face changed at that, something guarded came over her expression, like a curtain falling across a window.

"That's not up to me."

"Who is it up to? Ben?"

She gave a derisory snort at that.

"Enjoy."

As she turned to leave, she caught sight of herself in the little mirror on the back of the en suite door.

"Fuck, I've got blood on my face. Why didn't you say? If he knows you attacked me . . ." She went into the little toilet to splash and wipe her face.

But it wasn't just the blood she wiped away. When she came out, I froze. With that one simple act, I realized who she was.

In wiping away the blood she had wiped both her eyebrows clean off, leaving a smooth, skull-like forehead that was instantly, unbearably recognizable.

The woman in cabin 10 was Anne Bullmer.

- CHAPTER 26 -

I was too stunned to say anything. I just sat there, openmouthed with shock.

The girl looked from me, back to her reflection in the en suite mirror, and realized what she'd done. An expression of annoyance crossed her face for a moment, but then she seemed to shrug it off and stalked out of the room, letting the door swing shut behind her. I heard a key scrape in a lock, and then another door bang farther away.

Anne Bullmer.

Anne Bullmer?

It seemed impossible that she could be the same gaunt, gray, prematurely aged woman I'd seen and spoken to. And yet—her face was unmistakable. The same dark eyes. The same high, jutting cheekbones. The only thing I couldn't understand was how I'd missed it before.

If I hadn't seen her, midtransformation, I would never have believed how much her hair and the delicately penciled eyebrows changed her face. Without them she looked oddly featureless and smooth. It was impossible not to think of death and illness when you looked at that bone-pale sweep of skin, and the scarf tied tight around her skull only emphasized that fragility—painfully underscoring the lines of her neck and the shape of the bones beneath.

But her sleek black brows and the vibrant mass of dark hair changed all that beyond recognition. With it she became young, healthy, *alive*.

I realized, when I'd spoken to Anne Bullmer before, I had been so mesmerized by the trappings of her illness that I'd never really looked at the woman beneath. I had tried *not* to look in fact. I had just seen the distinctive, draping clothes, the missing eyebrows, the distractingly smooth skull beneath those delicate scarves . . .

The hair must be a wig—I had no doubt about that. There was no room under those thin silk scarves Anne wore for those thick dark tresses.

But was she sick? Well? Dying? Faking? It didn't make sense.

I tried to think back to what Ben had told me—four years of chemo and radiotherapy. Could you really fake that, even with private doctors in your pay and enough money to enable you to hop from one health system to another every few months? Maybe.

At least this explained one thing—how she had got on board, and what had happened to her after that splash in the night. She'd simply pulled off her wig, put on her scarf, and resumed her life as Anne Bullmer. It also explained how she had access to every part of the ship—to the passkeys and the staff areas, and this secret locked vault down in the belly of the boat. When your husband was the owner, nothing was out of bounds, presumably.

But the thing that puzzled me most was *why*? Why dress up in a wig and a Pink Floyd T-shirt and spend the afternoon hanging out in an empty cabin? What was she doing there? And if it was so secret, why answer the door at all?

As the last question ran through my head, I had a sudden flash of myself knocking on the door—one, two, three . . . pause, and another bang, and the way the door had been snatched open as if someone had been waiting for that final knock. It was an odd knock, idiosyncratic.

The kind of knock you might use if you were arranging a code. Was it possible I had, completely accidentally, stumbled on a prearranged signal for the woman in the cabin—Anne Bullmer—to open the door?

If only. If only I'd just knocked twice like any normal person—or even once. I would never have known she was there, never have put myself in this position where I had to be locked up—silenced . . .

Silenced. It was an uncomfortable thought, and the word stuck in my head, reverberating there like an echo.

I had to be silenced. But silenced for how long? Locked up here until . . . what? Some prearranged deadline had passed?

Or silenced . . . permanently?

Supper was white fish in a sort of cream sauce, with boiled potatoes. It was cold, congealing around the edges, but I was hungry. Before I ate I looked at the pill in my hand, wondering what to do. It was half my normal dose. I could take the whole pill now, or I could split it, and start building up a reserve in case . . . but in case what? I could hardly escape, and if Anne decided to stop dispensing the pills, I would run out long before she took pity on me.

In the end, I gulped down the whole thing, reasoning that I had a deficit to make up. I could start biting them in half tomorrow, if it seemed important. I felt better almost immediately, though I knew, logically, that it couldn't be the pills. They didn't absorb that fast, and the effect took a while to build up in my system. Whatever I was experiencing was completely placebo-based. At this point, though, I didn't care. I would take what I could get.

Then I started picking at the lukewarm supper. As I sat on the bunk, chewing the tepid, gluey potato slowly, in an effort to make it less unappealing, I tried to rearrange the pieces of the puzzle I had assembled so painstakingly inside my head.

I knew now what that derisive snort meant when I had said *Who is it up to? Ben?*

Poor Ben. I felt a rush of guilt that I had been so quick to judge him, and then another rush, this time of anger. I'd been so focused on Anne's chance mention of a male accomplice that it had never occurred to me that Anne herself might have been the one to run quickly down the spa stairs while her varnish was supposed to be drying and scrawl those words. Stupid, *stupid* Lo.

But stupid Ben, too. If he hadn't spent so many years belittling my feelings and if he hadn't been so eager to spill the beans to Nilsson, instead of supporting my story, then I might not have been so quick to jump to conclusions.

I knew now who *he* was. It must be Richard Bullmer. He owned the boat. And of all the men on the ship, I could imagine him planning and carrying out a murder better than anyone else. Certainly better than fat, fussy Alexander or the lumbering, bearlike Nilsson.

Except that no murder had taken place. Why did I have to keep reminding myself of that fact? Why was it so hard to grasp?

Because you're here, I thought. Because whatever you saw—whatever happened in that cabin—it was important enough that they would lock you up here and prevent you from going to see the police at Trondheim. What had happened? It must be something so high-stakes that they simply couldn't afford to let me talk about it. Was it smuggling? Were they throwing something overboard to an accomplice?

It'll be you next, you stupid bitch, said the voice inside my head, and an image of myself falling through deep water shot through me, like an electric shock deep in my skull.

I winced and gritted my teeth, forcing myself to swallow another glutinous mouthful of potato. The ship heaved, and nausea swilled around in the pit of my stomach.

What *was* going to happen to me? There were only two possibilities—they were going to let me go at some point. Or they were going to kill me. And somehow, the first one didn't seem very likely anymore. I knew so much. I knew about Anne. I knew she wasn't nearly as ill as she pretended. And they could not afford for me to get out and tell my story—a story of kidnap, imprisonment, and bodily harm—though would anyone believe me?

I touched my fingers to my cheek, where the blood was still caked from where she'd whacked me into the doorframe. I felt suddenly gross—dirty and sweaty and blood-smeared. Anne—judging by her previous timings—wouldn't be back for hours.

There wasn't much I could do to improve my lot, stuck in this two-meter coffin. But at least I could keep myself clean.

The jet was nothing like the one in my suite upstairs. Even turned up full it was a tepid trickle, but I stood underneath it for so long I felt my fingers wrinkle into mush. The clotted blood on my hand dissolved into the water and I shut my eyes and felt the warmth pour through me, seeping into my muscles.

When I climbed out I felt better, more like myself, washed clean of some of the fear and violence that had marked the last few days. It was putting my clothes back on that made me really realize how far I'd sunk. They stank—not to put too fine a point on it—and were stained with blood and sweat.

I lay down on the bunk and shut my eyes, listening to the steady thrum of the engine and wondering where we were. It was Wednesday night—or maybe even Thursday morning now. From what I could remember we had only a little over twenty-four hours of this trip left. And then what? When the boat got into Bergen on Friday morning, the other passengers would leave and with them would go my last hope of someone realizing what had happened.

For twenty-four hours I was probably safe. But after that . . . Oh God, but I couldn't think about that.

I pressed my hands into my eyes, listened to the blood roaring in my head. What should I do? What *could* I do?

If Anne was telling the truth, hurting her wouldn't achieve anything. There was another locked door the other side of this one, and very likely other codes on the exits. For a minute I wondered if I got out into the corridor, could I find and smash a fire alarm before Anne caught up with me? But it seemed like too long a shot. From what I'd seen of Anne's strength and quickness, I was unlikely to get that far.

No. My best chance was simple—I had to get Anne on my side.

But how? What did I actually know about her?

I tried to think about what I knew about Anne Bullmer—her fantastic wealth, her lonely upbringing, trailing around the boarding schools of Europe. It was no wonder it had taken me so long to make the connection. The rake-thin, sad-eyed woman in her gray silk wraps and designer headscarves—yes, somehow that fit with what I'd been told. But I could not make one word of what Ben had said connect with the girl in the Pink Floyd T-shirt, with her mocking dark eyes and cheap mascara. It was like there were two Annes. Same height, same weight, but that was where the similarity ended.

And then . . . something clicked.

Two Annes.

Two women.

The gray silk robe that matched her eyes . . .

I opened my eyes and swung my legs over the side of the bunk, groaning with my own stupidity. Of course—of *course*. If I hadn't been half-dead with fear and panic and the pain in my head, I would have seen it. How could I not have thought of it?

Of course there were two Annes.

Anne Bullmer was dead—had been since the night we left England.

The girl in the Pink Floyd T-shirt was very much alive, and had been impersonating her ever since.

Same height, same weight, same broad cheekbones—it was only the eyes that didn't match, and they had taken a calculated risk that no one would remember the features of a woman they'd barely met. No one on board knew Anne before the trip. Richard had even told Cole not to take any photographs of her, for Christ's sake! Now I understood why. It wasn't to protect a woman self-conscious about her appearance. It was so there would be no compromising photographs for his wife's friends and family to puzzle over afterwards.

I shut my eyes, my fingers gripping my hair so hard that it hurt, tugging painfully on my scalp, trying to work out what must have happened.

Richard Bullmer—it must have been him—had smuggled the woman in cabin 10 on board somehow. She was in that cabin before the rest of us ever came on the ship.

The day we set sail she had been waiting for the word, for instruction from Richard, to clear her cabin and get ready. I thought back to what I'd seen over her shoulder—a silk robe strewn across the bed, makeup, Veet in the bathroom—*waxing strips*. Christ—how could I have been so stupid? She had been shaving and ripping off her body hair, ready to impersonate a woman with cancer. But instead of Richard with his prearranged knock, *I* had come along, inadvertently given the signal, and she'd seen me instead.

What the hell must she have thought? I replayed again the fright and irritation in her face as she'd tried to shut the door and I'd stopped her. She'd been desperate to get rid of me but trying to act as unsuspiciously as possible. Far better that I just remembered a strange woman lending a mascara than started telling tales of a fellow guest slamming the door in my face.

And it had nearly worked. It had *so* nearly worked.

Did she tell Richard when he came? I couldn't be sure, but I thought not. He had seemed so normal at that first night's dinner—the perfect host. And besides, it was her blunder, and he didn't look like the kind of man you'd want to confess a mistake to. More likely she just crossed her fingers and hoped to get away with it.

Then she had packed her things, cleared the room, and waited.

After drinks that first night, Anne, somehow, had been taken to cabin 10. Was she alive, lured there by some cock-and-bull story? Or was she already dead?

Either way, it didn't really matter, because the end result was the same. While Richard was back in Lars's cabin, establishing his alibi with an uninterrupted poker game, the woman in cabin 10 had bundled the real Anne overboard and hoped that the body would never be found.

And they would have got away with it, if I—frightened and traumatized from the burglary—hadn't heard the splash and jumped to a conclusion that was so wrong, it was almost completely right.

So who was she? Who was this girl who had hit me, and fed me, and locked me up here like an animal?

I had no idea. But I knew one thing—she was my best hope of getting out of here alive.

- CHAPTER 27 -

All that night I lay awake, trying to work out what I should do. Judah and my parents would not be expecting me home until Friday and would have no reason to suspect anything was wrong until then. But the other passengers must know that I hadn't returned to the ship. Would they have raised the alarm? Or had Bullmer given them some story to explain my disappearance—unavoidably detained in Trondheim, perhaps? Decided to return home unexpectedly?

I wasn't sure. I tried to think who might be concerned enough to ask questions. I had little hope of Cole, Chloe, or most of the others making a fuss. They didn't know me. They had no contact details for any of my family. They would very likely accept whatever Bullmer told them.

Ben, then? He knew me well, enough to know that an early-morning flit to Trondheim without a word wasn't in character. But I wasn't sure. Under normal circumstances I was fairly certain he'd have contacted Judah or my parents with his concerns, but the way I had left things with him wasn't exactly normal circumstances. I had all but accused him of being complicit in a murder, and aside from his justifiable anger, he probably wouldn't be surprised at my disappearing off the ship without a word of good-bye.

Out of all the guests, Tina seemed like my best bet, and I was crossing my fingers that she would contact Rowan when I failed to return. But it seemed very slim odds to hang my life on.

No. I had to take matters into my own hands.

By the time morning came I hadn't slept, but I knew what I had to do, and when the knock came, I was ready.

"Come in," I said. The door cracked open, and the girl put her head cautiously around the doorframe. She saw me sitting quietly on the bed, washed and clean, holding the book in my lap. "Hey," I said.

She put down the tray of food on the floor. She was dressed as Anne this time, wearing a headscarf, her eyebrows not penciled in, but she didn't move like Anne, she moved like the girl I'd seen before, dumping the tray down impatiently and straightening up with none of the meditative grace she'd shown when impersonating Richard's wife.

"Hey yourself," she said, and her voice was different, too—the crystalline consonants elided and blurred. "You finished with that?" She nodded at the book.

"Yes, can you swap it for another one?"

"Yeah, I guess. What do you want?"

"I don't mind. Anything. You choose."

"Okay." She held out her hand for *The Bell Jar* and I handed it over, and then steeled myself for what I had to do next.

"I'm sorry," I said awkwardly. "About the tray."

She gave a smile at that, a flash of straight white teeth, a glint of mischief in her dark eyes.

"That's all right. I don't blame you; I'd have done the same. You've got a rubber one this time, though. Fool me once, and all that."

I looked down at the breakfast lying on the floor. It was true. The brittle melamine tray was gone, replaced by one made of thicker, grippy plastic, like the kind you serve drinks on in bars.

"I can't complain, I guess." I forced a smile. "I earned it."

"Your pill's on the saucer. Remember—good behavior, yeah?"

I nodded, and she turned to leave. I gulped. I had to stop her, say something. *Anything* that might prevent me from being condemned to another day and night here alone.

"What's your name?" I said desperately.

She turned back, her face suspicious.

"What?"

"I know you're not Anne. I remembered, about the eyes. On the first night Anne had gray eyes. You don't. Other than that it's very convincing. You're a really good actress, you know."

Her face went completely blank and for a minute I thought that she was going to slam out of the room and leave me here for another twelve hours. I felt like a fisherman, reeling in a huge fish on a delicate line, my muscles tense with the effort but trying not to jerk or show the strain.

"If I've got it wrong—" I began cautiously.

"Shut up," she said, fierce as a lioness. Her face was completely transformed, savage with anger, her dark eyes full of rancor and distrust.

"I'm sorry," I said humbly. "I didn't . . . Look, does it matter? I'm not going anywhere. Who would I tell?"

"Fuck," she said bitterly. "You're digging your grave, do you get that?"

I nodded. But I had known that for a few days now—whatever the girl tried to tell herself—whatever *I* tried to tell myself—there was only one way I was leaving this room.

"I don't think Richard will let me leave," I said. "You know that, right? So name or no name, it doesn't really matter."

Her face, beneath the expensive headscarf, was white. When she spoke her voice was bitter.

"You fucked it all up. Why couldn't you leave well enough alone?"

"I was trying to help!" I said. I didn't mean it to sound the way it came out, but in the little room it sounded frighteningly loud. I swallowed, and spoke more quietly. "I was trying to help *you*, don't you get that?"

"Why?" she said. It was half a question, half a cry of frustration. "Why? You barely knew me—why did you have to keep digging?"

"Because I knew what it was like to be you! I know—I know what it's like to wake up in the night, afraid for your life."

"But that's not me," she snarled. She stalked across the little cabin. Close up I could see that her eyebrows had just the faintest brush of regrowth. "It *was never me*."

"It will be, though," I said, holding her gaze so she couldn't look away. I couldn't afford to release her from the knowledge of what she was doing. "When Richard's got Anne's money—what do you think his next move will be? Making himself safe."

"Shut up! You have no idea what you're talking about. He's a good man. He's in love with me."

I stood up, level with her. Our eyes were locked, our faces just inches apart in the tiny space.

"That's bullshit and you know it," I said. My hands were shaking. If this went wrong she might lock the door and never come back, but I had to make her face up to the reality of the situation—both for my sake and hers. If she walked away now, we were very likely both dead. "If he was in love with you he wouldn't be beating you up and forcing you to dress up as his dead wife. What do you *think* this charade is all about? Being with you? It's not about you. If it was, he'd have got a divorce and walked off into the sunset with you—but she'd have taken her money with her. She was heir to a billion-pound dynasty. Those kinds of people don't risk marriage without a prenup."

"Shut up!" She put her hands over her ears, shaking her head. "You don't know what you're talking about. Neither of us wanted to be in this situation!"

"Really? You think it's coincidence he fell in love with someone who bears a startling resemblance to Anne? He planned this from the beginning. You're just a means to an end."

"You know nothing about it," the girl snarled. She turned away from me, walked to where the window would have been if I had one, and back. There was nothing of Anne's weary serenity in her expression now—it was naked fear and fury.

"All the money, without the controlling wife—I think he had that carrot waved in front of his nose by Anne's illness, and suddenly found he liked the idea: a future without Anne, but with the money. And when the doctors gave her the all clear, he didn't want to let go of it—is that right? And then he saw you—and a plan started to form. Where did he pick you up—a bar? No, wait." I remembered the photo on Cole's camera. "It was at his club, right?"

"You know nothing about it!" the girl shouted. "NOTHING!"

And before I could say anything else, she turned on her heel, unlocked the door with a trembling hand, and slammed out of the room, *The Bell Jar* still clutched beneath her arm. The door banged shut behind her, and I heard her key scraping shakily in the lock. Then farther away another bang, and then it was still.

I sat back on the bunk. Had I made her doubt Richard enough to put her trust in me? Or was she going upstairs right now to tell him this whole conversation? There was only one way to find out, and that was by waiting.

But as the hours slipped away and she didn't come back, I started to wonder how long that wait would be.

And when she didn't reappear with supper, and hunger began to claw at my stomach, I began to suspect I'd made a horrible mistake.

- CHAPTER 28 -

It's terrifying how long the hours can feel when you have no clock, no means of telling the time, and no way of knowing if anyone will come for you.

I lay for a long time, staring at the bunk above me, running over the conversation in my head and trying to work out if I'd just made the worst mistake of my life.

I'd gambled on establishing some kind of bond with the girl, forcing her to face up to what she was doing—and it was starting to look like I'd failed.

The hours dragged on and still no one came. My hunger grew more and more distracting. I wished I hadn't given her back the book, there was nothing in the cabin I could distract myself with. I began to think about solitary confinement—how prisoners went slowly crazy, heard voices, begged for release.

At least the girl had left the electricity on, although I wasn't sure it was an act of mercy—she had been so furious when she left the room she'd probably have switched it off just to punish me. More likely she'd just forgotten. But that small fact—the idea that I could choose my environment even in such a minor way—helped.

I showered again and licked the dried croissant jam off the plate. I lay on the bed and shut my eyes, and tried to remember things—the layout of the house I grew up in. The plot of *Little Women*. The color of Jude's—

But no. I pushed that away. I couldn't think of Judah. Not here. It would break me.

In the end—more as a way of taking charge of the situation than because I really thought it would help—I turned out the light and lay, staring into the blackness, trying to sleep.

I'm not sure if I did sleep. I dozed, I guess. Hours passed, or seemed to. No one came, but at some point in the long darkness, I was jerked awake and sat up, my pulse spiking, trying to fathom what was different. A noise? A presence in the dark?

My heart was thumping as I slipped out of bed and felt my way by touch to the door, but when I flicked on the light nothing was different. The cabin was empty. The tiny en suite as bare as ever. I held my breath, listening, but there were no footsteps in the corridor outside, no voices or movements. Not a sound disturbed the quiet.

And then I realized. The quiet. *That* was what had woken me. The engine had stopped.

I tried to count the days on my fingers, and although I couldn't be sure, I was fairly certain it must now be Friday the twenty-fifth. And that meant that the ship had arrived at its last port, Bergen, where we were due to disembark and catch planes back to London. The passengers would be leaving.

And then I'd be alone.

The thought brought panic rushing through my veins. I don't know why—maybe it was the idea that they were so close—sleeping, most likely, just a few feet above my head and yet there was nothing, *nothing* I could do to make them hear. And soon they would pack their cases and leave, and I would be alone in a boat-shaped coffin.

The thought was too much to bear. Without thinking, I grabbed the bowl that had held yesterday's breakfast and banged it against the ceiling as hard as I could.

"Help!" I screamed. "Can anyone hear me? I'm trapped, please, please help!"

I stopped, panting, listening, hoping desperately that with the sound of the engine no longer masking my cries, someone might hear.

There was no answering thump, no muffled shout filtering back through the floors. But I heard a sound. It was a metallic grinding, as if something was scraping the outside of the hull.

Had someone heard? I held my breath, trying to still my thumping heart, beating so loud it threatened to drown out the faint sounds from outside the ship. Was someone coming?

The grinding came again. . . . I felt the ship's side shudder, and I realized suddenly what it was. The gangway was being lowered. The passengers were disembarking.

"Help me!" I screamed, and I banged again, only now I was noticing the way the plastic ceiling deadened and absorbed the sound.

"Help me! It's me, Lo. I'm here! I'm on the boat!"

No answer, just the breath tearing in my throat, my blood in my ears.

"Anyone? Please! Please help!"

I put my hands to the wall, feeling the thumps against the gangway being transmitted down through the hull and into my hands. The impact of goods trolleys . . . and luggage . . . and departing feet.

I could feel all this. But I could not hear it. I was deep below the water—and they were up above, where any faint vibrations that I could make with my plastic bowl would be drowned out by the sound of the wind and the screech of the gulls and the voices of their fellow passengers.

I let the bowl fall from my hands to the floor, where it bounced and rolled across the thin carpet, and then I dropped to the bed, and I crouched there, my arms wrapped around my head, my head pressed into my knees, and I began to weep, great choking tears of fear and desperation.

I had been afraid before. I'd been scared half out of my wits.

But I had never despaired, and it was despair that I was feeling now.

As I knelt on the thin, sagging mattress, sobbing into my knees, pictures passed through my head: Judah reading the paper, my mother doing the crossword, her tongue between her teeth—my father, mowing the lawn on a Sunday, humming tunelessly. I would have given anything to see one of them in this room, just for a moment, just to tell them I was alive and loving them.

But all I could think of was them waiting for my return. And their despair as I didn't arrive. And finally the endless sentence of waiting, waiting without hope, for someone who would never come.

From: Judah Lewis

To: Judah Lewis, Pamela Crew and Alan Blacklock

BCC: [38 recipients]

Sent: Tuesday, 29 September

Subject: Lo—an update

Dear All,

I'm very sorry to be sending this news in an e-mail, but I'm sure you'll understand that these last few days have been very difficult and we've had trouble responding to everyone's concern and enquiries.

Up until now we didn't really have anything concrete to share, and this has resulted in a lot of hurtful speculation on social media. However, we have now received some news. Unfortunately, it's not what we were hoping for, and Lo's parents, Pam and Alan, have asked me to send this update to her close friends and immediate family on behalf of them as well as myself, as some details seem to have been leaked to the press already, and we didn't want anyone to find this out from the Internet.

There is no easy way to say this—early this morning Scotland Yard asked me to identify some photographs they received from the Norwegian police team handling the case. They were photographs of clothes, and the garments are Lo's. I recognized them immediately. The boots in particular are vintage and very distinctive, and unmistakably hers.

We are obviously in pieces at this discovery, but we are holding on and waiting to find out what the police can tell us—this is all we know at present as the body is still in Norway and the Norwegian police have not shared any information on when we may be able to see it. In the meantime we would please ask you to use your discretion in talking to the media—if you have anything to add to the investigation, I can give you the names of the officers at Scotland Yard handling the case at the UK end. We also have a family liaison officer who is helping us deal with media enquiries, but some of the stories that are running are upsetting and untrue and we'd like to ask you all for your help in respecting Lo's privacy.

We are just devastated at this turn of events and trying to come to terms with what it means, so please bear with us, and know that we'll update you as soon as we can.

Judah

PART SEVEN

- CHAPTER 29 -

She didn't come.

The girl didn't come.

The hours ticked past, blurring into one another, and I knew that somewhere on the other side of the metal coffin of the hull people were talking and laughing and eating and drinking, while I lay here unable to do anything except breathe, and count down the seconds, minute by minute, hour by hour. Somewhere outside the sun was rising and falling, the waves were lifting and rocking the hull, and life went on, while I sank into the darkness.

I thought of Anne's body again, floating through the depths of the sea, and I thought with bitterness that she was lucky—at least it had been quick. One moment of suspicion, one blow to the head—and that was it. I was beginning to fear that, for me, there would be no such mercy.

I lay on the bed, hugging my knees to my chest, and I tried not to think about my hunger, about the pains that were gnawing in the pit of my stomach. My last meal had been breakfast on Thursday and I thought at the least it must be late Friday now. I had a raging headache and stomach cramps, and when I stood to use the toilet I felt weak and light-headed.

The nasty little voice in the back of my head spoke, needling. *What do you think it's like to starve to death? Think it's a peaceful way to go?*

I shut my eyes. *One. Two. Three. Breathe in.*

It takes a long time. It'd be quicker if you could manage not to drink. . . .

An image came into my mind—myself, thin and white and cold, curled beneath the threadbare orange blanket.

"I choose not to think about these images," I muttered. "I choose to think about . . ." And then I stopped. What? *What?* None of Barry's tutorials had focused on what happy images to choose when you were being held prisoner by a murderer. Was I supposed to think about my mum? About Judah? About everything I loved and held dear and was about to lose?

"Insert happy image here, you little fucker," I whispered, but the place I was inserting it probably wasn't the one Barry had in mind.

And then I heard a sound in the corridor.

I leaped upright, and the blood rushed from my head so that I almost fell, and only just managed to lower myself to the bunk before my legs buckled beneath me.

Was it her? Or Bullmer?

Oh shit.

I knew I was breathing too fast, I could feel my heart speeding up and the tingling in my muscles, and then my vision began to fragment into little scraps of black and red—

And then everything went black.

"Fuck, fuck, fuck . . ."

One word, over and over, being whispered in a panicked, tearful monotone from somewhere close.

"Oh Jesus, just wake up, will you?"

"Wh—" I managed. The girl gave a kind of teary gasp of relief.

"Shit! Are you okay? You gave me such a scare!"

I opened my eyes, saw her worried face looming over mine. There was a smell of food in the air and my stomach groaned painfully.

"I'm sorry," she said rapidly, helping me to sit up against the steel bunk edge, with a cushion behind my back. I could smell alcohol on her breath, schnapps, or maybe vodka. "I didn't mean to leave you so long, I just . . ."

"S'the day?" I croaked.

"What?"

"Wh . . . what day is it?"

"Saturday. Saturday the twenty-sixth. It's late, nearly midnight. I've brought you some dinner."

She held out a piece of fruit and I snatched it, feeling almost sick with hunger, and tore into it, barely even noticing that it was a pear until the taste exploded in my mouth, almost unbearable in its intensity.

Saturday—nearly Sunday. No wonder I felt so awful. No wonder the hours had seemed to stretch out forever. No wonder my stomach was even now cramping and griping as I gulped down the pear in huge, wolfish chunks. I had been locked up here without food or contact for . . . I tried to do the maths. Thursday morning to Saturday evening. Forty-eight . . . sixty . . . sixty-something hours? Was that really right? My brain hurt. My stomach hurt. *Everything* hurt.

My stomach shifted and cramped again.

"Oh God." I tried to scramble to my feet, my legs weak and shaky. "I think I'm going to be sick."

I stumbled to the tiny en suite, anxiously shadowed by the girl, who put out a hand to steady me as I elbowed my way through the narrow doorway, and then fell to my knees and vomited sourly into the blue-stained pan of the toilet. The girl seemed to feel my wretchedness for she said, almost timidly, "I can get you another one, if you want. But there's some kind of potato thing as well. That might be better for your stomach. The cook called it pittypanny or something. I can't remember."

I didn't reply, just knelt over the bowl, bracing myself for the next heave, but it seemed to be gone, and at last I wiped my mouth and then stood slowly, pulling myself up by the handrail and testing the strength in my legs. Then I walked unsteadily back to the bunk. The cubes of fried potato looked and smelled divine. I picked up a fork and ate, more slowly this time, trying not to gulp the food. The girl watched me as I ate.

"I'm sorry," she said again. "I shouldn't have punished you like that."

I swallowed a mouthful of the tepid, salty potato pieces, feeling the caramelized skin crunch between my back teeth.

"What's your name?" I said at last.

She chewed her lip, looked away, and then sighed.

"I probably shouldn't tell you, but what does it matter? Carrie."

"Carrie." I took another mouthful, rolling the word around as I chewed. "Hi, Carrie."

"Hi," she said, but there was no warmth or life in her voice. She watched me eat for a moment longer and then scooted slowly back across the floor of the cabin and slumped against the opposite wall.

We sat in silence for a while, me eating methodically, trying to pace myself, she watching me. Then she gave a small exclamation, felt in her pocket, and pulled something out.

"I nearly forgot. Here you go." It was a pill, wrapped in a scrap of tissue. I took it, almost wanting to laugh with relief. It seemed pathetically hopeful, the idea that this tiny little white dot could make me feel better about my situation. And yet . . .

"Thanks," I said. I put it on the back of my tongue, took a gulp of the juice on the tray, and swallowed it.

At last the plate was empty, and I realized, as I scraped up the last of the potato, Carrie still watching me from across the room, that it was the first time she had waited while I ate. The thought made me bold enough to try something, maybe something stupid, but the words came out before I could stop them.

"What's going to happen to me?"

She said nothing, only levered herself to her feet, shaking her head slowly and dusting down her cream silk trousers. She was painfully thin, and I wondered, briefly, whether that was all part of the part for impersonating Anne or whether she was naturally that skinny.

"Is he—" I swallowed. I was pushing my luck, but I had to know. "Is he going to kill me?"

She still didn't answer, just picked up the tray and made for the door, but as she turned to pull it shut behind her, I saw there was a tear, welling up, about to spill. She paused for a second, the door almost shut, and I thought for a minute that she was about to say something. But instead, she just shook her head again, sending the tear tracing across her cheek, and then she wiped it away, almost angrily, and the door slammed shut behind her.

After she had gone I stood, holding on to the bunk, steadying myself, and then I saw it, on the floor, another book. This one my copy of *Winnie-the-Pooh.*

Pooh has always been my comfort read, my go-to book in times of stress. It's a book from the time before I started getting afraid, when there were no threats that were not Heffalumps, and I, like Christopher Robin, could conquer the world.

I had almost not packed it. But at the last moment, when I was shoving clothes and shoes into my case, I had seen it there, resting on my night table, and I'd put it in as a kind of protective charm against the stresses of the trip.

For the rest of the night I lay on the bunk with the book open on the pillow beside me, running my fingers over the worn dust cover, but I knew the words by heart, too well perhaps, and somehow they failed to exert their familiar magic. Instead, I found myself running over the conversation with Carrie again and again, and thinking about what lay in wait for me.

There were only two ways I was getting out of here—one was alive and the other was dead, and I knew which way I wanted it to be. In which case my choice was simple: to leave with Carrie's help, or without.

A few days ago, a few hours ago, I would have said unhesitatingly that my only real option was without—after all, she had beaten me, imprisoned me, starved me, even. But after tonight, I wasn't so sure. Her hands as she helped me to sit, the way she had waited as I ate, watching every mouthful, her face full of sadness . . . her eyes as she turned to leave . . . I didn't think she was a killer, not by choice, anyway. And something had happened these last few days that had made her realize that. I thought of the long, nightmarish wait for her to come, the way the hours had ticked past so slowly for me, my hunger growing and growing inexorably. But now, for the first time, I thought that perhaps the hours had been as slow and torturous for her, too, and perhaps she, too, had come face-to-face with something she was not ready for. She must have imagined me down here, growing weaker and weaker, clawing at the door. Until at last her resolve broke and she ran down with a stolen plate of lukewarm food.

What must she have thought when she opened the door and found me slumped on the floor—that she had come too late? That I had collapsed, maybe from hunger, maybe from sheer exhaustion?

And suddenly perhaps she knew—that she couldn't live with another death, not one that she'd caused.

She hadn't wanted me to die, I was utterly certain of that. And I doubted if she could kill me, not if I kept reminding her of the fact that I was here because of her, because I had fought for her and tried to help her.

Bullmer on the other hand . . . Bullmer, who had lived through his wife's chemo, counting her money and planning her death, only to be cheated out of it at the eleventh hour . . .

Yes. Bullmer, I could imagine all too clearly, would kill. And he probably wouldn't lose a single hour of sleep over it.

Where was he? Had he left the ship, establishing an alibi while Carrie starved me to death? I wasn't sure. He had taken good care to isolate himself far away from Anne's death; I couldn't imagine he would allow himself to be implicated in mine.

As I was pondering this, I heard the slow grinding roar of the ship's engine start up. It hummed for a while, and then I felt the whole boat rock and shift, and I knew that we were moving again, out of Bergen harbor, the darkness swallowing the ship as we sailed out into the North Sea.

- CHAPTER 30 -

The engine had stopped again when I woke up, but I could feel the shifting mass of water all around us. I wondered where we were—in the fjords, perhaps. I imagined the walls of dark rock rising up all around us, framing a narrow slip of bleached sky above, and sinking down below into the deep blue sea. I knew that some of the fjords could be more than a kilometer deep—unimaginably deep and cold. A body sunk into those kinds of depths might very easily never be found.

I was just wondering what time it was when there was a knock at the door, and Carrie appeared with a tray of muesli and a mug of coffee.

"I'm sorry it's not more," she said as she put the tray down. "Now that the passengers and crew have all left, it's got harder to take food without making the cook suspicious."

"The crew have left?" The words dismayed me, though I couldn't quite put my finger on why.

"Not all of them," Carrie said. "The captain's still here, along with some of his people. But all the passenger-facing staff have gone into Bergen with Richard for some kind of team-building-review thing."

Richard. So Bullmer wasn't on the boat. Maybe that explained Carrie's change in attitude. With Bullmer gone . . .

I began to eat the muesli, slowly, and as before she sat and watched me, her eyes sad beneath their savagely epilated brows.

"You didn't pluck your eyelashes?" I said between mouthfuls. She shook her head.

"No, I couldn't quite bring myself. My eyelashes are a bit skimpy without mascara anyway, but I thought if anyone noticed, I'd claim they were false."

"Who—"

I stopped. I'd been going to say "Who killed her?" but suddenly I couldn't bring myself to voice that question. I was too scared that it might be Carrie. And anyway, my best hope was in persuading her that she *wasn't* a killer, not reminding her that she'd done it once and could do it again.

"What?" she asked.

"I . . . What did you say, to my relatives, I mean? And the other passengers? Do they think I'm in Trondheim?"

"Yes. I put my wig back on and left the boat with your passport. I picked a time when the stewards were all preparing breakfast and it was a member of the sailing crew on duty at the gangway—lucky you didn't go on the tour of the bridge, you didn't meet any of them. And lucky we've both got dark hair. I don't know what I would have done if you were a blonde—I don't have a blond wig. And then I rejoined the boat as Anne, and hoped they wouldn't notice that Anne got on but had never actually got off."

Lucky. It wasn't the word I'd have chosen. So the paper trail was complete—a record of me leaving the boat and never returning. No wonder no police had turned up to search the vessel.

"What was the plan?" I said quietly. "If I hadn't seen you? What was supposed to happen?"

"I would still have got off at Trondheim," she said bitterly. "But this time as Anne. And then I'd have put my wig on, changed my clothes, drawn on my eyebrows, and disappeared into the crowd as just another anonymous backpacker. The trail would have ended in

Trondheim—an unstable woman, facing death, disappearing without a trace . . . And then, when everything had died down, Richard and I were going to 'meet,' fall in love, publicly this time—do it all over again for the cameras."

"Why did you *do* it, Carrie?" I asked despairingly, and then bit my tongue. Now wasn't the time to antagonize her. I needed to get her on my side and I wasn't going to do that by making her feel accused. But I couldn't hold it in anymore. "I just don't understand."

"Nor do I, sometimes." She put her hands over her face. "It wasn't supposed to *be* like this."

"So tell me," I said. I put my hand out, almost timidly, and let it rest on her knee, and she flinched as though she was expecting to be struck. I realized how frightened she was—how much of that vicious energy had come from terror, not hate.

"Carrie?" I prodded. She looked away and spoke towards the orange curtain, as if she couldn't face me.

"We met at the Magellan," she said. "I was a waitress there while I was trying to make it as an actress. And he—he just swept me off my feet, I suppose. It was like something out of *Fifty Shades*, penniless me, and him, falling in love, showing me this life I'd never dreamed of. . . ."

She stopped, swallowed.

"I knew he was married, of course—he was completely honest about that. So we could never see each other in public, and I couldn't tell anyone about him. Their marriage had been over almost before it started—she was horribly cold and controlling, and they lived separate lives, her in Norway and him in London. He hasn't had an easy life, you know—his mother left when he was a baby, and his father died when he was barely out of school. It seemed so unfair that Anne, the person who should have loved him most of all, couldn't even bear to be with him! But she was dying, and he couldn't bring himself to divorce a woman with just months to live—it seemed too cruel, and he kept talking about afterwards, when she died, when we'd be together . . ." Her voice trailed off, and for a minute I thought that was it, she was going to get up and go, but she started speaking again, the words coming faster now, as if she was unable to stop herself.

"One night he had this idea—he said that I should dress up as his wife and go to the theater, so that we could be out in public together. He gave me one of her kimonos, and I watched a film of her talking, so I knew how to carry myself and how to act, and I hid my hair under a swimming cap, with one of her scarves on top. And we pulled it off—we sat in a box, just the two of us, and drank champagne and, oh, it was amazing. Like a game, fooling everyone.

"We did it once or twice more, only when Anne was passing through London, so people wouldn't be suspicious, and then a few months later he had this idea—it seemed crazy at first, but he's like that, you know? Nothing is impossible—he truly makes you believe that. He said that he had a press trip coming up, that Anne was due to be there for the first night, but that she was getting off the boat late that night and going home to Norway. And he said, what if I stayed on and pretended to be her? He could smuggle me on board, and we could be a *real* couple—together, in public, for a whole week. He promised me I could pull it off, he said that no one on board had actually met her, and he would make sure no one photographed me so there wouldn't be any chance of getting caught afterwards. The boat was stopping in Bergen at the end of the trip, so people would just assume Anne had stayed on for a few extra days, and then I could change into my own clothes on the last day and go home as me. He arranged for one of the other guests not to turn up so there was an empty cabin and he said the only thing—" She stopped. "The only thing was, I'd have to cut my hair, to be convincing. But it seemed . . . it seemed worth it. To be with him."

She swallowed, and when she spoke again, it was more slowly.

"On the first night I was just getting into my clothes as Anne, when Richard came to the cabin. He was beside himself. He said that Anne had found out about the affair and had gone mad, lashing out at him. He'd pushed her away to try to protect himself, and she had stumbled and hit her head on the coffee table. When he tried to revive her he—he found—" She faltered, but carried on. "He found she was dead.

"He didn't know what to do—he said that if there was a police investigation, my presence on board would come out and no one would believe his version of the fight. He said that both of us would be prosecuted, him as a murderer, me as an accessory to a premeditated plot. He said it would come out—the fact that I'd been dressing up as Anne. He said that Cole had a photograph of me in Anne's clothes. He persuaded me—" She stopped again, emotion choking her voice. "He persuaded me the only thing to do was to tip Anne's body overboard and carry on with the plan. If she went missing in Bergen, nothing could be traced back to us. But it wasn't *supposed* to happen like this!"

Objections crowded to the tip of my tongue, screaming to be unleashed. How could Anne have got off the boat on the first night when we weren't due to arrive in Norway until the following day? And how could she get off without her passport, without the crew knowing that she'd left? It didn't make sense—the only explanation was that Richard had never been intending for Anne to walk down that gangplank of her own volition, and Carrie must know that herself. She wasn't stupid. But I'd seen this kind of willful blindness before, women who insisted their boyfriends weren't cheating in the face of all the evidence, people working for horrendous employers who'd persuaded themselves they were just following orders and doing what was necessary. There seemed to be no limit to the capacity of people to believe what they wanted to see, and if Carrie had argued herself into accepting Richard's twisted version of the facts in the face of all logic, she wasn't likely to listen to me.

Instead, I took a deep breath, pushed back the protests clamoring in my head, and asked the question that everything hinged on.

"What's going to happen to me?"

"Fuck!" Carrie stood up, raking her hands across her head so that the headscarf slipped, showing the shaven scalp beneath. "I don't *know*. Stop asking me, please."

"He's going to kill me, Carrie." He was going to kill us both, I was fairly sure of that now, but I wasn't sure if she was ready to hear that. "Please, *please*, you can get us both out of here, you know you can. I'll give evidence—I'll say that you saved me, that—"

"First"—she broke in, face hard—"I'd never betray him. I *love* him. You don't seem to get that. And second, even if I went along with you, I'd end up on a murder charge."

"But if you testified against him—"

"No." She cut me off. "No. That's not going to happen. I love him. And he loves me. I know he does."

She turned away, towards the door, and I knew that it was now or never, that I had to *try* to make her see the truth of what she was involved in, even if she walked away and I ended up starving to death down here in my metal coffin.

"He's going to kill you, Carrie," I spoke to the back of her head as she reached the door. "You know that, right? He's going to kill me, and then kill you. This is your last chance."

"I love him," she said. There was a crack in her voice.

"So much that you helped him kill his wife?"

"I didn't kill her!" she shouted, the anguished cry painfully loud in the cramped space. She stood with her back to me, her hand on the door handle, and her whole narrow body shook, like a child racked by sobs. "She was already dead—at least, that's what he said. He left her body in the cabin in a suitcase, and I wheeled it to cabin ten when you were all at dinner. All I had to do was throw the whole thing over the side while he was playing poker. But . . ."

She stopped, turned back round, slumped to the ground, her head bowed to her knees.

"But what?"

"But the case was incredibly heavy. I think he'd weighted it with something, and I banged it against the doorframe getting it into the suite. The lid sprang open and that's when"—she gave a sob—"oh God, I don't know anymore! Her face—it was all bloody, but just for a second—I—I thought her eyelids fluttered."

"Jesus." I went cold with horror. "You mean—you didn't throw her over alive, did you?"

"I don't know." She buried her face in her hands. Her voice was cracked, high and reedy, with a tremor like someone on the verge of hysteria. "I screamed—I couldn't help it. But I touched the blood on her face, and it was *cold*. If she'd been alive, the blood would have been warm, wouldn't it? I thought perhaps I'd just imagined it, or it was some kind of involuntary movement—they say that happens, don't they? In morgues and stuff. I didn't know what to do—I just shut the case! But I can't have fastened it properly, because when I threw it over the side, the catch burst open and I saw her face—her face in the water— Oh God!"

She stopped, her breath coming fast and choking, but just as I was trying to grapple with the horror of what she might have done, think of what I could possibly say in reply to her confession, she spoke.

"I haven't been able to sleep, ever since, you know? Every night I lie there, thinking about her, thinking about how she could have been alive."

She looked up at me, and for the first time I saw her feelings naked in her eyes—the guilt and fear she'd been trying so desperately to hide ever since that first night.

"This isn't what was supposed to happen," she said brokenly. "She was supposed to die at home, in her own bed—and I—and I—"

"You don't have to do this." I spoke urgently. "Whatever happened with Anne's death, you can stop this now. Can you really live with killing me? One death on your conscience has driven you half-crazy, Carrie. Don't make it two—I'm begging you—for both of us. *Please*, let me go. I won't say anything, I swear. I'll—I'll tell Judah I got off in Trondheim and must have blacked out. No one would believe me anyway! They didn't believe me when I said a body went over the side—why would this be any different?"

I knew why: because of DNA. Fingerprints. Dental records. The traces of Anne's blood that must remain on the glass screen and somewhere in Richard's cabin.

But I didn't say any of that, and Carrie didn't seem to have thought of it. Her panic seemed to have been excised along with her tumbling, spewed-out confession, and her breathing had slowed. Now, her face, as she stared at me, was tearstained but calm, and oddly beautiful now that her hysteria had passed.

"Carrie?" I said timidly, hardly daring to hope.

"I'll think about it," she said. She got to her knees, picked up the tray, and turned for the door. As she did, her foot knocked against the copy of *Winnie-the-Pooh*, and she looked down. Something in her face changed, and she picked it up, riffling the pages with her free hand.

"I loved that book as a kid," she said. I nodded.

"Me too. I must have read it a hundred times. That bit at the end, with the ring of trees . . . it always makes me sob."

"My mum used to call me Tigger," she said. "She used to say, you're like Tigger, you are, no matter how hard you fall, you always bounce back." She gave a shaky laugh and then tossed the book onto the foot of the bunk, making an obvious effort to snap back to practicalities. "Listen, I might not be able to bring you supper tonight. The cook's getting suspicious. I'll do my best, but if I can't, then I'll bring you something extra for breakfast, okay?"

"Okay," I said, and then, moved by some impulse, "thank you."

I thought about it after she left—the stupidity of thanking a woman who was keeping you captive, buying your compliance by withholding food and drugs. Was I developing Stockholm syndrome?

Maybe. Although if I was, she had a considerably more advanced case than I did. Maybe that was closer to the truth—we weren't captor and captive, but two animals in different compartments of the same cage. Hers was just slightly larger.

That day passed agonizingly slowly. After Carrie had left I paced the room, trying to ignore my growing hunger, and my growing fear of what would happen if Carrie didn't face up to the reality of Richard's plan.

I was absolutely certain that he had never intended Carrie to live much beyond establishing Anne's departure at Bergen. When I shut my eyes, pictures rippled in front of them—Anne's face, glassy-eyed with terror as Carrie let the suitcase fall. Carrie, walking innocently along some alleyway in Norway, a figure coming up behind her.

And now me. . . .

To distract myself I thought about home and Jude, until the pages of *Winnie-the-Pooh* blurred in front of me, and the familiar well-worn phrases dissolved into a flood of tears that left me too exhausted to do anything but lie there.

I was just beginning to lose hope of supper, and conclude that Carrie hadn't been able to get any food after all, when there was a sound from the outer door and the noise of rushed footsteps in the corridor outside. I was expecting her to knock, but instead I heard the key in the lock and she flung the door open. It was obvious as soon as she came into the room that she wasn't carrying any food, but all that went out of my head when I saw her panicked expression.

"He's coming," she burst out.

"What?"

"Richard. He's coming back tonight—it was supposed to be tomorrow, but I just got a message, he's coming back tonight."

Tuesday, 29 September

TELEGRAPH WEBSITE

BREAKING NEWS: Second body found in search for missing Briton Laura Blacklock.

PART EIGHT

- CHAPTER 31 -

"He—he's coming back?" My mouth was dry. "What does that mean?"

"What do you think it means? We've got to get you off the boat. They're docking to pick up Richard in about thirty minutes. After that . . ."

She didn't have to say anymore. I swallowed, my tongue sticky against the roof of my mouth.

"I— How . . . ?"

She pulled something out of her pocket and held it up, and for a moment I didn't understand. It was a passport, but not mine: hers.

"It's the only way." She pulled off the headscarf, revealing her shaven head beneath, bristly with regrowth, and then began to strip.

"What are you *doing*?"

"You're going to walk off this boat as Anne and get on a plane as me. Understand?"

"What? You're crazy. Come with me!"

"I can't. How the fuck am I going to explain this to the crew? Here's my friend who's been hiding out in the hold?"

"Tell them! Tell them the truth!"

She shook her head. She was down to her underwear now, shivering in spite of the fuggy heat of the stale air in the cabin.

"And say what? Hi, I'm a total stranger, the woman you think I am got pushed off the boat? No. I have no idea if I can trust any of them. At best he's their employer. At worst . . ."

"So what then?" I was half hysterical. "You'll stay here and let him kill you, too?"

"No. I've got a plan. Just stop arguing and take my clothes." She held them out, a bundle of silks that felt featherlight in my hands when I took them. Her skinniness was shocking, her bones practically poking through her skin, but I couldn't look away. "Now give me yours."

"What?" I looked down at myself, at the stained, sweaty jeans and the T-shirt and hoodie I'd been wearing for almost a week now. "These?"

"Yes. Hurry *up*!" Her voice was edgy. "What size are your feet?"

"Six," I said, my voice muffled as I stripped off my T-shirt.

"Good. Mine, too." She pushed the espadrilles she was wearing towards me and I kicked off my boots and began to peel off my jeans. We were both down to our underwear now, me awkwardly trying to cover myself, she completely focused as she began to pull on my discarded clothes. I pulled the silk tunic over my head, feeling the expensive fabric whisper cool against my skin. She pulled an elastic band off her wrist and handed it silently across.

"What's this for?"

"Pulling back your hair. It's not ideal. You'll have to be *very* careful with the headscarf, but it's the best I can do. We don't have time to shave your head, and in any case, if you're going to skip the country under my passport, it's probably better that you have real hair for passport control. We don't want to give them a reason to look twice at the photo."

"I don't understand. Why can't I just go as me? The police must be looking for me, surely?"

"For starters, Richard has your passport. And he has a lot of friends around here—not just in business, he knows people high up in the Norwegian police force as well. We have to get you far away from him before he puts two and two together. Get out. Get away from the coast. Cross the border into Sweden. And when you do get on a plane, don't fly to London. He'll be expecting that. Go via somewhere else—Paris, maybe."

"You're being ridiculous," I said, but her alarm had infected me. I shoved my feet into the espadrilles, and the passport into the pocket of the kimono. Carrie was zipping up my vintage leather boots. I felt a faint pang of regret—those boots were the single most expensive piece of clothing I owned. It had taken me weeks, and a fair amount of encouragement from Judah, to pluck up the courage to shell out for them. But the boots felt like a small sacrifice in exchange—potentially—for my life.

At last we were almost fully dressed—just the headscarf lay on the bunk between us.

"Sit," Carrie said brusquely, and I sat on the edge of the bunk while she stood beside me and swathed the beautiful printed scarf around my head. It was green and gold, blazoned with a pattern of intertwined ropes and anchors, and I had a sudden, distracting flash of Anne—the real Anne—floating down into the blue-green depths, her white limbs tangling in the detritus of a thousand wrecks, caught forever.

"There you go," Carrie said at last. She slid in a couple of pins, holding the edge of the scarf in place, and then looked at me critically, up and down. "It's not perfect—you're not thin enough—but you'll pass in poor light. Thank God I've not met most of the sailing crew."

She looked at her watch and then said, "Right. Last thing. Hit me."

"What?" Her words made no sense. Hit her with what?

"Hit me. Hit my head against the bunk."

"What?" I was starting to sound like an echo—but I couldn't help it. "Are you crazy? I'm not going to hit you!"

"*Hit me,*" she said furiously. "Don't you get it? This has to be convincing. This is my only chance of Richard believing I wasn't in on it. It has to look like you attacked me, overpowered me. *Hit me.*"

I took a deep breath and slapped her on the cheek. Her head whipped back, but it wasn't hard enough, I could tell it wasn't, even as she looked sourly round at me, rubbing her cheek.

"Oh, for Christ's sake. Do I have to do everything?"

She took a deep breath, and then, before I realized quite what she was about to do, she smacked her head into the side of the bunk.

I screamed. I couldn't help it. Blood started welling from the shallow cut the metal edge had made, dripping down her—my—white T-shirt and puddling on the floor. She staggered back, gasping in pain and holding her hands to her skull.

"*Jesus!*" she whimpered. "Fucking hell, that hurt. Oh God." She fell to her knees, her breath coming short and sharp, and for a second I thought she was about to faint.

"Carrie!" I said in panic, dropping to my knees beside her. "Carrie, are you—"

"Don't kneel in it, you stupid bitch!" she screamed, pushing my hand away. "Do you want to ruin everything? You can't have blood on your clothes! What the hell would the crew say? Oh Christ, oh God, why won't it stop bleeding?"

I got awkwardly to my feet, half tripping on the trailing kimono, and for a moment I just stood there, trembling. Then I came to my senses and ran to the bathroom to get a thick wad of tissue.

"Here you go." My voice shook. She looked up, ruefully, and then took the tissue and pressed it to the cut. Then she sank back onto the bunk, her face gray.

"Wh-what should I do?" I asked. "Can I help you?"

"No. The only thing that can help me is if Richard believes you beat me up so badly I couldn't have stopped you. Hopefully this'll do the job. Now get out," she said hoarsely. "Before he comes back and this is all for nothing."

"Carrie, I— What can I do?"

"Two things," she said, her teeth gritted against the pain. "First, give me twenty-four hours before you go to the police. Okay?"

I nodded. It wasn't what I'd meant, but I felt I couldn't refuse her that, at least.

"Second, *get the fuck out*." She groaned. Her face was now so white that I was frightened, but there was a fierce determination in her expression. "You tried to helped me, didn't you? That's what got you in this mess. Now this is the only thing I can do to help you. So don't make it a waste of my time. Get the fuck out!"

"Thank you," I croaked. She didn't say anything, just waved a hand towards the corridor. As I got to the door, she spoke.

"The key to the suite's in your pocket. You'll find about five thousand kroner in a purse on the dressing table. It's a mixture of Norwegian, Danish, and Swedish, but there's nearly five hundred pounds' worth, I think. Take the whole thing—it's got credit cards and ID. I don't know the PIN for the cards—they're not mine, they're Anne's, but you might find somewhere that'll let you sign. You'll have to ask someone to lower the gangway so you can get off the boat—unless they've already got it out for Richard. Tell them that he just phoned and you're going to meet him en route."

"Okay," I whispered.

"Change your clothes, and get away from the port as soon as you can. That's it." She shut her eyes and lay back. The chunk of paper pressed to her temple was already soaked with red. "Oh, and lock me in when you go."

"Lock you in? Are you sure?"

"Yes, I'm sure. It has to be convincing."

"But what if he doesn't come and find you?"

"He will." Her voice was flat. "It's the first thing he'll do if he finds me missing. He'll come and check on you."

"Okay . . ." I said reluctantly. "Wh-what's the PIN for the door?"

"The door?" She opened tired eyes. "What door?"

"You said there was a second locked door outside this one. With a PIN panel."

"I lied," she said wearily. "There's no door. I just said that so you wouldn't jump me. Just keep climbing."

"I— Thank you, Carrie."

"Don't thank me." Her eyes were closed again. "Just pull this off—for both of us. And don't look back."

"Okay." I moved towards her, I don't know why—to hug her, maybe. But her chest was spattered with fresh blood, with more coming from the wound at her temple. And she was right—bloodstains on my gown wouldn't help anyone, least of all her.

It was the hardest thing I'd ever done—turning my back on a woman who looked like she was bleeding to death, all because of me. But I knew what I had to do—for both of us.

"Good-bye, Carrie," I said. She didn't answer. I fled.

The corridor outside was narrow and hot as hell, even hotter than the stuffy little cabin I had left. There was a heavy clasp across the door, drilled roughly into the plastic, and a thick padlock with a key sticking out of it. I snapped it across, swallowing against the guilt that was constricting my throat, and then hesitated, my fingers over the key. Should I take it? I left it. I didn't want Carrie to spend a moment longer in there than she had to.

The cabin door was at one end of the drab beige corridor. At the other was a door marked NO ENTRY—AUTHORIZED CREW ONLY and then, past that, a flight of stairs. I took one stricken look back at the locked cabin door, behind which Carrie lay bleeding, and then I ran for the stairs and began to climb.

Up and up I climbed, my heart beating in my chest, my legs shaky with disuse. Up the service stairs, drably carpeted and edged with metal. I felt my hand slip with sweat on the plastic banister, and in my mind's eye I saw the dazzling glare of the Great Staircase, the glint of crystal, the feel of the polished mahogany rail beneath my fingers, smooth as silk. I felt a laugh bubble up inside me, as irrational as the time I giggled through my grandmother's funeral, my fear and fright turning to a kind of hysteria.

I shook my head and pushed on, up the next flight, past doors marked MAINTENANCE and STAFF ONLY.

I kept climbing, until I reached a huge steel door with a bar on the inside, like a fire escape. I stood for a moment, panting from the long climb, feeling the cold sweat pooling at the base of my spine. What was on the other side?

Behind me lay Carrie, curled on the bunk in that airless coffin of a room. My stomach turned, and I forced myself to put that picture out of my mind and focus, coldly and deliberately, on the steps that lay ahead. I had to get out—and then as soon as I was safe I could . . . but what? Call the police, in defiance of Carrie's request?

As I stood there, my hand on the door, I had a searing flashback to that night in my flat—to cowering inside my own bedroom, too scared to open the door and confront whatever—whoever—was on the other side. Perhaps it would have been better if I'd kicked down the locked door, burst out and confronted him, even if it meant being beaten bloody. I could be in the hospital right now, recovering, Judah at my side, not trapped in this waking nightmare.

Well, the door wasn't locked now.

I shoved my hand against the release and pushed it open.

- CHAPTER 32 -

The light. It hit me like a slap, leaving me blinking and dizzy, gaping at the rainbow prisms of a thousand Swarovski crystals. The service door led directly out onto the Great Staircase, where the chandelier blazed, day and night, a giant "fuck you!" to economy and restraint and global warming, not to mention good taste.

I steadied myself on the polished wooden handrail and looked left and right. There was a mirror at the turning point of the stairs, throwing back the reflected glare of the chandelier, multiplying the dancing light again and again, and as I turned I caught sight of myself in it and for a moment I did a double take, my heart leaping into my throat—for there in the glass was Anne, her head swathed in gold and green, her eyes hunted and bruised.

I looked like what I was—a fugitive. I forced myself to stand up straighter, and walk slowly, in spite of wanting to scurry like a terrified rat.

Hurry, hurry, hurry, snarled the voice in the back of my head. *Bullmer's coming. Get a move on!* But I kept my pace slow and steady, remembering Anne's—Carrie's—stately walk, the way she measured each pace like someone conserving their strength. I was heading towards the front of the ship, where cabin 1 was, and in my pocket my fingers closed over the cabin key, feeling its reassuring hardness under my sweaty fingers.

And then I came to a dead end, stairs leading up to the restaurant, no way through into the prow. *Fuck.* I had taken a wrong turn.

I turned back, trying to remember the route I had taken when I went to see Anne—Carrie—that night before Trondheim. God, was it really only last week? It felt like an age, a different life. Wait—it was supposed to be right at the library, not left. Wasn't it?

Hurry, for God's sake, hurry!

But I kept my pace steady, kept my head up, trying not to look back, not to imagine the hands snatching at my flowing silk robes, dragging me back down below. I turned right, then left, then past a storeroom. This looked right. I was sure I remembered the photograph of the glacier.

Another turn—and another dead end, with stairs leading up to the sundeck. I wanted to sob. Where were the fucking *signs*? Were people supposed to find cabins by telepathy? Or was the Nobel Suite deliberately hidden away so that the hoi polloi couldn't bother the VIPs?

I bent over, my hands on my knees, feeling my muscles trembling beneath the silk, and I breathed slowly, trying to make myself believe I could do this. I would not be still wandering the halls, sobbing, when Richard came up the gangplank.

Breathe in. . . . One. . . . Two. . . . Barry's soothing voice in my head gave me a surge of anger, enough to propel me upright, set me walking again. Stick it, Barry. Stick your positive thinking somewhere painful.

I was back at the library, and I tried again, this time turning left at the storeroom. And suddenly I was there. The door to the cabin was ahead of me.

I felt in my pocket for the key, feeling the adrenaline zipping up and down every neuron in my body. What if Richard was already back?

Don't be the loser cowering behind the door again, Lo. You can do this.

I shoved the key in the door and opened it, faster than fast, ready to drop and run if there was someone in the room.

But there was not. It was empty, the doors to the bathroom and adjoining bedroom standing wide.

My legs gave way, and I sank to my knees on the thick carpet, something very close to sobs rising in my throat. But I wasn't home and dry. I wasn't even halfway there. Purse. Purse, money, coat, and then off this horrible boat forever.

I closed the door behind me, stripped the kimono off, hurrying now that there was no one to see my feverish movements, and in my bra and knickers searched through Anne's drawers. The first trousers I tried were jeans, and impossibly tight, I couldn't get them halfway up my thighs, but I found a pair of Lycra sports leggings I could get into, and an anonymous black top. Then I put the kimono back on over the top, belted it tight, and adjusted the headscarf in the mirror where it had slipped.

I wished I could wear dark glasses, but glancing out the window I saw it was pitch-black—and the clock on Anne's bedside table said quarter past eleven. Oh God, Richard would be back any minute.

I pushed my feet back into Carrie's espadrilles, and then looked around for the purse she had described. There was nothing on the immaculately polished dressing table, but I opened a couple of the drawers at random, wondering if the maid might have put it away for safekeeping. The first drawer was empty. The second I tried had a clump of patterned headscarves, and I was about to close it again, when I noticed there seemed to be something beneath the pile of soft silks, a hard, flat shape among the gossamer-thin wraps. I pushed them aside—and my breath caught in my throat.

Nestled beneath was a handgun. I had never seen one in real life before, and I froze, half expecting it to go off without even being touched, questions clamoring at the back of my skull. Should I take it? Was it loaded? Was it *real*? Stupid question—I doubted anyone would bother to keep a replica handgun in their cabin.

As for whether I should take it . . . I tried to imagine myself pointing a gun at someone, and failed. No, I couldn't take it. Not least because I had no idea how to use it and was more likely to shoot myself than anyone else, but more because I *had* to get the police to believe and trust me, and turning up to a station with a stolen, loaded gun in my pocket was the best way to ensure I was locked up, not listened to.

Half reluctantly, I pulled the scarves back over the gun, shut the drawer, and resumed looking for the purse.

I found it at last in the third drawer down, a brown leather wallet, rather worn, laid carefully on top of a file of papers. Inside were half a dozen credit cards and a wad of bills—I didn't have time to count them, but they looked like easily the five thousand kroner Carrie had mentioned, maybe more. I slid it into the pocket of the leggings, beneath the kimono, and then took one last look round the room, ready to leave. Everything was as I'd found it, except for the purse. It was time to go.

I took a deep breath, readying myself, and then opened the door. And as I did so, I heard voices in the corridor. For a minute I wavered, wondering whether to brazen it out. But then one of the voices said, with a touch of flirtation, "Of course, sir, anything I can do to ensure your satisfaction. . . ."

I didn't wait to hear any more. I shut the door with a stealthy click, dimmed the lights, and stood in the darkness with my back to the solid wood, my heart going a mile a minute. My fingers were cold and prickly, and my legs felt weak, but it was my heart—my heart, racing crazily out of control, a panicked stampede of a beat—that threatened to overwhelm me. Fuck fuck fuck, I couldn't have a panic attack now!

Breathe, Laura. One. . . . Two. . . .

Shut the fuck up! I had no idea whether the scream was inside my head, but somehow, with a huge effort, I managed to peel myself away from the door and stumble to the veranda. The door slid open, and I was outside, the cold of the September night shocking against skin that hadn't felt fresh air for days.

I stood for a moment, my back to the glass, feeling my pulse in my temples and my throat, and my heart banging against my ribs, and then I took a deep breath and edged to one side, to where the veranda curved around the corner of the boat. I was out of sight of the window now, my back to the cold steel hull of the boat, but I saw the flash of light as the door to the corridor opened, and then the lamps in the cabin itself blazed on, illuminating the glass wall of the veranda. *Don't come out; don't come out,* I prayed, as I cowered in the corner of the veranda, waiting for the click and slide of the glass. But nothing happened.

I could see the reflection of the room in the glass barrier. The image was cut in half where the glass ended at rib height, and the reflection was jumbled with ghosts thrown up by the double and triple layers of glass. But I could see a man in the room, moving around. The dark silhouette of his shape moved off in the direction of the bathroom and I heard the noise of taps and the flush of a toilet, then the television came on, its blue-white flicker instantly recognizable in the glass. Above its sound, I heard the noise of a phone call, and Anne's name, and I held my breath. Was he asking about Carrie's whereabouts? How long before he went looking?

The phone call seemed to end, or at least he stopped talking, and I saw his shape move again as he threw himself onto the white expanse of the bed, a dark sprawl across its bright rectangle.

I waited, growing colder now, shifting from foot to foot to try to keep myself even a little warm, but not daring to move too much for fear he would see the movement reflected back at him from the same barrier I was using to spy on him. The night was unbelievably beautiful, and for the first time since I had come out here, I looked around.

We were deep inside one of the fjords, the rocky sides of the valley rising up all around us, the waters beneath black and still and unfathomably dark and deep. Far across the fjord I could see the lights of small settlements, and the lanterns of boats moored out on the still waters, but the overriding thing was the stars—clear and white and almost unbearably lovely. I thought of Carrie, down below, trapped and bleeding like an animal in a snare. . . . Please, dear God, let her be found. I couldn't bear it if something happened to her. I would be responsible for locking her down there, leaving her to her crazy plan.

I waited, shivering helplessly now, for Richard to fall asleep. But he did not. At least he dimmed the lights slightly, but the television continued to blast away, the flickering images turning the room shades of blue and green, with sudden cuts to black. I shifted my weight again, pushing my chilly hands beneath my arms. What if he fell asleep in front of the TV? Would I know? But even if he did fall asleep, properly and deeply, I was not sure if I could summon up the courage to enter the room with a murderer, tiptoe through it while his sleeping form lay there just inches away.

What was the alternative, then? Wait until he went in search of Carrie?

And then I heard something, something that made my heart seem to stop, and then stutter back to life, twice as fast. The boat's engine was starting up.

Panic washed over me like a cold sea wave and I tried to think—we weren't moving yet. There was a chance the gangway was still down. I would have heard it being raised. I remembered from when we set out from Hull that the engine had hummed and thrummed for a good long time before we actually departed. But it was a ticking clock. How long did I have? Half an hour? A quarter? Perhaps less, given there were no passengers on board, no reason to hang about.

I stood there, frozen in agonized indecision. Should I make a run for it? Was Richard asleep? I couldn't tell from the reflection in the balcony barrier—it was too blurred and indistinct.

Craning my head and moving as stealthily as I dared, I peered around the edge of the veranda door and into the silent room—but just as I did, he shifted and reached for a glass, and I whipped my head back, my heart thumping.

Fuck. It must be one a.m. Why wasn't he asleep? Was he waiting for Carrie? But I had to get off the ship. I *had* to.

I thought of the veranda windows, how they could be opened from the outside, how someone very brave—or very stupid—might scale the high glass wall between the verandas and gain entry to an empty cabin. Once inside I could just let myself out of cabin 2 and then make a break for the gangway. I didn't care what story I had to spin when I got there. Somehow I would get off this boat, if not for me, then for Anne, and Carrie. No—fuck it.

For *me.*

I was getting off this boat for me—because I had done nothing to deserve this apart from being in the wrong place at the wrong time, and I was damned if Bullmer was going to add me to the list of women he had screwed over.

I looked down at myself, at the flowing, slippery lines of the kimono, impossible to climb in, and I untied the belt and shrugged off the soft silk. It fell to the floor with barely a whisper, and I picked it up, balled up the fabric as tight as I could, and then tossed it over the privacy screen, where it landed with a soft, barely perceptible *flump.*

Then I looked up at the glass screen, towering above me, and swallowed.

I was never going to be able to climb the privacy screen itself, that was clear. At least not without some serious equipment and/or a ladder. But the barrier over the sea—that I probably could climb. It was rib height, and I was flexible enough to get one leg up and over and pull myself to sit astride it, and from there I could use the privacy screen to stand up.

There was just one problem. It was over the sea.

I'm not phobic about water—at least, I never used to be. But as I looked over the edge at the dark waves, sucking hungrily at the ship's prow, I felt my stomach shift and roll in a way not unlike seasickness.

Shit. Was I really going to do this? Apparently, yes.

I wiped my sweaty palms on the back of the Lycra leggings and took a deep breath. It wouldn't be easy—I wasn't fooling myself. But it *was* possible. Carrie had done it, after all, to get into my cabin. If she could do it, so could I.

I flexed my fingers, and then very slowly I hooked one leg up onto the glass overlooking the sea, and using all the strength in my weak caged-hen muscles, I pulled myself up so I was sitting astride the wall of glass. To the left of me was the cabin, its curtains pulled back, the veranda doors framing me in full view for anyone who turned their head to see. To my right was a sheer drop to the waters of the fjord below—I had no idea how far, but from this angle it looked like the equivalent of a two- or three-story house. I was not sure which side was more frightening—I just had to hope that my movements didn't attract Richard's attention. I swallowed and gripped the slippery glass with my legs, trying to get my courage up for the next step. I hadn't done the hard bit yet. That was coming.

Shaking with fear and exertion, I got one foot up in front of me, and I gripped the edge of the frosted privacy screen and hauled myself to standing. Now, all I had to do was edge my body weight out, round the seaward side of the privacy glass, and swing myself to safety on the other side.

All. Yeah. Right.

I took a deep breath, feeling my cold, sweaty fingers slip on the glass. There was no bloody *purchase*. Every other part of this boat was pimped up, couldn't they have spared a little bling for the privacy glass? Just a few rhinestones, some fancy etching, *something* to give my fingers an edge to hang on to?

I put one foot out, edging it round the high wall of glass . . . and I instantly knew the espadrilles had been a mistake.

I had left them on, thinking that something to protect my feet and give me extra purchase on the glass would be no bad thing, but as my weight swung out over the water, I felt the sole of my supporting foot slip against the sharp edge.

I gasped, and my fingers tightened desperately on the glass in front of me. If sheer willpower could have held me steady, I would have made it. I felt one nail break, then two—and then the glass seemed to be pulled out from between my scrabbling hands with a suddenness that left me unable to do anything—even scream.

I felt the wind against my cheek for a brief, terrifying instant, my hair flapping in the darkness, my hands still clutching at the air—I was falling, falling backwards towards the fathomless waters of the fjord.

I hit the blackness of the sea with a sound like a gunshot, a fierce, smacking blow that knocked all the breath from my lungs.

I felt the air bubbling from my lungs as I plummeted through the stone-cold chill, I felt the icy water strike through to my bones, and as I plunged deeper into fathomless black, I felt a silky current rise from far below me, grip my feet, and pull.

- CHAPTER 33 -

I didn't scream. I didn't have time. I was twenty, thirty, forty feet down in icy black water before I had time to draw a breath.

I don't remember what I felt as I fell—only the bone-cracking smack as I hit the sea, and the paralyzing cold of the water. But I do remember the gut-churning panic as the current seized me, deep, deep below.

Kick, I told my legs, feeling the breath sob in my throat. And I kicked. In the black and the cold, I kicked, first because I didn't want to die, and then as the black cold began to grip, because there was nothing else I could do, because my lungs were screaming and I knew that if I didn't break the surface soon, I would be dead.

The current pulled and tugged at my legs with slippery fingers, trying to drag me deep into the darkness of the fjord, and I kicked and kicked with increasing desperation and despair. In the dark, with the swirling currents of the fjord all around, it was almost impossible to tell which way was up. What if I was driving myself further into the depths? And yet, I didn't dare stop. The instinct to survive was too strong. *You're dying!* shouted a voice in the back of my head. And my legs had no other response except to kick, and kick, and kick.

I shut my eyes against the salt sting, and against my closed lids lights began to spark and shimmer, terrifyingly close to the shards of light and dark that fragmented my vision when I had a panic attack.

But amazingly, unbelievably, when I opened my eyes again, I could see something. A pale, luminous shimmer of the moonlight on water.

For a second I almost didn't believe it, but it was coming closer . . . and closer, and the tug of the current on my body was loosening, and then I broke the surface with a breath that sounded closer to a scream, water streaming down my face, coughing and sobbing, and coughing again.

I was very close to the hull of the ship, close enough to feel the throb of the engines like a pulse through the water, and I knew that I had to start swimming. Not just because it was totally possible to die of hypothermia in really not-very-cold seas, but more urgently because if the ship started moving while I was this close, nothing short of divine intervention would save me, and I'd had bad luck enough these past few days to make me think that if there was a God up there, he didn't like me very much.

Shivering, I trod water and tried to get my bearings. I had surfaced at the front of the boat, and I could see the string of lights at the quayside and what I thought might be the dark shape of a ladder, although my streaming eyes made it hard to be sure.

It was hard to make my body obey; I was shaking so convulsively that I could barely control my limbs, but I forced my arms and legs to start moving, and gradually I began to swim towards the lights, coughing against the waves that slapped my face, feeling the chill of the water striking through to my bones, forcing myself to breathe slowly and deeply, though every part of my body wanted to gasp and pant at the physical assault of the cold. Something soft and yet solid bumped against my face as I swam, and I shuddered, but it was more with cold than revulsion. I could worry about dead rats and decaying fish when I got to shore. Right now, the only thing I cared about was surviving.

I could not have fallen in more than twenty or thirty yards from the quay, but now it seemed to be much farther. I swam and swam, and at times I could swear the lights of the shore were getting farther away, and other times they seemed almost close enough to grasp—but at last I felt the rusted iron of the ladder bang against my numb fingers, and I was climbing and slipping and slipping and climbing up the ladder, trying not to shiver loose my grip as I hauled my wet and shuddering bones up the rungs.

At the edge of the quay I collapsed onto the concrete, gasping and coughing and shaking, and then I got to my hands and knees and looked up, first at the *Aurora* and then towards the little town in front of me.

It wasn't Bergen. I had no idea where we were, but it was a small town, barely even a village, and this late at night there was not a soul about. The smattering of cafés and bars that lined the quayside were all closed. There were a few lights in shop windows, but the only establishment I could see that looked as if I might stand a chance of finding someone to open the door was a hotel overlooking the quay.

Trembling, I got to my feet, lurched over the low chain that fenced off the sheer drop to the sea, and half walked, half staggered across the quayside towards the hotel. The *Aurora*'s engine had picked up a notch, and there was an urgency to it now. As I crossed the seemingly endless concrete apron of the quay, it rose again in pitch, and there was the sound of sloshing water, and as I glanced fearfully behind me, I saw the boat begin to pull slowly away, its prow pointing out into the fjord, its motors grinding and thrumming as it inched slowly away from the shore.

I looked quickly away, filled with a kind of superstition, as if just turning to look at the boat could attract the attention of the people on board.

As I reached the steps up to the hotel door, the sound of the engine picked up, and I felt my legs give way as I banged, banged, banged on the door. I heard a voice saying "Please, please, oh please somebody come . . ." And then the door opened and the light and warmth flooded out, and I felt myself helped upright and over the threshold to safety.

Some half hour later I was huddled in a wicker armchair, wrapped in a synthetic red blanket, in the dimly lit, glassed-in terrace overlooking the bay. I had a cup of coffee in my hands, but I was too tired to drink it, and I could hear voices in the background, speaking in . . . Norwegian, I supposed it must be. I was overwhelmingly tired. I felt as if I hadn't slept properly in days—which perhaps I hadn't, and my chin kept nodding onto my chest and then jerking back up as I remembered where I was, and what I'd escaped from. Had it been real, that nightmare of the beautiful boat, with its coffin-like cell, far beneath the waves? Or was this all one long hallucination?

I was half dozing and half watching the still black lights of the bay, the *Aurora* a distant speck far up the fjord, moving west, when I heard a voice over my shoulder.

"Miss?"

I looked up. It was a man wearing a slightly skewed name tag reading ERIK FOSSUM—GENERAL MANAGER. He looked as if he had been dragged from his bed, his hair rumpled and his shirt buttons awry, and he passed a hand over an unshaven chin as he sat down in the armchair opposite me.

"Hello," I said, wearily. I'd gone through my story with the man at the desk—at least as much of it as I thought safe to give, and as much as his English would permit. He was obviously the night porter, and he looked and sounded more Spanish or Turkish than Norwegian, although his Norwegian seemed to be better than his English, which was fine when it came to stock phrases about checking in and opening hours, but not up to a garbled tale of mixed identity and police.

I had seen him showing the only ID I had with me—Anne's—to the manager, and heard his low, guarded tones, and heard my own name repeated several times.

Now the man sitting opposite me folded his fingers and smiled, slightly nervously.

"Miss—Black Lock, is that right?" He pronounced it as two words. I nodded.

"I don't completely understand—my night manager tried to explain—how do you have Anne Bullmer's credit cards? We know Anne and Richard well; they stay here sometimes. Are you a friend?"

I put my hands over my face, as if I could press back the tiredness that was threatening to overwhelm me.

"I—it's a really long story. Please, can I use your phone? I have to contact the police."

I had made up my mind as I hung, dripping and exhausted, over the polished check-in desk. In spite of my promise to Carrie, this was my only chance to save her. I didn't for one second believe that Richard would let her live. She knew too much, had screwed too much up. And without the headscarf I had no chance of passing myself off as Anne, and without Carrie's passport I had no chance of posing as Carrie, and both were lost somewhere in the bay, fathoms down. Only Anne's purse had survived, miraculously still in the pocket of the Lycra stretch pants as I crawled up the ladder, out of the water.

"Of course," Erik said sympathetically. "Would you like me to phone them? They may not have an English speaker on duty at this time of night. I must warn you, we don't have a police station in the town, the nearest one is a few hours away in the next . . . what's the word. The next valley. It will probably be tomorrow before someone can come out."

"Please tell them it's urgent, though," I said wearily. "The sooner, the better. I can pay for a bed. I have money."

"Let's not worry about that," he said with a smile. "Can I get you another drink?"

"No. No, thanks. Just please tell them to come *soon*. Someone's life could be in danger."

I let my head rest, heavy on my hand, my eyelids almost closing as he went back to the front desk, and I heard the sound of a phone receiver being lifted, and the *beep-beep-beep-beep . . . beep-beep-beep* of a number being dialed. It sounded like a long one. Maybe the Norwegian number for 999 was different? Or perhaps he was calling the local station.

It rang. Someone at the other end picked up and there was a brief exchange. Through the haze of exhaustion I heard Erik saying something in Norwegian out of which I could only pick the word *hotel* . . . then a pause and then another burst of Norwegian. Then I heard my own name, given twice, and then Anne's.

"*Ja, din kone, Anne*," Erik said, as if the person on the other end had not heard correctly, or had not believed what he'd heard. Then more in Norwegian, and then a laugh, and finally. "*Takk, farvel, Richard*."

My head jerked up from my supporting hand, and every part of me went suddenly cold and still.

I looked out to the ships in the bay, to the *Aurora*, its lights disappearing in the far, far distance. And . . . was it my imagination? It looked as if the ship had stopped.

I sat for a moment longer, watching its lights, trying to measure them against the landmarks of the bay, and at last I was almost sure. The *Aurora* was no longer moving west up the fjord. It was turning around. It was coming back.

Erik had hung up, and was dialing another number now.

"*Politiet, takk*," he said as someone answered.

For a moment I couldn't move, frozen with the realization of what I'd done. I hadn't believed Carrie's assertions about Richard's web of influence, not really. I'd dismissed them as the paranoia of a woman too beaten down to believe in the possibility of escape. But now . . . now those fears seemed all too real.

I set the coffee cup gently down on the table, let the red blanket fall to the floor, and, very quietly, I opened the terrace door and slipped outside, into the night.

- CHAPTER 34 -

I ran, up through the winding streets of the little town, my breath tearing in my chest, stones cutting into my bare feet and making me wince with pain. The streets petered out, and the streetlights began to disappear, but I ran on in the dark and the cold, stumbling through invisible puddles and over wet grass and graveled paths, until my feet grew too numb for me to even feel the cuts and the stones.

Even then I kept going—desperate to put as many miles as possible between myself and Richard Bullmer. I knew that I could not keep this up, that at some point I was going to have to give in—but my only hope was to keep going as long as possible, until I found myself some kind of shelter.

Finally, I could not run anymore. I let myself drop back to a kind of gasping, limping jog, and then as the lights of the village grew smaller in the distance, I slowed to a walk, a painful, stumbling walk, along a winding dark road that twisted into the darkness, climbing up the side of the fjord. Every few hundred yards I looked back over my shoulder, down into the valley, to the shrinking speckle of lights of the little portside town, and to the dark slick of the fjord waters, where the lights of the *Aurora* were coming closer. They were unmistakable now. I could see the ship clearly, and I could see, too, light beginning to tinge the sky above me.

Dawn must be coming already—God, what day did that make it? Monday?

But something seemed wrong, and after a few minutes I realized what it was. The lights were not to the east but to the north. What I could see was not dawn but the eerie green and gold streaks of the northern lights.

The realization made me laugh—a bitter, mirthless choke that sounded shockingly loud in the still night air. What was it Richard had said? Everyone should see the northern lights before they died. Well, now I had. But it just didn't seem that important anymore.

I had stopped for a moment, watching the shifting glory of the aurora borealis, but now at the thought of Richard I began walking again. With each step, I remembered Carrie's frantic exhortations to get running and get out—her hysterical assertions about the reach of Richard's influence.

It didn't seem so hysterical now.

If *only* I had believed her—I should never have shown Anne's ID at the hotel, or trusted Erik with even the few details I'd given him. But I just hadn't quite believed that anyone, however wealthy, could have the kind of reach Carrie believed. Now I realized I was wrong.

I groaned, at my own stupidity, at the cold that was striking through my thin, damp clothes. Most of all at the fact that I'd left the wallet on the desk. Stupid, stupid, stupid. That was five thousand wet, soggy, but still usable kroner, and I'd left them there for Richard as a little golden hello when he turned up at the hotel. What was I going to do? I had no ID, nowhere to sleep, no means of buying so much as a bar of chocolate, let alone a train ticket. My best hope was finding a police station, but how? Where? And did I dare tell them the truth when I got there?

I was just considering this when I heard the roar of an engine behind me and turned to see a car coming round the bend, frighteningly fast, clearly not expecting anyone to be out here at this time of night.

I scrambled for the verge, lost my footing, and fell, sliding down a length of scree that left me bloodied and scraped, my leggings in tatters, and came to a halt with a splash in a pebbly ditch that seemed to be some kind of stream or drainage channel down to the fjord below. The car itself had screeched to a halt on the road some five or six feet above me, the headlamps pointing out into the valley, and the smoke from the exhaust billowing red in the rear lights.

I heard the crunch of feet on the road above. Richard? One of his men? I *had* to get away.

I tried to stand on my ankle, felt it give, and then tried again, more carefully this time, but the pain made me give a sob.

At the sound, a figure, lit from behind so that I could see his shape only in silhouette, peered over the edge of the road, and a voice said something in Norwegian. I shook my head. My hands were trembling.

"I d-don't speak Norwegian." I tried to keep the sob out of my voice. "Do you sp-speak English?"

"Yes, I speak English," the man said in a heavily accented voice. "Give me your hand. I will help you out."

I hesitated, but there was no way I could get out of the ditch without help, and if the man really intended to hurt me he could just as easily climb down here and attack me in the shelter of the ditch. Better to get out, where I could at least run if I had to.

The lights of the car shone in my eyes, blinding me, and I put my hand up, shielding them against the glare, but all I could see was a dark shape, and a halo of blond hair beneath some kind of cap. It wasn't Richard, at least, that I was sure of.

"Give me your hand," the man said again, with a touch of impatience this time. "Are you hurt?"

"No, I'm n-not hurt," I said. "At least, my ankle hurts, but I don't think it's broken."

"Put the leg there." He pointed at a rock about a foot out of the ditch, "and I will pull you up."

I nodded, and with a feeling that I might be doing something very stupid, I set my good foot to the rock and leaned upward with my right hand.

I felt the man grab hold of my wrist, his grip immensely strong, and with a grunt he began to pull, bracing himself against a rock at the edge of the ditch. The muscles and sinews in my arm were screaming in protest, and when I tried to put my weight on my bad foot, I cried out, but at last, with a painful, scrambling rush, I was up and out of the ditch, and standing trembling on the edge of the verge.

"What are you doing out here?" the man said. I couldn't see his face, but there was concern in his voice. "Are you lost? Have you had an accident? This road leads directly up the mountain, it's no place for a tourist."

I was trying to think of how to answer, when I realized two things.

The first was that he was carrying something in a holster at his hip, the shape of it silhouetted against the car lights. And the second was that the car itself was a police car. As I stood there, frozen, trying to think what to say, I heard the crackle of a radio pierce the night.

"I—" I managed.

The policeman took a step forward, tipping his cap so that he could see me more clearly, and frowned.

"What is your name, Miss?"

"I—" I said, and then stopped.

There was another crackle from his radio and he held up a finger.

"One moment, please." He put his hand to his hip, and I saw that what I had taken for a gun was actually a police radio in a holster, hanging next to a pair of handcuffs. He spoke briefly into the receiver and then climbed into the driver's side of the car and began a longer conversation on the car radio.

"*Ja*," I heard, and then a burst of conversation I didn't understand. Then he looked up at me through the windscreen, and his eyes met mine, his gaze puzzled. "*Ja*," he said again, "*det er riktig*. Laura Blacklock."

Everything seemed to slow down, and I knew with a cold certainty that it was now, or not at all. If I ran now, I might be making a mistake. But if I didn't, I might not live to find out, and I could not afford to take that risk.

I hesitated for just one second more, and then I saw the policeman replace the radio receiver and reach for something in his glove compartment.

I had no idea what to do. But I had not believed Carrie before, and it had nearly cost me everything.

Screwing my courage for the pain I knew was coming, I began to run—not up the road as before but down, cross-country, scrambling headlong down the vertiginous side of the fjord.

- CHAPTER 35 -

It was growing light when I realized that I could go no farther, that my muscles, exhausted beyond endurance, just simply would not obey me. I was no longer walking, I was stumbling as if I were drunk, my knees buckling when I tried to climb over a fallen tree stump.

I had to stop. If I didn't, I would fall where I stood, so deep in the Norwegian countryside that my body might never be found.

I needed shelter, but I had left the road a long time back, and there were no houses to be seen. I had no phone. No money. I didn't even know what time it was, although it must be close to dawn.

A sob rose in my dry throat, but just at that moment, I saw something loom from between the sparse trees—a long, low shape. Not a house—but some kind of barn, perhaps?

The sight gave my legs a last shot of energy, and I staggered out from between the trees, across a dirt track, through a gate in a wire fence. It *was* a barn—although the name seemed almost too grand for the shack that lay in front of me, with its rickety wooden walls and corrugated iron roof.

Two shaggy little horses turned their heads curiously as I trudged past, and then one of them returned to drinking from what I saw, with a leap of my heart, was a trough of water, its surface pink and gold in the soft dawn light.

I staggered to the trough, falling on my knees in the short grass beside it, and cupping the water in my hands I drank great gulps of it down. It was rainwater, and it tasted of mud and dirt and rust from the metal trough, but I didn't care. I was too thirsty to think about anything except slaking my parched throat.

When I'd drunk as much as I could, I straightened up and looked around me. The shed door was shut, but as I put my hand to the latch, it swung open and I went cautiously through, shutting the door behind me.

Inside there was hay—bales and bales of it—some tubs that I thought might be feed or supplements, and, hanging on the wall on pegs, a couple of horse blankets.

Slowly, drunk with weariness, I pulled the first one down and laid it over the deepest pile of hay—not even thinking about rats or fleas, or even Richard's men. There was surely no way they could find me here, and I had got to the stage where I almost didn't care—if they would just let me rest, they could take me away.

Then I lay down on the makeshift bed and drew the other blanket over the top of me.

And then I slept.

"H*allo?*" The voice in my head spoke again, painfully loud, and I opened my eyes to a blinding light, and a face gazing into mine. An elderly man with a full white beard and a strong resemblance to Captain Birdseye was peering at me with rheumy hazel eyes, and a mix of surprise and concern.

I blinked and scrambled backwards, my heart thudding painfully, and then tried to get to my feet, but my ankle gave a wrench of pain and I stumbled. The man took my arm, saying something in Norwegian, but without thinking I jerked it savagely out of his grip, and fell back onto the floor of the barn.

For a few minutes we just looked at each other, him taking in my scrapes and cuts, me looking at his lined face and the dog barking and circling behind him.

"*Kom*," he said at last, getting painfully to his knees and holding out his hand with cautious calm, as if I were a wounded animal that might snap at any provocation, and not a human at all. The dog barked again, hysterically this time, and the man shouted something over his shoulder that was clearly *quiet, you!* or something to that effect.

"Who—" I licked dry lips and tried again. "Who are you? Where am I?"

"Konrad Horst," the man said, pointing at himself. He pulled out his wallet and flicked through until he found a photo of an elderly lady with rosy cheeks and a bun of white hair, cuddling two blond-haired little boys.

"*Min kone*," he said, enunciating slowly. And then, pointing to the children, something that sounded like "*Vorry bon-bon*."

Then he pointed out of the barn door at an extremely elderly Volvo standing outside.

"*Bilen min*," he said, and again, "*Kom*."

I didn't know what to do. There *was* something reassuring about the photos of his wife and grandchildren—but even rapists and killers had grandkids, right? On the other hand, maybe he was just a nice old man. Maybe his wife would speak English. At the very least they'd likely have a phone.

I looked down at my ankle. I didn't have much choice. It had swollen to twice its usual size, and I wasn't sure I could even hobble as far as the car, let alone make it to an airport.

Captain Birdseye held out his arm and made a little gesture.

"*Pleese?*" he rumbled interrogatively, as if giving me a choice. But it was an illusion. I had no choice.

I let him help me to my feet, and I got into the car.

• • •

It was only as we drove that I realized quite how far I had run the night before. You couldn't even see the fjord from this wooded fold of the hillside, and the Volvo must have jolted down several miles of rutted track before we reached the semblance of a road.

We were turning onto the tarmac when I noticed something in the little well beneath the radio—a mobile phone. It was very, very ancient, but it was a phone.

I put out my hand, hardly able to breathe.

"May I?"

Captain Birdseye looked across, and then grinned. He put the phone in my lap but then tapped the screen, saying something in Norwegian. As soon as I looked at the phone, I realized what he was saying. There was no reception at all.

"*Vente*," he said loudly and clearly, and then slowly, in what sounded like heavily accented English, "Wait."

I held the phone in my lap, watching the screen with a lump in my throat as the trees flashed past. But something didn't make sense. The date on the phone showed the twenty-ninth of September. Either I was miscounting, or I had lost a day.

"This," I pointed at the date on the phone. "Today, is it really the twenty-ninth?"

Captain Birdseye glanced at the screen and then nodded.

"*Ja, tjueniende*. Toos-day," he said, enunciating the word very slowly, but he didn't need to. The pronunciation was close enough to the English for me to be in no doubt about what he was saying. Tuesday. Today was *Tuesday*. I had been asleep in that little hut for a full day and a night.

I was just computing that, and trying not to think about how worried Judah and my parents must be, when we turned into the driveway of a neat little blue-painted house, and something flickered in the corner of the phone's screen—a single bar of reception.

"Please?" I held it up, my heart suddenly beating so hard in my throat that the words felt choked and strange in my mouth. "Can I call my family in England?"

Konrad Horst said something in Norwegian that I didn't understand, but he was nodding, and so, with fingers that shook so hard I could hardly find the right keys, I pressed +44 and dialed the number of Judah's mobile phone.

- CHAPTER 36 -

We said nothing for the longest time, either of us. We just stood in the middle of the airport like two fools, holding each other, Judah touching my face and my hair and the bruises on my cheek like he truly couldn't believe it was me. I suppose I was probably doing the same to him, I can't remember.

All I could think was *I'm home. I'm home. I'm home.*

"I can't believe it," Judah kept saying. "You're okay."

And then the tears started, and I began to cry into the harsh scratchy wool of his jacket, and he didn't say anything at all, just held me like he'd never let me go.

At first I hadn't wanted the Horsts to call the police, but I couldn't make them understand that, and after I'd spoken to Judah and he had promised to call Scotland Yard with my story—a story so improbable that I almost didn't believe it myself—I began to accept that not even Richard Bullmer could buy his way out of this one.

When the police arrived, they took me to a health center first, to get treatment for my cut feet and wrenched ankle and to have my medication represcribed. It seemed to take forever, but at last the doctors pronounced me fit enough to leave, and the next thing I knew, I was being driven to a police station up the valley, where an official from the British Embassy in Oslo was waiting.

Again and again I found myself reciting the story of Anne, and Richard and Carrie, and each time it sounded more and more implausible to my own ears.

"You have to help her," I kept saying. "Carrie—you have to go after the boat."

The official and the police officer exchanged a look, and the policeman said something in Norwegian. I knew, suddenly, that whatever it was they were holding back, it was not good news.

"What?" I asked. "What is it? What's wrong?"

"The police have found two bodies," the embassy official said at last, his voice awkward and formal. "The first in the early hours of Monday morning, dredged up by a fishing boat, the second later on Monday, recovered by police divers."

I put my head in my hands, grinding my fingers into my eyes, watching the pressure build and bloom as flames and sparks on the insides of my lids. I drew a deep breath.

"Tell me." I looked up. "I have to know."

"The body recovered by divers was a man," the embassy official said slowly. "He had been shot through the temple, the police believe it may have been a self-inflicted wound. He had no ID on him, but they are presuming it to be the body of Richard Bullmer. He was reported missing from the *Aurora* by the crew."

"And . . ." I swallowed. "And the other?"

"The other was a woman, very slim, with shorn hair. The police will have to conduct a postmortem, but the preliminary findings are that she was drowned. Miss Blacklock?" He looked around, nervously, as if unsure what to do. "Are you all right, Miss Blacklock? Can someone get her a tissue, please? Please don't cry, Miss Blacklock, you're all right now."

But I couldn't speak. And the worst of it was that he was right, I *was* all right, but Carrie was not.

It should have been a comfort that Bullmer had killed himself, but I couldn't find any. I just sat there, crying into the tissue they gave me, and thinking of Carrie and everything she'd done to me and for me. Whatever the rights and wrongs, she had paid with her life. I hadn't been fast enough to save her.

- CHAPTER 37 -

The taxi from the airport took us back to Judah's. We didn't discuss it, exactly, but somehow I couldn't face my basement flat. I'd had enough of being shut up in lightless rooms, and Judah seemed to realize that.

In his living room he tucked me up on the couch with a blanket, as if I were a small child, or someone recovering from an illness, and he kissed me very gently on my forehead, like I might break.

"I can't believe you're home," he said again. "When they showed me your boots in that photo . . ."

His eyes welled up, and I felt my own throat scratch with tears.

"She took them," I said croakily. "So I could pretend to be her. She—"

But I couldn't finish.

Judah held me for a long time, and then when he could speak he swallowed and said, "You—you've got a lot of messages, you know. People have been calling me because your voice mail got full. I've been writing them down."

He felt in his pocket, and handed me a list, and I scanned down it. Most of them were names I would have expected . . . Lissie . . . Rowan . . . Emma . . . Jenn . . . One or two were a surprise.

Tina West said one, in Judah's handwriting. *Very relieved you're safe. No need to call back.*

Chloe Yansen (I assumed that was Judah's phonetic spelling of Jenssen.) *Hopes you're okay. Please call if there is anything she or Lars can do.*

Ben Howard. No message.

"God, Ben." I felt a stab of guilt. "I'm surprised he's speaking to me. I more or less accused him of being behind all this. Did he really call?"

"That's not the half of it," Judah said, and I saw him wipe his eyes surreptitiously on his T-shirt. "He was the one who raised the alarm. He called me from Bergen trying to find out if you'd made it home okay, and when I said I hadn't heard from you since Sunday, he told me to call the UK police and tell them it was a matter of urgency. He said he'd been raising hell since Trondheim and no one on the crew would listen to him."

"Don't make me feel worse." I put my hands over my face.

"Hey, he's still a self-important little shit," Judah said. He gave me his endearing smile, and I saw with a pang that his tooth had re-rooted. "And he did give a pretty crappy interview to the *Mail*, which made it sound like you two had barely just broken up."

"Okay," I said, with a slightly shaky laugh. "That makes me feel a bit better about accusing him of murder."

"Look, do you want a cup of tea?"

I nodded, and he got up and made his way to the kitchen. I took a handful of tissues out of a box on the coffee table and wiped my eyes, then picked up the remote control and turned on the television, trying for some semblance of normality.

I was just scrolling through the channels, looking for something reassuring and familiar—a *Friends* rerun, maybe, or *How I Met Your Mother*—when I stopped dead, my heart in my mouth.

My eyes were fixed on the television screen—at the man staring out at me.

It was Bullmer.

His eyes were locked onto mine, his mouth quirked in that asymmetric smile, and for a second I thought I might be hallucinating. I drew a breath, ready to scream for Judah, ask him if he could see the face staring out of the screen at me like a nightmare—but then the screen cut back to a newsreader, and I realized what was happening. It was a report of Bullmer's death.

". . . breaking news of the death of British businessman and peer Lord Richard Bullmer. Lord Bullmer, who was the majority shareholder in the troubled Northern Lights Group, has been found dead after being reported missing just hours earlier from his luxury yacht the *Aurora* off the coast of Norway."

The screen cut again, this time to Richard standing on a podium as he gave some kind of address.

His lips were moving, but his speech was muted, so that the newsreader could carry on narrating the story over the top of the images, and as the camera zoomed in on his face, I found myself turning down the volume, leaving the couch and kneeling in front of the TV, my face just inches from his.

When the talk came to an end, Richard bowed, and the camera went close up on his face, and he looked straight out of the screen and gave me his characteristic little wink—so that my stomach turned, and my skin crawled.

I picked up the remote with shaking hands, ready to exorcise him from my life once and for all, when the camera panned, and I saw a woman seated in the front row, smiling and applauding, and I paused, my finger hovering over the off button. She was extraordinarily beautiful, with a long river of dark gold hair and broad cheekbones, and for a moment I couldn't think where I had seen her before. And then . . . I realized.

She was Anne. Anne as she had been before Richard was through with her, young and beautiful and alive.

As she applauded, she seemed suddenly to realize that the cameras were on her, and her eyes flickered towards the lens, and I saw something there, although whether it was my imagination or not, it was hard to tell. It seemed to me that there was something sad in her expression, something a little trapped and afraid. But then she smiled more broadly and put her chin up, and I saw that this was a woman who would never capitulate, never give way, a woman who would fight to the last.

Then the picture changed and we were back in the newsroom, and I turned off the screen and went back to the couch. I drew the blanket over me and turned my face to the wall, listening to Judah making tea in the next room . . . thinking.

The clock on Judah's bedside table showed gone midnight. We were lying together, his chest molding to my spine, his arm around me, holding me close, as if he didn't trust me not to disappear in the night.

I had waited until I thought he was asleep before I let myself cry, but when a particularly big sob shook my ribs, he spoke, soft and low against my ear.

"Are you okay?"

"I thought you were asleep." My voice came out cracked and hoarse with tears.

"Are you crying?"

I wanted to deny it, but my throat had closed up and I couldn't speak, and anyway, I'd had enough of lies and pretending.

I nodded, and he put his hand up, feeling the wetness on my cheeks.

"Oh, honey." I heard the movement of his throat as he swallowed. "It'll be . . . you don't have to . . ."

He stopped, unable to continue.

"I can't stop thinking about her," I said against the ache in my throat. It was easier not looking at him, speaking to the quiet darkness and the slivers of moonlight across the floor. "I can't accept it; it's all wrong."

"Because he killed himself?" Judah asked.

"Not just that. Anne. And . . . and Carrie."

Judah said nothing, but I knew what he was thinking.

"Say it," I said bitterly. He sighed, and I felt his chest rise and fall against my spine, his breath warm against my cheek.

"I probably shouldn't say this, but I can't help but feel . . . glad."

I twisted round under the sheets to look at him, and he held up a hand.

"I know, I know it's wrong, but what she did to you . . . honestly, if it had been up to me, I wouldn't have dredged her out. I'd have left her there for the fishes. It's probably a good thing it wasn't my decision."

I felt anger rise up inside me, anger on behalf of Carrie, beaten and bullied and lied to.

"She died because of me," I said. "She didn't have to let me go."

"Bullshit. You were only there because of her. She didn't have to kill a woman and lock you up."

"You don't know that. You don't know what goes on in other people's relationships."

I thought of Carrie's terror, of the bruises on her body, of her belief that she would never escape Richard. She had been right. Judah said nothing, and I could not see his expression in the dark, but I felt his silent disagreement.

"What," I demanded, "you don't believe me? You don't think people can be sucked into doing something out of fear, or inability to see any other way out?"

"No, it's not that," Judah said slowly. "I believe that. But I still think, in spite of it all, we're responsible for our own actions. We all get scared. But you can't tell me that you'd do that to another person, no matter how tough things seemed—lock them up like that, imprison them—no matter how scared you were."

"I don't know," I said. I thought of Carrie, of how brave she had been, and how fragile. I thought of the masks she wore to hide the terror and loneliness inside. I thought of the bruise on her collarbone, and the fear in her eyes. I thought of how she had given up everything for me.

"Listen." I sat up and wrapped the sheet around me. "That job you were talking about, before I left. The one in New York. Did you turn it down?"

"Yes, I mean, well, no . . . I'm going to. I haven't called them yet. After you went missing, it kind of slipped my mind. Why?" Judah's voice was suddenly uneasy.

"Because I don't think you should. I think you should take it."

"What?" He sat up, too, and a shaft of moonlight fell across his face, showing me an expression full of shock, anger. For a minute he didn't seem to know what to say, then the words came pouring out. "What the *hell*? Why? Where has this come from?"

"Well, this is a chance in a lifetime, right? It's the post you've always wanted." I twisted the sheet around my fingers, cutting off the blood until they went numb and cold. "And let's face it, there's nothing holding you here, is there?"

"Nothing holding me here?" I heard him swallow, saw his fists clench and unclench against the white sheets. "I have *everything* holding me here, at least I thought I did. I—am—are you breaking up with me?"

"What?" Now it was my turn for shock. I shook my head and took his hands, rubbing my fingers across the sinews and the bones of his knuckles, hands that I knew by heart. *Fuck*. "Jude, no. Not in a million years. I'm saying—I'm trying to ask . . . Let's go. Together."

"But—but *Velocity*—your job. Rowan's maternity cover. This is your big chance. I can't screw that up for you."

"It's not my big chance." I sighed. I slid down beneath the sheets, still holding Judah's hands in mine. "I realized that when I was on the boat. I've spent, what, nearly ten years working at *Velocity*, while Ben and everyone else took risks, went on to bigger and better stuff, and I didn't. I was too scared. And I felt like I owed *Velocity* for standing by me when things were bad. But Rowan's never going to leave—she'll be back in six months, maybe less, and I've got nowhere to go. And the truth is, even if I did pull myself up the ladder, it's not what I want anymore. I never wanted it—I realized that on board the boat. God knows I had enough time to think about it."

"What do you mean? It's—ever since we met, it's all you've talked about."

"I think I lost sight of what I wanted. I don't want to end up like Tina and Alexander, traveling from country to country and only seeing five-star hotels and Michelin restaurants. Yes, Rowan's been to half the luxury resorts in the Caribbean, but in return she spends her life reporting the stories that people like Bullmer want her to tell, and I don't want that, not anymore. I want to write about the things people *don't* want you to know. And if I'm going to start pulling my way up from the bottom again, well, I can freelance from anywhere. You know that."

A thought came to me, and I let out a shaky, involuntary laugh.

"I could write a book! *My Floating Prison: True-Life Hell on the Seven Seas*."

"Lo." Judah took my hands, his eyes wide and dark in the moonlight, and painfully beseeching. "Lo, stop, stop joking. Are you serious about this?"

I took a deep breath. Then I nodded.

"I've never been more serious in my life."

Afterwards, Judah lay in my arms, his head in the crook of my shoulder in a way that I knew would give me a cramp eventually, but I couldn't bear to pull away.

"Are you awake?" I whispered. He didn't answer for a moment, and I thought that he had fallen asleep, in that way he had of slipping out of consciousness between one breath and the next, but then he stirred, and spoke.

"Just."

"I can't sleep."

"Shh . . ." He rolled over in my arms, touching my face. "It's okay, it's all over."

"It's not that . . . it's . . ."

"Are you still thinking about her?"

I nodded in the darkness, and he sighed.

"When you saw her body," I started, but he shook his head.

"I didn't."

"What do you mean? I thought the police sent you photographs to identify?"

"It wasn't a body—I wish it *had* been, if I'd seen it was Carrie's corpse, not yours, I wouldn't have spent two days in hell, thinking you were dead. It was just clothes. Photographs of clothes."

"Why did they do that?" It seemed an odd decision—why ask Judah to identify the clothes, and not the body?

I felt Judah's shoulders lift in the darkness in a shrug.

"I don't know. At the time I assumed it was because the body was too bashed up, but I spoke to the FLO in charge of the case after you called—I wanted to find out how the hell they could have got it so wrong—and she spoke to the Norwegians and seemed to think it was because the clothes were found separately."

Huh. I lay there, trying to puzzle it out. Had Carrie kicked off the boots and hoodie to try and swim for it, in a desperate attempt to get away from Bullmer?

I was almost afraid to go to sleep, expecting to be haunted by Carrie's reproachful face, but when I finally closed my eyes it was Bullmer's face that rose up in front of me, laughing, his black hair riffled by the wind as he tumbled down, down from the deck of the *Aurora*.

I opened my eyes, my heart thumping, trying to remember that he was gone—that I was safe, that Judah was lying in my arms and the whole nightmare was over and done with.

But it wasn't. Because I just didn't believe what had happened.

It wasn't just Carrie's death that I couldn't accept—it was Bullmer's. Not because I thought he should have lived, but because his death, out of all of it, just didn't make *sense.* Carrie's suicide I could have believed, but not his. Try as I might, I couldn't imagine that man, with his cold, fierce determination, giving up. He had fought so hard, played his cards with such cold daring. Would he really throw in his hand, just like that? It didn't seem possible.

But it was. And I had to accept that. He was gone.

I shut my eyes again, pushing his specter away from me, and I curled my body around Judah's, and I thought, very deliberately, about the future, about New York, and about the leap of faith I was about to make.

For a moment I saw a sharp, flashing image imprinted on the darkness of my closed lids: myself poised on the very edge of a high, high place, balancing on a rail, the dark waves below.

But I had no fear. I had fallen before, and I'd survived.

STANDARD

Thursday, 26 November

MYSTERY WOMAN IN AURORA DROWNING IDENTIFIED

Almost two months after the shocking discovery of two bodies at sea, one of them British businessman and peer Richard Bullmer, Norwegian police have today released a statement announcing the identity of the body dredged up by fishermen in the North Sea to be that of his wife, Anne Bullmer, heiress to the billion-pound Lyngstad fortune.

The body of Lord Bullmer was found several hundred miles away by police divers searching the coastal waters near Bergen, in Norway, after the peer was reported missing from his boat, the exclusive boutique cruise liner the *Aurora*.

NOT SUICIDE

The English-language statement confirms the previous announcement by Norwegian police that the cause of Lady Bullmer's death was drowning, while Lord Bullmer's death was due to a gunshot wound to the temple. However, the document contradicts earlier reports of Lord Bullmer's suicide, stating simply that the injury was "not self-inflicted," according to the findings of the local pathologist.

The discovery of a gun, recovered alongside Lord Bullmer's body and wrapped in clothing belonging to missing British journalist Laura Blacklock, led to initial allegations that his death was connected to her disappearance some days before.

Miss Blacklock was later found alive and well in Norway, but her parents have called for a police inquiry after they were left for several days believing that the body had been identified as that of their missing daughter. Scotland Yard stressed that the body had never at any stage been identified as Miss Blacklock, but admitted that the finding of Miss Blacklock's clothes had been "poorly communicated" to the family. They blamed the failings on "cross-force communication issues" with the Norwegian police handling the case, and have said that they are in private contact with the Blacklock family over the incident.

In answer to the *Standard*'s inquiry, a Norwegian police spokesperson stated that although they have interviewed Miss Blacklock in connection with the case, they are not considering the Briton as a suspect in either death, and that their investigations are continuing.

BANKING LIVE CHAT

6 DECEMBER, 4:15

Hi, welcome to our online customer services live chat.

You are speaking with Ajesh from online personal banking.

How can I help you today, Miss Blacklock?

Hi, I'm e-mailing because I've received an odd credit to my account. I wanted to check if you had any info on the sender. Thanks. Lo.

Hi, Miss Blacklock, sure, I can look into that.

Is it okay if I call you Laura?

Yep, that's fine.

What is the transaction you are concerned about, Laura?

It's the one two days ago, dated 4 Dec., for 40,000 Swiss francs.

Let me check that for you.

I have your details here—is it the transaction with the reference "Tiggers bounce"?

Yes, that's correct.

I have checked the sort code, it's a Swiss bank account based in Bern. I'm sorry to say I do not have any information on the identity of the bank account holder. It is a numbered account.

Does the reference convey anything?

It's fine, thanks. No worries. I'm pretty sure it's from a friend, I just wanted to check.

Thanks for looking into it.

You're welcome. Is there anything else I can help you with today, Laura?

No, that's fine. Thanks. And good-bye.

ACKNOWLEDGMENTS

Many thanks to all the people who have helped me along the road with *The Woman in Cabin 10.* Writing is an odd, solitary pursuit, but publishing is most definitely a team sport, and I am very grateful to have such dedicated, funny, and downright nice people involved with my book at Scout in the United States and Harvill in the United Kingdom.

First thanks must go to the two Alisons, Alison Hennessey and Alison Callahan, for being tactful, insightful, and fearless editors, and generally proving that three brains are most definitely better than one.

Also at Scout Press, I must thank Nina Cordes, Meagan Harris, Jen Bergstrom, Liz Psaltis, Melanie Mitzman, Carolyn Reidy, Louise Burke, Wendy Sheanin, Erica Nelson, Jennifer Robinson, and everyone else at Simon & Schuster who has helped to bring *The Woman in Cabin 10* to the public—you make me very proud to be a Scout author.

My agent, Eve White, and her team always have my back, and I am always astounded by and grateful for the generosity of the brilliant community of crime writers, online and off.

My friends and family know how much I love them, so I won't repeat it here—but I do!

Turn the page for an exclusive sneak peek of Ruth Ware's third novel

THE LYING GAME

Coming July 2017 from Scout Press

The Reach is wide and quiet this morning, the pale blue sky streaked with pink mackerel-belly clouds, the shallow sea barely rippling in the slight breeze, and so the sound of the dog barking breaks into the calm like gunshots, setting flocks of gulls crying and wheeling in the air.

Plovers and terns explode up as the dog bounds joyously down the river bank, scampering down the runnelled side, where the earth turns from spiky grassy dunes to reed-specked mud, where the water wavers between salt and fresh.

In the distance the Tide Mill stands sentinel, black and battered against the cool calm of the morning sky, the only man-made structure in a landscape slowly crumbling back into the sea.

"Bob!" The woman's voice rings out above the volley of barks as she pants to catch up. "Bob, you rascal. Drop it. Drop it, I say. What've you found?"

As she draws closer, the dog tugs again at the object protruding from the mud, trying to pull it free.

"Bob, you filthy brute, you're covered. Let it go. Oh God, it's not another dead sheep, is it?"

It's the last heroic yank that sends the dog staggering back along the shore, something in its jaw. Triumphant, he scrambles up the bank to lay the object at the feet of his owner.

And as she stands, looking dumbstruck, the dog panting at her feet, the silence returns to the bay like a tide coming in.

RULE ONE

TELL A LIE

The sound is just an ordinary text alert, a quiet *beep beep* in the night that does not wake Owen, and would not have woken me except that I was already awake, lying there, staring into the darkness, the baby at my breast snuffling, not quite feeding, not quite unlatching.

I lie there for a moment thinking about the text, wondering who it could be. Who'd be texting at this hour? None of my friends would be awake . . . unless it's Milly gone into labor already . . . God, it can't be Milly, can it? I'd promised to take Noah if Milly's parents couldn't get up from Devon in time to look after him, but I never really thought . . .

I can't quite reach the phone from where I'm lying, and at last I unlatch Freya with a finger in the corner of her mouth, and rock her gently onto her back, milk-sated, her eyes rolling back in her head like someone stoned. I watch her for a moment, my palm resting lightly on her firm little body, feeling the thrum of her heart in the birdcage of her chest as she settles, and then I turn to check my phone, my own heart quickening slightly like a faint echo of my daughter's.

As I tap in my pin, squinting slightly at the brightness of the screen, I tell myself to stop being silly—it's four weeks until Milly's due, it's probably just a spam text, *Have you considered claiming a refund for your payment protection insurance*?

But, when I get the phone unlocked, it's not Milly. And the text is only three words.

I need you.

It is 3:30 a.m., and I am very, very awake, pacing the cold kitchen floor, biting at my fingernails to try to quell the longing for a cigarette. I haven't touched one for nearly ten years, but the need for one ambushes me at odd moments of stress and fear.

I need you.

I don't need to ask what it means—because I know, just as I know who sent it, even though it's from a number I don't recognize.

Kate.

Kate Atagon.

Just the sound of her name brings her back to me, like a vivid rush—the smell of her soap, the freckles across the bridge of her nose, cinnamon against olive. Kate. Fatima. Thea. And me.

I close my eyes and picture them all, the phone still warm in my pocket, waiting for the texts to come through.

Fatima will be lying asleep beside Ali, curled into his spine. Her reply will come around 6:00 a.m., when she gets up to make breakfast for Nadia and Samir and get them ready for school.

Thea—Thea is harder to picture. If she's working nights she'll be in the casino, where phones are forbidden to staff and shut up in lockers until their shifts are finished. She'll roll off shift at eight in the morning, perhaps? Then she'll have a drink with the other girls, and then she'll reply, wired up with a successful night dealing with punters, collating chips, watching for card sharps and professional gamblers.

And Kate. Kate must be awake—she sent the text, after all. She'll be sitting at her dad's worktable—hers now, I suppose—in the window overlooking the Reach, with the waters turning pale gray in the predawn light, reflecting the clouds and the dark hulk of the Tide Mill. She will be smoking, as she always did. Her eyes will be on the tides, the endlessly shifting, eddying tides, on the view that never changes and yet is never the same from one moment to the next—just like Kate herself.

Her long hair will be drawn back from her face, showing her fine bones, and the lines that thirty-two years of wind and sea have etched at the corners of her eyes. Her fingers will be stained with oil paint, ground into the cuticles, deep beneath the nails, and her eyes will be at their darkest slate blue, deep and unfathomable. She will be waiting for our replies. But she knows what we'll say—what we've always said, whenever we got that text, those three words.

I'm coming.

I'm coming.

I'm coming.

"I'm coming!" I shout it up the stairs, as Owen calls something down above Freya's sleepy squawking cries.

When I get up to the bedroom he's holding her, pacing back and forth, his face still pink and crumpled from the pillow.

"Sorry," he says, stifling a yawn. "I tried to calm her down but she wasn't having any of it. You know what she's like when she's hungry."

I crawl onto the bed and scoot backwards into the pillows until I'm sitting against the headboard, and Owen hands me a red-faced, indignant Freya, who takes one affronted look up at me and then lunges for my breast with a little grunt of satisfaction.

All is quiet, except for her greedy suckling. Owen yawns again, ruffles his hair, and looks at the clock, and then begins pulling on his underwear.

"Are you getting up?" I ask in surprise. He nods.

"I might as well. No point in going back to sleep when I've got to get up at seven anyway. Bloody Mondays."

I look at the clock. Six a.m. It's later than I thought. I must have been pacing the kitchen for longer than I realized.

"What were you doing up, anyway?" he asks. "Did the bin lorry wake you?"

I shake my head.

"No, I just couldn't sleep."

A lie. I'd almost forgotten how they feel on my tongue, slick and sickening. I feel the hard, warm bump of my phone in my dressing gown pocket. I'm waiting for it to vibrate.

"Fair enough." He suppresses another yawn and buttons up his shirt. "Want a coffee, if I put one on?"

"Yeah, sure," I say. Then, just as he's leaving the room, "Owen—"

But he's already gone and he doesn't hear me.

Ten minutes later he comes back with the coffee, and this time I've had time to practice my lines, work out what I'm going to say, and the semi-casual way I'm going to say it. Still I swallow and lick my lips, dry-mouthed with nerves.

"Owen, I got a text from Kate yesterday."

"Kate from work?" He puts the coffee down with a little bump, it slops slightly and I use the sleeve of my dressing gown to mop the puddle, protecting my book, giving me time to reply.

"No, Kate Atagon. You know, I went to school with her?"

"Oh, *that* Kate. The one who brought her dog to that wedding we went to?"

"That's right. Shadow."

I think of him. Shadow—a white German shepherd with a black muzzle and soot-speckled back. I think of the way he stands in the doorway, growls at strangers, rolls his snowy belly up to those he loves.

"So . . . ?" Owen prods, and I realize I've stopped talking, lost my thread.

"Oh, right. So she's invited me to come and stay, and I thought I might go."

"Sounds like a nice idea. When would you go?"

"Like . . . now. She's invited me now."

"And Freya?"

"I'd take her."

Of course, I nearly add, but I don't. Freya has never taken a bottle, in spite of a lot of trying on my part, and Owen's. The one night I went out for a party, she screamed solidly from 7:30 p.m. to 11:58, when I burst through the doors of the flat to snatch her out of Owen's limp, exhausted arms.

There's another silence. Freya leans her head back, watching me with a small frown, and then gives a quiet belch and returns to the serious business of getting fed. I can see thoughts flitting across Owen's face . . . That he'll miss us . . . That he'll have the bed all to himself . . . Lie-ins . . .

"I could get on with decorating the nursery," he says at last. I nod, although this is the continuation of a long discussion between the two of us—Owen would like the bedroom, and me, back to himself and thinks that Freya will be going into her own room imminently, when she turns six months. I . . . don't. Which is partly why I've not found the time to clear the guest room of all our clutter and repaint it in baby-friendly colors.

"Sure," I say.

"Well, go for it, I reckon," Owen says at last. He turns away and begins sorting through his ties. "Do you want the car?" he asks over his shoulder.

"No, it's fine. I'll take the train. Kate will pick me up from the station."

"Are you sure? You won't want to be lugging all Freya's stuff on the train, will you? Is this straight?"

"What?" For a minute I'm not sure what he's on about, and then I realize—the tie. "Oh, yes, it's straight. No, honestly, I'm happy to take the train. It'll be easier; I can feed Freya if she wakes up. I'll just put all her stuff in the bottom of the pram." He doesn't respond, and I realize he's already running through the day ahead, ticking things off a mental checklist just as I used to do a few months ago—only it feels like a different life. "Okay, well, look, I might leave today if that's all right with you."

"Today?" He scoops his change off the chest of drawers and puts it in his pocket, and then comes over to kiss me good-bye on the top of my head. "What's the hurry?"

"No hurry," I lie. I feel my cheeks flush. I hate lying. It used to be fun—until I didn't have a choice. I don't think about it much now, perhaps because I've been doing it for so long, but it's always there, in the background, like a tooth that always aches and suddenly twinges with pain.

Most of all, though, I hate lying to Owen. Somehow I always managed to keep him out of the web, and now he's being drawn in. I think of Kate's text, sitting there on my phone, and it feels as if poison is leaching out of it, into the room—threatening to spoil everything.

"It's just Kate's between projects, so it's a good time for her and . . . well, I'll be back at work in a few months, so it just feels like now's as good a time as any."

"Okay," he says, bemused but not suspicious. "Well, I guess I'd better give you a proper good-bye kiss then."

He kisses me, properly, deeply, making me remember why I love him, why I hate deceiving him. Then he pulls away and kisses Freya.

She swivels her eyes sideways to regard him suspiciously, pausing in her feed for a moment, and then she resumes sucking with the single-minded determination that I love about her.

"Love you, too, little vampire," Owen says affectionately. Then, to me, "How long is the journey?"

"Four hours, maybe? Depends how the connections go."

"Okay, well, have a great time, and text me when you get there. How long do you think you'll stay?"

"A few days?" I hazard. "I'll be back before the weekend." Another lie. I don't know. I have no idea. As long as Kate needs me. "I'll see when I get there."

"Okay," he says again. "Love you."

"I love you, too." And at last, that's something I can tell the truth about.

I can remember to the day, almost to the hour and minute, the first time I met Kate. It was September. I was catching the train to Salten, an early one, so that I could arrive at the school in time for lunch.

"Excuse me!" I called nervously up the station platform, my voice reedy with anxiety. The girl ahead of me turned around. She was very tall and extremely beautiful, with a long, slightly haughty face like a Modigliani painting. Her waist-length black hair had been bleached gold at the tips, fading into the black, and her jeans were ripped across the thighs.

"Yes?"

"Excuse me, is this the train for Salten?" I panted.

She looked me up and down, and I could feel her appraising me, taking in my Salten House uniform, the navy-blue skirt, stiff with newness, and the pristine blazer I had taken off its hanger for the first time that morning.

"I don't know," she said at last, turning to a girl behind her. "Kate, is this the Salten train?"

"Don't be a dick, Thee," the girl said. Her husky voice sounded too old for her—I didn't think she could be more than sixteen or seventeen. She had light brown hair cut very short, framing her face, and when she smiled at me, the nutmeg freckles across her nose crinkled. "Yes, this is the Salten train. Make sure you get into the right half, though; it divides at Hampton's Lee."

Then they turned, and were halfway up the platform before it occurred to me, I hadn't asked which was the right half.

I looked up at the announcement board.

"Use front seven carriages for stations to Salten," read the display, but what did *front* mean? Front as in the closest to the ticket barrier, or front as in the direction of travel when the train left the station?

There were no officials around to ask, but the clock above my head showed only moments to spare, and in the end I got onto the farther end, where the two other girls had headed for, and dragged my heavy trunk after me into the carriage.

It was a compartment, just six seats, and all were empty. Almost as soon as I had slammed the door the guard's whistle sounded, and, with a horrible feeling that I might be in the wrong part of the train completely, I sat down, feeling the scratchy wool of the train seat harsh against my legs.

With a clank and a screech of metal on metal, the train drew out of the dark cavern of the station, the sun flooding the compartment with a suddenness that blinded me. I put my head back on the seat, closing my eyes against the glare, and as we picked up speed I found myself imagining what would happen if I didn't turn up in Salten, where the housemistress would be awaiting me. What if I were swept off to Brighton or Canterbury or somewhere else completely, or worse—what if I ended up split down the middle when the train divided, living two lives, each diverging from the other all the time, growing further and further apart from the me I should have become.

"Hello," said a voice, and my eyes snapped open. "I see you made the train."

It was the tall girl from the platform, the one the other had called Thee. She was standing in the doorway to my compartment, leaning against the wooden frame, twirling an unlit cigarette between her fingers.

"Yes," I said, a little resentful that she and her friend had not waited to explain which end to get. "At least, I hope so. This is the right end for Salten, isn't it?"

"It is," the girl said laconically. She looked me up and down again, tapped her unlit cigarette against the doorframe, and then said, with an air of someone about to confer a favor, "Look, don't think I'm being a bitch, but I just wanted to let you know, people don't wear their uniforms on the train."

"What?"

"They change into them at Hampton's Lee. It's . . . I don't know. It's just a thing. I thought I'd tell you. Only first-years and new girls wear them for the whole journey. It kind of makes you stand out."

"So . . . you're at Salten House, too?"

"Yup. For my sins."

"Thea got expelled," a voice said from behind her, and I saw that the other girl, the short-haired one, was standing in the corridor, balancing two cups of tea. "From three other schools. Salten's her last-chance saloon. Nowhere else would take her."

"At least I'm not a charity case," Thea said, but I could tell from the way she said it that the two were friends, and this goading banter was part of their act. "Kate's father is the art master," she told me. "So a free place for his daughter is all part of the deal."

"No chance of Thea qualifying for charity," Kate said. *Silver spoon*, she mouthed over the top of her teas, and winked. I tried not to smile.

She and Thea shared a look and I felt some wordless question and answer pass between them, and then Thea spoke.

"What's your name?"

"Isa," I said.

"Well, Isa. Why don't you come and join me and Kate?" She raised one eyebrow. "We've got a compartment of our own just up the corridor."

I took a deep breath and, with the feeling that I was about to step off a very high diving board, I gave a short nod. As I picked up my case and followed Thea's retreating back, I had no idea that that one simple action had changed my life forever.

It's strange being back at Victoria. The Salten train is new, with open-plan carriages and automatic doors, not the old-fashioned slam-door thing we used to take to school, but the platform has hardly changed, and I realize that I have spent seventeen years unconsciously avoiding this place—avoiding everything associated with that time.

Balancing my takeaway coffee precariously in one hand, I heave Freya's pram onto the train, put my coffee on an empty table, and then there's the same long, struggling moment there always is, as I attempt to unclip the cot attachment—wrestling with clasps that won't undo and catches that won't let go. Thank God the train is quiet and the carriage almost empty, so I don't have the usual hot embarrassment of people queueing in front or behind, or pushing past in the inadequate space. At last—just as the guard's whistle sounds again, and the train rocks and sighs and begins to heave out of the station—the final clip gives, and Freya's cot jerks up, light in my hands. I stow her safely, still sleeping, opposite the table where I left my coffee.

I take my cup with me when I go back to sort out my bags. There are sharp images in my head—the train jerking, the hot coffee drenching Freya. I know it's irrational—she's on the other side of the aisle. But this is the person I've become since having her. All my fears—the ones that used to flit between dividing trains, and lift doors, and strange taxi drivers, and talking to people I didn't know—all those anxieties have settled to roost on Freya.

At last we're both comfortable, me with my book and my coffee, Freya asleep, with her blankie clutched to her cheek. Her face, in the bright June sunshine, is cherubic—her skin impossibly fine and clear—and I am flooded with a scalding drench of love for her, as painful and shocking as if that coffee had spilled across my heart. I sit, and for a moment I am nothing but her mother, and there is no one in the world except the two of us in this pool of sunshine and love.

And then I realize that my phone is buzzing.

Fatima Chaudhry, reads the screen. And my heart does a little jump.

I open it up, my fingers shaking.

I'm coming, it reads. *Driving down tonight when the kids are in bed. Will be with you 9/10ish.*

So it's begun. Nothing from Thea yet, but I know it will come. The spell has broken—the illusion that it's just me and Freya, off on a seaside holiday for two. I remember why I am really here. I remember what we did.

I'm on the 12:05 from Victoria, I text back to the others. *Pick me up from Salten, Kate?*

No reply, but I know she won't let me down.

I shut my eyes. I put my hand on Freya's chest so I know she is there. And then I try to sleep.

I wake with a shock and a belting heart to the sound of crashing and shunting, and my first instinct is to reach out for Freya. For a minute I am not sure what has woken me but then I realize: the train is dividing; we are at Hampton's Lee. Freya is squirming grumpily in her cot, she looks like she may settle if I'm lucky—but then there's another shunt, more violent than the first set, and her eyes fly open in offended shock, her face crumpling in a sudden wail of annoyance and hunger.

"Shh . . ." I croon, scooping her up, warm and struggling from the cocoon of blankets and toys. "Shh . . . it's okay, sweetie pie. It's all right, my poppet. Nothing to worry about."

She is dark-eyed and angry, bashing her cross little face against my chest as I get my top undone and feel the by-now routine, yet always alien, rush of the milk letting down.

As she feeds, there is another bang and a crunch, and then a whistle blows, and we begin to move slowly out of the station, the platforms giving way to sidings, and then to houses, and then at last to fields and telegraph poles.

It is heart-stoppingly familiar. London, in all the years I've lived there, has been constantly changing. It's like Freya, never the same from one day to the next. A shop opens here; a pub closes there.

Buildings spring up—the Gherkin, the Shard—a supermarket sprawls across a piece of wasteland and apartment blocks seem to seed themselves like mushrooms, thrusting up from damp earth and broken concrete overnight.

But this line, this journey—it hasn't changed at all.

There's the burned-out elm.

There's the crumbling World War II pillbox.

There's the rickety bridge, the train's wheels sounding hollow above the void.

I shut my eyes, and I am back there in the compartment with Kate and Thea, laughing as they pull school skirts on over their jeans, button-up shirts and ties over their summery tops. Thea was wearing stockings; I remember her rolling them up her impossibly long, slender legs, and then reaching up beneath the regulation school skirt to fasten her suspenders. I remember the hot flush that stained my cheeks at the flash of her thigh, and looking away, out across the fields of autumn wheat, with my heart pounding as she laughed at my prudery.

"You'd better hurry," Kate said lazily to Thea. She was dressed, and had packed her jeans and boots away in the case resting on the luggage rack. "We'll be at Westridge soon. There's always piles of beachgoers there; you don't want to give a tourist a heart attack."

Thea only stuck out her tongue, but she finished hooking her suspenders and smoothed down her skirt just as we pulled into Westridge station.

Sure enough, just as Kate had predicted, there was a scattering of tourists on the platform, and Thea let out a groan as the train drew to a halt. Our compartment door was level with a family of three beach-trippers: a mother, a father, and a little boy of about six with his bucket and spade in one hand and a dripping choc ice in the other.

"Room for three more?" the father said jovially as he opened the door and they clambered in, slamming the door behind them. The little compartment felt suddenly very crowded.

"I'm so sorry," Thea said, and she did sound sorry. "We'd love to have you, but my friend here"—she indicated me—"she's out on day release, and part of the terms of her probation is no contact with minors. The court judgment was very specific about that."

The man blinked, and his wife gave a nervous giggle. The boy wasn't listening; he was busy picking bits of chocolate off his T-shirt.

"It's your child I'm thinking of," Thea said seriously. "Plus, of course, Ariadne really *doesn't* want to go back to the young offenders institute."

"There's an empty compartment next door," Kate said, and I could see she was trying to keep her face straight. She stood and opened the door out onto the corridor. "I'm so sorry. We don't want to inconvenience you, but I think it's for the best, for everyone's safety."

The man shot us all a suspicious look and then ushered his wife and little boy out into the corridor.

Thea burst into snorts of laughter as they left, barely waiting even until the compartment door had slid shut, but Kate was shaking her head.

"You do not get a point for that," she said. Her face was twisted with suppressed laughter. "They didn't believe you."

"Oh, come on!" Thea took a cigarette out of a packet in her blazer pocket and lit it, taking a deep drag in defiance of the NO SMOKING sign on the window. "They left, didn't they?"

"Yes, but only because they thought you were a fucking weirdo. That doesn't count!"

"Is . . . is this a game?" I said uncertainly.

There was a long pause.

Thea and Kate looked at each other, and I saw that wordless communication pass between them again, like an electric charge flowing from one to another, as if they were deciding how to answer. And then Kate smiled, a small, almost secretive smile, and leaned forwards across the gap between the bench seats, so close that I could see the dark streaks in her gray-blue eyes.

"It's not *a* game," she said. "It's *the* game. It's the Lying Game."

The Lying Game.

It comes back to me now as sharp and vivid as the smell of the sea, and the scream of gulls over the Reach, and I can't believe that I had almost forgotten it—forgotten the tally sheet Kate kept above her bed, covered with cryptic marks for her elaborate scoring system. This much for a new victim. That much for complete belief. The extras awarded for elaborate detail, or managing to rehook someone who had almost called your bluff. I haven't thought of it for so many years, but in a way, I've been playing it all this time.

I sigh and look down at Freya's peaceful face as she suckles, her complete absorption in the moment of it all. And I don't know if I can do it. I don't know if I can go back.

What has happened, to make Kate call us so suddenly and so urgently in the middle of the night?

I can only think of one thing . . . and I can't bear to believe it.

It is just as the train is drawing into Salten that my phone beeps for the last time, and I draw it out, thinking it will be Kate confirming my lift. But it's not. It's Thea.

I'm coming.

The platform at Salten is almost empty. As the sound of the train dies away, the peace of the countryside rolls back in, and I can hear the noises of Salten in summer—crickets chirping, the sound of birds, the faraway noise of a combine harvester across the fields. Always, before, when I arrived here there would be the Salten House minivan waiting, with its navy and ice-blue livery. Now the car park is hot dust and emptiness, and there is no one here, not even Kate.

I wheel Freya down the platform towards the exit, my heavy bag weighing down one shoulder, and wondering what to do. Phone Kate? I should have confirmed the time with her. I'd been assuming she got my message, but what if her phone was out of charge? There's no landline at the Mill anyway, no other number I can try.

I put the brake on the pram and then pull out my phone to check for text messages and find out the time. I'm just tapping in my code when I hear the roar of an engine, funneled by the sunken lanes, and I turn to see a car pulling into the station car park. I was expecting it to be the huge disreputable Land Rover Kate drove down to Fatima's wedding seven years ago, with its bench seats and Shadow sticking his head out the window, tongue flapping. But it's not. It's a taxi. For a minute I'm not sure if it's her, and then I see her, struggling with the rear passenger door, and my heart does a little flip-flop, and I'm no longer a civil service lawyer and a mother, I'm just a girl, running down the platform towards my friend.

"Kate!"

She's exactly the same. Same slim, bony wrists; same nut-brown hair and honey-colored skin; her nose still tip-tilted and sprinkled with freckles. Her hair is longer now, held back in a rubber band, and there are lines in the fine skin around her eyes and mouth, but otherwise she is Kate, my Kate, and as we hug, I inhale, and her own particular scent of cigarettes and turpentine and soap is just as I remember. I hold her at arm's length and find myself grinning, stupidly, in spite of everything.

"Kate," I repeat foolishly, and she pulls me into another hug, her face in my hair, squeezing me so I can feel her bones.

And then I hear a squawk and I remember who I am, the person I've become—and all that's passed since Kate and I last met.

"Kate," I say again, the sound of her name on my tongue so perfect, "Kate, come and meet my daughter."

I pull back the sunshade and pick up the wriggling, cross little bundle, and hold her out.

Kate takes her, her expression full of trepidation, and then her thin, mobile face breaks into a smile.

"You're beautiful," she says to Freya, and her voice is soft and husky just as I remember. "Just like your mum. She's lovely, Isa."

"Isn't she?" I look at Freya, staring up, bemused, into Kate's face, blue eyes fixed on blue eyes. She reaches out a chubby hand towards Kate's hair but then stops, mesmerized by some quality of the light. "She's got Owen's eyes," I say. I always longed for blue eyes as a child.

"Come on," Kate says at last, speaking to Freya, not me. She takes Freya's hand, her fingers stroking the silken baby pudge, the dimpled knuckles. "Let's get going."

"What happened to your car?" I say as we walk towards the taxi, Kate holding Freya, me pushing the pram, with the bag inside it.

"Oh, it's broken down again. I'll get it fixed but I've got no money, as usual."

"Oh, Kate."

Oh, Kate, when are you going to get a proper job, I could ask. When are you going to sell the Mill, go somewhere people appreciate your work instead of relying on the dwindling supply of tourists who want to holiday in Salten. But I know the answer. Never. Kate will never leave the Tide Mill. Never leave Salten.

"Back to the Mill, ladies?" the taxi driver calls out his window, and Kate nods.

"Thanks, Rick."

"I'll sling the pram in the back for you," he says, getting out. "Folds, does it?"

"Yes." I'm struggling with the clips again, and then I realize. "Damn, I forgot the car seat. I brought the cot attachment instead, I was thinking she could sleep in it."

"Ah, we won't see no police down here," Rick says comfortably, pushing the boot shut on the folded pram. "'Cept Mary's boy, and he's not going to arrest one of my passengers."

It wasn't the police I was worried about, but the name snags at me, distracting me.

"Mary's boy?" I look at Kate. "Not Mark Wren?"

"The very same," Kate says, with a dry smile, so that her mouth creases at one side. "Sergeant Wren, now."

"I can't believe he's old enough!"

"He's only a couple of years younger than us," Kate points out, and I realize she's right. Thirty is plenty old enough to be a policeman. But I can't think of Mark Wren as a thirty-year-old man—I think of him as a fourteen-year-old kid with acne and a fluffy upper lip, stooping to try to hide his six-foot-two frame. I wonder if he still remembers us. If he remembers the Game.

"Sorry," Kate says as we buckle in. "Hold her on your lap—I know it's not ideal."

"I'll drive careful," Rick says, as we bounce off, out of the rutted car park and into the sunken lane. "And besides, it's only a few miles."

"Less across the marsh," Kate says. She squeezes my hand and I know she's thinking of all the times she and I made that trip, picking our way across the salt marsh to school and back. "But we couldn't do that with the buggy."

"Hot for June, in't it?" Rick says conversationally as we round the corner, and the trees break into a flash of bright dappled sunlight, hot on my face. I blink, wondering if I packed my sunglasses.

"Scorching," I say. "It wasn't nearly so warm in London."

"So what brings you back then?" Rick's eyes meet mine in the mirror. "You was at school with Kate, that right?"

"That's right," I say. And then I stop. What did bring me back? A text? Three words? I meet Kate's eyes and I know there's nothing she can say now, not in front of Rick.

"Isa's come down for the reunion," Kate says unexpectedly. "At Salten House."

I blink, and she gives my hand a warning squeeze, but then we bump across the level crossing, the car shaking and bouncing over the rails, and I have to let go to hold Freya with both hands.

"Very posh, them Salten House dinners are, so I hear," Rick says comfortably. "My youngest does a bit of waitressing up there for pocket money, and I hear all sorts. Canapés, champagne, the works."

"So I hear," Kate says. "I've never been to one before, but it's fifteen years since our class graduated, and I thought this year might be the one to go to."

Fifteen? For a minute I think she's got the maths wrong, but then I realize. It's seventeen years since we left, after GCSEs, but if we'd stayed on for sixth form, she'd be right. For the rest of our class it will be their fifteen-year anniversary.

We swing round the corner of the lane and I hold Freya tighter, my heart in my mouth, wishing I'd brought the car seat. It was *stupid* of me not to think of it.

"You come down here much?" Rick says to me in the mirror.

"No," I say. "I—I haven't been back for a while. You know what it's like." I shift awkwardly in the seat, knowing I am gripping Freya too tight but unable to loosen my hold. "It's hard to find the time."

"Beautiful bit of the world," Rick throws back. "I can't imagine living anywhere else, meself, but I suppose it's different if you wasn't born and bred here. Where are your parents from?"

"They are—were—" I stumble, and I feel Kate's supportive presence at my side and take a breath. "My father lives in Scotland now, but I grew up in London."

We rattle over a cattle grid, and then the trees open up and we are out on the marsh.

And suddenly it's there. The Reach. Wide and gray and speckled with reeds, the wind-rippled waters reflecting the lazy streaks of sun-bleached cloud above, and the whole thing is so bright and clear and wide that I feel a lump in my throat.

Kate is watching my face, and I see her smile.

"Had you forgotten?" she asks softly. I shake my head.

"Never." But it's not true—I had forgotten. I had forgotten what it was *like*. There is nothing, nowhere like the Reach. I have seen many rivers, crossed other estuaries. But none as beautiful as this, where the land and the sky and the sea bleed into one another, soaking each other, mingling and mixing until it's hard to know which is which, and where the clouds end and the water starts.

The road is dwindling down to a single lane, and then to a pebbled track, with grass between the tire marks.

And then I see it—the Tide Mill: a black silhouette against the cloud-streaked water, even shabbier and more drunken than I remember. It's not a building so much as a collection of driftwood thrown together by the winds, and looking as if it might be torn apart by them at any point. My heart lurches in my chest, and the memories come unbidden, beating at the inside of my head with feathered wings.

Thea, swimming naked in the Reach in the sunset, her skin turned gold in the evening light, the long black shadows of the stunted trees cutting across the flame-colored water and turning the Reach to tiger-striped glory.

Kate, hanging out the mill window on a winter's morning, when the frost was thick on the inside of the glass and furring the reeds and bulrushes, throwing open her arms and roaring her white breath to the sky.

Fatima, lying out on the wooden jetty in her tiny bathing suit, her skin turned mahogany with the summer sun and a pair of giant sunglasses reflecting the flickering light off the waves as she basked in the heat.

And Luc—Luc—but here my heart contracts and I can't go on.

We have come to a barred gate across the track.

"Better stop here," Kate says to Rick. "We had a high tide last night and the ground up ahead is still soft."

"You sure?" He turns to look over his shoulder. "I don't mind giving it a whirl."

"No, we'll walk." She reaches for the door handle and holds out a tenner, but he waves it away.

"Your money's no good here, duck."

"But, Rick—"

"Rick, nothing. Your dad was a good man, no matter what others in this place say, and you done well to stick it out here with the gossips. Pay me another day."

Kate swallows, and I can see she is trying to speak but can't, and so I speak for her.

"Thank you, Rick," I say. "But *I* want to pay. Please."

And I hold out ten pounds of my own.

Rick hesitates, and I put it in the ashtray and get out of the car, holding Freya in my arms while Kate retrieves my bag and the buggy from the boot. At last, when Freya is safely strapped in, he nods.

"All right. But listen, you ladies need a lift anywhere, you call me, understand? Day or night. I don't like to think of you out here with no transport. That place"—he jerks his head at the Mill—"is going to fall down one of these days, and if you need a ride somewhere, you don't hesitate to call me, tenner or no tenner. Got it?"

"Got it," I say, and I nod.

There is something comforting in the thought.

After Rick drives away, we look at each other, each unaccountably tongue-tied, feeling the hot sun beating down on the top of our heads. I want to ask Kate about the message, but something is stopping me.

Before I have made up my mind to speak, Kate turns and opens the gate, closing it behind us, as I make my way down towards the short wooden walkway that joins the Tide Mill to the shore.

The mill itself sits on a little spit of sand, barely bigger than the building itself, which I suppose was once joined to the bank. At some point, when the mill was being constructed, a narrow channel was dug away, severing the mill from the land and funneling the rising and falling tide past the water wheel that used to sit in the channel. The wheel is long gone, only a stump of blackened wood sticking out at right angles from the wall shows where it once stood, and in its place is a wooden walkway, bridging the ten feet of water that separates the mill from the shore. Seventeen years ago I remember running across it, all four of us at a time sometimes, but now I can't quite believe we trusted our weight to it.

It is narrower than I remember, the slats salt-bleached and rotten in places, and no handrail has been installed in the years since I last saw it, but Kate starts across it fearlessly, carrying my bag. I take a deep breath, trying to ignore the images in my head (slats giving way, the pram falling into the salt water) and I follow, my heart in my throat as I bounce the wheels across the treacherous gaps, only exhaling when we reach the comparative safety of the other side.

The door is unlocked, as it always is, always was. Kate turns the handle and stands back, letting me pass—and I wheel Freya up the wooden step and inside.

It's seven years since I last saw Kate, but I have not been back to Salten for more than twice that. For a moment it is like I have stepped back in time, and I am fifteen, the ramshackle beauty of the place washing over me for the first time. I see again the long, asymmetrical windows with their cracked panes, overlooking the estuary, the vaulted roof that goes up and up to the blackened beams above, the staircase drunkenly twisting around the space, hopping from landing to rickety landing until it reaches the three bedrooms lodged high in the rafters. I see the smoke-blacked stove with its snaking pipe, and the long, low sofa with its broken springs, and most of all the paintings, paintings everywhere. Some I don't recognize, they must be Kate's, but intermingled are a hundred that are like old friends or half-remembered names.

There, above the rust-stained sink in a gilt frame is Kate as a baby, her face round with chub, her concentration fierce as she reaches for something just out of view.

There, hanging between the two long windows is the unfinished canvas of the Reach on a winter's morning, crackling with frost, and a single heron swooping low above the water.

Beside the door that leads to the outside toilet is a watercolor of Thea, her features dissolving at the edges of the rough paper.

And over the desk I catch sight of a pencil sketch of me and Fatima, arms entwined in a makeshift hammock, laughing, laughing, like there is nothing to fear in all the world.

It's like a thousand memories assault me all at once, each of them with clutching fingers pulling me back into the past—and then I hear a loud bark, and I look down to see Shadow, bounding up to me, a flurry of white and gray. I fend him off, patting his head as he butts it against my leg, but he is not part of the past, and the spell is broken.

"It hasn't changed!" I say, knowing I sound foolish. Kate shrugs and begins to unbuckle Freya from her pram.

"It has a bit. I had to replace the fridge." She nods at one in the corner that looks, if anything, older and more disreputable than its predecessor. "And I had to sell a lot of Dad's best paintings, of course. I filled the gaps with mine, but they're not the same. I had to sell some of my favorites—the plover's skeleton, and the one of the greyhound on the sands . . . but the rest, I couldn't bear to let these go."

She looks over the top of Freya's head at the pictures that remain, and her gaze caresses each one.

I take Freya from her arms and bounce her over my shoulder, not saying what I am thinking, which is that the place feels like a museum, like those rooms in the houses of famous men, frozen at the moment they left it. Marcel Proust's bedroom, faithfully reconstructed in the Musée Carnavalet. Kipling's study preserved in aspic at Bateman's.

Only here there are no ropes to hold the viewer back, only Kate, living on, in this memorial to her father.

To hide my thoughts I walk to the window, patting Freya's warm, firm back, more to soothe myself than her, and I stare out over the Reach. The tide is low, but the wooden jetty overlooking the bay is only a few feet above the lapping waves, and I turn back to Kate, surprised.

"Has the jetty sunk?"

"Not just the jetty," Kate says ruefully. "That's the problem. The whole place is sinking. I had a surveyor come and look at it, he said there's no proper foundations, and that if I were applying for a mortgage today I'd never get one."

"But—Wait, hang on, what do you mean? Sinking? Can't you repin it—underpin, that's what I mean. Can't you do that?"

"Not really. The problem is it's just sand underneath us. There's nothing for the underpinning to rest on. You could postpone the inevitable, but eventually it's just going to wash away."

"Isn't that dangerous?"

"Not really. I mean, yes, it's causing some movement in the upper stories, which is making the floor a bit uneven, but it's not going to disappear tonight if that's what you're worried about. It's more stuff like the electrics."

"*What?*" I stare at the light switch on the wall, as if expecting sparks to start flying at any moment. Kate laughs.

"Don't worry, I had a massive fuck-off circuit breaker installed when things started getting dicey. If anything starts to fizz it just trips. But it does mean that the lights have a tendency to go off at high tide."

"This place can't possibly be insured."

"Insured?" She looks at me like I've said something quaint and eccentric. "What the hell would I do with insurance?"

I shake my head, wondering.

"What are you *doing* here? Kate, this is mad. You can't live like this."

"Isa," she says patiently, "I can't leave. How could I? It's completely unsellable."

"So don't sell it—walk away. Give the keys to the bank. Declare yourself bankrupt if that's what it takes."

"I can't leave," she says stubbornly, and goes across to the stove to turn the handle on the gas bottle and light the little burner. The kettle on top starts to hiss quietly as she gets out two mugs and a battered canister of tea. "You know why."

And I can't answer that because I do. I know exactly why. And it's the very reason I've come back here myself.

"Kate," I say, feeling my insides tighten queasily. "Kate—that message . . ."

"Not now," she says. Her back is towards me, and I can't see her face. "I'm sorry, Isa, I just—it wouldn't be fair. We need to wait, until the others are here."

"Okay," I say quietly. But suddenly, I'm not. Not really.

SCOUT PRESS READERS GROUP GUIDE

THE WOMAN IN CABIN 10

RUTH WARE

This readers group guide for The Woman in Cabin 10 *includes an introduction, discussion questions, and ideas for enhancing your book club. The suggested questions are intended to help your reading group find new and interesting angles and topics for your discussion. We hope that these ideas will enrich your conversation and increase your enjoyment of the book.*

INTRODUCTION

From the *New York Times* bestselling author of *In a Dark, Dark Wood* comes another riveting thriller filled with twists and turns.

Travel journalist Lo Blacklock has just been given the assignment of a lifetime: to travel the North Sea on the inaugural voyage of the *Aurora*, a luxury cruise ship. Between the plush cabins, elegant guests, and sparkling dinner parties, Lo's trip is nothing short of amazing. But as the week progresses, Lo hears what can only be described as a nightmare: a woman in the cabin next to her being thrown overboard. The problem? None of the passengers on deck are missing, so the ship continues sailing as if nothing has happened, despite Lo's increasingly desperate attempts to raise the alarm.

Filled with surprising twists and turns, *The Woman in Cabin 10* proves once again that Ruth Ware is a writer at the top of her game.

TOPICS AND QUESTIONS FOR DISCUSSION

1. What's the effect of having Lo's e-mails and various news reports interspersed throughout Lo's narration? In what ways do they help you better understand what's happening aboard the *Aurora*?

2. When Lo first enters the ship, she says, "I had a sudden disorienting image of the *Aurora* as a ship imprisoned in a bottle—tiny, perfect, isolated, and unreal" (p. 37). In what ways does this statement foreshadow the events that take place on the ship? Describe the *Aurora*. In what ways do you think life on the ship may seem unreal? Discuss the book's title. Why do you think Ware chose it? Did the title influence your reading of the novel? If so, how?

3. Who is Carrie? Did you like her? Why or why not? Describe her relationship with Lo. In what ways, if any, are the two women

alike? How do Lo's feelings about Carrie change as Lo gets to know her? Did your opinion of Carrie change as you read?

4. Lo questions Alexander about eating fugu during dinner aboard the *Aurora*, and he tells her that the fact it is poisonous is "what *makes* the experience" (p. 74). What does Alexander mean by his statement? Lo seems dubious about the appeal of it. Does Lo strike you as someone who takes risks? Were you surprised by any of her risky actions aboard the *Aurora*? Which ones, if any?

5. After Lo's flat is burglarized, she calls *Velocity*'s assistant features editor, Jenn, and tells her about it. Lo says, "I told her what happened, making it sound funnier and more farcical than it really had been" (p. 13). Why do you think Lo underplays the break-in? How might this make her feel more in control? Have you ever underplayed an event of significance in your life?

6. When Lo panics on one of her first nights aboard the *Aurora*, she says, "I imagined burying my face in Judah's shoulder and for a second I nearly burst into tears, but I clenched my teeth and swallowed them back down. Judah was not the answer to all this" (p. 49). Why is Lo so resistant to accepting help from Judah? Do you think that she's right to be reticent? Describe their relationship. Do Lo and Judah support each other?

7. When Nilsson challenges Lo's claim that she's seen something happen in the cabin next to hers, she tells him, "Yes, someone broke into my flat. It has *nothing to do with what I saw*" (p. 141). Did you believe her? Did you think that the break-in made Lo more jumpy and distrustful? Give some examples to support your opinion.

8. When Lo first speaks to Richard Bullmer, she notices that he gives her "a little wink" (p. 79). What is the effect of this gesture? What were your initial impressions of Bullmer? Did you like him, or were you suspicious of him? After a prolonged conversation with Bullmer, Lo says, "I could see why [he] had got to where he had in life" (p. 194). Describe his manner. What does Lo think accounts for his success?

9. Archer tells Lo that self-defense is "not about size, even a girl like you can overpower a man if you get the leverage right" (p. 73). Is Lo able to do so? What kind of leverage does she have? What different kinds of power and leverage do the people on the *Aurora* use when dealing with each other? How did you react?

10. Judah tells Lo that "I still think, in spite of it all, we're responsible for our own actions" (p. 334). Do you agree? In what scenes did you think the deception and violence that occurred were justified? In what scenes did you think they were not justified?

11. When Lo sees the staff quarters on the *Aurora,* she says, "the rooms were no worse than plenty of cross-channel ferries I'd traveled on. . . . But it was the graphic illustration of the gap between the haves and have-nots that was upsetting" (p. 113). Contrast the guest quarters to those of the crew. Why does Lo find the discrepancy so unsettling? Much of the crew seemed unwilling to speak to Lo. Do you think this was caused by the "gap between the haves and have-nots"? Or some other reason?

12. Lo tells Judah, "You don't know what goes on in other people's relationships" (p. 333). Describe the relationships in *The Woman in Cabin 10.* Did you find any particularly surprising? Which ones, and why?

13. Bullmer tells Lo, "Why wait? . . . One thing I've learned in business—now almost always *is* the right time" (p. 190). Do you agree with his philosophy? In what ways has this attitude led to Bullmer's success? Does this attitude present any problems aboard the *Aurora*? Do you think Lo shares the same life philosophy as Bullmer? How would you describe Lo's philosophy on life?

14. Describe Lo's relationship with Ben. She tells him "[e]verything I hadn't told Jude. What it had been like . . . that I was vulnerable in a way I'd never thought I was before that night" (p. 82). Why does Lo share all this information with Ben rather than Jude? Did you think that Ben had Lo's best interests at heart? Why or why not? Were you surprised to learn of their history?

ENHANCE YOUR BOOK CLUB

1. Ware's debut novel, *In A Dark, Dark Wood*, received rave reviews when it was first published and was named a best book of the year by NPR and Shelf Awareness. Read *In a Dark, Dark Wood* with your book club, then compare and contrast the two books. In what ways are they similar? How has Ware's writing style evolved since she published her debut novel?

2. Richard Bullmer tells his guests, "The aurora borealis is something that everyone should see before they die" (p. 64). Look at pictures of the northern lights with your book club. Do you find them as breathtaking as Richard Bullmer does? Would you travel to see the northern lights as the guests of the *Aurora* plan on doing?

3. Lo says, "*Pooh* has always been my comfort read, my go-to book in times of stress" (p. 277). Why might *Pooh* bring Lo comfort? Do you have any "comfort reads"? Share them with your book club, and describe what you find so comforting about the books.

4. To learn more about Ruth Ware, read about her other writings, and connect with her online, visit her official website at www.ruthware.com.

PRAISE FOR RUTH WARE'S

INSTANT *NEW YORK TIMES* BESTSELLER

"WICKEDLY GOOD . . . Ware plays fair, bamboozling us with red herrings while expertly pacing her plot."
—***The Seattle Times***

"By the book's latter stages, readers may think they have it all figured out. **THEY SHOULD THINK AGAIN."**
—***The Wall Street Journal***

"ESPECIALLY TIMELY, given that the terror of isolation is at its heart."
—***Booklist*** **(starred review)**

"In Ruth We Trust . . . **COME FOR THE AGATHA CHRISTIE VIBES,** stay for the insane ending."
—**theSkimm**

"ENGROSSING."
—***Shelf Awareness***

"A CLASSIC WHODUNIT that solidifies Ware's reputation as the contemporary Agatha Christie." —***BuzzFeed***

"Tempestuous . . . [a] claustrophobic, adrenaline-fueled **CAT-AND-MOUSE GAME."**
—***Publishers Weekly***

"Ware's fans will **DEVOUR THIS IN A SITTING."**
—***Library Journal*** **(starred review)**

"Ruth Ware's **HITCHCOCKIAN THRILLERS** have yet to disappoint." —***PopSugar***

"A CLAUSTROPHOBIC SPINE-TINGLER." —*PEOPLE*

Praise for Ruth Ware's instant *New York Times* bestseller

"[Ware] sets the bar higher in *One by One* by burying her principal players in an Alpine chalet beneath an avalanche. . . . Readers will recognize the obvious homage to Agatha Christie's *And Then There Were None*, but with enough ingenious twists to make this whodunit another triumph for Ware."

—*The New York Times Book Review*

"Not only do Ware's novels wink at Christie in a saucy way, but Ware herself is turning out to be as ingenious and indefatigable as the Queen of Crime."

—Maureen Corrigan, *The Washington Post*

"A claustrophobic spine-tingler."

—*People*, "Best Books of Fall 2020"

"Ware manages to make a retreat in a chalet in the wide-open French Alps feel claustrophobic, nerve-wracking and deadly . . . The author's choice of telling the story in dueling narratives —Liz, a former Snoop employee who was invited to join in the retreat; and Erin, one of the chalet's two staff members —enhances the steadily escalating pace of the book."

—*USA Today*

"Wickedly good . . . Ware plays fair, bamboozling us with red herrings while expertly pacing her plot."

—*The Seattle Times*

"Especially timely, given that the terror of isolation is at its heart . . . This is *And Then There Were None* rendered for the twenty-first century."

—*Booklist* (starred review)

"In Ruth We Trust. . . . Come for the Agatha Christie vibes, stay for the insane ending."

—theSkimm

"A classic whodunit that solidifies Ware's reputation as the contemporary Agatha Christie . . . Suspense builds until it culminates in a terrifying game of cat-and-mouse that will keep you racing through the remaining pages."

—*BuzzFeed*, "13 New Thrillers That Will Make You Lose Sleep This Fall"

"Engrossing . . . One of Ware's strengths is propelling the story in a way that keeps readers trapped inside its pages, and armchair travelers can enjoy being whisked away to a location that's both breathtaking and deadly."

—*Shelf Awareness*

"Ruth Ware is often described as the new Agatha Christie . . . [S]he is a revitalizer, bringing the genre to a new audience with her modern preoccupations and addictive style."

—*Air Mail*

"Tempestuous . . . [a] claustrophobic, adrenaline-fueled cat-and-mouse game."

—*Publishers Weekly*

"Ware's gifts for characterization, plot, and pacing shine here . . . Ware's fans will devour this in a sitting."

—*Library Journal* (starred review)

"Ware has the perfect combination of light touch and complex plotting while also offering up the twists and reveals appreciated by Christie fans."

—*The Amazon Book Review*,
"The best mysteries and thrillers of September"

"Hilarious, well plotted, and vintage Ware, this one is not to be missed."

—*CrimeReads*

"Ruth Ware's Hitchcockian thrillers have yet to disappoint."

—*PopSugar*

"Ware does what she does best: Gives us a familiar locked-door mystery setup and lets the tension and suspicion marinate until they reach fever pitch. Another win for Ware . . . Simply masterful."

—*Kirkus*

"*The Turn of the Key* was not her first book, but its sweep of starred reviews and awards sets up *One by One* to be a most anticipated thriller of 2020."

—*Library Journal*

"Read this back-to-back with Christie's *And Then There Were None*, and you will witness the evolution of a literary form over the space of eight decades as Ware proves she's more than deserving of all those comparisons to the Queen of Crime."

—*BookPage*

"A gripping thriller that shows how toxic workplace culture can get and will keep you guessing through the very last page."

—*Good Housekeeping*

"Ware has quickly earned herself a place atop the psychological thriller world in recent years, and *One by One*, which brings in elements of the traditional mystery, is an exciting new addition to her body of work."

—*CrimeReads*, "Most Anticipated Crime Books of 2020"

"What begins as an interesting story of corporate intrigue soon morphs into something else entirely, a novel as chilling as the chalet where it is set. The pulse-pounding concluding act especially makes this a deeply satisfying thriller, perfect for cold evenings ahead."

—*The Free Lance-Star*

"Ware is a modern-day Agatha Christie, and in *One by One*, she combines a beloved premise with her signature scruffy characters and chilling atmosphere."

—*Bust*

ONE BY ONE

RUTH WARE

SCOUT PRESS

New York London Toronto Sydney New Delhi

Scout Press
An Imprint of Simon & Schuster, Inc.
1230 Avenue of the Americas
New York, NY 10020

This book is a work of fiction. Any references to historical events, real people, or real places are used fictitiously. Other names, characters, places, and events are products of the author's imagination, and any resemblance to actual events or places or persons, living or dead, is entirely coincidental.

First Scout Press trade paperback edition May 2021

SCOUT PRESS and colophon are registered trademarks of Simon & Schuster, Inc.

For information about special discounts for bulk purchases, please contact Simon & Schuster Special Sales at 1-866-506-1949 or business@simonandschuster.com.

The Simon & Schuster Speakers Bureau can bring authors to your live event. For more information or to book an event, contact the Simon & Schuster Speakers Bureau at 1-866-248-3049 or visit our website at www.simonspeakers.com.

Interior design by Jaime Putorti

Manufactured in the United States of America

10 9 8 7 6 5 4 3 2 1

Library of Congress Cataloging-in-Publication Data is available.

ISBN 978-1-5011-8881-7
ISBN 978-1-5011-8882-4 (pbk)
ISBN 978-1-5011-8883-1 (ebook)

To Ali, Jilly, and Mark, who first showed me the Hidden Valley.

From the "About Us" page of the Snoop company website:

Hey. We're snoop. Come meet us, message us, snoop on us—whatever. We're pretty cool. Are you?

Topher St. Clair-Bridges

Who's the daddy? Well, if anyone's got a claim, it's Toph. snoop cofounder (along with ex-girlfriend, model/artist/professional badass @evalution), it all started here. If he's not at his desk, he's probably riding the moguls in Chamonix, losing his mind in Berlin's Berghain, or just hangin'. Come find him on snoop at @xtopher or hit him up via his PA Inigo Ryder—the only dude who gets to tell Topher what to do.

Listening to: Oscar Mulero / Like a Wolf

Eva van den Berg

From Amsterdam to Sydney, New York to London, Eva's career has taken her all over the world—but right now home is Shoreditch, London, where she lives with her husband, financier Arnaud Jankovitch, and their daughter, Radisson. In 2015 she cofounded snoop with her then life partner @xtopher—their idea born of a single desire: to maintain their connection across 5000 km of ocean. Topher and Eva have since uncoupled, but their connection remains: snoop. Make your own connection with Eva on @evalution, or via her personal assistant Ani Cresswell.

Listening to: Nico / Janitor of Lunacy

Rik Adeyemi

head of beans

Rik's the money man, the bean counter, the keeper of the keys—you get the picture. He's been keepin' snoop real since the very first days, and he's known Toph for even longer. What can we say? snoop's a family affair. Rik lives with his wife, Veronique, in Highgate, London. You can snoop him at @rikshaw.

Listening to: Willie Bobo / La Descarga del Bobo

Elliot Cross

chief nerd

Music may be snoop's beating heart, but code is its DNA and Elliot is the maestro of code. Before snoop was a hot pink logo on your phone, it was just lines of Java on someone's screen—and that someone was Elliot. Best friends with Toph since before they could shave, he's cooler than any tech-head has a right to be. snoop him on @ex.

Listening to: Kraftwerk / Autobahn

Miranda Khan

friends czar

Miranda is into killer heels, sharp fashion, and really *great* coffee. Between savoring Guatemalan carbonic maceration and surfing Net-a-Porter, she's snoop's smile to the world. Wanna write us up, hit us up, haul us over the coals, or just say hi? Miranda's the place to start. snoop knows you can never have enough followers—or enough friends. Make Miranda one of yours at @mirandelicious.

Listening to: Madonna / 4 Minutes

Tiger-Blue Esposito

head of cool

The epitome of chill, Tiger keeps her trademark zen state with the help of daily yoga, mindfulness and—of course—a steady stream of snoop through her oversize headphones. When she's not pulling a Bhujapidasana or relaxing into an Anantasana (that's a side reclining leg lift to the uninitiated) she's polishing snoop's cogs to make sure we look our very best, and getting the word out. Chill with her on @blueskythinking.

Listening to: Jai-Jagdeesh / Aad Guray Nameh

Carl Foster

law man

There's no two ways about it—Carl keeps us on the straight and narrow, making sure that wherever we snoop, we're doing it on the right side of the law. A graduate of University College, London, Carl did his pupillage at Temple Square Chambers. Since then he's worked in a variety of international firms, mostly in the entertainment industry. He lives in Croydon. snoop him on @carlfoster1972.

Listening to: The Rolling Stones / Sympathy for the Devil

Taken from the BBC News website:

Thursday, 16th January

4 BRITONS DEAD IN SKI RESORT TRAGEDY

The exclusive French ski resort of St Antoine was rocked by news of a second tragedy this week, only days after an avalanche killed six and left much of the region without power for days.

Now, reports are emerging that in one remote ski chalet cut off by the avalanche, a 'house of horror' situation was unfolding, leaving four Britons dead and two hospitalised.

The alarm was only sounded when survivors trekked more than three miles through the snow to radio for help, raising questions of why the French authorities did not work to re-establish power and mobile phone coverage more quickly following Sunday's avalanche.

Local police chief Etienne Dupont refused to comment, except to say that 'an investigation is in progress', but a spokesperson at the British embassy in Paris said, 'We can confirm that we have been informed of the deaths of four British citizens in the Savoie department of the French Alps and that the local police are treating these incidents as a linked

murder inquiry at this stage. Our sympathies are with the friends and families of the victims.'

The families of the deceased have been informed.

Eight survivors, also thought to be British, are said to be helping the police investigation.

This year has been marked by unusually heavy snowfalls. Sunday's avalanche is the sixth since the beginning of the ski season, and brings the total of fatalities in the region to twelve.

FIVE DAYS EARLIER

LIZ

Snoop ID: ANON101

Listening to: James Blunt / You're Beautiful

Snoopers: 0

Snoopscribers: 0

I keep my earbuds shoved into my ears on the minibus from Geneva Airport. I ignore Topher's hopeful looks and Eva, glancing over her shoulder at me. It helps, somehow. It helps to shut out the voices in my head, *their* voices, pulling me this way and that, pummeling me with their loyalties and their arguments to and fro.

Instead, I let James Blunt drown them out, telling me I'm beautiful, over and over again. The irony of the statement makes me want to laugh, but I don't. There's something comforting in the lie.

It is 1:52 p.m. Outside the window the sky is iron gray, and the snowflakes swirl hypnotically past. It's strange. Snow is so white on the ground, but when it's falling, it looks gray against the sky. It might as well be ash.

We are starting to climb now. The snow gets thicker as we gain height, no longer melting into rain when it hits the window but sticking, sliding along the glass, the windscreen wipers swooshing it aside into rivulets of slush that run horizontally across the passenger window. I hope the bus has snow tires.

The driver changes gear; we are approaching yet another hairpin bend. As the bus swings around the narrow curve, the ground falls away, and I have a momentary feeling that we're going to fall—a lurch of vertigo that makes my stomach heave and my head spin. I shut my eyes, blocking them all out, losing myself in the music.

And then the song stops.

And I am alone, with only one voice left in my head, and I can't shut it out. It's my own. And it's whispering a question that I've been asking myself since the plane lifted off the runway at Gatwick.

Why did I come? *Why?*

But I know the answer.

I came because I couldn't afford not to.

ERIN

Snoop ID: N/A
Listening to: N/A
Snoopers: N/A
Snoopscribers: N/A

The snow is *still* falling—fat white flakes drifting lazily down to lie softly over the peaks and pistes and valleys of St. Antoine.

Three meters have fallen in the last couple of weeks, and there's more forecast. A snowpocalypse, Danny called it. Snowmaggedon. Lifts have been closed, and then reopened, and then closed again. Currently almost every lift in the entire resort is closed, but the faithful little funicular that leads up to our tiny hamlet is still chugging away. It's glassed in, so even the heaviest dump doesn't affect it; the snow just lies like a blanket over the tunnel rather than clogging the rails. Which is good—because on the rare occasions it does shut down, we're totally cut off. There's no road up to St. Antoine 2000, not in winter, anyway. Everything, from the guests in the chalet, right through to every scrap of food for breakfast, lunch, and dinner, has to come up in the funicular. Unless you've got the money for a helicopter transfer (which, believe me, is not unheard of in this place). But the helicopters won't fly in poor conditions. If a blizzard comes in, they stay safely down in the valley.

It gives me a strange feeling if I think about it too much—a kind of claustrophobia that's at odds with the wide-open vistas from the chalet. It's not just the snow; it's a hundredweight of unwelcome memories bearing down on me. If I stop for more than a minute or two, the images start to come unbidden, crowding into my mind—numb fingers scrabbling through hard-packed snow, the sheen of sunset on blue skin, the glint of frosted lashes. But fortunately I've got no time to stop today. It's gone one o'clock and I'm still cleaning the second-to-last bedroom when I hear the shuddering sound of the gong from downstairs. It's Danny. He shouts my name and then something I can't make out.

"What?" I call down, and he shouts again, his voice clearer this time. He must have come out into the stairwell.

"I *said*, 'Grub's up.' Truffled parsnip soup. So get your lazy arse down here."

"Yes, chef," I shout back mockingly. I quickly dump the contents of the bathroom bin into my black sack, change the bin liner, and then jog down the spiral stairs to the lobby, where the delicious smell of Danny's soup greets me, along with the sound of "Venus in Furs" emanating from the kitchen.

Saturday is both the best day of the week and the worst. Best, because it's changeover day—there are no guests, and Danny and I have the chalet to ourselves, free to laze in the pool, steam in the outdoor hot tub, and play the music we like at the volume we want.

Worst, because it's changeover day, which means nine double beds to change, nine bathrooms to clean (eleven, if you count the loo downstairs and the shower room by the pool), eighteen ski lockers to sweep and Hoover, not to mention the living room, the dining room, the den, the snug, and the outdoor smoking area, where I have to pick up all the disgusting butts the smokers always strew around in spite of the prominent bins and buckets. At least Danny takes care of the kitchen, though he has his own to-do list. Saturday night is always a big dinner. Got to put on a show for the new guests, don't you know.

Now, we sit down together at the big dining room table, and I read through the information Kate emailed this morning as I spoon Danny's soup into my mouth. It's sweet and earthy, and there are tiny little crunchy bits scattered over the top—shaved parsnip roasted in truffle oil, I think.

"This soup is really good," I say. I know my job here. Danny rolls his eyes in a *Well, duh* gesture. If there is one thing about Danny, he's not modest. But he is a great cook.

"Think they'll like it tonight?" He's fishing for more compliments, of course, but I can't blame him. Danny's an unashamed diva about his food and, like any artiste, he enjoys appreciation.

"I'm sure they will. It's gorgeous, really warming, and . . . um . . . complex." I am striving to pin down the particular savory quality that makes the soup so good. Danny likes compliments to be *specific*. "Like autumn in a bowl. What else are you doing?"

"I've got amuse-bouches." Danny ticks the courses off on his fingers. "Then the truffled soup for starter. Then venison haunch for the carnies and mushroom ravioli for the veggies. Then crème brûlée for dessert. And then the cheese."

Danny's crème brûlée is his showstopper, and it's to die for. I've literally seen guests come to blows over a spare portion.

"Sounds perfect," I say encouragingly.

"As long as there aren't any fucking stealth vegans this time," he says morosely. He's still reeling from last week, when one of the guests turned out to be not just vegan but gluten intolerant as well. I don't think he's forgiven Kate yet.

"Kate was *really* clear," I say, cajoling. "One lactose intolerant, one gluten-free, three veggies. No vegans. That's it."

"It won't be," Danny says, still enjoying his martyrdom. "One of them will be low-carbing or something. Or a fruitarian. Or a breatharian."

"Well, if they're a breatharian, they won't be bothering you, will they?" I say reasonably. "They've got all the air they could want up here."

I wave an arm at the huge window that dominates the south side of the room. It overlooks the peaks and ridges of the Alps, a panorama so breathtaking that even though I live here now, I still find myself stopping mid-stride on certain days, almost winded by its beauty. Today the visibility is poor, the clouds are low, and there's too much snow in the air. But on a good day you can see almost to Lake Geneva. Behind us, to the northeast of the chalet, rises the Dame Blanche, the mountain that forms the highest peak of the St. Antoine valley, overshadowing everything.

"Read out the names," Danny says, around a mouthful of soup, only he says it more like *read aht the names*. His accent is pure sarf London, though I know in reality he grew up in Portsmouth. I'm never quite sure how much is all part of the act. Danny's a performer, and the more I get to know him, the more I'm fascinated by the complicated mix of identities beneath the surface. The cheeky Cockney geezer he puts on for the guests is just one of them. On nights out in St. Antoine I've seen him pivot from note-perfect Guy Ritchie to a gloriously flaming RuPaul, all in the space of five minutes.

Not that I can talk. I'm putting on my own act. We all are on some level, I suppose. That's one of the joys of coming here, to a place like this, where everyone is passing through. You get to have a fresh start.

"I need to get it right this time," he says, breaking into my thoughts. He puts a minuscule grind of fresh black pepper onto his soup and tastes it, then looks approving. "Can't afford another fucking Madeleine. Kate'll have my guts for garters."

Kate is the area rep and is in charge of coordinating all the bookings and logistics for all six of the company's chalets. She likes us to greet the clients by their names right from day one. It's what marks us out from the big-chain operators, she says. The personal touch. Only it's harder than it sounds, week in, week out. Last week Danny made friends with a woman called Madeleine, only when the feedback forms came in, it turned out there was no one called Madeleine in the group. Or any woman with a name beginning with *M*. He's still got no idea who he was talking to all week.

I run my finger down the list Kate sent last night.

"So it's a corporate party this time. Tech company called Snoop. Nine people, all in separate rooms. Eva van den Berg, cofounder. Topher St. Clair-Bridges, cofounder. Rik Adeyemi, head of beans. Elliot Cross, chief nerd."

Danny snorts out his soup through his nose, but I carry on.

"Miranda Khan, friends czar. Inigo Ryder, Topher's 'boss.' Ani Cresswell, chief Eva-tamer. Tiger-Blue Esposito, head of cool. Carl Foster, law man."

By the time I'm finished, Danny is actually crying with laughter and his soup has gone down the wrong way.

"Is that really what it says?" he manages, between coughs. "Head of beans? Tiger—what the fuck else? I didn't think Kate had a sense of humor. Where's the real list?"

"That *is* the real list," I say, trying not to laugh at the sight of Danny's screwed-up face, shining with tears. "Have a napkin."

"What? Are you shitting me?" he gasps, and then sits back, fanning himself. "Actually, I take that back. Snoop's that sort of place."

"You've heard of them?" I'm surprised. Danny isn't normally the sort of person with his finger on the button that way. We get all types here, lots of private parties, the odd wedding or anniversary, but a surprising number of corporate retreats too—I guess the price tag is easier to swallow if your company is paying. There's a lot of law firms, hedge funds, and Fortune 500 companies. This is the first time Danny's heard of one of the companies and I haven't. "What do they do?"

"Snoop?" Now it's Danny's turn to look surprised. "Have you been living in a fucking cave, Erin?"

"No, I'm just—I've never heard of them. Are they a media company?" I don't know why I chose that. Media seems like the kind of industry that would have a Tiger-Blue Esposito.

"No, they're an app." Danny looks at me suspiciously. "Have you *really* not heard of them? You know—Snoop—the music app. It lets you—well, snoop on people. That's kind of it."

"I have literally no idea what you're on about."

"Snoop, Erin," Danny says, more acidly this time, like if he keeps saying it, I'll smack my forehead and go, *Oh yeah,* that *Snoop!* He pulls out his phone and scrolls down the apps to one that looks like two eyes on a hot-pink background. Or maybe two cogs, it's hard to see on the logo. He presses it, and the screen goes bright pink, then black, blazoned with *snoop. Real people, real time, real loud* in fuchsia letters.

This time the two *o*'s of the name are the wheels of a cassette tape.

"You like hook it up to your Spotify account or whatever," Danny explains, scrolling through menus as he does, as if lists of random celebrities will make everything clear. "And it makes your listening public."

"Why would anyone want to do that?" I say blankly.

"It's a quid pro quo, innit?" Danny says, sounding impatient. "The whole point is no one wants to listen to you, but if you join, you get to listen to other people. *Voyeurism for your ears* is what Snoop calls it."

"So . . . I can see what . . . I don't know . . . Beyoncé is listening to? If she were on there."

"Yup. And Madonna. And Jay-Z. And Justin Bieber. And whoever else. Slebs love it—it's the new Instagram. It's like, you can connect, yeah? But without actually giving away too much information."

I nod slowly. I can actually kind of see the attraction of that.

"So it's basically famous people's playlists?"

"Not playlists," Danny says. "Because the whole point is that it's real time. You get what they're listening to *right now*."

"What if they're asleep?"

"Then you don't get anything. They don't appear in the search bar if they're not online and listening, and if you're snooping on someone and they stop listening, their feed goes dead and you get the option to shunt along to someone else."

"So if you're snooping on someone and they pause a song to answer the phone—"

Danny nods.

"Yeah, it just cuts off."

"That's a really terrible idea."

He laughs and shakes his head.

"Nah, you're not getting it. The whole point is . . ." He stops, trying to formulate something unquantifiable into words. "The whole point is the connection. You're actually listening to the same thing at the same moment as they are—beat for beat. You know that wherever she is in the world, Lady Gaga is listening to the exact same thing you are. It's like"—inspiration strikes, and his face lights up—"it's like, you know when you're first going out with someone, and you're sharing a set of headphones, one earpiece in their ear, one earpiece in yours?"

I nod.

"Well, it's like that. You and Lady Gaga, sharing her earphones. It's really powerful. When you're lying there in bed, and they switch off, and you know that somewhere they're probably doing the exact same thing as you, rolling over, falling asleep . . . it's pretty intimate, you know? But it's not just celebrities. If you're in a long-distance relationship, say, you can snoop your bloke and listen to the same song at the same time. Assuming you know his Snoop ID of course. I keep mine locked down."

"Okay . . ." I say slowly. "So . . . like . . . your feed is public, but no one knows it's you?"

"Yeah, so I have like two followers, because I've not bothered to hook up any of my contact list. Mind you, some of the most popular Snoopees are totally incognito. There's this one guy in Iran, HacT, he's called. He's in the top ten Snoopees pretty much every month. Well, I say in Iran, but there's no actual way of knowing. That's just what it says on his Snoop biog. He could be from Florida."

An alert pings on his phone, and he brings it up.

"Ah, yeah, see? This is someone I'm subscribed to, Msaggronistic. She's this French Canadian chick in Montreal, she listens to some really cool punk stuff. That alert was telling me she's come online and she's playing . . ." He scrolls down the notification. "The Slits, apparently. Not sure that's my cup of tea, but that's the thing, it might be. I just don't know."

"Right." I'm not sure I'm any the wiser really, but it's sort of making sense.

"Anyway," Danny says. He gets up and starts clearing our plates. "That's what I meant, these tech start-ups, you could actually imagine them calling their head of finance 'chief bean counter' or whatever the fuck he was called. They'd think it was edgy or something. Coffee?"

I look at my watch—2:17.

"I can't. I've got a couple of rooms still to do, then the pool."

"I'll bring you one up."

I stand and stretch, working the kinks out of my neck and shoulders. It's physical work, cleaning. I never realized how much before I started this job. Heaving Hoovers up and down stairs, scrubbing toilets and tiles. Doing nine rooms on the trot is a workout.

I'm finishing the pool when Danny comes in with a cup of coffee. He's wearing his usual trunks—the smallest, tightest ones I've ever seen in real life. They are banana yellow, and when he turns around to put my coffee down on the lounger, you can see that he has *BAD BOI* written across his butt in scarlet letters.

"Don't make *any* splashes," I warn him, as he stands poised at the edge of the pool, his arms outstretched. "I'm not mopping again."

He says nothing, just sticks out his tongue, and then does a perfect, splash-free dive into the shallow end of the pool. It's not really deep enough for diving, but he skims the bottom and comes up safely at the far end.

"Come on, the bloody place is clean enough. Get in."

I waver. I haven't Hoovered the dining room, but I don't know if anyone would be able to tell.

I look at my watch—3:15. The guests are supposed to arrive at 4:00 p.m. I'm cutting it fine.

"Oh, all right, then."

It's our weekly ritual. A ten-minute dip after all the chores are done, like a way of reclaiming our territory, reminding ourselves who's actually in charge in this place.

My bikini is on under my clothes, and I pull off my sweaty T-shirt and stained cleaning jeans, and ready myself to dive. I'm just about to push off when I feel a hand grab my ankle and yank me forward, and with a shriek, I pitch into the pool.

I surface, spluttering, raking hair out of my eyes. There is water *everywhere.*

"You fucking imbecile! I said no splashes!"

"Chill." Danny is laughing uproariously, the water like jewels on his dark skin. "I'll mop it, I swear."

"I'll bloody kill you if you don't."

"I'll do it! I said so, didn't I? I'll do it while you dry your hair." He points to his buzz-cut scalp, reminding me that he's got a head start on me in that department.

I punch him on the shoulder, but I can't stay mad at him, and for the next few minutes we swim and wrestle, and fight like puppies, until at last we're both drenched and gasping for air and have to stop to catch our breath.

Danny pulls himself out of the water, grinning and panting, and pads off to the changing room to get dressed and greet the guests.

I should follow him, I know it. There is plenty still left to do, jobs to complete, tasks to finish. But for a moment, just a moment, I let myself float, spread-eagled on the clear blue water. I touch my fingers to the scar that runs across my cheek, tracing the dented line where the skin is thin and still tender, and I gaze up at the gray sky through the glass roof above, watching as the snowflakes come spiraling down.

The sky is the *exact* color of Will's eyes.

The clock is ticking down to the arrival of our guests, and I can hear Danny beginning to mop the changing rooms. I should get out, but I can't. I can't look away. I just lie there, my dark hair fanning out around me, floating, gazing up. Remembering.

LIZ

Snoop ID: ANON101
Listening to: Snooping EDSHEERAN ✓
Snoopers: 0
Snoopscribers: 0

We are quite high in the mountains now. The minibus makes its way up through little Alpine villages that would look like picture postcards, except the sky is a threatening slate color, not blue. The slushy rain down in the valley has turned into huge white flakes, and the driver has the windscreen wipers on full, swishing them aside as fast as they fall. Beneath us the wet black tarmac has turned into frozen gray ridges, and the tires are making a strange rattling sound as they pass over them. Either side of the road, huge mud-spattered drifts have been thrown up by the snow plow. It feels like we are driving through a tunnel. It gives me a strange hemmed-in feeling, and I look down at my phone, flicking through the apps to try to distract myself before coming back to Snoop.

After I left the company, I deleted the app. I wanted everything about Snoop behind me, and I didn't like the idea of Topher, Eva, and the others keeping tabs on me through the software. But a few weeks later, I found myself downloading it again. There is a reason it has just tipped a hundred million users: it's addictive. But this time my profile is locked down as tight as it will go, and there is a junk email address attached to the account so that even Elliot, who has access to all the behind-the-scenes information, can't know it's me. It's not that I'm paranoid. I don't imagine he sits there searching the user records for *Liz Owens* every few days. I'm just quite a private person. That's normal, isn't it?

Topher says something over his shoulder to me. I pull my earbuds out.

"Sorry, what did you say?"

"I said, 'Drink?'" He holds out an open bottle of champagne.

I shake my head.

"No. Thanks."

"Suit yourself." He takes a swig directly from the bottle, and I try not to shudder. He swallows, wipes his mouth, then says, "I hope the weather clears up. We won't get much skiing in at this rate."

"Can't you ski in the snow then?" I ask.

He laughs, like he thinks I'm an idiot.

"Well, you can, but it's not much fun. It's like running in the rain. Have you never been skiing?"

"No." I realize I'm chewing the dead skin at the side of my nail, and I make myself drop my hand. I have a sharp flash of my mother's worried voice. *Liz, please don't do that, you know Daddy doesn't like it.* I raise my own voice, shutting it out. "I mean, not really. I did dry-slope skiing once at school, but I don't think it's really the same."

"You'll love it," Topher says, with that infuriating confidence. The truth is, of course, that he has no way of knowing whether I will love skiing. But somehow when he makes these pronouncements, you believe him. When he says, *Your money will be completely safe*, or *It's an amazing investment*, or *You'll never get these terms again*, you trust him. You sign that check. You make that deposit. You put everything into his hands.

It is why he is who he is, I suppose. That million-dollar confidence. Ugh.

I don't say anything in response. But he's not waiting for an answer. He gives me a big, flashing grin and takes another gulp of Krug, then turns back to the driver.

"We must be almost there, is that right?"

"Comment?" the driver says in French.

Topher smiles with exaggerated patience and repeats himself, more slowly this time.

"Almost. There?"

"Presque," the driver says brusquely.

"Nearly," I translate under my breath, and then wish I had not.

"I didn't know you spoke French, Liz," Eva says. She turns around to look at me. She is smiling. She says the words like she is handing out gold stars.

There's a lot you don't know about me, Eva, I think.

"GCSE," I mutter instead. "Not very good."

"You are such a dark horse," Eva says admiringly. I know she is trying to flatter me, but her words have a patronizing edge considering English is her second language, after Dutch, and she is fluent in German and Italian as well.

Before I am expected to reply, the minibus comes to a halt, the tires squeaking in the snow. I look around. Instead of the chalet I was expecting, there is a dark opening into the snowy hill and a sign reading *Le funiculaire de St. Antoine.* A ski lift? Already?

I am not the only one who's puzzled. Carl, the thickset lawyer, is looking alarmed too. The driver gets down from the front and starts heaving out cases.

"Are we walking from here or what?" Carl says. "Didn't bloody pack my snowshoes!"

"We're staying in St. Antoine 2000," Topher's assistant says. His name, I discovered on the plane, is Inigo. He is American, blond, and extremely good-looking. He is speaking to Carl, but also to the rest of us. "This is St. Antoine le Lac, but there are a lot of little hamlets scattered around, some of them just a couple of chalets. The one we're staying in is at nearly seven thousand feet—I mean, two thousand meters," he says hurriedly, as Eva raises an eyebrow. "It's got no road access, so we have to travel the last part of the journey in this funicular railway." He nods at the dark opening, and as my eyes adjust, I can see a turnstile inside, and a bored-looking man in uniform playing with his phone in a little booth.

"I've got your tickets," Inigo adds, holding up a sheaf of paper.

He hands them out as we climb down from the minibus onto the soft snow, and we stand, holding them, looking up. I flex my fingers nervously inside my pockets, feeling, rather than hearing, the joints click. It is 4:07 p.m., but the clouds are so thick with snow that the entire sky is dark. We each take a case, with the driver bringing up the rear, and then there is an uncomfortable wait for the funicular. It is invisible, somewhere far up the tunnel, though we can hear the thrum of the huge steel cable as it approaches.

"How are you doing, Liz?" a voice says behind me, and I turn to see Rik Adeyemi, Snoop's financial controller. He has an empty bottle of champagne under one arm. Rik is one of the few people I recognize, apart from Eva, Topher, and Elliot. He grins, huffing a white cloud into the cold air, and claps me firmly on one shoulder. It hurts. I try not to wince. "Long time no see!"

"I'm all right," I say. My voice sounds stiff, prim. I hate myself for it, but I can't help it. It always comes out that way when I am nervous. And Rik has always made me nervous. It is partly his height. I don't relate well to men in general, particularly tall men who loom over me. But it's not just that. Rik is so . . . polished. Much more than Topher, although they both come from the same world. Literally. He, Topher, and Elliot met at boarding school. Apparently Elliot was always a genius, even then. It's a long way from Campsbourne Secondary in Crawley, where I went to school. I know I am a creature from another planet to them. Weird. Awkward. *Working class.*

I clench my fingers, making the joints crack, and Rik winces and then gives an awkward laugh.

"Good old Liz," he says. "Still doing that old clicking thing?"

I don't reply. He shifts his weight from one foot to the other, absently adjusting his silver Rolex as he does, staring up the track, in the direction of the invisible carriage lumbering towards us.

"How are you doing, anyway?" he asks, and I want to roll my eyes.

You just asked that, I think. But I say nothing. I am learning that it's okay to do that sometimes. In fact it is quite fun to watch people's reactions.

Rik's eyes flick to me, waiting for my socially conditioned "Fine," and when it doesn't come, he shoves his free hand in his pocket, looking distinctly disconcerted.

Good. Let him wait.

ERIN

Snoop ID: LITTLEMY
Listening to: Offline
Snoopscribers: 0

"Littlemy?" Danny says, looking over my shoulder as I type in my brand-new username. He pronounces it like two words—*litt lemy.* "What the fuck does that mean?"

"Not Lit Lemmy. Little My. It's a character from the Moomins."

"The moo you what?"

"The Moomins! It's a series of children's—Look, never mind," I say, seeing his baffled expression. "What's yours?"

"I'm not telling you," he says, affronted. "You might snoop on me."

"Oh, so you're allowed to know mine, but I'm not allowed to know yours?"

"Too bloody right. What are you going to listen to?"

I click a profile at random. NeverMindTheHorlix. It's someone the app suggested from my contact list, and although I don't know who it is for sure, I think it might be a girl I went to school with. "Come and Get Your Love" by Redbone fills the room. I've never heard of the band, but I know the song.

"Someone's been watching *Guardians of the Galaxy*," Danny mutters with a touch of derision, but his hips are twitching in time to the beat as he walks across the room to peer out into the snow. He's only there for a second before he swings back round, grabbing a bottle of champagne from the cooler on the coffee table and popping the cork with a sound like a gunshot.

"They're here, I can see the funicular coming up."

I nod and shove my phone into my pocket. No time for chat now. This is action stations.

Ten minutes later I am standing in the open doorway of Chalet Perce-Neige, tray of glasses in one hand, watching a little group staggering and sliding down the path from the funicular to the porch. None of them are wearing suitable shoes, and they've not mastered how to walk in snow, with short steps and your weight thrown forward, not back. One of them, a very good-looking black guy, is carrying what looks like—yes, it is. It's an empty bottle of Krug. Great. They're already drunk.

A tall blond man reaches me first, in his early thirties, handsome in a *Don't I know it* kind of way.

"Hi. Topher, Snoop founder," he says, grinning in a way that is clearly meant to charm the socks off me. His breath smells of alcohol, and his voice is every boarding school boy I've ever met. He looks faintly familiar although I can't place the connection—but maybe it's just the fact that if you were casting for the CEO of a hip internet start-up, he's exactly what you'd choose.

"Good to meet you," I say. "I'm Erin, your chalet host for the week. Champagne?"

"Well, since you insist . . ." He takes a glass of champagne off the tray and knocks it back in one. I make a mental note that next time I prepour drinks for this party, I'll use prosecco. There is no way they'll be able to taste the difference, throwing them back like that.

"Thanks." He replaces the empty glass on the tray and stares around him. "Great location, by the way."

"Thanks, we like it," I say. The others are coming up behind him now. A stunningly beautiful woman with caramel-tanned skin and white-blond hair is picking her way through the snow.

"Eva van den Berg," Topher says as she comes level with us, "my partner in crime."

"Hi, Eva," I say. "We're delighted to welcome your group to Chalet Perce-Neige. Do you want to leave your bags here and head inside to warm up?"

"Thanks, that would be great," Eva says. When she speaks there's a tinge of something not quite English in her inflection.

Behind her one of the men slips in the snow and launches into a grumbling rant under his breath, and she says, quite carelessly over her shoulder, "Do shut the fuck up, Carl."

I blink, but Carl doesn't seem to notice anything out of the ordinary and simply rolls his eyes, picks himself up, and follows his colleagues into the warmth.

Inside the lobby a fire is roaring in the big enameled wood burner. The guests shake the snow off their coats and rub their hands in front of the fire. I set down the tray of glasses within easy reach and unfurl the list of guests and room numbers. I glance around the room, mentally trying to match people to names.

Eva and Topher I've got already. Carl Foster, the guy who slipped in the snow, is a stocky white man in his forties with a buzz cut and a pugnacious expression, but he's cheerfully downing champagne in a way that suggests he's not brooding on the moment outside the door. Judging by her surname, Miranda Khan is probably the very elegant Asian woman over by the stairs. She's wearing six-inch heels and she's talking to the guy with the Krug, who's swapped the empty bottle for a full glass along the way.

"Oh, Rik," I hear her say, a touch of flirtation in her voice. "You *would* say that."

Rik Adeyemi. I put another mental tick on my list of names. Okay, so that's five of them. The four remaining guests are more of a puzzle. There's a slim woman in her midtwenties with ombré tips to her short hair, holding, for some reason, a rolled-up yoga mat under her arm. There's a boy in his early twenties with a strong resemblance to a young Jude Law. He seems to be American from what I heard of his accent when he took a glass of champagne. Behind him is a girl with fluffy yellow hair that cannot possibly be her real shade. It's the color of buttercups and the texture of dandelion fluff. She is wearing huge round spectacles and looking wonderingly around the lobby, and combined with her hair, the impression is of a particularly adorable baby chick. She must be either Ani or Tiger. She's about the furthest thing from a tiger I could possibly imagine, so I put her down as a probable Ani.

The ninth and last guest is a tall, awkward-looking man, staring out the window with his hands in his pockets. His standoffishness compares strangely with the other guests, who are all chatting companionably with the easy back-and-forth that you get only from people who've worked or socialized together for a long time.

No, wait. There is one other guest who's standing alone. A woman, in her late twenties, standing hunched in an inconspicuous corner by the fire, as if hoping no one will speak to her. She's wearing dark clothes, and she blended into the shadows so well that I didn't notice her at first. She's almost . . . the word that comes to mind is *cowering*, and although it feels too strong, it's the only one that really fits. Her uneasiness is in sharp contrast to the rest of the group, who are already laughing and refilling their glasses, in defiance of the advice about acclimating to altitude. But it's not just her body language that sets her apart—it's everything. She's the only one wearing clothes that look more H&M than D&G, and though she's not the only one wearing glasses, the others look like they're wearing props provided by a Hollywood studio. Hers look like National Health Service castoffs. She reminds me of a bird too, but not a fluffy little chick. There is nothing cute about her. This woman looks more like an owl—a hunted, panicked owl caught in the headlights of an oncoming car.

I'm about to go over to her, offer her a glass of champagne, when I realize there are none left on the tray. Did I put out the wrong number?

I look around again, counting. There are ten people in the lobby, not nine.

"Um . . . excuse me," I say quietly to Topher, "is one of your party staying elsewhere?"

He looks uncomprehendingly at me.

"I've only got nine guests on the list," I explain. "You seem to be ten. It's not a problem exactly—we can sleep up to eighteen—but there are only nine rooms, so I'm just wondering . . ."

I trail off.

Topher claps a hand to his forehead and turns to Eva.

"Fuck," his voice is very low, almost mouthing the words rather than saying them. "We forgot Liz."

"What?" she says, rather irritably, shaking her curtain of silky hair back. She's unwinding a long linen scarf from round her neck. "I didn't catch what you said."

"We forgot *Liz,*" he says, more emphatically this time. Her jaw drops, and she looks over her shoulder at the girl by the fireplace before mouthing a silent echoed *fuck* at her business partner.

Topher draws us both into a corner away from the other guests and beckons to the young Jude Law look-alike. As he comes closer the likeness fades, but the impression of startling good looks only intensifies. He has olive skin; sharp, Slavic cheekbones; and the most extraordinary topaz-blue eyes I've ever seen.

"Inigo," Topher hisses as the boy approaches. "Inigo, we forgot Liz."

Inigo looks at Topher blankly for a moment and then the words sink in, and the color drains out of his cheeks.

"Oh my God." His accent is American, Californian at a guess, though I'm not very good at placing Americans. He puts his hand over his mouth in horror. "Topher, I'm—I'm such a dick."

"It's not your fault," Eva says acidly. "Topher's the one who forgot her when he drew up the original list of names. But of all the people—"

"If you're so damn efficient," Topher growls between gritted teeth, "maybe you should have got Ani to do some of the legwork instead of leaving Inigo to do all the heavy lifting."

"It's fine—" I break in hurriedly. This isn't going the way it was supposed to. The first day is supposed to be rest and relaxation—unwinding in the hot tub, drinking vin chaud, and appreciating Danny's cooking. Mundane reality isn't supposed to surface until later, when the PowerPoint presentations come out. "Honestly, we can cater for more. The only issue is how we rearrange the bedrooms. We've only got nine guest rooms, which means two people will have to share."

"Let me see the list," Topher says, frowning.

"No, let *me* see the list," Eva snaps. "You've already screwed this up once, Topher."

"Fine," Topher says irritably, and Eva takes the piece of paper, running her finger down it. As she does, I notice there are what seems to be like burn holes in her sweater—it looks like she's been doing welding in it, but something tells me it came off the peg like this, and probably with a hefty price tag.

"Liz could share with Ani," Inigo says helpfully, but Eva shakes her head.

"No, absolutely not. Liz can't be the one to share or it'll be obvious what happened."

"What about Carl?" Topher mutters. "No one gives a fuck about him. He could share with someone."

"Who?" Eva says. "Rik's never going to agree to share a room, is he? And as for Elliot—" She jerks her head at the awkward-looking guy standing with his back to the others.

"Yes, okay," Topher says hastily. "I can see that's not going to work."

Both their gazes travel thoughtfully to Inigo, who is staring worriedly down at the list. Feeling their eyes upon him, he looks up.

"Did I miss something?"

"Yes," Eva says briskly. "You're sharing with Carl. Now run along and break the news to him."

Inigo's face falls.

"I'll have to switch the rooms around," I say, mentally running through the list of which rooms can fit a second bed. "Liz will have to go into Inigo's old room, that's the smallest, is that okay? And then Miranda can have Carl's, and then Carl and Inigo can share Miranda's old room; that's one of the few that can take an extra bed."

"Where *is* Miranda?" Topher says, looking around. I glance over at the stairs. Rik is now talking to the fluffy chick—definitely Ani, I have deduced—and tall, elegant Miranda has disappeared. Eva sighs.

"Damn, she's probably already gone up to her room. Well, she won't be impressed at being downgraded, but she'll have to put up with it. Let's go and find her before she unpacks."

"I'll come with you," I say. "Someone will have to move the cases."

From somewhere, I feel a headache begin behind my eyes. Suddenly, this feels like the start of a very long week.

LIZ

Snoop ID: ANON101
Listening to: Offline
Snoopscribers: 0

Something happened on arrival. I don't know what, but I saw Eva, Topher, and Inigo huddled in the corner of the lobby with the chalet girl. And I heard my name, I'm certain. They were talking about me. *Whispering* about me.

All I can think about is what they were saying, and why they were glancing over their shoulders and scheming.

Oh God, I hate this.

No. That's not true. I don't hate *all* of this. This place—this incredible chalet, with its pool and its views and its sheepskin throws and velvet sofas—this place is a dream come true. I don't think I have ever set foot in anywhere so luxurious, at least not since leaving Snoop. If I was here alone, I would be perfectly happy, more than happy in fact. I would be pinching myself.

I hate *them.*

When at last I'm alone in my room, I sink onto the hand-stitched quilt, lie back on the feather-stuffed pillows, and shut my eyes.

I ought to be prowling around the room, taking in the glorious panoramic view of the mountains, testing out the spa settings on the bath, marveling at my luck in being here. But I'm not. Instead, I am lying here with my eyes closed, replaying that awful, awkward moment downstairs over and over again.

I should be used to it. Used to them forgetting about me, taking me for granted, ignoring me. I had a whole year of that at Snoop. A year of people going out for drinks after work and not inviting me. Twelve months of "Oh, Liz, would you reserve a table for four at Mirabelle?" and knowing that that four didn't include me. One full year of invisibility. And I was fine with that—more than fine, actually. I was quite comfortable.

Now, three years after I left, everything has changed. I am very, *very* visible. And somehow Topher and Eva's scrutiny and their efforts to charm me are worse than being ignored.

It is 5:28 p.m., French time. I have about ninety minutes before dinner. An hour and a half to wash and change and try to find *something* in my suitcase that won't make me look like a frump compared to Eva's new assistant and that Tiger girl from marketing.

I don't even consider competing with Eva and the other woman with the high heels—what was her name? Miranda. They are not just out of my league, they're out of my pay grade. Eva was a catwalk model, and even before Snoop started to take off, her budget for shoes was higher than my whole salary. I have always known that we were operating on different levels. But it would be nice if I could go down to dinner looking like I belong in the same room with the others.

I unzip my sagging wheelie case and rummage through the layers of clothes I stuffed in there early this morning. At last, halfway down, I find a dress that might do. I drag it over my head and then I stand in front of the mirror, smoothing down the material, staring at myself. The dress is black and stretchy, and I bought it because I read some piece in *Elle* that said every woman needed a little black dress and this was the cheapest one in the feature.

But somehow it doesn't look like the dress in that photoshoot. It is crumpled from my case, and although I've only worn it two or three times, the material has gone into bobbles under the arms, giving it a tired, charity-shop look. There are what look like cat hairs all over the back, even though I don't own a cat. Maybe they've come off my scarf.

I know that a girl like Tiger would probably pick this dress up in a thrift shop and accessorize it with something ridiculous like a chain-mail vest and biker boots and walk out looking like a million dollars.

If I wore a chain-mail vest, it would pinch the skin under my arms and clank when I walked, and strangers would laugh and say, "Taking up jousting, love?" And it would rust where my sweat seeped into the links, and stain my clothes, and I would hate myself even more than I do already.

I am still standing there, gazing blankly at myself in the mirror, when there is a knock at the door.

My stomach flips. I can't face them. I can't face any of them.

"Who—who is it?" I call. My voice breaks on the last syllable.

"It's Erin, I'm your chalet host," I hear faintly through the wood. "Just wanted to check you have everything you need?"

I open the door. The girl who greeted us earlier is standing there. I didn't get a chance to really look at her when we arrived, but now I do. She is pretty and tanned, with shiny chestnut hair, and she is wearing a neat white blouse tucked into dark blue jeans. She looks self-possessed, assured, everything I am not.

Only one thing is out of place—the thin, pink tracing of a long scar that runs across her right cheekbone, disappearing into her hair. It stretches as she smiles at me, and I'm . . . surprised, I suppose. She looks like the kind of person who would cover such a thing up with makeup. But . . . she hasn't.

I want to ask her how she got it, but it doesn't feel like the kind of question you can just blurt out. Once upon a time I just would have asked. Now I have learned the hard way, that that kind of directness makes people think you are weird.

"Hi," she says, still smiling. "I'm Erin. I just wanted to check everything was okay with your room and to let you know there will be predinner drinks in the foyer this evening at six forty-five, followed by a short presentation."

"A presentation?" I tug at the hem of the dress. "About the resort?"

"No, a business presentation, I think. Was it not on your schedule?"

I rummage in my case and pull out the creased and folded itinerary Inigo emailed a few days ago. I have spent practically every spare second since poring over it, trying to figure out how this week is going to play out, so I know full well there is nothing listed for the first night, but I still need to reassure myself I'm not going crazy.

"There's nothing listed," I say. I can't prevent a note of accusation creeping into my voice. The girl shrugs.

"Probably a last-minute addition? Your colleague—Ani, is that right?—she just asked me to set up the projector in the den."

It is on the tip of my tongue to blurt out that Ani isn't my colleague. I have never worked with her. In fact I barely know any of them apart from the four original founders, Rik, Elliot, Eva, and Topher.

But I am too busy trying to figure out what this means.

Ani is Eva's assistant. So this presentation must be something Eva has hatched up. And Eva is the most strategic person I know. She would never leave anything off an agenda by accident. Which means she has done this on purpose. She is executing some kind of plan.

But what?

"Do you know what it's about?" I ask. "The presentation?"

"No, sorry. The timing is literally all I know. Drinks at six forty-five, presentation at seven."

"And . . . what should I wear?" I don't want to ask her, but I'm starting to feel desperate.

The girl smiles, but there is puzzlement behind her expression.

"How do you mean? We're really informal at Perce-Neige, no one dresses for dinner. Just wear whatever you feel comfortable in."

"But that's what they always say!" The words burst from me, in spite of myself. "They say, 'Oh, just wear whatever you want,' and then when you turn up there's some secret dress code that everyone seems to know apart from me. I go too smart and they're all in jeans and I look like I've tried way too hard, or I wear something casual and they're all in suits and dresses. It's like everyone else has the key to this and I don't!"

As soon as the words are out, I want to take them back. I feel naked, unbearably exposed. But it is too late. They cannot be unspoken.

She smiles again. Her expression is kind, but I see the pity in her eyes. I feel the blood creeping up into my cheeks, turning my face hot and red.

"It's really relaxed," she says. "I'm sure most people won't even change. You'll look lovely whatever you wear."

"Thanks," I say miserably. But I don't mean it. She is lying, and we both know it.

ERIN

Snoop ID: LITTLEMY
Listening to: Snooping XTOPHER ✔
Snoopers: 1
Snoopscribers: 1

As the various members of the party assemble in the foyer, the song that keeps running through my head is not the Chilean R & B I was listening to before they came in (yes, I was snooping on Topher), but the Beautiful South's "Rotterdam (or Anywhere)." Okay, not everyone is blond. But everyone is most certainly beautiful. Almost absurdly so. There is Eva's assistant, cute little Ani with her heart-shaped face and buttercup hair. Topher's PA, Inigo, now sporting a bronze five-o'clock shadow that makes his cheekbones look like he stepped off a film set. Even Carl the lawyer, who is probably the least conventionally attractive of the party, with his bullish expression and stocky frame, has a definite magnetism.

"*Thicc,*" Danny whispers appreciatively into my ear as he passes me with a tray of canapés. "I would, wouldn't you?"

"Carl? Uh, no," I whisper back, and Danny laughs, a deep throaty laugh, deliciously infectious.

"Who then? Coder dude over there?"

He nods at Elliot, who is standing in the same spot he chose on arrival, deliberately not making eye contact with anyone. I laugh and shake my head, but it's not because I find Elliot unattractive. Okay, he looks rather like an awkward schoolboy, but he still manages to be sexy in a geek-chic kind of way. He has the kind of body that looks as if his bones are too big for his skin, all jutting wrists and angled cheekbones, and knobbly ankles protruding from too-short trousers. But his lips are surprisingly sensuous, and when one of his colleagues maneuvers past him, she slips an arm around his midriff in a way that looks . . . well, it looks intimate. And Elliot doesn't flinch away as I thought he might.

"Come on," Topher calls over the sound of voices. "Let's get this party started. Carl, Inigo, surely one of you can figure out this speaker system? Jesus, no one would think we were a tech company."

From nowhere, music starts up. David Bowie, "Golden Years," filtering out of the Bluetooth speakers. I'm not sure who put it on, but it's an apt choice, almost to the point of irony. There is a definite gilded quality to this group. Nothing's going to touch them.

"Hey." The girl who pushed past Elliot has woven her way through the group to where Danny and I are standing. She is swaying in time to the beat and wearing a very short sweaterdress that exposes slim, toned legs, made more diminutive by her Doc Martens boots. For a minute I can't place her, and I have a flutter of panic, but then I clock the ombré hair and nose ring. She is the woman who was holding the yoga mat when she arrived, and the realization enables me to remember her name. Yoga. Tiger. Tiger-Blue Esposito. Head of cool.

"Hi, Tiger," I say. I hold out the tray of cocktails I'm holding. "Can I offer you a drink? This is a bramble gin martini, or on the left is a marmalade old-fashioned."

"Actually I came over to get something to eat." She gives me a beguiling smile, showing very white, even teeth and a dimple in her peach-soft cheek. Her voice is throaty—reminding me of a cat's purr, and her odd name seems suddenly rather apt. "Sorry, I know it's bad manners to hog the canapés straight out of the kitchen door, but the last tray was too good and I'm starving. They didn't serve any food on the plane, so all I've had since breakfast is Krug." She pauses for a second and then gives a surprisingly earthy laugh. "Oh, who am I kidding. I'm just pathologically greedy."

"Don't apologize," Danny says. He holds out the tray, where his carefully handmade canapés stand in rows like little battalions. "I like a girl with a good appetite. These are Gouda-filled profiteroles"—he points to the tiny, feather-like puffs on the left of the tray—"and these on the right are quails' eggs with smoked ricotta."

"Are they both veggie?" Tiger asks, and Danny nods.

"Gluten-free?"

"Only the quails' eggs."

"Great," Tiger says. The dimple flashes again, and she picks up a quail egg and pops it directly into her mouth, closing her eyes voluptuously as she chews. "Oh my God," she says as she swallows. "That was a canapé-shaped orgasm. Can I have another?"

"Sure," Danny says with a grin. "But save room for your tea."

She takes another, stuffs it into her mouth, and then says thickly, "Okay, save me from myself, take the tray away before I go full Homer Simpson and start drooling on the floor."

Danny gives a little mock bow and moves over towards Elliot, and Tiger looks after him appreciatively. I can't blame her. Danny is kind, a great cook, and cute as hell.

"Tiger," a clipped, monied voice says behind us, and I turn my head to see the PR woman, Miranda, stalking her way across the room. Her black hair is loose, a dark satin curtain down her back, and she's wearing a stunning black silk jumpsuit, cinched in to show an enviably tiny waist, and midnight-blue velvet stilettos. I notice with a wince that the pointed heels are leaving little divots in the polished wood floor, but I can't really say anything. Instead, I hold out the tray of drinks. Miranda takes a glass without looking at me and dumps a half-eaten smoked duck skewer in the space left.

"We need to talk," she says to Tiger. Her voice is high and sharp, her accent cut-glass, a few vowels away from full Princess Margaret.

"Sure," Tiger says good-naturedly. She swallows and wipes her mouth. "Hey, have you tried the quails' eggs? They're to die for."

"Never mind that, Tigs, listen, we need to put some time aside to discuss the comms strategy on Elliot's geosnoop release. I've just had that pushy little shit from *Unwired* on the phone asking about it."

"What?" Tiger looks taken aback. "How did that get out? It's not even in beta yet, is it?"

"I have no idea, but I suspect Elliot blabbed about it. He's never been able to stick to an embargo, and he's been telling anyone who'll listen how 'cool' it's going to be." She makes air quotes as she says the word. "I think I've shut *Unwired* down for the moment, but it's going to get out sooner or later and I have significant concerns about how it's going to go over in the press. I don't need to tell you that privacy on social is a big buzzword right now. I'm not sure if anyone's clocked the change in user-end permissions yet, but it's only a matter of time before they do. Christ, will someone please shut down that godawful racket?"

She looks round at me, pressing her fingers to her temple, and I realize she's talking about the music.

"One of the guests put it on," I say, trying not to sound defensive, "but I'll adjust the volume."

"I'm thinking we need two approaches," Miranda continues as I move away in search of the remote control for the speakers. "A plan A, which assumes a deliberate timed release, i.e., marketing, PR, social buzz, and so on. Basically all the stuff we'd already sketched out. But then a plan B in case of an early leak, in which case the question then is whether we bring forward aspects of the marketing campaign to support our narrative. It's absolutely *essential* we control the conversation on social."

They launch into technicalities as the discussion fades away int› the background babble. I locate the remote underneath a dirty napkin, turn the volume down a notch, and then glance at the clock on the mantelpiece. It's 6:55. They should be moving through shortly, but someone seems to be missing.

"Ah, about fucking time!" a man's voice says over my shoulder, and I turn to see Topher standing behind me. "Bloke could die of thirst waiting for service around here." He shakes his blond hair out of his eyes, then sweetens the rudeness with a grin that's just the right side of charming.

"So sorry!" I hold out the tray, masking my irritation with a polite smile. "Bramble martini?" Topher takes one and knocks it back with alarming speed. I restrain the urge to tell him that they are about 50 percent gin. "Carl?" I hold out the tray to his colleague, who nods heavily and takes the last old-fashioned.

"Cheers. Though I don't need any more booze if I'm being honest, it's food I'm after. Any more of them cheesy puffs going around? I'm bloody starving."

"Cheesy puffs!" Topher scoffs. "That's not how you maintain a ski-ready physique, Carl my dude."

He pats Carl's ample midriff, straining beneath a plaid shirt.

"Carb-loading, mate," Carl says, with a wink at me. "Essential part of my training regimen."

"Danny's circulating with the canapés; I'm sure he'll be over in just a sec," I say, though I can see over Carl's shoulder that Danny has been cornered by Elliot, who is methodically picking off the Gouda profiteroles one by one and putting them into his mouth like they are crisps. I hope there are some more in the kitchen.

Topher has seen it too, and now he leans past me to grab Elliot's shoulder.

"Elliot, my man. Stop hogging the server. Carl is carb-loading," he says, and I take the opportunity to slip away and check on the rest of the room.

It's 7:05 according to the clock above the fire, but when I count heads, only nine guests are present. Someone is late, and I'm not the only one who has noticed. Eva is tapping her foot and looking anxiously around.

"Where the fuck is Liz?" I hear her hiss at Inigo, who whispers something apologetic under his breath. Then his face brightens, and he touches Eva's arm.

Eva looks up towards the gallery landing. I follow her gaze to see Liz there, standing at the top of the spiral staircase. She has her arms crossed around herself, and her awkwardness makes Elliot look almost at ease.

"Liz!" Eva calls, welcoming. "Come down, have a drink."

Slowly, almost reluctantly, Liz descends the stairs. She's wearing the lumpish, unflattering black dress that I saw when I encountered her in her room earlier, and my heart sinks for her. It's cut all wrong for her shape, making her look like a bunch of potatoes in a sock, and you can tell from the way she's holding herself, plucking at her VPL, that she knows it. At the foot of the stairs she pauses and flexes her finger joints, like a kind of nervous tic. It makes a crackle like wood popping on a hot fire, surprisingly unpleasant.

I am about to step forward with a drink, but to my surprise, Topher forestalls me. He grabs a bramble martini from my tray and rushes forward, holding it out towards Liz with a puppy-dog expression of eagerness on his face.

It is so out of character that I blink.

Who *is* this woman? Why are they so keen to keep her happy? It's almost like . . . I frown, wondering. It's almost like they're afraid of her.

But that's absurd.

LIZ

Snoop ID: ANON101
Listening to: Offline
Snoopscribers: 0

They are all waiting, crowding around the bottom of the stairs as I reach the foyer—Eva, Topher, Inigo, Rik. Eva is wearing a long dress of white wool that I think is probably cashmere and which makes me feel like a frump. Topher is wearing jeans and an open-neck shirt. He is brandishing a martini glass in my face.

"Cocktail, Liz?" he says, flashing a smile.

"No, thanks," I say.

"Come on," Topher says. His voice is his very best cajoling charm. "It's a special occasion—all the gang back together!"

I should smile, but I do not feel like smiling. My dress is too tight. I wore Spanx underwear to try to make it fit better, but it is pinching, and my stomach hurts. And the music is too loud.

"Thanks, but I've got a headache," I say. I do not want to tell Topher the truth—that I do not drink alcohol anymore. He might wonder why—what has changed since I left Snoop.

"Oh, you poor thing," Topher says. "Let me get you something, I've got some ibuprofen in my room. Inigo—"

"No, thanks," I say again. My heart is beating in a weird fluttery way that is making me feel slightly sick. "I don't want any painkillers. I think I need a glass of water."

"It's probably the altitude," Eva says solicitously. "And the dry air. It's very easy to get dehydrated up here. You're so sensible not to drink alcohol."

Topher frowns at Inigo and jerks his head towards the kitchen. Inigo nods and hurries off. I suppose he has gone to get me water. This feels so wrong. It used to be me Topher barked at. And honestly, I preferred that. I preferred being invisible.

When Inigo comes back, Topher grabs the glass off him and says to the others, "Let's give Liz some space." Then he ushers me over to a small sofa where he gestures for me to sit down. I can't see any way out, so I do. Topher sits beside me, too close, and takes one of my hands.

I feel my sense of panic rise.

I know what he's going to say.

"Liz, I just wanted to tell you," he begins.

I look around, panicked. My heart keeps skipping beats. I wonder if I might have some kind of heart defect. Topher is talking about how proud he is of having given me my start, about the way I stood out at the interview, about the contribution I made to Snoop, about our "journey together."

His words are drowned out by the janglingly loud background music and a weird hissing in my ears. But I don't need to listen to his words to know what he is really saying.

I stood up for you.

I gave you your chance.

You wouldn't be here without me.

You owe me.

And he's right. I know he's right. That's the worst thing. Because I'm about to betray all of that.

He's being so nice that I want to be sick. But at the same time I can smell the booze on his breath and feel the heat of his body shoved up against mine, and all I can think of is my father, lowering over me.

I am about to nervously crack the joints in my fingers when a voice comes into my head unbidden. *If you make that disgusting sound one more time . . .*

I flinch, in spite of myself.

"And that makes me so proud," Topher is finishing.

I have no idea what to say. Before I can come up with anything, there is a high ringing noise from the far side of the foyer. It is Eva's assistant, Ani. She is wearing a silk dress that looks like it is made of two scarves tied together, and she is standing on her tiptoes and tapping two champagne flutes together. It makes a *ting ting ting* sound that echoes around the foyer.

Everyone falls quiet, apart from Elliot. He is still speaking to Rik. His deep bass monotone booms around the silent lobby.

"—server problems with the geosnoop rollout, if we can't—"

Rik nudges Elliot, who looks around. He breaks off midsentence, his face confused.

Beside me, Topher has gone completely stiff, and his expression is taken aback. This must be Eva's presentation. But it looks as if Topher knew nothing about it.

Suddenly I know what this is. I know what is happening. This is an ambush.

No. That's not the right word.

This is a coup.

ERIN

Snoop ID: LITTLEMY
Listening to: Offline
Snoopscribers: 1

"Snoopers!" Eva is saying, in a high-pitched, artificially jolly voice. She is standing on the bottom step of the spiral staircase, though she doesn't need the extra height, and she looks amazing in her flawless cashmere sheath, like a tall flute of champagne. "I know this wasn't on the agenda, but Ani and I wanted to welcome you all here and begin the week with a few highlights from the Snoop journey, just to remind you all how amazing you are, and how far we've come, and what you, all of you, have contributed to the phenomenon that is Snoop. Will you come into the den for a few minutes? You can bring your drinks."

There is a general shuffling and a weird feeling of electricity in the air that I can't quite pin down.

Looking around the room, I can see from the reactions of everyone here, and the expressions on their faces, that the group divides into three camps.

First, there is Eva's little coterie—which seems to comprise Rik and Ani. They knew about this, and were waiting for her cue. They were gathering round even before she made the announcement, and now that she has spoken they look tense, as if ready for battle.

Then there is a middle ground of people who are surprised, but pleasantly so, and looking forward to the diversion with a cheerful obliviousness. That group includes Tiger, Miranda, and the lawyer, Carl. They are picking up their drinks, chatting away, seemingly quite unaware of the tensions flowing around them.

And finally there is Topher's little group, who are also surprised—but not in a good way. His assistant, Inigo, looks like a kid who has stepped in a dog mess in new shoes and is about to get shouted at by his dad. Techy Elliot is standing in the corner with his arms folded, and he looks mulish. He is tapping his foot and glaring through his glasses like he's just been bluffed in a poker game. Topher himself has risen from the couch where he was talking to Liz, and he looks positively alarmed. It's the first time I've seen his boyish charm properly ruffled, and I realize that beneath the charisma and the projected confidence, there's something else. I'm just not sure what. Is his smooth surface hiding a frightened little boy inside? Or is it something very different, more dangerous perhaps? For a minute I think I see a flicker of anger cross his face.

Finally there is Liz. And I am not sure what camp she is in. She doesn't fit into any of them—but I think she does know what's going on. Her face is blank, her glasses reflecting the overhead light so that I can't see her expression. But she doesn't look happy. In fact she's got her arms wrapped round herself like she's fending off a blow.

"Hold on a second, Eva—" Topher says, with an attempt at his customary tone of command, but it's too late; Eva is ushering the others swiftly into the den, and he has no choice but to follow with Elliot, or get left behind. "Eva, what the f—"

And then the door shuts behind them.

LIZ

Snoop ID: ANON101
Listening to: Offline
Snoopscribers: 0

As Ani ushers us inside, I feel a twinge of panic. The den is small and dark. The windows are covered with blinds. The only light is coming from the doorway, and from a projection of the Snoop logo being beamed onto a blank wall. The image is bright pink, and it turns the faces of the others a strange, cooked color, like hot ham. I settle myself onto a sofa, and as the door swings softly shut, I feel the atmosphere close around me like a fist.

It is an atmosphere I haven't felt for nearly three years.

Money. Privilege. *Ambition.*

The scent of it is as real as Topher's expensive bespoke cologne, the same brand I used to have to order in from a little Paris perfumery in the rue des Capucines, stammering through his order in my bad schoolgirl French. I can smell it now, though he is over on the other side of the room.

I get a sudden wave of anxiety.

I think I might throw up.

"Tiger," Eva says, when everyone has found a place to sit. "Would you lead us through a short meditation?"

"Sure!" Tiger says. Her voice is slightly husky. I think she always sounds like that, but it makes me want to clear my own throat. I resist the urge to cough as she looks around the group. "Make yourselves comfortable everyone—whatever that means to you. That could be sitting, leaning, standing, embracing."

I can't stop myself from shuddering at the last word, but my reaction is better than the snort of derision I hear from Carl. Eva shoots him a look that could kill, and he covers it by shifting on his floor cushion. The filling inside squeaks and hisses as it resettles.

Tiger closes her eyes.

"Shut your eyes," she whispers, "and take a moment, everyone, to center yourselves."

There is silence in the room now. I shut my eyes, but it doesn't help the feeling of being trapped, in fact if anything it worsens it. I can feel the warmth of Inigo's shoulder to my left and Rik's thigh pressing against mine to the right. They can't help touching me—the sofa is too small for three—but it doesn't make me feel any less tense. I am sweating. My palms are sticky. My whole body is rigid with discomfort. I do not want to be here. I do *not* want to be here.

"Take a moment to thank yourself," Tiger says, her voice low and soft. "Thank your body for bringing you here, your bones for carrying you, your muscles for supporting you, your mind for freeing you."

I don't want to thank anyone for this. I want to get *out.* There is another rustle as Carl shifts uncomfortably, and suddenly I can't cope with the claustrophobia anymore. I open my eyes a crack, trying to dispel some of the discomfort. I am about to shut them again when I see I'm not the only one peeking. Opposite me, Topher's eyes open for a moment. He scans the room, trying to figure out what the hell is going on. Our eyes meet. *I see you.* He raises a single eyebrow. I shut my eyes quickly.

"Take a moment to thank the universe," Tiger-Blue continues. "For the gift that is your being; for the gift that is your being *here*; for the gift that is this place, the majesty of the mountains shared with us for just a few days."

Beside me I can hear Inigo's breathing. It is fast and shallow. When I glance over it looks like his teeth are gritted, and a muscle is jumping in his cheek. He is hating this as much as me, and clearly he did not know this was happening any more than Topher did. I know from my own PA days how Topher reacts to being out of the loop. Someone is going to get both barrels later. I feel sympathy for Inigo, but my main emotion is relief that it is not going to be me.

"And take a moment to thank Snoop," Tiger intones. "That thing that we are, and that is bigger than all of us. For all that we are—for all that we have—for bringing people into contact, and music into our lives. For the simple miracles it makes happen every day."

Thank God I don't work for Snoop anymore is all I can think.

I don't know if she is finished or not, but there is a short silence. I can feel a pulse beating in my throat. Just when it has stretched out to something almost unbearable, Eva speaks.

"Thank you Tiger-Blue, that was beautiful. And it brings me to what I wanted to say, which is thank *you* all for coming here, and for all that you've done for me, for Topher, for Snoop, and for music. Thank you for the music."

"Hear, hear," Topher says. Eyes snap open around the room, and he raises his glass so that we all have to drink, whether we want to or not. I sip my water.

"Now, you'll forgive me for springing this on you, but I couldn't let the week begin without a little celebration of our triumphs, of what *you've* achieved over the last four years," Eva says. She does not look at me when she says it, but it is impossible for me not to realize I am the odd one out here. I am the only person not currently employed by the company.

"Ani?" Eva says. And Ani nods and presses something on the laptop balanced on her knees. There is a crackle from the speakers.

Music begins to blast out, uncomfortably loud. Moving images begin to light up the wall opposite.

I should be watching the film—but I can't concentrate. The music is too loud. It is making my skull hurt. The images are too bright. They are zipping past too quickly. There is a kind of desperate, hectic intensity. My headache, which had been slowly fading, is back and pulsing in my temples. It feels as if a band is tightening around my forehead.

Figures and graphs flicker across the screen—profit and loss, users' profiles, expansion rates, competitors. I press my fingers to my eye sockets, shutting out the flashing images, but I can't shut out the thumping music as it segues from one song to another in a frenetic sample of Snoop's greatest hits.

Eva is talking over the music. She is speaking about social media reach and key influencers. The rest of the group is silent. I can feel Topher's simmering resentment from the other side of the room, even with my eyes closed.

And then the music cuts out. I feel a weight lifted off my shoulders, like someone has stopped screaming in my ears. I open my eyes. There is a single chart on the projector, overlaying the Snoop logo. It is full of figures. Eva is taking us through each set, explaining what they mean. Percentages, projections, ongoing costs—and then I hear it. The word we have all been dancing around for almost twelve hours.

Buyout.

I feel the band around my scalp squeeze unbearably tight. I am not ready for this.

She is talking about the offer. She is explaining what it could mean in terms of company expansion, employee opportunities—but she is barely halfway down the second table of figures when Topher interrupts.

"No, no, just fucking no, Eva."

"I beg your pardon?"

He stands up. His face obscures part of the projection so that his profile is beamed black and sharp onto the wall and the figures overlay his face like some sort of grotesque tattoo.

"This is half the story, and you know it. Where would we be if we'd given up our IP to Spotify like they wanted back at the beginning? Nowhere, that's where. We'd be some other tin-pot little streaming app no one's heard of and—"

"Topher, this is completely different." Eva is standing in the shadow, away from the projector beam. Her voice sounds pissed off, but also as if she is trying her best to sound reasonable. "You know it is."

"Different how? I'm not going to end up like fucking Friendster."

"If we try for another funding round we're more likely to end up like Boo.com at this rate," Eva snaps back. Then she takes a deep breath. I can see that she's trying to rein in her anger. "Look, Toph, you have some valid points, but I don't think now is the time or place—"

"Not the time or place?" He is crackling with anger.

I feel sick. I have a violent flashback to my childhood, my father standing over my mother, his voice raised. I squeeze my eyes tighter shut. I feel myself begin to shake.

"*You* were the one who decided to kick off the week with your little propaganda film—"

"Guys."

There's a lurch of cushions to my right, and Rik stands up. I open my eyes. He is picking his way through the cushions and glasses to put himself physically between them.

"I think Eva was just trying—"

"I know exactly what Eva was trying to do," Topher shouts. I fight the urge to put my hands over my ears. "She's trying to get her shot in first. Well, fuck that."

"Topher." Eva sounds close to tears, though I am not sure if she is. It's very difficult to know whether her upset is real or a strategic distraction. If she is acting, it is very convincing. "Toph, *please.* This was supposed to be a celebration—"

"It was supposed to be a fucking ambush—" Topher says.

"No, absolutely not, never." Her words carry conviction. But she has overreached herself with that statement. Everyone in the room knows that she is lying, and there is a rustle as people shift uncomfortably, refusing to meet one another's eyes.

"Guys!" Rik says desperately. "Guys, *please*, this isn't how we should be starting this week. We need to come out of this with a result everyone's happy with."

"Happy?" Topher rounds on him. "Happy? At this rate we'll be lucky to come out of it with everyone alive."

And with that he slams down his empty glass onto the coffee table and storms out of the room.

ERIN

Snoop ID: LITTLEMY
Listening to: Loyle Carner / Damselfly
Snoopers: 2
Snoopscribers: 3

I have my headphones in when Topher comes barreling out of the den and snatches a bottle of whiskey from the honesty bar in the lobby. I'm caught unawares, laying the table, tapping my feet to the beat. I wasn't expecting them to break for another ten minutes, and as I pull the earbuds hastily out, I catch the tail end of his remark.

"—can add this to the bill of that Dutch bitch."

Holy shit. What has gone down inside the den? For a minute I stand there, looking after Topher's retreating back, and then the rest of the group comes filing out, their expressions subdued, and I have to start showing them to their places at the table.

The big glass door in the lobby is still swinging to and fro from where Topher stormed out into the snow. Where on earth is he going? He was wearing jeans and a shirt, and it's minus eleven outside right now. There are no restaurants or bars in our little hamlet. St. Antoine 2000 is not much more than a handful of chalets. People who want to eat out in the evening have to go down to St. Antoine le Lac, which has all the shops and restaurants and cafés you could wish for. It's an easy ski down—a long blue run right into the center of the village. But the only way back up at this time is the funicular, and that closes at 11:00 p.m.

Someone puts music on the big main speakers in the dining room, The 1975, jangly and bright, perhaps in an attempt to raise the mood. But as I begin to serve up Danny's amuse-bouches—miniature wild mushroom gratins in little china spoons—Topher's absence is like a twinging nerve. The gratins go down well—as Danny's food always does—but I'm clearly not the only person stressing over Topher, and the atmosphere is strained. There is an empty space at the foot of the table where Topher should be, flanked by Inigo and Miranda, who exchange worried glances every time another course comes and goes without him reappearing.

Elliot, his back to the wall, eats with his head down, talking to no one, and spooning food into his mouth like it's a race. "Spooning" is literal. The starter is the truffled parsnip soup, so the spoon makes sense, but when I try to clear the cutlery away for the main course, Elliot snatches the spoon back and glares at me, like he caught me trying to steal his watch. When the venison arrives he attacks it with the soup spoon, ignoring the fork and steak knife to either side of his plate. In between courses he sits with his head bowed, staring at the knots and whorls of the wooden table, blanking Tiger to his left, who chatters away to Miranda as if this is perfectly normal, and Carl to his right, who ignores him back, pointedly angling his body away from Elliot towards Ani and Eva.

Eva, at the head of the table, picks at her food, looking at her watch and out the window at the falling snow, her face showing all the anxiety I am trying to conceal. When Carl makes some innocuous remark to her, she snaps back with a viciousness that makes me wince, though he seems to accept it as par for the course.

Liz looks pale and frankly miserable, like a rabbit in the headlights, and refuses all offers of wine. At one point Rik tries to talk to her. I don't know what he says, I don't hear the opening, but she shakes her head violently, and when he opens his mouth again, she bursts out "Excuse me, I'm going to the loo," pushing her chair back with a violence that makes it clatter against the tiled floor.

After she is gone Eva glares down the table at Rik, mouthing something that I can't quite read but which I think may have been *I told you so.*

Even Danny's crème brûlée fails to revive the evening, and after supper the group scatters, with pleas of headaches, early nights, and emails to send. As I pass through the lobby on my way to replenish the wood burner in the living room I notice that two more bottles are gone from the honesty bar.

The mystery of one at least is solved when I go through to the living room to find Rik and Miranda huddled in the corner of the big squashy sofa, a depleted bottle of Armagnac on the table between them, and some kind of Cuban jazz filtering out of the speaker system, presumably from either Rik's or Miranda's phone. Rik sees me clocking the bottle and flashes a smile.

"You don't mind, do you? We'll add it to the book at the end of the evening."

"Not at all," I say truthfully. "It's how the system is supposed to work. Can I get you anything else? Cheese? Coffee? Petits fours? Danny makes these incredibly moreish chocolate-dipped prunes that go really well with a glass of brandy."

Rik looks at Miranda and raises one eyebrow, in a kind of wordless exchange that speaks more about their relationship than anything physical. There is something going on here. They are more than just colleagues, whether they realize that themselves or not.

It is Rik who answers for them both.

"No, we're fine, thanks."

"No problem," I say. "Just let me know if you change your mind."

I begin to stack logs into the fire, and Rik leans closer to Miranda and recommences their conversation as if I'm not there.

"Did you see the *look* she gave me when I brought up the shares to Liz? I had to check it hadn't burned a hole in my shirt."

"I know." Miranda puts her head in her hands. "But, Rik, honestly, what were you thinking? Eva made it crystal clear—"

"I know, I know—" Rik says. He rubs his hand over his short hair, shaking his head in frustration. "But I was ticked off by Eva acting like she's the fucking Liz whisperer. I've known Liz as long as she has. We got on pretty well before all this blew up."

"What *did* happen?" Miranda says. "It was all before my time, I've never understood."

"You've got to understand, it was all just running on a shoestring in those days. It was a joke, those first six months. None of us were getting paid, not that Elliot gave a shit, I don't think he'd spend any money at all if Topher didn't make him. He's been like that ever since school. But the rest of us *did* mind. Eva was running through her modeling savings like no tomorrow. Topher had finally pissed his parents off so much they'd cut him off without a penny, and he was sofa surfing with old school friends. I was working days at KPMG and nights at Snoop, and right at the bottom of my overdraft. And Liz was just this secretary who answered an advert online and was happy to work for a shit wage. I mean, even then, she dressed like some kind of sister wife, but she was efficient, and she didn't make a fuss about working out of a crappy rented office with no air-con in South Norwood."

"I didn't mean that, I meant how did she end up being the one casting—"

"I'm coming to that. We were about two weeks off launching when we finally ran out of cash. We were just broke—flat broke—not a single avenue left. Credit cards, overdrafts, friends and family—we'd wrung them all dry, and we were about ten grand short of what we needed to keep the lights on. Topher had even sold his Ferrari, but it just wasn't enough. For about four days it looked like we were going to the wall—we had bills rolling in and contracts we'd signed, and we were getting 'letters before action' and bailiff notifications left, right, and center. And then out of nowhere, little Liz pipes up that her grandmother just died and left her ten thousand pounds.

And she says she'll put it into the company. Only she wants security. Not interest—she wants shares in the company, and not just any shares—but voting shares. Well, we left it to the lawyers to argue the split, but the end result was thirty percent shares to Topher, thirty percent to Eva, nineteen to Elliot, nineteen to me, and two percent to Liz."

"Two percent?" Miranda says. "Of a company that hadn't raised any capital and was barely solvent? It doesn't sound like much security for ten grand."

"Some people might agree," Rik says dryly. "But she's getting the last laugh. That ten grand will be worth around twelve million if the buyout goes ahead."

In my shock, I drop a log. It clatters to the slate hearth, knocking over a little pottery jar that holds firelighters. The jar smashes with a noise that sounds almost absurdly loud, and I catch my breath, ready to apologize, but Rik and Miranda don't seem to have even noticed, and as I resume stacking the logs more carefully, they are still talking.

"Holy shit," Miranda says, and she's laughing, but in a slightly shocked way, as if this is the first time she's heard the numbers. "I mean I knew the buyout offer was good but . . ." She looks like she's doing sums in her head. "So if Liz is getting twelve, then that makes your share—"

"You can do the maths," Rik says, and there's a grin pulling at the side of his face. "But that's the point. *If* the buyout goes ahead. The investors are getting antsy, and I don't think they're going to stand for another round of funding. If Topher just keeps on like this and runs us all into the ground—"

"Yup. Gotcha," Miranda says, a little bitterly. "Back where we started, in the insolvency courts. But then, surely, it's a no-brainer for Liz, isn't it? Okay, Elliot will vote with Topher, we all know that. But if Liz uses her brain and votes with you and Eva, then ka-ching." She makes a money-rubbing gesture with her fingers.

"Yeah, it's just a pity Eva's such a fucking bitch," Rik says, half under his breath. "She doesn't make it easy to do the right thing, sometimes."

I'm trying not to eavesdrop, but it's hard not to overhear what they're saying, even above the music, and by the time I have finished clearing up the pottery shards, I know more than I ever expected about Eva's bullying of the junior staff, Topher's instability, and Snoop's precarious financial position. It's almost a relief when they move on to other topics—plans for tomorrow's skiing, the crap Wi-Fi, Rik's wife, who seems to be causing him some grief. At some point one of them turns up the volume on the music so that I can no longer hear their words clearly.

But as I stand, feeling the small of my back complain after the long day of lifting and bending, I do hear the tail end of Miranda's reply to something Rik said.

"Well, you're probably right. But in that case, we'll just have to *make* her, won't we?"

The words stay with me as I close the door quietly behind me and move out into the lobby, to stare out at the still-falling snow.

We'll just have to *make* her.

Who are they talking about? Liz? Eva? Or someone else completely, Rik's wife, maybe?

On the face of it, there's nothing remarkable about her words. It's a phrase you might hear any day of the week. So why does the cool determination in Miranda's voice stick in my head?

LIZ

Snoop ID: ANON101
Listening to: Snooping XTOPHER ✔
Snoopers: 0
Snoopscribers: 0

It is 11:02 p.m. I am up in my room. I am in bed, in my dressing gown, but I am not asleep. I am snooping Topher. Not because I want to listen to his music, which is always weird experimental club stuff, but because I am trying to work out whether he is all right.

There is no check-in function on Snoop. As far as location goes, the only way of knowing where people live is if they choose to list their location in the brief paragraph of description attached to each username. Still, some part of me had been hoping that his music choices would give me an insight into his psyche.

I don't know what I imagined. Sad guitar solos. An infinite loop of "All by Myself." What he is actually playing is an endless stream of angry Spanish punk rock. Or it could be Portuguese. It sounds annoyed, but that is as much as I can tell. On the plus side he is listening to *something* and is therefore presumably alive. Though on reflection, I realize I can't even be sure of that. There's nothing to say his phone isn't just streaming to a frozen ditch. After a few minutes I minimize the app with a sigh.

The memory of our conversation on the sofa downstairs is still with me, like a hangover. I know what Topher was trying to do. He was trying to guilt-trip me. Trying to remind me of everything I owe him.

The thought should make me feel angry, and it does, in a way. He is an arrogant public school boy who got lucky with a great idea and, more crucially, a mummy and daddy who were prepared to bankroll him—at least for the first few years. He is everything I'm not. Rich. Entitled. Confident.

But underneath my anger there are some uncomfortable facts. The fact that he took a chance on a gawky, awkward twentysomething, who no one ever looked at twice. The girl from Crawley, smelling of charity shops and hand-me-downs and desperation—he looked past all that and saw the person inside—the *real* me, dogged, determined, prepared to give 110 percent.

Most important, when I offered to put my grandmother's money into Snoop, *he* was the one who told me to stick out for shares, not repayment interest. Rik, Eva, they both tried to persuade me against it. They talked about the uncertainty of the returns—the possibility that Snoop might fold without ever making a profit. But Topher told me that shares would be in my own best interests. And he was right.

Topher is the reason I'm here today. I still do not know whether I should be grateful to him for that, or blame him. Both, maybe.

That girl—Erin—told us that the funicular stops at eleven. So if he caught it, he should be here soon. But that is the question. Did he catch it?

I move restlessly to look out the window, at the snowflakes still whirling down. The forecast was predicting lows of minus twenty tonight. People die in cold like that.

The knock at the door makes me jump. I tighten the belt on my dressing gown and walk over. My heart is thumping as I turn the lock.

It is Eva.

"Liz," she says. "May I come in?" She has changed out of the white woolen dress she wore at dinner. Now she is wearing stretchy yoga pants that make her legs look extremely long. Her scent trails after her like an oil slick. It is strong and a little sickly. I think it might be Poison.

"Um . . . okay," I say. I feel a little ambushed and resentful. I do not really want her in my room, but I am not sure how I can say that without sounding strange.

She pushes past me and goes over to the window, where she stands looking out across the valley with her back to me. I notice that my closet door is ajar, showing a rail full of dowdy, unironed clothes and my two cases. The biggest suitcase is sticking out slightly, preventing the door from shutting. I nudge it with my foot and close the gap.

Eva turns, just as the door clicks shut.

"Are you okay?" she asks abruptly.

I am taken aback by the question, unsure what to reply. It is probably just a figure of speech, but still, I am not used to people, least of all Eva, caring what I think. It makes me feel strangely exposed. I cannot think what to say, but it doesn't matter, Eva is speaking.

"I wanted to apologize for springing that presentation on everyone, but I was afraid that if I put it on the agenda, Topher would find a way to get his side in first—"

Oh. She has come to try to persuade me again.

"Eva, please." My headache, which had subsided after dinner, starts up again. It throbs in time with my heartbeat. "Please, I don't want to do this now."

"Don't worry." She takes my hands in hers. They are cold and strong. "I totally understand. I'd be torn in your shoes too. You feel loyalty to Topher, I get that, I do. We all do. But we both know . . ."

She trails off. She does not need to finish.

And in fact, she does not really need to make her case. The facts make it for her.

There are twelve million reasons to vote with Eva. She doesn't need to make it twelve million and one.

"I know," I say. It's a whisper. "Eva I know, it's just that Topher . . ."

Topher, who gave me my first-ever chance, who told me to hold out for the shares in the first place. How can I tell him I am betraying him? What will he *do*? For the first time, I realize; I am frightened.

"Liz, you *know* what you want to do, what you *need* to do . . . ," Eva says, and her voice is cajoling, like she is talking to a scared child. "Come on, haven't I always had your back? Haven't we always taken care of each other?"

I remember Rik's question at dinner tonight, the question that made me push back my chair and leave the room. *So, Liz, how are you going to spend your share bonus?* It was so brash, so bold, so full of assumptions.

Eva is more subtle. She knows that the money terrifies me in a way. Because for someone like me, who grew up having to hoard every last penny my dad didn't spend on the slots, it is an unimaginable sum. Ridiculous. Transformative. *Life* changing.

Eva knows that the thing that will persuade me is not the money—but something else. Something much more personal, between her and me; an appeal to the past we share. I was her assistant once too, back in the days when Snoop could only afford one. In a different way, I owe as much to Eva as I do to Topher. More.

But really, she knows what Rik knows, what Carl knows, what everyone apart from Topher and Elliot seems to accept: that it is not a choice at all.

There is only one sane answer to the question in front of me. My loyalty to Topher is being weighed against not just twelve million pounds, but against something else entirely—the prospect of a very different life to the one I am used to. In the end, what is at stake is my freedom. Freedom from work, from worry, from watching every step—freedom from this.

"I know, Eva," I say. My voice is very low. "I know. It's just . . . it's hard."

"I understand," she says. She presses my hand again. Her fingers are cold against mine, and very insistent in the message her grip is conveying. "And I know it's hard. I feel that loyalty to Toph too, of course I do. But I can count on you, yes?"

"Yes," I say. My voice is almost inaudible, even to myself. "Yes, you can count on me."

"Good." She smiles, her wide, beautiful smile. It is a smile that once beamed out from a thousand billboards and catwalks all across Europe. It is like *Thank you, Liz, I know what that means. And you can count on me too. We'll take care of each other, won't we?*

I nod, and she gives me a perfunctory hug and leaves the room.

When she's gone I open the window to get rid of her scent. I lean out, and I let the anxiety locked inside my chest explode into something huge and almost overwhelming. I imagine the meeting, the vote, me raising my hand in support of the buyout, and the expression on Topher's face as he registers my betrayal . . . And then I imagine what will happen if I don't, and I feel utterly sick.

Because Eva is right. There *is* only one choice. I know what I have to do. I just have to find the courage.

And once I have made up my mind, a strange kind of peace descends on me.

It will be okay. It will all be okay.

I shut the window. I climb back into bed and I switch off Snoop. Then I lie, quite still, listening instead to the whisper of the snow falling onto my balcony outside. Obliterating everything.

ERIN

Snoop ID: LITTLEMY
Listening to: Snooping ITSSIOUXSIE ✔
Snoopers: 5
Snoopscribers: 7

When my alarm goes off, I struggle up out of a deep, disturbing dream—a nightmare of digging, digging, digging through hard-packed snow, my hands numb with cold, my muscles shaking, hot blood running down my neck. I know what I'm going to find—and I'm both yearning for it and dreading it. But I wake up before I reach my goal.

It's a relief to open my eyes and find myself in my own little room, my phone alarm screeching into the silence, until I grope my way to the snooze button and shut it off. The clock reads 6:01, and I lie there for a minute, blinking, still half asleep, and trying to throw off the uneasy feeling the dream has left.

Just because it's a weekend doesn't mean it's not an early start. Danny and I swap, so that one of us gets up at six to fire up the coffee machine, get breakfast started, and clear up from the night before, while the other has what passes for a lie-in. Today it's my turn for the early shift, and I can't stop yawning as I stumble out of bed and pull on my clothes. Some people find they get insomnia at altitude. Not me. If anything it's the reverse.

As I pass Topher's door I pause, trying to hear if he's inside. Did he get home okay? I didn't hear him come in, but I left the front door unlocked, and when I came down at midnight to check, there were wet footprints in the foyer.

I stand there, holding my breath, when suddenly a huge snore rips through the silence, and I let out a shuddering laugh. *Someone* is in there at any rate, even if it's not Topher.

Downstairs is quiet, last night's log fire just glowing embers behind the wood burner's glass door. I open up the vents and stick another log on top of the ashes, and then I begin clearing up the debris of the night before.

Snoop is no worse than a lot of the other groups that stay here, but I don't know why today I feel particularly jaded as I pour thirty-year-old brandy down the sink and pick melted Camembert out of the dining room rug. Someone has been smoking inside too, in defiance of the rules—there is a cigarette butt stubbed out in a dish of Danny's painstakingly made petits fours. That's what sets my teeth on edge, I think. I remember him making those miniature Florentines; mixing them, baking them, carefully dipping each one into precisely tempered chocolate, laying them out to set. Treating them like the little masterpieces they were. And now someone has used them as a makeshift ashtray.

It takes me a while to shake off the cloud of anger, but by 7:00 a.m. my mood has lifted a little. The rooms are clean, the fire is crackling, the oven is on for sausages, and the bircher muesli is standing in a big crystal bowl on the side, along with huge pitchers of fresh-squeezed juices and jugs of milk and cream. There is still no noise from above, which means I can afford ten minutes to sit down with a coffee and my phone. Normally I'd be checking the snow forecast, or scrolling through Twitter—but today I find myself opening up Snoop and idly flipping through lists of my favorite artists, figuring out who's online, who's listening to what, as I sip my coffee. There are some amazing people on here, proper celebs mixed with people who are just fascinating personalities, and Danny's right, there's something incredibly addictive about pressing play on the song they are actually listening to at this precise moment, knowing that you are beat for beat in sync with each other. It's midnight in NYC and lots of the people I snoop on are playing late-night come-down music, which is not what I'm looking for at this time of day, but then I hit a cool little vein of British celebrities who all seem to be up and listening. Why are they awake six a.m. UK time? Couldn't they sleep? Maybe they always get up at this time.

I'm washing up the serving bowls that are too big for the dishwasher, tapping my feet to "Rockaway Beach" by the Ramones, when the sound begins to break up. As I'm digging my phone out of my pocket to check the headphone connection, the song drops out completely. Damn. I stare at the screen. The Wi-Fi is still showing a strong signal, but when I click on the Snoop tab a little pop-up message appears. *We can't get no satisfaction. (Please check your internet connection.)*

I sigh, turn off the app, and begin washing up again, this time in silence, but before I have done more than a couple of plates, there's a tap on the window to my right, and I look across to see Jacques from the bakery down the valley, holding a stack of baguettes and a giant bag of croissants. I pull off my rubber gloves and open the door, breathing white into the cold morning air.

"Salut, ma belle," he says around his cigarette as he hands the bread over, and then he takes a long drag of his Gitane and blows the smoke over his shoulder.

"Hi, Jacques," I say in French. My French isn't perfect, but I can hold a conversation. "Thanks for the bread. What do you say to the forecast?"

"Ah, well, it isn't pretty," he says, also in French, taking another long, thoughtful drag and looking up at the sky. Jacques is one of the very few people who actually grew up here. Almost everyone else is an incomer, either a tourist or a seasonal worker. Jacques has lived here all his life; his father owns the bakery in St. Antoine le Lac, and Jacques will be taking over for good in few years when his dad retires.

"Do you think there will be the possibility to ski today?" I ask.

Jacques shrugs.

"Perhaps, in the morning. But the afternoon . . ." He holds his hand out and makes the rocking motion the French use to signify that something might go one way or the other. "There's heavy snow coming. You see the color of those clouds over La Dame?"

La Dame means La Dame Blanche—the big peak that looms over the whole valley, casting a near permanent shadow over the chalet. Now, as I look up at the top, I see what he means. The clouds that gather up there are ugly and dark.

"But it's not just that," Jacques says. "It's the wind. It makes it difficult for the guys in the avalanche-control teams. They can't get out to start the small falls, you know?"

I nod. I've seen them doing it on fine days, after big dumps—setting off small charges to safely release the buildup of snow on the upper slopes before it can get to critical mass. I'm not sure how they do it exactly—sometimes they seem to use helicopters, other times it looks more like some sort of gun. Either way, I can imagine that the wind makes it too hazardous and unpredictable.

"You think that there is a danger of falls?" I ask, trying to hide my uneasiness.

Jacques shrugs again.

"Serious ones? Unlikely. But there will be slopes closed this afternoon for sure, and I wouldn't plan any off-piste skiing."

"I don't ski off-piste," I say shortly. Well, not anymore.

Jacques doesn't respond to that, he just looks thoughtfully up at the slopes and then blows out a ring of smoke. "Well, I must be going. See you later, Erin."

And he crunches off through the soft-fallen snow towards the funicular. I feel my stomach shift with the lingering chill from my dream as I watch him go, and then I turn back, into the warmth of the kitchen.

Inside, I am stacking the bread on the table when the sound of a croaky, sleep-hoarse voice comes from behind my shoulder, making me jump.

"Monsieur Bun the boulanger's son?"

It's Danny, leaning against the counter, squinting at the bright morning lights.

"Jesus." I put a hand on my chest. "You startled me. Yes, it was Jacques. He says there's going to be more snow."

"You're shitting me." Danny rubs a hand over his stubble. "There's not going to be any more of the stuff left up there. Will we get any skiing in?"

"I think so. This morning he reckons. He says the runs will probably be shut in the afternoon—avalanche risk."

"It's already on orange," Danny says, referring to the colored scale published by Météo France. Orange is level three—"considerable risk" of avalanche occurring—and means off-piste skiing is inadvisable, and some of the steeper slopes are probably going to be shut. Red is level four and is when the whole resort starts to close. Black is level five and means risk to settlements and roads. Black is like, *Make sure your last meal is a good one*, but the control teams don't let it get to that point if they can help it.

I'm gathering up the tray of coffee cups when Danny speaks again, his voice casual.

"Who's Will?"

The question is a shock—enough to make me stumble, and two of the cups slide off the tray and shatter on the floor. By the time Danny and I have gathered up the shards, I'm composed enough to answer.

"What do you mean? There's no one here called Will."

"You were dreaming last night, shouting about someone called Will. I heard you through the wall. It woke me up."

Fuck.

"Huh, weird." I keep my voice light, and just a little puzzled. "Sorry about that. Nightmare I guess."

And then before he can pursue the question, I leave the room. I carry the tray through to the dining room with hands that are only slightly trembling and begin laying out the breakfast things on the big wooden table. I'm setting out the last jars of preserve when I hear the click of heels on the stairs and look up to see Eva coming into the lobby. She looks pissed off.

"Hi," I say.

"Hi, what's happened to the internet?" she says without preamble. My heart sinks. Shit. I'd hoped it was a temporary thing.

"Oh God, I'm so sorry. Is it still down?"

"Yes, and the mobile reception is terrible."

"I'm ever so sorry, it's something to do with the snow. It happens occasionally. I think it means a wire's snapped in the snow or a repeater's gone down or something. It's not uncommon after very heavy falls, and we've certainly had enough of that recently."

I wave my hand at the window where the snow is halfway up the glass in some parts.

"I don't need the science bit, what I want to know is when will it be back up?"

Her tone is sharp and unapologetically annoyed. It's the voice of someone used to saying "Jump" and getting the answer "How high?" Which doesn't bother me in itself—in some ways I prefer people who are clear about their expectations, rather than smiling at you all week and then giving you a shitty write-up on their feedback forms. But in this instance I can't help, and something tells me Eva isn't going to like that fact.

"I don't know," I say. I fold my arms. "I'm sorry. They usually get it up and running in a few days, but I can't say with more certainty than that."

"Fuck." She is annoyed and not trying to hide it, but the expression on her face is something more than that, there's a level of stress and upset here that's out of proportion.

"I'm sorry," I say again. "I wish I could do something more concrete. Is it a problem with work?"

"Work?" She looks up at that, and then shakes her head and gives a bitter little laugh. "God no. All my work problems can be summed up in one word—*Topher*. No, this is home. It's—" She sighs, and then runs her hand through her silky white-blond curtain of hair. "Oh, it probably doesn't sound like a big deal, but I always Skype my daughter, Radisson, every morning when I'm away. It's our little ritual, you know? I have to travel so much, and I'm not always able to be there as much as I'd like. But the one thing I always do is say good morning to her over breakfast, and I feel like a complete shit that I can't do it today. I managed to get through on the phone to my partner, but you know, with little kids they don't really understand phones. She's only eighteen months. She needs to see a face."

"I can understand that," I say softly. "It must be really hard being away from her."

"Thanks," Eva says shortly. She blinks and then turns away, under the pretense of filling up a cup at the steaming tea urn. I think she is pissed off with herself for showing that she's only human, but it makes me like her a bit more. Underneath that icy facade is a person, apparently.

Then she picks up a tea bag, puts it into the cup of boiling water, and walks away back to her room without another word.

Topher, Rik, and Carl are the next guests down, about half an hour later, and my heart does a little jump of relief at the sight of the three of them. Well—at the sight of Topher, to be more accurate. He looks bleary-eyed and hungover, but he's here, which is as far as my responsibility to the group goes.

"So you weren't the only dirty stay out," Carl is saying to Topher as they enter the room. "Inigo came crawling back to our room at five a.m."

"Oh Christ," Topher says. He rolls his eyes. "Not that again. Eva should know better."

Eva? Her name gives me a little prickle of reaction, though I can't say why, exactly. It's none of my business after all. Perhaps it's coming straight after her obvious distress at not being able to talk to her family. Is Topher right, or just stirring up trouble?

"Hashtag cougar," Carl says with a grin. He walks across to the breakfast buffet I have laid out, picks up a warm croissant, and dunks it straight into the glass mason jar containing Danny's golden homemade apricot preserve. Then takes a huge bite, grinning through the crumbs.

"Hashtag?" Rik says disdainfully. He's wearing a black merino polo neck and looks like a page ripped from a high-end men's knitwear catalog. "Cougar? Have I woken up in a frat house in 2005?" Then he turns to me with a deliberately charming smile that crinkles the skin at the corners of his mouth. "I'd love an espresso, please, Erin. If that's okay."

Carl glares at him with a force I can feel over the other side of the room.

It should have come across as a dick move—a younger, fitter, better-looking man taking the piss out of his less-hip colleague. But I get the impression that Rik's issue isn't really with Carl's choice of words but more with his choice of conversation topic. It's funny, I'm starting to like Rik more and more. There is something about the way he relates to Eva—and Miranda actually—that is very different to Carl's and Topher's sniggering boys' club attitude. Much more likable.

"So, skiing today?" The voice comes from the top of the stairwell, and I look up to see Miranda making her way down the spiral. Her dark hair is tied back in a bun, and she looks ready for business. She clocks me dispensing Rik's espresso and says, "Good morning, Erin, mine's an almond-milk cortado, please. What's the forecast?"

"More snow in the afternoon," I say. "In fact, some people are saying they expect the avalanche rating to rise, which means more closures. If you want to ski, do it this morning is my advice."

"Eva won't be pleased," Carl says. "She's got this morning packed with presentations."

"Eva will have to lump it," Topher says sourly. He pops two white pills into his mouth and washes them down with a gulp from his stainless-steel water bottle, then massages the bridge of his nose. "I didn't come all this way to sit in a board room all week listening to her bore on about investor expectations. She can push her little bits of paper around this afternoon."

"I'm sure she won't mind rescheduling," Miranda says mildly. "It'll be good for everyone to blow off some steam. I certainly can't wait to get my skis on."

She has the look of a skier. Lean but strong. Topher looks like a boarder, and I'm unsurprised when he says, "What's the off-piste like round here, Irene? Any good powder?"

It takes me a beat, then I realize he's referring to me, at the same time as Miranda hisses, "She's called *Erin*," in Topher's direction.

I smile, trying to convey that I don't mind. Irene, Eileen, Emma— it's all the same. When you're staff, you're not really a person. Topher would probably treat a robot with high-quality AI with the same level of polite disinterest.

"The snow must be amazing right now," Rik says. "Can you show us some good off-piste routes, Erin?"

I feel the blood drain from my face, and I'm trying to think what to say when I'm saved from answering by Danny, who comes out at that moment carrying a huge platter of bacon rolls.

"Erin's too much of a wuss to go out of bounds," he says with a grin. "But I can show you some cool little routes if you want. Not today though."

"Why not today?" Topher says, frowning.

"The avalanche risk is too high," I say, trying to regain my composure. "But it should be better later in the week when they've had the chance to set off some controlled explosions."

In truth I have absolutely no idea whether it'll be better, but no one likes a pessimist, and they've got to get up there and clear the buildup *some* time.

"Well that's a plan then," Topher says briskly. He picks up a bacon roll and takes a bite.

"What's a plan?"

The voice comes from the direction of the living room and we all turn to see Eva standing there. She's holding a massive sheaf of files and a laptop and looks ready to go.

"Erin says that the only skiing today is likely to be in the morning," Rik says quickly, "so we thought we'd get the finance presentation out of the way now, and then move the rest of the stuff to the afternoon." He speaks rather fast, and I have the impression he's attempting to head off Topher from saying the same thing but with less diplomacy.

Eva pauses in the doorway. She looks like she's trying to decide how to feel about this, whether to make a fuss. Then she looks at her watch, and shrugs.

"Fine. It's nearly eight thirty. Shall we get going on the presentation? It shouldn't take more than half an hour, so we won't be far off the first lift if we leave straight after that."

"Sooner the better, as far as I'm concerned," Topher says. "We can take breakfast into the den with us. Where the fuck are the others?"

"I'm here." It's a voice from the doorway, and we look across to see Tiger entering the room. "Sorry, have I kept you?" She looks pale and rumpled, her short ombré hair sticking out in all directions as if she hasn't brushed it yet this morning.

"Yes," Topher says, at the same time as Miranda says, "No, you're not the only one missing."

"Ready to milk some pow, Tiger?" Topher asks. I hear a noise from the direction of the kitchen where Danny has stifled a derisive snort, and I busy myself over the espresso machine to hide my own expression.

"Sorry?" Tiger says. She rubs her eyes as if the morning light is hurting her. "I didn't catch that."

"Are you ready to get on your board?"

"Oh, yes, sure."

"You look worse than Topher," Eva says bluntly, and Tiger laughs, with an uncertain look at Topher.

"I didn't sleep well. I had awful insomnia all night."

"It's the altitude," Eva says. "It affects some people that way. I always take sleeping pills for the first few nights."

I don't hear Tiger's reply, because Topher pulls me to one side.

"Are all the hire skis here?"

"All waiting for you in the locker room," I say. The ski shop is down in the village, so we pick up the gear for the skiers. Most people here have brought their own though. It's only Liz, Ani, and Carl who have hired equipment. "Before you go, let me show you the best route back to the chalet. It's a really great run, but it's a bit counterintuitive, looking at the map. You actually have to cut across a little bit between two runs."

"Is that safe?" Carl says, sounding alarmed. "You just said it was too dangerous to go out of bounds."

"Oh, no," I hasten to reassure him. "It's totally safe, it's a very well-trodden path. It's not off-piste in that sense. But it's just not shown as a route on the lift map, so unless you know to peel off through the trees, you get taken right down Blanche-Neige into St. Antoine le Lac and have to come back up the funicular."

"Is it safe for beginners?" Carl says, still looking anxious.

"The cut-through? Absolutely. It's the equivalent of a green run. Have you skied at all?"

"Yeah, but not for years." He looks over his shoulder. Topher and the others have gone through into the den to begin the meeting, and we are alone. "Strictly entre nous," he says, rather bitterly, lowering his voice, "I'd rather have poked my fucking eyes with cocktail sticks than gone on a skiing holiday. But this is what you get for working for a company like Snoop. Topher's a snowboarding nut, Eva's practically a pro skier, and what they say goes. The rest of us have to lump it."

I nod, as if he's making small talk, but in truth this insight into Snoop's inner workings is weirdly fascinating. There may be five shareholders, but in day-to-day life it seems that Topher and Eva call the shots pretty autocratically.

It makes it all the more interesting that for once, the balance of power is out of their hands. One of them is *not* going to get their way over this buyout. The question is, which one?

LIZ

Snoop ID: ANON101
Listening to: Offline
Snoopscribers: 0

"Okay," Rik says. He clicks off the PowerPoint slide and turns on the lights. "That's it. I think everyone can go and get into their ski gear now."

I rub my eyes, feeling the sudden brightness searing the back of my skull. My headache is back again. I stand up, pulling my tights straight. Around me there is the rustle of beanbags and the noise of sofa springs as everyone else gets to their feet.

"Just a second," Topher puts in. His voice is smooth. "Can the shareholders stay back for a sec?"

I feel something in my stomach drop away. There is a murmur of assent. Ani, Inigo, Carl, Miranda, and Tiger rise and begin to file out.

Within a few seconds it's just Topher, Eva, Rik, Elliot . . . and me.

Oh God. I feel my breath coming fast. Oh God, oh God, oh God . . . they're going to ask and I'm going to have to—to have to—

"Look," Eva is saying, "I think the cold, hard reality of Rik's figures wasn't lost on any of us. It's a pretty stark picture. Our overheads—"

"I don't want to go over all that again," Topher says dismissively, as if the profit and loss sheets Rik just took us through were totally irrelevant. "We can all read a spreadsheet, and Rik made his points very ably. Before we head out, I think it would be really helpful to take an indicative vote, so we know where we stand."

My breath quickens. The headache behind my eyes intensifies until the edges of my vision begin to fray.

"But, Topher," Eva is saying, "you know perfectly well that we don't have full information yet; that's the point of this week, to weigh up all—"

"And it's why I said *indicative*," Topher interrupts, a touch of aggression creeping into his voice. "This is nonbinding, Eva. It's just a show of hands to see where we are. It's possible we're already close to an agreement."

Eva says nothing. She glances at me, and I know what she is thinking, and I know she can't figure out how to head Topher off from this. He is like a mule when he puts his mind to something. He just pushes, and pushes, and pushes . . .

Elliot also says nothing, of course, but we all know what his silence means—support for Topher. It's what it always means. Elliot doesn't care about anything except for code. For everything else, he defers to Topher.

"Rik?" Eva says. Her tone is brittle.

"Why not?" Rik says. His acquiescence surprises me.

"So," Topher says, in a slightly mollifying voice. "As before, in a *nonbinding* show of hands, who's in favor of the buyout?"

"Me," Rik says.

"And me," Eva adds. There is a long silence, and I can feel the tension as they wait. When Topher speaks again, there is satisfaction in his tone, like a cat that's got the cream.

"Great, and who's against?"

"Me." Elliot's deep monotone makes the word sound like a full stop.

"And me, obviously," Topher says. There is another pause, and then he says, as if attempting to sound more casual than he really is. "And . . . um, what's your vote, Liz?"

I swallow. There is something hard stuck in my throat, and I realize that I haven't spoken since I got up this morning. No one talked to me at breakfast. No one asked my opinion at the meeting. I don't know if I can trust my voice when I speak.

"Liz?" Eva says. I can tell that she is trying not to pressure me, but at the same time, the edge in her tone shows clear.

"I—" There is a crack in my voice, it is croaky with disuse. I swallow again, vainly forcing down the obstacle that feels like it is choking me. "I don't know."

"Come on, Liz," Rik says, and though he is trying to sound jolly and supportive, there is impatience in his tone as well. "You must have an idea of how you feel. Do you want twelve million, yes or no? It's not a hard question."

"*Or*," Topher says, and the sharpness makes me flinch, "do you want shares worth potentially much more if we retain control and go public."

"If we retain control and manage to remain *solvent*," Rik shoots back.

"For fuck's sake, Rik—" Topher snaps, and I feel the panic in my chest begin to explode like a slow but inexorable chemical reaction. Before it can escape, Eva stands up, holding out her hands, putting herself physically between them.

"Guys, guys, come on. We've got plenty of time to go through the question of a public offering, now's not the time. Liz, am I to take it that you can't give us an indication right now?"

I can't bring myself to speak, I just make a swing of my head that could be yes, or could be no. Eva smiles, and crosses the room to take my hand. She squeezes it reassuringly, the scent of her perfume druglike and headily overwhelming in the small room.

"No problem, okay, well in view of that, I suggest we all head up to our rooms to get ready, and we can go through the issues Rik raised in more detail after lunch. Agreed?"

There are nods and murmurs of assent, and then Topher, Elliot, and Rik file out.

I stand up, my legs shaking, and I'm about to follow them when Eva stops me.

"Liz, hold up a second. Are you okay?"

I can't speak for a minute, and then I manage.

"I'm—I'm sorry, Eva, I know we talked about this last night, and I promise, I am—I am going to do it—it's j-just—"

"Of course," Eva says, and she puts a hand on my arm. I think it's meant to be reassuring, but the effect is to prevent me edging towards the door. "I completely understand."

"It's just—" I glance out the door, checking Topher isn't within earshot. But he is gone, thank God. "It's just, it's hard to come out and say it, you know?"

"I get that. There's a lot of loyalty between you. And I understand what you're saying; he's going to see it as a betrayal, no matter how reasonable your decision is."

"I'm—" I swallow. The truth is I'm frightened, but I don't want to say that to Eva. It sounds absurdly dramatic. "I'm just—"

Eva's looking at me with concern, and I know why. She's wondering if I will go through with our agreement. But I have made up my mind now. I grope again for that fatalistic peace that descended on me last night. I try to remember how it felt—that certainty, that calm resolve. My heart steadies a little. I can be as determined as Topher, when I make up my mind.

"You don't need to worry," I say, and my voice is stronger. "I'm not going to let you down. I just—I need to bite the bullet."

Eva's face clears, and she pats my arm sympathetically, giving it a little squeeze to show that we are in this together.

"Look, he'll be pissed off," she says. "I can't pretend that's not the case. And I can't say I'm relishing this either. But he'll get over it. He'll understand."

The thing is, he won't. As we file out of the little room to change into ski clothes and get our stuff together, that's what I realize. He definitely won't understand. There is no way of seeing what I'm about to do as anything other than a huge betrayal. But I have no choice. That's what I just have to keep telling myself. I have no choice. I have to see this through.

ERIN

Snoop ID: LITTLEMY
Listening to: Offline
Snoopscribers: 10

"Right," I call to the little group standing in front of the chalet, fiddling with bindings. "Let me explain the lay of the land a bit. The track in front of us, leading off to the left, is the one you took from the funicular railway. You can retrace your steps back up the hill, which would get you back to the funicular and the long blue run down into St. Antoine."

"Blanche-Neige, right?" Topher puts in, and I nod.

"That's right. It's a really nice run. *However,* getting back up there would require a fair amount of sidestepping uphill, so assuming you want to ski out, the only downhill route is this path down through the woods." I indicate a little path that winds along the side of the chalet and disappears through the pines behind us. "It leads onto the bottom of the green run, Atchoum, and from there to the Reine telecabine."

"Telecabine?" Inigo asks, and I remember the Americans use different terms.

"Oh, sorry, the what-do-you-call-it. The bubble lift. Are there any complete beginners here?"

"M-me!" Liz calls, nervously. "I've only skied once before. Dry slope. I wasn't very good."

"Okay, well don't worry, the path is a little bit steep for the first few meters but then it levels out and really all you've got to do is point your skis forward and slide the whole way. You can snowplow the first section if you want, but I wouldn't recommend it, you want a bit of speed for the flat. I suggest the experienced skiers go first, then the snowboarders, you're going to have a bit of trouble on the flat section, and then I'll bring up the rear with anyone who's slightly less confident. After the flat part the path joins the green piste and there's a very gentle descent to the lift."

"Give us a tow," Topher says to Eva, with a grin, and she rolls her eyes and sticks a pole out behind her. I point them in the right direction and watch as they schuss off along the little narrow path between the trees. When they get to the flat, Eva breaks out into a beautiful skating motion, pulling Topher along behind her, and I watch her as she goes, her scarlet ski jacket flickering in between the trees. Whoever it was who described her as practically an Olympian is right; she's a very good skier. Better than me, and I'm no slouch. Topher, from the way he handled the steep little descent at the beginning, not easy on a board, is evidently in his element.

Rik goes next, he's clearly an experienced skier, even if he lacks Eva's flair. Then Miranda, who snowplows the first steep section in defiance of my advice, grinds to a halt on the flat, and has to stump along looking embarrassed. I would guess she's competent rather than excellent, probably knows the basics but is a little too cautious to be really good. Next comes Inigo in a grass-green jacket that somehow makes his azure eyes look even bluer. He swooshes down with an elegant economy and passes Miranda, kindly putting a hand in the small of her back to help her regain her momentum. He's obviously been skiing since childhood, no mistaking that relaxed grace. Then Tiger, who turns out to be a very good snowboarder. She doesn't have Topher's advantage of a pull from Eva, but she makes it look easy.

Carl shoots off with a look of grim determination on his cherry-pink face that says, *Fuck it, might as well be hung for a sheep as a lamb*. He manages to get one ski stuck in a soft bank almost at once and falls over with a painful-sounding *crunch*, but he hauls himself up uncomplainingly, gets himself back in position, and this time makes it without incident. Next up is Ani. She is wearing a bright blue jacket and white salopettes that look fresh off the peg, and her buttercup hair is sticking out around her hood. The effect is somewhere between adorable toddler and children's TV presenter. She gives me a wry smile.

"I maybe should have put my hand up as a complete beginner," she says apologetically. "I'm really not very good!"

"Don't worry," I say encouragingly. "There's literally nothing that can go wrong on this bit, and the advantage of a heavy dump of snow is that at least it's soft when you fall over."

She grins at me, shoves off with her poles, giving a little squeak of alarm as the path falls away, and she almost tips backwards in surprise, wheeling with her poles. But she regains her balance somehow, and with a laugh she's off through the trees to where the others are waiting just out of sight.

Finally it's just me and Liz. In contrast to Ani's game enthusiasm she looks hot and stressed, and overdressed—she's clearly wearing far too many layers for such a nice day and is already visibly sweating. I'm annoyed with myself for not checking the gear of the inexperienced skiers, but it's probably better for her to be overdressed rather than under, and in any case, it's too late to tell her to take some off. I'm just about to give her a pep talk when something strikes me.

"Hang on, where's Elliot?"

"Oh," Liz looks embarrassed. "Didn't Topher tell you? He doesn't really . . . join in."

"Oh." I'm surprised somehow. I kind of had the idea that Snoop was one of those companies where joining in wasn't exactly optional.

Carl certainly gave that impression. Liz must have read my expression.

"I know . . . He's not the only person who'd rather be in their room, but somehow he's the only one who gets away with it. But that's what you get for being Topher's best friend, I guess."

"Have they known each other long?"

"They were at boarding school together," Liz says. The talk is helping, I realize. She's lost the look of pinched anticipation. "Along with Rik."

"Christ, talk about the old boys' network," I say, before I can help myself, and then blush. Out here, in my salopettes, it's harder to remember I'm Erin the ski chalet host, not just Erin the skier. But Liz doesn't seem offended. She even gives me a very small smile.

"I know, right?" she says. Then she reddens, as if she's been unspeakably daring.

Encouraged by her unbending slightly, I decide it's time to go.

"Okay, well, we'd better catch up with the others. Are you ready? I'll go in front, so don't worry, you're never going to get out of control. If you do, you'll just slide gently into me."

"I still . . ." Her face looks pinched again, staring at the narrow path with something like dread. "It just looks so *steep*."

God, she really isn't a natural skier. I make up my mind.

"I tell you what, give me your poles."

She hands them over, obediently like a child, and I clamp them under one arm and stick my own out behind me.

"Now hold on to these, okay? Got it? One in each hand."

She nods, and I push us off, very gently, using my thigh muscles to slow our descent.

With Liz's weight behind me, pressing on my poles, the easy little schuss is much harder work than usual, but we make it to the flat, and I follow Eva's example, skating along, pulling Liz behind me, listening to her panting breath.

At last we come out of the trees and glide down the slope to the bubble lift, where the others are waiting for us, standing just outside the turnstiles, underneath a painted wooden sign reading *LA REINE TC.*

"This lift is easy," I say to Liz, reassuringly, under my breath. "No skiing on or off to worry about, you take your skis off and walk on."

"Oh . . . phew." Her expression clears a little bit, and then she glances up at the top of the mountain where the clouds are gathering. "What's the rundown like?"

"There's two stations. If you get off at the first station, it's easy. You're halfway up the mountain and you can pick either the green run, Atchoum, back down to the bottom of the lift, or the blue, which peels off down to St. Antoine le Lac. If you stay on the lift it goes right up to the top of the mountain. There are amazing views when it's sunny but, well." I wave my arm at the clouds that are already closing in. "Anyway, from the top station you have the choice of two runs, La Sorcière, which is a black run off to the left that follows the path of the lift, or the top part of Blanche-Neige. That's a blue, but in poor conditions it can feel a bit more like a red. If you're not very experienced, then I'd recommend sticking to the first station, just until you get the feel of your skis, anyway. You could always have a go at the second station after lunch."

"Okay," Liz says, and she looks up at the mountain, but I can feel her doubt from here. "Will you be with us all day?"

"Just for the first couple of runs. I'll show you the way back to the chalet, and then I'm afraid I've got to go and help Danny with lunch."

Liz says nothing at that, but from the way she clutches her ski poles like grim death, I can tell she's not keen on being abandoned.

"It'll be fine," I tell her, with more assurance than I actually feel. "You're not the only beginner, Ani isn't very good, nor is Carl. And even Miranda doesn't look very confident."

Liz says nothing. She just unclips her bindings and pulls off her skis. But the look on her face is anything but happy.

LIZ

Snoop ID: ANON101
Listening to: Offline
Snoopscribers: 0

It is almost noon. We have been skiing all morning. The wind is mounting. Erin disappeared back to the chalet long ago, leaving me alone with Topher and Eva and the other adrenaline junkies. We have done the green run, Atchoum, back to the bottom of the bubble twice, and a long blue down into St. Antoine, then back up the funicular. My legs feel like jelly with being continually on edge. My face is stinging with cold, and my armpits are damp with sweat inside my many layers. My breath comes fast, misting my scarf with wetness, and I am simultaneously freezing and much too hot.

We gather, panting at the bottom of the Reine lift, and I can hear the relief in Ani's voice when she whispers, "Yay! Lunch!"

And then Topher says, as I *knew* he would, "Come on, time for one more before we break for the afternoon. Let's go up to the top of La Dame. Second stop on the bubble lift. Which of you pussies is with me?"

My heart begins thumping in my chest.

"Wouldn't it be better to stop before we're all too tired?" Miranda says. I can tell she does not want to do this, but she also doesn't want to be the party pooper. "I mean, it's the first day, and we've got all week to get skiing in."

"I agree," Ani says. She lifts her ski goggles. Beneath, her face is red and blotchy with a mixture of cold and exertion. She looks tired. "Plus, I just, like, really think it's too big a run for me."

"It's a fucking blue," Topher says dismissively. "Come on! It'll be fun. There's a black that peels off from the top, La Sorcière, and the blue is just the top section of that run we did before, Blanche-Neige. We can split into two groups and take whichever one you fancy. Blue for the babies, black for the big boys and girls."

"Topher," Eva says, wagging her finger, but her annoyance is pretend. She looks in her element, tall and slim on her improbably long skis. She is wearing a bright red ski jacket—scarlet silk that looks like a splash of blood against the white snow—and the sight gives me a weird pang, because I remember buying that jacket for her, back when I was her assistant. I got sent out to Harrods with her credit card and instructions to pick it up. I remember it so clearly, like it was yesterday.

I think, suddenly, of the fairy tale for which the blue run is named—Blanche Neige—Snow White. Skin as white as snow, lips as red as blood, hair as black as ebony. The hair is wrong. Eva's hair is almost as white as snow too. But today it is tucked into a black beanie, making the comparison almost spookily accurate.

"Come on . . . ," Topher cajoles. "We can't get back from here to the chalet anyway, it's all uphill, so unless you want an hour of sidestepping, we might as well go to the middle station. Just a little bit farther doesn't make much difference . . . does it?" He lifts his goggles and turns the full force of his charm on Ani. "Ani? Give this old man one last wish?"

Ani gives a little sigh. Then she caves like wet snow.

"Oh . . . okay. I suppose you only live once. You'll make sure I get down in one piece, won't you, Inigo?"

He smiles and nods.

"Miranda?" Topher says, smiling at her with all his considerable persuasive force. When he turns it on, it is not hard to understand how he got where he did. There's something about Topher that is very, very hard to say no to. "Miraaaanda . . . ?"

"Fine," Miranda says, rather grumpily. "If we've got to go up anyway, I suppose it won't make much difference."

And then Topher turns to me.

"Liz?"

So here it is, then. Why do I always seem to end up being this person—the person everyone else's fun hinges on, the person who's required to make a decision. I can feel myself shrinking beneath their gaze—but I have no choice.

"Fine," I say, but my voice sounds strained and tense, even to me.

"Okay!" Eva says briskly. "Right, let's regroup at the top, and if anyone gets lost, we'll meet at the shortcut back to the chalet—does everyone remember where the path splits off? That big pine Erin showed us, the one with the fluorescent padding."

There are nods and murmurs of assent.

And then it is happening. People are unclipping their bindings and shuffling forward in stiff heavy ski boots, clutching poles and skis, shoving through the turnstile barrier. There is no queue at all. The weather is too poor for that. All the sensible French are huddled in cafés having vin chaud and raclette, and we are the only people heading up the mountain, on this lift at least. I feel my heart do that sickening skipping rhythm as the bubble looms nearer and I shuffle ahead, pushing past Ani with an assertiveness that's out of character for me. I cannot afford to get left behind.

The bubble glides down the last part of the track, slowing dramatically as it enters the shelter of the lift terminal, and our little group surges forward and begins to clamber in as the plexiglass doors slide back. There are four seats inside each bubble, and I watch, counting under my breath as Topher, Rik, and Miranda climb in—and then it's my chance. The lift is almost at the barrier where the door will start to close, but I go for it, lumbering towards the doors with my boots clomping on the rubber tiles. I shove my skis roughly in the pigeonholes outside, their bindings tangling with Topher's snowboard—the doors are closing.

"Come on, Liz!" Miranda shouts encouragingly, and I scramble through the gap, sitting down, panting as the doors glide shut and the bubble shoots away up the mountain. Yes. I have done it. I am over the first hurdle.

I squeeze in beside Miranda, crushing my bulky jacket into the narrow gap, and she laughs.

"Liz, how many layers are you wearing? You look like the Michelin Man."

Topher gives a grin.

"Don't knock it, Miranda. Liz might have the last laugh when we get to the top."

He nods at the window, and I realize he is right. As the lift climbs, you can literally feel the weather getting colder. The condensation on the inside of the bubble begins to bead, and then freeze, spreading into beautiful frost flowers as the lift climbs, and climbs, past the midway station, where the doors slide open invitingly, but no one moves.

Then out again, and up, past the tree line, and up, up, into the clouds. I can feel the little bubble being buffeted by the wind, feel it swaying on its wire, and I have a sudden thrill of fear at what is awaiting us at the top. Oh God, am I *really* going to do this? Can I really go through with it? Suddenly I am not sure if I can. My stomach is sick and clenching with nerves. I have never felt so scared in my life of what I'm about to do. But I have to go through with it. I *have* to.

And then the doors are sliding back and we are stumbling out into a cold so profound that it strikes right through all my layers, even inside the relative shelter of the lift terminal.

We clip on our skis and slide out—into a white wilderness.

It is snowing—hard. The wind is fierce and vicious, driving the snow into our eyes and noses, making everyone fumble to pull down their goggles and pull up their scarves. Between that and the cloud that has descended to wreathe the mountain, the visibility is not the miles the brochures promised, it is meters.

I know that there should be two runs coming off from here. To the left is the black run Topher wants to do, La Sorcière. To the right is the top part of the blue run, Blanche-Neige. They meet at the second station of the bubble lift, but Blanche-Neige takes its time, curving round the mountain in gentle loops. La Sorcière, on the other hand, follows a more direct route, zigzagging down the mountain beneath the bubble lift. *Direct* is an understatement. We passed over the run in the lift a few minutes ago, and it looked like a sheer sheet of ice, like the side of a hill, even seen from forty feet up in the air.

I push off, wobbling as I clear the ice from my goggles with my mittens. Ahead is a snow-covered sign that might once have been two arrows but is now nothing but an indistinct white lump. To the left there is a kind of tennis-net thing cutting off the access. By the time I see this, I'm sliding towards it.

"Help!" I shout. There is nothing any of the others can do, and I ricochet into the net, feeling its springiness catch me across the middle. I flail for a moment, my poles pinwheeling, and then I teeter ungracefully to the ground in a clatter of skis.

Rik comes sliding across, laughing, and helps me up.

"You were lucky," he yells in my ear over the shriek of the wind, pointing to the snow-blasted *piste fermée* sign tacked over the net. "That's La Sorcière. You could have been skiing your first black if they hadn't closed the piste! Or worse."

He is right. Beyond the net is a steep run, dropping almost vertically away. It curves around the mountain and beyond the edge of the curve is . . . nothing. If I had shot off the edge at speed, there would have been nothing anyone could do. I could have been plummeting to my death in the valley a thousand feet below before anyone had a chance to stop me. The thought of that fall makes my stomach lurch with nerves over what I'm about to do.

I am too out of breath to reply, but I let him haul me to my feet and then guide me back to the others who are standing in a little huddle at the top of the blue piste.

"They've closed La Sorcière," Rik calls across to Topher, who nods bitterly.

"I saw. Fucking pussies."

"Should we wait?" I hear Miranda shout. Her voice is barely audible beneath the howling of the storm. "It's fucking freezing!"

"I think we have to," Rik says. "We can't go without Ani and Carl, they're not very experienced."

"They've got the others to babysit them," Topher grumbles, but Rik shakes his head.

"What if they come up separately and try to follow? Look." He points down the mountain where a bubble lift is emerging from the clouds, a single figure inside, or maybe two sitting close together. It's impossible to make out at this distance. It might not even be one of our party. It is so far below that the figure looks absurdly small.

I am shaking. My heart is pounding. I can't go through with this. But I have to. This might be my last chance—I have to say something. Now. *Now*.

"I can't do this," I force out. Topher looks across at me, as if surprised I've spoken.

"What did you say?"

"I can't do this," I say louder. I am breathing very fast, and my voice is high and squeaky with a barely contained fear. My pulse is going a mile a minute. "I can't. I just can't. I'm not going to ski down. I *can't*, Topher."

"Well, how do you plan to get to the bottom," Topher says sarcastically. "Toboggan?"

"Hey, hey." Rik has been trying to consult his phone, but now he looks up. "What's going on here?"

"I can't do it," I say desperately, as if, if I just keep repeating this one phrase, everything will slot into place. Maybe it still will. Maybe it will all be okay. "I can't. I can't ski down in this. I'm going to die, I know I will. You can't make me do it."

"Liz, it'll be fine." Rik puts a hand on my arm. "I'll take care of you, I promise. Look, you can snowplow all the way down if you want to. I'll guide you, you can hold my sticks."

"I. Can't. Do. It," I repeat doggedly. If I keep reciting this mantra, it will be okay. They can't *make* me ski with them. I *know* Topher. He's not a patient man. Very soon he will get pissed off with trying to persuade me and give up.

"Fuck," Topher says irritably. He wipes the snow from his googles and looks at Rik. "So what, then?"

"Liz—" Rik begins, and I feel that hard thing rise up in my throat, choking me, like it did at the meeting. The bubble with the single figure in it reaches the terminal. I think I am going to be sick. It's now or never.

"I can't do it!" I scream, and suddenly, out of nowhere, I am crying. The noise astonishes me—great ugly sobs, racking me. I lift up my goggles to scrub at my eyes with my frozen gloves, and the wind is so cold I can feel the tears running down my nose, freezing as they reach the tip. I swipe away the frozen drops, feeling them crackle against my skin. "I can't fucking do it!"

"Okay, okay!" Rik says hastily. "Liz, don't panic, it'll be fine. Look, we'll sort this out."

There is a schussing sound behind us and we turn to see a figure skiing down the slope towards us. It is Inigo, his green jacket unmistakable even with his goggles down and his scarf pulled up. Behind him, Tiger has shuffled out onto the bank immediately outside the lift. She is sitting on the snow, fastening her snowboard bindings.

"I'm going back," I say, gulping down my sobs. I point down the mountain, where the empty bubble lift Inigo came up in is returning back to the valley. "I'm going to talk to the lift attendant, make him let me back in. I'll explain I can't do it, that it's all been a mistake."

"Liz, this is fucking ridiculous," Topher explodes.

"What's the matter?" Inigo's voice is muffled from behind his scarf, barely recognizable.

"It's Liz," Topher says angrily. "She's having some kind of existential crisis."

But I'm not. I'm calm now. There is another bubble lift coming up the mountain, with another figure inside it. I can do this. I know what I need to do, and no one can stop me. I begin to sidestep up the slope.

"Liz," Rik calls, "are you sure?"

"Yes," I yell back, though I'm not even certain they can hear me over the wind now. "I'm quite sure. I'll meet you back at the chalet."

And as I step inside the terminal building and the bubble lift doors open, a sense of peace enfolds me. I know what I have to do, and it's going to be okay. Everything's going to be okay.

ERIN

Snoop ID: LITTLEMY

Listening to: Offline

Snoopscribers: 10

It's nearly half past one. They said they'd be back by one at the latest, and Danny is shouting expletives from the kitchen as the minutes tick past and his risotto clogs.

At one forty-five he sticks his head out the door with a face like thunder, and I shake my head.

"There's only one thing I hate more than fucking stealth vegans and that's wankers," he growls, and disappears, the swing door clacking behind him.

And then, suddenly, there's the clatter of ski boots on tiles, and I hurry into the lobby to hear noises from the ski entrance, the unmistakable sounds of people clumping along a hard floor, clanging open the heated ski lockers that line the corridor.

"Eva?" someone calls irritably. "Eva, where the fuck are you?"

No answer.

Then the insulated door to the lobby swings open and Topher comes in wearing ski gear and thick socks, looking pissed off.

"Oh, it's you," he says shortly when he sees me. "Where the fuck is Eva?"

"Eva?" A retort about his rudeness hovers on the tip of my tongue, but I swallow it back. "Sorry, Topher, I have no idea."

He stops, halfway to the stairs.

"You mean she's not here?"

"No, you're the first back."

He stands there, quite still, the expression on his face wavering between irritation and concern. Then he calls over his shoulder.

"Miranda, she's not here."

"You're kidding." Miranda is the next out of the door. Her face is bright pink, with the painful flush that always follows extreme cold. "Huh. Well . . . I guess at least that means we didn't freeze our arses off for no reason. But what do you think could have happened?"

"Maybe the lift closed before she could get on, and she skied back down into St. Antoine to get the funicular?" Topher says, but Carl has come out now and is shaking his head.

"She got on before me, mate. She was on that lift, I'd swear to it."

"And I saw her," Ani says. They gather in the lobby, sweaty and confused, melting snow dripping from their jackets. "I told you, Carl and I were coming up in the lift and I *saw* her skiing down."

"What's the matter?" Rik says, coming through in his turn, shaking the snow off his black salopettes. Miranda turns to him, and now her face is definitely worried.

"Eva's not here."

"She's not here?" Rik's expression is blank. "But—but that's not possible. There's nowhere else she could be."

They all begin talking at once, offering up different theories, many of them totally impossible based on the geography of the resort.

"Hold up, hold up," I say, and amazingly they all fall silent. Somehow, they want leadership, and I am the closest thing to it. "Start from the beginning. When was the last time you were all together as a group?"

"At the bottom of the Reine ski lift," Ani says, promptly. "We had a discussion about whether to break for lunch there, or do one last run. Topher made the point that it was uphill from the ski lift to the chalet, so we had to do *a* run, and we agreed to go up to the top station and do either La Sorcière or Blanche-Neige, depending on ability."

I bite back my reply to this. La Sorcière is a bitch of a run. I've been skiing all my life, and there's no *way* I'd do it in this weather. Even Blanche-Neige with this visibility is no joke for inexperienced skiers. Not for the first time it strikes me that Topher is kind of a jerk.

"But when we got up there Liz had some kind of breakdown," Topher says bitterly.

"Toph," Rik says sharply, with a jerk of his head towards the ski door, and I look over Topher's shoulder to see Liz plodding wearily across from the boot room. She is covered in snow and looks utterly exhausted, even more so than the others.

"When we got to the top the weather was pretty extreme, and Liz decided to take the lift back down," Miranda says smoothly, but looking at Topher's mutinous face I can well imagine the discussion that decision must have entailed. Part of me is amazed at Liz's strength of mind, that she didn't let herself be bullied into trying the run. But fear can make people amazingly resilient.

"The rest of us waited up there for the others," Topher says. "But Eva never came."

"But she *did*," Ani puts in. "We saw her, Carl and I. Didn't we?" She nudges Carl, who nods.

"Yeah, no doubt about it, mate. We saw her get on the bubble a few lifts ahead of us."

"A few?" Topher says. "How's that? There was no queue at all."

Carl reddens.

"Well, look, there's no point in beating about the bush. I—well I fluffed getting on the bubble if you must know. Ani and I were supposed to be getting in after Eva, but I tripped over my bindings. Fell over, and the lift doors closed, and Eva went up with my skis still stuck in the rack. It took me a few minutes to get myself sorted again, and then Ani and I caught the next lift after that."

"Could she have got confused and got off at the first station?" Miranda says with a frown, but Ani shakes her head.

"No, that's what I'm trying to tell you. I saw her, when we were coming up in the bubble. It goes right over that black piste—the really steep one that Topher wanted to do."

"La Sorcière," I put in, and Ani nods.

"That's the one. And I saw a skier coming down it. She stopped for a second on the ridge and kind of raised her hand, waving at me. And I realized, it was Eva."

"How could you tell at that distance?" Rik says, sceptically. "It could have been anyone."

"I recognized her red jacket. It's, like, really distinctive. No one else here has one like it, and we were the only people on that lift."

I look around the circle, and she's right. Topher is in mustard and khaki, Rik and Carl are both in black. Miranda is in a kind of purple jumpsuit. Inigo has a green jacket and black salopettes. Tiger is wearing kind of shabby surfer chic that looks like an eighties denim bomber jacket and cargo pants, but that I suspect is actually pretty expensive snowboard gear. Liz is wearing a faded navy-blue all-in-one that's too big for her and looks as though it was borrowed from a friend. And Ani herself is wearing the bright sea-blue jacket and white salopettes that I noticed earlier. None of them could possibly be mistaken for Eva.

"When we got off at the top my skis were waiting," Carl says. "She must have taken them off the lift and then skied off."

"Didn't you notice she wasn't at the top?" I ask, and Rik shakes his head, looking rueful.

"No, the visibility was really poor and well . . . look, if you must know there was a bit of . . . well, argy bargy at the top."

Argy bargy? What the hell does that mean? I'm about to ask when Miranda butts in.

"You might as well say it plainly, Rik. The lift attendant came out to tell us the avalanche warning had gone up to red, and they were closing the whole mountain, but half the party ignored the warning and deliberately skied off before they could get the nets out."

"I'm so sorry." Inigo at least has the grace to look embarrassed. "It was a total misunderstanding. I thought he was saying now or never, so I, uh, pushed off."

"So wait, some of you skied home," I say slowly, "and some of you took the bubble back down?"

Nods all round the circle.

"Naturally we stopped for a bit at the big pine by the shortcut back to the chalet to see if anyone was catching up, but when we saw people traveling back down in the bubble, we skied down to the bottom of the lift," Topher says. "So we waited there for another twenty minutes, only for the bastards in charge of the resort to close *that* lift too. At that point we concluded Eva had fucked off back to the chalet, but since we were now downhill from the chalet with no functioning lift, we had no choice but to ski down to St. Antoine and get the funicular back up."

"Okay . . . okay . . . ," I say, trying to make sense of it. "So the last time anyone is absolutely certain they saw her, she was skiing La Sorcière?"

Ani nods, turning to Carl for confirmation, who says, "That's the size of it."

"But La Sorcière was closed," Topher explodes. "That was the whole fucking problem."

The whole fucking problem is that your colleague and cofounder is missing in extreme weather conditions, I think, but I don't say it. I am thinking about La Sorcière, about its treacherous, icy slopes, and the way the loose powder builds up on the sheet ice beneath, making every turn a throw of the dice between a painful skid and a mini avalanche. I'm thinking of its brutal moguls, hidden by the drifting snow between, and the impossibility of even seeing the icy hummocks beneath their blanket of snow, let alone judging those knee-juddering turns in bad visibility.

Most of all, I'm thinking of the sheer drop at the side of the run. A precipice lies just meters from the side of the piste in places; in conditions like this, you could simply sail off the edge into nothingness. *That* is why they shut La Sorcière first, out of all the runs in the resort. Not because they're risk averse, or health and safety nuts, or don't trust experienced skiers to navigate it, but because the twists and turns are a death trap in low visibility. But then I remind myself that the worst section of the drop is right at the start of the run, and Ani saw her skiing farther down. It's a small comfort, but I'll take whatever comfort I can get right now.

"Has anyone tried her mobile?" I say. Inigo nods.

"Several times. There's no reception."

Danny comes out of the kitchen at that point, looking royally pissed off. *What about my fucking risotto?* he mouths at me over the heads of the guests, and I hurry across to him.

"Eva's missing," I tell him in a low voice, and his expression switches instantly from irritation to concern.

"What, really missing? Not just gone AWOL?"

"I don't know; it's hard to tell. They've all acted like complete fuckwits. They split up, no one kept track of who was in which party, and Eva seems to have gone off by herself to ski La Sorcière."

"Alone?" Danny's jaw drops. "But, there's a red avalanche warning. Why the hell didn't the pisteurs shut the run?"

"Apparently they did. She must have ducked under the netting or something, or somehow got lost and traversed across to the wrong run." Though I can't think quite how that could have happened. There is no obvious interconnection between Blanche-Neige and La Sorcière. That's part of the problem with the black run. It is hemmed in by a sheer cliff on one side, and a sheer drop on the other. There is no way out once you're going down, it's all twists and turns. "I don't know. But Ani is pretty convinced she and Carl saw Eva skiing down it. I mean, I know she's good, but that's just foolhardy in weather like this."

Danny's face is really grave now.

"And no one's seen her since?"

I shake my head.

"Do you think we should call the PGHM?" I ask. This is the specialist branch of mountain police who operate in the higher mountain ranges—a combination of gendarmes and mountain rescue.

"I dunno," Danny says. He pushes his bandanna up his forehead and rubs fretfully at the furrow between his brows, trying to think. "It's not impossible she's just got lost and gone down the wrong route. With the lifts shut it'd take her a while to get back. I reckon they'll tell us to give it a few hours before we panic. Should we try the ski pass office first? Maybe they can tell us if her pass has been used on any lifts?"

I want to kiss him. It's not just a good idea, it's a great one. But when I go to the phone in the lobby and dial the number on the back of the lift pass, I get only the insistent beep-beep signal of a busy line.

I go back to the little group huddled in the lobby, who are looking hot in their ski gear, and increasingly worried.

"We think the best thing is to check in with the lift pass office and see if Eva's used her pass anywhere. I've tried phoning, but the line's engaged, so rather than hanging around here, I think I'm going to hop down on the funicular and talk to the office in person."

"I'll go," Topher says immediately.

"Do you speak French?"

I know the answer before I ask the question, and his face changes to chagrin as he shakes his head.

"I totally get why you want to help," I say, trying to be gentle, "but I think it would be better for someone who speaks French to go. If she's not used her pass, that's probably the point where we need to report her missing to the police, and we'll definitely need a fluent speaker for that. You should all change into dry clothes and get some food into you, and I'll be back really soon. Meantime, keep trying her number."

They all nod, soberly.

"I'd better tell Elliot," Topher mutters, and I remember with a shock of surprise that Elliot was the only member of the group not skiing. He is still holed up in his room, presumably working on his coding update, or whatever he's doing up there alone.

They all disperse, talking quietly under their breaths to one another, and I grab my coat from the locker and hurry back to Danny to explain the plan.

"So you'll have to serve up alone, is that okay?"

He nods.

"Yeah, of course."

He disappears into the kitchen to begin plating up.

I put on my coat and open the front door.

LIZ

Snoop ID: ANON101
Listening to: Offline
Snoopscribers: 0

I am upstairs in my room changing out of my skiing clothes when it happens. At first it is just a noise, and then I feel the ground begin to shake, like an earthquake.

I turn to look out the window. I see what looks like a wall of snow coming down the valley towards us. But not a wall—that implies something solid. This is something else. A boiling mass that is air and ice and earth all rolled together.

I scream. I do the only thing I can, even though it is stupid. I fall to my knees with my arms over my head, as if that pathetic gesture might protect me.

I stay there shaking for a long time, before I dare to get up, my legs trembling. Did it miss us? Did it stop?

From far away I can hear other voices, shouts, screams, cries.

Somehow, I force my legs to work, and I stumble out into the corridor.

"Jesus Christ!" Topher is shouting. He is running towards the stairs. "What the hell just happened?"

"Erin!" I hear from below. It is a bellow of fear from a voice I don't recognize, and then I realize—it is the chef, Danny, calling for his friend. "Erin!"

The corridor is full of terrified people. There is a smoke alarm going off, shouts of panic.

Down in the lobby the chef is struggling with the front door, which has cracked and bowed beneath the weight of packed snow pressed up against it.

"Don't open the bloody door!" Topher yells. "You'll let all the snow in!"

Danny turns on him. His face is full of fury.

"My fucking friend is out there," he spits over the scream of the alarm. "So if you want to stop me, mate, come and try."

He shoves again. The door gives with a shriek of protest, and a mass of snow and ice comes skittering into the lobby. The doorway is still blocked four feet deep, but Danny clambers up the bank and over the top, sinking into the debris. The last I see of him is his legs as he staggers off into the storm.

"Oh my God," Miranda is saying. She is holding on to Rik like she is drowning. "Oh my God. Oh my God. What if Eva's still out there?"

There is no answer. I don't think anyone can bring themselves to say what they are thinking—which is that if Eva is still out there, she is dead. She must be.

And maybe Erin too.

"Is the building safe?" Rik says, with sudden practicality. "We don't want to stay here if it's about to collapse."

"I'll go and turn off that alarm," Tiger says, and she disappears into the kitchen. I hear her dragging a chair across tiles, and then the alarm stops. There is a sudden, shocking silence.

"Okay," Topher says. His voice is shaking, but it is so natural for him to take charge that he slips into the role. "Um, we should—we should check. We should check the building."

"The kitchen side isn't too bad," Tiger says as she comes back into the lobby. "I looked out the window. There's a couple of windows broken in the den but the snow isn't particularly high. It'll be the living room side that's suffered, and the pool extension."

"We should go upstairs," Topher says. "Get an overview."

Tiger nods, and we all troop upstairs to look out one of the upper windows. What we see makes my knees go weak. We have been *extremely* lucky.

The long single-story building to the rear of the chalet, which housed the swimming pool, has been crushed and obliterated. The roof has caved in like an empty eggshell. Beams and planks are sticking out of the huge snowdrift that has engulfed the extension. But the chalet itself is still standing. There is a mass of snow, sticks, and rubble piled up against the north side, but the structure has held firm. Just a few meters more, and Perce-Neige would have been matchsticks, like the swimming pool building. I can't see any of the other chalets. The path to the funicular is covered with fallen trees and rumpled snow. The funicular itself is out of sight in the gusting snow. Erin is nowhere to be seen.

And then I notice a movement around the side of the building. It is Erin. She is holding onto Danny and they are limping over the uneven, debris-covered surface, stumbling on the hard-packed lumps of snow scattered across what used to be the track to the funicular.

They go out of sight beneath the shadow of the building. From downstairs I hear the screech of the buckled front door scraping against the tiles, and Erin's sob of pain as she squeezes over the drift and down, inside the house.

"Is it broken?" I hear Danny saying, breathlessly. As if instructed, we all file down the spiral stairs to stand in a concerned circle around Erin.

"Is she okay?" Miranda asks, frowning.

"What do you think?" Danny snaps. Erin doesn't seem able to speak, but she holds up her hand. I'm not sure what she means, but her signal clearly conveys something to Danny, and he shakes his head angrily and stamps off to the kitchen.

"I'm gonna get you some ice," he calls back over his shoulder. "See if we can get the swelling down."

"I've got some arnica in my bag," Tiger calls after him. I cannot hear Danny's reply. It does not sound complimentary.

"I don't think arnica is going to cut it, Tig," Rik says quietly.

Erin is slumped on the floor of the lobby. Her face is gray. She looks like she is going into shock.

"What happened?" Tiger crouches beside her, putting her hand on her arm. Erin looks up at her. She blinks dazedly. She looks like she is unsure why she is here.

"Erin? Are you okay?"

"I don't know," Erin manages. Her voice is shaking. "I was walking towards the f-funicular and I heard this n-noise and then it was like—it was like the mountain just came and *swallowed* the lift."

"You mean—the funicular is gone?"

There is horror in Tiger's voice, but her tone only echoes the shock I can see reverberating around the room.

"Not gone," Danny says, coming back with a bag of frozen peas. He scowls around the group. "But . . . yeah, buried. A big chunk of glass has been stove in. *Shit.* There might have been people in there."

"We should, like, call 999?" Ani says, and Topher nods emphatically.

"Seventeen," Erin says tiredly.

"What?"

"Seventeen," Danny echoes. "That's the French number for the police. But I reckon you should try one-one-two. That's the international number, they'll have English speakers."

Ani takes out her phone and then frowns.

"I've got no reception."

"Transmitter's probably down," Danny says shortly. He is pressing the peas very gently onto Erin's ankle. Her face has gone a strange yellowish white and her eyes are closed. "Try the phone on the desk."

Ani nods and goes across to the landline phone on the desk next to the stairs, but when she picks up the receiver her face falls.

"There's no dial tone."

"Fuck." Carl speaks for the first time. His broad face is red. He looks angry. "Fucking hell, that's all we need. Avalanche took the line out I guess. Has *anyone* got any reception? Anything at all?"

There's a momentary shuffle. Everyone feels for their phones. I get out mine too. The reception bars are grayed out.

"Nothing," Topher says. Others are shaking their heads.

"No, wait." It's Inigo, his voice cracking with excitement. "I just got a bar! I've got one bar!"

He dials and then waits, holding up his hand for silence. We all stay totally still, listening.

"Hello?" he says. And then "Hello? Hello? Shit, they can't hear me!"

"Go upstairs," Miranda says sharply. "You might get better reception with the extra height."

Obediently Inigo climbs the spiral staircase and goes to stand at the end of the corridor, at the long window that overlooks the valley, as if the visibility might somehow translate into better reception.

"Hello?" we can hear him saying, and then "Yes," and "Okay," and "Chalet Blanche-Neige," followed by some information about our situation. There are long pauses, and many times he says "Can you repeat that? I'm sorry, the reception is really poor, you're breaking up. Hello? Hello?"

At last he comes back down looking grave.

"I lost reception in the end, but I spoke to the police operator, and I think I managed to give them all the details before I got cut off."

"Did you tell them about Eva?" Topher shoves in, and Inigo nods.

"Yes, I told them that we lost our friend right before the avalanche and we don't know if she's still out on the mountain."

"Is someone coming to rescue us?"

"I don't know," Inigo says, and he looks for a minute like what he is—a PA who has failed to get the result his boss wanted. "They said they're under enormous strain, there are people trapped on lifts and stuff. I'm not sure—" His voice falters a little at Topher's expression. "I'm not sure that people with food and shelter are their priority right now. They've got my number. They said they'd be in touch as soon as possible with more information."

"You mean we're fucking stranded?" Topher explodes. "The fucking funicular's down, Eva's missing, and we're trapped in this godforsaken chalet with an injured woman—" He indicates Erin. "We should be their top priority!"

Inigo says nothing, he just shrugs helplessly.

"Could one of us ski down?" Rik says, but Inigo shakes his head.

"No, they were really clear about that. We should stay where we are. There could be more falls."

"Well, we can't just stay here," Topher says angrily.

"You won't be skiing on that piste, mate," Danny says, looking up from where he's tending Erin.

"I'll have you know," Topher says, "I'm a boarder, and a damn good one."

"You could be Shaun White, mate, you still wouldn't be going down there. You didn't see it—it looked like a boulder field. There's no piste left."

"So we're stuck?" Topher says, furious disbelief in his tone. "And they're doing nothing at all, while Eva could be out there under a thousand tonnes of snow?"

No one answers. No one wants to say the fact that is obvious to all of us—if that is the case, there's nothing he or any of us can do.

ERIN

Snoop ID: LITTLEMY
Listening to: Offline
Snoopscribers: 10

I'm sitting in the kitchen, shaking. Danny has gone to get the first aid kit, and in truth I'm grateful to be alone for a few minutes. It gives me time to get myself back together.

That noise—that horrific, deafeningly soft roar that has haunted my dreams for three years—for a moment I thought it was some kind of flashback, like PTSD. And then I glanced over my shoulder and it was real. A wall of white engulfing the valley.

And the strange thing was, I felt nothing but peace, as it came towards me. It felt like justice. It felt like retribution. It felt completely right.

For a moment I thought about opening my arms and letting it swallow me. Only it didn't. It didn't swallow me. It spat me back out. To this.

"I'm gonna fucking kill them all." The swing door bangs back, and it's Danny, stomping in with the first aid box in his hand. "Fucking wankers every last one of them. You could've been killed, and he's busy worrying about when his airlift is coming. You know he's out there right now trying to get through to a private helicopter firm?"

"They won't do anything, even if he gets through," I say. I change my position on the makeshift footrest Danny has set up in the corner of the kitchen, trying to ignore the pain shooting up and down my leg as I move it. "They can't—not in this weather. Look at it."

I wave a hand at the window, where the wind has picked up into a full-blown blizzard.

"Get those peas off your ankle," Danny says brusquely, "they've defrosted anyway."

I hold out my leg meekly as he lifts off the soggy bag of peas and straps an ice-pack sleeve around my throbbing ankle. It hurts, but in a weird kind of way, I welcome the pain. It anchors me, reminding me that I'm here, alive.

Danny has found an old FM radio, and while he cooks, I sit quietly, listening to the accounts of the rescue attempts. The realization that keeps shivering up and down my spine is how incredibly lucky we have been—all of us. At least eight buildings have been totally crushed by the avalanche. Four were lift stations that were confirmed empty, since the lifts had been closed earlier that day. Two were cafés that are believed to have been closed at the time the avalanche hit. The remaining three were chalets. One, much farther down near St. Antoine le Lac, has been evacuated. Minor injuries, no fatalities. No one knows about the other two. Amid questions about responsibility and whether the resort authorities should have acted earlier, the newscaster emphasizes again and again how fortunate it was that so many pistes and lifts were shut. Even the funicular had only four people in it, and they have been safely evacuated down the smashed, glassed-in tunnel, but the announcer has already said, ominously, that it is going to take "many days to assess the repairs." Not even complete the repairs, assess them.

Given that, a mangled swimming pool seems like getting off pretty lightly. If it wasn't for Eva, we would be counting our blessings.

But the knowledge that she's still missing is like a dark, spreading poison, gnawing at the edge of everything. When I shut my eyes, I can see her—buried in darkness, growing colder and colder with every moment that passes, wondering if anyone is coming. If she's lucky, the close-packed snow will suffocate her quickly. If she's not . . .

The thought makes me feel suddenly weak with fear.

"How much food have we got?" I ask Danny, trying to distract myself from my thoughts, and he shakes his head dismissively.

"Plenty. Don't worry about that. Tony Stark down there might have to go without fresh milk for a few days, but the store cupboard's got enough in it for a siege."

There's always the possibility that Eva got bored of waiting for everyone, skied down into St. Antoine hours ago, and is absolutely fine, just unable to contact us. But as the hours tick on, that's starting to look more and more unlikely. The landline and the internet are still both down, and the mobile reception has only worsened since the avalanche. The remaining masts presumably buckled beneath a hundredweight of snow, but Inigo's phone continues to get a few erratic bars every now and again. He's had a text from home—just one—and managed to reply saying he was okay. Wouldn't Eva have texted to say she was all right when all this kicked off? Wouldn't she have found a way, *somehow,* to get word through?

LIZ

Snoop ID: ANON101
Listening to: Offline
Snoopscribers: 0

It is 3:11 p.m. when the electricity dies. I am sitting up in my room, trying to shut out the noises from downstairs, when the room is suddenly plunged into darkness. I fumble for my phone, wondering if a bulb has blown. Then I hear shouts of annoyance coming from up and down the corridor. It is not just me.

"Did your electricity just go off?"

It is Topher's voice, right outside my bedroom. For a moment I think he's talking to me, but then I hear an answering deep rumble: Elliot.

"Fuck," Topher says, in response. "That's all we need."

I open the door to find the rest of the group congregating on the landing, discussing what to do by the light of their mobile phone torches. In the end, we traipse downstairs to consult Erin and Danny. I hang back as Topher knocks irritably on the kitchen door. He is grumbling under his breath about the fucking arse end of nowhere.

"What?" Danny answers. His expression is belligerent.

"Hello," Topher says, abruptly changing his tone. He is out to charm now. He is not stupid. He knows he has got to get these people on his side. The effect is impressive. It is like a switch being flipped. "*So* sorry to disturb, but our electricity's gone out."

"You and me both, mate," Danny says shortly.

"And, is there anything one can do?" Topher asks. He's stressed, and I can tell because his accent has become indefinably more monied.

"Not really. The backup generator was in the pool house." Danny waves a hand at the debris just visible from the kitchen window. Topher swears. His charm is slipping.

"So we just wait and freeze to death?"

"Not freeze," Danny says. "We've got plenty of wood. You can start by putting a log on the living room fire."

Topher opens his mouth like he is about to say something. Then he seems to think better of it and closes it again. He turns and walks slowly back through to the darkened living room. The rest of us follow.

In the lounge, Topher flings himself onto the sofa while Miranda lights candles. Rik opens up the stove, stirs the embers, and puts another two logs on top.

"Great," Carl says. "Bloody great. This is all we need. We're gonna be fucking ice cubes by the time they find us."

"We'll be fine," Miranda says shortly, her voice clipped and annoyed. "It's Eva we need to worry about."

Eva. In all the commotion, I had almost succeeded in forgetting about her. My stomach crunches with mingled guilt and anxiety.

There is a long, horrible pause while no one asks the questions that are running in their heads. What has happened to her? Was she caught up in that avalanche? Is she dead?

"Wouldn't she have, like, phoned, if she were okay?" Ani says at last, breaking the silence. Her usual diffidence is even more pronounced. "I know there's not much signal, but just . . . like . . . a text, even?"

“She might not have been able to get through,” Miranda says, but I can tell she is trying to persuade herself, more than being convinced by her own argument.

Elliot is standing in the corner of the room, looking out at the darkening snow, and then he says something to Topher in his deep, abrupt voice and leaves. Topher gets up from the sofa and follows him without a word.

I frown, watching them go, watching their shadows leap and flicker in the light from the guttering candles. Where are they going? There is something in Topher’s expression I don’t like. A sense of sudden purpose. And it gives me a jolt of unease.

ERIN

Snoop ID: LITTLEMY
Listening to: Offline
Snoopscribers: 10

"This is bad, Erin." Danny is rummaging through tins at the back of the darkened kitchen. As I watch him, he straightens up, running his hands over his close-cropped hair. "This is very, very bad."

"It'll be okay," I say, but the truth is, I'm lying, and I know it. My ankle has puffed up to twice its usual size and still won't bear my weight properly. We have no lighting, and the only heat is from the woodstoves. Danny can't even microwave a frozen curry for dinner. And Eva—but I can't think about that now. I push the image of her white, cold face away from me, locking it behind the door in my mind where I keep images like that, frozen in ice. I have to hold on to the possibility that she's okay, that she made it down into the village and just hasn't been able to get through on the phone. God knows, the reception is bad enough.

"Your foot could be broken for all we know," Danny says, but I shake my head, with a confidence I don't feel.

"I don't think it's broken. I think it's just badly sprained."

"How the fuck would you know?" Danny asks, and then holds up a hand. "Never mind, I forgot you're a bloody doctor. Tell me again what you're doing cleaning up after posh wankers for minimum wage?"

I could give about eight different answers to this. I could remind him that I'm not a doctor, I'm a medical school dropout. I could tell him the truth about what brought me to St. Antoine. I could give him a lecture on greenstick fractures. But I don't need to say any of this because he's gone back to looking through the tins.

"I could heat up soup or something on the woodburner," he's saying, his brow furrowed as he tries to read a label with the aid of his mobile phone. "Jesus, what a carve-up."

The knock makes us both jump, and we stare at each other, and then Danny goes to the door. It's Topher again, but he's wearing a very different expression to the ingratiating one he used to ask us to magically fix the lights. He looks . . . I'm not sure. I don't know him well enough to tell. He could be pissed off, or gravely worried.

"Yes?" Danny says abruptly, but I heave myself to my feet and hobble past him. There is a reason Danny doesn't deal much with front of house. He's got no tact and no patience. But the fact is that however bad the situation is, Topher and Snoop are still our guests, and we still need to behave like we're representing the company.

"Topher," I say, and then I see Elliot hovering behind him. "Elliot, how can I help?"

"Elliot thinks he's found Eva," Topher says without preamble.

"*What?*" It's the last thing I'd expected. Questions jumble through my mind. Where? *How?* "Is she okay?"

"We don't know." Topher pushes past me and Danny and unfolds a laptop, putting it down on the stainless-steel kitchen work top. It lights up the circle of faces with an unearthly glow as he taps in a password. A screen of garbled code comes up. It means nothing to me.

"To be precise," it's Elliot's deep monotone, "we know the location of her phone."

"Her phone?"

"One of the reasons I didn't want to agree to the buyout," Topher begins, "is because Elliot's been working on a major update to help monetize Snoop. We're calling it geosnooping in beta, but that probably won't be the final name. As you may know, Snoop is as anonymous as you want it to be at the moment—you can't tell where someone is, all you've got to go on is what they declare in their profile."

"Right," I say slowly.

"But Elliot's been working on an upgrade that will allow people to view other Snoopers within a fifty-meter radius. You won't know exactly where they are, but you'll know they're close to you."

"Okay, I get that."

"It hasn't gone live yet. But as part of the preparations for rolling it out we changed the permissions Snoop requires to give the app access to your location. Basically Snoop knows that information whether you choose to display it or not—it's part of the data profile we share with stakeholders to create income."

"Right . . . ," I say again, trying to get him to cut to the chase. I don't care about the inner workings of Snoop, and I think I know where this is going. "Are you saying you used this information to find out Eva's location?"

"Yes. Elliot's been able to hack into the back end and get the GPS coordinates of Eva's phone."

"It's here," Elliot says, pulling up a GPS map, where a red flag shows the location of the coordinates he's tapped into the search bar.

As soon as I see the pin, my heart sinks down into my stomach, and I feel myself going cold with dread.

"Where is it exactly?" Topher is saying, but his voice sounds very far away now. Danny suddenly puts a hand to his mouth, and I know that he has just figured out what I already knew.

The pistes are marked on Elliot's maps, but not the elevations, and without the simplified three-dimensional rendering of the resort's official piste map, it's not very easy to put together the geography of the peaks and valleys. Eva's little dot is showing very close to the La Sorcière run. So close in fact that she could almost be *on* the run.

But she's not. Because if you've skied the run, as I have, many times, what you know is that there is a sheer drop to the side of La Sorcière. A drop that falls hundreds, maybe thousands of feet into a deep, inaccessible valley. Somehow, in the blinding snow, Eva must have done exactly what I feared in the first place—she has skied over the edge.

"If we can give these coordinates to search and rescue—" Topher is saying, with the kind of blithe confidence that only the CEO of a major international company could muster, but I interrupt.

"I'm sorry, Topher, I'm so sorry—"

"What do you mean?"

"This—" I swallow, I try to find a way of putting the news that's not too brutal. "This dot, it's off the side of the piste."

"Eva's an excellent skier," Topher says confidently. "Off-piste, even in this weather—"

"No, you don't understand. I'm not talking about a bit of loose snow. I mean she's skied *off* the piste. Off the edge. La Sorcière—" I swallow. There is no way of saying this nicely. "That section of La Sorcière runs alongside a sheer drop. A very steep one."

Topher looks at me blankly, unable, or unwilling, to understand what I'm trying to tell him.

"What do you mean?" he says at last.

"Topher, if Eva is really where that dot is showing, she's dead."

I regret the starkness as soon as the words have left my mouth, but they are said, and they can't be unsaid.

Topher's face goes white. Then he turns to Elliot.

"How accurate is this positioning?"

"GPS is typically accurate to about five meters," Elliot says. He looks . . . God, I don't know. Unperturbed almost? Can that be possible? Surely not. No one could be that callous. Even if they were, wouldn't they at least try to feign some kind of concern? "But you can get interference—bounced signals and so on. I'm not totally sure how the mountains would affect it. It's not impossible it's a few meters off."

"So, what, ten meters? She could be on the piste," Topher says, desperately, but we can all see, looking at the map's scale, that that's not possible. Even fifty meters wouldn't put her back on the run. "Or—or she could have dropped her phone skiing down."

"If she'd dropped it, I think it would be on the run," I say very quietly.

"She could have thrown it off the edge, for fuck's sake!" Topher cries.

No one responds to this. It's true, of course, but the obvious response is *why*, and no one can bring themselves to say it, not even Elliot, who simply nods in acceptance of the fact that Topher's remark is essentially correct. All we have found is Eva's phone. It's just very hard to work out how it could have got where it is now without Eva.

"Fuck," Topher says. He gropes his way to the footrest I was using to prop up my injured foot and sits, as though his legs will no longer hold him up. *"Fuck."*

"If she's dead," Elliot says flatly, "what does that mean for Snoop? Is Eva's husband a shareholder now? Will he get a vote on the buyout?"

"Fuck!" Topher looks wild-eyed, as if he can't believe what's happened. "Arnaud? I—I don't know! Jesus, Elliot, how can you—"

He breaks off . . . I can see his brain ticking. Even now, below his grief, he is still Snoop's founder as much, if not more, than he is Eva's friend.

"I suppose—I remember now, when we set it up. There was something about this. It was supposed to stop the company passing out of control of the original shareholders without their agreement. I'm pretty sure that shareholders can't sell or give away their shares—they can only offer them for sale to Eva and me. I mean—"

He stops. Swallows.

"To me."

LIZ

Snoop ID: ANON101
Listening to: Offline
Snoopscribers: 0

Eva is dead.

I don't know how the word gets out, but once the whispers start they are like frost creeping across a window. Soon everyone knows. In the living room Miranda and Tiger are exchanging urgent whispers.

"I know," I hear Miranda hiss. "But we have to figure out *some* kind announcement for when we're back online, Tiger. There's no way we can keep a lid on news this big, and if it leaks, it'll be worse in the long run."

"I can't believe it." Ani comes to sit beside me on the couch. Her face is swollen and blotched, even in the dim light from the stove and candles. "Have you heard?"

I nod. I don't trust my voice. In spite of everything, in spite of all that's happened and all the years since I left Snoop, my feelings are still too raw.

"I can't believe it!" Ani repeats desperately. "Oh God, this is awful. Poor, poor Eva. Rik says they may not even be able to recover a body. Oh God poor *Arnaud.* And he doesn't even know. How will he tell

Radisson? How do you explain to a child of that age that Mummy's never coming home?"

Radisson. The name stabs me like a knife. I had almost forgotten that Eva had had a child in the years since we worked together.

"I don't know," I say hoarsely.

"Fuck knows what this means for the buyout," Carl says morosely from the other end of the room, and Ani rounds on him.

"Carl! How can you even *think* about that?"

"I know." Carl holds up his hands. "Look, I'm not being selfish here, *I* won't be getting any million-dollar payouts, will I. I'm not talking about the money, I'm talking about the safety of the company. I'm still chief legal officer at Snoop and I have to think about this stuff. Snoop doesn't poof out of existence because Eva's had an accident. All our employees don't go away. I've got a duty to them and to the company. I'd be saying the same if it was me who skied off a cliff. Well, I mean, assuming I could still talk."

"Carl's right." Rik comes up behind us unexpectedly, looming out of the shadows, and puts his hand on his colleague's shoulder. His face, in the candlelight, looks uneasy. "However crassly he's phrased it. Eva's death is a tragedy—there's absolutely no doubt about that—but in the coldest possible way, it's got very little to do with Snoop. The company is a completely separate entity to any of us—even Eva and Topher. The buyout offer is still on the table. The clock's still ticking. We still have to come up with an answer. Eva's death doesn't change that."

"Well . . . it does change one thing, doesn't it, mate?" Carl says. There is something in his voice I don't quite like. It is a kind of grimness. Rik looks puzzled.

"Sorry, I'm not sure what you're getting at? Eva's shares you mean? They'll go to her husband I assume."

"Except they won't," Carl says flatly.

"What? I don't understand what you mean. Even if Eva's intestate, Arnaud would still stand to get everything, and he'll certainly want to accept the buyout now, won't he?"

"Shareholders agreement," Carl says. When Rik still looks blank, he spells it out. "When the company was set up there was a clause in the original paperwork to say that no one could pass their shares to an outsider. You're a shareholder mate, didn't you know this?"

"*What?*" Rik says, more forcefully. "No, I didn't know this! Why the fuck would anyone think that was a good idea?"

"It's quite common," Carl says with a shrug. "In fact I'd go as far as saying it's good practice. Stops the company passing into the hands of twats and plonkers. Means the original founders can't be forced out without their consent, that kind of thing. Topher and Eva set it up that way so this sort of thing couldn't happen—you know, if someone gets divorced and has to give up half their assets, you don't necessarily want their loony ex to have voting rights."

"So what the fuck are you saying?" Rik says. He looks horrified. "Eva's shares disappear on her death?"

"Nah, they still exist. But Arnaud has to sell them to Topher."

"To *Topher*? Why not to the rest of us?"

"Because this agreement predates you and Elliot coming on board," Carl says shortly. "This is how they set it up back when it was just the two of them. It was never updated when they issued more shares."

"So . . . Topher will have to buy out Arnaud?" Miranda says. She comes to sit beside Rik, her brow furrowed. "Except, well . . ." She stops, significantly, and exchanges a look with Rik.

"Except he can't," Rik says bluntly. "He doesn't have enough liquidity. I don't think that's any big secret, is it? So what does that mean?"

"There's an insurance policy to cover the cost. At least there should be, assuming they kept up the payments. They'll have to be independently valued, and Arnaud'll get whatever the valuers thresh out, I imagine. No idea how they'll take the buyout into consideration. That's for the insurers to decide I suppose."

"So wait, what you're saying is . . ." Rik looks thunderstruck. "What you're telling me—"

"Is Topher's voting share just got increased to sixty percent. Yup, that's about the size of it," Carl confirms.

There is deathly silence in the room.

Miranda looks stricken.

Rik turns and walks out the door.

ERIN

Snoop ID: LITTLEMY
Listening to: Offline
Snoopscribers: 10

The news of Eva's death is like a pebble thrown into a pond. No, not a pebble—a rock. First there is the god-awful, bone-shaking impact, and then the ripples of reaction, radiating out from that original catastrophe, and then rebounding, interacting, magnifying, and negating one another.

As Danny and I serve out soup to the guests in the silent, candlelit dining room, I can't help watching them, the way they're trying to make sense of Eva's disappearance in their own individual ways.

Some of them are in deep denial. Inigo, for instance, refuses to believe the GPS evidence. "She could still be down in St. Antoine," he keeps repeating. "GPS is wrong all the time and anyway, even if her phone is somewhere—what does that prove?"

Some of them seem to have been struck dumb by the tragedy. Tiger hardly eats. She just sits, head bowed over her untouched soup, letting the noise of the group wash over her as if the others aren't even there.

Some of them look stunned. Ani seems only half aware of what's going on; she crumbles her bread and makes inane remarks to no one in particular. Liz looks white and shocked, and barely speaks.

But some of them don't seem to be affected at all. Elliot, for instance, is spooning his soup with a poker face and much gusto, as if the tragedy had never happened. His lack of reaction is almost disturbing, though when Ani bursts out, "Elliot, don't you *care*?" he looks genuinely surprised.

"Of course I care," he says. "I still have to eat dinner."

It's Topher who my gaze keeps returning to. Topher, who has lost a partner, and gained a company.

For Snoop is now in Topher's complete control, that seems pretty clear, and for all his wild-eyed grief in the kitchen earlier, he doesn't seem that shaken by the news that he is now the majority shareholder in a billion-dollar company. In fact, he seems to have taken it in his stride, feeding on it almost, as if his personality has expanded to fill the vacuum left by Eva's absence. As I clear the soup bowls and refill the wineglasses—at least wine doesn't need cooking or refrigeration—he picks up his glass and downs it, laughing wildly as he does. He has been drinking a lot, throwing back glass after glass as he regales the silent Tiger with some tale of his and Eva's exploits when they first started the company. And the thing is, I can see it—I see the reason why they made this man CEO. I see the confidence that led him to think he could take a wild, improbable idea in a crowded market—and make it into a billion-dollar proposition. Something I never quite understood before—*how* someone would have the chutzpah to do this, and all before their thirtieth birthday—is suddenly plain.

Rik on the other hand seems to have shrunk. He looks bewildered, punch-drunk, like a man who's lost everything which, in a sense, I suppose he has. With Topher in charge, that billion-dollar buyout is melting away, leaving him with . . . what? Shares in a company he tried to sell out from under the founder? A position under a leader he doesn't trust? I can't see him surviving much longer in his post when they get back to the UK, best friend or no best friend. Topher doesn't strike me as the kind of man who would forgive or forget the kind of coup Rik and Eva were attempting to pull.

What's more impressive is that Carl and Miranda, who might easily have switched loyalties when they saw which way the wind was blowing, have instead both rallied around Rik. Do they really believe Snoop is doomed without Eva at the helm? Either way, they are not siding with Topher, that much is plain. Instead they sit either side of Rik, like chess pieces guarding their king.

But it feels like the match is over. They have lost their queen. For once more there is a space at the table, an empty place. Not Topher's this time, but Eva's, her empty chair a constant painful reminder of what has happened, not letting anyone forget, even for a second.

The chalet is still relatively warm in spite of the power cut and the temperature drop outside. Its thermal insulation and triple glazing means that the heat from earlier in the day is still enough to make the bedrooms bearable, while the two log burners downstairs keep the living room and dining room toasty.

Nevertheless, I distribute extra blankets and duvets before bed, limping from door to door with a torch clamped under my elbow, clutching armfuls of the spare bedding we keep for emergencies, along with thermos flasks of hot chocolate.

I'm about to knock on the second-to-last door when Danny, trailing behind me with a stack of blankets, says, "Erin, mate—" with a warning note in his voice.

And I stop. It's Eva's door.

And somehow that one simple thing catches me like a blow to the stomach, a reminder of the reality of what has happened here. An avalanche. A *death*. Will Perce-Neige ever recover from these twin disasters? It's hard to imagine people reading news like this in their Sunday paper and then turning to book a holiday, but then, St. Antoine isn't the first alpine resort to experience tragedy in the form of an avalanche. It happens almost every year, in fact there was another, similar fall just up the road earlier in the season.

"Mate?" Danny says, and I realize I have stopped stock-still, lost in thought.

"Sorry," I say stupidly. "I—I wasn't keeping track—I—"

"You all right?" Danny asks uneasily. "You should be sitting down, I'm not happy about you walking on that ankle."

"I'm fine," I say shortly. The truth is that my ankle is hurting. A lot. Danny's probably right, and I shouldn't be putting weight on it. But I can't bear to sit alone and silent in the darkness of the staff quarters, feeling it throb, thinking about what's happened and what's going to happen. I'm better off working; somehow the endless tasks keep my thoughts at bay. Plus, more practically, guest interaction isn't Danny's strong suit. They've forgiven him for his tactlessness in the wake of the avalanche, at least I hope they have, but our roles are firmly back in place now. We're here to be polite, good hosts, even in these circumstances. Perhaps *especially* in these circumstances. It feels like everything is crumbling—and our ordained roles are the only thing we have left to hang on to. Danny and I *must* remain in charge. If we don't keep that authority, if we let Topher take over—well, I don't like to think about how the situation could play out.

There's just one door left. Topher's. And I hitch my armful of blankets a little higher before I knock.

He's drunk, I can tell that when the door opens. He's wearing a robe, open to the waist in spite of the cold, and holding a bottle. And he's not alone. With the overhead light out, I can't see who's inside, but I've got a horrible feeling it might be little Ani, who didn't open her door when I knocked a few minutes ago. I want to tell her the answer to her distress over Eva doesn't lie in Topher's bed—but I can't. It's none of my business. She's the same age as me, she's a guest, not a friend, and I have no right to tell her what to do, even if I think she's making a fairly huge mistake.

"Ellen," he slurs. "Why hello. What brings you to my room at this late hour? It's a bit late to be tucking people in."

"Extra blankets," I say with my best cheerful smile. "Just in case the temperature drops overnight. Can't have you all freezing to death on my watch."

"I'll tell you a secret . . ." Topher leans in, confidentially, his robe gaping to show a smattering of dark blond chest hair. "The best survival kit is a naked woman."

Oh, ffs.

I can feel my smile thin.

"Well, I'm afraid the service doesn't extend to that."

"I've already got that part sorted," he says, but he reaches out for the blankets I'm holding, swaying slightly as he does.

I'm about to turn and leave when he says, out of the blue, "Don't I know you?"

"I don't think so," I say firmly.

"No, I do . . . I've seen you somewhere before. Did you waitress in London before you came here?"

"Sadly, no."

"I do," he persists. "I *know* you. I've thought it since I first arrived."

"Mate, she said she doesn't know you, and you're pissed," Danny breaks in, pushing past my shoulder to stand in front of me. Topher steps forward too, his expression turning ugly in less time than it takes for me to think, *Oh shit.*

Danny bunches his fists, the tendons in his neck standing out like cords, and for a minute the two men just stand there, chest to chest. I feel my heart thudding. Danny *cannot* hit Topher. He will get fired.

But Topher knows when he's on thin ice, and it's he who steps back, with a laugh that's just the right side of ingratiating.

"My mistake. *Mate.*"

And then he closes the door, and Danny and I are left standing, looking at each other, wondering how much longer this can go on, before the ice cracks.

LIZ

Snoop ID: ANON101
Listening to: Offline
Snoopscribers: 1

When I wake up, it is *cold*. That is the first thing I notice. It is a sharp contrast to yesterday, when I woke with a dry mouth and the feeling of having slept all night in a room a few degrees warmer than my bedroom at home.

I reach out and take a sip of the water on my bedside table. It is chilled, as if it has been in the fridge.

Under the extra duvets Erin dropped off I am still relatively comfortable, but I am not looking forward to getting dressed. In the end I reach out and grab the complimentary toweling robe off the end of the bed, dragging it under the covers with me to warm up before I put it on. I remember doing the same thing in my childhood bedroom when I was growing up, pulling my school uniform under the covers to get dressed. The room was in a badly converted loft, and in winter it was almost like sleeping outdoors. When I woke in the morning and breathed out, there would be a cloud of white hanging in the air. At night the moisture used to condense on the sloping ceiling and then freeze, so that I would wake to little runnels of ice on the wall above me. This is not as bad as that. I am in a luxurious chalet, not a Victorian terrace in Crawley, for a start. But as far as temperature goes, it is still painfully chilly.

I pick up my phone and peer at the screen. It is 7:19. The battery is down to 15 percent but I barely have time to worry about that fact because I am distracted by something.

I have a notification.

At some point in the night my phone has managed to connect to the internet. The reception is gone now, the bars grayed out to zero, but that notification is still there, proving that at least for a moment, there was a flicker of connection.

The second surprise is that it is from Snoop. I never get notifications from Snoop. You only get a notification if you get a new subscriber to your feed, and I never do.

Only . . . now I have. At some point in the night, someone snooped me. I'm not even sure how, since I wasn't listening to anything. I had no idea that was possible. Although maybe when the Wi-Fi connected it somehow restarted my stream where I left off, just for a minute?

The realization gives me an odd feeling. There is no way to know who it was—you can only see who is snooping you in real time; once they log off the connection is severed, only the number remains. Then I dismiss the issue from my mind. In all probability it was a bot or a server glitch, or someone mistyping the ID of someone they actually wanted to follow.

Downstairs the rooms are quiet but considerably warmer, and there's a pile of what I imagine must be yesterday's croissants keeping warm by the woodburner in the lobby, and two big thermos flasks sitting on the hearth.

I pick up a croissant and go through to the living room to warm my hands at the fire while I eat it. I assume I am alone. But then something catches my eye and I turn to see Elliot, seated in an armchair, bent over his laptop. The sight surprises me for two reasons—one, his laptop is on and seems to be plugged in. And two, Elliot almost never comes out of his room except for meals. In fact, when I was working at Snoop, he didn't even leave his office for those. He got whoever was doing work experience to bring him takeout—the same thing every day, black coffee and three Pret cheese-and-bacon croissants. It must have been very inconvenient when they stopped serving croissants all day and moved them to the breakfast menu. I find myself wondering what he did. Changed his lunch? Somehow I can't imagine that. Maybe he started sending the work experience person out at 10:00 a.m.

I don't normally talk to Elliot. He is very hard to make conversation with, though perhaps that is not my fault. Eva once told me that he divides women into ones he would like to sleep with and ones who are not of interest to him. I am definitely in the latter category. But now I pluck up my courage.

"Hi, Elliot."

"Hello, Liz." He says it flatly, but I know him well enough to know that's not a measure of his enthusiasm. He greets everyone like that, even Topher, who is probably his favorite human being out of anyone.

"How come your laptop is working?"

"I always carry a battery pack." He holds it up, a chunky thing the size of a brick that is plugged into the power port of his computer. Of course. How like Elliot to leave nothing to chance.

"But you've got no internet, right?"

"No," he agrees. "But I don't need it for coding."

"What are you working on?"

"The geosnoop update." His normally pale face flushes with excitement a little bit, and he launches off into a long explanation I don't completely follow about geotracking, ad partners, information storage, GDPR, and the technical challenges of making all those elements work with the law and the existing Snoop interface. I nod along, feigning more interest than I really feel. The only thing I really care about is the fact that he used this technology to find Eva. Somehow that seems unbearably poignant—that her own app may be what leads search and rescue to her body.

"I see," I say at last, as Elliot grinds to a halt. "It sounds very . . . exciting." I try to make my voice sound convincing, but Elliot doesn't really seem to care. It's not like he ever shows much expression of his own feelings.

"Now if you don't mind, I need to work," he says abruptly, with the directness that is so disconcerting.

"Sorry," I say. "I thought maybe you came down to chat."

"I came down because it's too cold to type in my room," he says, and then he puts his headphones on, and his fingers begin to clatter across the keyboard once more.

I should be offended. I feel like I ought to be. But I'm not. He may be direct to the point of rudeness, but right now, there is something reassuring about that. With Elliot, there are no secret codes to unravel, no hidden meanings, no weight of expectation. If he wants you to know something, he says it. If he wants something to happen, he tells you. Just at the moment, there is something comforting about it, in contrast to the smoke-and-mirror world of Topher and Eva, where you never know quite where you stand. Sometimes, back in the early days at Snoop, they would remind me of my parents—the way it would all be sweetness and light in front of visitors, and then screaming and threats when the company had left. At least when Elliot says, "Have you got a problem with that?" you know he genuinely wants an answer.

When my father said it, there was only one answer you were allowed to give: *No, Daddy*. And then get out of the way as fast as possible, before the blow landed.

I'm nibbling on the edge of the croissant, staring into the flames of the woodburner, when a noise behind me makes me jump. The croissant falls to the floor in a shower of crumbs. I pick it up. Then I turn to see Rik and Miranda coming into the room. Rik looks like he hasn't slept.

"How are you?" he says to me abruptly, as he sits beside me. I'm taken aback, not sure what to answer. It's the perfect illustration of the difference between Rik and Elliot. If Elliot were asking I would know what he meant—only Elliot would likely never ask, because he would understand the impossibility of the question. But when Rik asks, it becomes a puzzle to decode. What does he mean? Does he want to know how I feel about Eva's death? How can I sum that up in a simple answer? Or is he just asking in the meaningless way that people do, only wanting the answer *fine*?

"I'm . . . I'm okay," I say cautiously. "Considering."

"Really?" Rik looks at me, surprised. "You're a bigger person than me." He glances across at Elliot and then lowers his voice, though Elliot is still wearing his big noise-canceling headphones, and I doubt he can hear a thing. "Having that kind of money dangled under your nose and then snatched away . . ."

Suddenly the real meaning of his question is clear. He wants to talk about Topher. About what this shift in power means for the buyout.

"I . . . I hadn't really thought about it," I say, and it's the truth . . . in a way. I would be lying if I claimed I hadn't wondered what would happen now that Topher controls the company. But somehow the money never felt that real to me. I never felt I had earned it. It doesn't feel like I had anything taken away—just like I had a strange dream, and then woke up to reality. Only, this—the avalanche, Eva's death—this doesn't feel like reality either. More like waking from a dream to find yourself in an equally surreal nightmare.

"But hadn't you made plans? Banked on the money?"

"Not really," I say, slowly. "To be honest, I hadn't really come to terms with the idea that it was going to happen anyway."

"Jesus." Rik says. He looks annoyed. I think I've said the wrong thing, but I don't know how. A sense of panic sets in. It is the same sense I always got with my father. That I would do or say the wrong thing. That he would take it out on my mother. "Could you cut the Mother Teresa act, Liz? We've lost everything. Don't you get that?"

"W-we haven't lost everything though, surely? I mean, we've still got the shares."

"The shares!" Rik gives a short, barking laugh. "Liz, did you listen to the P and L figures I gave out yesterday? We'll be lucky if Snoop makes it to the year-end at the rate Topher's going, and without Eva to reassure investors, that's only going to get worse."

"But, the update," I say, although I know I am scrabbling for reassurance now. "Elliot's geosnooping thing—isn't the whole point of that to make Snoop more profitable?"

"From a revenue point of view, we've already got that information, we've had it since the permissions changed last year. How Elliot integrates it into the app may make a difference to the user experience, but user satisfaction has never been our problem, the issue has always been monetizing that. From an investor perspective, rolling out the geosnoop update won't make a difference—all the added value is already there. And anyway"—he glances over his shoulder at Elliot, who is still typing away—"I've got concerns about that update. I don't think people realize how much information Snoop is gathering on them. I think when this update makes the level of tracking visible, we might have a backlash on our hands."

"One of Snoop's USPs has always been its light touch," Miranda says, coming in from the lobby with a cup of coffee in her hand. She takes a sip and makes a face. I think it is the taste of the coffee that she is reacting to. Though it could be the prospect of the update. "People like the fact that you can be as anonymous as you want, it's part of what keeps celebrities coming back. I'm not sure how many people clocked the change in permissions and really realized what it meant, because nothing changed at the user end. But this update is going to make it very obvious. Users will see exactly how much Snoop knows about their movements. I told Topher and Elliot at the time that there was a big PR risk with all of this, but they're both so focused on the cool techy side of it—"

She stops and glances again at Elliot. He is still head down, tapping away with his earphones on.

"Anyway, never mind. This probably isn't the time or place to have this discussion. It's too . . . soon." She sits beside me and Rik and takes another sip of coffee, then puts the cup aside. "How *are* you?" she says to me. I can hardly prevent myself from rolling my eyes. It seems like everyone is asking that question, when what they really want to know is, *What are you thinking.*

I am saved from answering by Elliot, who stands unexpectedly, clicking his laptop closed, and pulling off his headphones. He looks . . . tense. Which is unusual. He doesn't show emotion easily.

"Okay, Elliot?" Miranda says brightly. I can tell she is wondering how much Elliot heard of our conversation.

"Erin's put out coffee in the lobby if you want it," she adds, but he ignores the remark.

"Do you know where Toph is? I need to speak to him."

"He's still in his room, I think," Rik says. He is frowning. I can imagine him running over our conversation in his head, trying to work out if he said anything incriminating and what Elliot might be about to pass back to Topher. "But wait," he adds, as Elliot heads purposefully towards the stairs. "I wouldn't go up there, I think he's got . . . company—"

But it is too late. Either Elliot didn't hear, or he doesn't care. He doesn't reply to Rik's warning. The last we hear of him is his heavy footsteps, thumping up the spiral staircase towards the bedrooms.

ERIN

Snoop ID: LITTLEMY
Listening to: Offline
Snoopscribers: 10

"Oh, hey, Erin."

I'm putting out another thermos of coffee when Ani trails into the dining room, smiling. She looks like she's not slept a lot. *I hope you know what you're doing*, I want to tell her, but I don't.

"Morning, Ani. Can I get you coffee? The espresso machine isn't working, but Danny's managed to rig up a kettle on the woodburner so we've got hot French press.

"Ooh, yes please," Ani says. "Could you take a cup up to Topher?"

"Sure."

"Oh, I mean, unless . . . how's your ankle?" she adds, flustered at having slipped so easily back into guest-and-server mode. "I can take it up if you're not—"

She stops. Everyone has been thrown off-kilter by the strangeness of our setup here. Are we fellow survivors, or still holidaymakers and staff? I don't know myself, but I do know that it's going to be easier for everyone if we stick to the normal protocols. Someone needs to be in charge, and to be perfectly honest, I'd prefer it if that someone were me, not Topher.

"It's loads better, thanks," I lie. "I can manage the stairs, no problem."

"But you shouldn't have to," Ani says, making up her mind. "I'll take it up."

"Are you sure?"

"Yes, totally. I'll take one for Elliot too. He must be freezing up there."

She pours out three cupfuls and carries them carefully up the spiral staircase to the bedrooms.

By 10:00 a.m. everyone is awake, and Danny and I make the decision to summon all the guests into the lobby for a meeting. There's no real news, and the weather is still too unpredictable for a helicopter to land on our narrow slice of mountainside, but local radio reports have been saying that search and rescue for casualties is ongoing, and that EDF are working on restoring power to outlying hamlets. We are not the only people trapped without electricity, by the sound of it. In fact we're considerably better off than some. But it feels like a good idea to reassure everyone that progress is being made, and to stress that we have enough food and water to see us through until they either restore the funicular, or get a helicopter up to airlift us out.

We also have to discuss the elephant in the room—Eva's death. Although the rumor has gone around the group and everyone seems to have learned of Elliot's conclusions, neither Danny nor I have formally acknowledged the issue. I've been putting it off, unable to face the reality of what has happened, but the time has come that we really *have* to make an announcement, make it clear that we're trying our best to contact the authorities and alert them to what's happened, but at the same time put to rest any false hopes, dispel any fantasies that she's going to come limping over the horizon at any moment.

Danny beats the gong in the lobby, sending its deafening crescendo ringing around the rafters, and when at last everyone is gathered I tap a spoon against a coffee cup and wait for silence.

"Hi, um, hi everyone. Sorry for dragging you out of your rooms like this, but Danny and I just wanted to give you an update on our situation. Danny spent the morning trekking out to our two closest chalets, which unfortunately—or perhaps fortunately, for the inhabitants—seem to be unoccupied. One is very badly damaged, but it doesn't look like anyone was there at the time of the avalanche. The other one was out of the path of the fall so it's fine, but again, there's no one home. We were hoping to find someone with a two-way radio or a satellite phone, but it's not looking good so far. There's one more chalet up at this level, but it's about three miles away, so Danny's going to wait until the weather clears before he heads out to check on that one."

"And have you managed to make contact with search and rescue?" Rik says.

"Yes and no," I say. "As you know, Inigo made contact yesterday and told them about our situation, but we haven't been able to get through since, and without access to a satellite phone, I don't think that's going to happen until the power is restored. The power cut seems to have wiped out the remaining mobile phone reception. But the key thing is that they *do* know we're here. We know from what Inigo said that we're on their list, we just have to be patient while they work through the more critical rescues."

"Do they know about Eva though?" The question comes from Tiger, her voice even more husky than usual, as if she is holding back a strong emotion, and a silence falls over the room as I try to answer it.

"Inigo told them that she's missing yes. But they don't know the latest. However—"

I stop and swallow. I knew this would be hard, but this is ridiculously hard. I see Liz's eyes, luminous with distress, reflecting back at me from the other side of the room; Topher's anguished face; Ani shading her eyes with a hand to hide the sudden tears that Tiger's question has provoked. I take a breath, steady myself on the arm of a chair, trying to take the weight off my ankle, give myself space to find the right words. What I want to try to tell them is that even if we *can* get Elliot's information to the search and rescue team, it's not going to help. Eva's already dead, and now she's probably under thousands of tonnes of snow as well. There is no chance of anyone rescuing her alive; in fact, there's not even any certainty that they will be able to recover her body. Some of the high passes never melt, even in summer. If Eva is buried at the bottom of one of the steep ravines, well, that's it. There aren't enough resources and money in the world to make that recovery.

"The position she's in—" I stop, swallow again, but before I can find words to go on, Carl is interrupting.

"How do we know she's definitely there though?" His expression is truculent. "I mean this whole place has shit phone reception. How can Elliot say those coordinates are right?"

I look around for Elliot. Where is he?

"My understanding is that GPS doesn't rely on phone reception," I fumble, still desperately scanning the room for his face, willing him to step in and explain the technicalities of how Snoop gets its geolocation information. I am way out of my depth here. "I mean obviously you have to relay the positioning, you can't do that without some kind of information exchange, but the GPS coordinates themselves don't rely on mobile towers for accuracy, they're . . . satellite, I think? Is that right, Elliot?" But I can't see him. "Where *is* Elliot?"

Other people are looking around now, asking themselves the same question.

"He was up in his room when I last saw him," Ani says, frowning. "He was working on something. He's probably got his headphones on, didn't hear the gong. I'll go and get him."

She turns and runs lightly up the spiral staircase and we hear her footsteps receding down the corridor towards Elliot's room, and the rat-a-tat on his door.

No answer. She knocks again, more loudly, and then calls, "Elliot?" through the wood.

There is a pause. I imagine her cautiously opening the door, venturing forwards to tap Elliot on the shoulder . . . but my mental picture is broken into shards by a scream. And not just a little shriek of surprise either. This is a full-throated panic-cry.

With my injured ankle, I'm not first up the stairs. Topher, Rik, Danny, and Miranda are ahead of me, and Liz and Carl both jostle past me halfway up. By the time I reach the first floor I can hear Ani's sobbing cries of "Oh God, he's dead, he's dead!" and Topher's brusque, impatient, "Stop being hysterical."

When I finally make it to the end of the corridor and push my way into Elliot's room, everything looks completely normal, except for two things.

Elliot is lying slumped across the little desk by the window. He is facedown in a pool of black coffee, spilled from a cup tipped on its side.

Next to his desk, on a towel on the floor, is his computer, and it has been smashed to pieces.

LIZ

Snoop ID: ANON101
Listening to: Offline
Snoopscribers: 1

Elliot is dead. You can tell that without even touching him. There is something about the unnatural way he is slumped, one arm hanging limp, the spilled coffee pooling around his face and in his eyes.

But it is not only that. It is what has happened to his computer that makes it clear. Elliot would have died before he let anyone touch that computer.

It has been—*wrecked* doesn't seem the right word. It has been *obliterated.* The keyboard has been ripped off, revealing the inner workings of the device. The screen has cracked, and a dark stain is spreading across the LCD. And finally, the hard drive has been pulled out, cracked open, and bent and twisted beyond all recognition.

"What—" Topher's face is white and stark. He looks more frightened than I have ever seen him. "What's happened? Oh my God, oh God, oh Jesus—he wanted to tell me something and I didn't—I wouldn't let—oh God . . ."

He stumbles from the room. He looks like he might be sick.

Ani appears struck completely dumb by the discovery. She simply stands there, gaping, tears streaming silently down her face, until Tiger takes her arm and leads her away.

It is Erin who speaks.

"Everyone, out."

"What?" Carl says it stupidly. He looks like a boxer who has taken too many blows to the head.

"Out. Out of the room. This is a crime scene."

She goes across to Elliot, puts two fingers to his neck, pulls Elliot's eyelids back, and then shakes her head very slightly at Danny.

"Well, what are you waiting for?" Danny says to the rest of the room. He sounds almost angry. "Didn't you hear what she said? Get out."

We file out. Erin takes a staff key from her pocket and locks the door behind us. Her face is outwardly calm, but I think underneath it she is holding down panic.

"Inigo," she says, "I know I don't need to tell you this, but please keep checking for reception with your phone. It's absolutely imperative that we get hold of the police, now."

"Uh, yes, of course." Inigo looks as stunned as Carl. "I'll go now, and check. I left it downstairs."

"What can we do?" Miranda says blankly to Erin. "What can we do?"

"Nothing," Erin says. Her face is grim now. "There is nothing we can do. Try to keep it together until the search and rescue come."

ERIN

Snoop ID: LITTLEMY
Listening to: Offline
Snoopscribers: 10

In the kitchen, Danny stands with his back to the door as if his weight can shut out the reality of what we left behind us, and he stares at me with an expression of horror.

"Fuck," he says. And I can't think of anything to say in reply. Because what else is there to say? This is . . . this is bad. This is beyond bad. And I can't make sense of it.

"Danny, what the hell is going on?"

"I have no fucking clue, mate. Did he commit suicide?"

"Maybe." I realize how little we know about these people—any of them. After all, Elliot could have been under any kind of pressure, and Danny and I would never have known. But that's the thing—we *don't* know. We have no idea what is happening here.

I put my hands to my head as if I can forcibly keep it together with the pressure of flesh on bone. Oh God, it feels like everything is falling apart.

"He wasn't hurt," I say, trying to figure it out as I speak. "I mean, I couldn't see any physical injuries, it didn't look like anyone had attacked him. Which means . . . I suppose he must have taken something. Don't you think?"

"Drugs? Injectables? Pills?"

"I don't know. I don't *know*. Holy fuck. Danny, what do we do?" The reality—if you can call it that—of our predicament is sinking in. We are stuck here—very stuck, in my case, with my wrenched ankle—in a chalet with a group of people we barely know, and two of them have died in the last twenty-four hours. Eva—Eva's death was a tragic accident. One of those horrible, awful lightning strikes that can occur in even the most tranquil places. But Elliot—surely there is no way his death can be anything but murder or suicide. A brain aneurism—a massive stroke—a heart attack—any of those might kill near enough instantly. But they don't explain the smashed-up computer.

"Was he *definitely* dead?" Danny asks.

"Definitely." I can't suppress a shudder as I think of it.

"Are you sure?" Danny is grasping at straws, and I think he knows it, but he can't stop himself asking. "Are you absolutely certain, mate?"

"Danny, I may have dropped out of med school without a degree, but I've seen enough dead bodies to know one. I promise you, he was dead. Dilated pupils, absent pulse, the works." I don't mention the puddle of piss under the chair. Danny doesn't need to know about that.

"But how?" Danny says. He looks like he might be sick. "How the fuck did someone get to him, if that's what happened? Something in the coffee?"

"Maybe, I don't know."

"Should we go and, you know . . . check?"

"I don't *know*," I say again, more forcefully this time. My head is spinning, trying to figure out the right course of action. "The police will want to—I mean, we shouldn't disturb the scene. But maybe if we knew what it was—"

I look down at the key in my hand and make up my mind.

"We'll go and check. We won't touch anything, we'll just look."

Danny nods, and together we make our way quietly up the service stairs to the first floor, trying not to let the others see where we're heading.

We don't discuss our decision to stick together, but I know we are both thinking the same thing. If Elliot didn't commit suicide, then someone in this group is a murderer. And that is a very scary idea indeed. Could one of those sleek, monied hipsters downstairs *really* have murdered someone? I try to imagine gentle Tiger with her slim hands around Elliot's neck, or Topher whacking him with an empty bottle of whiskey—and I feel suddenly sick.

The staff key grates in Elliot's locked door and then turns, and Danny and I tiptoe inside the room. It is very cold, and it smells of spilled coffee, and something else, more acrid: that stench of urine, which I recognize from my hospital days.

Danny hangs back, by the door, as if he can't bring himself to come any closer to Elliot's body. So it's clearly up to me. I swallow. Very, very cautiously, trying not to disturb anything, I move forward towards the desk. Elliot is still lying in the same slumped, unnatural position, his face in the puddle of cold black coffee. I already moved him slightly to check for signs of life, but I want to avoid disturbing the scene any further. So without touching him, or anything else, I lean over and try to peer inside the empty, fallen cup. It's difficult, without moving it; the angle is all wrong. I go round to the other side of the desk—and suddenly, there I can see it.

Shit. Danny was right.

"There's something in the cup," I tell Danny, who is not coming any closer than he can help. "Something white."

"Sugar?"

"No, definitely not. It's . . . chalky."

"Fuck."

I straighten up and Danny and I look at each other, trying to figure out what this means. His black eyes are very, very worried.

"I think this rules out suicide," I say, with immense reluctance. I am keeping my voice low. I don't want anyone but Danny to know I'm in here.

"Do you think?" Danny looks like he is desperate for an alternative. I can't blame him. "What if he was really bad at taking pills—don't you think someone might crush them?"

I shake my head.

"You didn't see him eating, Danny." I think of Elliot at dinner, spooning down his venison with concentrated ferocity, swallowing great gulps of it while barely chewing. "But it's not just the pills. Look at the computer."

"What do you mean? He could have smashed it up himself, couldn't he?"

I shake my head, pointing to the wreckage, strewn across one of the chalet's thick, fluffy white bath towels.

"Someone wrapped it in a towel before they destroyed it. Which means they didn't want to be heard. If it was Elliot smashing up his own laptop in a fit of frustration, he wouldn't have bothered to keep the noise down. And if he was trying to cover something up covertly, he'd just have reformatted the hard drive—why take the risk of smashing it up if you can just rewrite all the data? No, this was done by someone who couldn't log in. Someone who couldn't afford to be overheard."

We both stand, contemplating the smashed screen and broken pieces of hard drive. Danny doesn't say anything. I'm not sure there is anything he can say.

Then something else occurs to me.

"Were they *his* pills, do you think? Did he take any medication?"

"We'll have to ask the others." Danny looks like he's relishing the prospect about as much as a slug enema. "Jesus. How do we have that conversation?"

How do we discuss any of this. *Hey, guys, listen, there's a strong chance one of your colleagues is a murderer.*

But why? Why would anyone want to kill Elliot? His shares? His support for Topher? With Eva dead, is it possible someone is trying to undermine Topher's support?

None of that would explain the destruction of Elliot's computer, though. It is the computer that I keep coming back to. That vicious, efficient, stealthy act of destruction. That could not have been an accident. And I don't for a second believe it was Elliot.

There is only one plausible reason for this action—to hide something on the computer itself. Something Elliot knew. Something that got him killed.

I think of Topher's anguished wail, when we found Elliot's body: *Oh God, oh Jesus—he wanted to tell me something . . .*

I swallow.

"Danny, what if Eva's death wasn't an accident?"

LIZ

Snoop ID: ANON101
Listening to: Offline
Snoopscribers: 1

We sit, all of us, huddled around the woodburner in the living room. Except it is *not* all of us, that is the problem.

Now we are ten.

Now we are nine.

Now we are eight.

The words chant inside my head, a kind of gruesome countdown, edging closer to zero, one by one.

Suddenly I think I might vomit.

"Was it . . . ," Tiger speaks. Her voice is cracked and rough, as if she has been crying. "Was it . . . suicide?"

"No!" Topher's answer comes as quick as a gunshot. He stands up. He begins to pace. "Fuck no. Elliot? Never."

"So what?" Rik stands too, squaring up to Topher as if he is about to punch him. "What are you saying?"

Topher looks at him. I think he genuinely does not understand Rik's question.

"Use your head, Toph. If it's not suicide"—Rik's voice has an edge I have never heard before. He sounds . . . dangerous—"Then it's *murder*. Is that what you're saying, Topher? Is it?"

Topher's mouth falls open. Then he sits abruptly. He looks winded, almost as if Rik really had punched him.

"God. You're right. Oh my God." His face is ashen. "Elliot," he says brokenly. And then he begins to cry.

It is awful, watching him. None of us knows what to do. Rik looks at Miranda, whose face is aghast. Carl puts his hands up in a *Don't look at me, mate* gesture of repudiation. Inigo's expression is pure panic.

It is Tiger who steps up. She goes to sit beside Topher. She puts her hand on his arm.

"Topher," she says. Her voice is gentle. "We all feel his loss, but it must be incalculable for you, more than any of us. Coming on top of Eva's death—"

She stops. Not even Tiger can spin this as *what will be, will be.*

"Why?" Topher's mouth is square and ugly, tears running down his cheeks. He looks so far from the polished, urbane sophisticate I used to know; I am not sure if I can bear it. "Why would anyone do this to him? Why would they hurt Elliot?"

That, of course, is the $64,000 question.

We all look at one another. No one is sure what to say.

"Come on." Tiger takes Topher gently by the hand. She leads him from the room. "Let's go and splash your face with water."

As they leave, a sigh of released tension ripples round the room.

"Jesus," Carl says gruffly.

"But he's right," Rik says. "Why *would* anyone hurt Elliot? I mean, Eva, okay. But Elliot? It makes no sense at all. I know Topher doesn't want to hear it, but maybe he *did* commit suicide, uncomfortable as it is for all of us to face? Eva's disappearance and then on top of that the shock of the avalanche—he was quite a—" He stops. I think he is trying to work out how to phrase it without giving offense. "He was quite a quirky personality."

"I think that's a pretty offensive stretch, Rik," Miranda says wearily. "Yes, he had his eccentricities—we all do. But to go from that to—"

"No," Rik says defensively, "that's not what I meant. Jesus, I *liked* him. We were at school together, for goodness' sake. I'm just saying—look he was very hard to read. Still waters run deep and all that. There could have been a lot going on underneath."

"And what do you mean, you could understand someone wanting to hurt Eva?" Carl says suddenly.

Rik winces. He knows that he has made a misstep, not once, but twice.

"I didn't mean that either. Oh bloody hell, I'm putting my foot in it all over the fucking shop."

"So what *did* you mean?" It is Inigo. His voice is bitter, almost accusing. His interjection is so uncharacteristic that we all turn and stare at him.

Rik flushes.

"All I meant," he says carefully. I can tell he is picking his words now. "All I meant was Eva's death . . . it changed stuff."

"What *stuff*?"

Rik does not want to spell it out. I can see that he doesn't.

It is Carl who says it for him.

"Eva's death gave control of Snoop over to Topher, isn't that what you mean, mate?"

Rik cannot bring himself to reply, but he gives a small, tight nod.

There is a moment's long, shocked silence, as what he is saying sinks in around the circle.

Rik has joined the first two dots, but no one wants to go any further. They can already see the pattern that is forming.

Several people here had a powerful financial motive for Eva's death. Specifically Topher, and Elliot. Plus anyone else who was opposed to the buyout for their own private reasons.

Which means . . .

It means—

I feel the blood rush to my face. Suddenly I can't go on with this, can't sit here thinking the thoughts that are threatening to overwhelm me. I have to get out—get away.

I stand, and I run out of the room.

ERIN

Snoop ID: LITTLEMY
Listening to: Offline
Snoopscribers: 10

Danny and I are still standing outside Elliot's room when I hear the sound of running feet, and I turn to see Liz hurrying along the corridor. For a minute I think she is running towards us, and I tense, bracing myself for whatever has happened, but she stops halfway along the corridor, opens her bedroom door, and slams it behind herself. I hear the key scrape in the lock from the inside, and then nothing.

"Jeez," Danny says. He looks taken aback. "What's eating her?"

"Do you need to ask?" I whisper it. The doors here are thick, but you can hear through them if your room is quiet.

"Do you think she heard?" Danny lowers his voice too. "You know. What we were saying before." He doesn't repeat it, but the words I uttered just before Liz came barreling towards us still hang in the air between us. *Maybe Eva's death wasn't an accident.*

"I don't know," I mutter. "Let's get out of here. We can't talk here, and I need to think this through."

As we make our way down the corridor to the staff part of the building, where Danny and I have our private rooms, my mind is racing, ticking through possibilities. But it's only when we're safely in my little bedroom, the door closed behind us, that I feel able to voice them.

"What I just said—"

"Eva's death?" Danny looks troubled, but skeptical. "Yeah, how d'you make that out? Elliot, sure. There's some kind of hanky-panky there. But Eva? She skied a black run in a fucking blizzard and fell off the edge. It's a tragedy, but I can't see how it's anyone's fault."

"Listen," I say. I'm speaking very low, even though we're behind two sets of doors. Somehow it feels like I need to get these suspicions out in the open, like it might even be dangerous to keep quiet right now. Because if I'm right, it was Elliot's silence that killed him. "Listen, we're missing the important thing here. Whoever killed Elliot—"

"*If* he was killed," Danny breaks in.

"*If* he was killed," I echo impatiently, brushing his words away like irritating flies. "But the point is *if* he was killed, whoever killed him didn't just get rid of him, they got rid of his computer. Why would they do that? It's really hard work to destroy a hard drive—it takes a while, and they must have risked someone noticing their absence or hearing them do it."

"So . . . you're saying . . . he was killed for something on his computer?"

"Yes. He was killed for something he knew, but it must have been something he'd figured out from his computer data."

"Something about Snoop?"

"Maybe. Kind of. Look at the timing. Elliot is coding this geolocation update, whatever they're calling it. Then he realizes that the information he's got can lead him to Eva. That much we know. But what if he began to track back from that? What if he was looking at her movements before she died? What if there was something fishy about them, like perhaps she didn't shoot off the edge, but stopped for a chat with someone, and was pushed?"

"Holy fuck." Danny's face is stricken. "You're saying . . . someone in that group got rid of Eva and then killed Elliot to cover their tracks?"

"I don't want to believe it, but . . . I can't see what else makes sense." I feel sick even saying the words. "There is one other possibility, but I don't know if it's much better."

"Which is?"

"Well, Elliot is the only person without any kind of alibi the day Eva died. He was supposed to be here, working on his code, but there's no corroboration of that. It's not impossible he had something to do with her death. Maybe . . . maybe he couldn't live with that knowledge any longer."

"You're saying he topped himself out of guilt?"

"I'm saying it's a possibility."

"Okay, yeah, but even supposing he killed Eva to help Topher, then had an attack of conscience, why would he destroy his computer? If he's dead, why would he care about the evidence?"

I swallow. This is why this possibility isn't really any more comforting than the others.

"Because whatever was on there implicates someone else. Someone he's trying to protect."

"Flaming Nora." The words should sound funny, coming in Danny's deep, matter-of-fact voice. In fact, they're anything but. Actually I think I want to be sick.

"So you think I'm right?"

"I think . . ."

I can see Danny's brain processing furiously, trying to find holes in my logic and failing. He pulls off his bandanna irritably, scrubs his face with it. "Fucking hell. I don't know. I think you could be, and that's enough to give me the cold heaves. What do we do? We gotta tell someone, right?"

"Who can we tell? And what could they do even if we did?" I wave a hand at the window, where the vicious wind is whipping the snow past the glass with the scouring force of a sandstorm.

No one can go out in that, let alone fly a helicopter. You'd be mad to try.

"FUCK!" Danny bellows it, standing up and running his hands over his short hair like he can cudgel an idea out of his head.

"Shh!" I say frantically. "Be quiet! The others'll hear."

"But we have to tell them!" he says. "Don't we? I mean what's the alternative, we keep quiet and let some homicidal prick pick them off one by one?"

"We can't tell them!" My voice is a screaming whisper now. "Are you mad? Tell whoever's responsible for this that we might be onto them?"

"We can't *not* tell them!" Danny takes my arms, and for a minute I think he's going to shake me, like an actor in an old movie dealing with a hysterical woman, and I feel a desperate urge to laugh in spite of the predicament we're in, but he doesn't; he just stares into my face, his dark eyes very wide and as scared as I feel. But somehow seeing my own fear reflected back at myself, the realization that Danny's as terrified as me, and that we're in this together, it anchors me. I take a deep, shuddering breath, and Danny says quietly, "Erin, I'm shitting myself as much as you are. But I don't think I'm going to be able to go down there and act normal, knowing that one of those hipster wankers might be an honest-to-God murderer. Look at me—" He holds out a trembling hand. "I'm shaking like a bloody leaf. Whoever's done this, they're going to figure out that we *know* something, and if we haven't told anyone what we know, we'll end up the same way as Elliot. The best way to make ourselves safe is to *not* keep this a secret."

His words silence me. There is a kind of horrible logic in that.

"And besides," he adds, "I reckon we owe the others the chance to protect themselves. What if they know something they don't realize? What if they're the next people drinking coffee with a kick?"

I swallow. But his words have an undeniable truth behind them. Put like that, it's hard to justify not warning the seven innocent people in the chalet, even if that means giving the murderer a heads-up.

Murderer. The very word, hanging unspoken in my mouth, feels unreal. Is this actually happening? Are we really going to do this?

"Okay," I say at last. I look out of the window, at the storm, a sinking feeling beginning to churn in my gut at the thought of the meeting to come. "Okay . . . maybe you're right. So . . . what? How do we tell them? *What* do we tell them?"

"We tell them the truth," Danny says. His expression is set and grim now. "We say we think Eva's death may not have been an accident after all and that Elliot might've been killed for whatever he was about to tell Topher. We tell 'em to stay in pairs at all times, make their own drinks, eat nothing but stuff you and I serve them. We're the only people who can't possibly be suspected. We didn't know any of them before they came here. We weren't up on that mountain. We've got no connection to any of that group."

I nod. Only . . . and I can't bring myself to say this to Danny, not now . . . the problem is, in my case, it's not quite true.

LIZ

Snoop ID: ANON101
Listening to: Offline
Snoopscribers: 1

I am up in my room with my head in my hands, trying to block out the reality of what is happening, when I hear the sound of the gong in the foyer being struck.

My head jerks up.

I open my door cautiously. Erin's voice comes floating up the stairwell.

"—you could all come and gather in the lobby for a second. This won't take long, and then we'll serve lunch."

I am not ready to face the others. But whatever is going on down there, I have to know. Maybe the police have been in contact. Maybe we are about to be airlifted out.

I take a deep breath. I flex my fingers. I open the door of my room and walk downstairs.

The others are all waiting in the foyer, huddled around the woodstove. It has got noticeably colder now. The warmth leftover from yesterday's central heating has dispersed, and now only the two stoves downstairs are keeping the place from slowly freezing.

Erin is standing a few steps up on the spiral staircase. Her face is very white, and her scar looks more shocking than ever, a livid slash against her pale skin. Danny is at her shoulder like a lieutenant. I have to push past them to get to the ground floor. There are puddles on the wood in the foyer, where the piled-up snow is leaking in through the bowed front door, spoiling the polish.

When we are all gathered in front of them, looking up expectantly, Erin clears her throat.

"Okay, is everyone here?" She's counting heads, and I realize with a shudder that she is thinking of our abortive meeting this morning, which ended with the realization that Elliot was missing. I taste blood, and I realize I am chewing my cuticle again. *Disgusting little girl.* I flinch. I shove my hands in my pockets.

"We're going to serve lunch in the living room if that's okay, the dining room is starting to feel quite cold. It's salad—I know that's not the most appropriate, but without electricity Danny is very limited on what he can cook, and we need to finish up the fresh vegetables, now that the fridge is off."

There's a mild grumble from Topher, but Miranda glares at him, and everyone else nods. We know we are not in a position to complain.

"But . . . the real reason we asked you all here—" Erin stops. She looks a little bit sick. Like she is working herself up to say something she really doesn't want to say. Suddenly, I do not want to hear what she is about to say. "Danny and I, we . . ."

She looks over her shoulder at Danny. He gives her a look back. I am not sure if it is encouragement or impatience, but it seems to spur Erin on.

"We have some concerns," she finishes, in a rush, "about the manner of Elliot's death. We're pretty sure that he—that he was poisoned."

Little gasps come from all around the room. It is what they have all been thinking, but there is something horrifying about hearing the words spoken aloud.

"There are traces of crushed pills in his coffee," Erin says, "and while he may have taken an overdose deliberately, the sabotaged computer makes it at least possible—"

Danny mutters something. His voice is too low for me to hear, but Erin sighs. She tightens her fists at her sides.

"Maybe even *probable*, that Elliot was murdered. And that leads backwards to the possibility that Eva was killed too, and Elliot was murdered because of what he knew."

There is another ripple of reaction around the room, but it is not really surprise. She is only voicing what most people here had already begun to suspect. It is more like a kind of horror: these are no longer paranoid fears, but a potential reality.

"Danny and I debated this announcement long and hard," Erin continues, "because ultimately it's only speculation—we have no proof of any of this. It's still possible that Eva's death was an accident and Elliot's was suicide or an accidental overdose. However, the fact remains that two deaths have occurred and that is . . . well, *concerning* doesn't really cover it. So even while we hope this is overk—"

She stops. I realize that the word she was going to use was *overkill* but that she has thought better of it.

"Even while we hope this is overly cautious," she rephrases, "we would still urge everyone here to take precautions. If you know something that may endanger you, come and tell me and Danny as quickly as possible. Stay in pairs or groups at all times. That includes sleeping. Prepare your own drinks and don't leave them lying around. Only accept food from Danny or me. There's no need to be paranoid but—"

Carl breaks in. His short laugh sounds like the bark of a dog.

"No need to be paranoid? Are you having a giraffe?"

"I realize this is all—" Erin begins, but he cuts her off again.

"You're telling us there's a homicidal fucking maniac running around and the answer is to make our own coffee?"

"I'm not telling you anything of the kind," Erin says. Her voice is very level. "I am simply stating the facts of what's happened. Whether you concur with my conclusions and follow my advice is up to you."

"This is a fucking shitshow," Carl says angrily. "And I should sue the arse off you. Thousands of pounds to stay in a tin-pot little shit-hole with a psycho on—"

"Oi," Danny breaks in. He steps forward so he is close to Carl's face. "That's enough of that, mate. Erin and me are not responsible if you brought some psychotic fucker with you from the airport."

"Are you accusing Snoop employees of this?" Carl is practically shouting now. He and Danny are squaring up. "Because that, *mate*, is slander, and I'll see you in court."

"I'm not accusing Snoop employees of anything," Danny snarls, "I'm saying that we've hosted a hundred fucking holidays and it wasn't until you lot turned up—"

"Hey," Erin steps forward. She is speaking to both of them, but it is Danny's arm she takes. She shakes it gently. "*Hey.* This isn't helping."

"Carl," Tiger puts her hand on Carl's shoulder. "Come on, Erin's right. It's completely understandable that you're angry, but you need to channel that energy into a more positive place. Erin and Danny aren't at fault here. They're trying to help. C'mon. Deep breaths."

Carl is still muttering as he stalks to the other side of the room. He slumps on the sofa, arms folded, but I can see he knows Tiger is right.

"Inigo," Erin says now, "have you had *any* more luck with mobile reception?"

Inigo shakes his head.

"Nothing, sorry. And now I'm down to twelve percent battery, so I'm trying just to turn it on occasionally to check."

"Anyone else?" Erin says. There is an edge of desperation in her voice. There are headshakes all around the room. Most people must be out of battery now, anyway. I turned my phone off when it got to 4 percent.

"And what did they say when you spoke to them?" Erin asks, turning back to Inigo. He frowns.

"What do you mean?"

"I mean, did they give any timescales at all? Any indication of how they proposed to get to us? I know they didn't know the full extent of it then, but they knew we had someone missing, right? I would have thought we'd have been quite high up the list of priorities."

"I . . ." Inigo is frowning, as if he is trying to remember. "Yes, I mean, I told them Eva was missing and that we were trapped in our chalet at the top of the funicular. And I said . . . I told them about your ankle. And they just asked some questions about supplies and then said they would come out to us as quickly as possible."

"That was it? No timings at all?"

"N-no . . ." Inigo sounds uncertain. "I mean, the reception was really bad. I'm trying to remember, but I don't think it was mentioned."

"Okay," Erin says. There is an edge of frustration in her voice that her calm politeness doesn't quite mask. "That's understandable. Well, we'll just sit tight I guess. Okay, well, that's it, everyone. If you go through to the living room, Danny and I will bring lunch along very shortly."

Everyone begins to disperse. Carl is still muttering angrily. Tiger is talking to him soothingly. Miranda and Rik are the last to leave the lobby. I am directly in front of them. I can hear their low conversation as we file slowly into the lounge.

"I suppose Inigo did actually phone the police?" Rik speaks. His voice is barely above a mutter.

"What do you mean?" Miranda sounds surprised.

"Well . . . I mean . . . Erin seemed pretty concerned that we hadn't heard anything. And I can see her point. You'd have thought they'd have got *someone* up here, right? Even if it was just a scout."

"But we heard him, Rik, we heard him calling them."

"We heard his end of the conversation, yes. But how do we know he actually made the call? I mean it's a bit suspicious full stop that he managed to get reception when none of the rest of us did. What was that all about?"

Miranda doesn't answer that. But I notice that when we are all gathered in the living room, she takes the seat farthest away from Inigo, and she doesn't meet his eyes.

ERIN

Snoop ID: LITTLEMY
Listening to: Offline
Snoopscribers: 10

"Bollocks." I'm standing in the kitchen, watching Danny put the finishing touches to big bowls of salad. He's done an amazing job with tins and jars, but there is no way of masking the fact that the bread is stale and the lettuce has seen better days. Twenty-four hours without electricity is starting to take its toll on the freshness of the chilled food.

"What do you mean, bollocks?" Danny doesn't look up. He's crumbling crushed walnuts over a big plate of ripe, sliced pears and slightly overripe Bleu d'Auvergne cheese.

"I just . . . I feel like that didn't go so well?"

Danny tastes the dressing and then shrugs.

"I dunno. You were telling them something they didn't want to hear. What did you expect them to do—applaud?"

I shrug. I am not sure what to say.

At last Danny is ready, and we each pick up a couple of bowls and carry them out. As I limp after Danny, through the empty lobby, I see croissant crumbs from earlier today scattered across the thick sheepskin rug. There's not much I can do without any electricity for the Hoover, but in my current mood it feels like a sign of the way things are fraying at the edges, falling apart while Danny and I desperately try to keep the wheels on.

In the living room, the silence is deafening. There's no longer any friendly backdrop of music to mask the tensions in the group, only the soft roar of the log burner, and the patter of snow against the window. Rik and Miranda are sitting together, their arms touching. They seem to have abandoned all pretense of not being a couple, and as I draw closer I see that their hands are entwined in Miranda's lap.

Tiger is still talking to Carl in a low voice, as if she can calm him down.

Liz is sitting awkwardly on the edge of her seat. Her fingers are in her mouth, chewing at her nails, but as I enter the room she takes them out and flexes her hands nervously, cracking her knuckles. The little volley of clicks is very loud in the quiet room, and Ani, sitting between Liz and Topher, makes an involuntary grimace at the sound.

Only Inigo is by himself, and when I offer him the last bowl of salad, he waves it away with one hand.

"Thanks, but I'm not hungry."

"You've got to eat, Inigo," I say, but the look on his face worries me more than his appetite. The last thing we need is someone sinking into a depression.

"I'm not hungry." He says it with more force, and I put my hands up.

"Okay, okay. Not trying to strong-arm anyone. I'll leave it here, okay? If you don't want it, no pressure."

I am turning to go back to the kitchen when I hear his voice, very low.

"I feel like everyone is blaming me."

"Blaming you?" I say, in surprise. "Why on earth would they do that?"

"Because of what you said before—about not being able to get through to the police. I heard them." His voice drops to a whisper, and I have to bend closer to find out what's being said. "I heard Rik and Miranda, they were saying—" He stops, swallowing heroically, and I see there are tears in his eyes. "I think they think I was making it up. That I didn't talk to the police, or if I did that I didn't stress the urgency of the situation enough. But why?" He looks up, his extraordinary blue eyes swimming with tears. "Why would I do that? Unless I'd—unless I'd k-k—"

But he can't say it. *Unless I'd killed her.*

"I loved her," he says, his voice cracking on the last syllable. "That's what none of them understand. I *loved* her."

Oh shit. I remember the rumors of the first morning, Inigo coming to bed late, Topher's drawling, *Not that again. Eva should know better.*

"I loved her!" Inigo repeats, and I very, very much want to tell him to shut up. Because he seems to believe that this confession will exonerate him. But if anything, it's the reverse. Because you need a pretty powerful motive to kill someone—and one of those motives is money—that's the one we've all been assuming was at the bottom of this. And Inigo has no financial motive to kill Eva. Only Topher and Elliot fall into that camp, as far as we know. But the other thing that provokes people to kill is love. And Inigo's just put himself forward as the only candidate for that category.

"I'm sure you did," I say quietly, and then I watch as he stands and walks out of the room, unable to hold it together in front of his colleagues anymore.

In the kitchen I sink into my chair, prop my aching foot on Danny's makeshift footrest, and wait for him to come in through the service door.

"What was all that about with Inigo?" he asks, and I explain.

"Bloody hell." He runs his hand through his hair. "What a stupid little prick. What, with Eva shagging Inigo, and Topher getting his end away with Ani—haven't they heard of Me Too? You can't go around bonking your employees anymore. It's not right."

"It gives him a motive though, doesn't it?" I say reluctantly, and Danny shrugs.

"I dunno. I mean we could probably give them all motives if we needed to. Miranda could be madly in love with Inigo herself. Rik might be a raging incel who hates having a female boss. Who the fuck knows. I could come up with some old bollocks against all of them if I had to. If you ask me it's alibis we should be looking at. There must be some of them we can rule out."

"Not for Elliot's death. That could be anyone. We were all here—everyone was coming and going from the living room."

"Ani took him the coffee. And we all know she's got the hots for Topher."

"She took him *a* coffee, but we don't know if it was the same cup that killed him. You'd have to be pretty stupid to announce to the world you were taking up coffee to someone you were about to poison."

"Could be a double bluff," Danny says, a little feebly, but I can tell he's only playing devil's advocate. "But okay, sorting out alibis for Elliot's gonna be tricky, I can see that. What about Eva though? If we're accepting that Elliot was killed because he knew something about what happened to Eva . . ."

"Well . . ." I'm trying to think back, remember what everyone said about their whereabouts when we were discussing Eva's disappearance. "Ani and Carl saw Eva safe and sound halfway down La Sorcière. So if someone did kill her, they must have been on the mountain before Ani and Carl. *And* they must have been a good enough skier to intercept Eva halfway down that run. Right?"

"Riiight . . . ," Danny echoes, slightly doubtfully. "Although . . . if it comes to that, Carl never actually said he saw her. It was only ever Ani's word for it."

"Okay, but she *did* see her, she must have done. This was before Elliot's GPS information came out. Ani had no way of knowing that

Eva had gone down La Sorcière otherwise, surely? If she were lying, she'd have said that Eva went down Blanche-Neige, which is what you'd assume, and what anyone would say if they were trying to throw someone off the scent."

"Okay, I can buy that. So Ani and Carl are in the clear, is that your point?"

"Yes, and Liz, because she'd already gone down in the bubble lift. She left before Eva even arrived at the top. We're looking at the people who were at the top of the run before Eva—which means Topher, Rik, Tiger, Inigo, and Miranda."

"Not Miranda," Danny says unexpectedly, and I frown.

"Why not?"

"Well, if we're accepting Ani's sighting, Eva was killed about halfway down La Sorcière. Which means we're looking for someone who's good enough to ski that run."

I nod slowly. He's right. Which means . . . Well, it's actually a pretty small group of people in that case. Tiger. Inigo. *Maybe* Rik, though I'm not certain about that. He's good, but you wouldn't need to be just good, you'd need to be very good indeed. And Topher.

We keep coming back to Topher. Which is hardly surprising, because Topher has the strongest motive out of anyone here. And now he has opportunity as well.

"They got separated at the top, didn't they," I say, thinking aloud. "When the pisteurs closed Blanche-Neige. Some of them went back down in the bubble, and some of them skied it anyway. The people who took the bubble back down can't have had anything to do with it. Who was that?"

"I don't think they ever said." Danny's frowning now. "I know Topher and Inigo skied it, but I'm not sure about the others. Want me to ask?"

I nod, a little reluctantly. I should go out there myself, really. Danny's manner with the group is getting more and more terse. He was close to squaring off with Carl earlier, which is—well, it's just unthinkable. The last thing we need is a fight, added to this powder keg of grief and tension. But my ankle is hurting. A lot. And I can't bring myself to put weight on it right now.

When the door swings shut behind Danny, I feel in my pocket for the blister pack of ibuprofen and count the hours since I've had my last dose. Three. I should really wait another hour. Instead, quickly, before Danny comes back, I crack the foil and swallow down two more pills.

As I wash it down with a gulp of cold tea, the door swings open.

"Topher, Inigo, Tiger, and Rik skied Blanche-Neige," Danny says. "The rest of them went down in the bubble and met up with Liz, who was already waiting at the bottom."

"Okay. Well . . . if someone hung back they could probably have sidestepped back up to the top of the run and skied La Sorcière instead. But they'd have had to be quick. Very quick. Eva was a fast skier, and she was already halfway down the run when Ani saw her. That doesn't give someone much time to intercept her before she got to the bottom."

"Unless . . . unless . . ." Danny says. He's speaking slowly; I can almost see him figuring out the possibilities. "What if she'd fallen? What if they caught up with her, she's hurt herself or something, they're pretending to help her with her bindings and instead . . ."

I nod. There's a definite possibility in what he's saying. If this were opportunistic rather than planned . . . but then an objection occurs to me, and it's a big one.

"There's no drop on the bottom section of the run," I say. "There's no way someone could have pushed her off the edge."

"No, but if she was incapacitated somehow they could kill her and leave her body in the trees. Elliot said himself that he wasn't sure how the mountains affect the GPS signal. Maybe that's what he discovered—that she wasn't in the valley at all. Someone killed her on the piste."

"Maybe . . ." But Danny's comment has tipped off something in my mind. "But just a second, there's one other problem with all of this."

"What? I thought we were doing pretty well."

"It all hangs together except for one thing. How did anyone *know* Eva was skiing La Sorcière? We're talking as if someone went after her deliberately in the hopes of catching up with her. But no one saw her leave. No one knew she was skiing that run."

"Fuck, you're right." Danny frowns again, his dark brows knitting together. "How the fuck did they know to go after her?"

"The only person . . ." I'm thinking, putting two and two together. "The only person who *knew* she was on that run was Ani. What if she told someone what she saw?"

"If she told someone . . . ," Danny says slowly, but when he finishes his sentence, it's not what I expected him to say. "If she told someone, she could be in a fuck of a lot of danger. We have to find out who she told. And quick."

LIZ

Snoop ID: ANON101
Listening to: Offline
Snoopscribers: 1

"Fucking hell."

Topher is in my room. *Topher* is in my room. He is pacing, back and forth, back and forth between me and the door. He looks demented. I don't know what to do. My room has always been my refuge—the one place I could close the door and shut everyone else out—the smell of beer, the sound of my mother's sobs, my father's bellowing voice. *Go to your room, Elizabeth.* He meant it as a punishment. Instead, it was an escape.

Now my room has been invaded and my escape has been cut off.

"Fucking hell, Liz, this is a nightmare. They're all looking at me. They all think it's me!"

"Topher—"

I try to think what Tiger would do in this situation. Would she put her hand on his arm? Give him a hug? The latter makes me feel a bit ill, but I could try the arm.

I stick out my hand, awkwardly, but Topher is pacing. He just brushes straight past it like I was hailing a taxi and he was a driver with a passenger. I am not sure he even sees it. I go to chew my cuticles, then I shove my hand in my pocket to stop myself.

"God, I think I'm going mad. Oh Jesus, Eva. Eva!"

Topher stops and slumps onto my bed. He puts his face in his hands, and then to my horror, he begins to sob.

At least he's stationary now. I put my hand out, trying to remember how Tiger calmed Carl down. I let it drop onto his shoulder.

But then he gives a huge wrenching sob, almost like he might be about to be sick, and I snatch it away.

"Topher," I whisper. "Let me—" I look round the room, searching for inspiration. My eye falls upon the empty water glass by my bed. "Let me get you a glass of water."

I'm not sure if he hears me as I tiptoe into the corridor. I shut the door, leaning against it, breathing hard.

Oh god, this is not what I am good at.

I am good at filing, and taking notes, and making sure everything adds up. I am good at tidying up loose ends and keeping everything straight. I am task-oriented and time-conscious and detail-focused. And I am very, very good at making myself invisible.

In short, I was a perfect PA. But I am not cut out for this.

ERIN

Snoop ID: LITTLEMY
Listening to: Offline
Snoopscribers: 10

Danny and I should be washing up from lunch—it's no joke, with no dishwasher. The only hot water now comes from kettles we boil on the woodburning stove, and it's becoming a full-time task just to keep enough clean crockery to serve meals. The greasy crockery from lunch is piled high on the draining board, and cutlery is soaking in lukewarm water that's fast losing its heat. But important as it is to keep the guests fed, keeping them alive is more crucial, and neither of us wants to leave the other on their own, so there is no discussion over who will go and who will stay when I propose talking to Ani. That we will both tackle her is without question. The only thing in doubt is where and how.

"Now," Danny says firmly. "If she talked to the murderer, told them where Eva was, it's only a matter of time before they figure that out. And when they do . . ."

He trails off. I swallow. I know he's right.

"But, what if she's with one of the others?" I ask. "What's our excuse for talking to her alone?"

Danny shakes his head.

"No, we talk to her in front of everyone. It's better to get it on the table. If everyone knows the truth, great. They can't kill *all* of us."

He says it almost glibly, and a part of me finds myself wanting to laugh, hysterically. How has it come to this, that we're discussing murder like some kind of parlor game? But he's right. There's no sense in keeping whatever Ani has to say under wraps. The more people who know the truth, the better.

We don't have far to go to find her. We exit the kitchen and make our way through the chilly dining room, and there she is—sitting in the lobby in front of the woodburner, playing cards with Carl, Rik, and Miranda, her huge glasses pushed up on her forehead as she stares down at her hand.

"Three of a kind," Carl is saying smugly, as he lays down three kings.

"Hi," Danny says, a little brusquely, positioning himself in front of the group. "Can we talk for a moment?"

"Sure," Miranda says with a sigh, stacking her cards. "Carl's whipping our arses anyway, so please come and save us from another defeat." She runs a hand through her long dark hair, and then makes a face. I know how she is feeling. No hot water means no showers, and everyone is looking a little limp and grubby around the edges, including me and Danny. "Have you got news?"

The hope on her face gives me a momentary stab of guilt, as I realize what our purposeful entry must have looked like. I shake my head.

"No, I'm so sorry. Still nothing."

"Bloody hell," Rik says. "Still? Isn't this getting a little bit . . . concerning?"

"Well, I must admit, I would have hoped they'd be here by now."

I look out of the tall windows that span the double-height lobby. It's the middle of the afternoon, but the air is so dark with whirling snow that it looks like twilight, and I can't see the lights of St.

Antoine le Lac below, let alone the far-off mountain ranges. But then, the thought occurs to me uncomfortably, maybe they are without power down in Le Lac too. The batteries in Danny's radio have died, and we have no idea now what's happening down there. It could be much worse than we're imagining.

"It's more than twenty-four hours since the avalanche," Rik presses. "Shouldn't *someone* have been in contact by now?"

"I don't know," I say.

His concern is making me increasingly uneasy. Maybe he's right. Maybe there *is* something wrong.

"They're very stretched, I imagine."

"What are you getting at, mate?" Carl says sharply, looking across at his colleague. "You got a point to make, spit it out."

Rik exchanges a look with Miranda and then says, almost reluctantly, "Look, this isn't an accusation, please don't think that. But I'm just saying that it's . . . well, it's *unfortunate* that no one else managed to talk to the police, apart from Inigo."

"What do you mean?" Carl says, taken aback.

"I'm just saying . . . it would be nice to have corroboration of what went down. We only heard his side of the conversation. And it does seem a little . . . strange, that he's the only person who managed to get any reception."

"Are you saying he didn't call them?" Carl's eyebrows go up to his shaven hairline.

Rik says nothing, but he gives a little shrugging wince that could be yes or no, but functions effectively as an acknowledgment of the possibility.

"Fuck," Carl says. He breathes it out like some kind of prayer. "Faaaark."

Danny shoots me a startled, worried look, and I realize that I never told him about that part of my conversation with Inigo, and Rik's suspicions, perhaps because I never really believed they were true. Now I feel frighteningly naïve. What if Rik's right? What if *no one* is coming?

"What did you want to talk to us about?" Miranda says, bringing us back to our original mission, and I drag my mind back to the task in hand with an effort.

"Oh. Yes. Well, it was actually Ani we wanted to speak to—we had a quick question."

"Oh?" Ani looks up from her hand. "Yeah! I mean, sure, anything I can help with?"

"You want a bit of privacy?" Carl says, and he makes to half rise, but Danny shakes his head.

"Stay. Better to keep all our cards on the table, if you know what I mean."

Carl considers for a second, then sees the wisdom of what Danny's saying and gives a short nod, and sits again.

"Ani," I say, trying to think how to put this without causing undue alarm but being as clear as possible about what I mean. "You saw Eva skiing La Sorcière when you were coming up in the lift, is that right?"

"Yes," Ani says. "Definitely. I, like, already said that though . . . ?"

"Yes, but what I wanted to ask is, did you *tell* anyone at the time?"

"Oh . . ." She frowns, trying to think. "I don't remember. I might have said something to Carl. Like, *Oh, hey, there's Eva*. Do you remember, Carl?"

"To be quite honest, I don't," Carl says flatly. "I don't think you said anything, but hand on heart, I couldn't swear to it either way."

"Oh!" Ani says suddenly. She's flushing pink, and she looks like a child who's pleased they've come up with the answer you were prompting for. I realize, with a disquieting shift, that Ani thinks we are testing *her*, checking up on her story, and she's pleased she can give us corroboration. "Wait, I *did* tell someone. We came off the lift at the top, and Topher was talking about setting off, and Inigo said, 'But, like, we can't,' because of waiting for Eva, and I said, 'Gosh no, didn't she tell you? She's already left. I saw her skiing down the black run.' I'm not sure if Topher heard me, but Inigo *definitely* did. He can back me up."

He can back me up.

She's looking at me with wide, shining eyes, and her trust makes a lump come to my throat.

But Carl . . . Carl is looking at her with a kind of horror, and I know that he has joined the dots that Danny and I had already figured out.

"Bollocks to backing you up," he says abruptly. "Don't you get it?"

"Get what?" Ani says. She looks surprised, like we've taken away her gold star. She can't understand why Carl isn't pleased for her, happy that her story has checked out.

"Inigo *knew*," Carl says. "He knew where she was skiing. Eva. You told him how to find her."

"Oh my God," Ani says, and the color drains out of her face, leaving her translucent skin bone white, the blue of her veins showing through at the temple. "Oh my God, you're saying—you're saying—"

"I'm saying, someone went down that run and killed Eva. So question is, who knew she was skiing it?"

"Not Inigo!" Ani says, and her voice is a cry of anguish. "Not Inigo, no, he was—he and Eva—"

She stops, her hand over her mouth, as if she's said too much.

"Eva was shagging him," Carl says brutally. "Come on, love, we all know that. You don't have to be Sherlock bloody Holmes to get that far. But shagging someone isn't an alibi, you know that."

"No!" Ani stands up. The color has come back to her face, and she looks pink and furious. "*No.* I'm not having this! Eva's death—it was an accident. And Elliot—I just—no! I won't—I *can't* think like this. I can't!"

She lets the cards flutter from her hand, and stumbles from the room.

LIZ

Snoop ID: ANON101
Listening to: Offline
Snoopscribers: 1

I am standing outside my bedroom door, my back pressed to the wood, when someone comes up the stairs. I can't see who it is at first. With the lights out, the corridor is too dark. But as she comes closer, I see that it is Ani. She looks as if she has been crying.

My first instinct is to duck back inside my room—but I can't. Topher is in there. I am trapped. She is walking towards me. I am going to have to interact with her.

"Are you okay?" I say.

"They're—they're saying awful things," she gulps. "About Inigo. I don't believe it, Liz, I won't!"

"What kind of things?" There is a cold feeling in the pit of my stomach.

"That he—" She gulps again, and forces herself on. "That he *killed* Eva. That he didn't call the police."

"He didn't call the *police*? Are you saying no one's coming?"

"But he did!" Ani wails. "We saw him! It's completely unfair they're saying this stuff and not giving him the chance to defend himself. I've worked side by side with him for two years, for God's sake. I know him!" She pushes past me and bangs on his door.

Carl has pursued Ani up the stairs. The others are following. I see Rik, Danny—holding a torch—Miranda, last of all Erin, still limping.

"Ani, wait," Carl says. Just as he says it, my bedroom door opens so suddenly that I nearly fall backwards, because my weight is still resting against the wood. Topher shoves past me into the corridor. His face is still blotched from earlier but he is no longer crying.

"What's going on?" he asks abruptly.

"Inigo!" Ani is still banging on his door. There is no answer. "Where is he?"

"Oh God," Rik says. He looks at Miranda, and then at Erin. "You don't think—"

"Oh no, no," Danny says quickly. "We're not having another body. Not on my watch." He elbows past Ani, takes a staff key out of his pocket, and opens the door. Then he shines the torch into the room.

There is no one inside.

Over his shoulder I can see Carl's belongings, thrown untidily around, and Inigo's camp bed, the covers neatly smoothed and tucked.

In the center of the pillow is a folded piece of paper.

No one seems to know what to do, but then Erin hobbles past Danny into the room and picks it up.

"It's a note," she says, scanning it in the torchlight. Then her face goes blank. "Oh . . . fuck."

It is the first time I have heard her swear in front of us. Danny has lost it a few times, but Erin has always been completely professional. Now her face is white. She looks up at Danny and mouths something I can't decipher.

"What does it say?" Topher says authoritatively. Apart from a slight croakiness in his voice, you would never know he had been sobbing his heart out in my room a few minutes ago. "I have a right to know, I'm still CEO of this company."

He pulls the note from Erin's fingers. She does not resist. He reads it aloud.

"'Dear everyone, I have made a terrible mistake. I have gone to try to put it right. Please don't come after me. Inigo.'"

"Oh fuck," Miranda says, echoing Erin. "The idiot." She is standing in the doorway. Now she turns and looks out the long window at the end of the corridor, the window Inigo stood at to try to get reception. It is almost completely dark now. The snow is beating on the glass as if it is trying to get in. I cannot help an involuntary shiver at the sight. "I mean—look at it out there. He's going to kill himself."

"What does it actually mean though?" Erin asks. She looks bewildered. "The note I mean. Is he saying he *didn't* call the police but now he's gone to fetch them? Or has he gone after Eva?"

"Fuck knows," Carl says brusquely. "Stupid little plonker. Has he actually left already?"

"Good question," Danny says. "I'll check." He turns and walks quickly down the corridor taking the torch with him. The shadows close around us as he disappears. We hear him clattering on the spiral staircase, and then the bang of the door into the service part of the building where the ski lockers are. When he returns, he is walking more slowly, and his face is set. "Yes, he's left," he says as he comes closer to our group. "His skis are gone. So's his jacket."

"*Shit*," Carl says angrily. "Bloody little idiot. When did he go? Who saw him last?"

There are shrugs all around the group.

"I saw him at lunch," Miranda volunteers, and several other people nod.

"I saw him at lunch too," Erin says heavily. "He was . . . he didn't eat. He wasn't in a good state. He went off, I assumed to his room, but he might have gone to the ski lockers. Did anyone see him after lunch?"

Everyone shakes their head. Then Erin frowns.

"What about Tiger?"

We all look around at each other, and I can see a sinking dread mirrored on the faces of the others. Where *is* Tiger?

Without saying anything, Danny sets off in the direction of her room. We all follow him, like a flock of anxious sheep.

At the door he knocks. Nothing. I can feel the tension rising.

"Bollocks to this," Danny says roughly, and he sticks his staff key in the lock. The door springs open—and everyone crowds inside, jostling to see. I am at the back, my view blocked by Topher's broad shoulders. I hear Ani's anxious, "Tiger?"

And then I hear a sleepy voice saying, "Hey, what's happened?"

There's an audible exhalation, a mixture of relief and exasperation.

"Jesus, Tiger!" It's Miranda. Her accent is usually an upper-class drawl. Now she sounds sharp and annoyed. "Don't do that to us! Didn't you hear Erin's speech? Stick together!"

"I locked my door," Tiger says. Her normally unruffled voice sounds a little bit less serene than normal. "What's the matter?"

"Inigo's gone," Miranda says. And then, to my astonishment, something in her polished facade seems to crack, and she begins to cry.

ERIN

Snoop ID: LITTLEMY
Listening to: Offline
Snoopscribers: 10

We all go to bed very early, exhausted by a hideous, hideous day. Some people pair up, making sure everyone knows who they're with. Miranda and Rik aren't pretending anymore. After Miranda's breakdown outside Tiger's room earlier, they have been inseparable.

Now, Rik simply says bluntly, "I'll be sleeping in Miranda's room tonight," and there is not even a ripple of surprise.

What is perhaps more surprising is that Tiger and Ani pair up, leaving Carl and Topher as the two remaining single men. I had thought that Ani and Topher would have gone off together too . . . but something has changed between them since Elliot's death. What I can't figure out is who initiated the reserve. Elliot died having tried to tell Topher something, something Topher never gave him the chance to say. You don't have to be a genius to figure out that maybe there was a reason Topher didn't want him airing those suspicions.

But on the other hand, it was the fact that Topher was in bed with Ani that prevented Elliot from talking to Topher. It wouldn't be surprising if Topher, on some level, however irrationally, resented that fact. And Ani was, undeniably, the person who took up that coffee. Or at least *a* coffee, I remind myself. Though it was Topher who asked her to do it, from what she said to me in the kitchen. Assuming she was telling the truth. Jesus. I am talking myself in circles here.

It's Miranda who raises the question we'd all overlooked.

"What about Liz?"

There is an awkward silence as we all realize that, once again, everyone has forgotten about Liz. All eyes turn to her, and she seems to shrink into herself, wrapping her arms around herself as if she can protect herself from our stares.

"Do you want to, like, share with me and Tiger?" Ani says brightly, but Liz shakes her head.

"No, thanks, I'll be fine alone."

"Liz, no," Miranda says, with some concern, "I really *don't* think that's a good idea. Erin's right—we should stay together."

"Honestly," Liz says. There is something obstinate, mulish almost in her face. "I don't like sharing a room. I'll lock the door."

"Full disclosure," Danny says bluntly, "Erin and me, we've got staff keys. We can get in everywhere. Now, I'm not saying we're gonna come and bump you off in the night, but these doors ain't exactly Fort Knox, if you know what I'm saying."

"I'll put a chair under the doorknob," Liz says. She folds her arms, and I exchange a glance with Danny and a minute shrug. We can't *make* her take our advice.

"All right," Danny says at last. "Your funeral."

It's only after the words are spoken that he realizes how they sound.

LIZ

Snoop ID: ANON101
Listening to: Offline
Snoopscribers: 1

I know what they are thinking as we trail slowly off to our separate rooms. They are thinking I am mad. Perhaps they are right. As I shut and lock the door behind me, I can't help wondering if this is a terrible, dangerous idea, making myself the odd one out like this. What if it gives someone ideas?

But I cannot explain to them how much the thought of sharing a room with Tiger and Ani fills me with dread. It has been bad enough during the day, jostling with these faces from the past, hemmed into a nightmare with people I barely know.

I need my refuge. I need to be able to close the door behind me. The idea of spending the night on a mattress on Tiger's floor, listening to her soft breathing, and Ani shifting in her sleep—it makes me want to shudder.

I push a chair under the handle of the door, then get into bed, fully dressed. It is too cold to change. I am lying there, with my eyes closed, trying to relax my stiff muscles, trying to tell myself it's safe to fall into unconsciousness, when there is a noise at the door. I raise my head. Instantly my heart is racing at 150 beats a minute.

"Wh-who is it?" My voice is shaky with adrenaline.

I can barely hear the whisper through the thick wood.

"It's me, Ani."

"Hang on." I swing my legs out of bed and make my way over to the door, pulling away the chair. Then I open it cautiously.

Ani is standing outside. She is dressed in a thick pink sweater that comes down almost to her knees. Her eyes are huge in the darkness.

"Ani, what are you doing? You nearly gave me a heart attack."

"I'm sorry," she whispers. "I couldn't sleep, you know? I kept worrying about you, and I think Erin's right. We should, like, stick together? Please come in with me and Tiger."

"No, honestly, I'm fine," I say. Ani stands there in the dark corridor, twisting her fingers together. She is looking at me in a way I don't like. Her eyes are very wide and very worried. "I'm *fine*," I say more forcefully. "Go, Tiger will be wondering where you are."

"Tiger's already asleep," she says with a tremulous little laugh. "Out like a light and snoring. I don't know how she does it—she's so zen. And I just kept thinking about things, turning stuff over in my mind."

"I think she took a pill," I say. "She was talking about it at breakfast. But—what do you mean, thinking about stuff?"

"Oh . . . nothing." She gives that little shaky laugh again, but there is something in her eyes. It is pleading and concerned. I get a sudden lurch of apprehension.

"Ani, do you know something you've not told anyone?"

She shakes her head, but it's not really a decisive shake, it's more of a worried *Don't know.*

"Listen to me," I say. My voice is an urgent whisper. It is not like me to be so forceful, but I am very worried. "You heard what Erin said, if you know something, *tell* someone. Keeping secrets is the most dangerous thing you can do. Did you see something? Was it when Elliot came to Topher's room? Something about Inigo?"

"No, I didn't—" she says, with a catch in her voice. "I just—I keep feeling like there's something wrong . . . something I saw . . . I just—like, can't put my finger on it."

Oh God. My stomach is churning with unease. I have a horrible feeling that what Ani can't remember might be very, very important. It might be the clue to the killer's identity. It might be the one thing that gives them away.

"Ani, *tell* me," I plead. "Don't keep this to yourself."

Our eyes lock, and I see something there. Something that she *knows*. And suddenly I am very, very frightened.

"*Ani, please*," I say. I am begging, I know I am, and I no longer care. But she just shakes her head, her eyes as wide and as scared as I feel.

"I can't," she whispers. "I have to . . . I have to *think* . . ."

Then she disappears into the shadows, leaving me standing in the corridor, watching with foreboding as Tiger's door closes softly behind her. I wait, just to make sure, and then I hear the click as she turns the key in the lock, and I turn back to my room. There is nothing else I can do.

ERIN

Snoop ID: LITTLEMY
Listening to: Offline
Snoopscribers: 10

"Shit." Danny is lying on a mattress he's dragged into my room, his hands over his face. "Why did I say that about the bloody funeral? I'm so bleeding tactless! Their mates have just *died* and they probably think I'm making cracks about it."

"Honestly, Danny, I truly think that's the last thing anyone is worrying about."

I am so tired my eyes are scratching with it, and I'm sure Danny must feel the same, but I also know that there's no way I'm going to be able to fall asleep. Everything is too wrong. Danny's presence, comforting as it is, is too strange. The room is too cold. The situation is too dire. And I'm worried that if I do fall asleep, I'm going to have my recurring dream about digging through snow, that I'll wake up Danny, that he'll ask questions I can't answer.

Most of all I just feel incredibly scared.

It doesn't help that my foot is hurting again. A *lot*. I am starting to worry that maybe something is broken after all.

"Someone should have come," Danny says, into the silence, and I know what he's talking about.

"We don't *know* Inigo didn't phone."

"What did he mean then, about making a huge mistake?"

"I don't know, but it makes no sense, Danny. Why on earth wouldn't he phone? The only reason would be if he'd killed Eva, and if that's the case, we're safer without him, aren't we?"

"Maybe he did. Maybe he's getting a head start on the police. We don't know, do we?"

Danny's remark stops me in my tracks, and I can't honestly think what to say in reply. The truth is that I just don't think Inigo is a killer. He seemed gentle, and desperate, and genuinely sad about Eva. But then I think of all the newspaper pieces I've ever read about "perfectly nice guys" who killed their kids or their partners or a complete stranger. And I am forced to remind myself of what Danny was trying to get at—these people are strangers to us. Whatever odd intimacy this situation has created, it's illusory. We have known Inigo, like the rest of them, for less than three days.

There's another long silence, and for a while I think maybe Danny has drifted off to sleep, but then he gives a great sigh.

"Shit, what are we going to do, Erin?"

"I don't *know*." The three words encompass all the desperation I've been building up since Eva's disappearance. This is just unimaginably awful. First Eva, then Elliot, now Inigo. Our guests are disappearing one by one, like some bad horror movie. "If Inigo really has gone to get help—"

"I don't believe it," Danny says, with finality. "If he called the police like he claimed, then there's no need for him to go and get them. And if he *didn't* call them, why go and become the knight in shining armor all of a sudden? It doesn't make sense. He's not gone for the police. He's scarpered, and this is his way of covering it up."

His words make my stomach sink, but there's no denying the logic of what he said. The truth is, whether Inigo has disappeared or not, it doesn't change our predicament. We are stuck here, and we have no way of knowing whether Inigo will succeed in getting help—or even if he'll try. All the complicated analysis in the world can't change that. All we can do is sit and wait. Then, suddenly, an idea comes to me. "Wait, there's one thing we could do."

"What?"

"You could go. You could walk to Haut Montagne. Raise the alarm."

There's a long silence. Then Danny says flatly, "No."

"I know it's dangerous, but I can't go with my ank—"

"Fuck the danger," Danny breaks in. "I don't care about the bloody danger. But you're right—you can't go, and I'm not leaving you here with a bunch of psychopaths."

"We don't know anyone here is a psychopath—if it's true that Inigo—"

"I'm not leaving you," Danny says, and something about his tone makes it very clear: that's going to be his last word on the subject. I hear a rustle of covers as he turns sharply over in bed. "And that's that. Now go to sleep."

But it's a very long time before I do.

LIZ

Snoop ID: ANON101
Listening to: Offline
Snoopscribers: 1

I climb back into bed. I am so tense that I am not sure I will get to sleep, but when at last I do drift off, it is into the deep, dreamless sleep of complete exhaustion. When I wake up it is bitterly cold, and although my clothes feel crumpled and sweaty, I am grateful that I never took them off. Getting up would have been too painful. Even with my clothes on, it is too cold to face getting out of bed, and I shut my eyes and just lie there. My phone has died completely, so I have no idea what the time is.

It is then that the scream rips through the quiet. It is a long, loud one that goes on, and on.

I sit bolt upright, my heart thumping, and then I swing my legs out of bed and stand. The movement is much too fast. I feel the blood drain away from my head, and then return with a prickling rush. My heart is still pounding with adrenaline.

Out in the corridor I can hear doors banging. Voices are calling out in panic.

"It's coming from Tiger's room," I hear someone shout.

My hands are shaking as I fumble for my glasses and shove them onto my nose. It is so cold that my breath huffs white as I undo the door lock.

In the corridor Rik, Miranda, Topher, and Carl are crowded around Tiger's door. Miranda is wearing a beanie hat and gloves.

"Open up!" Topher is shouting. "What's the matter? Ani? Tiger? Open the door!"

The screaming has died into a low sobbing. It is impossible to tell who is making the sound.

I hear running feet, and then Danny the chef comes skidding around the corner of the corridor, wearing jogging pants and a crumpled sweatshirt.

"What the fuck's going on? What's all the shouting?"

"We heard screaming," Rik says tersely. "From Tiger and Ani's room. We can't get them to open the door."

"Stand aside," Danny says, reaching into his pocket for his passkey. His hand comes out empty. "Fuck, must have left it in my other trousers. Oi!" He bangs on the door. "Open up! We can't help you unless you open the door!"

There is a click. The door swings open.

With so many people in the way, I can't see who it is. But then I hear Miranda's startled voice say, "Tiger! What on earth is the matter!"

Tiger is sobbing so hard she can hardly get the words out.

"Ani, oh God, p-please help me. It's Ani. I think she's d-dead."

ERIN

Snoop ID: LITTLEMY
Listening to: Offline
Snoopscribers: 10

It takes me painfully long to hobble along the corridor. My ankle has puffed up overnight and it hurts to put weight on it. As I round the corner the sound of voices swells into a panicked hubbub.

"What's going on?" I ask, but no one's listening, they're crowding around Tiger and Ani's door. Tiger is crouched in the corridor, her arms wrapped around her head, sobbing hysterically. Liz is standing over her looking terrified, and occasionally placing a hand gingerly on Tiger's hair, like it's about to burst into flames.

"What's going on?" I say again, and this time Danny appears out of Tiger's room, his face gray.

"Fucking hell," he says. "They've got Ani."

"They've *got* her? Who's got her? What do you mean?" I can feel fear rising inside me.

"I mean, I'm pretty sure she's dead."

Oh God. Dread twists at my guts as I push past the others and into the room.

Ani is lying on a mattress on the floor. She's facedown, but when

I pull her shoulder to turn her over, she comes all of a piece, like a mannequin, her joints locked with rigor mortis. I don't need to feel her cold, waxen face to know that she's very, very dead.

Suddenly my legs won't hold me, and I stagger to Tiger's bed, which is still warm and rumpled. The room swims in and out of focus and I put my head between my knees, trying to hold it together.

"That can't have been Inigo," Danny says hoarsely. I shake my head in agreement. That much is clear. Oh God, what is this living nightmare we've found ourselves in.

"And then we were six," says a little voice from the doorway, and I look up to see Liz, her face a white mask of horror as she gazes at Ani's prone form.

"What?" Danny says. He looks bewildered, as if he didn't hear her right.

"Nothing," Liz says. She gives a shaking, tremulous laugh. It sounds like she's on the verge of hysterics. I know how she feels. And then she turns and disappears. I hear her door slam, and the lock grind into place. I don't blame her. A strong part of me would like to do the same. But I can't. I have to . . .

I stand, go over to the body, and very gently turn it again, this time forcing myself to look down at Ani's dead face.

She looks almost like she died in her sleep. *Almost.* Not quite. There's a tiny staining of blood on her lip where she must have bitten her tongue. And on her face, a few minute red dots. I know what they are, or rather, I know what they mean, but it takes a few minutes cudgeling my memory before my brain can come up with the medical term. *Petechiae.* First-year medical students don't come across much homicide—but I've seen enough textbook photographs to recognize it.

There are no marks on her neck, and no other wounds that I can see, apart from the tiny specks of blood on her lips. When I bend to lower her gently back to the position I found her, facedown, I see it has flecked the pillow too. A line sings in my head: *Lips as red as blood, skin as white as snow.*

"I think she was smothered," I say quietly to Danny. "Whoever did it either pressed her face down into the pillow, or they held something over her face and then turned her over afterwards. There's not much bruising and no defensive marks that I can see—she was probably asleep."

"Oh my God." Danny's face crumples into horror. He looks like a man decades older than his twenty-five years. "But, you're not telling me—Tiger?"

I shake my head, but I'm not disagreeing with him—I just have no idea what to say. I can't believe that gentle, zen-like Tiger could possibly have done this. But on the other hand—the door was locked. And could someone really have crept in and smothered Ani in her sleep without Tiger waking? I think back to her yoga-toned body, those slim, strong hands. The world seems to tilt and shift on its axis.

Out in the corridor, the others are waiting, pale and worried. Tiger has sobbed herself silent and is still crouched against the wall, Miranda's arm protectively around her. Liz is still locked in her room. Carl and Rik are standing with grim, drawn faces either side of the door like sentries. Topher is pacing, and he looks like a man possessed by demons. There is an expression on his face that frightens me.

"What. The. Fuck," he spits as Danny and I leave the room, closing the door behind us.

"Oi, mate," Danny puts up his hands, but I shush him. Five of these people are scared and grieving. One . . . But I can't think about that. It's too surreal, too horrible.

"Come down to the living room," I say. "I think we all need a drink."

It's barely 9:00 a.m., but downstairs I pour us all stiff whiskeys, and everyone drinks them without a murmur, except for Tiger, who is lying on the sofa, shivering, in a state of what I can only call near-catatonic shock.

"So," Rik says, as he puts down his glass. "What happened?"

"Just a second," Miranda says. "Where's Liz?"

I feel a wash of panic, followed by a wave of rationality. There is no way anyone can have killed Liz while we were all standing out in the corridor.

"I think she's in her room," I say. "I'll go and get her."

"Not alone you won't," Danny growls, and he follows me upstairs like a watchdog as I make my painful, limping way to knock at Liz's door.

"Wh-who is it?" I hear through the wood. She sounds as scared as I feel.

"It's me, Erin," I say. "And Danny. We—we need to talk about this, Liz. About what happened. We need to try to figure out what to do next. Can you come out?"

There is a scraping noise, and the door opens, very slowly, until Liz is standing there, white-faced and hollow-eyed. She looks terrified, like there is nothing in the world she would less rather do than go downstairs and face her fellow guests—and I can't blame her. I feel the same way. But we have to do it.

By the time we get downstairs, Miranda has built up the fire and Rik has poured everyone another round of very generous whiskeys. I want to say something about the advisability of adding more alcohol to this mix, but since I was the one who suggested a drink in the first place, I don't feel like I have the right to object.

"So, what happened?" Rik says again as he hands Liz a glass. His voice teeters on the edge of what sounds like aggression, but I think it's actually fear. "Don't tell me she just died in her sleep."

"She didn't," I say, very quietly, but they all fall instantly silent. "She had something called petechial hemorrhaging. Do you know what that means?"

There are headshakes all around the circle, apart from Carl, who nods.

"Little red dots, right? Yeah, I watch *CSI*. Shoot me."

"Exactly. Little red dots where blood vessels have broken in the skin. It usually means someone has died of some form of asphyxiation—choking or hanging. In this case, given there weren't any marks around her neck, I think Ani was probably smothered in her sleep."

"Oh my God." It's a long groan from Miranda. She puts her hands over her face.

"She—she knew something." It's Liz. She speaks very low, and I have to shush the others to hear what she's saying. "She came to my room last night, to try to persuade me not to sleep alone. When I asked why she was still awake, she said she had something on her mind, something she'd seen—I begged her to tell me—" She breaks off, her voice cracking. It's virtually the longest speech I've ever heard her make, and she looks like she's shrinking as all the eyes of the room turn to her.

"Oh, bloody hell." Danny's voice is angry, and he stands up, as if he can't contain his feelings. "What did Erin fucking say? If you know something *tell someone*."

"I know!" Liz says, her voice like a sob. "I begged her to say something, I really did—but she said she wasn't sure—"

"Tiger." Miranda is shaking Tiger now, gently. "Tiger, did Ani say *anything* to you last night, before she fell asleep?"

"I was asleep." Tiger's voice is broken, and very hoarse. It's hard to understand what she's saying, the words are cracked and fractured. I make out, "I'm so sorry . . . asleep . . . took a sleeping pill . . ."

"Wait, you take sleeping pills?" I say. I glance at Danny, who raises an eyebrow back, and I know he is thinking, as I am, of the crushed pills in Elliot's coffee. Tiger gives a huge sob.

"Not normally, but I couldn't sleep, I haven't been able to since I got here. It started the f-first day. Eva said it was the altitude. She gave me some of her pills."

"It's true," Miranda says. She glances round the circle, looking for support. "It was after breakfast that first morning, I remember the conversation. Rik, you heard her, didn't you?"

"I'm sorry," Rik says with a shrug. His voice is defensive. "I'm sure you're right, but I don't remember."

"Everyone was there," Miranda persists. "It was right before we went into the meeting room. Eva said to Tiger, you look like you haven't slept, and Tiger said, I actually didn't. And Eva said, it's the altitude. Remind me to give you some of my sleeping pills. Carl was there too, and Liz. And Topher."

"I don't remember either. I expect I was too busy thinking about the presentation," Topher says, rather brusquely. "What are you trying to say?"

He looks ruffled, like he thinks Miranda is trying to pin something on him. But I know why Miranda is pushing this. She knows that Tiger is the number one suspect for Ani's death. Tiger was in the room when Ani was smothered, and she slept through it. Which is pretty unlikely—unless you know that she was taking sleeping pills. Miranda is trying to show that everyone knew that fact. That anyone could have taken advantage of Tiger's drugged state to sneak in and kill Ani while Tiger slept. I admire her for it, in a way—she's standing by her colleague in the face of some pretty horrible evidence.

But there is still the question of the locked door.

"Who got to Ani's room first?" I ask.

"I did," Topher says. He is standing propped against the mantelpiece, now he folds his arms. "But it was locked. You saw that." He nods at Danny, who shrugs with corroboration.

"I tried the door, yeah. It was locked."

"So how did someone get in?" Topher demands. "Staff key? How many of those things are there?"

"Just two," I say. I hold up mine. "I had mine with me all night. I'm certain of it. Danny?"

But Danny is frowning, patting his pockets.

"I thought mine was in here. These were the clothes I was wearing yesterday. I thought . . . Hang on."

And without waiting for anyone else to accompany him, he jumps up and leaves the room.

"Danny!" I shout after him, but he calls back.

"I'll only be a sec."

There's a long silence. I find my heart beating uncomfortably fast, even though I know it's irrational. Everyone is in here. I'm looking at them right now. But this is starting to feel like *Lord of the Flies*.

When Danny comes back, his face is very grave, and the look he shoots at me tells me he's not relishing what he's about to say.

"Well, there ain't no point in sugarcoating this," he says. "My key's gone. Someone's half-inched it."

"Fuck." It's Rik, the word sounding like gunshot in the ensuing silence. "*Fuck.* You're saying someone has access to every room in the place now? None of us can lock our doors?"

"That's about the size of it," Danny says grimly.

"You," Topher spits, "are a fucking irresponsible *wanker*, you had a duty of care to us and—"

Danny stands up, putting himself on the same level as Topher, almost squaring up to him.

"Don't take that tone with me, mate."

"This is bloody convenient for you, isn't it? Before, if anyone managed to get access to any of the rooms you and Erin were prime suspects, now you've contrived—"

"I haven't contrived anything," Danny snarls back. "And don't you bring me and Erin into it. We ain't done nothing, and we never had any trouble until you lot turned up and started bumping each other off. We don't know any of you from Adam. So the fact that one of your employees nicked my key—"

"Well that's another thing," Topher says angrily. "Who exactly *is* Erin anyway, because she seems to be a little overqualified for a chalet girl if you ask me. Petrifical fucking whatever it was—is that part of the ski chalet training?"

Shit. I knew this was coming. I sigh and stand up too, favoring my good leg.

"No. No it's not. The truth is . . ." I glance at Danny, wondering what I can get away with. "The truth is, I went to medical school before I came here. I dropped out, but that's how I know about the petechiae."

"But that's not all, is it," Topher prods. "It's been bothering me since I got here. I *know* you. I know I do."

Fuck. *Fuck.*

There is no point in beating around the bush any longer.

"Yes, you probably do know me. My surname is FitzClarence. My friends all call me Erin, but that's my middle name."

"I fucking knew it!" Topher's voice is a shout of triumph. "I *knew* I knew you. Dorothea FitzClarence. I was at school with your brother, Alex—the one who—"

He breaks off, and I nod reluctantly, because there is nothing else I can do.

"*What?*" Danny says. He looks thunderstruck. "Erin, what is this bullshit? Dorothea—you what?"

"Let me introduce you," Topher says, with great malice, "to Lady Dorothea de Plessis FitzClarence, youngest daughter of the Marquess of Cardale."

LIZ

Snoop ID: ANON101
Listening to: Offline
Snoopscribers: 1

Looking around the circle of frowning faces, it is clear that I am not the only person who is very confused. Erin looks stricken. Topher looks delighted. But everyone else looks as baffled as I feel. What has just happened? What has this got to do with Ani's death?

There is no time to find out. Danny turns around so abruptly that he knocks over a chair. It falls with a clatter, smashing a whiskey glass.

"Danny," Erin says desperately.

"You fucking liar," he shoots over his shoulder. Then he leaves the room.

Erin gives a furious look at Topher.

"Thanks a bunch," she says, and then she is gone, hobbling after Danny.

"Ha," Topher says, sitting down in an armchair. There is a look of grim satisfaction on his face.

"Topher," Miranda says, bewildered. "What on earth was all that about? Ani is *dead* for goodness' sake. Have you forgotten that?"

"No," Topher says defensively, though I think the truth is that he had, just for a minute or two. "No, not at all. That's very hurtful of you to imply that, Miranda. But I'd had enough of that chippy chef throwing around accusations. We're not the only people hiding stuff."

"Speak for yourself, mate!" Carl splutters. "I'm not hiding anything! What the hell has it got to do with anything if Erin's a bit posher than she's been letting on?"

"Because she's got skin in this game too," Topher hisses angrily. "I'm fed up of them both acting so high and mighty."

"I remember Alex FitzClarence," Rik says slowly. "He was a couple of years below us. Didn't . . . didn't he die a few years ago?"

"That's him," Topher says. "He was a really good bloke actually. That wasn't my point—my point was simply that Erin is a bit more entangled in this than she's letting on. And what happened to Alex—" He stops. Suddenly his expression changes and he grips Rik's arm, so hard that Rik gives a little wince. He looks as if he has been given a very generous Christmas present. "Hang on a *second*. Alex died in an avalanche. With his best mate."

"What are you saying?" Rik is looking wary.

"I remember reading about it in the alumnae newsletter. Alex FitzClarence died in an avalanche in the alps with his best friend, Will Hamilton. The only survivor was Will's girlfriend, *Erin FitzClarence*."

"Topher." Miranda is looking as alarmed as Rik now. "Topher, what are you getting at?"

"I'm saying, this isn't the first time our little Erin has been involved in a fatal skiing accident."

ERIN

Snoop ID: LITTLEMY
Listening to: Offline
Snoopscribers: 10

"Danny!" There is no answer, but I know he's in there. "Danny, please, I'm sorry. Please let me explain." I bang on his door for maybe the twentieth or thirtieth time, but without much hope now. It's clear he doesn't want to open up.

Only then he does.

"This had better be good," he says, and his expression makes me quail, it's so angry.

"Danny, I'm sorry," I say again, desperately.

"You said you were going to explain." He folds his arms, his fury barely contained. "So go on then. Explain. Explain why you lied to me."

"I didn't lie to you—"

He begins to shut the door in my face.

"Hey!" I cry, and instinctively I shove my foot in the gap, forgetting that it's my bad ankle. The door crunches on it, and I let out a scream of pure agony. Danny claps his hands to his mouth.

"Holy shit, Erin, I'm sorry—I'm so, so sorry—it's fine!" he bellows, knowing that the others are probably jumping up in panic, attuned to the worst-case scenario. "Erin's fine, she just knocked her ankle."

"I'm fine," I call croakily, blinking away the sudden tears of pain that have started into my eyes, and whether they believe us, or they can't hear anything through the staff door, no one comes running.

Either way, something has broken in the deadlock between us, because Danny opens the door wider and jerks his head at his bed.

"You better come in. Take the weight off."

I hobble meekly inside and sit down.

There is a long silence.

"So?" Danny says at last. Every muscle in his body screams antagonism, but at least I've been offered the chance to explain.

"You're right," I say. "Even if I didn't lie to you, I didn't exactly tell you the truth."

"I thought we were friends," Danny says, and although the anger is fading from his kind, crumpled face, what's left is worse—bewildered hurt. "I thought—I thought you and me was on the same side."

"We were—we *are*," I say desperately. "This doesn't change anything. Everything I told you—about me, about dropping out of uni—it's all true. I just didn't tell you why."

"Why then?" Danny says. He folds his arms and leans back against his little chest of drawers, letting me know with his body language that this isn't going to be that easy. I've got a hole to dig myself out of.

I swallow. I haven't talked to anyone about this—not since the nightmare days and weeks after the accident. But I owe Danny the truth.

"It's true my dad's a marquess," I say. "But honestly, Danny, it sounds a hell of a lot grander than it is. He doesn't live in a castle. My family isn't particularly well-off. Alex went to boarding school, but I went to the local comprehensive because my parents couldn't afford two sets of fees; I'm no different from you."

He gives me a look at that, as if to say, *Fuck off are you*, and I wince, knowing he's right. Danny grew up on a council estate on the outskirts of Portsmouth, the only child of a single mum who struggled for years to make ends meet. He has pulled himself up by his bootstraps, with no help from anyone. However far the FitzClarence fortunes have fallen, our upbringings *were* different, and that's the truth. To pretend otherwise is pretty insulting.

"Okay, I'm sorry, that—that was clumsy. It's not what I meant. I just meant—I'm trying to explain—"

I stop. I put my head in my hands. This is all I need. Danny was the one person on my side, the one person I felt I could rely on. Have I really screwed all that up, thanks to Topher?

"When I was nineteen," I begin again, more slowly this time, "I went on a skiing holiday with my boyfriend, Will, and my brother, Alex, Will's best friend. We were skiing off-piste, and we were stupid. We got caught in a—" I swallow. I don't know how to talk about this, how to explain the horror of what happened. Words aren't enough.

"We got caught in an avalanche," I say at last, forcing the word out. "We triggered it. We were all wearing avalanche packs, but Alex didn't manage to set his off. Will's deployed, but it didn't save him, he was buried too deep, and I couldn't dig him out fast enough. I was the only person who survived."

I stop. I can't go on. I can't describe those nightmarish hours on the mountain, sobbing as I dug with numb bleeding hands through the hard-packed drifts to try to reach Will, who was trapped head down beneath a hundredweight of snow and ice. I dug and I wept, and I wept and I dug, using anything I could find in my pack—my lift pass, my water bottle, anything that could form a makeshift pick, for my poles and skis were long gone, ripped away from me somewhere far up the slope.

It was too late. I knew that. I had known it even before I began to dig, I think, and as the hours wore on, and the snow lay all around in unmoving silence, I somehow found the strength to accept it. But still I dug. Not just for Will, but for my own survival. Because Will had the

GPS locator beacon in his pack. And if I didn't activate it, I would die along with him.

The search and rescue eventually found us. Or rather, they found me. By the time they arrived I was hypothermic, cradling Will's dead body. Alex was not recovered until the following spring.

"I—I couldn't go back," I say, very quietly. "Do you understand that? I couldn't go back to my old life. It was completely meaningless. I went home to bury Will, and then I came back to the mountains—at first because I couldn't bear to leave without Alex, and then afterwards because . . ."

I stop. The truth is, I don't know why I stayed. Only that I couldn't stand to be at home, with the pity of all my friends suffocating me, and my parents' awful, crushing grief. And it seemed like a kind of penance to stay here, among the terrible austere beauty of the Alps, to keep forcing myself to look at the mountains that had killed Will and Alex.

"That's why you don't ski off-piste," Danny says hoarsely. He is looking at me very differently now. The anger has gone. There is only a kind of . . . pity left. It hurts to see it in his face, and I turn away, nodding.

"Yes, that's why. I still love skiing—which is perverse, I know. My parents think I'm crazy. My dad called me a masochist when I took this job. But I can't seem to bring myself to leave the mountains, and you can't live here year-round without skiing. But I don't think I'll ever go off-piste again."

"Fuck, Erin. Why didn't you tell me?" Danny asks, but he doesn't say it like he's expecting an answer. I think he knows that it wasn't that I didn't want to tell him—it was that I couldn't bear to say it. I couldn't bear to become a victim to him too.

There is a silence, and then he folds me in his arms, and I rest my face against his warm, muscled shoulder and I close my eyes and breathe in the good, Danny smell of him. I feel the tears soak into the worn softness of his sweater.

"So you're proper posh, eh?" he says, with a rumbling chuckle, and I give a shaky answering laugh, and lift my head, wiping the tears off my nose with my sleeve. "You belong down there, with that lot, not up here in the servants' quarters, with the hoi polloi."

"No, I *don't*." I say it more emphatically than I mean, and Danny laughs again, but I'm serious. "No, I mean it, Danny, I don't belong with them anymore. I'm not sure I ever did. What they stand for—"

I stop, thinking of Topher and his cushioned, monied existence—the way he has had everything handed to him on a plate, the way he's never had to scrap for anything, never had to swallow a snub from a boss, or pick up a stranger's dirty underwear, or do any of the myriad demeaning, boring jobs the rest of us take for granted.

They are arrogant, that's what I realize—maybe not Liz and Carl quite so much, but all of them to *some* degree. They are protected by the magic of their shares and their status and their IP. They think that life can't touch them—just like I used to do.

Only now it has. Now life has them by the throat. And it won't let go.

LIZ

Snoop ID: ANON101
Listening to: Offline
Snoopscribers: 1

"You're saying Erin is behind this?" Miranda's face is skeptical. She folds her arms, looking at Topher with narrowed dark eyes. Topher's expression is defensive.

"No. No, that's not what I said—I simply—"

"It's what you implied though," Miranda says. I realize something—Miranda does not like Topher. I don't know why I didn't notice this until now—perhaps it is the fact that she is so formal and polite. Now she is not bothering to hide her opinion.

"I'm just saying, once is bad luck, twice is a *hell* of a coincidence. How many skiing deaths can one person be involved in?"

"Oh, why don't we stop beating around the bush," Miranda says bitingly. "We all know why you're desperate to throw suspicion on other people."

"What are you suggesting?" Topher says, and his voice is suddenly dangerous.

"I'm not *suggesting* anything," Miranda says. She steps up to him. Even without her heels, they are almost exactly the same height. "I'm stating facts. Most people in this room stood to gain a lot of money before Eva died. Very few people had a motive for wanting her out of the way. You were one of those few."

Rik and Carl exchange an uneasy look. Neither of them jump in to defend Topher.

"One, that is fucking slander, and two, you are talking about my *best friend*," Topher begins furiously, but then Tiger lifts her head and says something. It's an almost inaudible croak, but all heads turn to her, and Topher stops midsentence.

"What did you say?" Miranda swings around, and Tiger struggles upright, brushing her hair away from her forehead. Her face is blotched red and white.

"She said something," she repeats, her voice still hoarse with tears.

"Who?" Rik comes and kneels beside her. His face is urgent, and he grabs Tiger's arm. His gesture seems to have been harder than he intended, because she winces a little. "Who said what?"

"Last night, Ani. I just remembered. She said something. She tried to wake me up, but I was—" She gulps, forcing back sobs. "She said, *I didn't see her.* If only I'd been able to wake up properly, if only I hadn't taken that sleeping pill—" She breaks off. Two huge tears roll down her face.

"Tiger," Miranda says uneasily. She crouches beside Rik. "Tiger, are you *sure* about this? Before you were saying you didn't wake up."

"I know, I know I said that, but I was wrong, I remember now. I remember her shaking me. I remember the words."

Miranda shoots a questioning look at Rik and he gives a minute shrug back.

"Well," Topher says. There's a touch of triumph in his voice. "Well, well, well. I didn't see *her*. Now who's got a reason to start slinging mud, Ms. Khan? After all, that sounds like it rules out half the room, doesn't it?"

"What does?" says a deep voice from the direction of the lobby.

We all look around. Danny and Erin are standing in the doorway, side by side. Erin looks as if she has been crying. I am not sure if they have made up completely, but it looks like they have patched their differences enough to put up a united front. Topher looks slightly annoyed.

"Tiger claims—" Miranda begins, but Tiger interrupts with an angry sob.

"I don't *claim* anything. I *heard* her, I'm sure of it. Ani tried to tell me something last night—she shook my shoulder and she said, *I didn't see her*. Only I couldn't wake up properly. But it fits—it fits with what Liz said, that Ani had something she was trying to figure out, something she wasn't sure of."

"*I didn't see her*," Erin repeats slowly. "Are you sure of that, Tiger?"

"*Yes*," Tiger says, more emphatically this time. "Yes, I was lying on the sofa just now trying to think back to last night, think whether I'd heard anything, and I remembered suddenly Ani coming over to me and shaking my shoulder. It was like a flashback."

"Which implies," Topher says smugly, "that we're looking for a woman. No? *Her*, that's what Tiger said. Ani was trying to figure something out about one of the women in the party."

He glares at Miranda.

"Not necessarily . . ." Danny says slowly. He is frowning. He scratches his head, thinking. "Maybe she wasn't talking about the killer. Ani was the only person who saw Eva on the slope. Isn't that right? Carl was the only other person on the bubble, and he didn't see her. Right?"

"Right," Carl says shortly. "But what are you saying?"

"I'm saying, what if Ani realized she'd made a mistake? What if Eva never skied that slope after all?"

"But she *did*," Miranda says, with exasperation. "Elliot's geotargeting proves that."

"It proves her phone is there," Danny says. "But the only evidence we ever had that Eva was with her phone on that slope was Ani's sighting. What if she realized she was wrong? What if . . . here, what about this—what if Eva faked her own death?"

That last suggestion causes a little excited ripple around the circle. Faces brighten. People want to believe this. Danny's suggestion is a solution that doesn't require a murderer, and everybody would desperately like that to be true.

But there is a problem. Two problems in fact. It is a solution that doesn't explain Elliot's or Ani's death. It does not hold up for a minute. As they would realize if they thought about it. But I can see they are *not* thinking.

Speaking up in front of the others makes my stomach curdle, but I have to say something. I can't not.

"Eva *was* on that slope," I say reluctantly. "I saw her too."

Every pair of eyes in the room turns to me. It feels like they are boring into me. My cheeks flush. I want to sink through the floor.

"What did you say?" It is Miranda, her voice almost accusing.

"I said, I saw Eva too. I was in the bubble lift on the way down, and I saw her skiing as well—further up the slope than Ani did, but I saw her. She was on La Sorcière. Ani wasn't mistaken. She must have been talking about something else."

"And you didn't think to mention this before?"

"I didn't—it didn't . . ." I trail off.

"Not something else. Some*one* else," Danny says flatly, and there is a moment's silence. Everyone's gaze travels around the room, going from one person to another. We are all realizing the same thing. If Tiger is right, there are very few people Ani could have been talking about. Topher folds his arms. *Your move*, his expression says to Miranda.

"Tiger are you *sure*," Miranda says. Now there is a note of desperation in her voice. "Are you absolutely certain Ani said *her*?"

"I'm sure," Tiger says stubbornly.

There is a long, long, silence. Miranda stands up and walks out of the room.

"I don't care," she shoots over her shoulder as she leaves. "I don't *care* what Ani said. There is one person in this room who had a motive for Eva's death. *One person*. Stop pretending that isn't the case!"

And then there's nothing but silence, and the *clack-clack* of her heels on the spiral staircase as she runs up to her room.

After she has gone, there is an extremely awkward silence. Topher is leaning against the mantelpiece, angry and flushed. Rik looks like a man being ripped in half. Tiger is slumped, with her hand over her face. Erin and Danny look intensely uncomfortable. Carl breaks the silence.

"Yeah, but she's right, isn't she?"

His voice seems to break some kind of spell, and Topher pushes himself upright and turns for the door.

"Fuck this," he says. "I'm not doing this anymore."

"What do you mean?" Rik turns to stare at him, puzzled. "You're not doing what?"

"*This*. I'm not sitting here like fucking frogs in a pressure cooker. I *didn't* kill Eva, no matter what Miranda and Carl want to believe, and I certainly didn't fucking kill my best friend or our PA. And I'm not hanging around waiting to prove it by being the next person killed. I'm out of here. I'm going to cross-country it down to St. Antoine le Lac."

"You're mad," Rik says instantly. "The piste is ripped to shreds, there's trees and rocks everywhere. And look at the weather for God's sake! You'll freeze to death."

Topher shrugs.

There is a short pause.

"You're mad!" Rik repeats desperately. And then, "I'm coming with you."

ERIN

Snoop ID: LITTLEMY
Listening to: Offline
Snoopscribers: 10

It's almost midday, and the group has spent the past hour or more discussing Topher's decision and going back and forth over the stupidity—or not—of the idea. Topher, for his part, is packing determinedly. So far he's got an avalanche pack, water, a torch, some energy bars, a rope, and he's looking for a shovel, though I'm not sure how he imagines he's going to use it. If there's another avalanche, a shovel in his pack isn't going to save him. But if he doesn't manage to get down to St. Antoine before nightfall, he's going to need some kind of shelter, so maybe it's not such a bad idea. There's worse survival tactics than a snow shelter.

Above all though, he seems set on simply getting away—no matter how stupid or risky the plan. Miranda's statement has unleashed something people were refusing to face before—Topher *is* the person who has benefited most from Eva's death. He's just been handed everything he wanted—sole control of Snoop. Rik and Liz, on the other hand, stand to lose millions of pounds if the buyout doesn't go through, and I can't imagine Miranda and Carl will survive this holiday with their posts intact. Whatever the facts, it's difficult to believe they can continue working for Topher after basically accusing their boss of murder. There are some things you don't come back from.

So I can understand why he feels he can't stay here—just as Inigo felt he had no choice but to leave when the group turned on him. What's more surprising is that Rik seems set on going too—though I don't honestly know how Topher feels about this. He has tried to dissuade Rik, but it's hard to deny that two people will stand a better chance than one. It's treacherous going out there, and if one person sprains an ankle, they'd be pretty much dead without a mobile phone. At least with two, you have a chance of sending for help.

By twelve fifteen, Rik and Topher are standing in the foyer, looking at the large-scale map of the resort that we have pinned to one of the walls and discussing potential routes, when Tiger comes down the spiral stairs. She's wearing her snowboarding gear, and she's looking determined.

"I'm coming with you too," she says, without preamble.

Topher frowns.

"Tiger—"

"No, don't try to stop me. I'm as good a boarder as you—and I'm better than Rik." She says it with no false modesty. "And I can't stay here after what—" She gulps, stops, tries again. "After wh-what happened—"

But she can't finish. I can see that beneath her oversize jacket, her small fists are clenched.

Rik and Topher look at each other, and I'm not sure what they're thinking. Tiger is still the person who had the best opportunity for killing Ani, that part is undeniable. The two of them were locked in a room together, and one of them didn't wake up. But she was also pretty firm about Ani's final words, words that deflected suspicion from Topher, which seems like strange behavior for a murderer. Plus Rik and Topher are two big, strapping blokes, each of them probably weighing almost twice as much as Tiger by themselves. If Tiger *were* the killer, it seems unlikely she could overpower one of them, let alone both. On the other hand, and I can almost see Rik and Topher calculating this in their heads, if one of *them* is a murderer, isn't it better to have a third-party witness?

The surrealness of this reasoning strikes me again, and I stifle a short, hysterical laugh, and then clap my hand over my mouth.

"What did you say?" Rik says, turning to me, frowning, and I shake my head. Tears are leaking out of my eyes, but I can't tell why.

"Nothing, I'm sorry. Ignore me."

"Fine, you can come," Topher says brusquely to Tiger, making up his mind.

"Rik." We all turn at the voice from above, and see Miranda coming down the spiral staircase too. Her expression is pale, but set. Rik's face falls. He knows what's coming, and he's already shaking his head.

"Rik, you can't do this," Miranda says. Her brittle voice seems to crack. She takes his arm, her fingers digging into his jacket. "This is incredibly stupid."

"Miranda, I'm sorry," Rik says. His deep voice is very quiet, he's trying to keep this between the two of them, but it's impossible, with the rest of us just feet away. "I don't want to go—but we can't stay here and get picked off one by one like this. I think Topher's right. We *have* to get to the police."

"But not with him." She's whispering, but the acoustics in this room are excellent. I can hear her, so I'm pretty sure Topher can. "Please, please, I'm begging you. Don't go with *him*. I'm frightened you won't come back."

"Mir—"

"We'll go together. I'll get my skis on—"

"You're not a strong enough skier," he whispers back. "Please, darling, believe me, I would if I could, but it's just too—"

"I won't stay here without you!"

"Oi, what about the other chalet?" We all turn to see Carl, standing in the living room doorway, his hands in his pockets. Miranda frowns, thrown off course.

"What other chalet?"

"That chef, Danny, wasn't he going to hike out to some chalet earlier? Before all this started."

I nod.

"He was," I say. "Chalet Haut Montagne. It's a big-chain chalet and much more likely to be occupied than the two closer ones, but it's a trek—a good three or four miles up the valley. That's why he left it until last."

"See?" Carl says triumphantly. "Three or four miles, that's nothing. You could walk that in a morning."

"I wouldn't call it nothing," I say cautiously. "For a start, you wouldn't be walking it, you'd have to snowshoe, and that's a really different skill. What with the avalanche, not to mention almost a week of uncleared snow . . . I'd say you'd be looking at a good three hours snowshoeing. Maybe more if you'd never done it."

"I reckon it's a better bet than the resort," Carl says flatly. "I mean, what's that, fifteen miles? And steep as fuck. You lose a ski on that boulder field, you're fucked."

"I'm not going to lose a ski," Topher snarls. "For a start, I'm a boarder, not a skier. Second, I'm halfway competent. And anyway—what happens if we get to the chalet and it's shut up? We're back to square fucking one. At least we *know* the resort has people who can help us. No, I've made my choice, and I'm sticking to it."

His irritation doesn't rub off on Carl, who just gives a shrug.

"Maybe it's not a choice."

There's a long puzzled silence.

"What are you saying?" Rik asks at last.

"I'm saying, it's not an either-or situation. Look, the strong skiers, that's you, Toph, and Tiger, try to make it to the village and raise the alarm there. The rest of us'll try for the chalet. Whoever makes it through, we'll send a party to rescue the other lot."

It's . . . it's actually not a bad plan. I can see Topher and Rik looking at each other, thinking it over, coming to the same conclusion. At last Topher nods, like Carl was asking him for permission, though I don't think he was. We are long past the point where Topher has that kind of authority.

"Yeah, okay," he says, a little sulkily, acceding to the inevitable.

"Miranda?" Rik says, and she gives an unhappy shrug.

"I—I guess. If you won't take me with you, it's better than sitting here."

"Liz?" Carl says. "How about it?"

For a second, Liz just blinks, like she is startled to be referred to by name. For a moment she does nothing at all—like a frightened animal frozen in the headlamp beam of Carl's attention.

Then she cracks the tiniest smile and gives a shaky, uncertain nod.

For the first time in a few days, I feel a flare of hope inside my chest.

Maybe it will be okay.

Maybe it will really all be okay.

LIZ

Snoop ID: ANON101

Listening to: Offline

Snoopscribers: 1

After so many days reacting to events, it feels good to have a plan. Up in my room I struggle into my faded blue jumpsuit and pull on ski socks and gloves. My helmet and goggles are down in the locker room. I will put those on when we are ready to go outside. One glance out of the window tells me that sunglasses won't be needed. It's midday, but almost dark. The sun is barely filtering through the clouds, and the wind is howling like something trying to get in.

When I am dressed, I feel, for the first time in a couple of days, hot and puffed out. It is strange to feel too warm again, after the growing chill of the chalet. I let myself sink to the bed and catch my breath for a few moments.

Now that it is almost over, I can look back on the living nightmare of the last few days. How has it come to this. *How?* Of all the ways I was expecting this week to go, I never imagined this unfolding horror.

In my mind I tick them off, a macabre school roll call.

Eva—dead.

Elliot—dead.

Inigo—gone, and goodness knows what has happened to him. Did he make it to St. Antoine? Or is he lying frozen with hypothermia in some isolated shack, far from the piste?

Ani—dead.

There's just six of us left. Me, Rik, Miranda, Carl, Tiger, and Topher.

Topher. It always comes back to him somehow. Because it is true what Miranda said—however much people try to ignore the fact, Topher has a very strong motive for Eva's death. In fact he has the best motive out of everyone here.

The thought should make my heart hurt. Topher—who hired me out of a pool of slick, skinny graduates and gave me my first chance. Topher—who stood up for me, stood by me, made sure I got those shares that have hung around my neck like an albatross ever since. Topher—the reason I am here.

And maybe it's because of that last one—but my heart doesn't hurt. I feel nothing—nothing at all.

Because Topher is the reason I have been dragged into this, into something I never wanted and never asked for. Topher and Eva between them, pushing me, pulling me, manipulating me like a chess piece in their battle for control of Snoop.

I know what Topher thought when he gave me those shares. He thought that he was handing over two percent of the company to someone he could control. I was his insurance policy, in case Eva and Rik ever ganged up on him. A way to tip the balance in his favor.

Topher thought I would be like putty in his hands. Soft. Malleable. Pliant. He thought that because of the kind of person he saw—someone meek and quiet, dressed in bad clothes, who never said boo to a goose.

In Topher's world, people are hard, polished shells, their shiny exteriors hiding the inadequacies and anxieties inside.

But Topher made a mistake. He didn't understand that some people are the other way around. But Eva . . . I think Eva did understand that. And perhaps it's what killed her in the end.

ERIN

Snoop ID: LITTLEMY
Listening to: Offline
Snoopscribers: 10

It is one o'clock. Everyone apart from Liz is gathered in the lobby wearing their ski gear. Topher's party is holding snowboards, skis, and poles. Miranda and Carl are equipped with a pair of snowshoes each. And my heart is thumping. Thumping because . . . maybe this is it. Maybe this long nightmare is finally over. Surely one group will be successful?

"What on earth is Liz doing?" Miranda says irritably. She has been on edge ever since Rik told her she couldn't go with him down to the village. The two-party idea makes sense, and she knows it does, but she would still prefer to be with Rik, and I can see the way her gaze keeps stealing across to him.

"I'm here," says a timid voice from the top of the stairs, and we all look up to see Liz standing at the top of the spiral staircase. She is wearing the oversize blue jumpsuit she had on the first day, and is clutching her ski poles in one mittened hand. A bobble hat is balanced on top of her head, and her glasses are misted. She looks hot and sweaty, but, like the rest of us, relieved to be finally doing something.

She starts down the stairs, and then it happens. Something—a pole? A trailing strap? catches in the banisters, and she stumbles. Her socked feet go out from under her. One hand grabs for the handrail, but the mitten has no grip and the wooden rail simply slides out from under the plasticky fabric.

As we watch, helpless, Liz tumbles forwards down the spiral staircase with a series of sickening thumps. And then she lands at the bottom, ominously quiet.

LIZ

Snoop ID: ANON101
Listening to: Offline
Snoopscribers: 1

I can't breathe.

I lie there, panic pulsing through me, trying to inhale and failing. I can hear myself making little strange gasps, like a fish stranded out of water.

"Liz!" It is Erin. She comes hobbling over. Her face is white. She crouches beside me. "Liz! Oh God, are you okay?"

I can't answer. I can't get my breath enough to say a word. I make a motion, half nodding, half shaking my head. Am I okay? I am not sure.

"Fucking hell." Carl falls to his knees next to me. "Liz?" He turns to the others. "Well, she's alive at least. Can you speak, Liz?" He says it very loudly, like I am hard of hearing.

"I think she's just very badly winded," Erin says. She strokes my forehead. I resist the urge to pull away. I am not sure if I could, anyway. "It's okay, don't fight it. Just try to breathe slowly. I'll count with you. One, two, three, four, five . . . and in. And now one, two, three, four, five, and out."

With Erin counting, slowly and rhythmically, I manage to take a breath. Then another. At last, shakily, I sit up.

"Are you okay?" Erin asks again. "Does anything hurt?"

"My knee," I manage. I pull up the leg of my jumpsuit, but I had forgotten my leggings underneath. You can't see anything, but my knee feels hot. When Erin squeezes it gently, a pulse of pain flares up my leg and I flinch.

"Fucking hell," Rik says shakily. "I thought for a minute there—"

He stops. He does not need to spell it out. I know exactly what he thought. I thought it too for a second. For a moment, we were almost five.

Erin helps me to stand up. I find I am shaking.

"Can you walk?" Erin asks. I nod and hobble a few steps. Behind me Carl's face is grim.

"Well, you can't manage four miles in snow, can you," he says. It's not a question.

"So we go alone?" Miranda says. Now it is Rik's turn to look uneasy. I know what he is thinking. Three people should be safe together. But if Carl is the murderer, he is sending Miranda out into the snow alone with a killer.

"I don't know—" he says, but Erin cuts in.

"Danny will go."

ERIN

Snoop ID: LITTLEMY
Listening to: Offline
Snoopscribers: 10

"Danny will go."

The words are out of my mouth before I have time to consider them, but as soon as I've said them, I know they make sense. It's not just about the maths of sending two people out into the snow together. Danny knows the way. Carl and Miranda don't.

"What?" The voice comes from behind me, and I turn around to see Danny standing there, looking mightily pissed off with me. "Erin, could we have a word, please?" he says, tightly. "In the kitchen?"

With a glance at Liz, who is white as a sheet and looks like she might keel over at any second, I follow him, and when the screen door swings shut behind us, Danny lets rip.

"Are you out of your fucking mind? We went over this. I am *not* leaving you here with a broken ankle and a psycho on the loose."

"I didn't mean just you," I say, trying to keep my voice low. It feels weird to be articulating our suspicions like this, within earshot of the group. "I meant the three of you should go. It's obvious—isn't it? I can't believe we didn't think of it before. Carl and Miranda have no idea where they're going—even with a map, the routes are covered up by the avalanche; it's more likely than not they'll end up wandering off into the forest and get lost. You know where the chalet is. You can speak French. And you know how to snowshoe. It makes complete sense. They stand a much better chance of getting there and back if you're with them. I'd be seriously worried about them setting out alone."

"Huh." Danny looks taken aback at this. He can see the logic in my argument. "So . . . what, you and that Liz bird stay here by yourselves?"

"That's right. I mean, think about it, Danny. She's not going anywhere with that twisted knee, she's as lame as I am. And she was never really a realistic prospect for the killer anyway. She can't ski, we know she was stuck on the bubble lift when Eva actually died, and out of everyone here, she has one of the strongest motives for *not* wanting Eva dead. I mean, who knows what might have happened to everyone else in a buyout situation—they were probably going to lose their jobs at the very least. But Liz had no job to lose—and she stood to gain several million quid if the deal went through. That's a pretty strong counterargument."

"Yeah . . . I can see that . . . ," Danny says slowly.

"Please," I say. I put my hand on his arm. "Danny, *please.* Get Miranda and Carl to that chalet and get word to the police about what's happening. We can't afford another death, and I don't trust Carl and Miranda by themselves."

"All right," Danny says, making up his mind. "You're probably right. I'll go and get my gear. But you lock up when we're gone, and don't answer the door to *anyone* except me or the gendarmes. You got that? I don't care if Topher comes crawling back with a sob story of Rik leaving him in the snow. I don't care if Tiger snaps a binding. You don't let them in. Any of them. And fuck knows what happened to Inigo, but I don't like the idea that he might be prowling around out there in the snow, waiting for everyone else to leave."

His words are like an unwelcome splash of cold water in the face. Inigo. We had assumed—*I* had assumed—that Inigo was out of the picture now. What if he's not?

Uneasiness shifts in my belly, but I put my chin up.

"We'll be fine. Even if someone does show up—which I doubt—there's two of us, and one of them. And they'll be outside in the snow, freezing their tits off."

"Yeah, well," Danny says darkly. "Just you stick to that, okay? I know you. Someone'll turn up, claim he's crawled eight miles through the snow with frostbite, and you'll open the door because you're soft. Don't be starting up with the bleeding-heart crap. Put yourself first."

I feel a sharp twinge of guilt—even though I haven't done anything—because Danny's right. That is exactly the kind of thing I would do. I try to imagine myself sitting in the warm, dry chalet while Inigo, or Topher, or even a complete stranger died slowly outside the front door, begging to be let in, and I just can't see it happening. I *would* crack. I *would* let them in. I know I would.

"We'll be fine," I say again, though my voice is a little bit less convincing, even to myself. "Just go and get back as fast as you can."

LIZ

Snoop ID: ANON101
Listening to: Offline
Snoopscribers: 1

After the others are gone, Erin locks and bolts the front door. She fixes it in place as securely as she can, but it is not perfect. It has been warped by the avalanche so that the bottom lock doesn't fasten properly and melted snow is leaking through the gap, but the lock at the top works. Then she checks the ski entrance, which is still buried by snow, and the door that used to lead out to the swimming pool.

"All safe and sound," she reports as she comes back into the lobby. Her smile is bright and slightly artificial. There is something a little bit oppressive about the silence now. It weighs heavy and feels like it is pressing in on us. "How are you feeling?"

"Uh—okay, I think." I rub the back of my head where I hit it on the banister and touch my knee gingerly through the padded salopettes. I wrenched it, but it is not as bad as I feared. Now that the first shock is wearing off, I can put my weight on it. "Still a bit wobbly, but I think it was mostly shock."

"What a pair," Erin says. She grins at me, the scar on her cheek twisting with the movement. "Me with my ankle, you with your knee. Couple of lame ducks."

"I know." I try for a laugh, but it doesn't sound quite right.

"I reckon it'll take Danny's party about six hours to get to Haut Montagne and back. And who knows about Topher's lot. I have no idea how badly bashed up the piste is. If it's not easily skiable, they could be days."

I nod. Clambering through waist-deep snow in ski boots is no joke. I know that.

"So I think we have at least six hours before we need to start worrying," Erin says. "The question is, how are we going to kill the time?"

ERIN

Snoop ID: LITTLEMY
Listening to: Offline
Snoopscribers: 10

It's gone three. After the others left, Liz and I ate a meager lunch of lukewarm tinned soup—the bread was stale, almost inedibly stale, but dipping it in the soup made it soft enough to chew—and we have been playing cards ever since. The chalet is completely, eerily silent. I never realized before how stifling silence could be, perhaps because Perce-Neige is so rarely quiet—it's always full of the noise of guest footsteps, playing children in the school holidays, the clatter of skis, the sound of Danny in the kitchen. While Topher and the others were here there was the constant jangle of someone playing music, and later the babble of conversation. Even on changeover days, there is the hum of the Hoover and the noise of Danny's radio.

Now, there is no music. Our phones are long since dead. The TV and radio sit silent with no electricity to power them. There is no sound at all apart from the crackle of the logs in the burner. Even the patter of snow outside is virtually silent, behind the triple glazing.

Every few minutes I glance out of the window, checking the weather. It . . . isn't great. There's no point in sugarcoating that. It's not as bad as it could have been. The wind has dropped at least. But the snow is still falling, and cloud has come rolling down the mountain, enveloping the chalet in a thick, frozen gray blur, so that visibility is down to a few feet. I am profoundly relieved that Danny is with Miranda and Carl, and knows where he's going. Even so, I'm starting to wonder, in earnest, whether he will be able to make it to Haut Montagne and back again before night falls in earnest. Maybe Liz and I will be stuck here alone overnight. It's not a completely comfortable thought.

As if echoing my unease, Liz flexes her fingers nervously—*crack, crack, crack.* The noise is like gunshots in the silence, and it puts my teeth on edge.

"How did you get involved with Snoop anyway?" I ask. I pitch my voice slightly too loud, trying to cover up the sound. Liz shifts in her chair. I can't tell if her knee is hurting her, or if it's the question that's made her uncomfortable.

"I just applied for a job. They were a start-up at the time—just Topher, Eva, Elliot, and Rik. I was their first . . . secretary, I suppose you'd call it. PA, maybe. They didn't have the weird job titles in those days."

She falls silent again, as if the uncharacteristically long speech has exhausted her. I'm about to ask another question when, to my surprise, she speaks again.

"I miss it. I miss them. It was fun . . . for a while."

"What made you leave?" I ask, but that's when the shutters come down again. Her face turns blank and unreadable.

"No reason," she says, looking down at her cards. "I just wanted a change."

In the silence I pick up a card, and put down a king. Liz picks it up, frowning. I have put my foot in it, but I'm not quite sure how. I think of Danny's remark about the incestuous nature of Snoop's workforce, Eva sleeping with Inigo, Topher with Ani. *Haven't they heard of Me Too?* Did something happen between Liz and Topher?

Something she is running from? But no, I don't think it's that. Of all the people in the company, Liz actually seems to get on best with Topher. And Topher, for all his faults, doesn't seem like the kind of man to pressure an employee into something sexual. Whatever was between him and Ani, I got the impression it was consensual.

But Ani ended up dead . . .

The words are a whisper in my ear, an uncomfortable reminder of the fact that Liz and I are not alone in this chalet—there are two bodies upstairs. And somewhere out there in the frozen peaks there is a third, Eva, and maybe a fourth, because who knows what happened to Inigo after he stumbled away into the snow. It feels like death is closing around us. It feels like Liz and I could be next.

But no. I shake myself. This is morbid—ridiculously so.

"Your turn," Liz says, and I look down and realize I have no idea when she made her move. I pick up a card from the draw pile at random and discard without really thinking about strategy.

"Rummy," Liz says, and she lays out a run of four spades and three kings. I force a smile.

"Well done."

Liz picks up the cards and deals again. I pick up my hand. It's a good one—three of a kind straight off. But I can't keep my mind on the cards.

"Eva's death . . . ," I say cautiously, and Liz looks up.

She's still wearing her oversize blue jumpsuit and I can't really blame her. Even with the woodstove, the chalet is now painfully cold, and I can see my breath when I speak.

"That . . . It must have been quite a shock. I suppose the buyout won't go through now? How did it feel—having all that money and then having it snatched away?"

I'm half expecting Liz to tell me that it's none of my business—and it's true, it's not. But we've gone long past the point of guest and chalet girl, and we both know it.

"It felt . . . strange . . . ," Liz says, slowly. The firelight is reflecting off her glasses, making her expression even harder to read than usual, but I can see her forehead crinkle as she frowns.

"Did you resent Topher?" I ask. "For quashing the sale? I think I would have."

But Liz is shaking her head.

"I never really wanted the money, to be honest. It never felt like mine. It was such a stupid sum, and for what?"

"Being in the right place at the right time, I guess?" I say with a laugh, but Liz doesn't smile back. She shakes her head again, although I'm not sure what she's denying. I can't blame her though. Whatever place we have ended up in, all of us, it's definitely not the right one.

Silence falls again. I look at my watch. Ten minutes to four. God, could this day pass any slower? Suddenly I can't sit any longer, and I stand, putting my weight carefully on my swollen ankle, and make my way over to the long window overlooking the valley.

It is almost completely dark outside now, but the chalet is dark too, and so I don't need to cup my hands to my eyes as I look out across the snow, wondering where Danny and the others are. Have they made it to Haut Montagne yet? And what about Topher and his party? I wish, harder than I've ever wished for anything before, that I had a phone with just a single bar of reception. Or a two-way radio. Or anything—*some* way of communicating with the outside world.

"Four aces," says Liz, over my shoulder, and I sigh, and turn back to the darkening room.

LIZ

Snoop ID: ANON101
Listening to: Offline
Snoopscribers: 1

It is 3:58. We are on our—I don't know. Twentieth game of rummy, perhaps. I have not been counting. Thoughts are chasing around my brain like rats. Questions like: *What is going to happen? When will they come? What will happen when the police get here?*

Erin glances up at the clock on the mantelpiece above the stove. I can tell that she is feeling the same way I am.

"One more round," she says, "and then I'll figure out something for supper. They should be there by now."

If they made it.

The words hang, unspoken, in the air, as Erin begins to deal.

It is more to drive the unsaid doubts away than because I really want to know that I say it.

"Topher said you were in an avalanche. What was it like?"

Erin looks up. I have caught her by surprise, and for a second her face is unguarded, horribly vulnerable. She looks like I have punched her. For a moment, I regret asking her. Then she composes herself. She deals out the last few cards before she speaks.

"I was. Three years ago. It was—" She stops, looks down at the remainder of the deck in her hand. "It was the worst thing that's ever happened to me."

"I'm sorry," I say. Then something occurs to me. "Even counting this weekend?"

She gives a laugh at that, a shaky mirthless one, and nods.

"Yes, unbelievably. Even counting this weekend. I can't explain how awful it was. The noise, the shock, the sense of powerlessness—" She falters, as if she is struggling to find the words. "I thought . . . I thought that it would have made it worse, you know? Being caught up in the same horror all over again. But in a strange way I . . . I think I've been expecting it to happen. Like I escaped the mountain once, so it would come back for me."

She stares into the darkness. She is facing me, so it should feel like she is staring at me, but I have the odd feeling that she is not, that she is looking *through* me, as if I am not there. It gives me a strange sensation. As if I am already gone.

"Is that when you—when you got your—" I can't say it. I just touch my face with my fingers, and she nods.

"Yes. I cut my face on something in the fall, probably my own ski."

"And is that why you left uni?" I ask, and she nods, very slowly.

"Yes. I can't really explain why, even now. I just—I felt like I'd become a different person, do you know what I mean?"

I nod too. I know exactly what she means. I have the impression that she is talking about this perhaps for the very first time.

"I had to dig him out."

Her voice is barely above a whisper. I have to strain to hear it.

"I wasn't carrying a GPS locator. I had to dig out my boyfriend to activate his beacon, knowing he was already dead."

She looks down, cuts the pack, deals the first card into the pickup pile, moving mechanically all the while.

Suddenly I do not want to talk about this anymore. I wish I had never asked the question. After all, I have my own secrets, my own subjects I do not want to discuss. What if Erin asks me about my past in return? What if she brings up Snoop again? About why I left? What if she asks about the friends I don't have, the schoolmates who bullied me for fourteen years, about the family I have cut myself off from?

I hear again my father's slurring voice, my mother's sobs . . . I taste blood. I am chewing my cuticles again. I stick my hands in the pockets of my jumpsuit.

But Erin does not ask about any of these things. She seems to be somewhere else completely, somewhere very far away. When she speaks, her voice has a strange quality to it. It is like a confession.

"It was my fault, you see," she says. She picks up her cards. Her hands are trembling a little. "I suggested we go. Off-piste skiing. I was the one who wanted to do it. I killed them." She swallows. "That changes a person."

She looks up at me, as if expecting me to understand. I have the most peculiar urge to take her hand and tell her that I know how she feels.

But that would be crazy. So I don't. Instead, I look down at my own cards. I pick up a three of hearts and discard a jack.

"Your move," I say.

ERIN

Snoop ID: LITTLEMY
Listening to: Offline
Snoopscribers: 10

I don't know what made me spill my past to Liz like that. It was the strangest thing. I've never talked to anyone about that time—not my parents, not Will's parents; even the coroner and the search and rescue team only wanted the bare facts, not to hear about my bewilderment and grief.

It's not that I didn't have the chance—my mother urged me to see a therapist, and I lost count of the number of friends who called me up, saying, *If you need to talk, I'm only a phone call away.* But I didn't want to talk. I didn't want to be that person. An object of pity. A victim.

Because I know how Topher and the others must feel, in a way. For I felt it too. And that's the thing I have never told anyone—that in the minutes and hours I spent searching for Will and Alex after the avalanche, it wasn't terror or fear that was uppermost in my mind but a kind of shocked disbelief, that this had happened to *me*, to *us*. I was not this person. I was not the person terrible things happened to. That was other people, other families. I was golden, slipping through life on a charm, insulated by the security of my family, my own good looks, and the luck of having found Will's love.

Because yes, that was luck. All of it. And I knew it. But it was also how it was supposed to be, because I was supposed to *be lucky*.

And now suddenly that luck had turned.

And after it did, I found that I couldn't stand to be there with the people still walking in that perpetual golden sun while I lived in a place that was black with guilt and grief. I couldn't stand to see the pity in their eyes.

It's almost completely dark in the living room now, and when I walk across to the clock over the mantelpiece, I see that it's getting on for 6:00 p.m. Danny and the others should have been at Haut Montagne about two hours ago. It's possible they could be starting back. It's possible they have managed to contact the police and a chopper is on its way.

Possible. Not certain. Possible.

It's equally possible the road is trashed and they are still trudging across icy rubble, or Haut Montagne was empty and shut up.

God, the possibilities are going to send me mad.

I don't know why, but with Danny and the others gone, it feels like the atmosphere of the chalet is closing around me and Liz. I can feel the weight of the snow pressing against the roof and the walls, feel the tonnes and tonnes still resting on the mountain side, waiting for another trigger. I can feel the darkness seeping through the rooms and corridors.

I know what the edge of endurance feels like, because I passed it once before—sitting frozen on a cold mountainside with the dead body of my lover, not knowing whether help was going to come. I passed it, and I survived. I came back. Back to safety. Back to normality.

But there are times when I feel myself being dragged back across that line into a place where nothing matters anymore, where every heartbeat drags you closer to the edge, and I think I am going to fall into the abyss again, and this time I won't be able to claw my way out.

When I shut my eyes I can see his face, Will's face, cold and white as marble, and peaceful, so terribly peaceful.

"Erin." The voice comes from very far away.

I shake my head.

"Erin."

I open my eyes. Liz is standing in front of me, looking anxious.

"Erin, are you okay? Should we get something to eat?"

I force myself to smile.

"Yes. Sure. Come through to the kitchen, and we'll see what we can find."

I lead the way, limping, and Liz follows me into the chilly darkened cavern of the kitchen, looking around her wonderingly as we enter, as if it's Aladdin's cave rather than a very ordinary professional kitchen.

"There's a t-tin of cassoulet here," I say, trying to read the label in the dim light. It's extremely cold away from the fire, and my teeth are trying to chatter. "At least I think it's c-cassoulet, it could be confit du canard. It's hard to tell. Will that do?"

"Sure," Liz says. She's still looking at me like she's concerned. "Are you all right, Erin?"

"I'm fine, I just—I'm just worried about D-Danny. I keep hoping we'll hear something."

Liz nods, and I realize she must be as worried as me, she's just hiding it better, under that calm, stolid exterior. I find myself wondering what she's thinking, and when the tin (it *was* cassoulet) is decanted into a pan and warming on top of the woodburning stove in the living room, I pluck up my courage to ask her the question I've been pondering but not quite daring to ask.

"Liz, what do you think happened? To Eva, I mean."

Her face crumples and I realize she is holding back the unthinkable just as hard as I am.

"I don't know. I've been thinking and thinking—I just—I can't believe any of it is true. It doesn't seem real. I keep wondering if Eva was just in an accident, but then what about Elliot and Ani?"

What indeed.

"What do you think Ani meant?" I say, stirring the beans slowly, feeling the heat of the fire at my face and the chill cold of the room at my back. "When she said, *She wasn't there.*" Or was it *I didn't see her*? I can't remember now, and that fact bothers me. I hear the rustle of waterproof fabric as Liz shrugs.

"I don't know. I keep going over and over it in my head. I thought at first she must have been talking about Eva, but it makes no sense. She was there, on the slope, I saw her too."

"Could it have been someone at the top?" I'm struggling to remember the exact wording now. Fuck. This could be important and I can't remember. "I'm wondering . . . when she got to the top of the bubble lift. Was someone already missing, someone other than Eva? Someone who had already skied after her?"

"But who?" Liz says. "There weren't that many women left at the top. I'd already gone down in the bubble. The two women left at the top were Tiger"—she ticks them off on her fingers—"in which case it seems very odd that she would report what Ani said. And Miranda—but she had no opportunity to go after Eva. She went down in the bubble with Ani."

"Maybe she didn't." My heart is suddenly thumping. "Maybe that's what Ani remembered. That Miranda *wasn't* in the lift. It's easy to get confused after all—there's a shuffle of bodies at the top, people heading for one telecabine, it's full, they go for another. Maybe that's what Ani realized, that Miranda never got on the lift?"

"What are you saying?" Liz looks uneasy. Her brows, behind the thick glasses, are knitted together and in the darkness I hear the *crack, crack, crack* of her knuckles as she nervously flexes her fingers.

"Maybe she's a better skier than she's letting on. It's quite easy to pretend to be worse than you are. Maybe she peeled off when everyone else was getting on the lift, and instead of going down in the bubble, she followed Eva down La Sorcière."

"I . . . I guess . . . ," Liz says slowly. She looks troubled.

I'm ladling the cassoulet out into two bowls when I realize something. If it's true, if what I'm guessing is correct, then I've sent Danny off with a killer. And my heart clutches like someone has put it in a vise.

Because yes, it's true, there are two of them and one of her. But the path to Haut Montagne passes along some pretty treacherous stretches. How hard would it be to wait until someone was close to the edge, and then give a little shove.

I have no proof of any of this, I remind myself, desperately. It's just a theory. It's *just* a theory.

But my throat is constricted, and my stomach is closed and sick, and suddenly I can't face eating the fast-cooling mess of beans and meat in front of me. I feel ill with the force of what I may have done.

Because I told him to go. With my instinct to organize, my certainty that I know what's best for others, I *told* Danny to go out into the snow alone with Miranda and Carl.

Is it true?

Have I sent another friend to his death?

LIZ

Snoop ID: ANON101
Listening to: Offline
Snoopscribers: 1

Erin hardly touches her supper. She has gone from being professional and friendly to something quite different in the space of about half an hour. I am at a loss to understand it. When I ask her about it she just mutters something about being worried about Danny, but I am not sure if that is completely true.

I eat most of her portion as well as my own. Then I get up and grope my way through to the kitchen to rinse the bowls under the cold tap. There is no point in trying to wash up. We are past things like that. This is starting to feel like survival. But when I turn the tap, nothing happens. I try the other. Still nothing.

When I get back into the living room, Erin is hunched over, staring into the fire. I sit beside her, gingerly flexing my knee, though it's feeling a lot better than it was.

"We've got a problem," I say.

She looks up, as if startled at the sound of my voice.

"What? What did you say?"

"We've got a problem," I repeat. "The water isn't working. I think the pipes have frozen."

"Fuck." She closes her eyes and rubs her face as if she is trying to wake herself from a nightmare, which I suppose in a way she is. "Well, there's nothing we can do except sit tight. Danny and the others *must* be there by now. We just have to make it until morning. If we can manage that without freezing to death."

Her words are unsettling, the more so because I realize that even with my snowsuit on, the chalet is almost unbearably cold now. My breath in the kitchen was a cloud of white. Upstairs must be subzero.

"Maybe . . . should we sleep down here?" I ask.

"I—I guess. Yes. I suppose it makes sense."

"I'll go and get my bedding," I say, making up my mind. Erin nods. "I'll make the sofas up into beds. They fold out."

I'm almost out of the room when she says, "Liz?"

And I look back, expectantly, wondering what she's about to say. "Yes?"

"Liz, I just wanted to say—thanks. Thanks for staying here with me. And I'm sorry it turned out like this."

"It's okay," I say, but somehow the words are hard to say. There is something in my throat—an unexpected kind of lump. "It's okay. It's not your fault."

And then I turn and hobble into the lobby and up the spiral stairs, before she can see the tears in my eyes.

ERIN

Snoop ID: LITTLEMY
Listening to: Offline
Snoopscribers: 10

When Liz's footsteps disappear along the corridor, I slump back in my seat with a sigh and run my hand over my face. *I'm sorry.* I don't know what possessed me to say that, except that out of everyone here, it's Liz I feel most sorry for. I'm not even sure why exactly—maybe because it was so plain, right from the start, that she never wanted to be here. Topher, Eva, however awful this weekend has turned out to be for both of them, they brought it on themselves in a way—choosing to come here, brandishing their money, pushing people around like little chess pieces in their battle for control of Snoop.

But Liz—Liz is just a pawn, like me, caught up in something she never asked for, never wanted.

And yet not once has she complained. Where Topher has grumbled about the crap food, and Carl has stamped and roared and threatened legal action, and Rik has blustered about health and safety and corporate responsibility, and Miranda has made accusations—

Liz has just trudged on, putting up with it all, even though under her self-effacing manner I'm sure she was as scared as anyone.

My ankle throbs as I force myself to standing, and I begin to move aside the sofa cushions, ready to pull out the mattress hidden inside the frame. But as I pick up the last cushion, I see something lying underneath it, right where Liz and I were sitting. It glitters in the firelight, and for a second I think it's a brooch or a piece of jewelry—but when I pick it up, I realize it's a key. A very familiar one.

It's a staff key.

Automatically I feel in my pocket, assuming it must have slid out of my jeans when I sat down, but mine is still there, hard and reassuring against my backside.

Only . . . it's not reassuring at all.

Because if my key is in my pocket it means . . . oh God, it means . . . this is Danny's key.

Danny's key that was stolen.

The key that was taken by the killer.

I stand there for a very long time, completely frozen, just looking down at the key in the palm of my hand and trying to cudgel my brain into figuring this out. Somehow, someone got hold of this key—probably during the kerfuffle over getting entry to Tiger's room, after Inigo's disappearance. It's not hard to imagine someone slipping it surreptitiously out of the lock while we were all preoccupied with checking if Tiger was okay. Whoever took it used it to gain entry to that same room in the middle of the night, and kill Ani. And then at some point after that, presumably this morning while we were all distracted by talking about the plan to ski down to the village, it slipped out of their pocket and fell between the sofa cushions.

The only question is: Who took it? Who was sitting on that space on the sofa this morning? Because I cannot for the life of me remember.

I shut my eyes, trying to picture the scene—Tiger lying on the sofa, sobbing, Miranda trying to comfort her, Rik handing out whiskeys . . . I need to place all the characters in the room, one by one, figure this out.

Danny and I were standing. I remember that clearly. Topher . . . Topher was leaning up against the mantelpiece. Miranda was kneeling on the floor by the coffee table. Liz was in one of the armchairs by the fire. Rik and Carl . . . they were on a sofa, but which one? I squeeze my eyes shut harder, and have a sudden vision of Rik leaning forward, filling up the whiskey glass at the far end of the table. It was the other sofa, the one beneath the window. Which means . . . I open my eyes.

It means Tiger was lying on the sofa where I found the key, her hip right on the point where the cushions join. It would make complete sense—the key could so easily have slid out of her pocket while she was lying there crying. Except . . . it makes no sense at all. Tiger is the only person who didn't need a key to kill Ani. She was already in the room. And if she wanted an alibi, she could have simply said she forgot to lock the door.

But no one else occupied that seat after the key went missing, apart from me . . .

And Liz.

As if hypnotized, my gaze drifts upwards, to the ceiling, where on the floor above Liz is moving around her room, gathering up duvets and pillows. I can hear the faint creak of the floor joists, and then the sound of her door shutting.

I hear the shush, shush as she drags the duvet along the corridor.

Then I hear the halting noise of her feet on the spiral stairs, going carefully this time; she does not want to slip again.

Then she appears in the doorway of the living room, her hands full of bedcovers, her face unreadable in the dim light, the firelight flickering off her big, owl-like glasses, and with a funny little pang I remember that very first day, the way she reminded me of an owl, paralyzed by the lights of an oncoming car.

She still looks like an owl, but suddenly the resemblance seems very different, and quite another kind of chill comes over me as I realize I was right all along—but so very, very wrong.

Because here is the thing. We think we know owls. They are the soft, friendly, blinking creatures of children's rhymes and stories. They may be wise, but they are also slow, and easily confused.

The problem is, none of that is true. Owls are not slow. They are fast—lightning fast. And they are not confused. In their own element—the dark—they are swift and merciless hunters.

Owls are raptors. Predators.

That was what I saw in Liz, right back on that very first day. I was just too blinded by my own preconceptions to recognize it.

In the dark, owls are not the hunted, but the hunter. And right now, it is dark.

"Hi," Liz says, and she smiles, an unreadable smile behind those blank, flickering lenses. "Are you all right?"

LIZ

Snoop ID: ANON101
Listening to: Offline
Snoopscribers: 1

When I come back down, my arms full of duvets and pillows, Erin is standing stock-still in the middle of the room, one hand on the sofa-bed frame, as if a thought has just occurred to her.

"Hi," I say. I throw the bedding into the armchair. Then, when she still doesn't move, I add, "Are you all right?" I don't know why I say that, except that she looks really odd. "Is the sofa bed stuck?"

"What?" She seems to shake herself. Then she gives a smile and a short laugh. "No, sorry. Just thinking. I was—I was thinking about Danny. They must be there by now. I was wondering if we'd hear from them tonight."

I glance up at the clock on the mantelpiece. It is so dark now that the hands are almost unreadable, but I think I can make out that it's nearly eight o'clock.

"I guess you're right. How long did you say it would take to get there?"

"I thought about three hours. But given Miranda and Carl have never snowshoed before, it might take longer. Still, they left just after one. Even allowing for rests and stuff, they ought to be at Haut Montagne easily by now. Maybe even on their way back, though I don't know if they'll snowshoe in the dark."

She gives the metal frame a tug. The sofa bed unfurls with a screech.

"I hope you're right." I move my pillows onto the mattress and then help Erin take the cushions off the other sofa and unfold the bed. "Losing the water feels like the last straw."

"We'll have to melt snow," Erin says. Her face looks white and strained in the dim light, but it's not surprising really. "I can't believe it's only been two days since the avalanche. It feels like forever."

"Two days?" For a second I don't believe her, and then I count up in my head, and I realize she's right. Two days and four hours. It feels like a lifetime ago. It *does* feel like we've been trapped here forever. And now it is almost over. The strange thing is, I am not sure I'm ready to face reality again. It is just dawning on me that what felt like captivity might actually be a kind of idyllic tranquility. Perce-Neige is a crime scene. And we are suspects. When we get back to the real world, we are going to have to face the full glare of publicity. There will be a police investigation, reporters, news stories. Interviews. I can see the headlines now: CHALET OF DEATH.

All sorts of things are going to come out of the woodwork.

Now it is my turn to stand, stock-still, staring into the darkness, thinking.

"I'll go and get my bedding," Erin says, into the silence. "Can you put another log in the stove?"

"Sure," I say, shaking myself back to the here and now. I watch her as she picks up a torch and passes through into the lobby, the thin beam spiraling around as she makes her way up the stairs, her hand going *click, click, click* on the banister as something hard, a ring perhaps, strikes against the metal.

Click. Click. Click.

I hear again my mother's breathless, nervous *Oh, Liz, you know Daddy doesn't like that . . .*

Tick. Tick. Tick. Disappearing into the darkness.

Perhaps it is the thought of the police, and everything that is going to come crashing down, but suddenly, I don't know why, it sounds like a clock, ticking down to zero.

ERIN

Snoop ID: LITTLEMY
Listening to: Offline
Snoopscribers: 10

My heart is hammering as I walk along the corridor to the staff section, and let myself into my bedroom. The room is totally dark, lit only by the narrow beam of the torch, but I don't want to risk the batteries giving way so I switch it off, and in the darkness I sink down onto my bed. I need to *think*.

My fist is clenched around the key, hard against my palm, like a physical reminder of the craziness of this situation, and now as I sit there, trying desperately to make myself understand this conundrum, I find that I'm holding it so hard that it's biting into my fingers, leaving dents I can still feel when I force my hand open.

What does it mean? What does it *mean*?

If Liz took that key . . . is she the killer? But *how*?

I cast my mind back, reliving the scrum in the corridor when Danny broke into Tiger's room. Liz was there, I'm certain. But I remember that while everyone else surged forward into the room, she hung back. I thought at the time it was because of her natural reserve—it seemed so in character, compared to the way everyone else thrust themselves forward, pushing to see what was going on. But now I wonder. Was she hanging back so that she could pocket the key, unobserved?

But *why*, that's what I can't understand. Liz cannot have killed Eva. Motive aside, she's one of the few people, along with Ani and Carl, who had no opportunity at all. She was stuck on the bubble lift going back down to the bottom of Blanche-Neige when Eva was seen skiing La Sorcière.

But the key. The key that is hard and jagged and incontrovertible in my hand, as if refusing to allow me to forget its evidence.

What about the key?

I rub my hand over my face, feeling the shiny scar tissue, the ever-present reminder of what I did, the price I paid for being too sure of myself, and I'm suddenly aware that I have been sitting here for—I'm not sure how long, but a long time. Too long. Suspiciously long. I have to get back downstairs, or Liz will know something is wrong.

I switch the torch back on and gather up an armful of duvets, and then, holding the torch in my teeth, balanced on top of the stack of pillows, I open the door with my free hand.

Liz is standing right outside, almost nose to nose with me, the torchlight reflecting off her glasses.

I scream, and the torch bounces off the pillows and falls to the floor with a thump, where it goes out.

My heart is hammering in my chest like a pneumatic drill.

"Jesus," I manage, my voice shaking. "Liz, you scared me."

I set the duvets down with trembling hands, and grope for the torch.

"Sorry," she says. It sounds like she's smiling, but I can't be sure in the darkness. There is something so flat about her voice, so hard to read. "You took so long. I got worried."

"I—" Oh fuck, what can I say? What excuse can I give? "I was just changing my top."

What. Why on *earth* did I say this? She'll be able to see I'm wearing the same clothes I was before. What a *stupid* lie.

I feel sick with nerves. I am a terrible liar. Even at school I could never do the two-faced "Oh, you look so lovely! I look like trash!" thing that the other girls did. The only time I can dissemble is when I'm in staff mode. Then I'm polite and cheerful to everyone, no matter how I really feel—not because I like them, but because they are guests, and I'm staff, and that's my job.

The thought calms me.

It's my job. I can do this. Liz is a guest, and it's my job to be sympathetic to her. I just have to channel that thought.

I switch on the torch, and I make myself smile.

"Shall we head down? It's really cold up here."

And Liz nods, and turns for the stairs.

LIZ

Snoop ID: ANON101
Listening to: Offline
Snoopscribers: 1

There is something wrong with Erin. I am not sure what. She said she was worried about Danny, but if that's the case, I don't know why her fears came on so suddenly. She was quite cheerful until about two hours ago. Then she got nervous and edgy.

We have been lying in the darkness for perhaps an hour or more, but she is not asleep. It's not just that she's not snoring—out of the corner of my gaze I can see her eyes are still open, reflecting the light from the fire's embers as she blinks. She is lying there in the darkness, silently watching me. She is thinking about something. But I do not know what.

What is she thinking?

I squeeze my eyes shut, trying to look as normal as possible.

A few minutes later I hear the creak of the mattress springs. Erin is cautiously swinging her legs out of bed.

"Where are you going?" I ask.

She jumps like a criminal caught in the middle of something, and puts her hand to her heart.

"God! Liz, you scared me."

"Sorry." I don't say anything else. From my experience, if you keep quiet, people get nervous. They talk. They fill the silence with their own conversation. You can find out a lot that way. Sure enough, after a pause, Erin answers my question without me having to restate it.

"I didn't mean to wake you. I couldn't sleep. I'm going to the t-toilet." She is shivering. I can hear her teeth beginning to chatter. It is very, very cold in the room now. The fire has died down to glowing ash.

"Okay." I roll over, pulling the covers up to my chin. "Don't forget the pipes are frozen."

"I kn-now." She opens the stove to put in another log. "I'll use one of the upstairs bathrooms. I think we've flushed both the d-downstairs loos already."

I don't say anything. I just watch her as she wraps her coat more tightly around her, and then pads up the stairs. Then I turn over and feel in my pocket for the key.

It is gone.

ERIN

Snoop ID: LITTLEMY
Listening to: Offline
Snoopscribers: 10

Bloody hell. My heart is pounding as I tiptoe up the staircase. I don't know where that lie about the toilets came from, but I've never been so thankful for frozen pipes. They have given me exactly what I needed—an excuse to go upstairs.

I have no idea what the truth is about the key. *Did* Liz take it? I don't dare to ask. Maybe someone else sat on that sofa when I wasn't around. Or maybe Liz found the key and picked it up but has been too scared to tell anyone in case they suspected her. There could be a dozen innocent explanations. Or there could be one, very damning one.

Either way, I could not lie there in the darkness listening to her soft, regular breathing a second more. I had to *do* something. And at last my subconscious overrode my racing thoughts to prod me about something I had totally forgotten.

Elliot's charging block. The giant external battery he was using to power his laptop, before he died and his computer was destroyed. If I can get to that battery and plug my dead phone in, maybe I can get a sliver of connection. It's worth a try. It's also not something Liz could possibly object to. And yet, for reasons I can't face examining, I don't want to tell her.

Why not? my brain whispers as I tiptoe along the corridor, in time with my steps. *Why not?*

Because I don't trust her.

Why not?

Because . . . I swallow, hearing the dry click of my jaw in the eerie silence. Because in my heart of hearts, I do think she could have killed Eva. I don't know *how*, but my fear over these last two hours has shown me something I would not have believed before tonight: I do think Liz has it in her to kill. It's not just the key—though that is concerning enough. The panic I felt when I opened the door of my room and saw her standing there, smiling blankly at me, her face hidden behind those silvery lenses—there was something deep and true and real about that panic. It told me something I had not admitted to myself before: I am afraid of Liz. She may be meek and quiet and almost painfully reserved, but behind that meekness, I believe there is steel, and yes, I think she could kill someone. I believe that in a way that I never believed it of Inigo, or even Topher, despite all the evidence piled up against him.

Out of everyone here, I believe Liz could kill in cold blood, and conceal that fact from us all. No one pays attention to her. And for a killer, that's a kind of superpower.

I am almost at Elliot's door. I am walking as silently as I can now, remembering the way Liz's steps along the corridor were audible in the room below. I take the passkeys out of my pocket, and choosing one, I insert it gently into the lock, turn it, and open Elliot's door, very, very quietly.

It creaks, just a little bit, and I hold my breath, hoping Liz didn't hear. But there is no sound from below. If she came up, I would have no excuse for being down this end of the building. The natural thing would be for me to use the staff bathroom, up the far end. Or, if I couldn't be bothered to walk that far, to access one of the guest bedrooms closer to the stairs. Not Elliot's. Not a room with a—

The smell hits me as I open the door. It's a smell I remember from the teaching hospital.

There is a dead body in this room—beneath the reek of urine and the incongruously homely smell of spilled coffee, it smells of death. Not badly, the room is too cold for that, but unmistakably. A fetid, animal kind of smell.

There is no way you would choose to use this room for anything, if you had another option.

The smell makes me gag, but I push the urge down and edge across the room to the far side of Elliot's desk. And there it is—sitting like a cinder block on the floor, a single red LED piercing the gloom. My heart gives a thump of relief. And almost at the same time I notice two things. The first is that a phone is plugged into the charging block, and it's switched on, and fully charged. Elliot left his phone charging. Of *course* he did.

But the second thing I see is that he has an Android, and mine is an iPhone. My phone is in my pocket, but I can't use his charger.

I want to kick myself. I should have collected my own charger first—that was incredibly stupid of me. Do I have time? Ordinarily it would take me less than a minute to run to the other end of the corridor, slam through the staff doors, and grab my charger from beside my bed. But now, I can't run. I can't slam through the doors. I can't afford to make a sound.

I make up my mind. I will try Elliot's phone first. You can dial some emergency numbers from the lock screen—I just have no idea whether 112 or 17 are among them.

I pick it up and the screen jumps into life, but with a lurch of disappointment I see there is still no reception—just an *x* by the grayed-out scale. I can't call anyone.

Still, there are a bunch of app notifications on the lock screen, and it's with a flicker of hope that I scroll down them, trying to figure out if the phone has connected at all during the past twenty-four hours. If it's getting even tiny blips of reception, that might be enough. If I can get into the phone I could send a text, which would just sit there in the outbox until the phone connected. I wouldn't have to do anything. Just wait for it to send.

And there it is. A WhatsApp from six hours ago. And below that, a notification from Snoop. *Anon101 is geoclose,* whatever that means. Geoclose? I've never had a notification like that on my Snoop account.

I have no time to worry about that now though. The question is how I get into the phone. I have three tries before it locks out, and then I'll have no choice but to go back and get my charger, and wait while my own phone powers up, which will take long enough to make Liz wonder where I am.

I'm racking my brains, trying to remember if Kate ever told me Elliot's date of birth, and if so whether to try the year, or the day and month, but when I bring up the lock screen, I come up short. It's not a pin pad, it's a thumb scanner.

My stomach drops with disappointment, but then I realize what this means, and I experience a different kind of lurch, this one of nauseated horror, as it dawns on me what I have to do next. Oh God. Can I do it? And if I can, what kind of person does that make me?

I glance across at the desk. I force myself to look at the shape I have been trying to ignore, let my eyes skitter across: Elliot. Elliot's body.

His hand is stretched out across the desk, and I feel my cheeks go hot and then cold and then hot again with a kind of deep piercing shame at what I am about to do. But I *have* to get inside that phone.

I stand up. I unplug the phone from the block, and I take a step across the room, closer to where Elliot is sprawled. And then another. And then I am standing by his desk, reaching for his hand—his cold, firm hand.

It is a little clammy, though that is mostly due to how cold the room is, and his arm is surprisingly heavy to maneuver, but the rigor has worn off, and it is without too much difficulty that I unfurl his fingers, and hold his long, bony thumb between my fingers, chill and firm as a joint of meat.

"I'm sorry," I whisper to him. "I'm so, so sorry."

And then I press the tip against the lock screen.

For a minute nothing happens and I feel a piercing, shooting sense of disappointment. Can the phone somehow tell? Does it work off body warmth? Does it know that this is a dead man, not a living owner?

There is only one way to find out. Feeling even sicker, I put down the phone and rub the cold, clammy tip of Elliot's thumb between my palms, chafing it roughly, trying to get a little of my own body heat into Elliot's skin.

It's surprisingly hard. My hands are cold too, and for a long time, all I can feel is the bone-deep chill of dead flesh against mine. But I persist, huffing on his thumb to try and warm him with my breath, and at last there does seem to be some perceptible difference in temperature. Before it can dissipate, I pick up the phone and press it quickly against the tip, holding my breath.

And then the display lights up, with the hot pink of the Snoop app's home screen. And I'm inside Elliot's phone.

I'm about to minimize Snoop and navigate to the text message app, when I stop. There is something really odd about Elliot's Snoop app.

He is being followed by 1.2 million people. Which is not that surprising, I guess. He's known to be one of the cofounders of the company, and his Snoop ID is public.

But the weird thing is that he's following only two people. One of them is Topher—I remember his avatar and ID from when I followed him myself—Xtopher and a photo of him balancing a spoon on his nose, with a little tick to show he's verified. *Snooping Xtopher for 3 years,* says the text beside his name. That's not the weird part.

The weird part is that the other person he's subscribed to is a totally anonymous user, Anon101. Anon has no picture, and when I click on the blank space where their avatar would have been, to take me through to their profile, there is nothing in their bio either. *Go away*, is the only line they've put in the "About" field, which maybe explains why they have only one follower. That's it.

But under *location*, there *is* an entry. A string of GPS coordinates and a tiny logo saying "beta" in brackets.

This must be the update Elliot was working on before he died—the geosnooping update that he and Topher were so excited about, the one that let them locate Eva. But who *is* Anon101 and why is Elliot following them? Is Anon Eva? But, no, that's ridiculous, not with one follower. And besides, I've snooped Eva. I can't remember what her ID was, but I remember her avatar—a snow leopard wearing Ray-Bans.

I click back to the previous screen.

Snooping Anon101 for 2 days says the text beside their name.

Elliot followed Anon101 right before he died.

My stomach is fluttering now, and my thumb hovers above the "Geosnoop (beta)" tab at the top of the menu. I remember that notification on the home screen now—the notification that I swiped aside so carelessly. *Anon101 is geoclose.*

I press the Geosnoop tab.

In your area: reads the text at the top of the menu. And then, underneath, there is a list of just two people.

Littlemy
Anon101

I am Littlemy. Which means . . . Anon101 must be . . . Liz.

LIZ

Snoop ID: ANON101
Listening to: Offline
Snoopscribers: 1

There is something wrong. Erin has not come back from her trip to the toilet. She has been gone a long time, but more than that, I can't hear anything at all. No doors opening. No footsteps on the stairs. No sound of water flushing. Has something happened? Has she fallen asleep?

I lie there chewing my lip, trying to work out what to do. I went after her last time. I was worried when she took so long over changing her top, but now I am not sure if that was a good idea. The panic on her face when she opened the bedroom door and saw me standing there, just about to knock, made me think I had made a mistake. And now I wonder, is that when her manner changed? Maybe she is frightened of me. Perhaps she thinks I'm a stalker.

People have a habit of pulling away from me. It is something I have noticed over the years. It started with the girls at school—they would be friendly at first, and I'd try to make overtures back—and then they would start to cool, for reasons I could never put my finger on. So I would try harder. Make more effort. But the more I tried, the more they seemed to grow cold, until at last everything I did just seemed to make them hate me more.

At primary school, the other girls weren't subtle about it. *Go away, Liz, you're so weird.* I heard it again and again. As we got older, the girls in my class pretended to be kinder, but underneath they were thinking the same things, beneath their *Oh, so sorry, we're saving this seat* or *My mum says I can only have three girls to the sleepover, really sorry, Liz.*

The girls were bad. The boys were worse. The worst of all was Kevin.

Even his name makes me shudder.

I *liked* Kevin. I thought that he might like me too. He had acne and his breath was a little stale, and he wasn't particularly handsome. He didn't seem as unattainable as some of the other boys. I got a book out of the library on how to make boys like you, but it was confusing and contradictory. *Laugh at his jokes,* it read. So I did. But then Kevin would look at me as if I were crazy and say, "What are you laughing at?"

Give him something to remind him of you. I gave him a pair of mittens I had knitted. I left them in his locker, but he never wore them. Later I found them in lost property.

Engineer chance meetings. I followed him around. I made sure that I was there, leaning against the lockers when he came out of the boys' toilets. I waited by his bus stop. One day I followed him home.

It was November and almost dusk. I didn't think he had noticed me, but he had. We had walked nearly two miles when he turned on me. "What do you want, you fucking weirdo?" he said, his voice cracking and breaking on the last word. Only he didn't say it. He came right up into my face and screamed it. I could smell his stale breath and feel his spit hitting me as he shouted.

It was dark. Rain had begun to fall. We were in a lonely part of the park. A small part of me wanted to kill him. But I didn't. Instead, I cowered away from him, cringing from his anger and then, when he pushed me and yelled, "Are you fucking desperate or what?" I ran. I was crying and shaking.

By the time I was hired at Snoop, I had learned my lesson. I kept myself to myself. I didn't try to make friends. I didn't trust anyone.

But Erin . . . somehow Erin seemed different. She was so friendly when we first arrived. I remember her sympathy when I asked her advice about the dress code, her kindness as she towed me to the ski lift that first day. She really seemed to like me. Now I am not so sure. What if she was pretending all along?

I want to go up there and ask her what she thinks of me, whether she is scared of me, what she is *doing* up there in the dark. But I don't know how she would feel about that. Maybe I could say I was worried about her. After all, three people have died. It's what a good friend would do. Look out for her. Check she was okay.

But would she see it that way? Would she *know* I was just being a good friend? Or would she give me that look again—that panicked, terrified look I saw in Kevin's eyes when he turned on me. The one I saw in Erin's eyes when she opened the door last time. The look that says, *You weirdo.* The look that says, *I'm scared.*

I am still dithering ten minutes later. At last I can't take the silence anymore. I *have* to know what she is doing.

I swing my legs out of bed and stand up. I'm still wearing my ski suit, so I'm not that cold. My knee still hurts, but I can put my weight on it now. Really I am very glad not to be snowshoeing to the other chalet. I mean, I would never have fallen down the stairs deliberately, that would be a really stupid idea. I could have been killed. But it worked out well.

Still, I go carefully on the stairs, holding the handrail. The wood is slippery beneath my socks, the treads themselves are hard to see in the darkness, and I definitely don't want another fall.

At the top of the stairs I pause, holding my breath, trying to listen. *Where* is she? In the staff quarters? I'm just about to turn left, to see if she's down that end of the corridor, when I hear a noise. It's a very slight one, but it is coming from the opposite direction—from the direction of the corridor that holds Miranda's, Elliot's, and my rooms. What would she be doing down there?

But before I can find out, I hear another noise from the same direction—this time unmistakable. It's the sound of a toilet flushing. The door to Miranda's room opens, and Erin comes out. She doesn't look that surprised to see me, this time, instead she just smiles.

"Hi, Liz." Her voice is slightly breathless. "Sorry, were you worried?"

"A bit." I frown at her. "What were you doing in Miranda's room?"

"I already flushed the staff toilet. I didn't think Miranda would mind, and it was the closest. Um, Liz, fair warning—" It's hard to tell in the darkness, but it looks like her face is a bit flushed. "Sorry, this is TMI, but I had a bit of an upset stomach. I think maybe the cassoulet wasn't heated through properly. That's why I—well, that's why it took me a bit longer."

"Oh!" I'm not sure what to say to that. Should I laugh? No, that would seem strange. I arrange my features into what I hope is a sympathetic smile. Then I worry that it might just look like a smile, so I frown instead. "Oh, gosh, poor you."

"I realize you probably didn't want to know that, but I thought I should warn you in case—well, I mean, we had the same supper—"

"Oh, I've been fine," I say hastily. It's the truth. I haven't had so much as a twinge. But then I've always had really good digestion.

"Oh, good," she says. There's relief in her face. "I'd hate to have given you food poisoning on top of everything else." She gives a shaky laugh, and then says, "Well, shall we?"

For a minute, I'm not sure what she's referring to, but then she nods at the stairs, and I understand what she's saying.

"Sure," I say. But then something stops me. "Actually, you head down. I need the toilet as well."

She nods, and begins to limp her way down the spiral staircase. I watch her go for a moment, and then I head down the corridor towards my own room. I unlock the door and slip inside, and go over to the built-in closet in the corner of my room. The door is ajar, which is how I left it. But, is it my imagination, or is it very slightly wider than it was before?

I stand stock-still for a long moment, looking at the door. It's cracked open maybe two inches. It looks like a lot. It looks like a wider gap than before. But I can't be sure.

Making up my mind, I open the door and pull out my suitcase, and then I unzip the lining. Inside, pressed flat against the base of the suitcase, behind the silky lining and a piece of card, should be a scarlet ski jacket. It's too dark to really see, and I left my torch downstairs, but when I poke my fingers through the narrow gap, I can feel it is there—its downy softness reassuring. I let out a sigh of relief and sit back on my heels.

Then I zip up the lining and replace the case inside the cupboard, and I stand painfully and go through to the bathroom. I might as well make my story convincing while I'm here.

But it's only when I'm halfway through peeling off my ski suit that something strikes me, something that stops me in my tracks.

That suitcase was on top of the stack, on *top* of my little wheelie cabin bag.

I left it the other way around. I am absolutely certain of it.

Someone has been inside my closet.

Erin? Or someone else?

My heart is thumping.

Slowly, very slowly, I pull up the zip of my jumpsuit, thinking hard, trying to figure out what to do.

Then I flush the toilet and walk back downstairs to try to figure out how much Erin knows.

ERIN

Snoop ID: LITTLEMY
Listening to: Offline
Snoopscribers: 10

From up above I hear Liz's toilet flush, and I hunker down underneath the duvet, hoping I can pretend to be asleep when she comes back. My mind is racing, trying to figure out what can possibly have happened.

Thank God I heard her coming up the stairs and was able to leave Elliot's room and nip two doors down to Miranda's. If she had found me coming out of Elliot's, I would have had to come clean. And the truth is, I am much too scared to do that.

What the hell does it all mean? Is Liz the killer? But *how*? Never mind motive, she has a cast-iron alibi. She was on the bubble lift going down the valley when Eva was killed.

Except . . .

Except no one actually *saw* her get on the lift.

I try to think back to that final run down the mountain as everyone had described it. Eva was coming up in the Reine bubble lift. Carl had fallen over at the bottom, trying to get on, and Ani was helping him. Everyone else was standing at the top of the blue run, Blanche-

Neige, huddled in the screaming wind, waiting for Eva, Carl, and Ani to arrive.

Then came Liz's refusal to ski, and Topher's bullying attempt to force her to do it.

Everyone agreed what happened next—Liz tore off her skis and walked back up the slope to the lift, to get on the bubble back down to the chalet.

But what if she hadn't? What if she had gone through the little shack housing the lift and straight out the other side, towards the black run, La Sorcière. Then, at the top of the run, right by the steepest part of the piste, she stood and waited.

I try to imagine how Liz could have lured Eva across. Maybe she pretended she had slid helplessly down the black run, towards the sheer drop. Maybe she faked a problem with her boot or her ski. Either way, she must have called to Eva, and then, when Eva was very close to her, and off guard, she pushed her off the precipice.

That would have been the riskiest part. Not the risk of being seen—the visibility was too bad for that, and the lift building would have been between them and the skiers standing on Blanche-Neige. But the risk of failing to push Eva over the edge. If Eva had managed to save herself, or worse, if she had grabbed hold of her attacker and taken her over the edge as well, everything would have been finished. But it worked. It must have done. And now Liz just had to give herself an alibi—by ensuring that Eva was seen to be safe and well *after* Liz was supposed to have gone back down in the lift.

I remember that huge, bulky ski suit, the way Liz was sweating, just standing around at the base of the lift. I even remember thinking that she was clearly wearing far too many layers, and wondering why, on such a nice day. Now I *know* why. It wasn't inexperience at all. It was planned.

It would not have been very hard to have a second ski jacket on underneath the first. It would have taken seconds to unzip the baggy blue jumpsuit, take off the scarlet ski jacket beneath, and put it on over the top. With her helmet, goggles, and dark-colored ski pants, anyone seeing her at a distance would take it for granted that she was Eva.

And so she set off to ski La Sorcière, stopping just to make sure that one person at least—faithful little Ani, far above her in the bubble lift—would be able to back up her story.

I think of Ani's last words to Tiger, her puzzled *I didn't see her.*

We all thought she was talking about Eva.

But what if . . . what if she were talking about Liz. Liz, who was supposed to be on the bubble going down the mountain, at the same time Ani was coming up. What if *that* was what Ani realized, that Liz never passed them going back down? That she never took the lift at all?

It is plausible. It is all horribly plausible. And it would very likely have worked if it weren't for one thing. Elliot's geosnooping app, covertly gathering data on everyone in the party.

Because Elliot wasn't stupid. As soon as he figured out that Eva had died, he would have looked at the movements of everyone else on the mountain that day. He would have known that the person who skied La Sorcière was not Eva but Anon101. Only even with all the info at his disposal, he could not be certain who Anon101 was.

So he followed Anon on Snoop. And he set about figuring it out by process of elimination. But he was killed before he could share his suspicions with Topher.

This theory explains almost everything. It explains why Elliot had to die, why his computer, with all the geosnooping data, was smashed up. It explains why Ani was killed.

There's only one thing it doesn't explain. *Why.*

Why Eva was killed in the first place.

Because Liz still doesn't have a motive.

Still, I remember Danny's words. *I dunno. We could probably give them all motives if we needed to.*

He's right. Alibi is the key, not motive. And I have just smashed Liz's alibi to pieces. There is one problem—if I'm right, that fact puts me next in line to be killed.

I am alone in an isolated chalet with a murderer, and there's nothing I can do.

LIZ

Snoop ID: ANON101
Listening to: Offline
Snoopscribers: 1

Who moved my suitcase?

The question gnaws at me like a rat as I walk slowly back downstairs. When I enter the living room I can see Erin is huddled under the duvet. Her eyes are closed, and she's breathing softly and rhythmically. But it seems to me—and I can't tell if I'm being paranoid here—that there is something a little fake about the way she is lying. Does anyone really look that composed in sleep?

"Erin," I whisper very softly. She stirs, her eyelids flickering momentarily, but she doesn't appear to wake.

I sit on the sofa bed beside her and try to think.

I *am* completely sure about the suitcase. At least I think I am. But I have not looked in that cupboard since Sunday. Anyone could have moved my case. Even if they moved it, that doesn't mean that they looked inside the lining. It could have been Elliot—gathering information before he took his suspicions to Topher. It could even have been something completely innocent.

I could kill Erin. That is not the issue. I could put a pillow over her face, just like I did with Ani, but here is the problem: If I kill Erin, everyone will know it was me. There is no one here for miles around. I would have no hope of persuading anyone that an unknown intruder broke in and smothered her in her sleep.

I killed Elliot and Ani because I had to. I acted quickly, on the spur of the moment, working with what I had to hand. With Elliot, that was Eva's sleeping pills, crushed into a cup of black coffee. He never suspected a thing when I offered him a refill. I guess that's all I ever was to him: someone to fetch the coffee.

For Ani, it was her own pillow, pressed over her nose and mouth. She died quietly, her struggles muffled by the thick duvet wrapped around her. I felt . . . well, I would like to say that I felt guilty for them both, but the truth is, I didn't really. Elliot brought it on himself, with his snooping and his prying. I did feel sorry for Ani. But she was in the wrong place at the wrong time. What I saw in her eyes when she stood, frozen in my doorway that night, was the sudden realization of what she had seen. What she had *not* seen. The empty glass spheres of the bubble lift, returning back down to the station, when one of them should have contained me.

She realized what it meant. I could tell that straightaway, from the moment our eyes locked and hers filled with sudden fear. She hurried back to her room, locking the door behind her. She probably felt safe. She didn't know I had a passkey.

But I don't feel guilty, even about Ani, because it's not my fault, any of this. *I* was in the wrong place at the wrong time too. I never asked for any of this. I was caught up in something I couldn't help, caught up in Topher's and Eva's own personal game of thrones—not even one of the major players, just a pawn for Eva to play against Topher when the time was right, my own past leveraged against me.

Because here's the thing—I am a *good* person. I never wanted any of this. I certainly don't want to kill anyone if I don't have to. If Erin didn't look inside that case, if she hasn't figured this out, well, I don't want to hurt her.

I don't need to act quickly. I have time to think about this. There is no way help can get here before morning. I can take my time to work out if she knows something, and if so, what I can do about it. It would have to be an accident, or look like an accident. Another slip on the stairs, maybe? A carbon monoxide leak with the stove? Though I am not sure how I would engineer that.

Slowly, I take off my glasses and lie down, but I don't shut my eyes. I lie there, facing Erin, watching her. Watching her sleep.

ERIN

Snoop ID: LITTLEMY
Listening to: Offline
Snoopscribers: 10

Liz is watching me. I don't dare to open my eyes more than a sliver, but under cover of tossing in my sleep I move my head a little, letting my eyelids flicker, and I can see her, lying there, staring unblinkingly into the darkness.

With her glasses off she looks quite different. The owlish, impenetrable look is gone, and she looks younger, but at the same time there is something even more unsettling about her blank, unwavering stare. When I close my eyes and settle back down with a little fake snore, I can sense her gaze boring into me.

I feel light-headed with fear. What am I going to do?

I try to force myself to breathe slowly—to think this through clearly. Am I in danger? Immediate danger? I don't know. If I am right, Liz has killed three people—but I don't think she is killing for fun. I still have no idea why Eva had to die, but Ani and Elliot were only killed when they had concrete information about Liz's guilt. If I can keep my suspicions under wraps until morning, I may be okay.

I squeeze my eyes shut, and I think about Elliot's phone, plugged back into the battery upstairs, with the text message I sent to Danny in the outbox, waiting for a thread of connection. "SOS, please send help. IT'S LIZ." A message I composed with trembling fingers, trying to walk the fine line between a message Danny would understand, a message that would act as a clue if something happens to me before morning, and a message that I could plausibly explain away if Liz somehow stumbles upon it.

I don't *think* she has access to Elliot's phone. But I don't know. That's the problem, I don't know anything. She was doing something up there when she claimed to be going to the toilet. She spent much too long in her room, and I could hear her pacing around, opening and closing doors. She walked into the loo and immediately flushed it, without even closing the door as far as I could tell, let alone sitting on the toilet.

She knows something. She suspects *something*. I just don't know what. All I know is that Ani was killed in her sleep, and so I don't dare to let myself drift off.

LIZ

Snoop ID: ANON101
Listening to: Offline
Snoopscribers: 1

Erin knows.

I was not sure at first, but as the time stretches out into what feels increasingly like an endless night, I am sure of it.

Because in spite of what I first assumed, she is *not* asleep. She is pretending to be asleep, but she is not. She is lying there with her eyes closed, and every now and again, when she thinks I am not watching, she opens her eyes just the smallest slit, to check if I am still awake. I see the glint of moonlight between her lashes, and then she squeezes them shut again and does a little fake snore.

It's so unfair. *God* it's so unfair!

I never asked for this. I never wanted any of it. I just wanted to be left *alone*.

It is all I've ever wanted. It's all I wanted from the girls at school, with their bitching and their teasing and their prying.

It's all I wanted at uni, with people badgering me to join up to clubs and attend freshers' formals.

It's all I wanted at Snoop. And at first they did—they left me alone, and you know what? It was fine!

And then it wasn't. It all unraveled. And that's why I hate them so much.

I hate Topher for dragging me into this, for saddling me with these shares like a millstone around my neck.

I hate Eva for meddling and meddling and meddling when she should have left well enough alone. I hated her *Are you okay?* and *Is there anything I can do?* and *We'll make this right, Liz, I swear.*

I hate Elliot for poking and prying and being too clever by half.

I hate Rik for just—for just being one of *them.* So entitled. So slick. Swimming with sharks and never getting hurt because he's one of *them.* Because he's a man, and a private-school boy, and so very, very charming.

And now I hate Erin too.

Lying there, with her fake little snores, and her half smile, when all the time she has been putting two and two together . . .

Only it is too late. What can I do? If only I had been sure of this earlier—I still have eight of Eva's sleeping tablets in my pocket. It would have been possible—not easy, but possible—to slip them into the cassoulet. I could have swapped our plates when Erin wasn't looking. Now it is too late. Though perhaps that has already occurred to her. Perhaps that was what she was really doing in the toilet, when she took so long and came up with that transparent food-poisoning story. Perhaps she was making herself sick.

Could I stage a break-in? Perhaps I could pretend that Inigo came back for us? It could work—but not if Inigo himself has an alibi. And the problem is that if Inigo *does* have an alibi and if Erin *doesn't* suspect me, then I would be exposing myself for no reason. I would be shooting myself in the foot.

I have to be very, very careful. I cannot afford a mistake.

But I have to know. I have to know what she knows.

"Erin," I whisper, very quietly. There is complete silence, but it is not quite the silence of someone fully asleep. It is more like the silence of someone thinking it over.

At last there is a sigh, and Erin says, "Yes?"

"You're still awake?"

"I can't sleep. I keep thinking about the others, wondering where they are."

It could be true. But then I think about that little slit of her eye, glinting at me in the dark. I don't think it is. I don't think that is what is keeping her awake. I play along.

"Are you worried about Danny?"

There is another long pause. I think she is trying to work out what to say. She is trying to figure out whether she needs to pretend to suspect someone else.

"A bit," she says at last. "I hoped he'd come back tonight, you know?"

I am about to say something else, I'm not sure what, something meaningless about being sure Danny is okay.

Only then, in the silence as I formulate my words, there is a double beep. Very faint, and coming from upstairs, but completely unmistakable.

It is a sound that sets my pulse racing even before I have pinned down what it is.

It is the sound of a text message coming through.

ERIN

Snoop ID: LITTLEMY
Listening to: Offline
Snoopscribers: 10

I can tell at once that Liz has heard. Her whole body goes stiff and alert, and she pushes herself up on her elbow, listening intently.

Fuck.

"What was that?" she says.

My heart is racing. I know bloody well what it was. It was Danny replying to Elliot's text message. It must be. Elliot's is the only phone in the house that still has any charge left on it. There must have been a blip of reception—the same sliver that allowed the notification from Snoop to come through.

But I keep my face carefully neutral.

"I have no idea—it sounded like a phone, don't you think? But that can't be right."

Liz is staring at me, like she's trying to figure out what's going on behind my face. Oh my god she *knows*. She definitely knows. She just isn't sure enough to act on her suspicions. I have to be very, very careful.

"It sounded like it was coming from upstairs," Liz says. She grabs her glasses and swings one leg out of bed.

"Yeah . . . ," I say it slowly, my mind racing. At all costs, I can't let her get into Elliot's room. If she sees that message, I am in big trouble. She already suspects me. It would be very hard to explain that message away. "Yeah, it did."

Could she kill me? I don't know. Her knee is as screwed as my ankle. Could she out-hobble me if it came to trying to get away? I am trying to think of a plan. Could I lure her outside somehow? Lock the door? But then I think of Danny's words, about Inigo turning up, begging to be let in, and I know he was right. I could never stand there and watch another human being freeze to death inches away, only a pane of glass separating us. I just couldn't. Not even Liz.

But I can't let her find that text message.

My mind is racing, trying to remember what I could see on Elliot's lock screen before I cleared it. Some people have their text messages show up in their entirety. Others only have the ID of the sender, or just *You have a text.* Which is Elliot? Why didn't I *check* before I unlocked the phone and cleared his notifications? Of course if it occurs to Liz to use Elliot's dead body to unlock the phone like I did, none of this matters.

"It sounds like it came from Miranda's room," I say slowly, trying to think how to put her off track.

"You think?" Liz says. Her face is skeptical. "I thought it sounded more like Elliot's. It'd be just like him to have some kind of superlong-charge battery."

My stomach flips. Of course. Of course she's right. She *knows* these people. And now I realize I'm trapped. I can't suggest we split up and *I* check Elliot's room, when I already said I think the sound came from Miranda's. I will have to go along with her suggestion.

"Should we . . . go and check?" I try to look doubtful. "It seems a bit disrespectful. Maybe we should rule out the other rooms first?"

Liz swings the other leg out of bed. She looks decisive.

"I think it's more important that we get to the phone while it still has reception," she says, reasonably, and I can't find a way of contradicting her because the thing is, she's right. That's exactly what I'd be saying too, if I hadn't sent that fucking text. "I understand if you don't want to come," she adds.

I waver. It's tempting. But I can't let her go up there alone. That would be worse. There may be some way I can get to the phone before she does, delete Danny's reply.

"Of course," I say instead, like I'm steeling myself to do something necessary. "Of course, you're right, I was just being squeamish. It's more important to get word out. Anyway, the door will be locked. You'll need my key."

"Of course," she echoes, and for a second, just a second, her hand strays towards her pocket, where the missing passkey must have been hidden, in a totally involuntary gesture that I would have missed if I hadn't been watching her every move. She catches herself before her hand makes contact, so that it just looks like she's adjusting her ski suit. But I know what she was thinking.

As we make our way up the stairs, I have a sharp, piercing sense of déjà vu, the number of times we have crept up these stairs in daylight or in darkness, to some horrible discovery. Only this time, I know what lies at the top of them, and I am the one who is fearing exposure.

My heart is racing as we approach Elliot's door, and when I reach into my pocket for the passkey, I find my hand is shaking.

"Are you okay?" Liz says. She has put her glasses back on, and they glitter in the darkness. "You don't have to come in if you don't want."

"I'm fine," I say, through gritted teeth. "Just cold."

And then I turn the key and we are inside Elliot's room, the stench of death somehow even worse than before, though I know, logically, that cannot be the case, not in the few hours since I was last here.

Liz gags, and puts her hand over her mouth, and her action gives me an excuse.

The battery block is down the side of the desk, hidden from the door. If I can get her to concentrate on the far side of the room . . .

"The smell's pretty bad," I say. "If you want to concentrate on the bed side of the room, I can take the desk."

She nods, and moves over to the other side of the room. I am busy going through the motions, opening drawers, pretending to search for a phone I know full well is just out of sight, when I hear something.

And then—

"Erin."

I look up, look towards the bed, but she's not there. She has come up behind me. And she has found the phone.

My heart starts beating so loudly I am sure that Liz will be able to hear.

Run, run, run, a voice in my ear is screaming. But I don't. I hold very still. Maybe I can still talk my way out of this. What does it say. What does it *say*?

I wish I could see the lock screen, but I can't. Liz is holding the phone in her hand, angling it towards her, so that all I can see is the light from the screen reflecting off her glasses.

"That sound . . . ," she says, very slowly. She looks up at me, a frown furrowed between the lenses of her spectacles. "It *was* a text message. And it was to you."

LIZ

Snoop ID: ANON101
Listening to: Offline
Snoopscribers: 1

I stare down at the screen, and then up at Erin's blank face.

This doesn't make sense. Or does it?

Messages: reads the lock screen, and then a little preview pane showing the first line of the message. *Fuck. Erin is that you?*

Erin is looking at me like a rabbit in a snare.

Elliot's phone is a thumb lock. It makes what I have to do next very easy.

I reach out, and grab his cold, heavy hand.

"No!" Erin yelps, and she reaches for the phone, but it is too late. I am in.

SOS, I read, feeling fury begin to kindle inside me, making my cheeks hot. *Please send help. IT'S LIZ.*

I stare up at Erin, looking her right in the eye, feeling my jaw fall open with shocked betrayal.

That bitch. That total bitch.

ERIN

Snoop ID: LITTLEMY
Listening to: Offline
Snoopscribers: 10

I see Liz's face change as she reads it and I know, instantly, there is no way of explaining my way out of this.

Her face goes white, and she stays very, very still, but I don't think it's fear that's paralyzing her. I think . . . I think it might be something else. I think it might be anger.

"You don't understand," I say weakly, but my voice is croaky, and I know there is no point in this. I don't know how I ever thought that text was ambiguous. Seeing Liz's face, I understand now, there is only one way for her to take it.

"You know," she says, and her voice is horribly calm. I want her to scream and shout—*anything* would be better than this icy chill.

But there's a kind of relief with her words, because now I can stop pretending. I can stop this horrible dance of *Does she know I know she knows*, and just face up to the truth.

"Yes, I know," I say quietly. And then I take a step backwards, and I sink down on Elliot's bed and put my face in my hands. Partly because my ankle is killing me, and the pain is starting to make me feel sick, and partly because my legs are shaking so hard I can't keep upright anymore.

She stands there, looking down at me, her face blank and unreadable behind those huge glasses. The light from Elliot's phone gives her face an eerie, up-lit glow. Behind her Elliot, the man she killed, lies sprawled across his desk—a terrifyingly immediate reminder of what she has done to protect her secret. The secret I now have. Oh God, what have I done? Danny, where are you?

"God, he *stinks*," she says at last, wrinkling up her face. She cracks her knuckles, *click, click, click*, but it no longer sounds nervy. It sounds like someone limbering up for a fight. "Let's get out of here. Come downstairs and we can talk this through."

As if in a dream—or maybe a nightmare—I follow her out of the room. She holds the phone out in front of her like a candle, illuminating the corridor, and when we get to the top of the stairs she says, "After you."

I hesitate.

I don't want to make her angry—but at the same time, there is no way I am going down that slippery, precarious staircase with her at my back. I'm just not.

Liz sees my hesitation and gives a mirthless laugh.

"Okay, I don't blame you. I'll go first. But you keep a step back, okay? I'm not having you pushing me down the steps either."

I nod. I don't mind keeping my distance. It would be almost as easy for her to snatch my ankle out from underneath me as it would be for me to kick her in the small of the back.

God, this is surreal.

I watch her as she makes her way carefully down the stairs, holding the handrail, the phone guiding the way like a faint will-o'-the-wisp.

Downstairs, she moves away from the foot of the stairs and feeds another log into the burner, making it flare so that the room is bright with its glow, and I hurry down while her back is turned, my heart beating quicker until I am on solid ground. Then she straightens up and shuts the glass door of the stove.

I am alone with a murderer. I am alone with a *murderer*. Maybe if I keep repeating the words to myself it will start to feel real?

LIZ

Snoop ID: ANON101
Listening to: Offline
Snoopscribers: 1

In a way, it is a relief to have it out in the open. I could tell there was something wrong, and I have always hated trying to read between the lines, second-guessing myself, attempting to parse a frown or a blank look or a pause that might be something or might be nothing.

Now we both know where we are. Which is a relief. But it is also a problem. Because I liked Erin. No, that's wrong. I shouldn't be using the past tense. Not yet.

I like her. I actually do really like her. I don't want to have to do this. But she did something really, *really* stupid when she sent that text, and now I have no choice. She's forced my hand, really. If anything this is *her* fault.

The sense of injustice boils up again. This is so un*fair.*

"I never wanted any of this, you know," I say to her as she sinks down onto one of the chairs, staring into the flames. She is shaking. I'm not sure if it's cold or shock.

"What?"

She looks up, and I feel anger bubble up inside me, and then I push it back down. Has she even been listening?

"I *said* I never wanted this." I sink down into the armchair opposite her. I stare at the fire, feeling its heat on my face. "I would never have killed any of them if I could help it. *I'm* just as much of a victim here."

She blinks—and for a minute it looks like she's going to say something, but then she seems to think better of it.

"Tell me about it," she says. And so I do.

ERIN

Snoop ID: LITTLEMY
Listening to: Offline
Snoopscribers: 10

I am lost in thought as Liz sits down opposite me, and it takes me a moment to realize she is talking. What she is saying doesn't make sense—some nonsense about *her* being the real victim in all of this.

I look up, and I meet her eyes, and I am overwhelmed with the urge to slap her, to shake her, to scream, *You? Are you kidding me? What about Eva? What about Elliot? What about fucking Ani, who never harmed a fly?*

But I don't.

Because I suddenly know what I have to do here.

I have to humor her. I have to keep her talking long enough for Danny to get back here with reinforcements. He has seen the text. He knows what it means. He will be doing everything he can to help me. I don't know what time it is, but it must be way after midnight. If I can just keep Liz talking long enough, I may be able to survive this. I may even be able to get justice for all the people she has killed.

Because I am a survivor, that's what Liz doesn't know about me. She sees a soft, posh girl from the same background as Topher and

Eva, someone who has never had to work for her living, to scrap for survival.

But that's not true. Not in my case. In spite of my family name, I *didn't* grow up with a silver spoon in my mouth, not in the way Topher and Eva did. I've always known that I was second best, and that I would have to fight for myself. I know what it's like to clean up other people's messes for a living.

But more than that, the most important thing about me, something Liz will never understand, *could* never understand, unless she had stood in my shoes: I looked death in the face once, and I turned him away.

I can do it again.

"Tell me about it," I say. There is a catch in my throat, and my voice is shaking with the effort of keeping it calm, when I feel anything but. But Liz doesn't seem to notice. Instead, she smiles. Incredibly, unbelievably, she smiles.

And she begins to speak.

LIZ

Snoop ID: ANON101
Listening to: Offline
Snoopscribers: 1

"You don't know what it was like, starting at Snoop," I say. It is easier not to look at Erin while I'm telling her this, so I look away again, into the fire, remembering that first day—opening the office door, and seeing them all, lounging around inside, laughing, bantering, so effortlessly, searingly cool. "It was like walking into a different world. Like something off the TV, where people were sleek and beautiful and witty. They were like a different species, and I wanted to be them so much. School—school was so horrible. I can't explain it. I knew I was different from the other girls in my class, I knew they all laughed at me. But somehow I thought when I got to my real life it would be different. I thought that maybe I was just an ugly duckling."

I swallow. It is strange saying all of this—unwrapping secrets I have carried for three years.

"But when I got to Snoop I realized that wasn't true—I wasn't going to magically grow into a swan overnight. Eva and Topher, even Elliot and Rik in a way, they had been different and special and beautiful right from the day they were born. And I wasn't. I was never going to be a swan. I had to accept that. But the thing is, I *was* good at my job. Really good. And Snoop was doing well. And I cared about it—about them. So when the firm had problems raising money just before the launch, I offered Topher and Eva my grandmother's money. I still remember the shock on their faces when I made the suggestion." I laugh, remembering Topher's expression when I spoke up in that meeting—as if his office chair had piped up, offering a solution to their finances. "I think they realized then that they'd underestimated me—that the girl who brought the coffee and took the minutes was a real human being who could understand a profit and loss sheet, and figure out when the company was in trouble. It was like they really *looked* at me for the first time. Eva offered to pay me back with interest, and it was a good rate too. I would have got back almost half as much again by the time it was all paid back. But Topher—Topher took me aside into his office and told me I should ask for shares, and hang out until I got them.

"I knew it was a risk. Rik spelled it out really carefully—I wouldn't see my money back for a long time, and if the firm went under, I'd lose everything. But Topher—you don't know what he's like. He's so charismatic. He makes you feel that you're *everything*, that he will take care of you, that your money could not be in safer hands. So that's what I went for in the end. I thought at the time that Topher was being generous. I thought he was looking out for me." I stare into the flames, feeling the brightness burning into my retinas, as if it can burn away the memories I have carried with me for years. "I didn't know then what I know now—that he had seen how it would pan out in the event of a disagreement, and thought I was someone he could pressure in the event of a split."

I stop. Suddenly this feels hard in a way I didn't think it would. It is good to spill all of this. Erin is a good listener in some ways, and it feels a little like lancing a boil—letting out all the poison that has festered away since that night. But it hurts too. And when

I swallow against the pain, my throat is dry. The sensation gives me an idea.

"Shall I make some tea?" I ask.

"Sorry?" Erin says. There is an incredulous note in her voice. I can't quite blame her—the question must have sounded slightly surreal in the midst of all this.

"Tea," I say. "I don't know about you, but I'm really thirsty."

"Tea?" Erin echoes, like someone speaking in a foreign language, and then she gives a shaky laugh. "Tea . . . would actually be great. It's exactly what I need right now."

We get up and limp together into the kitchen, where I find two cups, and Erin fetches the stovetop kettle and a packet of tea bags.

"There's no milk I'm afraid," she says as she puts the kettle under the tap. "It went off yesterday."

We both stand there, waiting for the kettle to fill, but there is no sound of rushing water. And then I remember. I can see from the sudden look of comprehension on Erin's face that she has remembered too.

"The pipes," she says unnecessarily. I nod.

"Should we get snow?" I ask.

"I . . . guess?" Erin says, but I can hear from the hesitation in her voice that she doesn't want to go outside. I can't say I exactly blame her. I don't really want to go out either. We both know that stepping outside the chalet would give the other person the chance to lock us out, where we would very likely freeze to death. But the snow is piled up against the front door, so if we do this right, neither of us needs to go outside.

"If you open the front door," I say, "and stand there with the kettle, I can chip bits off the drift by the door."

She nods, and I can see from her expression that she is grateful that I have taken on the more precarious role. The snow is piled up so high that you have to climb over the drift to get out, so it's fairly unlikely someone could just push you out of the door, but it is still possible.

"Thanks," she says, and together we troop through into the foyer, where Erin unlocks the bowing front door. I begin to dig at the hard-packed snow with a spoon, chipping off lumps, and putting them into the kettle Erin is holding out. At last we are both shivering with cold, but the kettle is full, and we shut the door and return to the living room, and the blazing fire, where Erin balances the kettle on the edge of the woodstove, and we both warm up our hands at the glass.

"You were saying," she prompts, as the kettle begins to hiss and sigh. "The shares?" Her words bring me back with a bump to our present reality. I finger the empty packet of sleeping pills in my pocket. I think about what I have to do.

ERIN

Snoop ID: LITTLEMY
Listening to: Offline
Snoopscribers: 10

Finding the kettle, getting the snow, all the little mundane practicalities of making the tea have let me push our situation to the back of my mind for a moment, but as the silence closes around us, I feel fear settle like a weight on the back of my neck. Liz is silent, her face blank and unreadable, her hands stuck out to the blaze, and somehow her silence is more terrifying than any speech. I find myself trying to work out what is going through her mind—is she figuring a way out of this? Or just thinking about what she has done?

The kettle hisses softly. Liz just sits there, staring at the kettle, one hand held out to the blaze, the other in her pocket, and suddenly I can't take it anymore.

"You were saying?" I blurt out.

Liz looks up. She looks at me appraisingly, in a way I don't like. She is crunching a piece of plastic in her pocket. The noise is loud in the silence and I think if she doesn't say something, I might scream.

And then she swallows and picks up her story again.

"The shares. Yes. So yes, there I am, twenty-two, a shareholder in this up-and-coming app—and Topher and Eva start treating me a bit more like a human being, now that I'm invested in the business. I mean, I've only got two percent. Even Elliot and Rik dwarf my share. But I *am* a shareholder. And one night, a few days after we signed the papers, there's this drinks party in this flashy London bar—I can't remember why, I think they were after a partnership with some streaming company, some kind of quid pro quo."

She stops. Something is coming, I can tell. I don't know what exactly, but it feels like Liz is gearing herself up for something, forcing herself on to a part of the story she doesn't want to spell out.

"They had an argument, over whether I should go. I remember Rik saying, *Do you think this is the image we want to project?* He didn't know I was listening, of course. They were in Eva's office, and I was listening in via the intercom. And Eva said, *For fuck's sake, Rik, it's not rocket science, I can make her presentable. And she's one of us on paper now, thanks to Toph, so she might as well look the part.* Then she paused and said, *Besides, Norland likes her type. He likes them young.* So I knew what was going on when Eva got me to come over to her house before the party and offered to lend me a dress, because she knew I was on a budget after pouring all my money into Snoop. When she said it like that it sounded perfectly reasonable, kind, even, but I knew the truth.

"Well, you've seen Eva. You know what she's like. There's probably only about three women in London who could squeeze into her jeans. But we found something, somehow, and Eva made up my face, and when we arrived at the bar and were introduced to the executives from the other company—I don't know—I actually started to feel like a real Snooper. Eva introduced me not as her PA but as *Liz, who is a minority shareholder*, and they talked to me with respect, and as the evening wore on I really started to believe this was it—this was the life I had been waiting for. I don't normally drink much, but I drank that night. I drank a lot—a lot of cocktails, and—"

She stops. The kettle is hissing and bubbling, and she picks it up gingerly by the handle and fills each of the cups, then drops a tea bag in the top.

I take the one she hands to me, looking down into it surreptitiously. I don't want to aggravate her suspicions, but given how Elliot died, it would be stupid of me not to check. The melted snow is a little cloudy, and the tea is starting to leach out of the bag and color the hot water, but I can still see the bottom of the cup and there's definitely nothing there. No pills, anyway.

"And?" I prompt, very gently, and then when she looks away, I say, "I'm sorry. I don't want to pry. If this is too painful—"

"No," she says, with a rush. "It's okay, honestly. I—it helps in a weird way, talking about it. I just haven't thought about it in so long. We all got very, very drunk. And somehow—I can't remember how—I ended up going with Eva . . . with one of the executives from the bar. It was just the three of us. Topher was going to come, I remember that, because he was in the taxi, but then at the last minute he bailed out and asked the driver to drop him off. We arrived at this house in Pimlico, and my God, it was amazing—it was so beautiful, this Georgian building, stories high, with a balcony right at the top overlooking the river . . ." She is staring past me now, as if she is looking at something I can't quite see. "He took us upstairs, and we went out onto the balcony, and he gave us champagne and we chatted for a while, and then Eva excused herself and went to the bathroom."

She breaks off. But I don't think it's because she can't go on. Not quite. It's because she is trying to work out what to say, *how* to say it.

"He tried to assault me," she says at last bluntly. "He had his hands down my top, I was trying to push him away. And I—I—"

She stops, she puts her hands to her face.

"I pushed him. I pushed him hard. I pushed him off the balcony."

"Oh my God," I say. Whatever I expected, it was not this. "Liz, I'm—I'm so sorry. I—"

The implications are buzzing in my head, even as I stammer out my pathetically inadequate attempts at sympathy.

She killed a man.

But it was self-defense.

But Liz is still talking, ignoring me, rushing on, as if she wants to be past this part of the narrative.

"I broke down when I realized what I'd done. But Eva—she—she was amazing. She came running, and when she saw what had happened she didn't ask any questions, she just got us both out of there, and when it came out in the paper, it was written up as a tragic accident. There were drugs and alcohol in his system and people, they just assumed that he fell I suppose, or that he threw himself over. No one ever mentioned that Eva and I were even there. It just goes to show what money and influence can buy, I guess."

She looks away at that, and then buries her face in her tea so that her glasses mist with steam.

"I couldn't stay after that," she says, very quietly. "I left Snoop—and I never looked back. I went to work somewhere completely different, a banking call center. It became like this horrible nightmarish episode in my life that was done and gone. Until the buyout happened. And I was dragged back into all of this."

"I'm so sorry," I say again, and it's true. I *am* sorry. Sorry for that poor kid dragged into a world she didn't understand.

But I still don't completely understand. She was assaulted. She was trying to get away from an attacker. And even if Liz didn't trust the court to believe that, and I can see why she wouldn't, why did Eva have to die? She kept Liz's secret.

And then, in a horrible, blinding flash, I get it.

Topher was the one who gave Liz those shares, on the tacit understanding that she would back him up if it ever came to a crunch like this. She owed him everything.

But Eva—Eva knew something about Liz that could ruin her. At the very least, she would be embroiled in a messy, public court case, and I know enough about Liz to know that that would be torture to her. At the worst, she might be looking at a manslaughter charge, and prison.

Whether she articulated it or not, Eva was the one who covered up what happened. She held that evidence in her hands. And she must have been holding that fact over Liz's head all these years.

No wonder Liz could never find the courage to say how she was planning to vote.

She could vote to betray her mentor, the man who hired her, stuck up for her, got her the shares in the first place.

Or she could vote against the person who held her life in her hands. The person who could send her to prison to rot.

When the realization comes, it's with a twisted lurch of sympathy for Liz.

I think of that poor, young girl—fresh out of university, swimming in waters far too strange and dangerous for her to navigate. Because Liz was the victim not of one horrible situation—but of two. Eva had helped her out of one nightmare, only to create another of her own making—blackmailing the girl she had professed to help.

Of course Liz did the sensible thing. She told Eva that she was voting with her. But what about next time? And the time after that? How could she live her life knowing that Eva had this secret to hold over her head anytime she needed something Liz was unwilling to give?

No. She needed to make herself safe forever. She needed to get rid of the person who had started all this, the only person who knew her secret.

She needed to kill Eva.

LIZ

Snoop ID: ANON101
Listening to: Offline
Snoopscribers: 1

"So that's it," I say at last. I put my tea to my lips for a long time, pretending to gulp it thirstily down.

Erin is staring at me, but I can't tell what her expression is. It looks slightly horrified—but that could be sympathetic horror at what I've been through. Does she believe me? I can't decide.

Don't you want to drink your tea? I want to ask, but I can't say that. It would sound suspicious. Instead, I raise my cup to my lips again, hoping to convey the message by subliminal suggestion. To my delight, it works. Erin picks up the cup. I see the muscles of her throat work as she swallows.

"So you had no choice," she says faintly, and I try to arrange my face in the expression I think she will expect to see. A kind of . . . pained regret. And it's true—I do regret this. That night, most of all.

"I never wanted any of this," I say. "I just feel like I've been swept up in something awful and horrible."

Erin shakes her head, but not like she is telling me she doesn't believe me. More like she's condemning whatever brought us here.

She is staring down into her cup. I can't see her face very well. That bothers me, but then she takes another sip of tea, and I begin to feel more relaxed.

I put my own cup to my lips too, in order not to seem suspicious. I'm careful not to actually swallow any of the liquid inside.

"I've worked out what you did," Erin says, as she puts the cup on her knees, nursing it with her hands. I can see from where I'm sitting that it's half empty, and I begin to feel more confident. "It was very clever. You had a ski jacket like Eva's. You met her at the top of the lift—"

She pauses, and I know why. She is trying not to spell out what I did, as if it will offend me in some strange way. But it's okay. I have to live with what happened, there is no point in not facing up to it.

I was waiting at the top of the lift when Eva got off, right by the barrier where I had pretended to lose control and almost ski over the edge with Rik earlier that day. Of course, I didn't lose control at all. It was a deliberate slide to give myself the chance to check out the edge up there. I wanted to see if it was as close as I remembered, to see if the barrier had been raised since my last visit, two years ago.

Nothing had changed. It was perfect.

The irony is I'm actually a very good skier. But Topher and Rik and the others were all too willing to believe that a girl from a Crawley comprehensive wouldn't know one end of a ski pole from the other. The truth, had they ever bothered to ask me, is that I loved skiing—right from the first time I went on a school trip, at age fifteen. I had never set foot on a ski slope before, but I remember the teacher saying admiringly, "You're a natural, Liz!"

And I was. I am not sporty, as a rule. I don't do well with anything that requires teamwork, or running in circles. I disliked getting red-faced and sweaty, everything jiggling unpleasantly under a sticky T-shirt, while girls shouted at me to pass the ball, no not that way, oh for God's sake Liz! Until I wanted to run away and hide from them all.

But skiing was different. Skiing is solo—and it is strategic. You have to think on your feet, making split-second decisions that could save your life or send you hurtling down a sheer slope at a hundred kilometers an hour.

I loved it.

I managed to go back again during my A-levels, and twice at university—the very cheapest trips I could manage: coach to Bulgaria, to stay in a Soviet-era concrete monolith; Ryanair to Romania, to a self-catering Airbnb with hot-air vents that smelled of ham. But it was worth it. It was worth the scrimping and the saving and the long nights spent crunched into economy coach seats, barreling down German autobahns in the middle of the night.

They did a corporate ski trip when I was at Snoop, wooing investors. Of course, they didn't invite me. But since I left Snoop, since I have been earning my own money, I have been back to the Alps every year, sometimes twice. And I have become a very, very good skier. Not quite as good as Eva, who has been skiing every year since she was a toddler. But almost. And I have been to St. Antoine twice. I know La Sorcière very well indeed.

When she got off the lift, I was over by the barrier. I called out to her, pretending that I was in some kind of difficulty, and when she skied over I waited until she was right next to me, bending over, looking at the binding of my boot, and then I gave her an almighty push, toppling her backwards over the shallow safety barrier.

The barrier caught her in the back of her knees and she went down like a skittle and landed in the thick, untouched snow, right on the edge of the precipice, her skis windmilling in the air. For a minute I didn't think it had worked. I thought she was going to stay, sprawled on the narrow ledge of snow, crawl her way back to the barrier, ask me what the hell I was playing at.

But then there was an imperceptible sound—like a sigh. The snow ledge began to shift and tilt, and a crack appeared at the top.

For a second I saw Eva, frozen in horror, looking up at me, holding out her arms like I was going to be her savior—and then the whole ledge gave way, and she was gone.

I waited for a moment, and then I unzipped my jumpsuit and pulled out the scarlet jacket I was wearing underneath. I put it on over the top of my navy blue ski suit, pulled my scarf up, and settled my goggles over my face. Then turned my skis to face down the run, and I began to ski La Sorcière.

I would be lying if I said it wasn't difficult. It was. Its twists and turns, full of sheer drops, heart-stopping hairpin bends and vertical ice sheets where I couldn't do anything but a kind of controlled fall. If I hadn't known the run well, I think it would have killed me. But I have never skied better.

I stopped halfway down to catch my breath and wait for the trembling in my legs to subside, and it was then that I saw Carl and Ani, traveling high above in the bubble. I looked up, safe in the knowledge that my goggles were pulled up and my hat was pulled down, and that no one could possibly tell who was wearing the distinctive scarlet ski jacket. I waved my ski pole, establishing my alibi, and Ani saw me, and waved back.

It was just my luck that she saw something else too: the empty bubble lifts making their way back to the valley floor. The bubble lifts that should have been taking *me* back to St. Antoine.

I saw the recognition in her eyes that night when she came to my room. I saw her literally put two and two together standing there in the doorway, the puzzlement changing to horror as she made her excuses. Suddenly she didn't want to speak to me anymore. She wanted to get away—figure out what to do, and short of putting a hand over her mouth and dragging her into my room, I couldn't think of any other alternative. So I let her go.

I knew then what I had to do. I thanked my lucky stars for Tiger's insomnia, and the instinct that had prompted me to pocket the passkey when Danny left it in the door earlier that day.

Although that wasn't luck really, was it. The truth is, I am not a lucky person. Yes, the Tiger thing went my way—but so much else has gone against me. And the passkey—that wasn't luck. That was *me.* A split-second decision that looked like it was about to save my skin.

Because the thing is, I may not be lucky. But I *am* good at thinking on my feet. Perhaps that is why I like skiing so much. It is the same skills, the same twisting and turning, the same heart-pounding excitement. The same drop in your stomach when you realize you've made a stupid mistake, and then the same lift of excitement when you realize you can maneuver your way out of it.

I felt bad about Ani though. Bad in a way that I didn't about Elliot. Elliot deserved what happened to him. He didn't have to poke, and pry. That was his choice. Ani's choice was no choice at all—she was in the wrong place at the wrong time, just like me. And that is a tragedy. But it's not my fault. I have to remember that. None of this is my fault.

"Wh-what did you say?" Erin asks me, and I realize I must have muttered some of those words aloud. I'm about to answer when I look at Erin more carefully. She appears almost . . . drunk. She is listing to one side.

"Nothing, don't worry. Are you tired?" I ask. I am trying not to sound too hopeful. She nods.

"Yes, I feel—" Her voice is slurred, and when she blinks, it is as if her facial muscles are moving in slow motion. "I feel really sh-strange."

"You must be exhausted," I say. I try to sound soothing, but my heart is beating faster with excitement. I put my untouched tea down on the table and wipe the dregs off my mouth, and I peer into Erin's cup. It is all but empty. "Why don't you lie down?"

"I feel strange . . . ," she says again, but her voice trails off. She lets me help her to lie horizontally on the sofa. Her body is heavy. I have no idea how many pills she has drunk. Three or four, maybe? I had eight left and I put them all into the kettle, trusting to the boiling water to dissolve them. I had no idea whether the heat would damage the chemicals, but I knew that Erin would be on the lookout for me tampering with her cup, and I was right—she watched me like a hawk as I put in the tea bag and poured out the water.

The kettle was my only chance—slipping the pills in one by one as I packed in the snow, relying on the white snow to camouflage the white pills, and the strong, unfamiliar taste of milkless tea to mask any odd taste. And, almost unbelievably, it seems to have worked. Erin has drunk the whole cup. Elliot had five, ground up in his cup, and it killed him. Erin is smaller and lighter, and she had about half the water, which means approximately four pills. Four should be enough, assuming the heat of the water hasn't degraded the active ingredient. I will have to make sure of that. I can't take her silence for granted. But first there is something I have to do. Something quite urgent.

With a sideways glance at Erin, who is lying sprawled on the sofa, drool coming out of the side of her mouth, I leave the living room. I run as quickly as I dare up the stairs to Elliot's room. The door is unlocked, and I open his phone again. Then I navigate to the text messaging app, and Erin's message to Danny. *SOS. Please send help. IT'S LIZ.*

His reply is still there. *Fuck. Erin is that you?*

The precipice is in front of me—and expertly, I swerve to avoid it.

No, I type. *I already told you—this is LIZ. Erin has just confessed everything—and she's talking about killing herself. PLEASE COME NOW.*

And then I press send.

ERIN

Snoop ID: LITTLEMY
Listening to: Offline
Snoopscribers: 10

I lie completely still, listening as Liz peers into my cup and then stands over me, breathing heavily. Then she seems to make up her mind, and I hear the soft sound of her socked feet retreating into the lobby and the creak as she begins to make her way up the stairs.

I hold still for as long as I can bear, and then I sit upright, wincing at every rustle of fabric, every squeak of the sofa springs.

My arm and thigh are drenched with tea—but thank God, Liz didn't seem to notice the spreading dampness on the sofa, only the empty cup.

The pills were in the kettle. I suspected as soon as I tasted the first gulp of tea—there was a strange, chemical acridity, and a very faint sweetness that must have come from the sugarcoating. And when I saw Liz putting the cup to her lips but only pretending to drink, I was certain of it. After that, I knew what I had to do. I had to pretend to drink too—taking advantage of the cover of darkness to slop the tea down my arm, onto the sofa, every time Liz turned away.

I had no way of knowing how long the pills should take to work—

but I had to gamble on Liz's ignorance too. She would have no way of knowing exactly what concentration I had taken, or how quickly it would take effect. Ten minutes? Fifteen? Whichever, she seemed to buy my performance of slipping into incoherence, and then unconsciousness.

Everything hinges now on whether she gave me enough to kill me. If she thinks she's given me a fatal dose, I'll be safe for a little while longer—at least until she comes back and notices I'm still breathing. But if she's only given me enough to knock me out, she'll be coming back very soon to finish me off. Will it be a pillow over the face like Ani, or a blow to the head, covered up as a fall down the stairs? Or something completely different?

Either way, I don't want to find out. I *have* to get away, and the sooner the better.

Holding my breath, listening out for any sound from above, I hobble as swiftly and quietly as I can through the lobby, to the door behind the stairs, the one that leads to the ski lockers. My own ski clothes are up in my room, and I can't risk trying to get to it, but my boots and skis are down in the storage lockers, and there should be enough spare clothing strewn around for me to put together an outfit that will at least keep me warm enough to ski in. I don't have nearly enough layers to survive a night in the open, and I can't walk on this ankle. I will *have* to get down to St. Antoine. But how? Skiing is the only option, and hope to God that the ski boot gives my ankle enough support to do it.

The door to the locker room opens with the gentle click, and I slide through, and close it with infinite care, my heart beating hard. It's very dark inside, the moonlight filtering faintly through a window almost completely blocked with snow, but my eyes are used to the darkness, and I'm able to pick out the vague shapes of jackets and ski pants hanging from pegs, and boots drying on their once-heated poles. Hastily, my heart thumping in my throat, I yank on a pair of salopettes. It's only when I look down at myself that I realize—they belonged to Ani. The thought that I'm literally stepping into a dead girl's clothes makes my stomach lurch with guilt. But I can't let myself get sentimental about this. Ani is gone—I can't save her. But maybe I can bring her killer to justice.

As I struggle into someone's ski jacket—Elliot's, I think, judging by the size—I remember Liz's self-pitying whine as she told me about everything that had happened. And the thing is, I could *almost* have bought it. I don't know for sure what happened on that balcony—but I could believe that part of it, the frightened girl, the desperate shove. And I could believe too her cornered fear as she realized that Eva had her trapped—and her terrified reaction.

But Elliot—no. And most of all Ani. Poor little Ani, killed as she slept for nothing more than having seen something Liz didn't want her to see.

Whatever Liz thinks about Eva, and that unnamed investor, and maybe even Elliot—Ani, out of everyone, *didn't* deserve this. She couldn't have.

Only a monster could have killed Ani.

It's Ani's face that I see before me now as I pull on wet ski socks, and search around for mittens.

Ani's face, speckled with the scarlet dots that give the lie to Liz's story.

Because Liz says that she never wanted Ani to die—but I know that's not true. Ani must have fought. She fought for every breath, so hard that blood vessels broke in her skin.

And Liz stood there, and pressed the pillow down over her face, all that long, long time.

You have to *want* someone to die to kill them by suffocation. You have to want it a *lot*.

It's Ani I'm thinking of as I open up my ski boot as wide as it will go. Ani, as I shove my foot inside, gritting my teeth as the pain in my ankle flares suddenly, bright and hot.

My breath is whimpering between my teeth, little sobs of pain coming in spite of the need for silence as I force my foot around the curve of the boot, hearing the bones in my feet click and grind in protest, feeling the swollen flesh squeezing against the hard plastic shell. But I have to do this. I *have* to.

Ani. Ani. Ani.

And then with a crunch, my foot slides into place. I'm sweating and shaking with the pain, cold perspiration on my upper lip. But my foot is in. And, miraculously, when I try to stand, the pain isn't as bad as I thought it would be; the top of the boot is tight enough that I'm taking some of my weight on my shin rather than my ankle. I ratchet the boot clips as tight as I can, praying that the support will keep the joint stable for long enough to make it down the valley. If I have broken a bone, I may end up lame for good after this—but it's better than dead.

Hastily, I shove my other foot into its boot and clip it up.

And then I hear a noise from the stairs.

My heart seems to stop. It's Liz coming down the spiral staircase.

For a second I freeze. I have everything I need—but can I get out the back entrance? The ski door faces the same way as the swimming pool, and it will have been blocked by the avalanche.

It opens inwards. At least . . . I'm pretty certain it does. I press my hands to my temples, trying to remember. Does it? If it opens outwards I'm screwed, regardless. But I'm sure it opens inwards. The question is whether I can dig my way out.

And then my eyes go to the narrow little window above the ski lockers. It's letter box–shaped, and although it's certainly long enough, it's probably only twelve inches high, less when you take into account the frame and the hinges. But it might be my best bet.

Wincing at every sound, I climb up onto the wooden bench, and from there I lean over the ski lockers and open the window. A freezing blast scours my face, but I can see that the aperture isn't blocked—the snow obscuring the glass was just drifting flakes sticking to the pane. There is a drift almost up to the top of the lockers—but that will cushion my fall.

I push my skis out first, one by one, listening as they tip into the soft snow with a *flump*. Then my poles. I pull on the borrowed mittens, and grab a helmet at random from the rack. It fits, thank God, because I don't have time to pick and choose. And then I climb up to lie flat along the top of the lockers. They rock precariously—but only for a moment.

I feel sick with nerves. From somewhere in the chalet I hear a cry of surprise—and then a shout of "Erin? . . . Erin, where are you?"

Liz has discovered that I'm gone.

I slide my legs out first. I am apprehensive about falling onto my bad ankle, but the alternative is dropping face-first into the snow, and I don't fancy that either. Okay, I'm wearing a helmet, but the fall could still break my neck, or if the drift is deep enough, I might plunge in vertically and suffocate before I could dig myself out. Feet first is safer.

It's a squeeze, but I am managing. One boot, sideways, my good leg first, then the other. The weight of the boot hanging off my bad ankle makes me gasp, but it's bearable, just.

And then the locker room door opens.

I can't see anything at first because she's holding a torch—Elliot's phone, I think—and it's shining full in my face. But I can see the shape of a figure in the doorway, and I know who it is before she runs towards me with a snarl of anger that sounds more animal than human.

I feel her hands grappling my arms, snatching, scratching, but her nails slide off the thick, smooth fabric, and there is nothing for her to catch hold of. I force my bum through the narrow gap, and then my body weight does the rest, dragging me after—until I stick, with a sickening jolt.

For a split second I can't work out what's happened. Has Liz shut the window? Has she grabbed my helmet? Then I realize.

Fuck. The helmet won't fit.

I am hanging from my neck, and I'm beginning to choke, the strap of the helmet is digging into my jaw and throat, and I'm twisting like a fish on a line. My mittened hands are at my neck, desperately trying to relieve the pressure of the strap. My feet are scrambling in the soft snow, frantic to get enough purchase to loosen the strain on my throat.

My foot finds something, loses it again, and then finds it once more, just for a second—just long enough for me to unclip the strap.

And then I fall, gasping and retching, into a heap of soft snow and painful obstructions that after a minute or two I identify as my own skis and poles.

There is no time to recover.

Liz is yanking furiously at the helmet, stuck in the aperture, trying to pull it free so that she can follow me. I expect her to shout or swear, but she doesn't, and somehow that's more terrifying. She says nothing, all I can hear is her grunting breath as she struggles to get the helmet out of the window. I *have* to get away before she pulls it free.

I manage to stumble to my feet, sinking into the snow as I do, and using my skis as crutches I stagger down the drift to the hard-packed snow.

There, I take a split-second inventory. Mittens—yes. Skis—yes, both. And my poles.

Scarf—gone. It must have got pulled off with the helmet. And no hat of course. I don't wear one now—the helmet is usually warm enough, but with the cold wind scouring my cheeks and face I know I'm going to regret that. Still, there is nothing I can do. I can't turn back. I have to make it down to St. Antoine, somehow.

I also have no avalanche pack.

Fuck. *Fuck.* Which way?

Slowly, painfully, I drag myself and my skis around to the side of the chalet, and survey the piste.

The long blue down into St. Antoine is a wreck—there is no other way to describe it. I saw the top of the run when Danny and I made our way painfully back from the crushed funicular—the avalanche has dumped everything straight down it—huge boulders, lift poles, tree trunks. It's not just unskiable—it's impassable. And the path through the woods to the green run, Atchoum, is totally inaccessible—the little copse has taken the full force of the avalanche and the trees are crushed and obliterated, buried under a hundred tonnes of snow.

But there is another way.

It's called the Secret Valley, or at least, that's what the English skiers call it. I don't think it has an official name—it's not a piste, just an unofficial route that you can *just* about ski if the conditions are right, and if you're very good and you enjoy a challenge. Besides, "piste" gives completely the wrong impression anyway—it conjures up the image of a flat apron of snow, with skiers crisscrossing each other with elegant turns. This is nothing like that. It's a long couloir between two sheer rock walls, formed by a deep crevasse in the mountains. It needs a lot of snow to blanket the jagged boulders at the bottom, and even when conditions are good, the path at the bottom is so narrow that it can only take a single skier, and in places if you reach out, you can touch both sides with your fingertips.

If I can get down to it, I think it will be passable—surely we've had enough snow to cover the worst of the jagged rocks, and it's out of the path of the main avalanche.

But it's not a run so much as an obstacle course—a twisting, turning slalom of boulders and tree trunks, hard enough to navigate in daylight, let alone with no light but the moon. It's also very prone to mini avalanches—the snow builds up on the ridges above, and breaks off without warning, deluging the skiers below.

That's not the worst part though. The worst part, the part that is making me hesitate, is that once you're down there—there is no way out. The sides of the crevasse rise higher, and higher, and there is no way of getting a helicopter or a blood wagon down to someone trapped there. You just have to keep going, until the chute spits you out among the trees at the top of the village.

It is my best chance. And Liz very likely doesn't know about it. There's no way of finding it unless someone shows you the entrance.

It's also my worst nightmare.

But I have no choice.

Holding my skis like a crutch, I begin to walk towards the head of the pass.

LIZ

Snoop ID: ANON101
Listening to: Offline
Snoopscribers: 1

Erin is missing.

I almost don't notice. When I first walk into the living room, I am so sure she will be there that it doesn't even occur to me to check. But then something catches at the corner of my vision—something that is not quite as I left it. When I turn around I see what has changed, the sofa is empty.

For a moment I just stand there, too puzzled to be worried. Has she woken up? Stumbled to the toilet?

"Erin?" I shout. I go back into the lobby. I stare around the dark space, shining my torch up the stairs, into the kitchen. "Erin, where are you?"

She cannot have gone far. She drank enough of those pills to knock her out for a week.

It is only when I go back into the living room that I see the dark spreading stain on the sofa. I touch it and sniff my fingers. It smells of *tea*. That is when I understand. She never drank the tea at all.

I don't often swear, but I do when I see this, and I realize how she tricked me.

I run. First to the door in the lobby, but the snow outside is untouched. She hasn't left the building by that route at any rate.

Then into the kitchen—but she is not there either.

I am halfway upstairs, ready to check the bedrooms, when I hear a noise. It is very faint, but it sounds like something falling onto the snow outside. It is coming from the back of the building, where the ski entrance is.

I make my way back down to the lobby and I open the door to the rear part of the building, where all the ski lockers are. It takes a moment for my eyes to get used to the darkness—and then I see something—or someone—moving at the far side of the room. It is Erin. She has climbed up on top of the ski lockers, and she is almost out of the window.

I hurl myself across the locker room, scramble up the bench she has placed below the window, ignoring the twinges in my knee, and grab hold of her helmet, which is just about to disappear through the window.

Then I realize why she is still there. The helmet won't fit through the gap. She is stuck. She is dangling from the helmet, horrible wheezing noises coming from her throat, kicking and kicking to try and get enough purchase on the snow to twist free.

But before I have had time to figure out what to do, there is a sudden jerk, and the weight on the helmet falls away. The catch has broken—or she has unclipped herself, I am not sure which. For a second she lies, gasping and winded in the snow, and then she staggers to her feet, picks up her skis, and begins to hobble off towards the front of the chalet and the path that leads up to the funicular.

I have to *follow* her, but the helmet is stuck in the frame, blocking it. It is only after a few minutes of fruitless tugging that I realize, this is stupid. Erin has her skis and poles. She is clearly intending to ski to St. Antoine—and I have to stop her.

I have to ski after her.

Letting go of the helmet, I turn back to the room. I am wearing my jumpsuit already. All I need are boots, skis, and mittens. *Fast,* before Erin gets away.

I have two realizations to comfort me—first, in the soft snow, she won't be able to hide her tracks. I will be able to tell exactly which way she has gone.

And second, I can ski faster than her. My wrenched knee has almost recovered, while her ankle has only been getting worse. I saw the way she hobbled back from the kitchen with the tea just a couple of hours ago. She couldn't put any real weight on it at all. I am pretty sure it is broken—and there is no way she can ski aggressively with a broken ankle. She will have to go slowly and carefully, and it will take her a long time to clamber over the broken-up snow at the beginning of the blue piste. I saw what it looked like after the avalanche—a mess of rubble and debris. It will take a while to pick her way through that, even if it clears further down. I will be able to catch up to her. *If* I act quickly.

I make up my mind. I ram my feet into my boots and grab my skis and poles from the rack. My mittens are in the pocket of my jumpsuit. But my helmet—where *is* my helmet? It's missing from the locker, and after a few seconds I realize: it's the one that Erin took, and it is wedged into the window.

I have another go at trying to free it, but it's useless, and I cast around for an alternative before realizing that I am wasting time. If Erin gets too much of a head start, even with her ankle, I won't catch her.

Shoving Elliot's phone into my pocket, I hoist my skis onto my shoulder and clack-clack my way back along the corridor to the lobby, where I open the door into the snow, and squeeze into the night.

It is unbelievably cold outside, and I realize that however chilly the chalet was without heating, it was actually doing a pretty good job of protecting us from the elements.

Now, out here, I don't know what the temperature is, but it can't be much over minus twenty. Maybe even less. The sky is clear, and the moon has that strange frost halo around it that you only get in extreme cold.

Shivering, even in my warm jumpsuit, I clip my boots into my ski bindings and then straighten up, looking around for Erin's tracks.

There they are—deep slashes of furrowed snow, dark against the moonlit white.

But they are not leading up the track to the smashed-up blue piste. They are going the other way, into the forest.

ERIN

Snoop ID: LITTLEMY
Listening to: Offline
Snoopscribers: 10

I had forgotten the beginning. Oh God, the beginning. It's like a sheer wall of thick, soft snow, hemmed in with trees, studded with boulders, narrowing to a steep path just a few feet wide. And taking the first step is basically like jumping off the edge of a cliff and trusting to the snow to hold you.

With two good legs I could do this—probably not elegantly, but I could do this. I'm rusty, but I've done enough off-piste skiing that I am pretty confident in my technique. I know how to manage the deep, dragging snow, how to navigate the heavy turns, how to avoid plunging into drifts and how to keep up momentum.

I know all that in theory. It's just that it's more than three years since I've skied off-piste. And I don't know if I can put any of it into practice with a broken ankle.

My heart is in my mouth. But Liz will have seen my tracks in the snow. She'll be following after me. I *have* to do this.

My downhill leg will be bearing most of my weight. I clip my ski boots into their bindings, and then turn and angle myself so that my good ankle is down the slope. Then, with a sick feeling, I tip off.

At first it goes okay. I schuss sideways in the fresh, fluffy snow, feeling like someone trying to swim with a duvet around their legs. But I'm heading rapidly towards the trees. I'm going to have to turn—onto my bad leg.

I manage an awkward kind of parallel turn, but I'd forgotten the physicality of skiing in thick drifts. The snow drags at my skis, nearly sending me over, but the real problem is the shock as I complete the turn and land on my bad leg. It sends prickles of pain up and down my spine, and I hastily turn back, trying to keep my sound leg down the slope.

But it's no good—I have to turn again to avoid a tree that looms out of the darkness, and this time my trailing ski catches in a drift, twisting my ankle with such excruciating force that I scream, the noise echoing off the steep walls of the valley. I land heavily on my bad leg, try to save myself with a flailing pole, and then—I don't know what happens after that. All I know is that my leg gives way and my pole sinks, and I am falling, tumbling in the soft snow, my arms around my head to try to protect myself from the half-buried boulders that stud the slope.

One ski is ripped off, my poles are wrenching at my wrists, I am upright, and then head down, then sliding bum first, then I somersault—and land with a bone-shaking jolt against a rock, at the bottom of the pass.

For a second I can't do anything except lie there, gasping, winded, trying not to shriek from the pain pulsing through my leg. But I have to move.

My spine makes a sound like crunching glass when I try to sit up, and I think I might throw up from the pain in my ankle—but I can see straight. I'm not concussed. At least, I don't think I am. And when I drag myself to kneeling the pain in my leg is intense, but it's still bearable. Just.

I pull myself to standing using one pole and then I rest for a moment, panting, shivering with shock and pain, forcing myself to breathe long and slow. It works . . . to a point. Then when I'm calm enough, I shake the snow out of my hair and collar and take stock. I have one ski still on, and I'm holding one of my poles. The other is leaning against a rock on the far side of the gully, and I hobble across and grab it with hands that are still shaking with adrenaline. Okay. This is good.

The other ski though . . . where is it? I could ski with one pole, but I can't do anything with only one ski. If I can't find the missing ski, I'm screwed.

And then I see it. The tip is sticking out of the snow a few feet up the cliff face I just fell down. I sigh, unclip my remaining ski, and crawl up the soft, shifting side of the crevasse to try to pull it out, but it's too deep, the bindings are stuck against something deep in the snow, and so I begin to dig with my mittened hands. And suddenly, out of nowhere, I am hit with a sickening, jolting flashback—the most vivid I've had since those first, awful days when I woke up sweating every morning, fresh from a relived nightmare.

Digging. Digging through the snow. Will's hair. The end of his ski. His cold, waxen face . . .

Nausea rises in my throat.

I push it away.

I scrabble at the snow with my fingers.

The snow in his eyelashes, the frozen tip of his nose . . .

I want to sob, but I can't. I can't afford to make any more noise than I already have. Liz could be very near.

The torn edge of his scarf. His blue lips—

And then I have the ski. The bindings are clear of the snow, and I can pull the rest of it out of the hole.

Every part of me is shaking as I slide back down the slope to where I left my other ski. My teeth are chattering, my hands are trembling so hard that I can't get them through the loops in my poles, and I have to try to force my boots into the bindings six or seven times before I finally hear the answering click and feel the firmness of the clasp.

When it's done I just stand for a moment, resting wearily on my poles, giving my poor, quivering muscles a moment's respite. I'm honestly not sure if it's pain, or exhaustion, or the memory of Will's and Alex's deaths that's getting to me most. Maybe it's all three. But I can't allow myself to rest. I *can't.*

There is a noise from the slope above me. It might be a marmot, or just the snow I disturbed shifting and falling in my wake, but I can't afford to stay to find out.

I push off with my poles, and begin to ski cautiously into the mouth of the pass.

LIZ

Snoop ID: ANON101
Listening to: Offline
Snoopscribers: 1

Have I made a mistake? Erin's tracks stop at the top of what looks like a sheer drop into a gully below. The ravine itself is in deep shadow, and I can't see the bottom. There could be anything down there—jagged rocks, a mountain stream, a thousand-foot drop . . .

And yet, when I peer closer, I can see marks in the snow. Something—or maybe someone—has been down here. I can't believe that anything except for a mountain goat could make it down this slope in one piece, but as my eyes adjust to the shadows, I can see two deep grooves in the snow that look like someone sat back on their skis, catching their breath, before making a turn.

I stand, hesitating, wondering what to do. Surely Erin hasn't skied down here with a broken ankle? Even for someone experienced in off-piste skiing, it looks like suicide.

But her tracks definitely lead here. And they definitely stop here. Did she climb down? No. Whoever went down there was wearing skis. Did she *fall* down? If she did, my problems may be solved.

Or is it some kind of elaborate trick?

I pause for a moment, looking up and down the valley, but I can't see how it could be a ruse. There are only two sets of tracks leading up to this cliff edge, Erin's and mine, and neither of them lead away. And she didn't have enough time to do anything Sherlock Holmes–like. If she had retraced her own footprints to lay a false trail, I would have met her coming the other way.

This *must* be a route down to St. Antoine. And somehow, Erin has managed to clamber down to it.

Well, if she can do it, so can I.

I am definitely not skiing down there. I don't care whether Erin did—I have not done enough off-piste skiing to trust myself on anything this steep. Instead, I unclip my skis and, holding them in one hand, I sit on the edge of the drop and lower myself down into the soft snow to try to walk down the precipice.

I know immediately that it was a mistake. Without skis to spread my weight, I sink deep, deep into the feathery drift. I scramble up, clawing for purchase, using my skis as a support, but as I struggle, the snow begins to shift underneath me. All of a sudden, it gives way, and we slither down the slope with terrifying speed—me, my skis, and a slippery, moving mass of snow. At first it is scary, but okay. I manage to stay upright, I can see where I am heading, and I am able to steer myself away from the trees, slow my descent—but then my boot catches on a rock. I can't stop myself. The weight of snow at my back is too great. I pitch forward. My skis are ripped from my hands. I am falling—falling in a terrifying white blur of snow and rocks and skis.

I have my arms wrapped around my head. I feel something hit my cheek, and my shoulder crunches against something hard. I think I scream. I think I am dying. This isn't how I wanted to die.

And then there is an almighty thump, and I realize I have stopped moving.

I am lying on my back, my head pointing down the slope, and

there is hot blood coming from my cheek. My shoulder is pulsing with pain. I think I may have broken my collarbone.

I try to pull myself to sitting, but the snow slithers treacherously beneath me, and I suppress a scream as I begin to fall again, but it grinds to a halt after just a few feet, and I lie, panting, sobbing with fear, before I realize that that last slide took me almost to the bottom of the slope. There is a path just a few feet below me. I can see one of my skis lying across it.

Slowly, painfully, I swivel myself around so that my boots are down the slope, and I let myself toboggan the last few feet. Then I am down. I am lying on the valley floor, practically crying with relief.

Everything hurts. I can taste blood in my mouth. But I am down. And now that I am at the shadowy bottom of the ravine, I can see that I was right, and the realization gives me a little pulse of excitement that helps take my mind off my throbbing shoulder.

Because I can see ski tracks in the snow leading away down the valley, towards St. Antoine. One set, pressed deep into the snow, marked with divots either side where the skier pulled themselves along with their poles.

Erin *was* here. And if I hurry, I can catch up.

ERIN

Snoop ID: LITTLEMY
Listening to: Offline
Snoopscribers: 10

This is harder than I could ever have believed. I remember doing this route in daylight—the sun sparkling from the frosted trees high up above, blazing back at us from the bright snow at our feet. I remember twisting, turning, laughing, leaping over half-buried boulders and dodging moguls.

I cannot see any of those now. Traps loom out of the darkness—tree branches that swipe at my face, jagged projections rearing up without warning so that I have to swerve with sickening force, my ankle screaming with every jolt and twist.

In a way, it helps that the gully is thick with fresh snow. It makes the skiing slow and arduous, and I have no tracks to guide me, but it means I don't have to constantly try to slow myself down. When I came this way last time, the route was hardpacked by skiers who had gone before me. I could see where they had twisted and turned, where they had misjudged an angle and wiped out against an unexpected tree, or plowed into a drift they didn't see coming. But at the same time, it made the going fast and furious, and with a track far too narrow for proper turns, most of my attention was taken up by trying to slow myself down to a safe pace.

The thick snow makes this much less of an issue. But it gives me an urgent problem. Liz will be coming up behind, skiing in my tracks, where I have already pressed down the snow. She will be going much faster. And she has my tracks to guide her.

I *have* to go faster. But if I do, I could end up killing myself.

I give myself a shove with my poles, ski around a tight turn, my ankle screaming with protest, and then thump over what must be a concealed hummock in the snow. The shock of agony that runs up my leg makes me cry out, and I wobble, and fall with a crash, thumping painfully into the rocky side of the couloir. For a few minutes I just lie there, panting, hot tears running down my face. I cannot believe how much this hurts. I don't dare open up the ski boot to find out what's inside, but I can feel my whole leg throbbing with my pulse. I don't know if I will be able to ski again, after this. I don't know if I will be able to *walk* again.

But Liz has killed three people already. I *have* to keep going.

I take a deep breath, and go to push myself up on my pole. But I can't do it. My muscles are shaking so hard, I can't make myself do it—I can't force myself to put weight on my leg again, it makes my whole body tremble when I think of doing it.

And then, from somewhere up the gully, I hear sounds. There's a cry—the sound of someone who has just been hit in the face by an unexpected branch, maybe—followed by the rough scrape of skis being forced into an emergency snowplow.

Liz is coming. And she is very close.

I have to do this. I *have* to do this.

I force my pole into the snow, and heave myself upright, sweating and shaking.

And then I push off.

LIZ

Snoop ID: ANON101
Listening to: Offline
Snoopscribers: 1

Where. Is. She.

Where. *Is.* She.

The words keep repeating inside my head as I twist and turn, doggedly following in Erin's tracks. She cannot have been that far ahead of me, and her ankle is in a much worse state than my knee. I *should* have caught up with her by now. But I haven't. And that fact is making me . . . not worried exactly. I am not at that point yet. But definitely frustrated.

Part of the frustration is because this is difficult skiing, more difficult than I had imagined it would be. Even after my eyes have got used to the moonlit dimness at the bottom of the crevasse, I can't see very much except for Erin's ski tracks, and I have no choice but to follow them blindly, as fast as I can, hoping that if she didn't mess up or wipe out, I won't either.

There is a long straight stretch coming up and I give myself a push with my poles and hunch down, making my body more aerodynamic. I feel the wind in my face, and then I thump into a mini mogul, invisible in the dim light. I feel air for a moment beneath my skis, and then I slam back down, all my weight on my bad knee in a way that makes me catch my breath. I ought to slow down, recover my balance, but before I can do so a tree branch comes out of nowhere, whipping me across the face so that I cry out.

I go into an instant, reflexive snowplow, the snow schussing beneath my skis, my heart thumping, and grind to a halt.

That was very close. If I hadn't been wearing goggles, that branch could have blinded me. As it is, it has opened the cut on my cheek again. I feel a ticklish trickle of hot blood run down my chin.

I cannot afford to stop though. I just have to be more careful. I push myself off again, peering into the darkness. I must be catching up. I *must* be.

Then, just a hundred meters further on, I hear it—the hissing sound of skis on snow. Someone up ahead is whisking around a tight turn, throwing up snow with the backs of their skis.

My pulse quickens, and I race to catch up.

ERIN

Snoop ID: LITTLEMY
Listening to: Offline
Snoopscribers: 10

It is very dark now, at the bottom of the gully. The rocky walls rise up so high that no moonlight makes it down, and there are tall pines leaning over the top, their canopy blocking out the sky. But I don't dare slow down.

This is the part of the run I remember the best. The part just before it shoots you out into the village. I must be almost there. Here is the long sliding turn that takes you up the side of the couloir, between two scraggly little saplings. I shoot up between them, trying to ignore the scream of my ankle, and the trembling thumps of my heart, flooded with more adrenaline than it knows how to cope with.

Then a swerve to the right.

And then—oh *fuck.*

I'm almost on it before I remember. What looks like a sheer rock wall, and a breakneck left turn, at a point in the path so narrow it's virtually impossible to slow yourself down.

Its blackness looms out of the dark, and I fling myself into a desperate sideways slide, my skis throwing up a glittering, hissing mist of crystals all around me. One ski catches on a rock and I almost lose control. My ankle is on fire with the pain, but I can't stop the frantic attempt to brake—if I hit the turn at this speed I won't just wipe out; without a helmet I will be dead.

I'm turning, I'm turning, my skis almost perpendicular to the slope—and then I'm round, and almost immediately I hit a tree root, my ankle gives way, and this time I do wipe out, in a tumbling flurry of skis and snow.

I have to get up. Liz is very near now. I can hear the hiss of her skis coming closer, the sound growing louder, funneled by the couloir. I *have* to get up. Only, when I try to push myself to standing, I can't do it. My ankle won't bear my weight. I try—and my knee goes out from under me. I try again, sobbing this time, no longer caring about the noise I'm making, and collapse into the snow, weeping and swearing.

She is almost here. She is coming, she is coming *fast.*

LIZ

Snoop ID: ANON101
Listening to: Offline
Snoopscribers: 1

I am very close to Erin now—and then I hear it. A cry from up ahead, and a clatter of skis. *Yes.* She has fallen!

I feel a surge of triumph, and it quickens my pace. This is going to be okay. I am going to catch her up! I don't think about what will happen when I do. Time for that later.

I crouch down again, I feel the wind in my face. This is it. I can *do* this.

I thump over a hummock, and I feel that same sense of exhilaration I did when I skied the black run, only this is even better. I am skiing by pure instinct now, like a bird, flying in a slipstream, wheeling and turning with effortless skill. It's almost—

And then it happens.

A wall of rock looming out of the darkness, just feet away.

I think I scream, I'm not sure—someone does.

I try, desperately, to snowplow—but the path is too narrow, and I'm not slowing down, I'm not slowing, I'm—

ERIN

Snoop ID: LITTLEMY
Listening to: Offline
Snoopscribers: 10

The sound when she hits is like nothing else I've ever heard.

It is the sound of skis snapping and bones breaking. It's the sound of flesh hitting rock.

It's wet and yielding, and it's hard as stone all at once.

Was she wearing a helmet? *Was she wearing a helmet?*

There is silence. Total, unbroken silence.

"Liz?" I call shakily, but there is no answer, not even a whimper.

I try to stand, but I can't. Pain roars up and down my leg and my ankle gives way.

I crouch on the snow, hunched on my side, trying not to throw up with the pain.

I know I should leave her, but I can't do that either.

I think of Danny's words before he left. *I know you . . . Don't be starting up with the bleeding-heart crap. Put yourself first.*

And I know he's right. But I can't do it. I can't leave her there to die, like Alex, like Will, alone in the snow.

I take off my poles. I unclip my ski boots from their bindings, and then I get onto my hands and knees and I begin to crawl, back up the pass, towards the turn.

LIZ

Snoop ID: ANON101

Listening to: Offline

Snoopscribers: 1

ERIN

Snoop ID: LITTLEMY
Listening to: Offline
Snoopscribers: 10

When I get there, the silence is complete.

Liz is lying on her side at the foot of the cliff, a crumpled heap of red, white, and blue. The blue is her jumpsuit, the white is the snow, and the red . . . the red is *everywhere.*

She has been bleeding out over the snow, but it has stopped now. In the time it took me to crawl the twenty feet back up the pass, Liz has died. There is no breath coming from between her broken lips. When I put my fingers to the side of her neck, the skin is warm and slick with blood, but there is no pulse, not even a flicker.

For a minute I think about trying the impossible—chest compressions, mouth-to-mouth . . . but when I turn her very gently onto her back, what I see makes me fall back, choked with horror. The left-hand side of her skull is smashed in like an egg, and there is brain matter on the snow.

I feel faintness wash over me, a great wave of revulsion and nausea that leaves me crouched and rocking on the ground, hugging my own knees, a tearing sound in my ears that I know must be my own sobs, but which sound like they are coming from someone else completely.

I don't know how much time passes. I only know that two things shake me out of my catatonic despair.

The first is that the sun is beginning to come up. The ravine is too deep for the rays to penetrate down here, but faint pink streaks of light are beginning to pattern the clouds above.

And the second . . . the second is that I can hear a buzzing.

For a minute I can't think what it is. It sounds like a phone, but I don't have one—my own phone is miles up in the mountains, back in Chalet Perce-Neige, with a battery as dead and cold as all the bodies Liz has left scattered behind her.

The buzzing stops, and then it starts again—and this time I realize. Liz. It's coming from Liz's pocket.

Her jumpsuit is soaked with frozen blood, but I know I have to do this, and I reach across, my arms stiff with cold, and touch her hip. I pull open the zip, my mittened fingers numb and clumsy, and something slithers out onto the snow, something bright as a jewel, with a jangling sound that makes tears start to my eyes.

It's Elliot's phone.

It is ringing.

And the caller is Danny.

ERIN

Snoop ID: LITTLEMY
Listening to: Pixies / Where Is My Mind
Snoopers: 8
Snoopscribers: 151

I don't know how long I lay there, side by side with Liz in the slushy puddle of her fast-freezing blood. I only know that when the rescuers finally trekked up the gorge with their stretchers, I was almost hypothermic, and I couldn't answer their questions.

It was Danny who kept me going through those long hours, his voice in my ear, talking, talking, telling me that they were on their way, that I just had to hang on, not to give up. But when the rescue party finally arrived and pried the phone from my frozen mitten, slicked over with a sheen of bloody ice, he couldn't tell them what had happened either.

It wasn't until two days later that I was finally able to piece it together for them—explain the abandoned chalet, the cryptic texts, and headlong flight down the treacherous couloir. But even I couldn't explain everything. Because, how do you explain someone like Liz?

To explain is to assign a reason for something, to make sense of behavior, to justify it, in a way.

And I cannot, *will* not justify what Liz did.

I am discharged from hospital after a few days, but I can't go home. Partly because I don't want to—I am twenty-two. I don't want to go back to my childhood bedroom, with its posters of long-forgotten bands, and its photographs, Will and Alex permanent ghosts hovering just out of the corner of my eye.

But partly because I literally *can't.* The police haven't finished processing the crime scene that Perce-Neige has become, and they've asked everyone concerned to remain in the area, at least until their preliminary investigations are complete. We aren't suspects—at least, I don't think we are, so there's nothing legally preventing us from returning to the UK. But it would look very bad to be impeding the investigation, and everyone knows that.

It's clearly impossible to go back to the chalet as long as it's a crime scene, so I accept with some relief the police's offer of accommodation at a hotel in St. Antoine le Lac. It is only when I arrive, plastic bag of belongings in my hand, that I realize what this offer means.

It's where they have put *everyone.* Topher. Rik. Miranda. Danny. Carl. Tiger. Even Inigo.

In fact it's Inigo that I see first when I step through the door into the reception area, and my mouth falls open.

"Inigo!"

I pull out my earbuds, and he turns from where he is inexpertly attempting to sort out internet access with the French-speaking receptionist. When he sees me, he flushes a deep unflattering red, so dark it's almost purple. The flush doesn't suit him, and it tones down his extraordinary good looks into something approaching normality.

"Um, excusez-moi, please," he says, awkwardly to the girl behind the counter. "Un moment. Je—I mean—I need to—God, Erin, what must you—let me take your bag."

He gestures at the crutch I'm using, at my ankle in its surgical boot, and grabs for the plastic bag I'm holding in my free hand.

"It's okay," I say, laughing, though the situation isn't really funny.

"My ankle's fine. I mean—it's not fine, it's broken, but I can walk again now that I've got a cast."

"No but still," he says wretchedly. He ushers me over to the 1970s woolen couch in the corner of reception and we sit down, facing each other, like awkward guests on a talk show. For the first time I see that he has a surgical dressing on his forehead, and two black eyes. Has he been in a fight? "Erin, you must have thought—you must think—I mean, God, I was a total idiot. I'm so sorry. I'm so, so sorry."

"Sorry for what?" I say, taken aback.

"For going off and leaving you all like that! I had no idea that Liz—that she—"

"Inigo, it wasn't your fault!"

"But it *was*. I mean not Liz—but if I hadn't been such an idiot with the phone call Ani might still, she might still—"

He stops, and I realize that he's very close to crying, and is trying desperately to master himself. I also realize that I have no idea what he's talking about. In fact I have no idea what the story is with Inigo at all. What *did* happen with the phone call? Why did he run off?

"Inigo, I have no idea what you're talking about," I say more gently. "What happened? *Did* you fake that phone call, after all? Why?"

"What?" It's his turn to look taken aback. "No! God no! How could you think such a thing?"

"Then why did you run away?"

"I told you! I left a note—because I made such a stupid mistake."

I suppress a sigh of irritation and wonder, not for the first time, whether Inigo was ever actually that good as a PA. How did Topher put up with him?

"Yes, but you never said what the mistake was," I spell out. "We all thought—" And then I stop. Inigo flushes again, even deeper this time, but he puts his chin up.

"I know. You all thought it was me. That's why I had to leave—to put things right. The mistake—God, I was so dumb. I told the police we were at Chalet Blanche-Neige."

For a minute I don't understand. Then my mouth falls open. I have a sudden, vivid flashback to Inigo on the phone to the police. Yes . . . *okay . . . Chalet Blanche-Neige.*

Blanche-Neige. Snow White. Perce-Neige. Snow drop. An easy mistake to make for someone who didn't speak French. But one that was fatal for Ani. Oh, Inigo, you *idiot.*

"I know Chalet Blanche-Neige," I say slowly. "It's about ten miles away, over the other side of the valley. Of course. Of *course*, that's why the police never came. You told them the wrong place."

Inigo nods, in miserable assent.

"It was such a stupid fucking mistake. And I realized the next day what I'd done, and I kept trying to get through to explain, but the line was just dead," he says brokenly. "So I knew the only thing I could do to try to put it right was ski down to the town, to tell the cops in person what had happened and where we were. So I left. I know it was stupid but I just felt so—so ashamed, and I wanted to put things right. I knew if I told anyone what I was doing they'd try to come and I didn't want them to, I didn't want to put anyone in danger because of my mistake. But instead—" He gulps, and I see tears brimming in his eyes. I know he is thinking, as I am, of Elliot, and of Ani, both of whom might still be alive if the police had come that afternoon, if they had known where to look. "Instead I got lost, skied into a *tree*, and woke up in hospital." He touches his forehead, the surgical bandage I saw when we sat down. For the first time I notice the rawness of the skin on his cheeks and fingers, the blackened tips of his ears, where frostbite must have set in. "If only I hadn't—" His voice breaks. "If I didn't—"

"Inigo, you couldn't have known," I say softly. "It was a mistake—just a terrible mistake." These are words people have been saying to me for months, years now. You couldn't have known what would happen, when you suggested skiing off-piste. It's not your fault. It was just a mistake—just a terrible mistake.

They are phrases that have always seemed meaningless. Now, suddenly, it is vital that Inigo believes them.

"It's *not your fault*," I say, urgently, putting every shred of conviction that I can muster into my words. I put out a hand to touch his, feeling his rough, blistered fingers. Inigo winces, but then looks up at me. He gives a weak smile. I don't know if he believes me. Maybe. Maybe not.

Ani and Elliott might still be alive if Inigo had said the right name. But he didn't.

Maybe he will learn to live with what happened, just as I did. Just as I do.

ERIN

Snoop ID: LITTLEMY
Listening to: Offline
Snoopscribers: 160

I don't see the others until dinnertime, when the hotel serves up a hearty, veggie-unfriendly dinner at 7:00 p.m. sharp. There is no reservation, no picking and choosing your meal or your time. This is family dining—you come down when the chef tells you and you get the plat du jour, or you don't eat. It's quite restful.

I'm in my room, curled up in bed, more than half asleep when I hear the dinner bell ring, and I get up painfully, feeling the aches and pains in my bones from the last few days, and rubbing the side of my cheek where it's imprinted with the wrinkles of the pillowcase. Then I step out into the corridor.

I'm limping along to the stairs when a door opens and another guest comes barreling out, almost knocking me over, making me drop my crutch. I bend over to retrieve it, feeling my ankle scream in protest, and when I straighten up I'm about to make an irritated remark, but then I see the guest's face. He is standing stock-still, just looking at me.

It's Danny.

"Danny!"

I fling my arms around him, but he just stands, unresponsive, and then, like ice thawing, he seems to melt, and his arms creep around me, holding me in a hug that is at first gentle, then firm, and then crushingly hard, almost as if he's trying to make himself believe I'm here and solid flesh.

"I never believed her," he says at last, his deep voice coming to me as much through his chest, where my face is pressed. "I never believed her. That text—I knew something was wrong. I set out straightaway—I've never walked so fast in my life—but you were gone. I thought you'd died. I thought—I thought—"

But he can't finish. He just gulps, pressing his face into the top of my hair, and I feel the wetness of his tears on my parting.

"I should never have fucking left!" he says, and his arms tighten. "I knew you wasn't safe to be left alone. I told you, don't do anything stupid. And what happens? Skiing off-piste with a broken ankle? You ain't Jason effing Bourne."

I shake my head, and tighten my grip, burying my face in his shoulder, trying to hide my shaking sobs. I love him—I love his attempts to lighten the atmosphere and make a joke of this, but I can't even pretend to laugh. All I can do is hold him and cry, and cry, and cry, for everything.

"Fucking hell," he is saying, his voice rough and soft in my ear, rocking me back and forth, back and forth. "You're okay, Erin. You're all right, pet."

And I want to believe him. But I'm not sure if it's true.

"You look like shit," he says at last, pulling back to look me up and down. I feel like he wants me to laugh, and part of me wants to. *You should have seen the other guy*. The riposte is on the tip of my tongue. But Liz is dead, and it doesn't feel funny. Instead, I just shrug and Danny's lip curls into something close to a snarl.

"Fucking bitch."

"Don't," I say. "Don't—you don't know what she—"

But I'm interrupted by the clanging of the dinner bell for the second time, and Danny rolls his eyes.

"Better go down. You ready?"

"Not really. You?"

"I'm fine, mate. You're the one who pulled off the Bear Grylls stuff."

I laugh, but my nerves are still jangling as I make my way slowly and awkwardly down the narrow stairs from my room, crutch clamped under one arm, the other supporting my weight with the rickety banister.

When I enter the dining room, they are all there—all the people who are left, at any rate. Topher, Tiger, Rik, Inigo, Miranda, and Carl—they are all seated around the long dining table, and when I come in, unsure of my reception, there is a collective intake of breath and then, to my surprise, Topher breaks the silence with a slow round of applause that is taken up first by Inigo, and then by Rik, Miranda, and all the others.

"Bloody hell," Carl says, jumping up from his place to help me with my crutch and my chair. "You look even worse than Inigo, and that's saying something."

My seat is next to Tiger, and she puts her arm around me as Carl pushes my chair in, holding me in a warm, one-sided hug.

"Erin," she says. "Are you okay? It must have been terrifying. I'm so sorry—we never should have left you."

"It's okay," I manage. My eyes are filling with tears. I can't think what to say. My ankle, inside the Aircast, is throbbing painfully, and I can feel their eyes on me. It's a welcome distraction when Danny pulls out the chair on my other side and slumps into it with a sigh.

"Smells like that bleeding cassoulet again," he says morosely. "It was bad enough last time." Somehow his irritation breaks the ice, and Inigo is smiling, a watery grin.

"Bit louder, mate," Carl says, as the young waitress—the same girl from reception—comes into the room carefully carrying three plates of thick pale stew on a tray, breathing heavily with concentration as she navigates round the corner of the table. "We want to be sure she spits in the right plate."

"Going by the stuff they served the other night, spit would probably improve it," Rik says under his breath.

"Shh," Miranda hisses severely, and Rik grins, and rubs the back of her neck with an easy intimacy that makes me think whatever their situation at home, these two will not be going back to England as just colleagues. Something has changed between them, something irrevocable, and Rik looks stronger, more determined than the person I met just a few days ago.

Topher, by contrast, looks like a pale, deflated version of the charismatic man who stepped off the funicular. It's not surprising in a way—he has lost his cofounder and his best friend, a terrible price to pay for regaining control of his own company, by any standards, and one that seems to have aged him, and scuffed away some of his confidence and sheen. He's still seated at the head of the table, though, and when the cassoulet is served he taps his fork on his glass, and clears his throat as we all look round expectantly.

"Um . . . look, this won't take long," he says, and then stops, and rubs his forehead wearily, seeming to have lost the thread of what he was about to say. "But I—well, I've had a couple of bits of news. I thought you deserved to know as soon as possible."

He takes a long swig from the glass of red wine at his side, and then grimaces, and wipes his mouth. I don't think it's the kind of vintage he's used to drinking.

"The first thing is, well, there's no easy way to say this." He swallows, his throat working. "The, er, the buyout offer has been withdrawn."

There is a murmur from round the table. It's a mixture of shock and concern, but there's not much surprise in people's voices. Rik and Miranda share a glance.

"What does that mean for the company valuation, if you take Snoop public?" Carl asks bluntly. Topher doesn't answer. Rik folds his arms, his mouth a thin line of annoyance.

"In the toilet, am I right? You don't need to bullshit here, Toph. You're not wooing investors. It's not surprising, is it? High-profile massacre on company time, one partner dead, arguably the one the investors liked more—"

"Rik!" It's Tiger speaking; she stands up, her chair screeching on the tiled floor, her face twisted, her air of serenity quite gone. "Rik for God's sake! Does this matter? Eva is dead. Elliot is dead. Ani is *dead*." Her voice cracks on the last word. "How can you give a fuck about share valuation?"

She is right, and Rik knows it. He sinks back in his seat, and shrugs slightly feebly.

"It's a fact," he says, but not like he's arguing with her, just like he's trying to backtrack on his own insensitivity. "That's all I was saying."

And the thing is, he's right. It *is* a fact, and an important one to the people who are losing their money, and the employees who may soon be losing their jobs when Snoop's bubble bursts. But Tiger is right too. It's a fact that pales into nothing compared to the loss of their colleagues.

"What was the second thing?" Miranda says. Her interjection, into the uneasy silence after Tiger's outburst, is unexpected, and Topher looks nonplussed for a moment. "A couple of bits of news, you said," she prompts. "What was the other thing?"

"Oh." Topher looks . . . I don't know. Sickened, almost. He rubs his face. "I got a letter. I mean an email. From Arnaud."

Arnaud? Danny glances at me, frowning, and then I remember. "Eva's husband," I whisper, and Danny's expression changes to comprehension and unease.

"Has he heard?" Rik says. He looks a little sick. Topher nods.

"The police told him. They haven't given him the full picture, just the basic facts, that she's been involved in a fatal skiing accident. Anyway, he sent me a file."

"A file?" Miranda's expression is confused. She's not the only one. "About Eva?"

"A folder. About lots of people. Letters. Photos. Videos. Eva asked him to send it all to me in the event of her death. Arnaud hasn't seen any of it, it was password protected, but I've been through it and . . . there's this one video . . ." He runs his hand through his mussed blond hair, tousling it, but it no longer looks like it's sticking up in a way that's been artfully tweaked into place, it just looks like a mess. "I don't know what the fuck to do with it, you know? Eva's dumped it in my lap, and the rest of it's bad enough but this—this thing—I feel like it's too much for one person."

He looks . . . the word comes to me. He looks lost.

"You want us to watch it too?" Rik says. "All of us?"

His glance flickers at me and Danny. He doesn't say it, but the implication is clear—is this private Snoop stuff? But to my surprise, Topher nods.

"All of you. It concerns everyone here."

Beside me, Danny is frowning, and I know how he feels. Something is about to be dumped onto us—and I don't understand what. Why is this to do with me and Danny? Did Eva send something to her husband before her death?

Topher pulls open his MacBook, clicks a link, and taps in a password. Then he angles the screen towards the rest of the table, and, with a glance at the door to the kitchen to check the waitress isn't hovering, he presses play.

For a minute it's hard to make out what I'm seeing. It seems to be footage from a mobile phone, but it's nighttime, and the resolution is grainy and poor. It looks like a garden—or no, a balcony, because I can see rooftops beyond. A man and a woman are standing there, talking, but although I can hear the breathing of the person filming, I can't hear anything from the couple talking on the balcony, which makes me think they are being filmed from inside, through glass.

The woman is leaning against the opposite wall, and her face is in shadow, making it impossible to tell who she is, but there is something about her stance that looks both familiar, and more than a little tipsy. She is steadying herself with a hand on the wall, and when the man leans in, offering her more champagne, the glass she holds out is definitely swaying.

The man, I don't recognize. I'm sure of that. He is standing with his back to the balcony parapet, so that I can only see his profile, but it's no one I know. He's handsome, in an obvious kind of way, and there is something a little patronizing about his expression, like he's enjoying talking down to this young woman in front of him, enjoying her homage. He lifts his glass to his lips and drains his drink, and then says something to the woman.

The woman shakes her head. She makes as if to move away, but the man puts his arm up on the wall over her head, blocking her in. She is hemmed in by his body on one side, and the wall of the house on the other. My heart begins beating faster for her. I know what is happening. I have been this woman. I know her panic. I know how much she will want to escape.

And then, very deliberately, he puts his hand on her breast.

I am screaming at her internally to kick his shins, knee him in the balls, get *away*.

But I have realized with a sinking feeling that I know this woman. And I know what she is about to do.

She squirms to one side trying to get out from under his grasp, but he blocks her, putting his other hand there to prevent her escape, and now he leans in, too close for me to see what he's doing, though I can imagine, I can imagine all too well. My heart is racing now, sickeningly fast. Why isn't the person holding the phone going to help?

The shove, when it comes, is no surprise to me, even though there is an audible gasp from the person filming, and from a few of the viewers in the dining room.

On screen, the man staggers back, against the low barrier of the balcony, winded. And then the next few seconds unfold so fast I can hardly make out what happens.

The woman steps towards him, and for a second I think she is about to help him up. But she doesn't. She pushes him again. And this time his legs go up, his glass slips from his hand, his arms windmill—and he is gone.

It's only when the woman turns to walk away that we see her face.

It's completely calm.

It is, of course, Liz.

ERIN

Snoop ID: LITTLEMY
Listening to: Offline
Snoopscribers: 160

There is complete silence around the table as Topher closes his laptop and puts it away. Carl is the first to speak.

"What the fuck did we just watch?"

"I think . . ." It's Miranda, speaking very slowly, her face drained of color. "I think . . . we just watched Liz murder someone."

"It's why Eva was killed," Topher says, and his voice is gravelly. "It must be, surely? Liz must have known she knew."

"But—that makes no *sense*," Miranda says, bewildered. "Why kill Eva when she knew she had footage?"

"I'm guessing she didn't know about the footage," Topher says. He looks indescribably weary, his face graven with the lines of a man ten years older than his actual age.

"She didn't," I say. My words drop into their silence like stones into a well, and they all turn to look at me, astonished.

"You knew about this?" Miranda says, and, very reluctantly, I nod.

"Yes, I knew. Liz confessed to me before—" I stop, I can't bring myself to say what happened, even though I've already been through it with the police: the endless night, the pills in the kettle, that nightmarish chase in the darkness, the horror of her lonely death. "Before I ran," I end, lamely.

"She fucking killed a man in cold blood," Carl says, and his voice is blank with shock.

"He assaulted her," Miranda says stiffly, but I don't listen to the argument that ensues. I am too busy trying to figure out something else.

Who was filming? And *why*?

There is only one explanation—it must have been Eva. She was the only other person there that night, by Liz's account. And she had the footage. She *must* have been the person hiding inside the flat, filming through the closed window. It's the only explanation that makes sense, and it ties in with Liz's account of the timings, Eva making an excuse to leave and go to the bathroom, right before it happened.

But . . . I am putting two and two together as the argument rages around me, Miranda's shrill voice rising over Carl's booming tones. Why would Eva be filming? Unless she knew, or at least had a very good idea, that Liz was going to be assaulted.

And then I remember Liz's words to me, repeating Eva. *Besides, Norland likes her type. He likes them young.*

Did . . . did Eva *send* Liz in there, knowing Norland would likely make a pass, knowing Liz would fight him off and then . . . what?

The pieces click into place, with a horrible finality.

Then Eva would have video of a man, a potential investor, sexually assaulting her employee.

She would have him where she wanted him.

Eva is a blackmailer—I knew that already. But somehow, this cruel, calculated setup is infinitely worse than anything I had imagined.

She sent Liz in there like a lamb to the slaughter. What she didn't know was that Liz was no lamb.

It's like Liz said, everyone at Snoop underestimated her.

Well, that was a mistake. And Eva's mistake killed her. And it killed Norland too. And now it's killed Liz.

"She knew." I say it quietly, and at first they don't hear me, and the argument carries on over my head, but then Tiger says, "What did you say, Erin?"

"She knew." When I repeat it, the others fall quiet, so that my words drop into the sudden silence like little bombs.

"Who? Liz?"

"Eva. She *knew* that guy would probably go for Liz. That's why she was filming. She told you, Rik, do you remember? *Norland likes her type. He likes them young.*"

Rik says nothing, but the expression on his face says more than any speech. He remembers. He remembers perfectly. And he understands. Still, I spell it out for the others.

"She dressed Liz up, and she took her up to his flat, knowing that Norland would quite likely make a pass at her and Liz would panic. And she would have it all on film."

"Fuuuck." It's Carl who speaks, and his face is ashen. "She told me once, when I asked her how she got so good at persuading investors. She said everyone has a button, you just have to find it, and then you press it as hard as you can, even if they squeal."

"That film was supposed to be her button," I say. "Only it didn't turn out how she planned."

"And all this time," Tiger says slowly. "All this time she was holding it over Liz's head. What do we *do*?"

"What can we do?" It's Topher. He stands up, runs his hands through his hair. "Fuck, this is horrible—that fucking file. And it's not just Liz. She had stuff on all sorts of people. It's like a fucking time bomb."

"Does Arnaud know?" Rik asks. Topher shakes his head.

"No, I haven't told him what the folder contained. If this gets out, it'll *end* Snoop. What do we do? A company built on blackmailing investors? We might have survived Eva's death, even the revelations about Liz. But if this gets out, we could all be going down." He looks across the table at Rik. "I mean *literally* going down. Like, you and me could be looking at prison time. How do we prove we didn't know about this?"

"We can't bury this!" Tiger's voice is horrified. "Topher, what are you suggesting? That we pretend we never saw this?"

"I'm just saying—" Topher's voice is desperate; he runs his hands through his tow-colored hair again, looking half crazed now. "I'm just saying, what good would it do to drag all of this out? Eva's dead. Liz is dead. Norland is dead. No one can get brought to justice. All we can do is hurt Arnaud and Radisson."

"And *Snoop*," Tiger says accusingly. "That's what you really mean, isn't it? This isn't about Arnaud, this is about protecting your position." Her usually tranquil voice has grown high with anger and distress. "What about Liz?"

"Liz is a murderer!" Topher cries.

"She's a victim!"

"She's a fucking psychopath," Carl puts in, matter-of-factly. "Was, I mean."

There is silence, while we all consider this.

Because here's the thing. They are all right. Liz *was* a victim. And just like she said, she never wanted any of this. She was just a poor, confused kid, in the wrong place at the wrong time. But I can't forget that second, extra push. And I can't forget little, trusting Ani. Perhaps Liz was both.

ERIN

Snoop ID: LITTLEMY

Listening to: The Verve / Bitter Sweet Symphony

Snoopers: 43

Snoopscribers: 164

It's still not resolved when dinner breaks up, and I climb awkwardly up the steep stairs to my room, leaving the voices of the others still raised in angry discussion and circular argument. It's a relief in fact to stick my headphones in and slump back on the bed with my ankle raised, thinking of nothing but the music in my head.

I barely hear the knock at the door, but something makes me pull out one earbud, and it comes again, a brisk *rap-rap*.

With a sigh, I swing my legs off the bed and hobble to the floor.

It's Danny. And he's holding a crutch.

"You left this, mate."

"Oh, of course." I smack my hand to my forehead. "I'm such an idiot. Thanks." He hands it over and there's a moment's awkward silence. "Do you want to come in?" I ask, waving a hand at my slightly meager room. "I know it's not exactly the Ritz, but I'm not sure I can face sitting with the others downstairs."

Slightly to my surprise, Danny shakes his head.

"Nah. I'm . . . well, I'm actually gonna go out. For a drink."

"With who?" I'm surprised. I'm even more surprised when Danny blushes.

"Eric. Landlady's son. He runs the bar up the road, you know, the one with the brass counter on the corner, the Petit Coin? Said . . . you know. 'Come in for a drink after supper.'"

"Danny!" I can't stop a smile spreading across my face. "That's awesome. Is he . . . ?"

Danny raises one eyebrow, drawing out the silence, making me blush, and then he puts me out of my discomfort.

"If you mean, does he like piña coladas, sources say yes."

"Ha. Well. Go you."

"You sure? I mean, you could come . . ." He trails off, but I'm laughing and shaking my head.

"No. No, thanks. No piña coladas for me, I'm going to have an early night."

"Okay. Good plan, Batman." He pauses, but he still doesn't leave. He just stands there, frowning down at his feet, tracing a pattern on the lurid carpet with his toe. "Fucking weird, wasn't it?"

"All the stuff with the film? Yeah. What do you think they'll do?"

"Fuck knows. I've been wondering if we should go to the police ourselves, but I dunno if there's much point."

I've been wondering the same thing, but I don't have any answers either, and in the end I just shrug.

Danny turns as if he's about to go, and I'm just about to close the door when he swings back as if he's thought better of something. He leans in, and I think he's going to whisper something in my ear, but instead, rather sweetly, and to my surprise, he gives me a kiss. His lips are full and soft against my cheekbone.

"Love you, mate," he says. I put my arms around him, and squeeze.

"Love you too, Danny. Now go. You've got piña coladas waiting."

ERIN

Snoop ID: LITTLEMY
Listening to: Carole King / Tapestry
Snoopers: 28
Snoopscribers: 345

It's just over three weeks later, and I'm sitting by the fire in the chalet, staring out of the tall window that overlooks the valley, listening to music and not thinking about anything in particular.

It's still strange being in the chalet without working. Both Danny and I are still employed, technically, but I don't know how much longer that can go on. After Perce-Neige was declared an official crime scene, its photo smeared all over the newspapers in half a dozen countries, it became very clear that even if the avalanche damage was repaired, it wasn't going to be possible to use it for a holiday destination for this season at least.

The remaining bookings for the year have been either cancelled, or hastily reallocated to the other properties owned by the skiing company, and now Danny and I are simply waiting to find out what will happen, pacing the empty rooms, looking at the place where Ani last sat, seeing Elliot's ghost, spooning stew into his mouth, hearing the *click-click-click* of Eva's heels on the parquet, and the slam of Liz's bedroom door.

I can't stay in this place. I know that now. But I can't keep running.

The smells from the kitchen are making my stomach rumble, and I'm just thinking about heaving myself out of my chair and clumping through to ask Danny what time he will be serving up, when my Snoop stream goes dead. For a minute I'm not sure what's happened. I wasn't snooping on anyone else, so the feed shouldn't cut out like that. It was *my* music.

I open up my phone to check on the app, but that's when I notice. There's an email notification. And it's from Kate. The subject line is *Some difficult news.* My stomach gives a lurching jolt.

"Danny," I shout, over the sound of pots and pans from the kitchen. There's no reply, and I am about to get up and walk through to show him the notification when he appears in the doorway, holding his own phone.

"Did you get it too?" he asks, and I nod my head.

"Yeah. I think we're both cc'd in. What does it say?"

"Open it and find out."

My gut is churning as I open the email and scan down the contents. *Difficult decision . . . not practical to reopen . . . eventual sale . . . sick pay . . . generous redundancy packages . . . four weeks' notice.*

"They're closing the chalet." I look up at Danny.

He nods solemnly.

"Yup. That's about the size of it. Have to say, I'm not exactly surprised, what plonker's gonna want to stay in a place where four guests got killed? I mean, it's not exactly home sweet home, is it, even if you take the banjaxed swimming pool out of the equation. What are you gonna do?"

"What am I going to do?" I stare back at him. It's stupid, because I've had three weeks to figure this out, but I'm no closer to deciding. Would I come back to work? Did I want to? Now it's not even a question.

"I don't know," I say at last. "What about you?"

"We could sue, you know," Danny says conversationally. "I mean, quote unquote generous redundancy package is all very well, but you were bloody near killed in the line of duty. I reckon that deserves something a bit more than a few weeks' pay and a box of fucking chocs."

"I don't want to sue," I say reflexively, without even thinking about it, but as the words leave my mouth I am sure of the rightness of them. I don't want to. It was hard enough going through all this once. I am not putting myself through it all again in a court of law, let alone dragging in Topher, Tiger, Rik, and everyone else to give evidence.

"Nah, neither do I really," Danny says, looking down at the screen, with a little sigh. "Coulda done with the squids though. Well, as me old ma would say, if wishes were horses and all that." He sighs again, and then says, "Shall I serve up? Butternut squash soup with hazelnut gremolata and charred fougasse."

"Sounds delicious," I say, trying for a smile. "I can't wait."

ERIN

Snoop ID: LITTLEMY
Listening to:
Snoopscribers:

After lunch Danny and I sit down in front of the TV and I get out my phone. I've become slightly addicted to watching my Snoopscribers tick upwards. There's nothing like news getting around that you've been almost killed to send your numbers rocketing. And I like checking up on Topher, Rik, and the others too. Rik's username is Rikshaw and he doesn't have nearly as many Snoopers as Topher, but I like his music taste a lot more. He was listening to some amazing Cuban rap the other day.

But when I open up the app, there's nothing there, just a blank home page.

For a second I think I've accidentally logged out, but no—I'm still signed in, and there is my profile picture in the top right, Little My from the Moomins scowling out of the screen. But there is nothing in my recently played list, no suggestions of people to follow, no Snoopscriber list—in fact even my numbers have disappeared. Is the internet down again? But I remember when that happened before, and it wasn't like this. Have I been *banned*?

"Danny," I say. Danny is scrolling through Netflix. He speaks, without looking away from the screen.

"That's my name, don't wear it out."

"Danny, is your Snoop working?"

"Yeah, why?" he says, and then opens up the app to check. "No, wait, what? I've lost all my subscriptions and all my favorites. What's going on?"

"I don't know. Has this ever happened before? Have we been banned?"

"No . . ." Danny is scrolling through menus. "No, I don't think so . . . I mean, there's nothing they can ban you *for*. It's not like Twitter where you can post far-right shit. There's nothing you can do apart from follow people. I think . . . I think this did happen before, ages ago, when they were starting up and they didn't have enough servers. I remember a few days where the whole app just crashed, and it was like this. Just a blank screen. Maybe they're having server problems their end?"

"Maybe."

I pull up Google, and type in *is snoop down*.

Article after article comes up. *BREAKING* reads the first one. *British tech start-up Snoop files for administration.*

And another one: *Snoop users received a rude shock when they logged into their favorite app today to be met with a blank screen, after the company shut down servers following a declaration of bankruptcy by founder and CEO Topher St. Clair-Bridges.*

"Fuck." I can see from his face and the way he looks up at me that Danny has just made the same search, and is reading the same article—or one just like it. "Fuck, they've gone under. Rik was right."

I let out a long breath, and a tension that I didn't realize I had been holding rolls off me. It's not that I'm glad that Snoop has gone bankrupt—far from it. The thought of Inigo, Tiger, Carl, and all the rest of them out of a job, not to mention all the people I never met behind the scenes—that gives me zero pleasure. But it sets my mind at rest over a decision that has been gnawing at the back of my mind for three weeks now. What to do about Eva's video.

Because that was the one question that we never resolved before the Snoop team left St. Antoine. On the one hand, there was Topher's strenuous argument that telling the truth would make no one better off, and would damage Snoop beyond repair, and probably cost dozens of innocent people their jobs.

But on the other hand, that equation was precisely what made keeping the secret so uncomfortable. We were not doing what was *right,* we were doing what was *profitable,* a fact that Tiger stressed again and again in the increasingly bitter arguments that repeated themselves the last few nights of their stay in the hotel in St. Antoine.

"Are you telling me," Topher raged, "that if it weren't for Snoop you'd put Eva's family through all that? Would you deliberately add another body to Liz's account, open all those old wounds that poor man's family thought they laid to rest years ago, torment Arnaud with something he never needs to know? Is all of that really worth sacrificing for the truth to come out when everyone concerned is already dead?"

"No!" Tiger cried. "But that's the point, we're not weighing all that against the truth, we're weighing *Snoop* against the truth, that's what makes this so problematic! Topher, you can't go through life expecting everyone to sacrifice every principle they have for your company's vision—it doesn't *work* like that. It just makes you sound like an arrogant entitled—"

"Entitled, entitled, fucking entitled!" Topher shouted over her. "I am so bloody sick of that word! It's become a fucking stick to beat white men with. Do you know what entitled actually *means,* Tiger? It means you *deserve* something, that you are legally *due it,* for whatever reason. Think about that next time you talk about someone being entitled."

And then he stormed out.

Now, three weeks later, I do think about it. I think about what *entitled* really means. About the fact that the unknown executive's family are entitled to know the truth about their son and brother. About the fact that Eva's innocent baby daughter is entitled to grow up without the shadow of her mother's actions hanging over her. And I think about the fact that the dead are entitled to be left in peace.

Topher is entitled, and that's the truth. Entitled in the way that Tiger meant. He has gone through life taking, and taking, and taking, just as Eva did. They used people like their own personal chess pieces. Employees, investors, friends, relations—they took and they took from all of them. And they never accepted responsibility for the harm they caused.

I think about what responsibility means.

I think about guilt.

I think about moving on.

ERIN

I am up in my room, packing, when the email comes through. I don't know what I was expecting—Kate, maybe, with some last-minute details about our redundancy packages, or HR with some more legal disclaimers to sign. It's neither of those. And I don't recognize the email address.

But the subject line reads *Sorry,* and so I click through.

I scan first to the bottom of the email to see who it's from—and the name there makes me do a double take. Topher. What the hell is he emailing me for?

I frown. Then I scroll back up to read what he's actually sent.

Dear Erin.

I expect by now you'll have seen in the papers that Snoop has gone under. Fucking vulture capitalists. When you're hot they can't get their tongues far enough down your throat—and when you actually need them, you might as well have herpes.

If Eva was here she'd be saying I told you so, I expect, but she's not—and so I can't even give her that small satisfaction.

I got your email off the user database before we got locked out. I know. Don't shop me. But listen, I wanted to say . . . oh fuck it. I don't know. I'm sorry, or some bullshit like that. I'm sorry for everything that happened to you, but mainly, I'm sorry for being such a fucking prick about Alex and Will. I keep thinking back to that afternoon at the chalet when I realized who you were, and—well, look, I can't take the words back, but I never apologized for saying them in the first place, so that's what this is about.

I'm not very good at saying sorry. I haven't had much practice, to tell you the truth, so I'll just come out with it. Sorry. Alex and Will—they were good blokes. They didn't deserve to have that happen to them, and nor did you. And I'm fucking sorry for what I implied—I don't know how much you overheard, you were out of the room at the time, but I said some pretty shitty stuff in the heat of the moment, and I'm not proud of that.

Because here is the thing—now that the dust has settled, and I've had some time to come to terms with stuff, I get it. I get what losing people like that does to you. Eva—Elliot—they weren't blood, but they were the nearest thing to it. Elliot and I came up through the prep school system together and Eva—I don't know. It's hard to explain. Even after we broke up, we never really severed that connection.

So I get it now. I get why you didn't tell us. I get why you couldn't leave.

I think about them all the time. About Elliot, being post-mortemed in some French morgue. About Eva, still up there, frozen in the mountain passes like Sleeping Beauty. And about Ani too, I guess. Fuck.

Anyway—that's all really. I just wanted to say it one last time.

Sorry.

Topher

x

PS I just wanted to tell you, that file—I handed it all to the police. It felt like the right thing to do in the end. And for what it's worth, I did it last week. Before all this happened. It's not why Snoop went under—I'd like to say it was, but it wasn't. But I wanted you to know.

When I look up from the screen, I'm surprised to find my cheeks are wet. And although I don't know what to say, I hit reply and sit, for a long time, my fingers just hovering over the keys. And then I type. Just eight words. And I really, really hope they are true.

Dear Topher, it's going to be all right.

ERIN

"Oh, mate." Danny's arms are around my neck, his face is buried in my shoulder. "Gonna miss you, you stupid cow."

"I'm going to miss you too." I hug him back, feeling his strong shoulders, hard beneath his down jacket, smelling his permanent scent of French cooking—of simmering wine-rich stews, and melting butter, and sautéed garlic and all good things.

"You gonna be all right?"

I nod. Because for the first time in a long while . . . I think I am.

"I have to go home," I say, and I mean it this time. Not home, St. Antoine, but home to England, where Will's grieving parents and my own family have been waiting patiently for me to make peace with my ghosts.

I have been alone with them for so long, listening to the Will and Alex in my head, trying to come to terms with what happened, with what I did—trying to come to terms with the responsibility of having said those four little words, *Let's go off-piste.*

Lying there in the snow with Liz, feeling her life ebbing away beneath my fingers, I realized—I can't keep running anymore. And maybe that's okay.

"And are *you* going to be all right?" I ask. In the distance the coach is coming, I can hear the sound of its snow tires against the plowed road. "What are you going to do? Try for a job in one of the other chalets?"

"Oh," Danny says, and to my surprise, he's gone a little pink. The tips of his ears, just visible in spite of his beany hat, are tinged with rose. "Oh yeah, well, actually, I've got a place lined up."

"You have?"

"Yeah." He coughs, a little awkwardly. "Um, you remember that B and B the police put us in?"

"The one with the shit cassoulet? Of course I remember!"

"Yeah, well, they've sacked their chef. And, well, um, well, a mate put in a word for me."

"A mate?" I am grinning broadly now. "A *mate*? Would that mate by any chance be sexy Eric the landlady's son? Monsieur Piña Colada from Le Petit Coin?"

Danny is blushing so furiously that I can't help prodding him in the ribs, making him laugh.

"Oh, Danny! What did you have to do to earn that?"

"Never you mind." Danny's cheeks are glowing, and he's half glowering, half grinning back, but I can see the happiness radiating out of him. "Bit of nepotism never did no one any harm."

"I very much doubt it was nepotism," I say. "One taste of your cassoulet and Eric would be mad not to snap you up."

I want to know more. I want to know everything, but now the bus is nearly here, and there's no time. I kiss Danny on the cheek and he picks up my other bag and when the coach draws up, he hands it to the guy in charge of loading the luggage.

"Look after her," he says in French to the driver as I make my way carefully up the steps. I don't need a crutch anymore, but my ankle is still in the Aircast. "She's not as tough as she looks."

"Bien sur," the driver calls back, and winks at me.

I am sliding into my seat when I hear Danny calling something through the thick window, and I pop open the little vent at the top of the pane and kneel up on the seat to look down at him.

"What is it?"

"I forgot to say—download Choon!"

"Choon?"

"It's the new Snoop, mate. Only better. *C, H,* double *O, N.*"

"Choon. Got it," I call back. And then the coach begins moving and I shut the window. It picks up speed, and I'm waving to Danny, and he's waving to me, and kissing his hand, and I feel a tear tracing down my cheek.

He's calling something through the glass, but I can't hear what.

"I can't hear you!" I shout. My face is crumpling. I swipe at the tears on my cheek, feeling the tight ripple of the fading scar slick beneath my knuckles. "I love you!" But we're too far up the road, and I know he didn't hear either.

I sink back into my seat, feeling my heart ache for everyone I've lost, everything I'm leaving behind in the mountains. Another tear rolls down my face, and for a minute I think I'm not going to be able to hold it back—the tears are going to come whether I want them to or not, and I'm going to bawl my heart out on the bus. But then my phone gives a single beep.

It's a text message. From Danny.

CHOON, mate. Oh—and my ID, it's DANNYBOI. Luv ya.

ERIN

Choon ID: Little-My

Followers: 1

ACKNOWLEDGMENTS

Writing a book is for the most part a selfish, lonesome thing, but I cannot stress enough the extent to which publishing is a team effort—and the tireless teams of editors, publicists, marketers, designers, sales reps, rights people, production editors, and everyone else behind the scenes are the unsung heroes of the book world, along with the booksellers and librarians who take care of our efforts after they have left the doors of the publishing house. The fact that this book made it from my head into your hands is down to them, and for that I cannot say a large enough thank you.

To Alison, Liz, Jade, Sara, Jen, Maggie, Noor, Sydney, Aimee, Bethan, Catherine, Nita, Kevin, Richard, Faye, Jessica, Rachel, Sophie, Mackenzie, Christian, Chloe, Anne, Anabel, Abby, Mikaela, Tom, Christina, Jane, Sophie, Jennifer, Kathy, Carolyn, and everyone at Simon & Schuster and PRH, my heartfelt thanks. And to the booksellers, librarians, bloggers, readers and reviewers—I cannot name you all, but you are the reason I keep getting to do this, and I thank you all every day.

While the characters and situations in this book are all my own invention, I was shameless in picking the brains of others to create

Snoop—so thank you to Joe, James, and James for giving me advice on everything from musical playlists to shareholders agreements.

To Eve and Ludo, I literally could not do this without you.

To Carmen Sane and my fabulous writer friends, you are funny, wise, wonderful, and filthy people and I would get a lot more work done without you but would have much less fun.

To Jilly, Ali and Mark—thank you for being the best skiing support team, media assistants, publicists, and drinking companions. And of course for making me ski the Secret Valley (though not at night).

And last and best thanks always to my dear family, for everything.

BOOK CLUB
FAVORITES
READER'S GUIDE

ONE BY ONE

RUTH WARE

This reading group guide for One by One *includes an introduction, discussion questions, and ideas for enhancing your book club. The suggested questions are intended to help your reading group find new and interesting angles and topics for your discussion. We hope that these ideas will enrich your conversation and increase your enjoyment of the book.*

INTRODUCTION

The #1 *New York Times* bestselling author of *The Turn of the Key* and *In a Dark, Dark Wood* returns with another suspenseful thriller set on a snow-covered mountain.

Getting snowed in at a beautiful, rustic mountain chalet doesn't sound like the worst problem in the world, especially when there's a breathtaking vista, a cozy fire, and company to keep you warm. But what happens when that company is eight of your coworkers . . . and you can't trust any of them?

An off-site company retreat meant to promote mindfulness and collaboration goes utterly wrong when an avalanche hits; the corporate food chain becomes irrelevant and survival trumps togetherness. Come Monday morning, how many members short will the team be?

TOPICS AND QUESTIONS FOR DISCUSSION

1. Erin and Danny have a strong and supportive relationship from the beginning of the book. Before opening the chalet to guests, they have a tradition of swimming together. Why do you think this is important for them to have this time alone? Have you ever had a confidant that you can rely on like Erin did with Danny?
2. Erin and Liz are both used to being outsiders. Why do you think the author chose these two characters be the ones to tell this story? What do you think the experience would look like through Danny's eyes? What about Eva's or Topher's perspectives?
3. Discuss the appeal of Snoop for users. Do you think you would use the app if it existed? What people would you follow?
4. The founders of Snoop disagree about whether or not to sell the company, with Liz as the deciding vote. If you were Liz, what would your decision be? Who of the founders do you find more trustworthy: Eva or Topher? Why?

5. Erin and Danny both begin *One by One* as the chalet's staff. However, once the avalanche traps them along with Snoop's staff, they are not quite sure how to proceed. Why do you think Erin and Danny continue to act as the chalet's caretakers? Discuss moments where Erin and Danny come into conflict with Snoop employees.
6. After the avalanche hits, Snoop employees also ignore the corporate food chain, and instead focus on survival. How did you feel about the alliances that people made? Who begins the book with the most power? How does that change throughout the book?
7. Many people almost uncover the murderer before they are also killed. Discuss how each character found out who the murderer was. How did the killer find out that *they* knew?
8. It quickly becomes clear that Snoop's corporate culture is toxic. How do you think Liz fit into this culture when she worked there? How do you think she fit into Snoop after she left as a shareholder? Were you surprised that Eva and Topher each had sexual relationships with their assistants?
9. Though Erin begins the book as an outsider, she comes from a very similar background to Topher. Did this come as a surprise to you? Why do you think she chose to stay close to the mountains after such a traumatic accident?
10. Snoop can track the location of its users while they use the app. However, the users are not yet aware of this technology. What do you think the public's reaction would have been? Discuss the ethical implications of tracking users without notifying them. Does the app helping to uncover the murderer change your opinion?
11. Liz had been taken advantage of often in her life, both in her own family and by her former colleagues at Snoop. How much did you agree with Liz's view of herself as a victim of circumstance?
12. Why do you think Topher felt it was important to message Erin after Snoop went under? What do you think of Erin's reply? Did you find Topher to be a sympathetic character? Why or why not?

ENHANCE YOUR BOOK CLUB

1. Snoop is an app that allows its users to anonymously listen to what music anyone is streaming in real time. In your book group invent an app that you wish existed. Give it a concept, a name, and even a logo.
2. Music plays a major role for the characters in *One by One.* Use the online playlist to enhance your reading experience. After reading the book, flip back to the character introductions with their song choices. Play the songs and have your book group guess which character it represents.
3. Author Ruth Ware's novels often focus on characters that are trapped in one location, such as fancy smart homes (*The Turn of the Key*), spooky cabins (*The Woman in Cabin 10*), or in this case, picturesque chalets. Have you read any other thrillers that take place in one location? What do you think of this as a device for a thriller?